W9-CZO-138

THE WARDEN

———

BARCHESTER TOWERS

THE WARDEN

—

BARCHESTER TOWERS

by

ANTHONY TROLLOPE

designed to be read as modern novels

THE BOOK LEAGUE OF AMERICA

New York

CONTENTS

THE WARDEN

CONTENTS

BARCHESTER TOWERS

viii   CONTENTS

THE WARDEN

CHAPTER I

HIRAM'S HOSPITAL

THE Reverend Septimus Harding was, a few years since, a beneficed clergyman residing in the cathedral town of ——. Let us call it Barchester. Were we to name Wells or Salisbury, Exeter, Hereford, or Gloucester, it might be presumed that something personal was intended, and as this tale will refer mainly to the cathedral dignitaries of the town in question, we are anxious that no personality may be suspected. Let us presume that Barchester is a quiet town in the west of England, more remarkable for the beauty of its cathedral and the antiquity of its monuments than for any commercial prosperity; that the west end of Barchester is the cathedral close, and that the aristocracy of Barchester are the bishop, dean, and canons, with their respective wives and daughters.

Early in life Mr. Harding found himself located at Barchester. A fine voice and a taste for sacred music had decided the position in which he was to exercise his calling, and for many years he performed the easy but not highly paid duties of a minor canon. At the age of forty a small living in the close vicinity of the town increased both his work and his income, and at the age of fifty he became Precentor of the cathedral.

Mr. Harding had married early in life, and was the father of two daughters. The eldest, Susan, was born soon after his marriage, the other, Eleanor, not till ten years later. At the time at which we introduce him to our readers he was living as Precentor at Barchester with his youngest daughter, then twenty-four years of age, having been many years a widower, and having married his eldest daughter to a son of the Bishop a very short time before his installation to the office of precentor.

Scandal at Barchester affirmed that had it not been for the beauty of his daughter, Mr. Harding would have remained a minor canon. But here probably Scandal lied, as she so often does, for even as a minor canon no one had been more popular among his reverend brethren in the close than Mr. Harding, and Scandal, before she had reprobated Mr. Harding for being made Precentor by his friend the Bishop, had loudly blamed the Bishop for having so long omitted to do something for his friend Mr. Harding. Be this as it may, Susan Harding, some twelve years since, had married the Reverend Dr. Theophilus Grantly, son of the Bishop, Archdeacon of Barchester, and Rector of Plumstead Episcopi, and her father became, a few months later, Precentor of Barchester Cathedral, that office being, as is not usual, in the Bishop's gift.

Now there are peculiar circumstances connected with the precentorship which must be explained. In the year 1434 there died at Barchester one John Hiram, who had made money in the town as a wool stapler, and in his will he left the house in which he died and certain meadows and closes near the town, still called Hiram's Butts and Hiram's Patch, for the support of twelve superannuated wool-carders, all of whom should have been born and bred and spent their days in Barchester. He also appointed that an almshouse should be built for their abode, with a fitting residence for a warden, which warden was also to receive a certain sum annually out of the rents of the said butts and patches. He moreover willed, having had a soul alive to harmony, that the precentor of the cathedral should have the option of being also warden of the almshouses, if the bishop in each case approved.

From that day to this the charity has gone on and prospered—at least the charity had gone on, and the estates had prospered. Wool-carding in Barchester there was no longer any, so the bishop, dean, and warden, who took it in turn to put in the old men, generally appointed some hangers-on of their own—worn-out gardeners, decrepit gravediggers, or octogenarian sextons, who thankfully received a comfortable lodging and one shilling and fourpence a day, such being the stipend to which, under the will of John Hiram, they were declared to be entitled. Formerly, indeed—that is, till within some fifty years of the present time—they received but sixpence a day, and their breakfast and dinner was found them at a common table by the warden, such an arrangement being in stricter conformity with the absolute wording of old Hiram's will. But this was thought to be inconvenient, and to suit the tastes of neither warden nor bedesmen, and the daily one shilling and fourpence was substituted with the common consent of all parties, including the bishop and the corporation of Barchester.

Such was the condition of Hiram's twelve old men when Mr. Harding was appointed Warden, but if they may be considered to have been well-to-do in the world according to their condition, the happy Warden was much more so. The patches and butts which in John Hiram's time produced hay or fed cows were now covered with rows of houses. The value of the property had gradually increased from year to year and century to century, and was now presumed by those who knew anything about it to bring in a very nice income, and by some who knew nothing about it, to have increased to an almost fabulous extent.

The property was farmed by a gentleman in Barchester, who also acted as the bishop's Steward—a man whose father and grandfather had been stewards to the bishops of Barchester, and farmers of John Hiram's estate. The Chadwicks had earned a good name in Barchester. They had lived respected by bishops, deans, canons, and precentors; they had been buried in the precincts of the cathedral; they had never been known as griping, hard men, but had always lived comfortably, maintained a good house, and held a high position in Barchester society. The present Mr. Chadwick was a worthy scion of a worthy stock, and the tenants living on the butts and patches, as well as those on the wide episcopal domains of the see, were well pleased to have to do with so worthy and liberal a steward.

For many, many years—records hardly tell how many, probably from the time when Hiram's wishes had been first fully carried out—the proceeds of the estate had been paid by the steward or farmer to the warden, and by him divided among the bedesmen, after which division he paid himself such sums as became his due. Times had been when the poor warden got nothing but his bare house, for the patches had been subject to floods and the land of Barchester butts was said to be unproductive, and in these hard times the warden was hardly able to make out the daily dole for his twelve dependents. But by degrees things mended. The patches were drained and cottages began to rise upon the butts, and the wardens, with fairness enough, repaid themselves for the evil days gone by. In bad times the poor men had had their due, and therefore in good times they could expect no more. In this manner the income of the warden had increased. The picturesque house attached to the hospital had been enlarged and adorned, and the office had become one of the most coveted of the snug clerical sinecures attached to our Church. It was now wholly in the bishop's gift, and though the dean and chapter, in former days, made a stand on the subject, they had thought it more conducive to their honor to have a rich precentor appointed by the bishop than a poor one appointed by themselves. The stipend of the Precentor of Barchester was eighty pounds a year. The income arising from the wardenship of the hospital was eight hundred, besides the value of the house.

Murmurs, very slight murmurs, had been heard in Barchester—few indeed, and far between—that the proceeds of John Hiram's property had not been fairly divided. But they can hardly be said to have been of such a nature as to have caused uneasiness to anyone. Still the thing had been whispered, and Mr. Harding had heard it. Such was his character in Barchester, so universal was his popularity, that the very fact of his appointment would have quieted louder whispers than those which had been heard. But Mr. Harding was an openhanded, just-minded man, and feeling that there might be truth in what had been said, he had on his installment declared his intention of adding twopence a day to each man's pittance, making a sum of sixty-two pounds eleven shillings and fourpence, which he was to pay out of his own pocket. In doing so, however, he distinctly and repeatedly observed to the men that though he promised for himself, he could not promise for his successors, and that the extra twopence could only be looked on as a gift from himself, and not from the trust. The bedesmen, however, were most of them older than Mr. Harding, and were quite satisfied with the security on which their extra income was based.

This munificence on the part of Mr. Harding had not been unopposed. Mr. Chadwick had mildly but seriously dissuaded him from it, and his strong-minded son-in-law, the Archdeacon, the man of whom alone Mr. Harding stood in awe, had urgently—nay, vehemently—opposed so impolitic a concession. But the Warden had made known his intention to the hospital before the Archdeacon had been able to interfere, and the deed was done.

Hiram's Hospital, as the retreat is called, is a picturesque building enough, and shows the correct taste with which the ecclesiastical architects of those days were imbued. It stands on the banks of the little river which flows nearly round the cathedral close, being on the side furthest from the town. The London road crosses the river by a pretty one-arched bridge, and, looking from this bridge, the stranger will see the windows of the old men's rooms, each pair of windows separated by a small buttress. A broad gravel walk runs between the building and the river, which is always trim and cared for. And at the end of the walk, under the parapet of the approach to the bridge, is a large and well-worn seat on which, in mild weather, three or four of Hiram's bedesmen are sure to be seen seated. Beyond this row of buttresses, and farther from the bridge, and also farther from the water, which here suddenly bends, are the pretty oriel windows of Mr. Harding's house and his well-mown lawn.

The entrance to the hospital is from the London road, and is made through a ponderous gateway under a heavy stone arch, unnecessary, one would suppose, at any time, for the protection of twelve old men, but greatly conducive to the good appearance of Hiram's charity. On passing through this portal, never closed to anyone from six A.M. till ten P.M., and never open afterward—except on application to a huge, intricately hung medieval bell, the handle of which no uninitiated intruder can possibly find—the six doors of the old men's abodes are seen, and beyond them is a slight iron screen, through which the more happy portion of the Barchester elite pass into the Elysium of Mr. Harding's dwelling.

Mr. Harding is a small man, now verging on sixty years but bearing few of the signs of age. His hair is rather grizzled than gray. His eye is very mild, but clear and bright, though the double glasses which are held swinging from his hand, unless when fixed upon his nose, show that time has told upon his sight. His hands are delicately white, and both hands and feet are small. He always wears a black frock coat, black knee breeches, and black gaiters, and somewhat scandalizes some of his more hyperclerical brethren by a black neck handkerchief.

Mr. Harding's warmest admirers cannot say that he was ever an industrious man—the circumstances of his life have not called on him to be so—and yet he can hardly be called an idler. Since his appointment to his precentorship, he has published, with all possible additions of vellum, typography, and gilding, a collection of our ancient church music, with some correct dissertations on Purcell, Crotch, and Nares. He has greatly improved the choir of Barchester which under his dominion now rivals that of any cathedral in England. He has taken something more than his fair share in the cathedral services, and has played the violoncello daily to such audiences as he could collect, or, faute de mieux, to no audience at all.

We must mention one other peculiarity of Mr. Harding. As we have before stated, he has an income of eight hundred a year, and has no family but his one daughter, and yet he is never quite at ease in money matters. The vellum and gilding of *Harding's Church Music* cost more than anyone knows except the author, the publisher, and the Reverend Theophilus Grantly, who allows none of his father-in-law's extravagances to escape him. Then he is generous to his daughter, for whose service he keeps a small carriage and pair of ponies. He is, indeed, generous to all, but especially to the twelve old men who are in a peculiar manner under his care. No doubt with such an income Mr. Harding should be above the world, as the saying is. But at any rate he is not above Archdeacon Theophilus Grantly, for he is always more or less in debt to his son-in-law, who has, to a certain extent, assumed the arrangement of the Precentor's pecuniary affairs.

CHAPTER II

THE BARCHESTER REFORMER

MR. HARDING has been now Precentor of Barchester for ten years, and, alas! the murmurs respecting the proceeds of Hiram's estate are again becoming audible. It is not that anyone begrudges to Mr. Harding the income which he enjoys and the comfortable place which so well becomes him, but such matters have begun to be talked of in various parts of England. Eager, pushing politicians have asserted in the House of Commons, with very telling indignation, that the grasping priests of the Church of England are gorged with the wealth which the charity of former times has left for the solace of the aged or the education of the young. The well-known case of the Hospital of St. Cross has even come before the law courts of the country, and the struggles of Mr. Whiston at Rochester have met with sympathy and support. Men are beginning to say that these things must be looked into.

Mr. Harding, whose conscience in the matter is clear, and who has never felt that he had received a pound from Hiram's will to which he was not entitled, has naturally taken the part of the Church in talking over these matters with his friend the Bishop, and his son-in-law the Archdeacon. The Archdeacon, indeed, Dr. Grantly, has been somewhat loud in the matter. He is a personal friend of the dignitaries of the Rochester Chapter, and has written letters in the public press on the subject of that turbulent Dr. Whiston, which, his admirers think, must well-nigh set the question at rest. It is also known at Oxford that he is the author of the pamphlet signed "Sacerdos," on the subject of the Earl of Guildford and St. Cross, in which it is so clearly argued that the manners of the present times do not admit of a literal adhesion to the very words of the founder's will, but that the interests of the Church for which the founder was so deeply concerned are best consulted in enabling its bishops to reward those shining lights whose services have been most signally serviceable to Christianity. In answer to this, it is asserted that Henry de Blois, founder of St. Cross, was not greatly interested in the welfare of the reformed Church, and that the masters of St. Cross, for many years past, cannot be called shining lights in the service of Christianity. It is, however, stoutly maintained, and no doubt felt, by all the Archdeacon's friends that his logic is conclusive, and has not, in fact, been answered.

With such a tower of strength to back both his arguments and his conscience, it may be imagined that Mr. Harding has never felt any compunction as to receiving his quarterly sum of two hundred pounds. Indeed, the subject has never presented itself to his mind in that shape. He has talked not infrequently, and heard very much, about the wills of old founders and the incomes arising from their estates, during the last year or two. He did even, at one moment, feel a doubt (since expelled by his son-in-law's logic) as to whether Lord Guildford was clearly entitled to receive so enormous an income as he does from the revenues of St. Cross. But that he himself was overpaid with his modest eight hundred pounds—he who out of that voluntarily gave up sixty-two pounds eleven shillings and four-pence a year to his twelve old neighbors—he who, for the money, does his Precentor's work as no precentor has done it before since Barchester Cathedral was built—such an idea has never sullied his quiet, or disturbed his conscience.

Nevertheless, Mr. Harding is becoming uneasy at the rumor which he knows to prevail in Barchester on the subject. He is aware that at any rate two of his old men have been heard to say that if everyone had his own, they might each have their hundred pounds a year and live like gentlemen, instead of a beggarly one shilling and sixpence a day; and that they had slender cause to be thankful for a miserable dole of twopence when Mr. Harding and Mr. Chadwick between them ran away with thousands of pounds which good old John Hiram never intended for the like of them. It is the ingratitude of this which stings Mr. Harding. One of this discontented pair, Abel Handy, was put into the hospital by himself. He had been a stonemason in Barchester, and had broken his thigh by a fall from a scaffolding while employed about the cathedral, and Mr. Harding had given him the first vacancy in the hospital after the occurrence, although Dr. Grantly had been very anxious to put into it an insufferable clerk of his at Plumstead Episcopi, who had lost all his teeth, and whom the Archdeacon hardly knew how to get rid of by other means. Dr. Grantly has not forgotten to remind Mr. Harding how well satisfied with his one and sixpence a day old Joe Mutters would have been, and how injudicious it was on the part of Mr. Harding to allow a radical from the town to get into the concern. Probably Dr. Grantly forgot at the moment that the charity was intended for broken-down journeymen of Barchester.

There is living at Barchester a young man, a surgeon, named John Bold, and both Mr. Harding and Dr. Grantly are well aware that to him is owing the pestilent, rebellious feeling which has shown itself in the hospital. Yes, and the renewal, too, of that disagreeable talk about Hiram's estates which is now again prevalent in Barchester. Nevertheless, Mr. Harding and Mr. Bold are acquainted with each other. We may say are friends, considering the great disparity in their years. Dr. Grantly, however, has a holy horror of the impious demagogue, as on one occasion he called Bold when speaking of him to the Precentor; and being a more prudent, far-seeing man than Mr. Harding, and possessed of a stronger head, he already perceives that this John Bold will work great trouble in Barchester. He considers that he is to be regarded as an enemy, and thinks that he should not be admitted into the camp on anything like friendly terms. As John Bold will occupy much of our attention, we must endeavor to explain who he is, and why he takes the part of John Hiram's bedesmen.

John Bold is a young surgeon who passed many of his boyish years at Barchester. His father was a physician in the city of London, where he made a moderate fortune, which he invested in houses in that city. The Dragon of Wantly inn and posting house belonged to him, also four shops in the High Street, and a moiety of the new row of genteel villas (so called in the advertisements) built outside the town just beyond Hiram's Hospital. To one of these Dr. Bold retired to spend the evening of his life, and to die, and here his son John spent his holidays, and afterward his Christmas vacation, when he went from school to study surgery in the London hospitals. Just as John Bold was entitled to write himself surgeon and apothecary, old Dr. Bold died, leaving his Barchester property to his son and a certain sum in the three per cents to his daughter Mary, who is some four or five years older than her brother.

John Bold determined to settle himself at Barchester and look after his own property, as well as the bones and bodies of such of his neighbors as would call upon him for assistance in their troubles. He therefore put up a large brass plate, with "John Bold, Surgeon" on it, to the great disgust of the nine practitioners who were already trying to get a living out of the bishop, dean, and canons, and began housekeeping with the aid of his sister. At this time he was not more than twenty-four years old, and though he has now been three years in Barchester, we have not heard that he has done much harm to the nine worthy practitioners. Indeed, their dread of him has died away, for in three years he has not taken three fees.

Nevertheless, John Bold is a clever man, and would, with practice, be a clever surgeon. But he has got quite into another line of life. Having enough to live on, he has not been forced to work for bread. He has declined to subject himself to what he calls the drudgery of the profession, by which, I believe, he means the general work of a practicing surgeon, and has found other employment. He frequently binds up the bruises and sets the limbs of such of the poorer classes as profess his way of thinking—but this he does for love. Now I will not say that the Archdeacon is strictly correct in stigmatizing John Bold as a demagogue, for I hardly know how extreme must be a man's opinions before he can be justly so called, but Bold is a strong reformer. His passion is the reform of all abuses; state abuses, church abuses, corporation abuses (he has got himself elected a town councilor of Barchester, and has so worried three consecutive mayors that it became somewhat difficult to find a fourth), abuses in medical practice, and general abuses in the world at large.

Bold is thoroughly sincere in his patriotic endeavors to mend mankind, and there is something to be admired in the energy with which he devotes himself to remedying evil and stopping injustice. But I fear that he is too much imbued with the idea that he has a special mission for reforming. It would be well if one so young had a little more diffidence himself, and more trust in the honest purposes of others—if he could be brought to believe that old customs need not necessarily be evil, and that changes may possibly be dangerous. But no, Bold has all the ardor and all the self-assurance of a Danton, and hurls his anathemas against time-honored practices with the violence of a French Jacobin.

No wonder that Dr. Grantly should regard Bold as a firebrand, falling, as he has done, almost in the center of the quiet, ancient close of Barchester Cathedral. Dr. Grantly would have him avoided as the plague, but the old Doctor and Mr. Harding were fast friends. Young Johnny Bold used to play as a boy on Mr. Harding's lawn. He has many a time won the Precentor's heart by listening with rapt attention to his sacred strains. And since those days, to tell the truth at once, he has nearly won another heart within the same walls.

Eleanor Harding has not plighted her troth to John Bold, nor has she, perhaps, owned to herself how dear to her the young reformer is, but she cannot endure that anyone should speak harshly of him. She does not dare to defend him when her brother-in-law is so loud against him, for she, like her father, is somewhat afraid of Dr. Grantly, but she is beginning greatly to dislike the Archdeacon. She persuades her father that it would be both unjust and injudicious to banish his young friend because of his politics. She cares little to go to houses where she will not meet him, and, in fact, she is in love.

Nor is there any good reason why Eleanor Harding should not love John Bold. He has all those qualities which are likely to touch a girl's heart. He is brave, eager, and amusing, well made and good-looking, young and enterprising. His character is in all respects good, he has sufficient income to support a wife, he is her father's friend, and above all, he is in love with her. Then why should not Eleanor Harding be attached to John Bold?

Dr. Grantly, who has as many eyes as Argus, and has long seen how the wind blows in that direction, thinks there are various strong reasons why this should not be so. He has not thought it wise as yet to speak to his father-in-law on the subject, for he knows how foolishly indulgent is Mr. Harding in everything that concerns his daughter. But he has discussed the matter with his all-trusted helpmate within that sacred recess formed by the clerical bed curtains of Plumstead Episcopi.

How much sweet solace, how much valued counsel, has our Archdeacon received within that sainted enclosure! 'Tis there alone that he unbends and comes down from his High Church pedestal to the level of a mortal man. In the world Dr. Grantly never lays aside that demeanor which so well becomes him. He has all the dignity of an ancient saint with the sleekness of a modern bishop. He is always the same, he is always the Archdeacon. Unlike Homer, he never nods. Even with his father-in-law, even with the Bishop and Dean, he maintains that sonorous tone and lofty deportment which strikes awe into the young hearts of Barchester and absolutely cows the whole parish of Plumstead Episcopi. 'Tis only when he has exchanged that ever-new shovel hat for a tasseled nightcap, and those shining black habiliments for his accustomed robe-de-nuit, that Dr. Grantly talks, and looks, and thinks like an ordinary man.

Many of us have often thought how severe a trial of faith must this be to the wives of our great church dignitaries. To us these men are personifications of St. Paul. Their very gait is a speaking sermon, their clean and somber apparel exacts from us faith and submission, and the cardinal virtues seem to hover round their sacred hats. A dean or an archbishop in the garb of his order is sure of our reverence, and a well-got-up bishop fills our very souls with awe. But how can this feeling be perpetuated in the bosoms of those who see the bishops without their aprons, and the archdeacons even in a lower state of dishabille?

Do we not all know some reverend, all but sacred, personage before whom our tongue ceases to be loud, and our step to be elastic? But were we once to see him stretch himself beneath the bedclothes, yawn widely, and bury his face upon his pillow, we could chatter before him as glibly as before a doctor or a lawyer. From some such cause, doubtless, it arose that our Archdeacon listened to the counsels of his wife, though he considered himself entitled to give counsel to every other being whom he met.

"My dear," he said, as he adjusted the copious folds of his nightcap, "there was that John Bold at your father's again today. I must say your father is very imprudent."

"He is imprudent—he always was," replied Mrs. Grantly, speaking from under the comfortable bedclothes. "There's nothing new in that."

"No, my dear, there's nothing new—I know that. But at the present juncture of affairs, such imprudence is—is—— I'll tell you what, my dear, if he does not take care what he's about, John Bold will be off with Eleanor."

"I think he will, whether Papa takes care or no. And why not?"

"Why not!" almost screamed the Archdeacon, giving so rough a pull at his nightcap as almost to bring it over his nose. "Why not!—That pestilent, interfering upstart, John Bold—the most vulgar young person I ever met! Do you know that he is meddling with your father's affairs in a most uncalled for—most——" And being at a loss for an epithet sufficiently injurious, he finished his expressions of horror by muttering "Good heavens!" in a manner that had been found very efficacious in clerical meetings of the diocese. He must for the moment have forgotten where he was.

"As to his vulgarity, Archdeacon," (Mrs. Grantly had never assumed a more familiar term than this in addressing her husband) "I don't agree with you. Not that I like Mr. Bold—he is a great deal too conceited for me. But then Eleanor does, and it would be the best thing in the world for Papa if they were to marry. Bold would never trouble himself about Hiram's Hospital if he were Papa's son-in-law." And the lady turned herself round under the bedclothes in a manner to which the Doctor was well accustomed, and which told him, as plainly as words, that as far as she was concerned the subject was over for that night.

"Good heavens!" murmured the Doctor again. He was evidently much put beside himself.

Dr. Grantly was by no means a bad man. He was exactly the man which such an education as his was most likely to form, his intellect being sufficient for such a place in the world, but not sufficient to put him in advance of it. He performed with a rigid constancy such of the duties of a parish clergyman as were, to his thinking, above the sphere of his curate, but it is as an archdeacon that he shone.

We believe, as a general rule, that either a bishop or his archdeacons have sinecures. Where a bishop works, archdeacons have but little to do, and vice versa. In the diocese of Barchester the Archdeacon of Barchester did the work. In that capacity he was diligent, authoritative, and, as his friends particularly boasted, judicious. His great fault was an overbearing assurance of the virtues and claims of his order, and his great foible an equally strong confidence in the dignity of his own manner and the eloquence of his own words. He was a moral man, believing the precepts which he taught, and believing also that he acted up to them, though we cannot say that he would give his coat to the man who took his cloak, or that he was prepared to forgive his brother even seven times. He was severe enough in exacting his dues, considering that any laxity in this respect would endanger the security of the Church, and could he have had his way, he would have consigned to darkness and perdition not only every individual reformer, but every committee and every commission that would even dare to ask a question respecting the appropriation of church revenues.

"They are church revenues. The laity admit it. Surely the Church is able to administer her own revenues." 'Twas thus he was accustomed to argue when the sacrilegious doings of Lord John Russell and others were discussed either at Barchester or at Oxford.

It was no wonder that Dr. Grantly did not like John Bold, and that his wife's suggestion that he should become closely connected with such a man dismayed him. To give him his dues, we must admit that the Archdeacon never wanted courage. He was quite willing to meet his enemy on any field and with any weapon. He had that belief in his own arguments that he felt sure of success, could he only be sure of a fair fight on the part of his adversary. He had no idea that John Bold could really prove that the income of the hospital was malappropriated. Why, then, should peace be sought for on such bad terms? What! Bribe an unbelieving enemy of the Church with the sister-in-law of one dignitary and the daughter of another—with a young lady whose connections with the diocese and chapter of Barchester were so close as to give her an undeniable claim to a husband endowed with some of its sacred wealth! When Dr. Grantly talks of unbelieving enemies, he does not mean to imply want of belief in the doctrines of the Church, but an equally dangerous skepticism as to its purity in money matters.

Mrs. Grantly is not usually deaf to the claims of the high order to which she belongs. She and her husband rarely disagree as to the tone with which the Church should be defended. How singular, then, that in such a case as this she should be willing to succumb! The Archdeacon again murmurs "Good heavens!" as he lays himself beside her, but he does so in a voice audible only to himself, and he repeats it till sleep relieves him from deep thought.

Mr. Harding himself has seen no reason why his daughter should not love John Bold. He has not been unobservant of her feelings, and perhaps his deepest regret at the part which he fears Bold is about to take regarding the hospital arises from a dread that he may be separated from his daughter, or that she may be separated from the man she loves. He has never spoken to Eleanor about her lover. He is the last man in the world to allude to such a subject unconsulted, even with his own daughter. And had he considered that he had ground to disapprove of Bold, he would have removed her or forbidden him his house, but he saw no such ground. He would probably have preferred a second clerical son-in-law, for Mr. Harding also is attached to his order, and, failing in that, he would at any rate have wished that so near a connection should have thought alike with him on church matters. He would not, however, reject the man his daughter loved because he differed on such subjects with himself.

Hitherto Bold had taken no steps in the matter in any way annoying to Mr. Harding personally. Some months since, after a severe battle, which cost him not a little money, he gained a victory over a certain old turnpike woman in the neighborhood, of whose charges another old woman had complained to him. He got the Act of Parliament relating to the trust, found that his protégée had been wrongly taxed, rode through the gate himself, paying the toll, then brought an action against the gatekeeper, and proved that all people coming up a certain by-lane, and going down a certain other by-lane, were toll-free. The fame of his success spread widely abroad, and he began to be looked on as the upholder of the rights of the poor of Barchester. Not long after this success, he heard from different quarters that Hiram's bedesmen were treated as paupers, whereas the property to which they were, in effect, heirs was very large; and he was instigated by the lawyer whom he had employed in the case of the turnpike to call upon Mr. Chadwick for a statement as to the funds of the estate.

Bold had often expressed his indignation at the malappropriation of church funds in general, in the hearing of his friend the Precentor, but the conversation had never referred to anything at Barchester, and when Finney, the attorney, induced him to interfere with the affairs of the hospital, it was against Mr. Chadwick that his efforts were to be directed. Bold soon found that if he interfered with Mr. Chadwick as steward, he must also interfere with Mr. Harding as warden, and though he regretted the situation in which this would place him, he was not the man to flinch from his undertaking from personal motives.

As soon as he had determined to take the matter in hand, he set about his work with his usual energy. He got a copy of John Hiram's will, of the wording of which he made himself perfectly master. He ascertained the extent of the property and as nearly as he could the value of it, and made out a schedule of what he was informed was the present distribution of its income. Armed with these particulars, he called on Mr. Chadwick, having given that gentleman notice of his visit, and asked him for a statement of the income and expenditure of the hospital for the last twenty-five years.

This was of course refused, Mr. Chadwick alleging that he had no authority for making public the concerns of a property in managing which he was only a paid servant.

"And who is competent to give you that authority, Mr. Chadwick?" asked Bold.

"Only those who employ me, Mr. Bold," said the Steward.

"And who are those, Mr. Chadwick?" demanded Bold.

Mr. Chadwick begged to say that if these inquiries were made merely out of curiosity, he must decline answering them. If Mr. Bold had any ulterior proceeding in view, perhaps it would be desirable that any necessary information should be sought for in a professional way by a professional man. Mr. Chadwick's attorneys were Messrs. Cox and Cummins, of Lincoln's Inn. Mr. Bold took down the address of Cox and Cummins, remarked that the weather was cold for the time of the year, and wished Mr. Chadwick good morning. Mr. Chadwick said it was cold for June, and bowed him out.

He at once went to his lawyer, Finney. Now Bold was not very fond of his attorney, but, as he said, he merely wanted a man who knew the forms of law and who would do what he was told for his money. He had no idea of putting himself in the hands of a lawyer. He wanted law from a lawyer as he did a coat from a tailor, because he could not make it so well himself, and he thought Finney the fittest man in Barchester for his purpose. In one respect, at any rate, he was right. Finney was humility itself.

Finney advised an instant letter to Cox and Cummins, mindful of his six and eightpence. "Slap at them at once, Mr. Bold. Demand categorically and explicitly a full statement of the affairs of the hospital."

"Suppose I were to see Mr. Harding first," suggested Bold.

"Yes, yes, by all means," said the acquiescing Finney. "Though perhaps, as Mr. Harding is no man of business, it may lead—lead to some little difficulties. But perhaps you're right. Mr. Bold, I don't think seeing Mr. Harding can do any harm." Finney saw from the expression of his client's face that he intended to have his own way.

CHAPTER III

THE BISHOP OF BARCHESTER

BOLD at once repaired to the hospital. The day was now far advanced, but he knew that Mr. Harding dined in the summer at four, that Eleanor was accustomed to drive in the evening, and that he might therefore probably find Mr. Harding alone. It was between seven and eight when he reached the slight iron gate leading into the Precentor's garden, and though, as Mr. Chadwick observed, the day had been cold for June, the evening was mild and soft and sweet. The little gate was open. As he raised the latch he heard the notes of Mr. Harding's violoncello from the far end of the garden and, advancing before the house and across the lawn, he found him playing—and not without an audience. The musician was seated in a garden chair just within the summerhouse, so as to allow the violoncello which he held between his knees to rest upon the dry stone flooring. Before him stood a rough music desk, on which was open a page of that dear, sacred book, that much-labored and much-loved volume of church music which had cost so many guineas. And around sat, and lay, and stood, and leaned ten of the twelve old men who dwelt with him beneath old John Hiram's roof. The two reformers were not there. I will not say that in their hearts they were conscious of any wrong done or to be done to their mild warden, but latterly they had kept aloof from him, and his music was no longer to their taste.

It was amusing to see the positions and eager, listening faces of these well-to-do old men. I will not say that they all appreciated the music which they heard, but they were intent on appearing to do so. Pleased at being where they were, they were determined, as far as in them lay, to give pleasure in return, and they were not unsuccessful. It gladdened the Precentor's heart to think that the old bedesmen whom he loved so well admired the strains which were to him so full of almost ecstatic joy, and he used to boast that such was the air of the hospital as to make it a precinct specially fit for the worship of St. Cecilia.

Immediately before him, on the extreme corner of the bench which ran round the summerhouse, sat one old man, with his handkerchief smoothly laid upon his knees, who did enjoy the moment, or acted enjoyment well. He was one on whose large frame many years, for he was over eighty, had made small havoc. He was still an upright, burly, handsome figure, with an open, ponderous brow, round which clung a few, though very few, thin gray locks. The coarse black gown of the hospital, the breeches and buckled shoes, became him well, and as he sat with his hands folded on his staff and his chin resting on his hands, he was such a listener as most musicians would be glad to welcome.

This man was certainly the pride of the hospital. It had always been the custom that one should be selected as being to some extent in authority over the others, and though Mr. Bunce—for such was his name, and so he was always designated by his inferior brethren—had no greater emoluments than they, he had assumed, and well knew how to maintain, the dignity of his elevation. The Precentor delighted to call him his subwarden, and was not ashamed, occasionally, when no other guest was there, to bid him sit down by the same parlor fire and drink the full glass of port which was placed near him. Bunce never went without the second glass, but no entreaty ever made him take a third.

"Well, well, Mr. Harding, you're too good, much too good," he'd always say as the second glass was filled. But when that was drunk and the half-hour over, Bunce stood erect, and with a benediction which his patron valued, retired to his own abode. He knew the world too well to risk the comfort of such halcyon moments by prolonging them till they were disagreeable.

Mr. Bunce, as may be imagined, was most strongly opposed to innovation. Not even Dr. Grantly had a more holy horror of those who would interfere in the affairs of the hospital. He was every inch a churchman, and though he was not very fond of Dr. Grantly personally, that arose from there not being room in the hospital for two people so much alike as the Doctor and himself rather than from any dissimilarity in feeling. Mr. Bunce was inclined to think that the Warden and himself could manage the hospital without further assistance, and that though the Bishop was the constitutional visitor, and as such entitled to special reverence from all connected with John Hiram's will, John Hiram never intended that his affairs should be interfered with by an archdeacon.

At the present moment, however, these cares were off his mind, and he was looking at his Warden as though he thought the music heavenly, and the musician hardly less so.

As Bold walked silently over the lawn, Mr. Harding did not at first perceive him, and continued to draw his bow slowly across the plaintive wires. But he soon found from his audience that some stranger was there and, looking up, began to welcome his young friend wth frank hospitality.

"Pray, Mr. Harding—— Pray don't let me disturb you," said Bold. "You know how fond I am of sacred music."

"Oh, it's nothing!" said the Precentor, shutting up the book and then opening it again as he saw the delightfully imploring look of his old friend Bunce. Oh, Bunce, Bunce, Bunce, I fear that after all thou art but a flatterer. "Well, I'll just finish it then. It's a favorite little bit of Bishop's. And then, Mr. Bold, we'll have a stroll and a chat till Eleanor comes in and gives us tea." And so Bold sat down on the soft turf to listen, or rather to think how, after such sweet harmony, he might best introduce a theme of so much discord to disturb the peace of him who was so ready to welcome him kindly.

Bold thought that the performance was soon over, for he felt that he had a somewhat difficult task, and he almost regretted the final leave-taking of the last of the old men, slow as they were in going through their adieus.

Bold's heart was in his mouth as the Precentor made some ordinary but kind remark as to the friendliness of the visit.

"One evening call," said he, "is worth ten in the morning. It's all formality in the morning. Real social talk never begins till after dinner. That's why I dine early, so as to get as much as I can of it."

"Quite true, Mr. Harding," said the other. "But I fear I've reversed the order of things, and I owe you much apology for troubling you on business at such an hour. But it is on business that I have called just now."

Mr. Harding looked blank and annoyed. There was something in the tone of the young man's voice which told him that the interview was intended to be disagreeable, and he shrank back at finding his kindly greeting so repulsed.

"I wish to speak to you about the hospital," continued Bold.

"Well, well, anything I can tell you I shall be most happy——"

"It's about the accounts."

"Then, my dear fellow, I can tell you nothing, for I'm as ignorant as a child. All I know is that they pay me eight hundred pounds a year. Go to Chadwick, he knows all about the accounts. And now tell me, will poor Mary Jones ever get the use of her limb again?"

"Well, I think she will, if she's careful. But, Mr. Harding, I hope you won't object to discuss with me what I have to say about the hospital."

Mr. Harding gave a deep, long-drawn sigh. He did object, very strongly object, to discuss any such subject with John Bold, but he had not the business tact of Mr. Chadwick and did not know how to relieve himself from the coming evil. He sighed sadly, but made no answer.

"I have the greatest regard for you, Mr. Harding," continued Bold, "the truest respect, the most sincere——"

"Thank ye, thank ye, Mr. Bold," interjaculated the Precentor somewhat impatiently. "I'm much obliged, but never mind that. I'm as likely to be in the wrong as another man—quite as likely."

"But, Mr. Harding, I must express what I feel, lest you should think there is personal enmity in what I'm going to do."

"Personal enmity! Going to do! Why you're not going to cut my throat, nor put me into the Ecclesiastical Court!"

Bold tried to laugh, but he couldn't. He was quite in earnest, and determined in his course, and couldn't make a joke of it. He walked on awhile in silence before he recommenced his attack, during which Mr. Harding, who had still the bow in his hand, played rapidly on an imaginary violoncello. "I fear there is reason to think that John Hiram's will is not carried out to the letter, Mr. Harding," said the young man at last, "and I have been asked to see into it."

"Very well, I've no objection on earth. And now we need not say another word about it."

"Only one word more, Mr. Harding. Chadwick has referred me to Cox and Cummins, and I think it my duty to apply to them for some statement about the hospital. In what I do I may appear to be interfering with you, and I hope you will forgive me for doing so."

"Mr. Bold," said the other, stopping and speaking with some solemnity, "if you act justly, say nothing in this matter but the truth, and use no unfair weapons in carrying out your purposes, I shall have nothing to forgive. I presume you think I am not entitled to the income I receive from the hospital, and that others are entitled to it. Whatever some may do, I shall never attribute to you base motives because you hold an opinion opposed to my own, and adverse to my interests. Pray do what you consider to be your duty. I can give you no assistance, neither will I offer you any obstacle. Let me, however, suggest to you that you can in no wise forward your views nor I mine by any discussion between us. Here comes Eleanor and the ponies, and we'll go in to tea."

Bold, however, felt that he could not sit down at ease with Mr. Harding and his daughter after what had passed and therefore excused himself with much awkward apology, and merely raising his hat and bowing as he passed Eleanor and the pony chair, left her in disappointed amazement at his departure.

Mr. Harding's demeanor certainly impressed Bold with a full conviction that he as warden felt that he stood on strong grounds, and almost made him think that he was about to interfere without due warrant in the private affairs of a just and honorable man. But Mr. Harding himself was anything but satisfied with his own view of the case.

In the first place, he wished for Eleanor's sake to think well of Bold and to like him, and yet he could not but feel disgusted at the arrogance of his conduct. What right had he to say that John Hiram's will was not fairly carried out? But then the question would arise within his heart—Was that will fairly acted on? Did John Hiram mean that the warden of his hospital should receive considerably more out of the legacy than all the twelve old men together for whose behoof the hospital was built? Could it be possible that John Bold was right, and that the Reverend Warden of the hospital had been for the last ten years and more the unjust recipient of an income legally and equitably belonging to others? What if it should be proved before the light of day that he, whose life had been so happy, so quiet, so respected, had absorbed eight thousand pounds to which he had no title, and which he could never repay? I do not say that he feared that such was really the case. But the first shade of doubt now fell across his mind, and from this evening, for many a long, long day, our good, kind, loving Warden was neither happy nor at ease.

Thoughts of this kind, these first moments of much misery, oppressed Mr. Harding as he sat sipping his tea, absent and ill at ease. Poor Eleanor felt that all was not right, but her ideas as to the cause of the evening's discomfort did not go beyond her lover and his sudden and uncivil departure. She thought there must have been some quarrel between Bold and her father, and she was half-angry with both, though she did not attempt to explain to herself why she was so.

Mr. Harding thought long and deeply over these things, both before he went to bed and after it as he lay awake questioning within himself the validity of his claim to the income which he enjoyed. It seemed clear at any rate that, however unfortunate he might be at having been placed in such a position, no one could say that he ought either to have refused the appointment first, or to have rejected the income afterward. All the world—meaning the ecclesiastical world as confined to the English Church—knew that the wardenship of the Barchester Hóspital was a snug sinecure, but no one had ever been blamed for accepting it. To how much blame, however, would he have been open had he rejected it! How mad would he have been thought had he declared, when the situation was vacant and offered to him, that he had scruples as to receiving eight hundred pounds a year from John Hiram's property and that he had rather some stranger should possess it! How would Dr. Grantly have shaken his wise head, and have consulted with his friends in the close as to some decent retreat for the coming insanity of the poor minor canon! If he was right in accepting the place, it was clear to him also that he would be wrong in rejecting any part of the income attached to it. The patronage was a valuable appanage of the bishopric, and surely it would not be his duty to lessen the value of that preferment which had been bestowed on himself! Surely he was bound to stand by his order!

But somehow these arguments, though they seemed logical, were not satisfactory. Was John Hiram's will fairly carried out? That was the true question. And if not, was it not his especial duty to see that this was done—his especial duty, whatever injury it might do to his order, however ill such duty might be received by his patron and his friends? At the idea of his friends, his mind turned unhappily to his son-in-law. He knew well how strongly he would be supported by Dr. Grantly if he could bring himself to put his case into the Archdeacon's hands, and to allow him to fight the battle. But he knew also that he would find no sympathy there for his doubts, no friendly feeling, no inward comfort. Dr. Grantly would be ready enough to take up his cudgel against all comers on behalf of the Church Militant, but he would do so on the distasteful ground of the Church's infallibility. Such a contest would give no comfort to Mr. Harding's doubts. He was not so anxious to prove himself right as to be so.

I have said before that Dr. Grantly was the working man of the diocese, and that his father, the Bishop, was somewhat inclined to an idle life. So it was, but the Bishop, though he had never been an active man, was one whose qualities had rendered him dear to all who knew him. He was the very opposite to his son. He was a bland and a kind old man, opposed by every feeling to authoritative demonstrations and episcopal ostentation. It was perhaps well for him, in his situation, that his son had early in life been able to do that which he could not well do when he was younger, and which he could not have done at all now that he was over seventy. The Bishop knew how to entertain the clergy of his diocese, to talk easy small talk with the rectors' wives, and put curates at their ease. But it required the strong hand of the Archdeacon to deal with such as were refractory either in their doctrines or their lives.

The Bishop and Mr. Harding loved each other warmly. They had grown old together, and had together spent many, many years in clerical pursuits and clerical conversation. When one of them was a bishop and the other only a minor canon, they were even then much together, but since their children had married, and Mr. Harding had become Warden and Precentor, they were all in all to each other. I will not say that they managed the diocese between them, but they spent much time in discussing the man who did, and in forming little plans to mitigate his wrath against church delinquents and soften his aspirations for church dominion.

Mr. Harding determined to open his mind and confess his doubts to his old friend, and to him he went on the morning after John Bold's uncourteous visit.

Up to this period no rumor of these cruel proceedings against the hospital had reached the Bishop's ears. He had doubtless heard that men existed who questioned his right to present to a sinecure of eight hundred pounds a year, as he had heard from time to time of some special immorality or disgraceful disturbance in the usually decent and quiet city of Barchester. But all he did, and all he was called on to do, on such occasions was to shake his head, and to beg his son, the great dictator, to see that no harm happened to the Church.

It was a long story that Mr. Harding had to tell before he made the Bishop comprehend his own view of the case, but we need not follow him through the tale. At first the Bishop counseled but one step, recommended but one remedy, had but one medicine in his whole pharmacopoeia strong enough to touch so grave a disorder. He prescribed the Archdeacon. "Refer him to the Archdeacon," he repeated as Mr. Harding spoke of Bold and his visit. "The Archdeacon will set you quite right about that," he kindly said when his friend spoke with hesitation of the justness of his cause. "No man has got up all that so well as the Archdeacon." But the dose, though large, failed to quiet the patient. Indeed, it almost produced nausea.

"But, Bishop," said he, "did you ever read John Hiram's will?"

The Bishop thought probably he had, thirty-five years ago, when first instituted to his see, but could not state positively. However, he very well knew that he had the absolute right to present to the wardenship, and that the income of the warden had been regularly settled.

"But, Bishop, the question is, who has the power to settle it? If, as this young man says, the will provides that the proceeds of the property are to be divided into shares, who has the power to alter these provisions?"

The Bishop had an indistinct idea that they altered themselves by the lapse of years, that a kind of ecclesiastical statute of limitation barred the rights of the twelve bedesmen to any increase of income arising from the increased value of property. He said something about tradition, more of the many learned men who by their practice had confirmed the present arrangement, then went at some length into the propriety of maintaining the due difference in rank and income between a beneficed clergyman and certain poor old men who were dependent on charity, and concluded his argument by another reference to the Archdeacon.

The Precentor sat thoughtfully gazing at the fire, and listening to the good-natured reasoning of his friend. What the Bishop said had a sort of comfort in it, but it was not a sustaining comfort. It made Mr. Harding feel that many others—indeed, all others of his own order—would think him right, but it failed to prove to him that he truly was so.

"Bishop," said he, at last, after both had sat silent for a while, "I should deceive you and myself too if I did not tell you that I am very unhappy about this. Suppose that I cannot bring myself to agree with Dr. Grantly —that I find, after inquiry, that the young man is right, and that I am wrong —what then?"

The two old men were sitting near each other—so near that the Bishop was able to lay his hand upon the other's knee, and he did so with a gentle pressure. Mr. Harding well knew what that pressure meant. The Bishop had no further argument to adduce. He could not fight for the cause as his son would do, he could not prove all the Precentor's doubts to be groundless, but he could sympathize with his friend, and he did so; and Mr. Harding felt that he had received that for which he came. There was another period of silence, after which the Bishop asked with a degree of irritable energy very unusual with him whether this "pestilent intruder" —meaning John Bold—had any friends in Barchester.

Mr. Harding had fully made up his mind to tell the Bishop everything, to speak of his daughter's love as well as his own troubles, to talk of John Bold in his double capacity of future son-in-law and present enemy, and though he felt it to be sufficiently disagreeable, now was his time to do it.

"He is very intimate at my own house, Bishop." The Bishop stared. He was not so far gone in orthodoxy and church militancy as his son, but still he could not bring himself to understand how so declared an enemy of the Establishment could be admitted on terms of intimacy into the house not only of so firm a pillar as Mr. Harding, but one so much injured as the Warden of the hospital.

"Indeed, I like Mr. Bold much, personally," continued the disinterested victim. "And to tell you the 'truth' "—he hesitated as he brought out the dreadful tidings—"I have sometimes thought it not improbable that he would be my second son-in-law." The Bishop did not whistle. We believe that they lose the power of doing so on being consecrated, and that in these days one might as easily meet a corrupt judge as a whistling bishop, but he looked as though he would have done so but for his apron.

What a brother-in-law for the Archdeacon! What an alliance for Barchester close! What a connection for even the episcopal palace! The Bishop, in his simple mind, felt no doubt that John Bold, had he so much power, would shut up all cathedrals and probably all parish churches; distribute all tithes among Methodists, Baptists, and other savage tribes; utterly annihilate the sacred bench, and make shovel hats and lawn sleeves as illegal as cowls, sandals, and sackcloth! Here was a nice man to be initiated into the comfortable arcana of ecclesiastical snuggeries, one who doubted the integrity of parsons, and probably disbelieved the Trinity!

Mr. Harding saw what an effect his communication had made, and almost repented the openness of his disclosure. He, however, did what he could to moderate the grief of his friend and patron. "I do not say that there is any engagement between them. Had there been, Eleanor would have told me. I know her well enough to be assured that she would have done so. But I see that they are fond of each other, and as a man and a father, I have had no objection to urge against their intimacy."

"But, Mr. Harding," said the Bishop, "how are you to oppose him it he is your son-in-law?"

"I don't mean to oppose him. It is he who opposes me. If anything is to be done in defense, I suppose Chadwick will do it. I suppose——"

"Oh, the Archdeacon will see to that. Were the young man twice his brother-in-law, the Archdeacon will never be deterred from doing what he feels to be right."

Mr. Harding reminded the Bishop that the Archdeacon and the reformer were not yet brothers, and very probably never would be, exacted from him a promise that Eleanor's name should not be mentioned in any discussion between the father Bishop and son Archdeacon respecting the hospital, and then took his departure, leaving his poor old friend bewildered, amazed, and confounded.

CHAPTER IV

HIRAM'S BEDESMEN

The parties most interested in the movement which is about to set Barchester by the ears were not the foremost to discuss the merit of the question, as is often the case. But when the Bishop, the Archdeacon, the Warden, the Steward, and Messrs. Cox and Cummins were all busy with the matter, each in his own way, it is not to be supposed that Hiram's bedesmen themselves were altogether passive spectators. Finney, the attorney, had been among them, asking sly questions and raising immoderate hopes, creating a party hostile to the Warden and establishing a corps in the enemy's camp, as he figuratively calls it to himself. Poor old men! Whoever may be righted or wronged by this inquiry, they at any rate will assuredly be only injured. To them it can only be an unmixed evil. How can their lot be improved? All their wants are supplied, every comfort is administered. They have warm houses, good clothes, plentiful diet, and rest after a life of labor, and above all, that treasure so inestimable in declining years, a true and kind friend to listen to their sorrows, watch over their sickness, and administer comfort as regards this world and the world to come!

John Bold sometimes thinks of this when he is talking loudly of the rights of the bedesmen whom he has taken under his protection, but he quiets the suggestion within his breast with the high-sounding name of justice. *"Fiat justitia ruat coelum."* These old men should, by rights, have one hundred pounds a year instead of one shilling and sixpence a day, and the Warden should have two hundred or three hundred pounds instead of eight hundred pounds. What is unjust must be wrong, what is wrong should be righted, and if he declined the task, who else would do it?

"Each one of you is clearly entitled to one hundred pounds a year by common law!" Such had been the important whisper made by Finney into the ears of Abel Handy, and by him retailed to his eleven brethren.

Too much must not be expected from the flesh and blood even of John

Hiram's bedesmen, and the positive promise of one hundred a year to each of the twelve old men had its way with most of them. The great Bunce was not to be wiled away, and was upheld in his orthodoxy by two adherents. Abel Handy, who was the leader of the aspirants after wealth, had, alas, a stronger following. No less than five of the twelve soon believed that his views were just, making with their leader a moiety of the hospital. The other three, volatile, unstable minds, vacillated between the two chieftains, now led away by the hope of gold, now anxious to propitiate the powers that still existed.

It had been proposed to address a petition to the Bishop as visitor, praying his lordship to see justice done to the legal recipients of John Hiram's charity, and to send copies of this petition and of the reply it would elicit to all the leading London papers, and thereby to obtain notoriety for the subject. This it was thought would pave the way for ulterior legal proceedings. It would have been a great thing to have had the signatures and marks of all the twelve injured legatees, but this was impossible. Bunce would have cut his hand off sooner than have signed it. It was then suggested by Finney that if even eleven could be induced to sanction the document, the one obstinate recusant might have been represented as unfit to judge on such a question—in fact, as being non compos mentis—and the petition would have been taken as representing the feeling of the men. But this could not be done. Bunce's friends were as firm as himself, and as yet only six crosses adorned the document. It was the more provoking as Bunce himself could write his name legibly, and one of those three doubting souls had for years boasted of like power, and possessed, indeed, a Bible in which he was proud to show his name written by himself some thirty years ago—"Job Skulpit." But it was thought that Job Skulpit, having forgotten his scholarship, on that account recoiled from the petition, and that the other doubters would follow as he led them. A petition signed by half the hospital would have but a poor effect.

It was in Skulpit's room that the petition was now lying, waiting such additional signatures as Abel Handy, by his eloquence, could obtain for it. The six marks it bore were duly attested, thus:

his	his	his
Abel+Handy,	Gregy+Moody,	Mathew+Spriggs,
mark	mark	mark

&c., and places were duly designated in pencil for those brethren who were now expected to join. For Skulpit alone was left a spot on which his genuine signature might be written in fair clerklike style. Handy had brought in the document and spread it out on the small deal table, and was now standing by it persuasive and eager. Moody had followed with an inkhorn, carefully left behind by Finney, and Spriggs bore aloft, as though it were a sword, a well-worn ink-black pen, which from time to time he endeavored to thrust into Skulpit's unwilling hand.

With the learned man were his two abettors in indecision, William Gazy and Jonathan Crumple. If ever the petition were to be forwarded, now was the time—so said Mr. Finney—and great was the anxiety on the part of those whose one hundred pounds a year, as they believed, mainly depended on the document in question.

"To be kept out of all that money," as the avaricious Moody had muttered to his friend Handy, "by an old fool saying that he can write his own name like his betters!"

"Well, Job," said Handy, trying to impart to his own sour, ill-omened visage a smile of approbation, in which he greatly failed, "so you're ready now, Mr. Finney says. Here's the place, d'ye see."—and he put his huge brown finger down on the dirty paper. "Name or mark, it's all one. Come along, old boy. If so be we're to have the spending of this money, why the sooner the better—that's my maxim."

"To be sure," said Moody. "We ain't none of us so young, we can't stay waiting for old Catgut no longer."

It was thus these miscreants named our excellent friend. The nickname he could easily have forgiven, but the allusion to the divine source of all his melodious joy would have irritated even him. Let us hope he never knew the insult.

"Only think, old Billy Gazy," said Spriggs, who rejoiced in greater youth than his brethren, but having fallen into a fire when drunk, had had one eye burnt out, one cheek burnt through, and one arm nearly burnt off, and who therefore in regard to personal appearance was not the most prepossessing of men, "a hundred a year, and all to spend. Only think, old Billy Gazy." And he gave a hideous grin that showed off his misfortunes to their full extent.

Old Billy Gazy was not alive to much enthusiasm. Even these golden prospects did not arouse him to do more than rub his poor old bleared eyes with the cuff of his bedesman's gown, and gently mutter he didn't know, not he, he didn't know.

"But you'd know, Jonathan," continued Spriggs, turning to the other friend of Skulpit's, who was sitting on a stool by the table, gazing vacantly at the petition. Jonathan Crumple was a meek, mild man who had known better days. His means had been wasted by bad children, who had made his life wretched till he had been received into the hospital, of which he had not long been a member. Since that day he had known neither sorrow nor trouble, and this attempt to fill him with new hopes was indeed a cruelty.

"A hundred a year's a nice thing, for sartain, neighbor Spriggs," said he. "I once had nigh to that myself, but it didn't do me no good." And he gave a low sigh as he thought of the children of his own loins who had robbed him.

"And shall have again, Jonathan," said Handy, "and will have someone to keep it right and tight for you this time."

Crumple sighed again. He had learned the impotency of wordly wealth, and would have been satisfied, if left untempted, to have remained happy with one and sixpence a day.

"Come, Skulpit," repeated Handy, getting impatient, "you're not going to go along with old Bunce in helping that parson to rob us all. Take the pen, man, and right yourself. Well," he added, seeing that Skulpit still doubted, "to see a man as is afraid to stand by hisself is, to my thinking, the meanest thing as is."

"Sink them all for parsons, says I," growled Moody. "Hungry beggars, as never thinks their bellies full till they have robbed all and everything!"

"Who's to harm you, man?" argued Spriggs. "Let them look never so black at you, they can't get you put out when you're once in—no, not old Catgut, with Calves to help him!" I am sorry to say the Archdeacon himself was designated by this scurrilous allusion to his nether person.

"A hundred a year to win, and nothing to lose," continued Handy, "my eyes!—Well, how a man's to doubt about sich a bit of cheese as that passes me. But some men is timorous—some men is born with no pluck in them—some men is cowed at the very first sight of a gentleman's coat and waistcoat."

Oh, Mr. Harding, if you had but taken the Archdeacon's advice in that disputed case when Joe Mutters was this ungrateful demagogue's rival candidate!

"Afraid of a parson," growled Moody, with a look of ineffable scorn. "I tell ye what I'd be afraid of—I'd be afraid of not getting nothing from 'em but just what I could take by might and right. That's the most I'd be afraid on of any parson of 'em all."

"But," said Skulpit, apologetically, "Mr. Harding's not so bad. He did give us twopence a day, didn't he now?"

"Twopence a day!" exclaimed Spriggs with scorn, opening awfully the red cavern of his lost eye.

"Twopence a day!" muttered Moody with a curse. "Sink his twopence!"

"Twopence a day!" exclaimed Handy. "And I'm to go, hat in hand, and thank a chap for twopence a day when he owes me a hundred pounds a year. No, thank ye, that may do for you, but it won't for me. Come, I say, Skulpit, are you a going to put your mark to this here paper, or are you not?"

Skulpit looked round in wretched indecision to his two friends. "What d'ye think, Bill Gazy?" said he.

But Billy Gazy couldn't think. He made a noise like the bleating of an old sheep, which was intended to express the agony of his doubt, and again muttered that he didn't know.

"Take hold, you old cripple," said Handy, thrusting the pen into poor Billy's hand. "There, so—ugh! you old fool, you've been and smeared it all. There—that'll do for you. That's as good as the best name as ever was written." And a big blotch of ink was presumed to represent Billy Gazy's acquiescence.

"Now, Jonathan," said Handy, turning to Crumple.

"A hundred a year's a nice thing, for sartain," again argued Crumple.

"Well, neighbor Skulpit, how's it to be?"

"Oh, please yourself," said Skulpit. "Please yourself and you'll please me."

The pen was thrust into Crumple's hand, and a faint, wandering, meaningless sign was made, betokening such sanction and authority as Jonathan Crumple was able to convey.

"Come, Job," said Handy, softened by success, "don't let 'em have to say that old Bunce has a man like you under his thumb—a man that always holds his head in the hospital as high as Bunce himself, though you're never axed to drink wine, and sneak, and tell lies about your betters, as he does."

Skulpit held the pen, and made little flourishes with it in the air, but still hesitated.

"And if you'll be said by me," continued Handy, "you'll not write your name to it at all, but just put your mark like the others." The cloud began to clear from Skulpit's brow. "We all know you can do it if you like, but maybe you wouldn't like to seem uppish, you know."

"Well, the mark would be best," said Skulpit. "One name and the rest marks wouldn't look well, would it?"

"The worst in the world," said Handy. "There—there." And stooping over the petition, the learned clerk made a huge cross on the place left for his signature.

"That's the game," said Handy, triumphantly pocketing the petition. "We're all in a boat now, that is, the nine of us. And as for old Bunce and his cronies, they may——" But as he was hobbling off to the door, with a crutch on one side and a stick on the other, he was met by Bunce himself.

"Well, Handy, and what may old Bunce do?" said the gray-haired, upright senior.

Handy muttered something and was departing, but he was stopped in the doorway by the huge frame of the newcomer.

"You've been doing no good here, Abel Handy," said he, "'tis plain to see that. And 'tisn't much good, I'm thinking, you ever do."

"I mind my own business, Master Bunce," muttered the other, "and do you do the same. It a'n't nothing to you what I does—and your spying and poking here won't do no good nor yet no harm."

"I suppose then, Job," continued Bunce, not noticing his opponent, "if the truth must out, you've stuck your name to that petition of theirs at last."

Skulpit looked as though he were about to sink into the ground with shame.

"What is it to you what he signs?" said Handy. "I suppose if we all wants to ax for our own, we needn't ax leave of you first, Mr. Bunce, big a man as you are. And as to your sneaking in here, into Job's room when he's busy, and where you're not wanted——"

"I've knowed Job Skulpit, man and boy, sixty years," said Bunce, looking at the man of whom he spoke, "and that's ever since the day he was born. I knowed the mother that bore him, when she and I were little wee things picking daisies together in the close yonder. And I've lived under the same roof with him more nor ten years, and after that I may come into his room without axing leave, and yet no sneaking neither."

"So you can, Mr. Bunce," said Skulpit, "so you can, any hour, day or night."

"And I'm free also to tell him my mind," continued Bunce, looking at the one man and addressing the other. "And I tell him now that he's done a foolish and a wrong thing. He's turned his back upon one who is his best friend, and is playing the game of others who care nothing for him, whether he be poor or rich, well or ill, alive or dead. A hundred a year? Are the lot of you soft enough to think that if a hundred a year be to be given, it's the likes of you that will get it?" And he pointed to Billy Gazy, Spriggs, and Crumple. "Did any of us ever do anything worth half the money? Was it to make gentlemen of us we were brought in here, when all the world turned against us and we couldn't longer earn our daily bread? A'n't you all as rich in your ways as he in his?" And the orator pointed to the side on which the Warden lived. "A'n't you getting all you hoped for—ay, and more than you hoped for? Wouldn't each of you have given the dearest limb of his body to secure that which now makes you so unthankful?"

"We wants what John Hiram left us," said Handy. "We wants what's ourn by law. It don't matter what we expected. What's ourn by law should be ourn, and by goles we'll have it."

"Law!" said Bunce, with all the scorn he knew how to command—"Law! Did ye ever know a poor man yet was the better for law, or for a lawyer? Will Mr. Finney ever be as good to you, Job, as that man has been? Will he see to you when you're sick, and comfort you when you're wretched? Will he——"

"No, nor give you port wine, old boy, on cold winter nights! He won't do that, will he?" asked Handy, and laughing at the severity of his own wit, he and his colleagues retired, carrying with them, however, the now powerful petition.

There is no help for spilt milk, and Mr. Bunce could only retire to his own room, disgusted at the frailty of human nature. Job Skulpit scratched his head. Jonathan Crumple again remarked, that, for sartain, sure a hundred a year was very nice—and Billy Gazy again rubbed his eyes, and lowly muttered that he didn't know.

CHAPTER V

DR. GRANTLY VISITS THE HOSPITAL

THOUGH doubt and hesitation disturbed the rest of our poor Warden, no such weakness perplexed the nobler breast of his son-in-law. As the indomitable cock preparing for the combat sharpens his spurs, shakes his feathers, and erects his comb, so did the Archdeacon arrange his weapons for the coming war, without misgiving and without fear. That he was fully confident of the justice of his cause let no one doubt. Many a man can fight his battle with good courage, but with a doubting conscience. Such was not the case with Dr. Grantly. He did not believe in the Gospel with more assurance than he did in the sacred justice of all ecclesiastical revenues. When he put his shoulder to the wheel to defend the income of the present and future precentors of Barchester, he was animated by as strong a sense of a holy cause as that which gives courage to a missionary in Africa, or enables a Sister of Mercy to give up the pleasures of the world for the wards of a hospital. He was about to defend the holy of holies from the touch of the profane, to guard the citadel of his Church from the most rampant of its enemies, to put on his good armor in the best of fights, and secure, if possible, the comforts of his creed for coming generations of ecclesiastical dignitaries. Such a work required no ordinary vigor, and the Archdeacon was therefore extraordinarily vigorous. It demanded a buoyant courage, and a heart happy in its toil, and the Archdeacon's heart was happy, and his courage was buoyant.

He knew that he would not be able to animate his father-in-law with feelings like his own, but this did not much disturb him. He preferred to bear the brunt of the battle alone, and did not doubt that the Warden would resign himself into his hands with passive submission.

"Well, Mr. Chadwick," he said, walking into the Steward's office a day or two after the signing of the petition as commemorated in the last chapter, "anything from Cox and Cummins this morning?" Mr. Chadwick handed him a letter, which he read, stroking the tight-gaitered calf of his right leg as he did so. Messrs. Cox and Cummins merely said that they had as yet received no notice from their adversaries, that they could recommend no preliminary steps, but that should any proceeding really be taken by the bedesmen, it would be expedient to consult that very eminent Queen's Counsel, Sir Abraham Haphazard.

"I quite agree with them," said Dr. Grantly, refolding the letter. "I perfectly agree with them. Haphazard is no doubt the best man, a thorough churchman, a sound Conservative, and in every respect the best man we could get. He's in the House, too, which is a great thing."

Mr. Chadwick quite agre

"You remember how completely he put down that scoundrel Horseman about the Bishop of Beverley's income, how completely he set them all adrift in the Earl's case." Since the question of St. Cross had been mooted by the public, one noble lord had become "*the Earl*," par excellence, in the Doctor's estimation. "How he silenced that fellow at Rochester! Of course we must have Haphazard, and I'll tell you what, Mr. Chadwick, we must take care to be in time, or the other party will forestall us."

With all his admiration for Sir Abraham, the Doctor seemed to think it not impossible that that great man might be induced to lend his gigantic powers to the side of the Church's enemies.

Having settled this point to his satisfaction, the Doctor stepped down to the hospital to learn how matters were going on there, and as he walked across the hallowed close and looked up at the ravens who cawed with a peculiar reverence as he wended his way, he thought with increased acerbity of those whose impiety would venture to disturb the goodly grace of cathedral institutions.

And who has not felt the same? We believe that Mr. Horseman himself would relent, and the spirit of Sir Benjamin Hall give way, were those great reformers to allow themselves to stroll by moonlight round the towers of some of our ancient churches. Who would not feel charity for a prebendary when walking the quiet length of that long aisle at Winchester, looking at those decent houses, that trim grassplat, and feeling, as one must, the solemn, orderly comfort of the spot! Who could be hard upon a dean while wandering round the sweet close of Hereford, and owning that in that precinct, tone and color, design and form, solemn tower and storied window, are all in unison, and all perfect! Who could lie basking in the cloisters of Salisbury, and gaze on Jewel's library and that unequaled spire, without feeling that bishops should sometimes be rich!

The tone of our Archdeacon's mind must not astonish us. It has been the growth of centuries of church ascendancy, and though some fungi now disfigure the tree, though there be much dead wood, for how much good fruit have not we to be thankful? Who without remorse can batter down the dead branches of an old oak, now useless, but, ah! still so beautiful, or drag out the fragments of the ancient forest, without feeling that they sheltered the younger plants, to which they are now summoned to give way in a tone so peremptory and so harsh?

The Archdeacon, with all his virtues, was not a man of delicate feeling, and after having made his morning salutations in the Warden's drawing-room, he did not scruple to commence an attack on "pestilent" John Bold in the presence of Miss Harding, though he rightly guessed that that lady was not indifferent to the name of his enemy.

"Nelly, my dear, fetch me my spectacles from the back room," said her father, anxious to save both her blushes and her feelings.

Eleanor brought the spectacles while her father was trying, in ambiguous phrases, to explain to her too-practical brother-in-law that it might be as well not to say anything about Bold before her, and then retreated. Nothing had been explained to her about Bold and the hospital, but with a woman's instinct she knew that things were going wrong.

"We must soon be doing something," commenced the Archdeacon, wiping his brows with a large, bright-colored handkerchief, for he had felt busy, and had walked quick, and it was a broiling summer's day. "Of course you have heard of the petition?"

Mr. Harding owned, somewhat unwillingly, that he had heard of it.

"Well!" The Archdeacon looked for some expression of opinion, but none coming, he continued. "We must be doing something, you know, we mustn't allow these people to cut the ground from under us while we sit looking on." The Archdeacon, who was a practical man, allowed himself the use of everyday expressive modes of speech when among his closest intimates, though no one could soar into a more intricate labyrinth of refined phraseology when the Church was the subject and his lower brethren were his auditors.

The Warden still looked mutely in his face, making the slightest possible passes with an imaginary fiddle bow, and stopping, as he did so, sundry imaginary strings with the fingers of his other hand. 'Twas his constant consolation in conversational troubles. While these vexed him sorely, the passes would be short and slow and the upper hand would not be seen to work—nay, the strings on which it operated would sometimes lie concealed in the musician's pocket, and the instrument on which he played would be beneath his chair. But as his spirit warmed to the subject—as his trusting heart, looking to the bottom of that which vexed him, would see its clear way out—he would rise to a higher melody, sweep the unseen strings with a bolder hand, and swiftly fingering the cords from his neck down along his waistcoat, and up again to his very ear, create an ecstatic strain of perfect music, audible to himself and to St. Cecilia, and not without effect.

"I quite agree with Cox and Cummins," continued the Archdeacon. "They say we must secure Sir Abraham Haphazard. I shall not have the slightest fear in leaving the case in Sir Abraham's hands." The Warden played the slowest and saddest of tunes. It was but a dirge on one string. "I think Sir Abraham will not be long in letting Master Bold know what he's about. I fancy I hear Sir Abraham cross-questioning him at the Common Pleas." The Warden thought of his income being thus discussed, his modest life, his daily habits, and his easy work, and nothing issued from that single cord but a low wail of sorrow. "I suppose they've sent this petition up to my father." The Warden didn't know, he imagined they would do so this very day. "What I can't understand is, how you let them do it, with such a command as you have in the place, or should have with such a man as Bunce. I cannot understand why you let them do it."

"Do what?" asked the Warden.

"Why, listen to this fellow Bold, and that other low pettifogger, Finney —and get up this petition, too. Why didn't you tell Bunce to destroy the petition?"

"That would have been hardly wise," said the Warden.

"Wise—yes, it would have been very wise if they'd done it among themselves. I must go up to the palace and answer it now, I suppose. It's a very short answer they'll get, I can tell you."

"But why shouldn't they petition, Doctor?"

"Why shouldn't they!" responded the Archdeacon in a loud, brazen voice, as though all the men in the hospital were expected to hear him through the walls. "Why shouldn't they? I'll let them know why they shouldn't. By-the-by, Warden, I'd like to say a few words to them all together."

The Warden's mind misgave him, and even for a moment he forgot to play. He by no means wished to delegate to his son-in-law his place and authority of warden. He had expressly determined not to interfere in any step which the men might wish to take in the matter under dispute. He was most anxious neither to accuse them nor to defend himself. All these things he was aware the Archdeacon would do in his behalf, and that not in the mildest manner, and yet he knew not how to refuse the permission requested. "I'd so much sooner remain quiet in the matter," said he, in an apologetic voice.

"Quiet!" said the Archdeacon, still speaking with his brazen trumpet. "Do you wish to be ruined in quiet?"

"Why, if I am to be ruined, certainly."

"Nonsense, Warden. I tell you something must be done. We must act. Just let me ring the bell, and send the men word that I'll speak to them in the quad."

Mr. Harding knew not how to resist, and the disagreeable order was given. The quad, as it was familiarly called, was a small quadrangle open on one side to the river and surrounded on the others by the high wall of Mr. Harding's garden, by one gable end of Mr. Harding's house, and by the end of the row of buildings which formed the residences of the bedesmen. It was flagged all round, and the center was stoned. Small stone gutters ran from the four corners of the square to a grating in the center, and attached to the end of Mr. Harding's house was a conduit with four cocks covered over from the weather, at which the old men got their water, and very generally performed their morning toilet. It was a quiet, somber place, shaded over by the trees of the Warden's garden. On the side toward the river there stood a row of stone seats, on which the old men would sit and gaze at the little fish as they flitted by in the running stream. On the other side of the river was a rich green meadow, running up to and joining the deanery, and as little open to the public as the garden of the dean itself. Nothing, therefore, could be more private than the quad of the hospital, and it was there that the Archdeacon determined to convey to them his sense of their refractory proceedings.

The servant soon brought in word that the men were assembled in the quad, and the Archdeacon, big with his purpose, rose to address them.

"Well, Warden, of course you're coming," said he, seeing that Mr. Harding did not prepare to follow him.

"I wish you'd excuse me," said Mr. Harding.

"For heaven's sake, don't let us have division in the camp," replied the Archdeacon. "Let us have a long pull and a strong pull, but above all a pull all together. Come, Warden, come, don't be afraid of your duty."

Mr. Harding was afraid. He was afraid that he was being led to do that which was not his duty. He was not, however, strong enough to resist, so he got up and followed his son-in-law.

The old men were assembled in groups in the quadrangle—eleven of them, at least, for poor old Johnny Bell was bedridden and couldn't come. He had, however, put his mark to the petition, as one of Handy's earliest followers. 'Tis true he could not move from the bed where he lay. 'Tis true he had no friend on earth but those whom the hospital contained, and of those the Warden and his daughter were the most constant and most appreciated. 'Tis true that everything was administered to him which his failing body could require, or which his faint appetite could enjoy, but still his dull eye had glistened for a moment at the idea of possessing a hundred pounds a year "to his own cheek," as Abel Handy had eloquently expressed it, and poor old Johnny Bell had greedily put his mark to the petition.

When the two clergymen appeared, they all uncovered their heads. Handy was slow to do it, and hesitated, but the black coat and waistcoat, of which he had spoken so irreverently in Skulpit's room, had its effect even on him, and he too doffed his hat. Bunce, advancing before the others, bowed lowly to the Archdeacon, and with affectionate reverence expressed his wish that the Warden and Miss Eleanor were quite well, "and the Doctor's lady," he added, turning to the Archdeacon, "and the children at Plumstead, and my lord." And having made his speech, he also retired among the others, and took his place with the rest upon the stone benches.

As the Archdeacon stood up to make his speech, erect in the middle of that little square, he looked like an ecclesiastical statue placed there as a fitting impersonation of the Church Militant here on earth. His shovel hat, large, new, and well-pronounced, a churchman's hat in every inch, declared the profession as plainly as does the Quaker's broad brim. His heavy eyebrows, large open eyes, and full mouth and chin expressed the solidity of his order. The broad chest, amply covered with fine cloth, told how well-to-do was its estate. One hand ensconced within his pocket evinced the practical hold which our Mother Church keeps on her temporal possessions, and the other, loose for action, was ready to fight if need be in her defense. And below these, the decorous breeches and neat black gaiters, showing so admirably that well-turned leg, betokened the stability, the decency, the outward beauty and grace of our church Establishment.

"Now, my men," he began, when he had settled himself well in his position, "I want to say a few words to you. Your good friend, the Warden here, and myself, and my lord the Bishop, on whose behalf I wish to speak to you, would all be very sorry, very sorry indeed, that you should have any just ground of complaint. Any just ground of complaint on your part would be removed at once by the Warden, or by his lordship, or by me on his behalf, without the necessity of any petition on your part." Here the orator stopped for a moment, expecting that some little murmurs of applause would show that the weakest of the men were beginning to give way, but no such murmurs came. Bunce himself even sat with closed lips, mute and unsatisfactory. "Without the necessity of any petition at all," he repeated. "I'm told you have addressed a petition to my lord." He paused for a reply from the men, and after a while Handy plucked up courage and said, "Yes, we has."

"You have addressed a petition to my lord, in which, as I am informed, you express an opinion that you do not receive from Hiram's estate all that is your due." Here most of the men expressed their assent. "Now what is it you ask for? What is it you want that you haven't got here? What is it——"

"A hundred a year," muttered old Moody, with a voice as if it came out of the ground.

"A hundred a year!" ejaculated the Archdeacon militant, defying the impudence of these claimants with one hand stretched out and closed while with the other he tightly grasped, and secured within his breeches pocket, that symbol of the Church's wealth which his own loose half-crowns not unaptly represented. "A hundred a year! Why, my men, you must be mad! And you talk about John Hiram's will! When John Hiram built a hospital for worn-out old men, worn-out old laboring men, infirm old men past their work, cripples, blind, bedridden, and suchlike, do you think he meant to make gentlemen of them? Do you think John Hiram intended to give a hundred a year to old single men who earned perhaps two shillings or half a crown a day for themselves and families in the best of their time? No, my men! I'll tell you what John Hiram meant. He meant that twelve poor old worn-out laborers, men who could no longer support themselves, who had no friends to support them, who must starve and perish miserably if not protected by the hand of charity—he meant that twelve such men as these should come in here in their poverty and wretchedness and find within these walls shelter and food before their death, and a little leisure to make their peace with God. That was what John Hiram meant. You have not read John Hiram's will, and I doubt whether those wicked men who are advising you have done so. I have,

I know what his will was, and I tell you that that was his will, and that that was his intention."

Not a sound came from the eleven bedesmen as they sat listening to what, according to the Archdeacon, was their intended estate. They grimly stared upon his burly figure, but did not then express, by word or sign, the anger and disgust to which such language was sure to give rise.

"Now let me ask you," he continued. "Do you think you are worse off than John Hiram intended to make you? Have you not shelter, and food, and leisure? Have you not much more? Have you not every indulgence which you are capable of enjoying? Have you not twice better food, twice a better bed, ten times more money in your pocket than you were ever able to earn for yourselves before you were lucky enough to get into this place? And now you sent a petition to the Bishop asking for a hundred pounds a year! I tell you what, my friends, you are deluded and made fools of by wicked men who are acting for their own ends. You will never get a hundred pence a year more than what you have now. It is very possible that you may get less. It is very possible that my lord the Bishop, and your Warden, may make changes——"

"No, no, no," interrupted Mr. Harding, who had been listening with indescribable misery to the tirade of his son-in-law. "No, my friends. I want no changes—at least no changes that shall make you worse off than you now are—as long as you and I live together."

"God bless you, Mr. Harding," said Bunce, and "God bless you, Mr. Harding, God bless you, sir. We know you was always our friend," was exclaimed by enough of the men to make it appear that the sentiment was general.

The Archdeacon had been interrupted in his speech before he had quite finished it, but he felt that he could not recommence with dignity after this little ebullition, and he led the way back into the garden, followed by his father-in-law.

"Well," said he, as soon as he found himself within the cool retreat of the Warden's garden, "I think I spoke to them plainly." And he wiped the perspiration from his brow, for making a speech under a broiling midday sun in summer, in a full suit of thick black cloth, is warm work.

"Yes, you were plain enough," replied the Warden in a tone which did not express approbation.

"And that's everything," said the other, who was clearly well satisfied with himself. "That's everything. With those sort of people one must be plain, or one will not be understood. Now I think they did understand me— I think they knew what I meant."

The Warden agreed. He certainly thought they had understood to the full what had been said to them.

"They know pretty well what they have to expect from us, they know how we shall meet any refractory spirit on their part, they know that we are not afraid of them. And now I'll just step into Chadwick's and tell him what I've done, and then I'll go up to the palace and answer this petition of theirs."

The Warden's mind was very full—full nearly to overcharging itself—and had it done so, had he allowed himself to speak the thoughts which were working within him, he would indeed have astonished the Archdeacon by the reprobation he would have expressed as to the proceeding of which he had been so unwilling a witness. But different feelings kept him silent. He was as yet afraid of differing from his son-in-law. He was anxious beyond measure to avoid even a semblance of rupture with any of his order, and was painfully fearful of having to come to an open quarrel with any person on any subject. His life had hitherto been so quiet, so free from strife. His little early troubles had required nothing but passive fortitude, his subsequent prosperity had never forced upon him any active cares—had never brought him into disagreeable contact with anyone. He felt that he would give almost anything—much more than he knew he ought to give—to relieve himself from the storm which he feared was coming. It was so hard that the pleasant waters of his little stream should be disturbed and muddied by rough hands, that his quiet paths should be made a battlefield, that the unobtrusive corner of the world which had been allotted to him, as though by Providence, should be invaded and desecrated, and all within it made miserable and unsound.

Money he had none to give, the knack of putting guineas together had never belonged to him. But how willingly, with what a foolish easiness, with what happy alacrity, would he have abandoned the half of his income for all time to come could he by so doing have quietly dispelled the clouds that were gathering over him—could he have thus compromised the matter between the reformer and the Conservative, between his possible son-in-law, Bold, and his positive son-in-law, the Archdeacon.

And this compromise would not have been made from any prudential motive of saving what would yet remain, for Mr. Harding still felt little doubt but he should be left for life in quiet possession of the good things he had, if he chose to retain them. No, he would have done so from the sheer love of quiet, and from a horror of being made the subject of public talk. He had very often been moved to pity—to that inward weeping of the heart for others' woes. But none had he ever pitied more than that old lord whose almost fabulous wealth, drawn from his church preferments, had become the subject of so much opprobrium, of such public scorn—that wretched clerical octogenarian Croesus whom men would not allow to die in peace, whom all the world united to decry and to abhor.

Was he to suffer such a fate? Was his humble name to be bandied in men's mouths as the gormandizer of the resources of the poor, as of one who had filched from the charity of other ages wealth which had been intended to relieve the old and the infirm? Was he to be gibbeted in the press, to become a byword for oppression, to be named as an example of the greed of the English Church? Should it ever be said that he had robbed those old men, whom he so truly and so tenderly loved in his heart of hearts? As he slowly paced, hour after hour, under those noble lime trees, turning these sad thoughts within him, he became all but fixed in his resolve that some great step must be taken to relieve him from the risk of so terrible a fate.

In the meanwhile, the Archdeacon, with contented mind and unruffled spirit, went about his business. He said a word or two to Mr. Chadwick, and then finding, as he expected, the petition lying in his father's library, he wrote a short answer to the men, in which he told them that they had no evils to redress, but rather great mercies for which to be thankful. And having seen the Bishop sign it, he got into his brougham and returned home to Mrs. Grantly and Plumstead Episcopi.

CHAPTER VI

THE WARDEN'S TEA PARTY

AFTER much painful doubting, on one thing only could Mr. Harding resolve. He determined that at any rate he would take no offense, and that he would make this question no cause of quarrel either with Bold or with the bedesmen. In furtherance of this resolution, he himself wrote a note to Mr. Bold the same afternoon, inviting him to meet a few friends and hear some music on an evening named in the next week. Had not this little party been promised to Eleanor, in his present state of mind he would probably have avoided such gaiety, but the promise had been given, the invitations were to be written, and when Eleanor consulted her father on the subject, she was not ill pleased to hear him say: "Oh, I was thinking of Bold, so I took it into my head to write to him myself. But you must write to his sister."

Mary Bold was older than her brother, and at the time of our story was just over thirty. She was not an unattractive young woman, though by no means beautiful. Her great merit was the kindliness of her disposition. She was not very clever, nor very animated, nor had she apparently the energy of her brother. But she was guided by a high principle of right and wrong, her temper was sweet, and her faults were fewer in number than her virtues. Those who casually met Mary Bold thought little of her, but those who knew her well loved her well, and the longer they knew her, the more they loved her. Among those who were fondest of her was Eleanor Harding, and though Eleanor had never openly talked to her of her brother, each understood the other's feelings about him. The brother and sister were sitting together when the two notes were brought in.

"How odd," said Mary, "that they should send two notes. Well, if Mr. Harding becomes fashionable, the world is going to change."

Her brother understood immediately the nature and intention of the peace offering, but it was not so easy for him to behave well in the matter as it was for Mr. Harding. It is much less difficult for the sufferer to be generous than for the oppressor. John Bold felt that he could not go to the Warden's party. He never loved Eleanor better than he did now, he had never so strongly felt how anxious he was to make her his wife as now, when so many obstacles to his doing so appeared in view. Yet here was her father himself, as it were, clearing away those very obstacles, and still he felt that he could not go to the house any more as an open friend.

As he sat thinking of these things with the note in his hand, his sister was waiting for his decision.

"Well," said she, "I suppose we must write separate answers, and both say we shall be very happy."

"You'll go, of course, Mary," said he, to which she readily assented. "I cannot," he continued, looking serious and gloomy. "I wish I could, with all my heart."

"And why not, John?" said she. She had as yet heard nothing of the new-found abuse which her brother was about to reform—at least nothing which connected it with her brother's name.

He sat thinking for a while till he determined that it would be best to tell her at once what it was that he was about. It must be done sooner or later.

"I fear I cannot go to Mr. Harding's house any more as a friend, just at present."

"Oh, John! Why not? Ah, you've quarreled with Eleanor!"

"No, indeed," said he. "I've no quarrel with her as yet."

"What is it, John?" said she, looking at him with an anxious, loving face, for she knew well how much of his heart was there in that house which he said he could no longer enter.

"Why," said he at last, "I've taken up the case of these twelve old men of Hiram's Hospital, and of course that brings me into contact with Mr. Harding. I may have to oppose him, interfere with him—perhaps injure him."

Mary looked at him steadily for some time before she committed herself to reply, and then merely asked him what he meant to do for the old men.

"Why, it's a long story, and I don't know that I can make you understand it. John Hiram made a will, and left his property in charity for certain poor old men, and the proceeds, instead of going to the benefit of these men, go chiefly into the pocket of the Warden and the bishop's Steward."

"And you mean to take away from Mr. Harding his share of it?"

"I don't know what I mean yet. I mean to inquire about it. I mean to see who is entitled to this property. I mean to see, if I can, that justice be done to the poor of the city of Barchester generally, who are, in fact, the legatees under the will. I mean, in short, to put the matter right, if I can."

"And why are you to do this, John?"

"You might ask the same question of anybody else," said he. "And according to that, the duty of righting these poor men would belong to nobody. If we are to act on that principle, the weak are never to be protected, injustice is never to be opposed, and no one is to struggle for the poor!" And Bold began to comfort himself in the warmth of his own virtue.

"But is there no one to do this but you, who have known Mr. Harding so long? Surely, John, as a friend, as a young friend, so much younger than Mr. Harding——"

"That's woman's logic all over, Mary. What has age to do with it? Another man might plead that he was too old. And as to his friendship, if the thing itself be right, private motives should never be allowed to interfere. Because I esteem Mr. Harding, is that a reason that I should neglect a duty which I owe to these old men? Or should I give up a work which my conscience tells me is a good one because I regret the loss of his society?"

"And Eleanor, John?" said the sister, looking timidly into her brother's face.

"Eleanor—that is, Miss Harding—if she thinks fit—that is, if her father—or rather, if she—or, indeed, he—if they find it necessary—— But there is no necessity now to talk about Eleanor Harding. This I will say, that if she has the kind of spirit for which I give her credit, she will not condemn me for doing what I think to be a duty." And Bold consoled himself with the consolation of a Roman.

Mary sat silent for a while, till at last her brother reminded her that the notes must be answered, and she got up and placed her desk before her, took out her pen and paper, wrote on it slowly:

Pakenham Villas, Tuesday morning

"My dear Eleanor,
    "I——"

and then stopped and looked at her brother.

"Well, Mary, why don't you write it?"

"Oh, John," said she, "dear John, pray think better of this."

"Think better of what?" said he.

"Of this about the hospital—of all this about Mr. Harding—of what you say about those old men. Nothing can call upon you—no duty can require you to set yourself against your oldest, your best friend. Oh, John, think of Eleanor. You'll break her heart and your own."

"Nonsense, Mary. Miss Harding's heart is as safe as yours."

"Pray, pray, for my sake, John, give it up. You know how dearly you love her." And she came and knelt before him on the rug. "Pray give it up. You are going to make yourself, and her, and her father miserable.

You are going to make us all miserable. And for what? For a dream of justice. You will never make those twelve men happier than they now are."

"You don't understand it, my dear girl," said he, smoothing her hair with his hand.

"I do understand it, John. I understand that this is a chimera—a dream that you have got. I know well that no duty can require you to do this mad—this suicidal thing. I know you love Eleanor Harding with all your heart, and I tell you now that she loves you as well. If there was a plain, a positive duty before you, I would be the last to bid you neglect it for any woman's love. But this—— Oh, think again before you do anything to make it necessary that you and Mr. Harding should be at variance." He did not answer as she knelt there, leaning on his knees, but by his face she thought that he was inclined to yield. "At any rate let me say that you will go to this party. At any rate do not break with them while your mind is in doubt." And she got up, hoping to conclude her note in the way she desired.

"My mind is not in doubt," at last he said, rising. "I could never respect myself again were I to give way now because Eleanor Harding is beautiful. I do love her. I would give a hand to hear her tell me what you have said, speaking on her behalf. But I cannot for her sake go back from the task which I have commenced. I hope she may hereafter acknowledge and respect my motives, but I cannot now go as a guest to her father's house." And the Barchester Brutus went out to fortify his own resolution by meditations on his own virtue.

Poor Mary Bold sat down and sadly finished her note, saying that she would herself attend the party, but that her brother was unavoidably prevented from doing so. I fear that she did not admire as she should have done the self-devotion of his singular virtue.

The party went off as such parties do. There were fat old ladies in fine silk dresses, and slim young ladies in gauzy muslin frocks. Old gentlemen stood up with their backs to the empty fireplace, looking by no means so comfortable as they would have done in their own armchairs at home. And young gentlemen, rather stiff about the neck, clustered near the door, not as yet sufficiently in courage to attack the muslin frocks, who awaited the battle drawn up in a semicircular array. The Warden endeavored to induce a charge, but failed signally, not having the tact of a general. His daughter did what she could to comfort the forces under her command, who took in refreshing rations of cake and tea, and patiently looked for the coming engagement. But she herself, Eleanor, had no spirit for the work. The only enemy whose lance she cared to encounter was not there, and she and others were somewhat dull.

Loud above all voices was heard the clear sonorous tones of the Archdeacon as he dilated to brother parsons of the danger of the Church, of the fearful rumors of mad reforms even at Oxford, and of the damnable heresies of Dr. Whiston.

Soon, however, sweeter sounds began timidly to make themselves audible. Little movements were made in a quarter notable for round stools and music stands. Wax candles were arranged in sconces, big books were brought from hidden recesses, and the work of the evening commenced.

How often were those pegs twisted and retwisted before our friend found that he had twisted them enough, how many discordant scrapes gave promise of the coming harmony! How much the muslin fluttered and crumpled before Eleanor and another nymph were duly seated at the piano. How closely did that tall Apollo pack himself against the wall, with his flute, long as himself, extending high over the heads of his pretty neighbors. Into how small a corner crept that round and florid little minor canon, and there with skill amazing found room to tune his accustomed fiddle!

And now the crash begins. Away they go in full flow of harmony together—up hill and down dale—now louder and louder, then lower and lower, now loud as though stirring the battle, then low as though mourning the slain. In all, through all, and above all, is heard the violoncello. Ah, not for nothing were those pegs so twisted and retwisted. Listen, listen! Now alone that saddest of instruments tells its touching tale. Silent, and in awe, stand fiddle, flute, and piano, to hear the sorrows of their wailing brother. 'Tis but for a moment. Before the melancholy of those low notes has been fully realized, again comes the full force of all the band. Down go the pedals. Away rush twenty fingers scouring over the bass notes with all the impetus of passion. Apollo blows till his stiff neckcloth is no better than a rope, and the minor canon works with both arms till he falls into a syncope of exhaustion against the wall.

How comes it that now, when all should be silent, when courtesy, if not taste, should make men listen—how is it at this moment the black-coated corps leave their retreat and begin skirmishing? One by one they creep forth, and fire off little guns timidly and without precision. Ah, my men, efforts such as these will take no cities, even though the enemy should be never so open to assault. At length a more deadly artillery is brought to bear. Slowly, but with effect, the advance is made, the muslin ranks are broken and fall into confusion, the formidable array of chairs gives way. The battle is no longer between opposing regiments, but hand to hand and foot to foot with single combatants, as in the glorious days of old, when fighting was really noble. In corners, and under the shadow of curtains, behind sofas and half-hidden by doors, in retiring windows and sheltered by hanging tapestry, are blows given and returned, fatal, incurable, dealing death.

Apart from this another combat arises, more sober and more serious. The Archdeacon is engaged against two prebendaries, a pursy full-blown rector assisting him, in all the perils and all the enjoyments of short whist. With solemn energy do they watch the shuffled pack and, all-expectant, eye the coming trump. With what anxious nicety do they arrange their cards, jealous of each other's eyes! Why is that lean Doctor so slow—cadaverous man with hollow jaw and sunken eye, ill beseeming the richness of his Mother Church! Ah, why so slow, thou meager Doctor? See how the Archdeacon, speechless in his agony, deposits on the board his cards and looks to heaven or to the ceiling for support. Hark how he sighs as with thumbs in his waistcoat pocket he seems to signify that the end of such torment is not yet even nigh at hand! Vain is the hope, if hope there be, to disturb that meager Doctor. With care precise he places every card, weighs well the value of each mighty ace, each guarded king and comfort-giving queen, speculates on knave and ten, counts all his suits, and sets his price upon the whole. At length a card is led, and quick three others fall upon the board. The little Doctor leads again while with lustrous eye his partner absorbs the trick. Now thrice has this been done—thrice has constant fortune favored the brace of prebendaries ere the Archdeacon rouses himself to the battle. But at the fourth assault he pins to the earth a prostrate king, laying low his crown and scepter, bushy beard, and lowering brow with a poor deuce.

"As David did Goliath," says the Archdeacon, pushing over the four cards to his partner. And then a trump is led, then another trump, then a king—and then an ace—and then a long ten, which brings down from the meager Doctor his only remaining tower of strength—his cherished queen of trumps.

"What, no second club?" says the Archdeacon to his partner.

"Only one club," mutters from his inmost stomach the pursy rector, who sits there red-faced, silent, impervious, careful, a safe but not a brilliant ally.

But the Archdeacon cares not for many clubs, or for none. He dashes out his remaining cards with a speed most annoying to his antagonists, pushes over to them some four cards as their allotted portion, shoves the remainder across the table to the red-faced rector, calls out "two by cards and two by honors, and the odd trick last time," marks a treble under the candlestick, and has dealt round the second pack before the meager Doctor has calculated his losses.

And so went off the Warden's party, and men and women arranging shawls and shoes declared how pleasant it had been, and Mrs. Goodenough, the red-faced rector's wife, pressing the Warden's hand, declared she had never enjoyed herself better—which showed how little pleasure she allowed herself in this world, as she had sat the whole evening through in the same chair without occupation, not speaking and unspoken to. And Matilda Johnson, when she allowed young Dickson of the bank to fasten her cloak round her neck, thought that two hundred pounds a year and a little cottage would really do for happiness—besides, he was sure to be manager some day. And Apollo, folding his flute into his pocket, felt that he had acquitted himself with honor. And the Archdeacon pleasantly jingled his gains, but the meager Doctor went off without much audible speech, muttering ever and anon as he went "three and thirty points!" "three and thirty points!"

And so they all were gone, and Mr. Harding was left alone with his daughter.

What had passed between Eleanor Harding and Mary Bold need not be told. It is indeed a matter of thankfulness that neither the historian nor the novelist hears all that is said by their heroes or heroines, or how would three volumes or twenty suffice! In the present case so little of this sort have I overheard that I live in hopes of finishing my work within three hundred pages, and of completing that pleasant task, a novel in one volume. But something had passed between them, and as the Warden blew out the wax candles and put his instrument into its case, his daughter stood sad and thoughtful by the empty fireplace, determined to speak to her father, but irresolute as to what she would say.

"Well, Eleanor," said he, "are you for bed?"

"Yes," said she, moving, "I suppose so, but Papa— Mr. Bold was not here tonight. Do you know why not?"

"He was asked, I wrote to him myself," said the Warden.

"But do you know why he did not come, Papa?"

"Well, Eleanor, I could guess, but it's no use guessing at such things, my dear. What makes you look so earnest about it?"

"Oh, Papa, do tell me," she exclaimed, throwing her arms round him and looking into his face, "what is it he is going to do? What is it all about? Is there any—any—any—" She didn't well know what word to use— "any danger?"

"Danger, my dear? What sort of danger?"

"Danger to you, danger of trouble, and of loss, and of— Oh, Papa, why haven't you told me of all this before?"

Mr. Harding was not the man to judge harshly of anyone, much less of the daughter whom he now loved better than any living creature, but still he did judge her wrongly at this moment. He knew that she loved John Bold, he fully sympathized in her affection. Day after day he thought more of the matter and, with the tender care of a loving father, tried to arrange in his own mind how matters might be so managed that his daughter's heart should not be made the sacrifice to the dispute which was likely to exist between him and Bold. Now, when she spoke to him for the first time on the subject, it was natural that he should think more of her than of himself, and that he should imagine that her own cares, and not his, were troubling her.

He stood silent before her awhile as she gazed up into his face, and then, kissing her forehead, he placed her on the sofa.

"Tell me, Nelly," he said (he only called her Nelly in his kindest, softest, sweetest moods, and yet all his moods were kind and sweet), "tell me, Nelly, do you like Mr. Bold—much?"

She was quite taken aback by the question. I will not say that she had forgotten herself and her own love in thinking about John Bold, and while conversing with Mary. She certainly had not done so. She had been sick at heart to think that a man of whom she could not but own to herself that she loved him, of whose regard she had been so proud, that such a man should turn against her father to ruin him. She had felt her vanity hurt that his affection for her had not kept him from such a course. Had he really cared for her, he would not have risked her love by such an outrage. But her main fear had been for her father, and when she spoke of danger, it was of danger to him and not to herself.

She was taken aback by the question altogether. "Do I like him, Papa?"

"Yes, Nelly, do you like him? Why shouldn't you like him? But that's a poor word. Do you love him?" She sat still in his arms without answering him. She certainly had not prepared herself for an avowal of affection, intending, as she had done, to abuse John Bold herself and to hear her father do so also. "Come, my love," said he, "let us make a clean breast of it. Do you tell me what concerns yourself, and I will tell you what concerns me and the hospital."

And then, without waiting for an answer, he described to her, as he best could, the accusation that was made about Hiram's will, the claims which the old men put forward, what he considered the strength and what the weakness of his own position, the course which Bold had taken and that which he presumed he was about to take. And then by degrees, without further question, he presumed on the fact of Eleanor's love, and spoke of that love as a feeling which he could in no way disapprove. He apologized for Bold, excused what he was doing—nay, praised him for his energy and intentions, made much of his good qualities, and harped on none of his foibles. Then, reminding his daughter how late it was, and comforting her with much assurance which he hardly felt himself, he sent her to her room with flowing eyes and a full heart.

When Mr. Harding met his daughter at breakfast the next morning, there was no further discussion on the matter, nor was the subject mentioned between them for some days. Soon after the party Mary Bold called at the hospital, but there were various persons in the drawing-room at the time and she therefore said nothing about her brother. On the day following, John Bold met Miss Harding in one of the quiet, somber, shaded walks of the close. He was most anxious to see her, but unwilling to call at the Warden's house, and had in truth waylaid her in her private haunts.

"My sister tells me," said he, abruptly hurrying on with his premeditated speech, "my sister tells me that you had a delightful party the other evening. I was so sorry I could not be there."

"We were all sorry," said Eleanor with dignified composure.

"I believe, Miss Harding, you understood why, at this moment——" And Bold hesitated, muttered, stopped, commenced his explanation again, and again broke down. Eleanor would not help him in the least. "I think my sister explained to you, Miss Harding?"

"Pray don't apologize, Mr. Bold. My father will, I am sure, always be glad to see you if you like to come to the house now as formerly. Nothing has occurred to alter his feelings. Of your own views you are, of course, the best judge."

"Your father is all that is kind and generous, he always was so. But you, Miss Harding, yourself——I hope you will not judge me harshly, because——"

"Mr. Bold," said she, "you may be sure of one thing. I shall always judge my father to be right, and those who oppose him I shall judge to be wrong. If those who do not know him oppose him, I shall have charity enough to believe that they are wrong through error of judgment. But should I see him attacked by those who ought to know him, and to love him, and revere him, of such I shall be constrained to form a different opinion." And then, curtsying low, she sailed on, leaving her lover in anything but a happy state of mind.

CHAPTER VII

THE "JUPITER"

THOUGH Eleanor Harding rode off from John Bold on a high horse, it must not be supposed that her heart was so elate as her demeanor. In the first place, she had a natural repugnance to losing her lover; and in the next, she was not quite so sure that she was so certainly in the right as she pretended to be. Her father had told her, and that now repeatedly, that Bold was doing nothing unjust or ungenerous. Why then should she rebuke him, and throw him off, when she felt herself so ill able to bear his loss? But such is human nature, and young-lady nature especially. As she walked off from him beneath the shady elms of the close, her look, her tone, every motion and gesture of her body, belied her heart. She would have given the world to have taken him by the hand, to have reasoned with him, persuaded him, cajoled him, coaxed him out of his project—to have overcome him with all her female artillery, and to have redeemed her father at the cost of herself—but pride would not let her do this, and she left him without a look of love or a word of kindness.

Had Bold been judging of another lover and of another lady, he might have understood all this as well as we do, but in matters of love men do not see clearly in their own affairs. They say that faint heart never won fair lady. It is amazing to me how fair ladies are won, so faint are often men's hearts! Were it not for the kindness of their nature, that seeing the weakness of our courage they will occasionally descend from their impregnable fortresses and themselves aid us in effecting their own defeat, too often would they escape unconquered if not unscathed, and free of body if not of heart.

Poor Bold crept off quite crestfallen. He felt that as regarded Eleanor Harding his fate was sealed unless he could consent to give up a task to which he had pledged himself, and which indeed it would not be easy for him to give up. Lawyers were engaged, and the question had to a certain extent been taken up by the public. Besides, how could a high-spirited girl like Eleanor Harding really learn to love a man for neglecting a duty which he had assumed! Could she allow her affection to be purchased at the cost of his own self-respect?

As regarded the issue of his attempt at reformation in the hospital, Bold had no reason hitherto to be discontented with his success. All Barchester was by the ears about it. The Bishop, the Archdeacon, the Warden, the Steward, and several other clerical allies, had daily meetings, discussing their tactics and preparing for the great attack. Sir Abraham Haphazard had been consulted, but his opinion was not yet received. Copies of Hiram's will, copies of wardens' journals, copies of leases, copies of accounts, copies of everything that could be copied and of some that could not, had been sent to him, and the case was assuming most creditable dimensions. But above all, it had been mentioned in the daily *Jupiter*. That all-powerful organ of the press in one of its leading thunderbolts launched at St. Cross had thus remarked:

"Another case, of smaller dimensions indeed, but of similar import, is now likely to come under public notice. We are informed that the warden or master of an old almshouse attached to Barchester Cathedral is in receipt of twenty-five times the annual income appointed for him by the will of the founder, while the sum yearly expended on the absolute purposes of the charity has always remained fixed. In other words, the legatees under the founder's will have received no advantage from the increase in the value of the property during the last four centuries, such increase having been absorbed by the so-called warden. It is impossible to conceive a case of greater injustice. It is no answer to say that some six or nine or twelve old men receive as much of the goods of this world as such old men require. On what foundation, moral or divine, traditional or legal, is grounded the warden's claim to the large income he receives for doing nothing? The contentment of these almsmen, if content they be, can give him no title to this wealth! Does he ever ask himself, when he stretches wide his clerical palm to receive the pay of some dozen of the working clergy, for what service he is so remunerated? Does his conscience ever entertain the question of his right to such subsidies? Or is it possible that the subject never so presents itself to his mind—that he has received for many years, and intends, should God spare him, to receive for years to come, these fruits of the industrious piety of past ages, indifferent as to any right on his own part, or of any injustice to others! We must express an opinion that nowhere but in the Church of England, and only there among its priests, could such a state of moral indifference be found."

I must for the present leave my readers to imagine the state of Mr. Harding's mind after reading the above article. They say that eighty thousand copies of the *Jupiter* are daily sold, and that each copy is read by five persons at the least. Four hundred thousand readers then would hear this accusation against him, four hundred thousand hearts would swell with indignation at the griping injustice, the barefaced robbery of the Warden of Barchester Hospital! And how was he to answer this? How was he to open his inmost heart to this multitude, to these thousands, the educated, the polished, the picked men of his own country? How show them that he was no robber, no avaricious, lazy priest scrambling for gold, but a retiring humble-spirited man who had innocently taken what had innocently been offered to him?

"Write to the *Jupiter*," suggested the Bishop.

"Yes," said the Archdeacon, more worldly wise than his father, "yes, and be smothered with ridicule, tossed over and over again with scorn, shaken this way and that as a rat in the mouth of a practiced terrier. You will leave out some word or letter in your answer, and the ignorance of the cathedral clergy will be harped upon. You will make some small mistake, which will be a falsehood, or some admission, which will be self-condemnation. You will find yourself to have been vulgar, ill-tempered, irreverent, and illiterate, and the chances are ten to one but that, being a clergyman, you will have been guilty of blasphemy! A man may have the best of causes, the best of talents, and the best of tempers; he may write as well as Addison, or as strongly as Junius; but even with all this he cannot successfully answer when attacked by the *Jupiter*. In such matters it is omnipotent. What the Czar is in Russia, or the mob in America, that the *Jupiter* is in England. Answer such an article! No, Warden, whatever you do, don't do that. We were to look for this sort of thing, you know, but we need not draw down on our heads more of it than is necessary."

The article in the *Jupiter*, while it so greatly harassed our poor Warden, was an immense triumph to some of the opposite party. Sorry as Bold was to see Mr. Harding attacked so personally, it still gave him a feeling of elation to find his cause taken up by so powerful an advocate. And as to Finney, the attorney, he was beside himself. What! To be engaged in the same cause and on the same side with the *Jupiter*, to have the views he had recommended seconded, and furthered, and battled for by the *Jupiter!* Perhaps to have his own name mentioned as that of the learned gentleman whose efforts had been so successful on behalf of the poor of Barchester! He might be examined before committees of the House of Commons, with heaven knows how much a day for his personal expenses—he might be engaged for years on such a suit! There was no end to the glorious golden dreams which this leader in the *Jupiter* produced in the soaring mind of Finney.

And the old bedesmen—they also heard of this article, and had a glimmering, indistinct idea of the marvelous advocate which had now taken up their cause. Abel Handy limped hither and thither through the rooms, repeating all that he understood to have been printed, with some additions of his own which he thought should have been added. He told them how the *Jupiter* had declared that their Warden was no better than a robber, and that what the *Jupiter* said was acknowledged by the world to be true. How the *Jupiter* had affirmed that each one of them—"each one of us, Jonathan Crumple, think of that!"—had a clear right to a hundred a year, and that if the *Jupiter* had said so, it was better than a decision of the Lord Chancellor. And then he carried about the paper, supplied by Mr. Finney, which, though none of them could read it, still afforded in its very touch and aspect positive corroboration of what was told them. And Jonathan Crumple pondered deeply over his returning wealth. And Job Skulpit saw how right he had been in signing the petition, and said so many scores of times. And Spriggs leered fearfully with his one eye. And Moody, as he more nearly approached the coming golden age, hated more deeply than ever those who still kept possession of what he so coveted. Even Billy Gazy and poor bedridden Bell became active and uneasy. But the great Bunce stood apart with lowering brow, with deep grief seated in his heart, for he perceived that evil days were coming.

It had been decided, the Archdeacon advising, that no remonstrance, explanation, or defense should be addressed from the Barchester conclave to the editor of the *Jupiter*, but hitherto that was the only decision to which they had come.

Sir Abraham Haphazard was deeply engaged in preparing a bill for the mortification of Papists, to be called the "Convent Custody Bill," the purport of which was to enable any Protestant clergyman over fifty years of age to search any nun whom he suspected of being in possession of treasonable papers or Jesuitical symbols. And as there were to be a hundred and thirty-seven clauses in the bill, each clause containing a separate thorn for the side of the Papist, and as it was known the bill would be fought inch by inch by fifty maddened Irishmen, the due construction and adequate dovetailing of it did consume much of Sir Abraham's time. The bill had all its desired effect. Of course it never passed into law. But it so completely divided the ranks of the Irish members, who had bound themselves together to force on the Ministry a bill for compelling all men to drink Irish whisky and all women to wear Irish poplins, that for the remainder of the session the Great Poplin and Whisky League was utterly harmless.

Thus it happened that Sir Abraham's opinion was not at once forthcoming, and the uncertainty, the expectation and suffering, of the folk of Barchester was maintained at a high pitch.

CHAPTER VIII

PLUMSTEAD EPISCOPI

THE reader must now be requested to visit the rectory of Plumstead Episcopi, and as it is as yet still early morning, to ascend again with us into the bedroom of the Archdeacon. The mistress of the mansion was at her toilet, on which we will not dwell with profane eyes, but proceed into a small inner room, where the Doctor dressed and kept his boots and sermons. And here we will take our stand, premising that the door of the room was so open as to admit of a conversation between our reverend Adam and his valued Eve.

"It's all your own fault, Archdeacon," said the latter. "I told you from the beginning how it would end, and Papa has no one to thank but you."

"Good gracious, my dear," said the Doctor, appearing at the door of his dressing-room with his face and head enveloped in the rough towel which he was violently using, "how can you say so? I am doing my very best."

"I wish you had never done so much," said the lady, interrupting him. "If you'd just have let John Bold come and go there, as he and Papa liked, he and Eleanor would have been married by this time, and we should not have heard one word about all this affair."

"But, my dear——"

"Oh, it's all very well, Archdeacon, and of course you're right—I don't for a moment think you'll ever admit that you could be wrong—but the fact is you've brought this young man down upon Papa by huffing him as you have done."

"But, my love——"

"And all because you didn't like John Bold for a brother-in-law. How is she ever to do better? Papa hasn't got a shilling, and though Eleanor is well enough, she has not at all a taking style of beauty. I'm sure I don't know how she's to do better than marry John Bold—or as well indeed," added the anxious sister, giving the last twist to her last shoestring.

Dr. Grantly felt keenly the injustice of this attack, but what could he say? He certainly had huffed John Bold, he certainly had objected to him as a brother-in-law, and a very few months ago the very idea had excited his wrath. But now matters were changed. John Bold had shown his power, and though he was as odious as ever to the Archdeacon, power is always respected, and the reverend dignitary began to think that such an alliance might not have been imprudent. Nevertheless, his motto was still "No surrender," he would still fight it out. He believed confidently in Oxford, in the bench of bishops, in Sir Abraham Haphazard, and in himself, and it was only when alone with his wife that doubts of defeat ever beset him.

He once more tried to communicate this confidence to Mrs. Grantly, and for the twentieth time began to tell her of Sir Abraham.

"Oh, Sir Abraham!" said she, collecting all her house keys into her basket before she descended. "Sir Abraham won't get Eleanor a husband, Sir Abraham won't get Papa another income when he has been worrited out of the hospital. Mark what I tell you, Archdeacon. While you and Sir Abraham are fighting, Papa will lose his preferment, and what will you do then with him and Eleanor on your hands? Besides, who's to pay Sir Abraham? I suppose he won't take the case up for nothing?" And so the lady descended to family worship among her children and servants, the pattern of a good and prudent wife.

Dr. Grantly was blessed with a happy, thriving family. There were, first, three boys, now at home from school for the holidays. They were called, respectively, Charles James, Henry, and Samuel. The two younger—there were five in all—were girls. The elder, Florinda, bore the name of the Archbishop of York's wife, whose godchild she was, and the younger had been christened Grizzel after a sister of the Archbishop of Canterbury. The boys were all clever, and gave good promise of being well able to meet the cares and trials of the world. And yet they were not alike in their dispositions, and each had his individual character, and each his separate admirers among the Doctor's friends.

Charles James was an exact and careful boy. He never committed himself. He well knew how much was expected from the eldest son of the Archdeacon of Barchester, and was therefore mindful not to mix too freely with other boys. He had not the great talents of his younger brothers, but he exceeded them in judgment and propriety of demeanor. His fault, if he had one, was an overattention to words instead of things. There was a thought too much finesse about him and, as even his father sometimes told him, he was too fond of a compromise.

The second was the Archdeacon's favorite son, and Henry was indeed a brilliant boy. The versatility of his genius was surprising, and the visitors at Plumstead Episcopi were often amazed at the marvelous manner in which he would, when called on, adapt his capacity to apparently most uncongenial pursuits. He appeared once before a large circle as Luther the reformer and delighted them with the perfect manner in which he assumed the character, and within three days he again astonished them by acting the part of a Capuchin friar to the very life. For this last exploit his father gave him a golden guinea, and his brothers said the reward had been promised beforehand in the event of the performance being successful. He was also sent on a tour into Devonshire, a treat which the lad was most anxious of enjoying. His father's friends there, however, did not appreciate his talents, and sad accounts were sent home of the perversity of his nature. He was a most courageous lad, game to the backbone.

It was soon known, both at home, where he lived, and within some miles of Barchester Cathedral, and also at Westminster, where he was at school, that young Henry could box well and would never own himself beat. Other boys would fight while they had a leg to stand on, but he would fight with no leg at all. Those backing him would sometimes think him crushed by the weight of blows and faint with loss of blood, and his friends would endeavor to withdraw him from the contest. But no, Henry never gave in, was never weary of the battle. The ring was the only element in which he seemed to enjoy himself, and while other boys were happy in the number of their friends, he rejoiced most in the multitude of his foes.

His relations could not but admire his pluck, but they sometimes were forced to regret that he was inclined to be a bully. And those not so partial to him as his father was observed with pain that though he could fawn to the masters and the Archdeacon's friends, he was imperious and masterful to the servants and the poor.

But perhaps Samuel was the general favorite, and dear little Soapy, as he was familiarly called, was as engaging a child as ever fond mother petted. He was soft and gentle in his manners, and attractive in his speech. The tone of his voice was melody, and every action was a grace. Unlike his brothers, he was courteous to all, he was affable to the lowly, and meek even to the very scullery maid. He was a boy of great promise, minding his books and delighting the hearts of his masters. His brothers, however, were not particularly fond of him. They would complain to their mother that Soapy's civility all meant something. They thought that his voice was too often listened to at Plumstead Episcopi, and evidently feared that as he grew up he would have more weight in the house than either of them. There was, therefore, a sort of agreement among them to put young Soapy down. This, however, was not so easy to be done. Samuel, though young, was sharp. He could not assume the stiff decorum of Charles James, nor could he fight like Henry, but he was a perfect master of his own weapons, and contrived, in the teeth of both of them, to hold the place which he had assumed. Henry declared that he was a false, cunning creature, and Charles James, though he always spoke of him as his dear brother Samuel, was not slow to say a word against him when opportunity offered. To speak the truth, Samuel was a cunning boy, and those even who loved him best could not but own that for one so young he was too adroit in choosing his words, and too skilled in modulating his voice.

The two little girls Florinda and Grizzel were nice little girls enough, but they did not possess the sterling qualities of their brothers. Their voices were not often heard at Plumstead Episcopi, they were bashful and timid by nature, slow to speak before company even when asked to do so. And though they looked very nice in their clean white muslin frocks and pink sashes, they were but little noticed by the Archdeacon's visitors.

Whatever of submissive humility may have appeared in the gait and visage of the Archdeacon during his colloquy with his wife in the sanctum of their dressing-rooms was dispelled as he entered his breakfast parlor with erect head and powerful step. In the presence of a third person he assumed the lord and master, and that wise and talented lady too well knew the man to whom her lot for life was bound to stretch her authority beyond the point at which it would be borne. Strangers at Plumstead Episcopi, when they saw the imperious brow with which he commanded silence from the large circle of visitors, children, and servants who came together in the morning to hear him read the word of God, and watched how meekly that wife seated herself behind her basket of keys with a little girl on each side as she caught that commanding glance—strangers, I say, seeing this, could little guess that some fifteen minutes since she had stoutly held her ground against him, hardly allowing him to open his mouth in his own defense. But such is the tact and talent of women!

And now let us observe the well-furnished breakfast parlor at Plumstead Episcopi, and the comfortable air of all the belongings of the rectory. Comfortable they certainly were, but neither gorgeous nor even grand. Indeed, considering the money that had been spent there, the eye and taste might have been better served. There was an air of heaviness about the rooms which might have been avoided without any sacrifice to propriety, colors might have been better chosen and lights more perfectly diffused, but perhaps in doing so the thorough clerical aspect of the whole might have been somewhat marred. At any rate, it was not without ample consideration that those thick, dark, costly carpets were put down, those embossed but somber papers hung up, those heavy curtains draped so as to half-exclude the light of the sun. Nor were these old-fashioned chairs, bought at a price far exceeding that now given for more modern goods, without a purpose.

The breakfast service on the table was equally costly and equally plain. The apparent object had been to spend money without obtaining brilliancy or splendor. The urn was of thick and solid silver, as were also the teapot, coffeepot, cream ewer, and sugarbowl. The cups were old, dim dragon china, worth about a pound a piece, but very despicable in the eyes of the uninitiated. The silver forks were so heavy as to be disagreeable to the hand, and the bread basket was of a weight really formidable to any but robust persons.

The tea consumed was the very best, the coffee the very blackest, the cream the very thickest. There was dry toast and buttered toast, muffins and crumpets, hot bread and cold bread, white bread and brown bread, homemade bread and bakers' bread, wheaten bread and oaten bread—and if there be other breads than these they were there. There were eggs in napkins, and crispy bits of bacon under silver covers. And there were little fishes in a little box, and deviled kidneys frizzling on a hot-water dish—which, by-the-by, were placed closely contiguous to the plate of the worthy Archdeacon himself. Over and above this, on a snow-white napkin spread upon the sideboard was a huge ham, and a huge sirloin, the latter having laden the dinner table on the previous evening. Such was the ordinary fare at Plumstead Episcopi.

And yet I have never found the rectory a pleasant house. The fact that man shall not live by bread alone seemed to be somewhat forgotten. And noble as was the appearance of the host, and sweet and good-natured as was the face of the hostess, talented as were the children, and excellent as were the viands and the wines, in spite of these attractions I generally found the rectory somewhat dull. After breakfast the Archdeacon would retire—of course to his clerical pursuits. Mrs. Grantly, I presume, inspected her kitchen—though she had a first-rate housekeeper, with sixty pounds a year—and attended to the lessons of Florinda and Grizzel, though she had an excellent governess with thirty pounds a year. At any rate she disappeared: and I never could make companions of the boys. Charles James, though he always looked as though there was something in him, never seemed to have much to say, and what he did say he would always unsay the next minute. He told me once that he considered cricket, on the whole, to be a gentlemanlike game for boys, provided they would play without running about. And that fives also was a seemly game so that those who played it never heated themselves. Henry once quarreled with me for taking his sister Grizzel's part in a contest between them as to the best mode of using a watering pot for the garden flowers, and from that day to this he has not spoken to me, though he speaks at me often enough. For half an hour or so I certainly did like Sammy's gentle speeches, but one gets tired of honey, and I found that he preferred the more admiring listeners whom he met in the kitchen garden and back precincts of the establishment. Besides, I think I once caught Sammy fibbing.

On the whole, therefore, I found the rectory a dull house, though it must be admitted that everything there was of the very best.

After breakfast on the morning of which we are writing, the Archdeacon, as usual, retired to his study, intimating that he was going to be very busy, but that he would see Mr. Chadwick if he called. On entering this sacred room he carefully opened the paper case on which he was wont to compose his favorite sermons, and spread on it a fair sheet of paper and one partly written on. He then placed his inkstand, looked at his pen, and folded his blotting paper. Having done so, he got up again from his seat, stood with his back to the fireplace and yawned comfortably, stretching out vastly his huge arms and opening his burly chest. He then walked across the room and locked the door, and having so prepared himself, he threw himself into his easy chair, took from a secret drawer beneath his table a volume of Rabelais, and began to amuse himself with the witty mischief of Panurge. So passed the Archdeacon's morning on that day.

He was left undisturbed at his studies for an hour or two, when a knock came to the door, and Mr. Chadwick was announced. Rabelais retired into the secret drawer, the easy chair seemed knowingly to betake itself off, and when the Archdeacon quickly undid his bolt, he was discovered by the Steward working, as usual, for that Church of which he was so useful a pillar. Mr. Chadwick had just come from London and was therefore known to be the bearer of important news.

"We've got Sir Abraham's opinion at last," said Mr. Chadwick as he seated himself.

"Well, well, well!" exclaimed the Archdeacon impatiently.

"Oh, it's as long as my arm," said the other. "It can't be told in a word, but you can read it." And he handed him a copy, in heaven knows how many spun-out folios, of the opinion which the Attorney General had managed to cram on the back and sides, of the case as originally submitted to him.

"The upshot is," said Chadwick, "that there's a screw loose in their case, and we had better do nothing. They are proceeding against Mr. Harding and myself, and Sir Abraham holds that under the wording of the will, and subsequent arrangements legally sanctioned, Mr. Harding and I are only paid servants. The defendants should have been either the Corporation of Barchester, or possibly the chapter, or your father."

"W—hoo," said the Archdeacon. "So Master Bold is on a wrong scent, is he?"

"That's Sir Abraham's opinion, but any scent almost would be a wrong scent. Sir Abraham thinks that if they'd taken the corporation, or the chapter, we could have baffled them. The Bishop, he thinks, would be the surest shot, but even there we could plead that the Bishop is only visitor, and that he has never made himself a consenting party to the performance of other duties."

"That's quite clear," said the Archdeacon.

"Not quite so clear," said the other. "You see the will says, 'My lord, the bishop, being graciously pleased to see that due justice be done.' Now, it may be a question whether in accepting and administering the patronage, your father has not accepted also the other duties assigned. It is doubtful, however. But even if they hit that nail—and they are far off from that yet— the point is so nice, as Sir Abraham says, that you would force them into fifteen thousand pounds' cost before they could bring it to an issue! And where's that sum of money to come from?"

The Archdeacon rubbed his hands with delight. He had never doubted the justice of his case, but he had begun to have some dread of unjust success on the part of his enemies. It was delightful to him thus to hear that their cause was surrounded with such rocks and shoals—such causes of shipwreck unseen by the landsman's eye, but visible enough to the keen eyes of practical law mariners. How wrong his wife was to wish that Bold should marry Eleanor! Bold! Why, if he should be ass enough to persevere, he would be a beggar before he knew whom he was at law with!

"That's excellent, Chadwick—that's excellent! I told you Sir Abraham was the man for us." And he put down on the table the copy of the opinion, and patted it fondly.

"Don't you let that be seen though, Archdeacon."

"Who?—I!—Not for worlds," said the Doctor.

"People will talk, you know, Archdeacon."

"Of course, of course," said the Doctor.

"Because if that gets abroad, it would teach them how to fight their own battle."

"Quite true," said the Doctor.

"No one here in Barchester ought to see that but you and I, Archdeacon."

"No, no, certainly no one else," said the Archdeacon, pleased with the closeness of the confidence. "No one else shall."

"Mrs. Grantly is very interested in the matter, I know," said Mr. Chadwick.

Did the Archdeacon wink, or did he not? I am inclined to think he did not quite wink, but that without such perhaps unseemly gesture he communicated to Mr. Chadwick with the corner of his eye intimation that, deep as was Mrs. Grantly's interest in the matter, it should not procure for her a perusal of that document. And at the same time he partly opened the small drawer above spoken of, deposited the paper on the volume of Rabelais, and showed to Mr. Chadwick the nature of the key which guarded these hidden treasures. The careful Steward then expressed himself contented. Ah! vain man! He could fasten up his Rabelais, and other things secret, with all the skill of Bramah or of Chubb, but where could he fasten up the key which solved these mechanical mysteries? It is probable to us that the contents of no drawer in that house were unknown to its mistress, and we think, moreover, that she was entitled to all such knowledge.

"But," said Mr. Chadwick, "we must of course tell your father and Mr. Harding so much of Sir Abraham's opinion as will satisfy them that the matter is doing well."

"Oh, certainly—yes, of course," said the Doctor.

"You had better let them know that Sir Abraham is of opinion that there is no case at any rate against Mr. Harding, and that as the action is worded at present, it must fall to the ground. They must be nonsuited if they carry it on. You had better tell Mr. Harding that Sir Abraham is clearly of opinion that he is only a servant, and as such, not liable. Or if you like it, I'll see Mr. Harding myself."

"Oh, I must see him tomorrow, and my father too, and I'll explain to them exactly so much. You won't go before lunch, Mr. Chadwick. Well, if you will, you must, for I know your time is precious." And he shook hands with the diocesan Steward and bowed him out.

The Archdeacon had again recourse to his drawer, and twice read through the essence of Sir Abraham Haphazard's law-enlightened and law-bewildered brains. It was very clear that to Sir Abraham, the justice of the old men's claim or the justice of Mr. Harding's defense were ideas that had never presented themselves. A legal victory over an opposing party was the service for which Sir Abraham was, as he imagined, to be paid, and that he, according to his lights, had diligently labored to achieve, and with probable hope of success. Of the intense desire which Mr. Harding felt to be assured on fit authority that he was wronging no man, that he was entitled in true equity to his income, that he might sleep at night without pangs of conscience, that he was no robber, no spoiler of the poor, that he and all the world might be openly convinced that he was not the man which the *Jupiter* had described him to be—of such longings on the part of Mr. Harding, Sir Abraham was entirely ignorant. Nor, indeed, could it be looked on as part of his business to gratify such desires. Such was not the system on which his battles were fought, and victories gained. Success was his object, and he was generally successful. He conquered his enemies by their weakness rather than by his own strength, and it had been found almost impossible to make up a case in which Sir Abraham, as an antagonist, would not find a flaw.

The Archdeacon was delighted with the closeness of the reasoning. To do him justice, it was not a selfish triumph that he desired. He would personally lose nothing by defeat, or at least what he might lose did not actuate him. But neither was it love of justice which made him so anxious, nor even mainly solicitude for his father-in-law. He was fighting a part of a never-ending battle against a never-conquered foe—that of the Church against its enemies.

He knew Mr. Harding could not pay all the expense of these doings—for these long opinions of Sir Abraham's, these causes to be pleaded, these speeches to be made, these various courts through which the case was, he presumed, to be dragged. He knew that he and his father must at least bear the heavier portion of this tremendous cost. But to do the Archdeacon justice, he did not recoil from this. He was a man fond of obtaining money, greedy of a large income, but openhanded enough in expending it, and it was a triumph to him to foresee the success of this measure, although he might be called on to pay so dearly for it himself.

CHAPTER IX

THE CONFERENCE

On the following morning the Archdeacon was with his father betimes, and a note was sent down to the Warden begging his attendance at the palace. Dr. Grantly, as he cogitated on the matter leaning back in his brougham as he journeyed into Barchester, felt that it would be difficult to communicate his own satisfaction either to his father or his father-in-law. He wanted success on his own side and discomfiture on that of his enemies. The Bishop wanted peace on the subject—a settled peace if possible, but peace at any rate till the short remainder of his own days had spun itself

ut. Mr. Harding required not only success and peace, but demanded also
hat he might stand justified before the world.

The Bishop, however, was comparatively easy to deal with, and before
he arrival of the other, the dutiful son had persuaded his father that all
vas going on well. And then the Warden arrived.

It was Mr. Harding's wont whenever he spent a morning at the palace
o seat himself immediately at the Bishop's elbow, the Bishop occupying a
uge armchair fitted up with candlesticks, a reading table, a drawer, and
ther paraphernalia, the position of which chair was never moved, summer
r winter. And when, as was usual, the Archdeacon was there also, he con-
ronted the two elders, who thus were enabled to fight the battle against
im together—and together submit to defeat, for such was their constant fate.

Our Warden now took his accustomed place, having greeted his son-
n-law as he entered and then affectionately inquired after his friend's
ealth. There was a gentleness about the Bishop to which the soft womanly
ffection of Mr. Harding particularly endeared itself, and it was quaint to
ee how the two mild old priests pressed each other's hands, and smiled and
nade little signs of love.

"Sir Abraham's opinion has come at last," began the Archdeacon. Mr.
Harding had heard so much, and was most anxious to know the result.

"It is quite favorable," said the Bishop, pressing his friend's arm. "I am
o glad."

Mr. Harding looked at the mighty bearer of the important news for
confirmation of these glad tidings.

"Yes," said the Archdeacon. "Sir Abraham has given most minute attention to the case. Indeed, I knew he would—most minute attention, and his
opinion is—and as to his opinion on such a subject being correct, no one
who knows Sir Abraham's character can doubt—his opinion is that they
haven't got a leg to stand on."

"But as how, Archdeacon?"

"Why, in the first place—— But you're no lawyer, Warden, and I doubt
you won't understand it. The gist of the matter is this—under Hiram's will
two paid guardians have been selected for the hospital, the law will say
two paid servants, and you and I won't quarrel with the name."

"At any rate I will not if I am one of the servants," said Mr. Harding.
"A rose, you know——"

"Yes, yes," said the Archdeacon, impatient of poetry at such a time.
"Well, two paid servants, we'll say, one to look after the men and the
other to look after the money. You and Chadwick are these two servants,
and whether either of you be paid too much, or too little—more or less in
fact than the founder willed—it's as clear as daylight that no one can fall
foul of either of you for receiving an allotted stipend."

"That does seem clear," said the Bishop, who had winced visibly at the
words servants and stipend, which, however, appeared to have caused no
uneasiness to the Archdeacon.

"Quite clear," said he, "and very satisfactory. In point of fact, it bein necessary to select such servants for the use of the hospital, the pay to b given to them must depend on the rate of pay for such services accordin to their market value at the period in question. And those who manag the hospital must be the only judges of this."

"And who does manage the hospital?" asked the Warden.

"Oh, let them find that out, that's another question. The action is brough against you and Chadwick. That's your defense, and a perfect and ful defense it is. Now that I think very satisfactory."

"Well," said the Bishop, looking inquiringly up into his friend's face who sat silent awhile, and apparently not so well satisfied.

"And conclusive," continued the Archdeacon. "If they press it to a jury which they won't do, no twelve men in England will take five minutes to decide against them."

"But according to that," said Mr. Harding, "I might as well have sixteer hundred a year as eight, if the managers choose to allot it to me. And a I am one of the managers, if not the chief manager myself, that can hardly be a just arrangement."

"Oh, well, all that's nothing to the question. The question is whethe this intruding fellow, and a lot of cheating attorneys and pestilent Dis senters, are to interfere with an arrangement which everyone knows i essentially just and serviceable to the Church. Pray don't let us be splitting hairs, and that among ourselves, or there'll never be an end of the caus or the cost."

Mr. Harding again sat silent for a while, during which the Bishop once and again pressed his arm, and looked in his face to see if he could catch a gleam of a contented and eased mind. But there was no such gleam, and the poor Warden continued playing sad dirges on invisible stringed instru ments in all manner of positions. He was ruminating in his mind on this opinion of Sir Abraham, looking to it wearily and earnestly for satisfaction, but finding none. At last he said, "Did you see the opinion, Archdeacon?"

The Archdeacon said he had not—that was to say, he had—that was, he had not seen the opinion itself, he had seen what had been called a copy, but he could not say whether of a whole or part. Nor could he say that what he had seen were the *ipsissima verba* of the great man himself. But what he had seen contained exactly the decision which he had announced, and which he again declared to be to his mind extremely satisfactory.

"I should like to see the opinion," said the Warden—"that is, a copy of it."

"Well, I suppose you can if you make a point of it, but I don't see the use myself. Of course it is essential that the purport of it should not be known, and it is therefore unadvisable to multiply copies."

"Why should it not be known?" asked the Warden.

"What a question for a man to ask!" said the Archdeacon, throwing up his hands in token of his surprise. "But it is like you. A child is not more innocent than you are in matters of business. Can't you see that if we ell them that no action will lie against you, but that one may possibly e against some other person or persons, that we shall be putting weapons nto their hands, and be teaching them how to cut our own throats?"

The Warden again sat silent, and the Bishop again looked at him wistfully. "The only thing we have now to do," continued the Archdeacon, is to remain quiet, hold our peace, and let them play their own game s they please."

"We are not to make known, then," said the Warden, "that we have onsulted the Attorney General, and that we are advised by him that the ounder's will is fully and fairly carried out."

"God bless my soul!" said the Archdeacon. "How odd it is that you vill not see that all we are to do is to do nothing! Why should we say nything about the founder's will? We are in possession, and we know hat they are not in a position to put us out. Surely that is enough for the resent."

Mr. Harding rose from his seat and paced thoughtfully up and down he library, the Bishop the while watching him painfully at every turn, and he Archdeacon continuing to pour forth his convictions that the affair vas in a state to satisfy any prudent mind.

"And the *Jupiter*?" said the Warden, stopping suddenly.

"Oh, the *Jupiter*!" answered the other. "The *Jupiter* can break no bones. You must bear with that. There is much of course which it is our ounden duty to bear, it cannot be all roses for us here," and the Archdeacon looked exceedingly moral. "Besides, the matter is too trivial, of oo little general interest, to be mentioned again in the *Jupiter*, unless we tir up the subject." And the Archdeacon again looked exceedingly knowing nd worldly wise.

The Warden continued his walk. The hard and stinging words of that newspaper article, each one of which had thrust a thorn as it were into his inmost soul, were fresh in his memory. He had read it more than once, word by word, and what was worse, he fancied it was as well known to everyone as to himself. Was he to be looked on as the unjust griping priest he had been there described, was he to be pointed at as the consumer of the bread of the poor, and to be allowed no means of refuting such charges, of clearing his begrimed name, of standing innocent in the world, as hitherto he had stood? Was he to bear all this, to receive as usual his now hated income, and be known as one of those greedy priests who by their rapacity have brought disgrace on their Church? And why? Why should he bear all this? Why should he die—for he felt that he could not live—under such a weight of obloquy? As he paced up and down the room he resolved in his misery and enthusiasm that he could with pleasure, f he were allowed, give up his place, abandon his pleasant home, leave the hospital, and live poorly, happily, and with an unsullied name on the small remainder of his means.

He was a man somewhat shy of speaking of himself, even before

those who knew him best and whom he loved the most. But at las
it burst forth from him, and with a somewhat jerking eloquence h
declared that he could not, would not, bear this misery any longer.

"If it can be proved," said he at last, "that I have a just and honest righ
to this, as God well knows I always deemed I had—if this salary or stipen
be really my due, I am not less anxious than another to retain it. I have th
well-being of my child to look to. I am too old to miss without some pai
the comforts to which I have been used, and I am, as others are, anxiou
to prove to the world that I have been right, and to uphold the plac
I have held. But I cannot do it at such a cost as this. I cannot bear thi
Could you tell me to do so?" And he appealed, almost in tears, to th
Bishop, who had left his chair and was now leaning on the Warden'
arm as he stood on the farther side of the table facing the Archdeacor
"Could you tell me to sit there at ease, indifferent and satisfied, whil
such things as these are said loudly of me in the world?"

The Bishop could feel for him and sympathize with him, but he coul
not advise him. He could only say: "No, no, you shall be asked to d
nothing that is painful, you shall do just what your heart tells you to b
right, you shall do whatever you think best yourself. Theophilus, don'
advise him, pray don't advise the Warden to do anything which is painful.

But the Archdeacon, though he could not sympathize, could advise
and he saw that the time had come when it behooved him to do so in
somewhat peremptory manner.

"Why, my lord," he said, speaking to his father—and when he calle
his father "my lord" the good old Bishop shook in his shoes, for he knev
that an evil time was coming. "Why, my lord, there are two way
of giving advice. There is advice that may be good for the present day
and there is advice that may be good for days to come. Now I canno
bring myself to give the former if it be incompatible with the other."

"No, no, no, I suppose not," said the Bishop, reseating himself and shading
his face with his hands. Mr. Harding sat down with his back to the farthe
wall, playing to himself some air fitted for so calamitous an occasion
and the Archdeacon said out his say standing, with his back to the empty
fireplace.

"It is not to be supposed but that much pain will spring out of thi
unnecessarily raised question. We must all have foreseen that, and the
matter has in no wise gone on worse than we expected. But it will be
weak—yes, and wicked also—to abandon the cause and own ourselves wrong
because the inquiry is painful. It is not only ourselves we have to look to
to a certain extent the interest of the Church is in our keeping. Should
it be found that one after another of those who hold preferment abandoned
it whenever it might be attacked, is it not plain that such attacks would
be renewed till nothing was left us? And that, if so deserted, the Church
of England must fall to the ground altogether? If this be true of many, i
is true of one. Were you, accused as you now are, to throw up the warden-

hip, and to relinquish the preferment which is your property, with the
main object of proving yourself disinterested, you would fail in that object,
you would inflict a desperate blow on your brother clergymen, you would
encourage every cantankerous Dissenter in England to make a similar
charge against some source of clerical revenue, and you would do your
best to dishearten those who are most anxious to defend you and uphold
your position. I can fancy nothing more weak, or more wrong. It is not
that you think that there is any justice in these charges, or that you doubt
your own right to the wardenship. You are convinced of your own honesty,
and yet would yield to them through cowardice."

"Cowardice!" said the Bishop, expostulating. Mr. Harding sat unmoved,
gazing on his son-in-law.

"Well, would it not be cowardice? Would he not do so because he is
afraid to endure the evil things which will be falsely spoken of him? Would
that not be cowardice? And now let us see the extent of the evil which
you dread. The *Jupiter* publishes an article which a great many, no doubt,
will read. But of those who understand the subject, how many will
believe the *Jupiter*? Everyone knows what its object is. It has taken up
the case against Lord Guildford and against the Dean of Rochester, and that
against half a dozen bishops; and does not everyone know that it would take
up any case of the kind, right or wrong, false or true, with known justice
or known injustice, if by doing so it could further its own views? Does
not all the world know this of the *Jupiter*? Who that really knows you
will think the worse of you for what the *Jupiter* says? And why care
for those who do not know you? I will say nothing of your own comfort,
but I do say that you could not be justified in throwing up in a fit of
passion—for such it would be—the only maintenance that Eleanor has.
And if you did so, if you really did vacate the wardenship and submit
to ruin, what would that profit you? If you have no future right to the
income, you have had no past right to it, and the very fact of your
abandoning your position would create a demand for repayment of that
which you have already received and spent."

The poor Warden groaned as he sat perfectly still looking up at the
hardhearted orator who thus tormented him, and the Bishop echoed the
sound faintly from behind his hands. But the Archdeacon cared little for
such signs of weakness, and completed his exhortation.

"But let us suppose the office to be left vacant, and that your own
troubles concerning it were over. Would that satisfy you? Are your only
aspirations in the matter confined to yourself and family? I know they
are not. I know you are as anxious as any of us for the Church to which
we belong. And what a grievous blow would such an act of apostasy give
her! You owe it to the Church of which you are a member and a minister
to bear with this affliction, however severe it may be. You owe it to
my father, who instituted you, to support his rights. You owe it to those
who preceded you to assert the legality of their position. You owe it

to those who are to come after you to maintain uninjured for them tha which you received uninjured from others. And you owe to us all th unflinching assistance of perfect brotherhood in this matter, so that up holding one another we may support our great cause without blushing an without disgrace."

And so the Archdeacon ceased, and stood self-satisfied, watching th effect of his spoken wisdom.

The Warden felt himself, to a certain extent, stifled. He would hav given the world to get himself out into the open air without speakin to or noticing those who were in the room with him, but this was impossi ble. He could not leave without saying something, and he felt himself con founded by the Archdeacon's eloquence. There was a heavy, unfeeling unanswerable truth in what he had said. There was so much practical but odious, common sense in it that he neither knew how to assent or t differ. If it were necessary for him to suffer, he felt that he could endur without complaint and without cowardice, providing that he was self satisfied of the justice of his own cause. What he could not endure wa that he should be accused by others and not acquitted by himself. Doubt ing, as he had begun to doubt, the justice of his own position in th hospital, he knew that his own self-confidence would not be restored becaus Mr. Bold had been in error as to some legal form. Nor could he b satisfied to escape because, through some legal fiction, he who received th greatest benefit from the hospital might be considered only as one of it servants.

The Archdeacon's speech had silenced him, stupefied him, annihilated hin —anything but satisfied him. With the Bishop it fared not much better He did not discern clearly how things were, but he saw enough to know that a battle was to be prepared for, a battle that would destroy his few remaining comforts and bring him with sorrow to the grave.

The Warden still sat, and still looked at the Archdeacon, till his thoughts fixed themselves wholly on the means of escape from his present position and he felt like a bird fascinated by gazing on a snake.

"I hope you agree with me," said the Archdeacon at last, breaking the dread silence. "My lord, I hope you agree with me." Oh, what a sigh the Bishop gave! "My lord, I hope you agree with me," again repeated the merciless tyrant.

"Yes, I suppose so," groaned the poor old man, slowly.

"And you, Warden?"

Mr. Harding was now stirred to action. He must speak and move, so he got up and took one turn before he answered.

"Do not press me for an answer just at present. I will do nothing lightly in the matter, and of whatever I do I will give you and the Bishop notice." And so without another word he took his leave, escaping quickly through the palace hall and down the lofty steps. Nor did he breathe freely till he found himself alone under the huge elms of the silent close. Here

walked long and slowly, thinking on his case with a troubled air,
d trying in vain to confute the Archdeacon's argument. He then went
me, resolved to bear it all—ignominy, suspense, disgrace, self-doubt,
d heartburning—and to do as those would have him who he still believed
ere most fit and most able to counsel him aright.

CHAPTER X

TRIBULATION

R. HARDING was a sadder man than he had ever yet been when he returned
his own house. He had been wretched enough on that well-remembered
orning when he was forced to expose before his son-in-law the publisher's
count for ushering into the world his dear book of sacred music—when
ter making such payments as he could do unassisted, he found that
was a debtor of more than three hundred pounds—but his sufferings
en were as nothing to his present misery. Then he had done wrong, and
knew it, and was able to resolve that he would not sin in like manner
ain; but now he could make no resolution and comfort himself by no
omises of firmness. He had been forced to think that his lot had placed
m in a false position, and he was about to maintain that position against
e opinion of the world and against his own convictions.

He had read with pity amounting almost to horror the strictures which
d appeared from time to time against the Earl of Guildford as master
St. Cross, and the invectives that had been heaped on rich diocesan digni-
ries and overgrown sinecure pluralists. In judging of them, he judged
niently. The old bias of his profession had taught him to think that
ey were more sinned against than sinning, and that the animosity with
hich they had been pursued was venomous and unjust; but he had not
e less regarded their plight as most miserable. His hair had stood on
d and his flesh had crept as he read the things which had been written.
e had wondered how men could live under such a load of disgrace,
w they could face their fellow creatures while their names were ban-
ed about so injuriously and so publicly. Now this lot was to be his. He,
at shy retiring man who had so comforted himself in the hidden obscurity
his lot, who had so enjoyed the unassuming warmth of his own little
rner—he was now to be dragged forth into the glaring day, gibbeted
fore ferocious multitudes. He entered his own house a crestfallen,
miliated man, without a hope of overcoming the wretchedness which
fected him.

He wandered into the drawing-room, where was his daughter, but he
uld not speak to her now, so he left it and went into the bookroom. He

was not quick enough to escape Eleanor's glance, or to prevent her from
seeing that he was disturbed, and in a little while she followed him. She
found him seated in his accustomed chair with no book open before him,
no pen ready in his hand, no ill-shapen notes of blotted music lying before
him as was usual, none of those hospital accounts with which he was so
precise and yet so unmethodical. He was doing nothing, thinking of nothing,
looking at nothing. He was merely suffering.

"Leave me, Eleanor, my dear," he said. "Leave me, my darling, for a
few minutes, for I am busy."

Eleanor saw well how it was, but she did leave him, and glided silently
back to her drawing-room. When he had sat awhile, thus alone and
unoccupied, he got up to walk again. He could make more of his thought
walking than sitting, and was creeping out into his garden when he
met Bunce on the threshold.

"Well, Bunce," said he, in a tone that for him was sharp, "what is it?
Do you want me?"

"I was only coming to ask after Your Reverence," said the old bedesman,
touching his hat—"and to inquire about the news from London," he
added after a pause.

The Warden winced, and put his hand to his forehead and felt bewildered.

"Attorney Finney has been there this morning," continued Bunce, "and
by his looks I guess he is not so well pleased as he once was, and it has
got abroad somehow that the Archdeacon has had down great news from
London, and Handy and Moody are both as black as devils. And I hope,"
said the man, trying to assume a cheery tone, "that things are looking up,
and that there'll be an end soon to all this stuff which bothers Your
Reverence so sorely."

"Well, I wish there may be, Bunce."

"But about the news, Your Reverence?" said the old man, almost whispering. Mr. Harding walked on, and shook his head impatiently. Poor
Bunce little knew how he was tormenting his patron. "If there was anything
to cheer you, I should be so glad to know it," said he, with a tone of affection
which the Warden in all his misery could not resist.

He stopped and took both the old man's hands in his. "My friend,"
said he, "my dear old friend, there is nothing, there is no news to cheer
me. God's will be done." And two small hot tears broke away from
his eyes and stole down his furrowed cheeks.

"Then God's will be done," said the other solemnly. "But they told
me that there was good news from London, and I came to wish Your
Reverence joy. But God's will be done." The Warden again walked on,
and the bedesman looking wistfully after him and, receiving no encouragement to follow, returned sadly to his own abode.

For a couple of hours the Warden remained thus in the garden, now
walking, now standing motionless on the turf, and then, as his legs got

weary, sitting unconsciously on the garden seats, and then walking again. Eleanor, hidden behind the muslin curtains of the window, watched him through the trees as he came in sight and then again was concealed by the turnings of the walk. And thus the time passed away till five, when the Warden crept back to the house and prepared for dinner.

It was but a sorry meal. The demure parlor maid, as she handed the dishes and changed the plates, saw that all was not right, and was more demure than ever. Neither father nor daughter could eat, and the hateful food was soon cleared away and the bottle of port placed upon the table.

"Would you like Bunce to come in, Papa?" said Eleanor, thinking that the company of the old man might lighten his sorrow.

"No, my dear, thank you, not today. But are not you going out, Eleanor, this lovely afternoon? Don't stay in for me, my dear."

"I thought you seemed so sad, Papa."

"Sad," said he, irritated. "Well, people must all have their share of sadness here, I am not more exempt than another. But kiss me, dearest, and go now. I will, if possible, be more sociable when you return."

And Eleanor was again banished from her father's sorrow. Ah! her desire now was not to find him happy but to be allowed to share his sorrows, not to force him to be sociable but to persuade him to be trustful.

She put on her bonnet as desired, and went up to Mary Bold. This was her daily haunt, for John Bold was up in London among lawyers and church reformers, diving deep into other questions than that of the wardenship of Barchester; supplying information to one Member of Parliament and dining with another; subscribing to funds for the abolition of clerical incomes; and seconding at that great national meeting at the Crown and Anchor a resolution to the effect that no clergyman of the Church of England, be he who he might, should have more than a thousand a year, and none less than two hundred and fifty. His speech on this occasion was short—for fifteen had to speak, and the room was hired for two hours only, at the expiration of which the Quakers and Mr. Cobden were to make use of it for an appeal to the public in aid of the Emperor of Russia—but it was sharp and effective. At least he was told so by a companion with whom he now lived much, and on whom he greatly depended—one Tom Towers, a very leading genius, and supposed to have high employment on the staff of the *Jupiter*.

So Eleanor, as was now her wont, went up to Mary Bold, and Mary listened kindly while the daughter spoke much of her father and, perhaps kinder still, found a listener in Eleanor while she spoke about her brother. In the meantime the Warden sat alone, leaning on the arm of his chair. He had poured out a glass of wine, but had done so merely from habit, for he left it untouched. There he sat gazing at the open window and thinking, if he can be said to have thought, of the happiness of his past life. All manner of past delights came before his mind, which at the time he had enjoyed without considering them—his easy days, his absence of all kind of hard work, his pleasant shady home, those twelve old neighbors whose welfare till now had been the source of so much pleasant care, the excellence of his children, the friendship of the dear old Bishop, the solemn grandeur of those vaulted aisles through which he loved to hear his own voice pealing. And then that friend of friends, that choice ally that had never deserted him, that eloquent companion that would always, when asked, discourse such pleasant music, that violoncello of his!

Ah, how happy he had been! But it was over now. His easy days and absence of work had been the crime which brought on him his tribulation. His shady home was pleasant no longer, maybe it was no longer his. The old neighbors whose welfare had been so desired by him were his enemies. His daughter was as wretched as himself, and even the Bishop was made miserable by his position. He could never again lift up his voice boldly as he had hitherto done among his brethren, for he felt that he was disgraced. And he feared even to touch his bow, for he knew how grievous a sound of wailing, how piteous a lamentation, it would produce.

He was still sitting in the same chair and the same posture, having hardly moved a limb for two hours, when Eleanor came back to tea and succeeded in bringing him with her into the drawing-room.

The tea seemed as comfortless as the dinner, though the Warden, who had hitherto eaten nothing all day, devoured the plateful of bread and butter unconscious of what he was doing.

Eleanor had made up her mind to force him to talk to her, but she hardly knew how to commence. She must wait till the urn was gone, till the servant would no longer be coming in and out.

At last everything was quiet, and the drawing-room door was permanently closed. Then Eleanor, getting up and going round to her father, put her arm round his neck, and said, "Papa, won't you tell me what it is?"

"What what is, my dear?"

"This new sorrow that torments you. I know you are unhappy, Papa."

"New sorrow! It's no new sorrow, my dear. We have all our cares sometimes." And he tried to smile, but it was a ghastly failure. "But I shouldn't be so dull a companion. Come, we'll have some music."

"No, Papa, not tonight, it would only trouble you tonight." And she sat upon his knee, as she sometimes would in their gayest moods, and with her arm round his neck she said: "Papa, I will not leave you till you talk to me. Oh, if you only knew how much good it would do to you to tell me of it all."

The father kissed his daughter and pressed her to his heart, but still he said nothing. It was so hard to him to speak of his own sorrows. He was so shy a man even with his own child!

"Oh, Papa, do tell me what it is. I know it is about the hospital, and what they are doing up in London, and what that cruel newspaper has said. But if there be such cause for sorrow, let us be sorrowful together. We are all in all to each other now. Dear, dear Papa, do speak to me."

Mr. Harding could not well speak now, for the warm tears were running down his cheeks like rain in May, but he held his child close to his heart and squeezed her hand as a lover might, and she kissed his forehead and his wet cheeks, and lay upon his bosom, and comforted him as a woman only can do.

"My own child," he said as soon as his tears would let him speak, "my own, own child, why should you too be unhappy before it is necessary? It may come to that, that we must leave this place, but till that time comes why should your young days be clouded?"

"And is that all, Papa? If that be all, let us leave it, and have light hearts elsewhere. If that be all, let us go. Oh, Papa, you and I could be happy if we had only bread to eat so long as our hearts were light."

And Eleanor's face was lighted up with enthusiasm as she told her father how he might banish all his care. And a gleam of joy shot across his brow as this idea of escape again presented itself, and he again fancied for a moment that he could spurn away from him the income which the world envied him, that he could give the lie to that wielder of the toma-hawk who had dared to write such things of him in the *Jupiter,* that he could leave Sir Abraham, and the Archdeacon, and Bold, and the rest of them with their lawsuit among them, and wipe his hands altogether of so sorrow-stirring a concern. Ah, what happiness might there be in the distance, with Eleanor and him in some small cottage and nothing left of their former grandeur but their music! Yes, they would walk forth with their music books and their instruments, and shaking the dust from off their feet as they went, leave the ungrateful place. Never did a poor clergy-man sigh for a warm benefice more anxiously than our Warden did now to be rid of his.

"Give it up, Papa," she said again, jumping from his knees and standing on her feet before him, looking boldly into his face. "Give it up, Papa."

Oh, it was sad to see how that momentary gleam of joy passed away, how the look of hope was dispersed from that sorrowful face as the remem-brance of the Archdeacon came back upon our poor Warden and he reflected that he could not stir from his now hated post. He was as a man bound with iron, fettered with adamant. He was in no respect a free agent, he had no choice. "Give it up!" Oh, if he only could! What an easy way that were out of all his troubles!

"Papa, don't doubt about it," she continued, thinking that his hesitation arose from his unwillingness to abandon so comfortable a home. "Is it on my account that you would stay here? Do you think that I cannot be happy without a pony carriage and a fine drawing-room? Papa, I never can be happy here as long as there is a question as to your honor in staying here, but I could be gay as the day is long in the smallest tiny little cottage if I could see you come in and go out with a light heart. Oh! Papa, your face tells so much! Though you won't speak to me with your voice, I know how it is with you every time I look at you."

How he pressed her to his heart again with almost a spasmodic pressure! How he kissed her as the tears fell like rain from his old eyes! How he blessed her, and called her by a hundred soft sweet names which now came new to his lips! How he chid himself for ever having been unhappy with such a treasure in his house, such a jewel on his bosom, with so sweet a flower in the choice garden of his heart! And then the floodgates of his tongue were loosed, and at length, with unsparing detail of circumstances, he told her all that he wished, and all that he could not do. He repeated those arguments of the Archdeacon, not agreeing in their truth, but explaining his inability to escape from them—how it had been declared to him that he was bound to remain where he was by the interests of his order, by gratitude to the Bishop, by the wishes of his friends, by a sense of duty which, though he could not understand it, he was fain to acknowledge. He told her how he had been accused of cowardice, and though he was not a man to make much of such a charge before the world, now in the full candor of his heart he explained to her that such an accusation was grievous to him—that he did think it would be unmanly to desert his post merely to escape his present sufferings, and that therefore he must bear as best he might the misery which was prepared for him.

And did she find these details tedious? Oh, no, she encouraged him to dilate on every feeling he expressed, till he laid bare the inmost corners of his heart to her. They spoke together of the Archdeacon as two children might of a stern, unpopular, but still respected schoolmaster, and of the Bishop as a parent kind as kind could be, but powerless against an omnipotent pedagogue.

And then, when they had discussed all this, when the father had told all to the child, she could not be less confiding than he had been. And as John Bold's name was mentioned between them, she owned how well she had learned to love him—had loved him once, she said, but she would not, could not, do so now. No, even had her troth been plighted to him, she would have taken it back again—had she sworn to love him as his wife, she would have discarded him, and not felt herself forsworn when he proved himself the enemy of her father.

But the Warden declared that Bold was no enemy of his, and encouraged her love, and gently rebuked, as he kissed her, the stern resolve she had made to cast him off. And then he spoke to her of happier days when their trials would all be over, and declared that her young heart should not be torn asunder to please either priest or prelate, dean or archdeacon. No, not if all Oxford were to convocate together and agree as to the necessity of the sacrifice!

And so they greatly comforted each other. In what sorrow will not such mutual confidence give consolation!—And with a last expression of tender love they parted, and went comparatively happy to their rooms.

CHAPTER XI

IPHIGENIA

WHEN Eleanor laid her head on her pillow that night, her mind was anxiously intent on some plan by which she might extricate her father from his misery, and in her warm-hearted enthusiasm, self-sacrifice was decided on as the means to be adopted. Was not so good an Agamemnon worthy of an Iphigenia? She would herself personally implore John Bold to desist from his undertaking. She would explain to him her father's sorrows, the cruel misery of his position. She would tell him how her father would die if he were thus dragged before the public and exposed to such unmerited ignominy. She would appeal to his old friendship, to his generosity, to his manliness, to his mercy. If need were, she would kneel to him for the favor she would ask.

But before she did this, the idea of love must be banished. There must be no bargain in the matter. To his mercy, to his generosity, she could appeal, but as a pure maiden, hitherto even unsolicited, she could not appeal to his love, nor under such circumstances could she allow him to do so. Of course when so provoked he would declare his passion. That was to be expected, there had been enough between them to make such a fact sure. But it was equally certain that he must be rejected. She could not be understood as saying "Make my father free and I am the reward." There would be no sacrifice in that. Not so had Jephthah's daughter saved her father, not so could she show to that kindest, dearest of parents how much she was able to bear for his good. No, to one resolve must her whole soul be bound. And so resolving, she felt that she could make her great request to Bold with as much self-assured confidence as she could have done to his grandfather.

And now I own I have fears for my heroine, not as to the upshot of her mission, not in the least as to that—as to the full success of her generous scheme, and the ultimate result of such a project, no one conversant with human nature and novels can have a doubt—but as to the amount of sympathy she may receive from those of her own sex. Girls below twenty and old ladies above sixty will do her justice, for in the female heart the soft springs of sweet romance reopen after many years and again gush out with waters pure as in earlier days, and greatly refresh the path that leads downward to the grave. But I fear that the majority of those between these two eras will not approve of Eleanor's plan. I fear that unmarried ladies of thirty-five will declare that there can be no probability of so absurd a project's being carried through, that young women on their knees before their lovers are sure to get kissed, and that they would not put themselves in such a position did they not expect it; that Eleanor is going to Bold only because circumstances prevent Bold from coming to her—that she is certainly a little fool, or a little schemer, but that in all probability she is thinking a good deal more about herself than her father.

Dear ladies, you are right as to your appreciation of the circumstances, but very wrong as to Miss Harding's character. Miss Harding was much younger than you are and could not therefore know, as you may do, to what dangers such an encounter might expose her. She may get kissed, I think it very probable that she will, but I give my solemn word and positive assurance that the remotest idea of such a catastrophe never occurred to her as she made the great resolve now alluded to.

And then she slept, and then she rose refreshed and met her father with her kindest embrace and most loving smiles. And on the whole their breakfast was by no means so triste as had been their dinner the day before. And then, making some excuse to her father for so soon leaving him, she started on the commencement of her operations.

She knew that John Bold was in London, and that therefore the scene itself could not be enacted today. But she also knew that he was soon to be home, probably on the next day, and it was necessary that some little plan for meeting him should be concerted with his sister Mary. When she got up to the house, she went as usual into the morning sitting-room, and was startled by perceiving, by a stick, a greatcoat, and sundry parcels which were lying about, that Bold must already have returned.

"John has come back so suddenly," said Mary, coming into the room. "He has been traveling all night."

"Then I'll come up again some other time," said Eleanor, about to beat a retreat in her sudden dismay.

"He's out now, and will be for the next two hours," said the other. "He's with that horrid Finney. He only came to see him, and he returns by the mail train tonight."

Returns by the mail train tonight, thought Eleanor to herself as she strove to screw up her courage—away again tonight! Then it must be now or never, and she again sat down, having risen to go.

She wished the ordeal could have been postponed. She had fully made up her mind to do the deed, but she had not made up her mind to do it this very day, and now she felt ill at ease, astray, and in difficulty.

"Mary," she began, "I must see your brother before he goes back."

"Oh, yes, of course," said the other. "I know he'll be delighted to see you." And she tried to treat it as a matter of course. But she was not the less surprised, for Mary and Eleanor had daily talked over John Bold and his conduct, and his love, and Mary would insist on calling Eleanor her sister, and would scold her for not calling Bold by his Christian name. And Eleanor would half-confess her love, but like a modest maiden would protest against such familiarities even with the name of her lover. And so

hey talked hour after hour, and Mary Bold, who was much the elder,
ooked forward with happy confidence to the day when Eleanor would
ot be ashamed to call her her sister. She was, however, fully sure that
ust at present Eleanor would be much more likely to avoid her brother than
o seek him.

"Mary, I must see your brother now, today, and beg from him a great
avor." And she spoke with a solemn air not at all usual to her. And then
he went on, and opened to her friend all her plan, her well-weighed scheme
or saving her father from a sorrow which would, she said, if it lasted,
ring him to his grave. "But, Mary," she continued, "you must now, you
now, cease any joking about me and Mr. Bold. You must now say no
nore about that. I am not ashamed to beg this favor from your brother, but
when I have done so, there can never be anything further between us!" And
nis she said with a staid and solemn air quite worthy of Jephthah's
aughter or of Iphigenia either.

It was quite clear that Mary Bold did not follow the argument. That
Eleanor Harding should appeal on behalf of her father to Bold's better
eelings seemed to Mary quite natural. It seemed quite natural that he
nould relent, overcome by such filial tears and by so much beauty. But,
o her thinking, it was at any rate equally natural that, having relented,
ohn should put his arm round his mistress's waist and say, "Now, having
ttled that, let us be man and wife, and all will end happily!" Why his
ood nature should not be rewarded when such reward would operate to
ne disadvantage of none, Mary, who had more sense than romance, could
ot understand, and she said as much.

Eleanor, however, was firm, and made quite an eloquent speech to sup-
ort her own view of the question. She could not condescend, she said,
o ask such a favor on any other terms than those proposed. Mary might,
erhaps, think her high-flown, but she had her own ideas, and she could
ot submit to sacrifice her self-respect.

"But I am sure you love him. Don't you?" pleaded Mary. "And I am
ure he loves you better than anything in the world."

Eleanor was going to make another speech, but a tear came to each
ye and she could not. So she pretended to blow her nose, and walked
o the window, and made a little inward call on her own courage, and
nding herself somewhat sustained, said sententiously,—"Mary, this is
onsense."

"But you do love him," said Mary, who had followed her friend to
ne window and now spoke with her arms close wound round the other's
aist. "You do love him with all your heart. You know you do, I defy you
o deny it."

"I——" commenced Eleanor, turning sharply round to refute the charge.
ut the intended falsehood stuck in her throat and never came to utter-
nce. She could not deny her love, so she took plentifully to tears, and
ant upon her friend's bosom and sobbed there, and protested that, love

or no love, it would make no difference in her resolve, and called Mary
a thousand times the most cruel of girls, and swore her to secrecy by
hundred oaths, and ended by declaring that the girl who could betray her
friend's love, even to a brother, would be as black a traitor as a soldier
in a garrison who should open the city gates to the enemy. While they
were yet discussing the matter, Bold returned, and Eleanor was forced
into sudden action. She had either to accomplish or abandon her plan
and having slipped into her friend's bedroom as the gentleman closed the
hall door, she washed the marks of tears from her eyes and resolved within
herself to go through with it. "Tell him I am here," said she, "and coming
in. And mind, whatever you do, don't leave us." So Mary informed her
brother, with a somewhat somber air, that Miss Harding was in the next
room and was coming to speak to him.

Eleanor was certainly thinking more of her father than herself as she
arranged her hair before the glass and removed the traces of sorrow from
her face. And yet I should be untrue if I said that she was not anxious to
appear well before her lover. Why else was she so sedulous with that
stubborn curl that would rebel against her hand, and smooth so eagerly
her ruffled ribands? Why else did she damp her eyes to dispel the red
ness, and bite her pretty lips to bring back the color? Of course she was
anxious to look her best, for she was but a mortal angel after all. But
had she been immortal, had she flitted back to the sitting-room on
cherub's wings, she could not have had a more faithful heart, or a truer
wish to save her father at any cost to herself.

John Bold had not met her since the day when she left him in dudgeon
in the cathedral close. Since that his whole time had been occupied in
promoting the cause against her father—and not unsuccessfully. He had
often thought of her, and turned over in his mind a hundred schemes
for showing her how disinterested was his love. He would write to her and
beseech her not to allow the performance of a public duty to injure
him in her estimation. He would write to Mr. Harding, explain all his
views, and boldly claim the Warden's daughter, urging that the untoward
circumstances between them need be no bar to their ancient friendship
or to a closer tie. He would throw himself on his knees before his mistress
He would wait and marry the daughter when the father had lost his
home and his income. He would give up the lawsuit and go to Australia
with her of course, leaving the *Jupiter* and Mr. Finney to complete the
case between them. Sometimes as he woke in the morning fevered and
impatient, he would blow out his brains and have done with all his cares—
but this idea was generally consequent on an imprudent supper enjoyed
in company with Tom Towers.

How beautiful Eleanor appeared to him as she slowly walked into
the room! Not for nothing had all those little cares been taken. Though
her sister, the Archdeacon's wife, had spoken slightingly of her charms
Eleanor was very beautiful when seen aright. Hers was not of those im

passive faces which have the beauty of a marble bust—finely chiseled features, perfect in every line, true to the rules of symmetry, as lovely to a stranger as to a friend, unvarying unless in sickness or as age affects them. She had no startling brilliancy of beauty, no pearly whiteness, no radiant carnation. She had not the majestic contour that rivets attention, demands instant wonder, and then disappoints by the coldness of its charms. You might pass Eleanor Harding in the street without notice, but you could hardly pass an evening with her and not lose your heart.

She had never appeared more lovely to her lover than she did now. Her face was animated, though it was serious, and her full dark lustrous eyes shone with anxious energy. Her hand trembled as she took his, and she could hardly pronounce his name when she addressed him. Bold wished with all his heart that the Australian scheme was in the act of realization, and that he and Eleanor were away together, never to hear further of the lawsuit.

He began to talk, asked after her health, said something about London being very stupid, and more about Barchester being very pleasant, declared the weather to be very hot, and then inquired after Mr. Harding.

"My father is not very well," said Eleanor.

John Bold was very sorry—so sorry! He hoped it was nothing serious, and put on the unmeaningly solemn face which people usually use on such occasions.

"I especially want to speak to you about my father, Mr. Bold. Indeed, I am now here on purpose to do so. Papa is very unhappy, very unhappy indeed, about this affair of the hospital. You would pity him, Mr. Bold, if you could see how wretched it has made him."

"Oh, Miss Harding!"

"Indeed you would—anyone would pity him. But a friend, an old friend as you are—indeed you would. He is an altered man. His cheerfulness has all gone, and his sweet temper, and his kind happy tone of voice. You would hardly know him if you saw him, Mr. Bold, he is so much altered, and—and—if this goes on, he will die." Here Eleanor had recourse to her handkerchief, and so also had her auditors, but she plucked up her courage and went on with her tale. "He will break his heart, and die. I am sure, Mr. Bold, it was not you who wrote those cruel things in the newspaper."

John Bold eagerly protested that it was not, but his heart smote him as to his intimate alliance with Tom Towers.

"No, I am sure it was not, and Papa has not for a moment thought so. You would not be so cruel. But it has nearly killed him. Papa cannot bear to think that people should so speak of him, and that everybody should hear him so spoken of. They have called him avaricious, and dishonest, and they say he is robbing the old men, and taking the money of the hospital for nothing."

"I have never said so, Miss Harding. I——"

"No," continued Eleanor, interrupting him, for she was now in the full flood tide of her eloquence, "no, I am sure you have not. But others have said so, and if this goes on, if such things are written again, it will kill Papa. Oh, Mr. Bold, if you only knew the state he is in! Now Papa does not care much about money."

Both her auditors, brother and sister, assented to this, and declared on their own knowledge that no man lived less addicted to filthy lucre than the Warden.

"Oh, it's so kind of you to say so, Mary, and of you too, Mr. Bold! I couldn't bear that people should think unjustly of Papa. Do you know he would give up the hospital altogether—only he cannot. The Archdeacon says it would be cowardly, and that he would be deserting his order, and injuring the Church. Whatever may happen, Papa will not do that. He would leave the place tomorrow willingly, and give up his house and the income and all, if the Archdeacon——" Eleanor was going to say "would let him," but she stopped herself before she had compromised her father's dignity, and giving a long sigh, she added—"Oh, I do so wish he would!"

"No one who knows Mr. Harding personally accuses him for a moment," said Bold.

"It is he that has to bear the punishment, it is he that suffers," said Eleanor. "And what for? What has he done wrong? How has he deserved this persecution? He that never had an unkind thought in his life, he that never said an unkind word!" and here she broke down, and the violence of her sobs stopped her utterance.

Bold, for the fifth or sixth time, declared that neither he nor any of his friends imputed any blame personally to Mr. Harding.

"Then why should he be persecuted?" ejaculated Eleanor through her tears, forgetting in her eagerness that her intention had been to humble herself as a suppliant before John Bold. "Why should he be singled out for scorn and disgrace? Why should he be made so wretched? Oh! Mr. Bold"—and she turned toward him as though the kneeling scene were about to be commenced—"oh! Mr. Bold, why did you begin all this? You, whom we all so—so—valued!"

To speak the truth, the reformer's punishment was certainly come upon him. His present plight was not enviable, he had nothing for it but to excuse himself by platitudes about public duty, which it is by no means worth while to repeat, and to reiterate his eulogy on Mr. Harding's character. His position was certainly a cruel one. Had any gentleman called upon him on behalf of Mr. Harding he could of course have declined to enter upon the subject, but how could he do so with a beautiful girl, with the daughter of the man whom he had injured, with his own love?

In the meantime Eleanor recollected herself, and again summoned up her energies.

"Mr. Bold," said she, "I have come here to implore you to abandon this proceeding." He stood up from his seat and looked beyond measure distressed. "To implore you to abandon it, to implore you to spare my father, to spare either his life or his reason, for one or the other will pay the forfeit if this goes on. I know how much I am asking, and how little right I have to ask anything. But I think you will listen to me, as it is for my father. Oh, Mr. Bold, pray, pray do this for us—pray do not drive to distraction a man who has loved you so well."

She did not absolutely kneel to him, but she followed him as he moved from his chair, and laid her soft hands imploringly upon his arm. Ah! at any other time how exquisitely valuable would have been that touch! But now he was distraught, dumfounded, and unmanned. What could he say to that sweet suppliant? How explain to her that the matter now was probably beyond his control, how tell her that he could not quell the storm which he had raised?

"Surely, surely, John, you cannot refuse her," said his sister.

"I would give her my soul," said he, "if it would serve her."

"Oh, Mr. Bold," said Eleanor, "do not speak so. I ask nothing for myself, and what I ask for my father it cannot harm you to grant."

"I would give her my soul if it would serve her," said Bold, still addressing his sister. "Everything I have is hers, if she will accept it—my house, my heart, my all. Every hope of my breast is centered in her. Her smiles are sweeter to me than the sun, and when I see her in sorrow as she now is, every nerve in my body suffers. No man can love better than I love her."

"No, no, no," ejaculated Eleanor, "there can be no talk of love between us. Will you protect my father from the evil you have brought upon him?"

"Oh, Eleanor, I will do anything. Let me tell you how I love you!"

"No, no, no," she almost screamed. "This is unmanly of you, Mr. Bold. Will you, will you, will you leave my father to die in peace in his quiet home?" And seizing him by his arm and hand, she followed him across the room toward the door. "I will not leave you till you promise me. I'll cling to you in the street, I'll kneel to you before all the people. You shall promise me this, you shall promise me this, you shall——" And she clung to him with fixed tenacity, and reiterated her resolve with hysterical passion.

"Speak to her, John, answer her," said Mary, bewildered by the unexpected vehemence of Eleanor's manner. "You cannot have the cruelty to refuse her."

"Promise me, promise me," said Eleanor. "Say that my father is safe. One word will do. I know how true you are. Say one word and I will let you go."

She still held him, and looked eagerly into his face, with her hair disheveled and her eyes all bloodshot. She had no thought now of herself, no care now for her appearance, and yet he thought he had never seen her half so lovely. He was amazed at the intensity of her beauty, and could hardly believe that it was she whom he had dared to love. "Promise me," said she. "I will not leave you till you have promised me."

"I will," said he at length, "I do. All I can do, I will do."

"Then may God Almighty bless you forever and ever!" said Eleanor. And falling on her knees with her face on Mary's lap, she wept and sobbed like a child. Her strength had carried her through her allotted task, but now it was well-nigh exhausted.

In a while she was partly recovered and got up to go, and would have gone had not Bold made her understand that it was necessary for him to explain to her how far it was in his power to put an end to the proceedings which had been taken against Mr. Harding. Had he spoken on any other subject, she would have vanished, but on that she was bound to hear him. And now the danger of her position commenced. While she had an active part to play, while she clung to him as a suppliant, it was easy enough for her to reject his proffered love and cast from her his caressing words. But now—now that he had yielded, and was talking to her calmly and kindly as to her father's welfare—it was hard enough for her to do so. Then Mary Bold assisted her, but now she was quite on her brother's side. Mary said but little, but every word she did say gave some direct and deadly blow. The first thing she did was to make room for her brother between herself and Eleanor on the sofa. As the sofa was full large for three, Eleanor could not resent this, nor could she show suspicion by taking another seat, but she felt it to be a most unkind proceeding. And then Mary would talk as though they three were joined in some close peculiar bond together, as though they were in future always to wish together, contrive together, and act together. And Eleanor could not gainsay this, she could not make another speech and say "Mr. Bold and I are strangers, Mary, and are always to remain so!"

He explained to her that though undoubtedly the proceeding against the hospital had commenced solely with himself, many others were now interested in the matter, some of whom were much more influential than himself; that it was to him alone, however, that the lawyers looked for instruction as to their doings, and, more important still, for the payment of their bills. And he promised that he would at once give them notice that it was his intention to abandon the cause. He thought, he said, that it was not probable that any active steps would be taken after he had seceded from the matter, though it was possible that some passing allusion might still be made to the hospital in the daily *Jupiter*. He promised, however, that he would use his best influence to prevent any further personal allusions being made to Mr. Harding. He then suggested that he would on that afternoon ride over himself to Dr. Grantly and inform him of his altered intentions on the subject, and with this view, he postponed his immediate return to London.

This was all very pleasant, and Eleanor did enjoy a sort of triumph in the feeling that she had attained the object for which she had sought this nterview. But still the part of Iphigenia was to be played out. The ;ods had heard her prayer, granted her request, and were they not to iave their promised sacrifice? Eleanor was not a girl to defraud them villfully, so as soon as she decently could she got up for her bonnet.

"Are you going so soon?" said Bold, who half an hour since would iave given a hundred pounds that he was in London and she still at Bar-chester.

"Oh, yes!" said she. "I am so much obliged to you. Papa will feel this o be so kind." She did not quite appreciate all her father's feelings. "Of course I must tell him, and I will say that you will see the Archdeacon."

"But may I not say one word for myself?" said Bold.

"I'll fetch you your bonnet, Eleanor," said Mary, in the act of leaving he room.

"Mary, Mary," said she, getting up and catching her by her dress, "don't ;o. I'll get my bonnet myself." But Mary, the traitress, stood fast by the loor and permitted no such retreat. Poor Iphigenia!

And with a volley of impassioned love, John Bold poured forth the feelings of his heart, swearing, as men do, some truths and many false-ioods. And Eleanor repeated with every shade of vehemence the "No, io, no" which had had a short time since so much effect. But now, alas! ts strength was gone. Let her be never so vehement, her vehemence was iot respected. All her "No, no, no's" were met with counterasseverations, ind at last were overpowered. The ground was cut from under her on every side. She was pressed to say whether her father would object, whether she herself had any aversion—aversion! God help her, poor girl! :he word nearly made her jump into his arms—any other preference—this she loudly disclaimed—whether it was impossible that she should love iim—Eleanor could not say that it was impossible—and so at last, all her defenses demolished, all her maiden barriers swept away, she capitulated, or rather marched out with the honors of war, vanquished evidently, palpably vanquished, but still not reduced to the necessity of confessing it.

And so the altar on the shore of the modern Aulis reeked with no sacrifice.

CHAPTER XII

MR. BOLD'S VISIT TO PLUMSTEAD

WHETHER or no the ill-natured prediction made by certain ladies in the beginning of the last chapter was or was not carried out to the letter, I am not in a position to state. Eleanor, however, certainly did feel herself to have been baffled as she returned home with all her news to her father. Certainly she had been victorious, certainly she had achieved her object, certainly she was not unhappy. And yet she did not feel herself triumphant. Everything would run smooth now. Eleanor was not at all addicted to the Lydian school of romance. She by no means objected to her lover because he came in at the door under the name of Absolute instead of pulling her out of a window under the name of Beverley. Yet she felt that she had been imposed upon, and could hardly think of Mary Bold with sisterly charity. "I did believe I could have trusted Mary," she said to herself over and over again. "Oh, that she should have dared to keep me in the room when I tried to get out!" Eleanor, however, felt that the game was up, and that she had now nothing further to do but to add to the budget of news which was prepared for her father that John Bold was her accepted lover.

We will, however, now leave her on her way and go with John Bold to Plumstead Episcopi, merely premising that Eleanor on reaching home will not find things so smooth as she fondly expected. Two messengers had come, one to her father and the other to the Archdeacon, and each of them much opposed to her quiet mode of solving all their difficulties—the one in the shape of a number of the *Jupiter*, and the other in that of a further opinion from Sir Abraham Haphazard.

John Bold got on his horse and rode off to Plumstead Episcopi, not briskly and with eager spur, as men do ride when self-satisfied with their own intentions, but slowly, modestly, thoughtfully, and somewhat in dread of the coming interview. Now and again he would recur to the scene which was just over, support himself by the remembrance of the silence that gives consent, and exult as a happy lover. But even this feeling was not without a shade of remorse. Had he not shown himself childishly weak thus to yield up the resolve of many hours of thought to the tears of a pretty girl? How was he to meet his lawyer? How was he to back out of a matter in which his name was already so publicly concerned? What, oh, what, was he to say to Tom Towers? While meditating these painful things he reached the lodge leading up to the Archdeacon's glebe, and for the first time in his life found himself within the sacred precincts.

All the Doctor's children were together on the slope of the lawn close to the road as Bold rode up to the hall door. They were there holding high debate on matters evidently of deep interest at Plumstead Episcopi, and the voices of the boys had been heard before the lodge gate was closed.

Florinda and Grizzel, frightened at the sight of so well-known an enemy to the family, fled on the first appearance of the horseman and ran in terror to their mother's arms. Not for them was it, tender branches, to resent injuries, or as members of a Church Militant to put on armor against its enemies. But the boys stood their ground like heroes, and boldly demanded the business of the intruder.

"Do you want to see anybody here, sir?" said Henry with a defiant eye and a hostile tone which plainly said that at any rate no one there wanted to see the person so addressed, and as he spoke he brandished aloft his garden water pot, holding it by the spout ready for the braining of anyone.

"Henry," said Charles James slowly, and with a certain dignity of diction, "Mr. Bold of course would not have come without wanting to see someone. If Mr. Bold has a proper ground for wanting to see some person here, of course he has a right to come."

But Samuel stepped lightly up to the horse's head and offered his services. "Oh, Mr. Bold," said he, "Papa, I'm sure, will be glad to see you. I suppose you want to see Papa. Shall I hold your horse for you? Oh, what a very pretty horse!" And he turned his head and winked funnily at his brothers. "Papa has heard such good news about the old hospital today. We know you'll be glad to hear it, because you're such a friend of Grandpapa Harding, and so much in love with Aunt Nelly!"

"How d'ye do, lads?" said Bold, dismounting. "I want to see your father if he's at home."

"Lads!" said Henry, turning on his heel and addressing himself to his brother, but loud enough to be heard by Bold. "Lads, indeed! If we're lads, what does he call himself?"

Charles James condescended to say nothing further, but cocked his hat with much precision and left the visitor to the care of his youngest brother.

Samuel stayed till the servant came, chatting and patting the horse, but as soon as Bold had disappeared through the front door, he stuck a switch under the animal's tail to make him kick, if possible.

The church reformer soon found himself tête-à-tête with the Archdeacon in that same room, in that sanctum sanctorum of the rectory, to which we have already been introduced. As he entered he heard the click of a certain patent lock, but it struck him with no surprise. The worthy clergyman was no doubt hiding from eyes profane his last much-studied sermon, for the Archdeacon, though he preached but seldom, was famous for his sermons. No room, Bold thought, could have been more becoming for a dignitary of the Church. Each wall was loaded with theology, over each separate bookcase was printed in small gold letters the names of those great divines whose works were ranged beneath. Beginning from the early Fathers in due chronological order, there were to be found the precious labors of the chosen servants of the Church down to the last pamphlet written in opposition to the consecration of Dr. Hampden. And raised above this were to be seen the busts of the greatest among the great: Chrysostom, St. Augustine, Thomas à Becket, Cardinal Wolsey, Archbishop Laud, and Dr. Philpotts.

Every appliance that could make study pleasant and give ease to the overtoiled brain was there: chairs made to relieve each limb and muscle, reading desks and writing desks to suit every attitude, lamps and candles mechanically contrived to throw their light on any favored spot, as the student might desire, a shoal of newspapers to amuse the few leisure moments which might be stolen from the labors of the day. And then from the window a view right through a bosky vista along which ran a broad green path from the rectory to the church, at the end of which the tawny-tinted fine old tower was seen with all its variegated pinnacles and parapets. Few parish churches in England are in better repair, or better worth keeping so, than that at Plumstead Episcopi, and yet it is built in a faulty style. The body of the church is low—so low that the nearly flat leaden roof would be visible from the churchyard were it not for the carved parapet with which it is surrounded. It is cruciform, though the transepts are irregular, one being larger than the other, and the tower is much too high in proportion to the church. But the color of the building is perfect; it is that rich yellow-gray which one finds nowhere but in the south and west of England, and which is so strong a characteristic of most of our old houses of Tudor architecture. The stonework also is beautiful, the mullions of the windows, and the thick tracery of the Gothic workmanship is as rich as fancy can desire. And though in gazing on such a structure one knows by rule that the old priests who built it built it wrong, one cannot bring oneself to wish that they should have made it other than it is.

When Bold was ushered into the bookroom, he found its owner standing with his back to the empty fireplace ready to receive him, and he could not but perceive that that expansive brow was elated with triumph, and that those full heavy lips bore more prominently than usual an appearance of arrogant success.

"Well, Mr. Bold," said he. "Well, what can I do for you? Very happy, I can assure you, to do anything for such a friend of my father-in-law."

"I hope you'll excuse my calling, Dr. Grantly."

"Certainly, certainly," said the Archdeacon. "I can assure you no apology is necessary from Mr. Bold—only let me know what I can do for him."

Dr. Grantly was standing himself, and he did not ask Bold to sit, and therefore he had to tell his tale standing, leaning on the table with his hat in his hand. He did, however, manage to tell it, and as the Archdeacon never once interrupted him or even encouraged him by a single word, he was not long in coming to the end of it.

"And so, Mr. Bold, I'm to understand, I believe, that you are desirous of abandoning this attack upon Mr. Harding."

"Oh, Dr. Grantly, there has been no attack, I can assure you."

"Well, well, we won't quarrel about words. I should call it an attack—most men would so call an endeavor to take away from a man every shilling of income that he has to live upon. But it shan't be an attack if you don't like it. You wish to abandon this—this little game of backgammon you've begun to play."

"I intend to put an end to the legal proceedings which I have commenced."

"I understand," said the Archdeacon. "You've already had enough of it. Well, I can't say that I am surprised. Carrying on a losing lawsuit where one has nothing to gain, but everything to pay, is not pleasant."

Bold turned very red in the face. "You misinterpret my motives," said he. "But however, that is of little consequence. I did not come to trouble you with my motives, but to tell you a matter of fact. Good morning, Dr. Grantly."

"One moment—one moment," said the other. "I don't exactly appreciate the taste which induced you to make any personal communication to me on the subject. But I dare say I'm wrong, I dare say your judgment is the better of the two. But as you have done me the honor—as you have, as it were, forced me into a certain amount of conversation on a subject which had better, perhaps, have been left to our lawyers—you will excuse me if I ask you to hear my reply to your communication."

"I am in a hurry, Dr. Grantly."

"Well, I am, Mr. Bold. My time is not exactly leisure time, and therefore, if you please, we'll go to the point at once. You are going to abandon this lawsuit?"—And he paused for a reply.

"Yes, Dr. Grantly, I am."

"Having exposed a gentleman who was one of your father's warmest friends to all the ignominy and insolence which the press could heap upon his name, having somewhat ostentatiously declared that it was your duty as a man of high public virtue to protect those poor old fools whom you have humbugged there at the hospital, you now find that the game costs more than it's worth, and so you make up your mind to have done with it. A prudent resolution, Mr. Bold. But it is a pity you should have been so long coming to it. Has it struck you that we may not now choose to give over? That we may find it necessary to punish the injury you have done to us? Are you aware, sir, that we have gone to enormous expense to resist this iniquitous attempt of yours?"

Bold's face was now furiously red, and he nearly crushed his hat between his hands, but he said nothing.

"We have found it necessary to employ the best advice that money could procure. Are you aware, sir, what may be the probable cost of securing the services of the Attorney General?"

"Not in the least, Dr. Grantly."

"I dare say not, sir. When you recklessly put this affair into the hands of your friend Mr. Finney, whose six and eightpences and thirteen and fourpences may, probably, not amount to a large sum, you were indifferent as to the cost and suffering which such a proceeding might entail on others. But are you aware, sir, that these crushing costs must now come out of your own pocket?"

"Any demand of such a nature which Mr. Harding's lawyer may have to make will doubtless be made to my lawyer."

"Mr. Harding's lawyer and my lawyer! Did you come here merely to refer me to the lawyers? Upon my word, I think the honor of your visit might have been spared! And now, sir, I'll tell you what my opinion is.

My opinion is that we shall not allow you to withdraw this matter from the courts."

"You can do as you please, Dr. Grantly. Good morning."

"Hear me out, sir," said the Archdeacon. "I have here in my hands the last opinion given in this matter by Sir Abraham Haphazard. I dare say you have already heard of this. I dare say it has had something to do with your visit here today."

"I know nothing whatever of Sir Abraham Haphazard or his opinion."

"Be that as it may, here it is. He declares most explicitly that under no phasis of the affair whatever have you a leg to stand upon—that Mr. Harding is as safe in his hospital as I am here in my rectory, that a more futile attempt to destroy a man was never made than this which you have made to ruin Mr. Harding. Here," and he slapped the paper on the table, "I have this opinion from the very first lawyer in the land, and under these circumstances you expect me to make you a low bow for your kind offer to release Mr. Harding from the toils of your net! Sir, your net is not strong enough to hold him. Sir, your net has fallen to pieces, and you knew that well enough before I told you. And now, sir, I'll wish you good morning, for I am busy."

Bold was now choking with passion. He had let the Archdeacon run on because he knew not with what words to interrupt him, but now that he had been so defied and insulted he could not leave the room without some reply.

"Dr. Grantly," he commenced.

"I have nothing further to say or to hear," said the Archdeacon. "I'll do myself the honor to order your horse." And he rang the bell.

"I came here, Dr. Grantly, with the warmest, kindest feelings——"

"Oh, of course you did, nobody doubts it."

"With the kindest feelings—and they have been most grossly outraged by your treatment."

"Of course they have! I have not chosen to see my father-in-law ruined. What an outrage that has been to your feelings!"

"The time will come, Dr. Grantly, when you will understand why I called upon you today."

"No doubt, no doubt. Is Mr. Bold's horse there? That's right. Open the front door. Good morning, Mr. Bold." And the Doctor stalked into his own drawing-room, closing the door behind him and making it quite impossible that John Bold should speak another word to him.

As John Bold got on his horse, which he was fain to do feeling like a dog turned out of a kitchen, he was again greeted by little Sammy.

"Good-by, Mr. Bold. I hope we may have the pleasure of seeing you again before long. I am sure Papa will always be glad to see you."

That was certainly the bitterest moment in John Bold's life. Not even the remembrance of his successful love could comfort him. Nay, when he thought of Eleanor, he felt that it was that very love which had brought

him to such a pass. That he should have been so insulted and be unable
to reply! That he should have given up so much to the request of a girl
and then have had his motives so misunderstood! That he should have
made so gross a mistake as this visit of his to the Archdeacon's! He bit
the top of his whip till he penetrated the horn of which it was made. He
struck the poor animal in his anger, and then was doubly angry with himself at his futile passion. He had been so completely checkmated, so palpably overcome! And what was he to do? He could not continue his action
after pledging himself to abandon it. Nor was there any revenge in that.
It was the very step to which his enemy had endeavored to goad him!

He threw the reins to the servant who came to take his horse, and rushed
upstairs into his drawing-room, where his sister Mary was sitting.

"If there be a devil," said he, "a real devil here on earth, it is Dr. Grantly."
He vouchsafed her no further intelligence, but again seizing his hat, he
rushed out and took his departure for London without another word to
anyone.

CHAPTER XIII

THE WARDEN'S DECISION

THE meeting between Eleanor and her father was not so stormy as that
described in the last chapter, but it was hardly more successful. On her
return from Bold's house she found her father in a strange state. He was
not sorrowful and silent as he had been on that memorable day when his
son-in-law lectured him as to all that he owed to his order, nor was he in
his usual quiet mood. When Eleanor reached the hospital, he was walking
to and fro upon the lawn, and she soon saw that he was much excited.

"I am going to London, my dear," he said as soon as he saw her.

"To London, Papa!"

"Yes, my dear, to London. I will have this matter settled in some way.
There are some things, Eleanor, which I cannot bear."

"Oh, Papa, what is it?" said she, leading him by the arm into the house.
"I had such good news for you, and now you make me fear I am too late."
And then, before he could let her know what had caused this sudden resolve, or could point to the fatal paper which lay on the table, she told
him that the lawsuit was over, that Bold had commissioned her to assure
her father in his name that it would be abandoned—that there was no further
cause for misery, and that the whole matter might be looked on as though
it had never been discussed. She did not tell him with what determined
vehemence she had obtained this concession in his favor, nor did she mention the price she was to pay for it. The Warden did not express himself
peculiarly gratified at this intelligence, and Eleanor, though she had not

worked for thanks and was by no means disposed to magnify her own good offices, felt hurt at the manner in which her news was received. "Mr. Bold can act as he thinks proper, my love," said he. "If Mr. Bold thinks he has been wrong, of course he will discontinue what he is doing, but that cannot change my purpose."

"Oh, Papa!" she exclaimed, all but crying with vexation. "I thought you would have been so happy—I thought all would have been right now."

"Mr. Bold," continued he, "has set great people to work—so great that I doubt they are now beyond his control. Read that, my dear." The Warden, doubling up a number of the *Jupiter*, pointed to the peculiar article which she was to read. It was to the last of the three leaders which are generally furnished daily for the support of the nation that Mr. Harding directed her attention. It dealt some heavy blows on various clerical delinquents; on families who received their tens of thousands yearly for doing nothing; on men who, as the article stated, rolled in wealth which they had neither earned nor inherited, and which was in fact stolen from the poorer clergy. It named some sons of bishops and grandsons of archbishops, men great in their way, who had redeemed their disgrace in the eyes of many by the enormity of their plunder. And then, having disposed of these leviathans, it descended to Mr. Harding.

"We alluded some weeks since to an instance of similar injustice, though in a more humble scale, in which the warden of an almshouse at Barchester has become possessed of the income of the greater part of the whole institution. Why an almshouse should have a warden we cannot pretend to explain, nor can we say what special need twelve old men can have for the services of a separate clergyman, seeing that they have twelve reserved seats for themselves in Barchester Cathedral. But be this as it may, let the gentleman call himself warden or precentor, or what he will—let him be never so scrupulous in exacting religious duties from his twelve dependents, or never so negligent as regards the services of the cathedral—it appears palpably clear that he can be entitled to no portion of the revenue of the hospital, excepting that which the founder set apart for him. And it is equally clear that the founder did not intend that three-fifths of his charity should be so consumed.

"The case is certainly a paltry one after the tens of thousands with which we have been dealing, for the warden's income is after all but a poor eight hundred a year. Eight hundred a year is not magnificent preferment of itself, and the warden may, for anything we know, be worth much more to the Church. But if so, let the Church pay him out of funds justly at its own disposal.

"We allude to the question of the Barchester almshouse at the present moment because we understand that a plea has been set up which will be peculiarly revolting to the minds of English churchmen. An action has been taken against Mr. Warden Harding, on behalf of the almsmen, by a gentleman acting solely on public grounds, and it is to be argued that Mr.

Harding takes nothing but what he receives as a servant of the hospital, and that he is not himself responsible for the amount of stipend given to him for his work. Such a plea would doubtless be fair if anyone questioned the daily wages of a bricklayer employed on a building, or the fee of the charwoman who cleans it. But we cannot envy the feeling of a clergyman of the Church of England who could allow such an argument to be put in his mouth.

"If this plea be put forward, we trust Mr. Harding will be forced as a witness to state the nature of his employment, the amount of work that he does, the income which he receives, and the source from whence he obtained his appointment. We do not think he will receive much public sympathy to atone for the annoyance of such an examination."

As Eleanor read the article her face flushed with indignation, and when she had finished it, she almost feared to look up at her father.

"Well, my dear," said he, "what do you think of that? Is it worth while to be a warden at that price?"

"Oh, Papa—dear Papa!"

"Mr. Bold can't unwrite that, my dear. Mr. Bold can't say that that shan't be read by every clergyman at Oxford—nay, by every gentleman in the land." Then he walked up and down the room while Eleanor in mute despair followed him with her eyes. "And I'll tell you what, my dear," he continued, speaking now very calmly, and in a forced manner very unlike himself, "Mr. Bold can't dispute the truth of every word in that article you have just read—nor can I." Eleanor stared at him as though she scarcely understood the words he was speaking. "Nor can I, Eleanor. That's the worst of all, or would be so if there were no remedy. I have thought much of all this since we were together last night"—and he came and sat beside her, and put his arm round her waist as he had done then—"I have thought much of what the Archdeacon has said, and of what this paper says, and I do believe I have no right to be here."

"No right to be warden of the hospital, Papa?"

"No right to be warden with eight hundred a year—no right to be warden with such a house as this, no right to spend in luxury money that was intended for charity. Mr. Bold may do as he pleases about his suit, but I hope he will not abandon it for my sake."

Poor Eleanor! This was hard upon her. Was it for this she had made her great resolve! For this that she had laid aside her quiet demeanor and taken upon her the rants of a tragedy heroine! One may work and not for thanks, but yet feel hurt at not receiving them, and so it was with Eleanor. One may be disinterested in one's good actions and yet feel discontented that they are not recognized. Charity may be given with the left hand so privily that the right hand does not know it, and yet the left hand may regret to feel that it has no immediate reward. Eleanor had had no wish to burden her father with a weight of obligation, and yet she had looked forward to much delight from the knowledge that she had freed him from his sorrows. Now such hopes were entirely over. All that she had done was of no avail. She had humbled herself to Bold in vain. The evil was utterly beyond her power to cure!

She had thought also how gently she would whisper to her father all that her lover had said to her about herself, and how impossible she had found it to reject him. And then she had anticipated her father's kindly kiss and close embrace as he gave his sanction to her love. Alas! she could say nothing of this now. In speaking of Mr. Bold, her father put him aside as one whose thoughts and sayings and acts could be of no moment. Gentle reader, did you ever feel yourself snubbed? Did you ever, when thinking much of your own importance, find yourself suddenly reduced to a nonentity? Such was Eleanor's feeling now.

"They shall not put forward this plea on my behalf," continued the Warden. "Whatever may be the truth of the matter, that at any rate is not true, and the man who wrote that article is right in saying that such a plea is revolting to an honest mind. I will go up to London, my dear, and see these lawyers myself, and if no better excuse can be made for me than that, I and the hospital will part."

"But the Archdeacon, Papa?"

"I can't help it, my dear. There are some things which a man cannot bear. I cannot bear that."—And he put his hand upon the newspaper.

"But will the Archdeacon go with you?"

To tell the truth, Mr. Harding had made up his mind to steal a march upon the Archdeacon. He was aware that he could take no steps without informing his dread son-in-law, but he had resolved that he would send out a note to Plumstead Episcopi detailing his plans, but that the messenger should not leave Barchester till he himself had started for London, so that he might be a day before the Doctor, who he had no doubt would follow him. In that day, if he had luck, he might arrange it all. He might explain to Sir Abraham that he, as warden, would have nothing further to do with the defense about to be set up. He might send in his official resignation to his friend the Bishop, and so make public the whole transaction that even the Archdeacon would not be able to undo what he had done. He knew too well the Archdeacon's strength and his own weakness to suppose he could do this if they both reached London together. Indeed, he would never be able to get to London if the Archdeacon knew of his intended journey in time to prevent it.

"No, I think not," said he. "I think I shall start before the Archdeacon could be ready. I shall go early tomorrow morning."

"That will be best, Papa," said Eleanor, showing that her father's ruse was appreciated.

"Why, yes, my love. The fact is, I wish to do all this before the Archdeacon can—can interfere. There is a great deal of truth in all he says. He argues very well, and I can't always answer him, but there is an old saying, Nelly: 'Everyone knows where his own shoe pinches!' He'll say that I want moral courage, and strength of character, and power of endurance, and it's all true. But I'm sure I ought not to remain here if I have nothing better to put forward than a quibble. So, Nelly, we shall have to leave this pretty place."

Eleanor's face brightened up as she assured her father how cordially she agreed with him.

"True, my love," said he, now again quite happy and at ease in his manner. "What good to us is this place, or all the money, if we are to be ill-spoken of?"

"Oh, Papa, I am so glad!"

"My darling child. It did cost me a pang at first, Nelly, to think that you should lose your pretty drawing-room, and your ponies, and your garden. The garden will be the worst of all—but there is a garden at Crabtree, a very pretty garden."

Crabtree Parva was the name of the small living which Mr. Harding had held as a minor canon, and which still belonged to him. It was only worth some eighty pounds a year and a small house and glebe, all of which were now handed over to Mr. Harding's curate. But it was to Crabtree glebe that Mr. Harding thought of retiring. This parish must not be mistaken for that other living, Crabtree Canonicorum, as it is called. Crabtree Canonicorum is a very nice thing. There are only two hundred parishioners, there are four hundred acres of glebe, and the great and small tithes, which both go to the rector, are worth four hundred pounds a year more. Crabtree Canonicorum is in the gift of the dean and chapter, and is at this time possessed by the Honorable and Reverend Dr. Vesey Stanhope, who also fills the prebendal stall of Goosegorge in Barchester Chapter, and holds the united rectory of Eiderdown and Stogpingum, or Stoke Pinquium, as it should be written. This is the same Dr. Vesey Stanhope whose hospitable villa on the Lake of Como is so well known to the elite of English travelers, and whose collection of Lombard butterflies is supposed to be unique.

"Yes," said the Warden, musing, "there is a very pretty garden at Crabtree. But I shall be sorry to disturb poor Smith." Smith was the curate of Crabtree, a gentleman who was maintaining a wife and half a dozen children on the income arising from his profession.

Eleanor assured her father that as far as she was concerned, she could leave her house and her ponies without a single regret. She was only so happy that he was going—going where he would escape all this dreadful turmoil.

"But we will take the music, my dear."

And so they went on planning their future happiness, and plotting how they would arrange it all without the interposition of the Archdeacon. At last they again became confidential, and then the Warden did thank her for what she had done, and Eleanor, lying on her father's shoulder, did find an opportunity to tell her secret. And the father gave his blessing to his child, and said that the man whom she loved was honest, good, and kindhearted, and right-thinking in the main—one who wanted only a good wife to put him quite upright—"a man, my love," he ended by saying, "to whom I firmly believe that I can trust my treasure with safety."

"But what will Dr. Grantly say?"

"Well, my dear, it can't be helped. We shall be out at Crabtree then."

And Eleanor ran upstairs to prepare her father's clothes for his journey, and the Warden returned to his garden to make his last adieus to every tree and shrub and shady nook that he knew so well.

CHAPTER XIV

MOUNT OLYMPUS

WRETCHED in spirit, groaning under the feeling of the insult, self-condemning, and ill-satisfied in every way, Bold returned to his London lodgings. Ill as he had fared in his interview with the Archdeacon, he was not the less under the necessity of carrying out his pledge to Eleanor, and he went about his ungracious task with a heavy heart.

The attorneys whom he had employed in London received his instructions with surprise and evident misgiving. However, they could only obey, and mutter something of their sorrow that such heavy costs should only fall upon their own employer—especially as nothing was wanting but perseverance to throw them on the opposite party. Bold left the office which he had latterly so much frequented, shaking the dust from off his feet, and before he was down the stairs, an edict had already gone forth for the preparation of the bill.

He next thought of the newspapers. The case had been taken up by more than one, and he was well aware that the keynote had been sounded by the *Jupiter*. He had been very intimate with Tom Towers, and had often discussed with him the affairs of the hospital. Bold could not say that the articles in that paper had been written at his own instigation. He did not even know as a fact that they had been written by his friend. Tom Towers had never said that such a view of the case, or such a side in the dispute, would be taken by the paper with which he was connected. Very discreet in such matters was Tom Towers, and altogether indisposed to talk loosely of the concerns of that mighty engine of which it was his high privilege to move in secret some portion. Nevertheless Bold believed that to him were owing those dreadful words which had caused such panic at Barchester, and he conceived himself bound to prevent their repetition. With this view he betook himself from the attorneys' office to that laboratory where, with amazing chemistry, Tom Towers compounded thunderbolts for the destruction of all that is evil and for the furtherance of all that is good, in this and other hemispheres.

Who has not heard of Mount Olympus—that high abode of all the powers of type, that favored seat of the great goddess Pica, that wondrous habitation of gods and devils from whence, with ceaseless hum of steam and never-ending flow of Castalian ink, issue forth eighty thousand nightly edicts for the governance of a subject nation?

Velvet and gilding do not make a throne, nor gold and jewels a scepter. It is a throne because the most exalted one sits there, and a scepter because the most mighty one wields it. So it is with Mount Olympus. Should a stranger make his way thither at dull noonday, or during the sleepy hours of the silent afternoon, he would find no acknowledged temple of power and beauty, no fitting fane for the great Thunderer, no proud façades and pillared roofs to support the dignity of this greatest of earthly potentates. To the outward and uninitiated eye, Mount Olympus is a somewhat humble spot, undistinguished, unadorned—nay, almost mean. It stands alone, as it were, in a mighty city, close to the densest throng of men but partaking neither of the noise nor the crowd, a small secluded, dreary spot, tenanted, one would say, by quite unambitious people, at the easiest rents. "Is this Mount Olympus?" asks the unbelieving stranger. "Is it from these small, dark, dingy buildings that those infallible laws proceed which Cabinets are called upon to obey, by which bishops are to be guided, lords and commons controlled, judges instructed in law, generals in strategy, admirals in naval tactics, and orangewomen in the management of their barrows?" "Yes, my friend—from these walls. From here issue the only known infallible bulls for the guidance of British souls and bodies. This little court is the Vatican of England. Here reigns a Pope, self-nominated, self-consecrated—ay and much stranger too, self-believing!—a Pope whom, if you cannot obey him, I would advise you to disobey as silently as possible; a Pope hitherto afraid of no Luther; a Pope who manages his own Inquisition, who punishes unbelievers as no most skilful Inquisitor of Spain ever dreamt of doing; one who can excommunicate thoroughly, fearfully, radically, put you beyond the pale of men's charity, make you odious to your dearest friends, and turn you into a monster to be pointed at by the finger!"

Oh, heavens! And this is Mount Olympus!

It is a fact amazing to ordinary mortals that the *Jupiter* is never wrong. With what endless care, with what unsparing labor, do we not strive to get together for our great national council the men most fitting to compose it. And how we fail! Parliament is always wrong. Look at the *Jupiter* and see how futile are their meetings, how vain their councils, how needless all their trouble! With what pride do we regard our chief Ministers, the great servants of state, the oligarchs of the nation on whose wisdom we lean, to whom we look for guidance in our difficulties! But what are they to the writers of the *Jupiter?* They hold council together and with anxious thought painfully elaborate their country's good. But when all is done, the *Jupiter* declares that all is nought. Why should we look to Lord John Russell, why should we regard Palmerston and Gladstone, when Tom Towers without a struggle can put us right? Look at our generals, what faults they make—at our admirals, how inactive they are. What money, honesty, and science can do is done, and yet how badly are our troops brought together, fed, conveyed, clothed, armed, and managed. The most excellent of our good men do their best to man our ships, with the assistance of all possible external appliances, but in vain. All, all is wrong! Alas! alas! Tom Towers, and he alone, knows all about it. Why, oh why, ye earthly ministers, why have ye not followed more closely this heaven-sent messenger that is among us?

Were it not well for us in our ignorance that we confided all things to the *Jupiter?* Would it not be wise in us to abandon useless talking, idle thinking, and profitless labor? Away with majorities in the House of Commons, with verdicts from judicial bench given after much delay, with doubtful laws, and the fallible attempts of humanity! Does not the *Jupiter,* coming forth daily with eighty thousand impressions full of unerring decision on every mortal subject, set all matters sufficiently at rest? Is not Tom Towers here, able to guide us and willing?

Yes indeed—able and willing to guide all men in all things, so long as he is obeyed as autocrat should be obeyed, with undoubting submission! Only let not ungrateful Ministers seek other colleagues than those whom Tom Towers may approve; let Church and State, law and physic, commerce and agriculture—the arts of war, and the arts of peace—all listen and obey, and all will be made perfect. Has not Tom Towers an all-seeing eye? From the diggings of Australia to those of California, right round the habitable globe, does he not know, watch, and chronicle the doings of everyone? From a bishopric in New Zealand to an unfortunate director of a Northwest passage, is he not the only fit judge of capability? From the sewers of London to the Central Railway of India, from the palaces of St. Petersburg to the cabins of Connaught, nothing can escape him. Britons have but to read, obey, and be blessed. None but the fools doubt the wisdom of the *Jupiter*. None but the mad dispute its facts.

No established religion has ever been without its unbelievers, even in the country where it is the most firmly fixed, no creed has been without scoffers, no Church has so prospered as to free itself entirely from Dissent. There are those who doubt the *Jupiter!* They live and breathe the upper air, walking here unscathed; though scorned—men born of British mothers and nursed on English milk who scruple not to say that Mount Olympus has its price, that Tom Towers can be bought for gold!

Such is Mount Olympus, the mouthpiece of all the wisdom of this great country. It may probably be said that no place in this nineteenth century is more worthy of notice. No Treasury mandate armed with the signatures of all the Government has half the power of one of those broad sheets which fly forth from hence so abundantly, armed with no signature at all.

Some great man, some mighty peer—we'll say a noble duke—retires to rest feared and honored by all his countrymen, fearless himself, if not a good man, at any rate a mighty man—too mighty to care much what men may say about his want of virtue. He rises in the morning degraded, mean, and miserable, an object of men's scorn, anxious only to retire as quickly as may be to some German obscurity, some unseen Italian privacy, or, indeed, anywhere out of sight. What has made this awful change? What has so afflicted him? An article has appeared in the *Jupiter*, some fifty lines of a narrow column have destroyed all His Grace's equanimity and banished him forever from the world. No man knows who wrote the bitter words. The clubs talk confusedly of the matter, whispering to each other this and that name, while Tom Towers walks quietly along Pall Mall with his coat buttoned close against the east wind, as though he were a mortal man and not a god dispensing thunderbolts from Mount Olympus.

It was not to Mount Olympus that our friend Bold betook himself. He had before now wandered round that lonely spot, thinking how grand a thing it was to write articles for the *Jupiter*, considering within himself whether by any stretch of the powers within him he could ever come to such distinction, wondering how Tom Towers would take any little humble offering of his talents, calculating that Tom Towers himself must have once had a beginning, have once doubted as to his own success. Towers could not have been born a writer in the *Jupiter*. With such ideas, half ambitious and half awe-struck, had Bold regarded the silent-looking workshop of the gods, but he had never yet by word or sign attempted to influence the slightest word of his unerring friend. On such a course was he now intent, and not without much inward palpitation did he betake himself to the quiet abode of wisdom where Tom Towers was to be found o' mornings inhaling ambrosia and sipping nectar in the shape of toast and tea.

Not far removed from Mount Olympus, but somewhat nearer to the blessed regions of the West, is the most favored abode of Themis. Washed by the rich tide which now passes from the towers of Caesar to Barry's halls of eloquence, and again back, with new offerings of a city's tribute, from the palaces of peers to the mart of merchants, stand those quiet walls which Law has delighted to honor by its presence. What a world within a world is the Temple! How quiet are its "entangled walks," as someone lately has called them, and yet how close to the densest concourse of humanity! How gravely respectable its sober alleys, though removed but by a single step from the profanity of the Strand and the low iniquity of Fleet Street! Old St. Dunstan, with its bell-smiting bludgeoners, has been removed. The ancient shops with their faces full of pleasant history are passing away one by one. The bar itself is to go—its doom has been pronounced by the *Jupiter*. Rumor tells us of some huge building that is to appear in these latitudes dedicated to law, subversive of the courts of Westminster and antagonistic to the Rolls and Lincoln's Inn. But nothing yet threatens the silent beauty of the Temple. It is the medieval court of the metropolis.

Here, on the choicest spot of this choice ground, stands a lofty row of chambers looking obliquely upon the sullied Thames. Before the windows, the lawn of the Temple Gardens stretches with that dim yet delicious verdure so refreshing to the eyes of Londoners. If doomed to live within the thickest of London smoke, you would surely say that that would be your chosen spot. Yes, you, you whom I now address, my dear, middle-aged bachelor friend, can nowhere be so well domiciled as here. No one here will ask whether you are out or at home, alone or with friends. Here no Sabbatarian will investigate your Sundays, no censorious landlady will scrutinize your empty bottle, no valetudinarian neighbor will complain of late hours. If you love books, to what place are books so suitable? The whole spot is redolent of typography. Would you worship the Paphian goddess, the groves of Cyprus are not more taciturn than those of the Temple. Wit and wine are always here, and always together. The revels of the Temple are as those of polished Greece, where the wildest worshiper of Bacchus never forgot the dignity of the god whom he adored. Where can retirement be so complete as here? Where can you be so sure of all the pleasures of society?

It was here that Tom Towers lived, and cultivated with eminent success the tenth Muse who now governs the periodical press. But let it not be supposed that his chambers were such, or so comfortless, as are frequently the gaunt abodes of legal aspirants. Four chairs, a half-filled deal bookcase with hangings of dingy green baize, an old office table covered with dusty papers which are not moved once in six months, and an old Pembroke brother with rickety legs for all daily uses; a despatcher for the preparation of lobsters and coffee, and an apparatus for the cooking of toast and mutton chops—such utensils and luxuries as these did not suffice for the well-being of Tom Towers. He indulged in four rooms on the first floor, each of which was furnished if not with the splendor with probably more than the comfort of Stafford House.

Every addition that science and art have lately made to the luxuries of modern life was to be found there. The room in which he usually sat was surrounded by bookshelves carefully filled, nor was there a volume there which was not entitled to its place in such a collection, both by its intrinsic worth and exterior splendor. A pretty portable set of steps in one corner of the room showed that those even on the higher shelves were intended for use. The chamber contained but two works of art: the one, an admirable bust of Sir Robert Peel by Power, declared the individual politics of our friend, and the other, a singularly long figure of a female devoted by Millais, told equally plainly the school of art to which he was addicted. This picture was not hung, as pictures usually are, against the wall. There was no inch of wall vacant for such a purpose. It had a stand or desk erected for its own accommodation, and there on her pedestal, framed and glazed, stood the devotional lady looking intently at a lily as no lady ever looked before.

Our modern artists, whom we style Pre-Raphaelites have delighted to go back not only to the finish and peculiar manner, but also to the subjects, of the early painters. It is impossible to give them too much praise for the elaborate perseverance with which they have equaled the minute perfections of the masters from whom they take their inspiration. Nothing probably can exceed the painting of some of these latter-day pictures. It is, however, singular into what faults they fall as regards their subjects. They are not quite content to take the old stock groups—a Sebastian with his arrows, a Lucia with her eyes in a dish, a Lorenzo with a gridiron, or the Virgin with two children. But they are anything but happy in their change. As a rule, no figure should be drawn in a position which it is impossible to suppose any figure should maintain. The patient endurance of St. Sebastian, the wild ecstasy of St. John in the wilderness, the maternal love of the Virgin, are feelings naturally portrayed by a fixed posture. But the lady with the stiff back and bent neck who looks at her flower, and is still looking from hour to hour, gives us an idea of pain without grace, and abstraction without a cause.

It was easy, from his rooms, to see that Tom Towers was a sybarite, though by no means an idle one. He was lingering over his last cup of tea, surrounded by an ocean of newspapers through which he had been swimming, when John Bold's card was brought in by his tiger. This tiger never knew that his master was at home, though he often knew that he was not, and thus Tom Towers was never invaded but by his own consent. On this occasion, after twisting the card twice in his fingers, he signified to his attendant imp that he was visible, and the inner door was unbolted and our friend announced.

I have before said that he of the *Jupiter* and John Bold were intimate. There was no very great difference in their ages, for Towers was still considerably under forty, and when Bold had been attending the London hospitals, Towers, who was not then the great man that he had since become, had been much with him. Then they had often discussed together the objects of their ambition and future prospects. Then Tom Towers was struggling hard to maintain himself, as a briefless barrister, by shorthand reporting for any of the papers that would engage him. Then he had not dared to dream of writing leaders for the *Jupiter*, or canvassing the conduct of Cabinet Ministers. Things had altered since that time.

The briefless barrister was still briefless, but he now despised briefs. Could he have been sure of a judge's seat, he would hardly have left his present career. It is true he wore no ermine, bore no outward marks of a world's respect, but with what a load of inward importance was he charged! It is true his name appeared in no large capitals, on no wall was chalked up "Tom Towers forever"—"Freedom of the Press and Tom Towers." But what Member of Parliament had half his power? It is true that in far-off provinces men did not talk daily of Tom Towers, but they read the *Jupiter*, and acknowledged that without the *Jupiter* life was not worth having. This kind of hidden but still conscious glory suited the nature of the man. He loved to sit silent in a corner of his club and listen to the loud chattering of politicians, and to think how they all were in his power—how he could smite the loudest of them, were it worth his while to raise his pen for such a purpose. He loved to watch the great men of whom he daily wrote and flatter himself that he was greater than any of them. Each of them was responsible to his country, each of them must answer if inquired into, each of them must endure abuse with good humor, and insolence without anger.

But to whom was he, Tom Towers, responsible? No one could insult him, no one could inquire into him. He could speak out withering words and no one could answer him. Ministers courted him, though perhaps they knew not his name, bishops feared him, judges doubted their own verdicts unless he confirmed them, and generals, in their councils of war, did not consider more deeply what the enemy would do than what the *Jupiter* would say. Tom Towers never boasted of the *Jupiter*, he scarcely ever named the paper even to the most intimate of his friends. He did not even wish to be spoken of as connected with it, but he did not the less value his privileges, or think the less of his own importance. It is probable that Tom Towers considered himself the most powerful man in Europe, and so he walked on from day to day, studiously striving to look a man, but knowing within his breast that he was a god.

CHAPTER XV

TOM TOWERS, DR. ANTICANT, AND MR. SENTIMENT

"Ah, Bold! How are you? You haven't breakfasted?"

"Oh, yes, hours ago. And how are you?"

When one Eskimo meets another, do the two, as an invariable rule, ask after each other's health? Is it inherent in all human nature to make this obliging inquiry? Did any reader of this tale ever meet any friend or acquaintance without asking some such question, and did anyone ever listen to the reply? Sometimes a studiously courteous questioner will show so much thought in the matter as to answer it himself by declaring that had he looked at you he needn't have asked, meaning thereby to signify that you are an absolute personification of health. But such persons are only those who premeditate small effects.

"I suppose you're busy?" inquired Bold.

"Why, yes, rather—or I should say rather not. If I have a leisure hour in the day, this is it."

"I want to ask you if you can oblige me in a certain matter."

Towers understood in a moment from the tone of his friend's voice that the certain matter referred to the newspaper. He smiled, and nodded his head, but made no promise.

"You know this lawsuit that I've been engaged in," said Bold.

Tom Towers intimated that he was aware of the action which was pending about the hospital.

"Well, I've abandoned it."

Tom Towers merely raised his eyebrows, thrust his hands into his trousers' pockets, and waited for his friend to proceed.

"Yes, I've given it up. I needn't trouble you with all the history, but the fact is that the conduct of Mr. Harding——. Mr. Harding is the——"

"Oh, yes, the master of the place, the man who takes all the money and does nothing," said Tom Towers, interrupting him.

"Well, I don't know about that, but his conduct in the matter has been so excellent, so little selfish, so open, that I cannot proceed in the matter to his detriment." Bold's heart misgave him as to Eleanor as he said this, and yet he felt that what he said was not untrue. "I think nothing should now be done till the wardenship be vacant."

"And be again filled," said Towers, "as it certainly would before anyone heard of the vacancy, and the same objection would again exist. It's an old story, that of the vested rights of the incumbent. But suppose the incumbent has only a vested wrong, and that the poor of the town have a vested right if they only knew how to get at it! Is not that something the case here?"

Bold could not deny it, but thought it was one of those cases which required a good deal of management before any real good could be done. It was a pity that he had not considered this before he crept into the lion's mouth in the shape of an attorney's office. "It will cost you a good deal, I fear," said Towers.

"A few hundreds," said Bold—"perhaps three hundred. I can't help that, and am prepared for it."

"That's philosophical. It's quite refreshing to hear a man talking of his hundreds in so purely indifferent a manner. But I'm sorry you are giving the matter up. It injures a man to commence a thing of this kind and not carry it through. Have you seen that?" And he threw a small pamphlet across the table, which was all but damp from the press.

Bold had not seen it nor heard of it, but he was well acquainted with the author of it—a gentleman whose pamphlets, condemnatory of all things in these modern days, had been a good deal talked about of late.

Dr. Pessimist Anticant was a Scotchman who had passed a great portion of his early days in Germany. He had studied there with much effect, and had learnt to look with German subtlety into the root of things, and to examine for himself their intrinsic worth and worthlessness. No man ever resolved more bravely than he to accept as good nothing that was evil, to banish from him as evil nothing that was good. 'Tis a pity that he should not have recognized the fact that in this world no good is unalloyed, and that there is but little evil that has not in it some seed of what is goodly.

Returning from Germany, he had astonished the reading public by the vigor of his thoughts, put forth in the quaintest language. He cannot write English, said the critics. No matter, said the public. We can read what he does write, and that without yawning. And so Dr. Pessimist Anticant became popular. Popularity spoilt him for all further real use, as it has done many another. While, with some diffidence, he confined his objurgations to the occasional follies or shortcomings of mankind, while he ridiculed the energy of the squire devoted to the slaughter of partridges or the mistake of some noble patron who turned a poet into a gauger of beer barrels, it was all well. We were glad to be told our faults and to look forward to the coming millennium, when all men, having sufficiently studied the works of Dr. Anticant, would become truthful and energetic. But the Doctor mistook the signs of the times and the minds of men, instituted himself censor of things in general, and began the great task of reprobating everything and everybody, without further promise of any millennium at all. This was not so well, and, to tell the truth, our author did not succeed in his undertaking. His theories were all beautiful, and the code of morals that he taught us was certainly an improvement on the practices of the age. We all of us could, and many of us did, learn much from the Doctor while he chose to remain vague, mysterious, and cloudy. But when he became practical, the charm was gone.

His allusion to the poet and the partridges was received very well. "Oh, my poor brother," said he, "slaughtered partridges a score of brace to each gun, and poets gauging ale barrels, with sixty pounds a year, at Dumfries, are not the signs of a great era!—perhaps of the smallest possible era yet written of. Whatever economies we pursue, political or other, let us see at once that this is the maddest of the uneconomic. Partridges killed by our land magnates at, shall we say, a guinea a head, to be retailed in Leadenhall at one shilling and ninepence, with one poacher in limbo for every fifty birds! Our poet, maker, creator, gauging ale, and that badly, with no leisure for making or creating—only a little leisure for drinking, and suchlike beer-barrel avocations! Truly, a cutting of blocks with fine razors while we scrape our chins so uncomfortably with rusty knives! Oh, my political economist, master of supply and demand, division of labor, and high pressure—oh, my loud-speaking friend, tell me, if so much be in you, what is the demand for poets in these kingdoms of Queen Victoria, and what the vouchsafed supply?"

This was all very well. This gave us some hope. We might do better with our next poet, when we got one. And though the partridges might not be abandoned, something could perhaps be done as to the poachers. We were unwilling, however, to take lessons in politics from so misty a professor, and when he came to tell us that the heroes of Westminster were naught, we began to think that he had written enough. His attack upon despatch boxes was not thought to have much in it, but as it is short, the Doctor shall again be allowed to speak his sentiments.

"Could utmost ingenuity in the management of red tape avail anything to men lying gasping—we may say, all but dead, could despatch boxes with never-so-much velvet lining and Chubb's patent be of comfort to a people in extremis, I also, with so many others, would, with parched tongue, call on the name of Lord John Russell; or, my brother, at your advice, on Lord Aberdeen; or, my cousin, on Lord Derby, at yours; being, with my parched tongue, indifferent to such matters. 'Tis all one. Oh, Derby! Oh, Gladstone! Oh, Palmerston! Oh, Lord John! Each comes running with serene face and despatch box. Vain physicians! Though there were hosts of such, no despatch box will cure this disorder! What! Are there other doctors' new names, disciples who have not yet burdened their souls with tape? Well, let us call again. Oh, Disraeli, great oppositionist, man of the bitter brow! Or, oh, Molesworth, great reformer, thou who promisest Utopia. They come, each with that serene face, and each—alas, me! alas, my country!—each with a despatch box!

"Oh, the serenity of Downing Street!

"My brothers, when hope was over on the battlefield, when no dimmest chance of victory remained, the ancient Roman could hide his face within his toga and die gracefully. Can you and I do so now? If so, 'twere best for us. If not, oh, my brothers, we must die disgracefully, for hope of life and victory I see none left to us in this world below. I for one cannot trust much to serene face and despatch box!"

There might be truth in this, there might be depth of reasoning, but Englishmen did not see enough in the argument to induce them to withdraw their confidence from the present arrangements of the Government, and Dr. Anticant's monthly pamphlet on the decay of the world did not receive so much attention as his earlier works. He did not confine himself to politics in these publications, but roamed at large over all matters of public interest, and found everything bad. According to him nobody was true, and not only nobody, but nothing. A man could not take off his hat to a lady without telling a lie. The lady would lie again in smiling. The ruffles of the gentleman's shirt would be fraught with deceit, and the lady's flounces full of falsehood. Was ever anything more severe than that attack of his on chip bonnets, or the anathemas with which he endeavored to dust the powder out of the bishops' wigs?

The pamphlet which Tom Towers now pushed across the table was entitled *Modern Charity*, and was written with the view of proving how much in the way of charity was done by our predecessors, how little by the present age, and it ended by a comparison between ancient and modern times very little to the credit of the latter.

"Look at this," said Towers, getting up and turning over the pages of the pamphlet, and pointing to a passage near the end. "Your friend the Warden, who is so little selfish, won't like that, I fear." Bold read as follows:

"Heavens, what a sight! Let us with eyes wide open see the godly man of four centuries since, the man of the Dark Ages—let us see how he does his godlike work, and, again, how the godly man of these latter days does his.

"Shall we say that the former one is walking painfully through the world, regarding, as a prudent man, his worldly work, prospering in it as a diligent man will prosper, but always with an eye to that better treasure to which thieves do not creep in? Is there not much nobility in that old man as, leaning on his oaken staff, he walks down the high street of his native town and receives from all courteous salutation and acknowledgment of his worth? A noble old man, my august inhabitants of Belgrave Square and suchlike vicinity—a very noble old man, though employed no better than in the wholesale carding of wool.

"This carding of wool, however, did in those days bring with it much profit, so that our ancient friend, when dying, was declared, in whatever slang then prevailed, to cut up exceeding well. For sons and daughters there was ample sustenance, with assistance of due industry, for friends and relatives some relief for grief at this great loss, for aged dependents comfort in declining years. This was much for one old man to get done in that dark fifteenth century. But this was not all. Coming generations of poor wool-carders should bless the name of this rich one, and a hospital should be founded and endowed with his wealth for the feeding of such of the trade as could not, by diligent carding, any longer duly feed themselves.

" 'Twas thus that an old man in the fifteenth century did his godlike work to the best of his power, and not ignobly, as appears to me.

"We will now take our godly man of latter days. He shall no longer be a wool-carder, for such are not now men of mark. We will suppose him to be one of the best of the good—one who has lacked no opportunities. Our old friend was, after all, but illiterate. Our modern friend shall be a man educated in all seemly knowledge. He shall, in short, be that blessed being, a clergyman of the Church of England!

"And now, in what perfectest manner does he in this lower world get his godlike work done and put out of hand? Heavens! In the strangest of manners. Oh, my brother! In a manner not at all to be believed but by the most minute testimony of eyesight. He does it by the magnitude of his appetite—by the power of his gorge! His only occupation is to swallow the bread prepared with so much anxious care for these impoverished carders of wool. That, and to sing indifferently through his nose once in the week some psalm more or less long—the shorter the better, we should be inclined to say.

"Oh, my civilized friends!—great Britons that never will be slaves—men advanced to infinite state of freedom and knowledge of good and evil, tell me, will you, what becoming monument you will erect to a highly educated clergyman of the Church of England?"

Bold certainly thought that his friend would not like that. He could not conceive anything that he would like less than this. To what a world of toil and trouble had he, Bold, given rise by his indiscreet attack upon the hospital!

"You see," said Towers, "that this affair has been much talked of, and the public are with you. I am sorry you should give the matter up. Have you seen the first number of *The Almshouse?*"

No, Bold had not seen *The Almshouse*. He had seen advertisements of Mr. Popular Sentiment's new novel of that name, but had in no way connected it with Barchester Hospital, and had never thought a moment on the subject.

"It's a direct attack on the whole system," said Towers. "It'll go a long way to put down Rochester, and Barchester, and Dulwich, and St. Cross, and all such hotbeds of peculation. It's very clear that Sentiment has been down to Barchester and got up the whole story there. Indeed, I thought he must have had it all from you. It's very well done, as you'll see. His first numbers always are."

Bold declared that Mr. Sentiment had got nothing from him, and that he was deeply grieved to find that the case had become so notorious. "The fire has gone too far to be quenched," said Towers. "The building must go now, and as the timbers are all rotten, why, I should be inclined to say the sooner the better. I expected to see you get some éclat in the matter."

This was all wormwood to Bold. He had done enough to make his friend the Warden miserable for life, and had then backed out just when the success of his project was sufficient to make the question one of real interest. How weakly he had managed his business! He had already done the harm, and then stayed his hand when the good which he had in view was to be commenced. How delightful would it have been to have employed all his energy in such a cause—to have been backed by the *Jupiter*, and written up to by two of the most popular authors of the day! The idea opened a vista into the very world in which he wished to live. To what might it not have given rise? What delightful intimacies, what public praise—to what Athenian banquets and rich flavor of Attic salt?

This, however, was now past hope. He had pledged himself to abandon the cause, and could he have forgotten the pledge, he had gone too far to retreat. He was now, this moment, sitting in Tom Towers' room with the object of deprecating any further articles in the *Jupiter* and, greatly as he disliked the job, his petition to that effect must be made.

"I couldn't continue it," said he, "because I found I was in the wrong."

Tom Towers shrugged his shoulders. How could a successful man be in the wrong! "In that case," said he, "of course you must abandon it."

"And I called this morning to ask you also to abandon it," said Bold.

"To ask me," said Tom Towers with the most placid of smiles, and a consummate look of gentle surprise, as though Tom Towers was well aware that he of all men was the last to meddle in such matters.

"Yes," said Bold, almost trembling with hesitation. "The *Jupiter*, you know, has taken the matter up very strongly. Mr. Harding has felt what it has said deeply, and I thought that if I could explain to you that he personally has not been to blame, these articles might be discontinued."

How calmly impassive was Tom Towers' face as this innocent little proposition was made! Had Bold addressed himself to the doorposts in Mount Olympus, they would have shown as much outward sign of assent or dissent. His quiescence was quite admirable. His discretion certainly more than human.

"My dear fellow," said he when Bold had quite done speaking, "I really cannot answer for the *Jupiter*."

"But if you saw that these articles were unjust, I think that you would endeavor to put a stop to them. Of course nobody doubts that you could, if you chose."

"Nobody and everybody are always very kind, but unfortunately are generally very wrong."

"Come, come, Towers," said Bold, plucking up his courage, and remembering that for Eleanor's sake he was bound to make his best exertion, "I have no doubt in my own mind but that you wrote the articles yourself. And very well written they were. It will be a great favor if you will in future abstain from any personal allusion to poor Harding."

"My dear Bold," said Tom Towers, "I have a sincere regard for you. I have known you for many years, and value your friendship. I hope you will let me explain to you, without offense, that none who are connected with the public press can with propriety listen to interference."

"Interference!" said Bold. "I don't want to interfere."

"Ah, my dear fellow, but you do. What else is it? You think that I am able to keep certain remarks out of a newspaper. Your information is probably incorrect, as most public gossip on such subjects is. But at any rate you think I have such power, and you ask me to use it. Now that is interference."

"Well, if you choose to call it so."

"And now suppose for a moment that I had this power, and used it as you wish. Isn't it clear that it would be a great abuse? Certain men are employed in writing for the public press, and if they are induced either to write or to abstain from writing by private motives, surely the public press would soon be of little value. Look at the recognized worth of different newspapers, and see if it does not mainly depend on the assurance which the public feel that such a paper is, or is not, independent. You alluded to the *Jupiter*. Surely you cannot but see that the weight of the *Jupiter* is too great to be moved by any private request, even though it should be made to a much more influential person than myself. You've only to think of this and you'll see that I am right."

The discretion of Tom Towers was boundless. There was no contradicting what he said, no arguing against such propositions. He took such high ground that there was no getting up onto it. "The public is defrauded," said he, "whenever private considerations are allowed to have weight." Quite true, thou greatest oracle of the middle of the nineteenth century, thou sententious proclaimer of the purity of the press. The public is defrauded when it is purposely misled. Poor public! How often is it misled! Against what a world of fraud has it to contend!

Bold took his leave, and got out of the room as quickly as he could, inwardly denouncing his friend Tom Towers as a prig and a humbug.

"I know he wrote those articles," said Bold to himself. "I know he got his information from me. He was ready enough to take my word for gospel when it suited his own views, and to set Mr. Harding up before the public as an impostor on no other testimony than my chance conversation. But when I offer him real evidence opposed to his own views, he tells me that private motives are detrimental to public justice! Confound his arrogance! What is any public question but a conglomeration of private interests? What is any newspaper article but an expression of the views taken by one side? Truth! It takes an age to ascertain the truth of any question! The idea of Tom Towers talking of public motives and purity of purpose! Why, it wouldn't give him a moment's uneasiness to change his politics tomorrow if the paper required it."

Such were John Bold's inward exclamations as he made his way out of the quiet labyrinth of the Temple. And yet there was no position of worldly power so coveted in Bold's ambition as that held by the man of whom he was thinking. It was the impregnability of the place which made Bold so angry with the possessor of it, and it was the same quality which made it appear so desirable.

Passing into the Strand, he saw in a bookseller's window an announcement of the first number of *The Almshouse*, so he purchased a copy, and hurrying back to his lodgings, proceeded to ascertain what Mr. Popular Sentiment had to say to the public on the subject which had lately occupied so much of his own attention.

In former times great objects were attained by great work. When evils were to be reformed, reformers set about their heavy task with grave decorum and laborious argument. An age was occupied in proving a grievance, and philosophical researches were printed in folio pages which it took a life to write and an eternity to read. We get on now with a lighter step, and quicker. "*Ridiculum acri Fortius et melius magnas plerumque secat res.*" Ridicule is found to be more convincing than argument, imaginary agonies touch more than true sorrows, and monthly novels convince when learned quartos fail to do so. If the world is to be set right, the work will be done by shilling numbers.

Of all such reformers Mr. Sentiment is the most powerful. It is incredible the number of evil practices he has put down. It is to be feared he will soon lack subjects, and that when he has made the working classes comfortable, and got bitter beer put into proper-sized pint bottles, there will be nothing left for him to do. Mr. Sentiment is certainly a very powerful man, and perhaps not the less so that his good poor people are so very good, his hard rich people so very hard, and the genuinely honest so very honest. Namby-pamby in these days is not thrown away if it be introduced in the proper quarters. Divine peeresses are no longer interesting, though possessed of every virtue, but a pattern peasant or an immaculate manufacturing hero may talk as much twaddle as one of Mrs. Ratcliffe's heroines and still be listened to. Perhaps, however, Mr. Sentiment's great attraction is in his second-rate characters. If his heroes and heroines walk upon stilts, as heroes and heroines, I fear, ever must, their attendant satellites are as natural as though one met them in the street. They walk and talk like men and women, and live among our friends a rattling, lively life— yes, live, and will live till the names of their calling shall be forgotten in their own, and Buckett and Mrs. Gamp will be the only words left to us to signify a detective police officer or a monthly nurse.

The Almshouse opened with a scene in a clergyman's house. Every luxury to be purchased by wealth was described as being there. All the appearances of household indulgence generally found amongst the most self-indulgent of the rich were crowded into this abode. Here the reader was introduced to the demon of the book, the Mephistopheles of the drama. What story was ever written without a demon? What novel, what history, what work of any sort, what world, would be perfect without existing principles both of good and evil? The demon of The Almshouse was the clerical owner of this comfortable abode. He was a man well stricken in years, but still strong to do evil. He was one who looked cruelly out of a hot, passionate, bloodshot eye, who had a huge red nose with a carbuncle, thick lips, and a great double, flabby chin which swelled out into solid substance like a turkey cock's comb when sudden anger inspired him. He had a hot, furrowed, low brow, from which a few grizzled hairs were not yet rubbed off by the friction of his handkerchief. He wore a loose unstarched white handkerchief, black, loose, ill-made clothes, and huge loose shoes, adapted to many corns and various bunions. His husky voice told tales of much daily port wine, and his language was not so decorous as became a clergyman. Such was the master of Mr. Sentiment's Almshouse. He was a widower, but at present accompanied by two daughters and a thin and somewhat insipid curate. One of the young ladies was devoted to her father and the fashionable world, and she of course was the favorite. The other was equally addicted to Puseyism and the curate.

The second chapter of course introduced the reader to the more especial inmates of the hospital. Here were discovered eight old men, and it was given to be understood that four vacancies remained unfilled through the perverse ill-nature of the clerical gentleman with the double chin. The state of these eight paupers was touchingly dreadful. Sixpence farthing a day had been sufficient for their diet when the almshouse was founded, and on sixpence farthing a day were they still doomed to starve, though food was four times as dear and money four times as plentiful. It was shocking to find how the conversation of these eight starved old men in their dormitory shamed that of the clergyman's family in his rich drawing-room. The absolute words they uttered were not perhaps spoken in the purest English, and it might be difficult to distinguish from their dialect to what part of the country they belonged. The beauty of the sentiment, however, amply atoned for the imperfection of the language, and it was really a pity that these eight old men could not be sent through the country as moral missionaries instead of being immured and starved in that wretched almshouse.

Bold finished the number, and as he threw it aside, he thought that that at least had no direct appliance to Mr. Harding, and that the absurdly strong coloring of the picture would disenable the work from doing either good or harm. He was wrong. The artist who paints for the million must use glaring colors, as no one knew better than Mr. Sentiment when he described the inhabitants of his almshouse, and the radical reform which has now swept over such establishments has owed more to the twenty numbers of Mr. Sentiment's novel than to all the true complaints which have escaped from the public for the last half-century.

CHAPTER XVI

A LONG DAY IN LONDON

THE WARDEN had to make use of all his very moderate powers of intrigue to give his son-in-law the slip and get out of Barchester without being stopped on his road. No schoolboy ever ran away from school with more precaution and more dread of detection, no convict slipping down from a prison wall ever feared to see the gaoler more entirely than Mr. Harding did to see his son-in-law as he drove up in the pony carriage to the railway station on the morning of his escape to London. It was mean, all this, and he knew that it was mean, but for the life of him he could not help it. Had he met the Archdeacon he certainly would have lacked the courage to explain the purpose which was carrying him up to London—to explain it in full.

The evening before he went, however, he wrote a note to the Archdeacon, explaining something. He said that he should start on the morrow on his journey, that it was his intention to see the Attorney General if possible, and to decide on his future plans in accordance with what he heard from that gentleman. He excused himself for giving Dr. Grantly no earlier notice by stating that his resolve was very sudden, and having entrusted this note to Eleanor with the perfect, though not expressed, understanding that it was to be sent over to Plumstead Episcopi without haste, he took his departure.

He also prepared and carried with him a note for Sir Abraham Haphazard, in which he stated his name, explaining that he was the defendant in the case of "The Queen on behalf of the Wool-Carders of Barchester *v.* Trustees under the will of the late John Hiram," for so was the suit denominated, and begged the illustrious and learned gentleman to vouchsafe to him ten minutes' audience at any hour on the next day. Mr. Harding calculated that for that one day he was safe. His son-in-law, he had no doubt, would arrive in town by an early train, but not early enough to reach the truant till he should have escaped from his hotel after breakfast, and could he thus manage to see the lawyer on that very day, the deed might be done before the Archdeacon could interfere.

On his arrival in town the Warden drove, as was his wont, to the Chapter Hotel and Coffeehouse near St. Paul's. His visits to London of late had not been frequent, but in those happy days when *Harding's Church Music* was going through the press he had been often there, and as the publisher's house was in Paternoster Row and the printer's press in Fleet Street, the Chapter Hotel and Coffeehouse had been convenient. It was a quiet, somber, clerical house, beseeming such a man as the Warden, and thus he afterward frequented it. Had he dared, he would on this occasion have gone elsewhere to throw the Archdeacon further off the scent, but he did not know what violent steps his son-in-law might take for his recovery if he were not found at his usual haunt, and he deemed it not prudent to make himself the object of a hunt through London.

Arrived at his inn, he ordered dinner, and went forth to the Attorney General's chambers. There he learnt that Sir Abraham was in Court, and would not probably return that day. He would go direct from Court to the House. All appointments were, as a rule, made at the chambers. The clerk could by no means promise an interview for the next day, was able, on the other hand, to say that such interview was, he thought, impossible, but that Sir Abraham would certainly be at the House in the course of the night, where an answer from himself might possibly be elicited.

To the House Mr. Harding went, and left his note, not finding Sir Abraham there. He added a most piteous entreaty that he might be favored with an answer that evening, for which he would return. He then journeyed back sadly to the Chapter Coffeehouse, digesting his great thoughts as best he might in a clattering omnibus, wedged in between a wet old lady and a journeyman glazier returning from his work with his tools in his lap. In melancholy solitude he discussed his mutton chop and pint of port. What is there in this world more melancholy than such a dinner? A dinner, though eaten alone, in a country hotel may be worthy of some energy. The waiter, if you are known, will make much of you, the landlord will make you a bow and perhaps put the fish on the table. If you ring you are attended to, and there is some life about it. A dinner at a London eating house is also lively enough, if it have no other attraction. There is plenty of noise and stir about it, and the rapid whirl of voices and rattle of dishes disperses sadness. But a solitary dinner in an old, respectable, somber, solid London inn, where nothing makes any noise but the old waiter's creaking shoes, where one plate slowly goes and another slowly comes without a sound, where the two or three guests would as soon think of knocking each other down as of talking to one another, where the servants whisper and the whole household is disturbed if an order be given above the voice—what can be more melancholy than a mutton chop and a pint of port in such a place?

Having gone through this, Mr. Harding got into another omnibus and again returned to the House. Yes, Sir Abraham was there, and was that moment on his legs, fighting eagerly for the hundred and seventh clause of the Convent Custody Bill. Mr. Harding's note had been delivered to him, and if Mr. Harding would wait some two or three hours, Sir Abraham could be asked whether there was any answer. The House was not full, and perhaps Mr. Harding might get admittance into the Strangers' Gallery, which admission, with the help of five shillings, Mr. Harding was able to effect.*

This bill of Sir Abraham's had been read a second time and passed into committee. A hundred and six clauses had already been discussed, and had occupied only four morning and five evening sittings. Nine of the hundred and six clauses were passed, fifty-five were withdrawn by consent, fourteen had been altered so as to mean the reverse of the original proposition, eleven had been postponed for further consideration, and seventeen had been directly negatived. The hundred and seventh ordered the bodily searching of nuns for Jesuitical symbols by aged clergymen, and was considered to be the real mainstay of the whole bill. No intention had ever existed to pass such a law as that proposed, but the Government did not intend to abandon it till their object was fully attained by the discussion of this clause. It was known that it would be insisted on with terrible vehemence by Protestant Irish members, and as vehemently denounced by the Roman Catholic, and it was justly considered that no further union between the parties would be possible after such a battle. The innocent Irish fell into the trap as they always do, and whisky and poplins became a drug in the market.†

A florid-faced gentleman with a nice head of hair, from the south of Ireland, had succeeded in catching the Speaker's eye by the time that Mr.

*How these pleasant things have been altered since this was written a quarter of a century ago!

†Again what a change!

Harding had got into the gallery, and was denouncing the proposed sacrilege, his whole face glowing with a fine theatrical frenzy.

"And is this a Christian country?" said he. (Loud cheers, countercheers from the ministerial benches. "Some doubt as to that," from a voice below the gangway.) "No, it can be no Christian country in which the head of the bar, the lagal adviser (loud laughter and cheers)—yes, I say the lagal adviser of the Crown (great cheers and laughter)—can stand up in his seat in this house (prolonged cheers and laughter), and attempt to lagalise indacent assaults on the bodies of religious ladies." (Deafening cheers and laughter, which were prolonged till the honorable Member resumed his seat.)

When Mr. Harding had listened to this and much more of the same kind for about three hours, he returned to the door of the House, and received back from the messenger his own note, with the following words scrawled in pencil on the back of it: "Tomorrow, 10 P.M.—my chambers. A.H."

He was so far successful. But 10 P.M.! What an hour Sir Abraham had named for a legal interview! Mr. Harding felt perfectly sure that long before that Dr. Grantly would be in London. Dr. Grantly could not, however, know that this interview had been arranged, nor could he learn it unless he managed to get hold of Sir Abraham before that hour. And as this was very improbable, Mr. Harding determined to start from his hotel early, merely leaving word that he should dine out, and unless luck were much against him, he might still escape the Archdeacon till his return from the Attorney General's chambers.

He was at breakfast at nine, and for the twentieth time consulted his Bradshaw to see at what earliest hour Dr. Grantly could arrive from Barchester. As he examined the columns, he was nearly petrified by the reflection that perhaps the Archdeacon might come up by the mail train! His heart sank within him at the horrid idea, and for a moment he felt himself dragged back to Barchester without accomplishing any portion of his object. Then he remembered that had Dr. Grantly done so, he would have been in the hotel looking for him long since.

"Waiter," said he, timidly.

The waiter approached, creaking in his shoes, but voiceless.

"Did any gentleman—a clergyman—arrive here by the night mail train?"

"No, sir, not one," whispered the waiter, putting his mouth nearly close to the Warden's ear.

Mr. Harding was reassured.

"Waiter," said he again, and the waiter again creaked up. "If anyone calls for me, I am going to dine out, and shall return about eleven o'clock."

The waiter nodded, but did not this time vouchsafe any reply, and Mr. Harding, taking up his hat, proceeded out to pass a long day in the best way he could, somewhere out of sight of the Archdeacon.

Bradshaw had told him twenty times that Dr. Grantly could not be at the Paddington station till 2 P.M., and our poor friend might therefore have trusted to the shelter of the hotel for some hours longer with perfect safety. But he was nervous. There was no knowing what steps the Archdeacon might take for his apprehension. A message by electric telegraph might desire the landlord of the hotel to set a watch upon him, some letter might come which he might find himself unable to disobey. At any rate, he could not feel himself secure in any place at which the Archdeacon could expect to find him, and at 10 A.M. he started forth to spend twelve hours in London.

Mr. Harding had friends in town had he chosen to seek them, but he felt that he was in no humor for ordinary calls, and he did not now wish to consult with anyone as to the great step which he had determined to take. As he had said to his daughter, no one knows where the shoe pinches but the wearer. There are some points on which no man can be contented to follow the advice of another—some subjects on which a man can consult his own conscience only. Our Warden had made up his mind that it was good for him at any cost to get rid of this grievance. His daughter was the only person whose concurrence appeared necessary to him, and she did concur with him most heartily. Under such circumstances he would not, if he could help it, consult anyone further till advice would be useless. Should the Archdeacon catch him, indeed, there would be much advice, and much consultation of a kind not to be avoided. But he hoped better things, and as he felt that he could not now converse on indifferent subjects, he resolved to see no one till after his interview with the Attorney General.

He determined to take sanctuary in Westminster Abbey. He went, therefore, again thither in an omnibus, and finding that the doors were not open for morning service, he paid his twopence and entered the Abbey as a sight-seer.* It occurred to him that he had no definite place of rest for the day, and that he should be absolutely worn out before his interview if he attempted to walk about from 10 A.M. to 10 P.M. So he sat himself down on a stone step and gazed up at the figure of William Pitt, who looks as though he had just entered the church for the first time in his life and was anything but pleased at finding himself there.

He had been sitting unmolested about twenty minutes when the verger asked him whether he wouldn't like to walk round. Mr. Harding didn't want to walk anywhere, and declined, merely observing that he was waiting for the morning service. The verger, seeing that he was a clergyman, told him that the doors of the choir were now open, and showed him into a seat. This was a great point gained. The Archdeacon would certainly not come to morning service at Westminster Abbey, even though he were in London, and here the Warden could rest quietly and, when the time came, duly say his prayers.

He longed to get up from his seat and examine the music books of the choristers, and the copy of the litany from which the service was chanted.

*Again, what a change!

to see how far the little details at Westminster corresponded with those at Barchester, and whether he thought his own voice would fill the church well from the Westminster precentor's seat. There would, however, be impropriety in such meddling, and he sat perfectly still, looking up at the noble roof and guarding against the coming fatigues of the day.

By degrees two or three people entered: the very same damp old woman who had nearly obliterated him in the omnibus, or some other just like her, a couple of young ladies with their veils down and gilt crosses conspicuous on their prayer books, an old man on crutches, a party who were seeing the Abbey and thought they might as well hear the service for their twopence, as opportunity served—and a young woman with her prayer book done up in her handkerchief who rushed in late and in her hurried entry tumbled over one of the forms and made such a noise that everyone, even the officiating minor canon, was startled, and she herself was so frightened by the echo of her own catastrophe that she was nearly thrown into fits by the panic.

Mr. Harding was not much edified by the manner of the service. The minor canon in question hurried in, somewhat late, in a surplice not in the neatest order, and was followed by a dozen choristers, who were also not as trim as they might have been. They all jostled into their places with a quick hurried step, and the service was soon commenced. Soon commenced and soon over, for there was no music, and time was not unnecessarily lost in the chanting.* On the whole Mr. Harding was of opinion that things were managed better at Barchester, though even there he knew that there was room for improvement.

It appears to us a question whether any clergyman can go through our church service with decorum, morning after morning in an immense building, surrounded by not more than a dozen listeners. The best actors cannot act well before empty benches, and though there is, of course, a higher motive in one case than the other, still even the best of clergymen cannot but be influenced by their audience. To expect that a duty should be well done under such circumstances would be to require from human nature more than human power.

When the two ladies with the gilt crosses, the old man with his crutches, and the still palpitating housemaid were going, Mr. Harding found himself obliged to go too. The verger stood in his way and looked at him and looked at the door, and so he went. But he returned again in a few minutes, and re-entered with another twopence. There was no other sanctuary so good for him.

As he walked slowly down the nave, and then up one aisle and then again down the nave and up the other aisle, he tried to think gravely of the step he was about to take. He was going to give up eight hundred a year voluntarily, and doom himself to live for the rest of his life on about a hundred and fifty. He knew that he had hitherto failed to realize

*Again the changes which years have made should be noted.

this fact as he ought to do. Could he maintain his own independence and support his daughter on a hundred and fifty pounds a year without being a burden on anyone? His son-in-law was rich, but nothing could induce him to lean on his son-in-law after acting, as he intended to do, in direct opposition to his son-in-law's counsel. The Bishop was rich, but he was about to throw away the Bishop's best gift, and that in a manner to injure materially the patronage of the giver. He could neither expect nor accept anything further from the Bishop. There would be not only no merit, but positive disgrace, in giving up his wardenship if he were not prepared to meet the world without it. Yes, he must from this time forward limit all his human wishes for himself and his daughter to the poor extent of so limited an income. He knew he had not thought sufficiently of this, that he had been carried away by enthusiasm, and had hitherto not brought home to himself the full reality of his position.

He thought most about his daughter, naturally. It was true that she was engaged, and he knew enough of his proposed son-in-law to be sure that his own altered circumstances would make no obstacle to such a marriage—nay, he was sure that the very fact of his poverty would induce Bold more anxiously to press the matter—but he disliked counting on Bold in this emergency, brought on, as it had been, by his doing. He did not like saying to himself, "Bold has turned me out of my house and income, and therefore he must relieve me of my daughter." He preferred reckoning on Eleanor as the companion of his poverty and exile, as the sharer of his small income.

Some modest provision for his daughter had been long since made. His life was insured for three thousand pounds, and this sum was to go to Eleanor. The Archdeacon, for some years past, had paid the premium, and had secured himself by the immediate possession of a small property which was to have gone to Mrs. Grantly after her father's death. This matter, therefore, had been taken out of the Warden's hands long since, as, indeed, had all the business transactions of his family, and his anxiety was therefore confined to his own life income.

Yes. A hundred and fifty per annum was very small, but still it might suffice. But how was he to chant the litany at the cathedral on Sunday mornings and get the service done at Crabtree Parva? True, Crabtree Church was not quite a mile and a half from the cathedral, but he could not be in two places at once. Crabtree was a small village, and afternoon service might suffice, but still this went against his conscience. It was not right that his parishioners should be robbed of any of their privileges on account of his poverty. He might, to be sure, make some arrangements for doing weekday service at the cathedral, but he had chanted the litany at Barchester so long, and had a conscious feeling that he did it so well, that he was unwilling to give up the duty.

Thinking of such things, turning over in his own mind together small desires and grave duties, but never hesitating for a moment as to the necessity

of leaving the hospital, Mr. Harding walked up and down the Abbey, or
sat still meditating on the same stone step, hour after hour. One verger went
and another came, but they did not disturb him. Every now and then
they crept up and looked at him, but they did so with a reverential stare, and
on the whole Mr. Harding found his retreat well chosen. About four
o'clock his comfort was disturbed by an enemy in the shape of hunger.
It was necessary that he should dine, and it was clear that he could not
dine in the Abbey. So he left his sanctuary, not willingly, and betook himself to the neighborhood of the Strand to look for food.

His eyes had become so accustomed to the gloom of the church that they
were dazed when he got out into the full light of day, and he felt confused
and ashamed of himself, as though people were staring at him. He hurried
along, still in dread of the Archdeacon, till he came to Charing Cross, and
then remembered that in one of his passages through the Strand he had seen
the words "Chops and Steaks" on a placard in a shop window. He remembered the shop distinctly. It was next door to a trunk-seller's, and there
was a cigar shop on the other side. He couldn't go to his hotel for dinner,
which to him hitherto was the only known mode of dining in London
at his own expense, and therefore he would get a steak at the shop in the
Strand. Archdeacon Grantly would certainly not come to such a place
for his dinner.

He found the house easily, just as he had observed it, between the trunks
and the cigars. He was rather daunted by the huge quantity of fish which
he saw in the window. There were barrels of oysters, hecatombs of
lobsters, a few tremendous-looking crabs, and a tub full of pickled salmon.
Not, however, being aware of any connection between shellfish and iniquity, he entered, and modestly asked a slatternly woman who was picking
oysters out of a great watery reservoir whether he could have a mutton
chop and a potato.

The woman looked somewhat surprised, but answered in the affirmative,
and a slipshod girl ushered him into a long back room filled with boxes for
the accommodation of parties, in one of which he took his seat. In
a more miserably forlorn place he could not have found himself. The room
smelt of fish, and sawdust, and stale tobacco smoke, with a slight taint of
escaped gas. Everything was rough, and dirty, and disreputable. The cloth
which they put before him was abominable. The knives and forks were
bruised, and hacked, and filthy, and everything was impregnated with fish.
He had one comfort, however. He was quite alone, there was no one there
to look on his dismay, nor was it probable that anyone would come to
do so. It was a London supper house. About one o'clock at night the
place would be lively enough, but at the present time his seclusion was
as deep as it had been in the Abbey.

In about half an hour the untidy girl, not yet dressed for her evening
labors, brought him his chop and potatoes, and Mr. Harding begged for

a pint of sherry. He was impressed with an idea, which was generally prevalent a few years since and is not yet wholly removed from the minds of men, that to order a dinner at any kind of inn without also ordering a pint of wine for the benefit of the landlord was a kind of fraud—not punishable indeed by law, but not the less abominable on that account. Mr. Harding remembered his coming poverty, and would willingly have saved his half-crown, but he thought he had no alternative, and he was soon put in possession of some horrid mixture procured from the neighboring public house.

His chop and potatoes, however, were eatable, and having got over as best he might the disgust created by the knives and forks, he contrived to swallow his dinner. He was not much disturbed. One young man, with pale face and watery fishlike eyes, wearing his hat ominously on one side, did come in and stare at him, and ask the girl, audibly enough, who that old cock was, but the annoyance went no further, and the Warden was left seated on his wooden bench in peace, endeavoring to distinguish the different scents arising from lobsters, oysters, and salmon.

Unknowing as Mr. Harding was in the ways of London, he felt that he had somehow selected an ineligible dining house, and that he had better leave it. It was hardly five o'clock. How was he to pass the time till ten? Five miserable hours! He was already tired, and it was impossible that he should continue walking so long. He thought of getting into an omnibus and going out to Fulham for the sake of coming back in another. This, however, would be weary work, and as he paid his bill to the woman in the shop, he asked her if there were any place near where he could get a cup of coffee. Though she did keep a shellfish supper house, she was very civil, and directed him to the cigar divan on the other side of the street.

Mr. Harding had not a much correcter notion of a cigar divan than he had of a London dinner house, but he was desperately in want of rest, and went as he was directed. He thought he must have made some mistake when he found himself in a cigar shop, but the man behind the counter saw immediately that he was a stranger, and understood what he wanted. "One shilling, sir—thank ye, sir—cigar, sir?—ticket for coffee, sir—you'll only have to call the waiter. Up those stairs, if you please, sir. Better take the cigar, sir—you can always give it to a friend, you know. Well, sir, thank ye, sir—as you are so good, I'll smoke it myself." And so Mr. Harding ascended to the divan, with his ticket for coffee but minus the cigar.

The place seemed much more suitable to his requirements than the room in which he had dined. There was, to be sure, a strong smell of tobacco, to which he was not accustomed, but after the shellfish, the tobacco did not seem disagreeable. There were quantities of books, and long rows of sofas. What on earth could be more luxurious than a sofa, a book, and a cup of coffee? An old waiter came up to him with a couple of magazines and an evening paper. Was ever anything so civil? Would he have a cup of coffee, or would he prefer sherbet? Sherbet! Was he absolutely in an Eastern divan, with the slight addition of all the London periodicals? He had, however, an idea that sherbet should be drunk sitting cross-legged, and as he was not quite up to this, he ordered the coffee.

The coffee came, and was unexceptionable. Why, this divan was a paradise! The civil old waiter suggested to him a game of chess. Though a chess-player, he was not equal to this, so he declined and, putting up his weary legs on the sofa, leisurely sipped his coffee and turned over the pages of his *Blackwood*. He might have been so engaged for about an hour, for the old waiter enticed him to a second cup of coffee, when a musical clock began to play. Mr. Harding then closed his magazine, keeping his place with his finger, and lay listening with closed eyes to the clock. Soon the clock seemed to turn into a violoncello, with piano accompaniments, and Mr. Harding began to fancy the old waiter was the Bishop of Barchester. He was inexpressibly shocked that the Bishop should have brought him his coffee with his own hands. Then Dr. Grantly came in with a basket full of lobsters, which he would not be induced to leave downstairs in the kitchen. And then the Warden couldn't quite understand why so many people would smoke in the Bishop's drawing-room. And so he fell fast asleep, and his dreams wandered away to his accustomed stall in Barchester Cathedral and the twelve old men he was so soon about to leave forever.

He was fatigued, and slept soundly for some time. Some sudden stop in the musical clock woke him at length, and he jumped up with a start, surprised to find the room quite full. It had been nearly empty when his nap began. With nervous anxiety he pulled out his watch, and found that it was half-past nine. He seized his hat and, hurrying downstairs, started at a rapid pace for Lincoln's Inn.

It still wanted twenty minutes to ten when the Warden found himself at the bottom of Sir Abraham's stairs, so he walked leisurely up and down the quiet inn to cool himself. It was a beautiful evening at the end of August. He had recovered from his fatigue. His sleep and the coffee had refreshed him, and he was surprised to find that he was absolutely enjoying himself, when the inn clock struck ten. The sound was hardly over before he knocked at Sir Abraham's door, and was informed by the clerk who received him that the great man would be with him immediately.

CHAPTER XVII

SIR ABRAHAM HAPHAZARD

Mr. Harding was shown into a comfortable inner sitting-room looking more like a gentleman's bookroom than a lawyer's chambers, and there waited for Sir Abraham. Nor was he kept waiting long. In ten or fifteen minutes he heard a clatter of voices speaking quickly in the passage, and then the Attorney General entered.

"Very sorry to keep you waiting, Mr. Warden," said Sir Abraham, shaking hands with him, "and sorry, too, to name so disagreeable an hour. But your notice was short, and as you said today, I named the very earliest hour that was not disposed of."

Mr. Harding assured him that he was aware that it was he that should apologize.

Sir Abraham was a tall thin man with hair prematurely gray, but bearing no other sign of age. He had a slight stoop, in his neck rather than his back, acquired by his constant habit of leaning forward as he addressed his various audiences. He might be fifty years old, and would have looked young for his age had not constant work hardened his features and given him the appearance of a machine with a mind. His face was full of intellect, but devoid of natural expression. You would say he was a man to use and then have done with, a man to be sought for on great emergencies but ill-adapted for ordinary services, a man whom you would ask to defend your property but to whom you would be sorry to confide your love. He was bright as a diamond, and as cutting, and also as unimpressionable. He knew everyone whom to know was an honor, but he was without a friend. He wanted none, however, and knew not the meaning of the word in other than its parliamentary sense. A friend! Had he not always been sufficient to himself, and now, at fifty, was it likely that he should trust another? He was married, indeed, and had children, but what time had he for the soft idleness of conjugal felicity? His working days or termtimes were occupied from his time of rising to the late hour at which he went to rest, and even his vacations were more full of labor than the busiest days of other men. He never quarreled with his wife, but he never talked to her. He never had time to talk, he was so taken up with speaking. She, poor lady, was not unhappy. She had all that money could give her, she would probably live to be a peeress, and she really thought Sir Abraham the best of husbands.

Sir Abraham was a man of wit, and sparkled among the brightest at the dinner tables of political grandees. Indeed, he always sparkled. Whether in society, in the House of Commons, or the courts of law, coruscations flew from him, glittering sparkles, as from hot steel—but no heat. No cold heart was ever cheered by warmth from him, no unhappy soul ever dropped a portion of its burden at his door.

With him success alone was praiseworthy, and he knew none so successful as himself. No one had thrust him forward, no powerful friends had pushed him along on his road to power. No, he was Attorney General, and would, in all human probability, be Lord Chancellor by sheer dint of his own industry and his own talent. Who else in all the world rose so high with so little help? A Premier, indeed! Who had ever been Premier without mighty friends? An archbishop! Yes, the son or grandson of a great noble, or else, probably, his tutor. But he, Sir Abraham, had had no mighty lord at his back. His father had been a country apothecary, his mother a farmer's daughter. Why should he respect any but himself? And so he glitters along through the world, the brightest among the bright. And when his glitter is gone, and he is gathered to his fathers, no eye will be dim with a tear, no heart will mourn for its lost friend.

"And so, Mr. Warden," said Sir Abraham, "all our trouble about this lawsuit is at an end."

Mr. Harding said he hoped so, but he didn't at all understand what Sir Abraham meant. Sir Abraham, with all his sharpness, could hardly have looked into his heart and read his intentions.

"All over. You need trouble yourself no further about it. Of course they must pay the costs, and the absolute expense to you and Dr. Grantly will be trifling—that is, compared with what it might have been if it had been continued."

"I fear I don't quite understand you, Sir Abraham."

"Don't you know that their attorneys have noticed us that they have withdrawn the suit?"

Mr. Harding explained to the lawyer that he knew nothing of this, although he had heard in a roundabout way that such an intention had been talked of, and he also at length succeeded in making Sir Abraham understand that even this did not satisfy him. The Attorney General stood up, put his hands into his breeches' pockets, and raised his eyebrows as Mr. Harding proceeded to detail the grievance from which he now wished to rid himself.

"I know I have no right to trouble you personally with this matter, but as it is of most vital importance to me, as all my happiness is concerned in it, I thought I might venture to seek your advice."

Sir Abraham bowed, and declared his clients were entitled to the best advice he could give them—particularly a client so respectable in every way as the Warden of Barchester Hospital.

"A spoken word, Sir Abraham, is often of more value than volumes of written advice. The truth is, I am ill-satisfied with this matter as it stands at present. I do see—I cannot help seeing—that the affairs of the hospital are not arranged according to the will of the founder."

"None of such institutions are, Mr. Harding, nor can they be. The altered circumstances in which we live do not admit of it."

"Quite true—that is quite true. But I can't see that those altered circumstances give me a right to eight hundred a year. I don't know whether I ever read John Hiram's will, but were I to read it now I could not understand it. What I want you, Sir Abraham, to tell me, is this—am I, as warden, legally and distinctly entitled to the proceeds of the property, after the due maintenance of the twelve bedesmen?"

Sir Abraham declared that he couldn't exactly say in so many words that Mr. Harding was legally entitled to, &c., &c., &c., and ended in expressing a strong opinion that it would be madness to raise any further question on the matter, as the suit was to be—nay, was—abandoned.

Mr. Harding, seated in his chair, began to play a slow tune on an imaginary violoncello.

"Nay, my dear sir," continued the Attorney General, "there is no further ground for any question. I don't see that you have the power of raising it."

"I can resign," said Mr. Harding, slowly playing away with his right hand, as though the bow were beneath the chair in which he was sitting.

"What! Throw it up altogether?" said the Attorney General, gazing with utter astonishment at his client.

"Did you see those articles in the *Jupiter?*" said Mr. Harding piteously, appealing to the sympathy of the lawyer.

Sir Abraham said he had seen them. This poor little clergyman, cowed into such an act of extreme weakness by a newspaper article, was to Sir Abraham so contemptible an object that he hardly knew how to talk to him as to a rational being.

"Hadn't you better wait," said he, "till Dr. Grantly is in town with you? Wouldn't it be better to postpone any serious step till you can consult with him?"

Mr. Harding declared vehemently that he could not wait, and Sir Abraham began seriously to doubt his sanity.

"Of course," said the latter, "if you have private means sufficient for your wants, and if this——"

"I haven't a sixpence, Sir Abraham," said the Warden.

"God bless me! Why, Mr. Harding, how do you mean to live?"

Mr. Harding proceeded to explain to the man of law that he meant to keep his precentorship—that was eighty pounds a year. And also that he meant to fall back upon his own little living of Crabtree, which was another eighty pounds. That, to be sure, the duties of the two were hardly compatible, but perhaps he might effect an exchange. And then, recollecting that the Attorney General would hardly care to hear how the service of a cathedral church is divided among the minor canons, stopped short in his explanations.

Sir Abraham listened in pitying wonder. "I really think, Mr. Harding, you had better wait for the Archdeacon. This is a most serious step—one for which, in my opinion, there is not the slightest necessity—and as you have done me the honor of asking my advice, I must implore you to do nothing without the approval of your friends. A man is never the best judge of his own position."

"A man is the best judge of what he feels himself. I'd sooner beg my bread till my death than read such another article as those two that have appeared, and feel, as I do, that the writer has truth on his side."

"Have you not a daughter, Mr. Harding—an unmarried daughter?"

"I have," said he, now standing also, but still playing away on his fiddle with his hand behind his back. "I have, Sir Abraham, and she and I are completely agreed on this subject."

"Pray excuse me, Mr. Harding, if what I say seems impertinent, but surely it is you that should be prudent on her behalf. She is young, and does not know the meaning of living on an income of a hundred and fifty pounds a year. On her account give up this idea. Believe me, it is sheer quixotism."

The Warden walked away to the window, and then back to his chair, and then, irresolute what to say, took another turn to the window. The Attorney General was really extremely patient, but he was beginning to think that the interview had been long enough.

"But if this income be not justly mine, what if she and I have both to beg?" said the Warden at last, sharply, and in a voice so different from that he had hitherto used that Sir Abraham was startled. "If so, it would be better to beg."

"My dear sir, nobody now questions its justness."

"Yes, Sir Abraham, one does question it—the most important of all witnesses against me—I question it myself. My God knows whether or no I love my daughter, but I would sooner that she and I should both beg than that she should live in comfort on money which is truly the property of the poor. It may seem strange to you, Sir Abraham, it is strange to myself, that I should have been ten years in that happy home and not have thought of these things till they were so roughly dinned into my ears. I cannot boast of my conscience when it required the violence of a public newspaper to awaken it, but now that it is awake, I must obey it. When I came here I did not know that the suit was withdrawn by Mr. Bold, and my object was to beg you to abandon my defense. As there is no action, there can be no defense. But it is, at any rate, as well that you should know that from tomorrow I shall cease to be the warden of the hospital. My friends and I differ on this subject, Sir Abraham, and that adds much to my sorrow, but it cannot be helped."

And as he finished what he had to say, he played up such a tune as never before had graced the chambers of any Attorney General. He was standing up, gallantly fronting Sir Abraham, and his right arm passed with bold and rapid sweeps before him, as though he were embracing some huge instrument which allowed him to stand thus erect, and with the fingers of his left hand he stopped, with preternatural velocity, a multitude of strings, which ranged from the top of his collar to the bottom of the lappet of his coat. Sir Abraham listened and looked in wonder. As he had never before seen Mr. Harding, the meaning of these wild gesticulations was lost upon him. But he perceived that the gentleman who had a few minutes since been so subdued as to be unable to speak without hesitation was now impassioned—nay, almost violent.

"You'll sleep on this, Mr. Harding, and tomorrow——"

"I have done more than sleep upon it," said the Warden. "I have lain awake upon it, and that night after night. I found I could not sleep upon it. Now I hope to do so."

The Attorney General had no answer to make to this, so he expressed a quiet hope that whatever settlement was finally made would be satisfactory, and Mr. Harding withdrew, thanking the great man for his kind attention.

Mr. Harding was sufficiently satisfied with the interview to feel a glow of comfort as he descended into the small old square of Lincoln's Inn. It was a calm, bright, beautiful night, and by the light of the moon, even the chapel of Lincoln's Inn and the somber row of chambers which surround the quadrangle looked well. He stood still a moment to collect his thoughts and reflect on what he had done, and was about to do. He knew that the Attorney General regarded him as little better than a fool, but that he did not mind—he and the Attorney General had not much in common between them. He knew also that others, whom he did care about, would think so too, but Eleanor, he was sure, would exult in what he had done, and the Bishop, he trusted, would sympathize with him.

In the meantime he had to meet the Archdeacon, and so he walked slowly down Chancery Lane and along Fleet Street, feeling sure that his work for the night was not yet over. When he reached the hotel he rang the bell quietly, and with a palpitating heart. He almost longed to escape round the corner and delay the coming storm by a further walk round St. Paul's Churchyard, but he heard the slow creaking shoes of the old waiter approaching, and he stood his ground manfully.

CHAPTER XVIII

THE WARDEN IS VERY OBSTINATE

"Dr. Grantly is here, sir," greeted his ears before the door was well open, "and Mrs. Grantly. They have a sitting-room above, and are waiting up for you."

There was something in the tone of the man's voice which seemed to indicate that even he looked upon the Warden as a runaway schoolboy just recaptured by his guardian, and that he pitied the culprit, though he could not but be horrified at the crime.

The Warden endeavored to appear unconcerned as he said, "Oh, indeed! I'll go upstairs at once," but he failed signally. There was, perhaps, a ray of comfort in the presence of his married daughter; that is to say, of comparative comfort, seeing that his son-in-law was there. But how much would he have preferred that they should both have been safe at Plumstead Episcopi! However, upstairs he went, the waiter slowly preceding him, and on the door being opened, the Archdeacon was discovered standing in the middle of the room, erect, indeed, as usual, but oh, how sorrowful! And on a dingy sofa behind him reclined his patient wife.

"Papa, I thought you were never coming back," said the lady. "It's twelve o'clock."

"Yes, my dear," said the Warden. "The Attorney General named ten for my meeting. To be sure ten is late, but what could I do, you know? Great men will have their own way."

And he gave his daughter a kiss, and shook hands with the Doctor, and again tried to look unconcerned.

"And you have absolutely been with the Attorney General?" asked the Archdeacon.

Mr. Harding signified that he had.

"Good heavens, how unfortunate!" And the Archdeacon raised his huge hands in the manner in which his friends are so accustomed to see him express disapprobation and astonishment. "What will Sir Abraham think of it? Did you not know that it is not customary for clients to go direct to their counsel?"

"Isn't it?" asked the Warden innocently. "Well, at any rate I've done it. Sir Abraham didn't seem to think it so very strange."

The Archdeacon gave a sigh that would have moved a man-of-war.

"But, Papa, what did you say to Sir Abraham?" asked the lady.

"I asked him, my dear, to explain John Hiram's will to me. He couldn't explain it in the only way which would have satisfied me, and so I resigned the wardenship."

"Resigned it!" said the Archdeacon in a solemn voice, sad and low but yet sufficiently audible—a sort of whisper that Macready would have envied, and the galleries have applauded with a couple of rounds. "Resigned it! Good heavens!" And the dignitary of the Church sank back horrified into a horsehair armchair.

"At least I told Sir Abraham that I would resign—and of course I must now do so."

"Not at all," said the Archdeacon, catching a ray of hope. "Nothing that you say in such a way to your own counsel can be in any way binding on you. Of course you were there to ask his advice. I'm sure Sir Abraham did not advise any such step."

Mr. Harding could not say that he had.

"I am sure he disadvised you from it," continued the reverend cross-examiner.

Mr. Harding could not deny this.

"I'm sure Sir Abraham must have advised you to consult your friends."

To this proposition also Mr. Harding was obliged to assent.

"Then your threat of resignation amounts to nothing, and we are just where we were before."

Mr. Harding was now standing on the rug, moving uneasily from one foot to the other. He made no distinct answer to the Archdeacon's last proposition, for his mind was chiefly engaged on thinking how he could escape to bed. That his resignation was a thing finally fixed on, a fact all but completed, was not in his mind a matter of any doubt. He knew his own weakness, he knew how prone he was to be led, but he was not weak enough to give way now, to go back from the position to which his conscience had driven him after having purposely come to London to declare his determination. He did not in the least doubt his resolution, but he greatly doubted his power of defending it against his son-in-law.

"You must be very tired, Susan," said he. "Wouldn't you like to go to bed?"

But Susan didn't want to go till her husband went. She had an idea that her papa might be bullied if she were away. She wasn't tired at all, or at least she said so.

The Archdeacon was pacing the room, expressing by certain noddings of his head his opinion of the utter fatuity of his father-in-law.

"Why," at last he said—and angels might have blushed at the rebuke expressed in his tone and emphasis.—"Why did you go off from Barchester so suddenly? Why did you take such a step without giving us notice, after what had passed at the palace?"

The Warden hung his head and made no reply. He could not condescend to say that he had not intended to give his son-in-law the slip, and as he had not the courage to avow it, he said nothing.

"Papa has been too much for you," said the lady.

The Archdeacon took another turn and again ejaculated "Good heavens!" —this time in a very low whisper, but still audibly.

"I think I'll go to bed," said the Warden, taking up a side candle.

"At any rate, you'll promise me to take no further step without consultation," said the Archdeacon. Mr. Harding made no answer, but slowly proceeded to light his candle. "Of course," continued the other, "such a declaration as that you made to Sir Abraham means nothing. Come, Warden, promise me this. The whole affair, you see, is already settled, and that with very little trouble or expense. Bold has been compelled to abandon his action, and all you have to do is to remain quiet at the hospital." Mr. Harding still made no reply, but looked meekly into his son-in-law's face. The Archdeacon thought he knew his father-in-law, but he was mistaken—he thought that he had already talked over a vacillating man to resign his promise. "Come," said he, "promise Susan to give up this idea of resigning the wardenship."

The Warden looked at his daughter, thinking probably at the moment that if Eleanor were contented with him, he need not so much regard his other child, and said, "I am sure Susan will not ask me to break my word, or to do what I know to be wrong."

"Papa," said she, "it would be madness in you to throw up your preferment. What are you to live on?"

"God, that feeds the young ravens, will take care of me also," said Mr. Harding with a smile, as though afraid of giving offense by making his reference to Scripture too solemn.

"Pish!" said the Archdeacon, turning away rapidly. "If the ravens persisted in refusing the food prepared for them, they wouldn't be fed." A clergyman generally dislikes to be met in argument by any Scriptural quotation. He feels as affronted as a doctor does when recommended by an old woman to take some favorite dose, or as a lawyer when an unprofessional man attempts to put him down by a quibble.

"I shall have the living of Crabtree," modestly suggested the Warden.

"Eighty pounds a year!" sneered the Archdeacon.

"And the precentorship," said the father-in-law.

"It goes with the wardenship," said the son-in-law. Mr. Harding was prepared to argue this point and began to do so, but Dr. Grantly stopped him. "My dear Warden," said he, "this is all nonsense. Eighty pounds or a hundred and sixty makes very little difference. You can't live on it—you can't ruin Eleanor's prospects forever. In point of fact, you can't resign. The Bishop wouldn't accept it. The whole thing is settled. What I now want to do is to prevent any inconvenient tittletattle—any more newspaper articles."

"That's what I want, too," said the Warden.

"And to prevent that," continued the other, "we mustn't let any talk of resignation get abroad."

"But I shall resign," said the Warden, very, very meekly.

"Good heavens! Susan, my dear, what can I say to him?"

"But, Papa," said Mrs. Grantly, getting up and putting her arm through that of her father, "what is Eleanor to do if you throw away your income?"

A hot tear stood in each of the Warden's eyes as he looked round upon his married daughter. Why should one sister who was so rich predict poverty for another? Some such idea as this was on his mind, but he gave no utterance to it. Then he thought of the pelican feeding its young with blood from its own breast, but he gave no utterance to that either—and then of Eleanor waiting for him at home, waiting to congratulate him on the end of all his trouble.

"Think of Eleanor, Papa," said Mrs. Grantly.

"I do think of her," said her father.

"And you will not do this rash thing?" The lady was really moved beyond her usual calm composure.

"It can never be rash to do right," said he. "I shall certainly resign this wardenship."

"Then, Mr. Harding, there is nothing before you but ruin," said the Archdeacon, now moved beyond all endurance. "Ruin both for you and Eleanor. How do you mean to pay the monstrous expenses of this action?"

Mrs. Grantly suggested that as the action was abandoned, the costs would not be heavy.

"Indeed they will, my dear," continued he. "One cannot have the Attorney General up at twelve o'clock at night for nothing. But of course your father has not thought of this."

"I will sell my furniture," said the Warden.

"Furniture!" ejaculated the other, with a most powerful sneer.

"Come, Archdeacon," said the lady, "we needn't mind that at present. You know you never expected Papa to pay the costs."

"Such absurdity is enough to provoke Job," said the Archdeacon, marching quickly up and down the room. "Your father is like a child. Eight hundred pounds a year!—Eight hundred and eighty with the house—with nothing to do. The very place for him. And to throw that up because some scoundrel writes an article in a newspaper! Well, I have done my duty. If he chooses to ruin his child I cannot help it." And he stood still at the fireplace and looked at himself in a dingy mirror which stood on the chimney-piece.

There was a pause for about a minute, and then the Warden, finding that nothing else was coming, lighted his candle, and quietly said, "Good night."

"Good night, Papa," said the lady.

And so the Warden retired, but as he closed the door behind him, he heard the well-known ejaculation,—slower, lower, more solemn, more ponderous than ever—"Good heavens!"

CHAPTER XIX

THE WARDEN RESIGNS

The party met next morning at breakfast, and a very somber affair it was—very unlike the breakfasts at Plumstead Episcopi.

There were three thin, small, dry bits of bacon, each an inch long, served up under a huge old plated cover. There were four three-cornered bits of dry toast, and four square bits of buttered toast. There was a loaf of bread, and some oily-looking butter. And on the sideboard there were the remains of a cold shoulder of mutton. The Archdeacon, however, had not come up from his rectory to St. Paul's Churchyard to enjoy himself, and therefore nothing was said of the scanty fare.

The guests were as sorry as the viands. Hardly anything was said over the breakfast table. The Archdeacon munched his toast in ominous silence, turning over bitter thoughts in his deep mind. The Warden tried to talk to his daughter, and she tried to answer him, but they both failed. There were no feelings at present in common between them. The Warden was thinking only of getting back to Barchester, and calculating whether the

Archdeacon would expect him to wait for him, and Mrs. Grantly was preparing herself for a grand attack which she was to make on her father, as agreed upon between herself and her husband during their curtain confabulation of that morning.

When the waiter had creaked out of the room with the last of the teacups, the Archdeacon got up and went to the window, as though to admire the view. The room looked out on a narrow passage which runs from St. Paul's Churchyard to Paternoster Row, and Dr. Grantly patiently perused the names of the three shopkeepers whose doors were in view. The Warden still kept his seat at the table and examined the pattern of the tablecloth, and Mrs. Grantly, seating herself on the sofa, began to knit.

After a while the Warden pulled his Bradshaw out of his pocket and began laboriously to consult it. There was a train for Barchester at 10 A.M. That was out of the question, for it was nearly ten already. Another at 3 P.M., another, the night mail train, at 9 P.M. The three o'clock train would take him home to tea, and would suit very well.

"My dear," said he, "I think I shall go back home at three o'clock today. I shall get home at half-past eight. I don't think there's anything to keep me in London."

"The Archdeacon and I return by the early train tomorrow, Papa. Won't you wait and go back with us?"

"Why, Eleanor will expect me tonight, and I've so much to do, and——"

"Much to do!" said the Archdeacon sotto voce, but the Warden heard him.

"You'd better wait for us, Papa."

"Thank ye, my dear! I think I'll go this afternoon." The tamest animal will turn when driven too hard, and even Mr. Harding was beginning to fight for his own way.

"I suppose you won't be back before three?" said the lady, addressing her husband.

"I must leave this at two," said the Warden.

"Quite out of the question," said the Archdeacon, answering his wife and still reading the shopkeepers' names. "I don't suppose I shall be back till five."

There was another long pause, during which Mr. Harding continued to study his Bradshaw.

"I must go to Cox and Cummins," said the Archdeacon at last.

"Oh, to Cox and Cummins," said the Warden. It was quite a matter of indifference to him where his son-in-law went.

The names of Cox and Cummins had now no interest in his ears. What had he to do with Cox and Cummins further, having already had his suit finally adjudicated upon in a court of conscience, a judgment without power of appeal fully registered, and the matter settled so that all the lawyers in London could not disturb it? The Archdeacon could go to Cox and Cummins, could remain there all day in anxious discussion, but what might be said there was no longer matter of interest to him who was so soon to lay aside the name of Warden of Barchester Hospital.

The Archdeacon took up his shining new clerical hat and put on his black new clerical gloves, and looked heavy, respectable, decorous, and opulent, a decided clergyman of the Church of England, every inch of him. "I suppose I shall see you at Barchester the day after tomorrow," said he.

The Warden supposed he would.

"I must once more beseech you to take no further steps till you see my father. If you owe me nothing"—and the Archdeacon looked as though he thought a great deal were due to him—"at least you owe so much to my father." Without waiting for a reply, Dr. Grantly wended his way to Cox and Cummins.

Mrs. Grantly waited till the last fall of her husband's foot was heard as he turned out of the court into St. Paul's Churchyard, and then commenced her task of talking her father over.

"Papa," she began, "this is a most serious business."

"Indeed it is," said the Warden, ringing the bell.

"I greatly feel the distress of mind you must have endured."

"I am sure you do, my dear." And he ordered the waiter to bring him pen, ink, and paper.

"Are you going to write, Papa?"

"Yes, my dear. I am going to write my resignation to the Bishop."

"Pray, pray, Papa, put it off till our return. Pray put it off till you have seen the Bishop. Dear Papa! For my sake, for Eleanor's!——"

"It is for your sake and Eleanor's that I do this. I hope, at least, that my children may never have to be ashamed of their father."

"How can you talk about shame, Papa?" Then she stopped while the waiter creaked in with the paper and slowly creaked out again. "How can you talk about shame? You know what all your friends think about this question."

The Warden spread his paper on the table, placing it on the meager blotting-book which the hotel afforded, and sat himself down to write.

"You won't refuse me one request, Papa?" continued his daughter. "You won't refuse to delay your letter for two short days? Two days can make no possible difference."

"My dear," said he naïvely, "if I waited till I got to Barchester, I might perhaps be prevented."

"But surely you would not wish to offend the Bishop?" said she.

"God forbid! The Bishop is not apt to take offense, and knows me too well to take in bad part anything that I may be called on to do."

"But, Papa——"

"Susan," said he, "my mind on this subject is made up. It is not without much repugnance that I act in opposition to the advice of such men as Sir Abraham Haphazard and the Archdeacon. But in this matter I can take no advice, I cannot alter the resolution to which I have come."

"But two days, Papa——"

"No—nor can I delay it. You may add to my present unhappiness by pressing me, but you cannot change my purpose. It will be a comfort to me if you will let the matter rest." Then, dipping his pen into the inkstand, he fixed his eyes intently on the paper.

There was something in his manner which taught his daughter to perceive that he was in earnest. She had at one time ruled supreme in her father's house, but she knew that there were moments when, mild and meek as he was, he would have his way, and the present was an occasion of the sort. She returned, therefore, to her knitting, and very shortly after left the room.

The Warden was now at liberty to compose his letter, and as it was characteristic of the man, it shall be given at full length. The official letter, which, when written, seemed to him to be too formally cold to be sent alone to so dear a friend, was accompanied by a private note; and both are here inserted.

The letter of resignation ran as follows:

"Chapter Hotel, St. Paul's
"London—August, 18—

"My Lord Bishop,

"It is with the greatest pain that I feel myself constrained to resign into Your Lordship's hands the wardenship of the hospital at Barchester, which you so kindly conferred upon me, now nearly twelve years since.

"I need not explain the circumstances which have made this step appear necessary to me. You are aware that a question has arisen as to the right of the warden to the income which has been allotted to the wardenship. It has seemed to me that this right is not well made out, and I hesitate to incur the risk of taking an income to which my legal claim appears doubtful.

"The office of precentor of the cathedral is, as Your Lordship is aware, joined to that of the warden. That is to say, the precentor has for many years been the warden of the hospital. There is, however, nothing to make the junction of the two offices necessary, and unless you or the dean and chapter object to such an arrangement, I would wish to keep the precentorship. The income of this office will now be necessary to me. Indeed, I do not know why I should be ashamed to say that I should have difficulty in supporting myself without it.

"Your Lordship, and such others as you may please to consult on the matter, will at once see that my resignation of the wardenship need offer not the slightest bar to its occupation by another person. I am thought in the wrong by all those whom I have consulted in the matter. I have very little but an inward and an unguided conviction of my own to bring me to this step, and I shall, indeed, be hurt to find that any slur is thrown on the preferment which your kindness bestowed on me by my resignation of it. I, at any rate for one, shall look on any successor whom you may appoint as enjoying a clerical situation of the highest respectability, and one to which Your Lordship's nomination gives an indefeasible right.

"I cannot finish this official letter without again thanking Your Lordship for all your great kindness, and I beg to subscribe myself

"Your Lordship's most obedient servant,
"SEPTIMUS HARDING
"Warden of Barchester Hospital,
and Precentor of the Cathedral."

He then wrote the following private note:

"My dear Bishop,

"I cannot send you the accompanying official letter without a warmer expression of thanks for all your kindness than would befit a document which may to a certain degree be made public. You, I know, will understand the feeling, and perhaps pity the weakness, which makes me resign the hospital. I am not made of caliber strong enough to withstand public attack. Were I convinced that I stood on ground perfectly firm, that I was certainly justified in taking eight hundred a year under Hiram's will, I should feel bound by duty to retain the position, however unendurable might be the nature of the assault. But as I do not feel this conviction, I cannot believe that you will think me wrong in what I am doing.

"I had at one time an idea of keeping only some moderate portion of the income—perhaps three hundred a year—and of remitting the remainder to the trustees. But it occurred to me, and I think with reason, that by so doing I should place my successors in an invidious position, and greatly damage your patronage.

"My dear friend, let me have a line from you to say that you do not blame me for what I am doing, and that the officiating vicar of Crabtree Parva will be the same to you as the warden of the hospital.

"I am very anxious about the precentorship. The Archdeacon thinks it must go with the wardenship. I think not, and that, having it, I cannot be ousted. I will, however, be guided by you and the dean. No other duty will suit me so well, or come so much within my power of adequate performance.

"I thank you from my heart for the preferment which I am now giving up, and for all your kindness, and am, dear Bishop, now as always

"Yours most affectionately,
"SEPTIMUS HARDING

"London,—August, 18—"

Having written these letters and made a copy of the former one for the benefit of the Archdeacon, Mr. Harding, whom we must now cease to call the Warden—he having designated himself so for the last time—found that it was nearly two o'clock, and that he must prepare for his journey. Yes, from this time he never again admitted the name by which he had been so familiarly known, and in which, to tell the truth, he had rejoiced. The love of titles is common to all men, and a vicar or fellow is as pleased at becoming Mr. Archdeacon or Mr. Provost as a lieutenant at getting his captaincy, or a city tallowchandler in becoming Sir John on the occasion of a Queen's visit to a new bridge. But Warden he was no longer, and the name of Precentor, though the office was to him so dear, confers in itself no sufficient distinction. Our friend, therefore, again became Mr. Harding.

Mrs. Grantly had gone out. He had therefore no one to delay him by further entreaties to postpone his journey. He had soon arranged his bag, and paid his bill, and, leaving a note for his daughter in which he put the copy of his official letter, he got into a cab and drove away to the station with something of triumph in his heart.

Had he not cause for triumph? Had he not been supremely successful? Had he not for the first time in his life held his own purpose against that of his son-in-law, and manfully combated against great odds—against the Archdeacon's wife as well as the Archdeacon? Had he not gained a great victory, and was it not fit that he should step into his cab with triumph?

He had not told Eleanor when he would return, but she was on the look-out for him by every train by which he could arrive, and the pony carriage was at the Barchester station when the train drew up at the platform.

"My dear," said he, sitting beside her as she steered her little vessel to one side of the road to make room for the clattering omnibuses as they passed from the station into the town, "I hope you'll be able to feel a proper degree of respect for the Vicar of Crabtree."

"Dear Papa," said she, "I am so glad."

There was great comfort in returning home to that pleasant house, though he was to leave it so soon, and in discussing with his daughter all that he had done, and all that he had to do. It must take some time to get out of one house into another. The curate at Crabtree should not be abolished under six months; that is, unless other provision could be made for him. And then the furniture! The most of that must be sold to pay Sir Abraham Haphazard for sitting up till twelve at night. Mr. Harding was strangely ignorant as to lawyers' bills. He had no idea, from twenty pounds to two thousand, as to the sum in which he was indebted for legal assistance. True, he had called in no lawyer himself. True, he had been no consenting party to the employment of either Cox and Cummins or Sir Abraham, he had never been consulted on such matters. The Archdeacon had managed all this himself, never for a moment suspecting that Mr. Harding would take upon him to end the matter in a way of his own. Had the lawyers' bills been ten thousand pounds, Mr. Harding could not have helped it, but he was not on that account disposed to dispute his own liability. The question never occurred to him. But it did occur to him that he had very little money at his banker's, that he could receive nothing further from the hospital, and that the sale of the furniture was his only resource.

"Not all, Papa," said Eleanor, pleadingly.

"Not quite all, my dear," said he. "That is, if we can help it. We must have a little at Crabtree—but it can only be a little. We must put a bold front on it, Nelly. It isn't easy to come down from affluence to poverty."

And so they planned their future mode of life, the father taking comfort from the reflection that his daughter would soon be freed from it, and she resolving that her father would soon have in her own house a ready means of escape from the solitude of the Crabtree vicarage.

When the Archdeacon left his wife and father-in-law at the Chapter Coffeehouse to go to Messrs. Cox and Cummins, he had no very defined idea of what he had to do when he got there. Gentlemen when at law, or in any way engaged in matters requiring legal assistance, are very apt to go to their lawyers without much absolute necessity. Gentlemen when doing so are apt to describe such attendance as quite compulsory, and very disagreeable. The lawyers, on the other hand, do not at all see the necessity, though they quite agree as to the disagreeable nature of the visit—gentlemen when so engaged are usually somewhat graveled to find nothing to say to their learned friends. They generally talk a little politics, a little weather, ask some few foolish questions about their suit, and then withdraw, having passed half an hour in a small dingy waiting-room in company with some junior assistant clerk and ten minutes with the members of the firm. The business is then over for which the gentleman has come up to London, probably a distance of a hundred and fifty miles. To be sure he goes to the play, and dines at his friend's club, and has a bachelor's liberty and bachelor's recreation for three or four days. And he could not probably plead the desire of such gratifications as a reason to his wife for a trip to London.

Married ladies, when your husbands find they are positively obliged to attend their legal advisers, the nature of the duty to be performed is generally of this description.

The Archdeacon would not have dreamt of leaving London without going to Cox and Cummins, and yet he had nothing to say to them. The game was up. He plainly saw that Mr. Harding in this matter was not to be moved. His only remaining business on this head was to pay the bill and have done with it. And I think it may be taken for granted that whatever the cause may be that takes a gentleman to a lawyer's chambers, he never goes there to pay his bill.

Dr. Grantly, however, in the eyes of Messrs. Cox and Cummins, represented the spiritualities of the diocese of Barchester, as Mr. Chadwick did the temporalities, and was therefore too great a man to undergo the half-hour in the clerk's room. It will not be necessary that we should listen to the notes of sorrow in which the Archdeacon bewailed to Mr. Cox the weakness of his father-in-law and the end of all their hopes of triumph. Nor need we repeat the various exclamations of surprise with which the mournful intelligence was received. No tragedy occurred, though Mr. Cox, a short and somewhat bull-necked man, was very near a fit of apoplexy when he first attempted to ejaculate that fatal word—resign!

Over and over again did Mr. Cox attempt to enforce on the Archdeacon the propriety of urging on Mr. Warden the madness of the deed he was about to do.

"Eight hundred a year!" said Mr. Cox.

"And nothing whatever to do!" said Mr. Cummins, who had joined the conference.

"No private fortune, I believe," said Mr. Cox.

"Not a shilling," said Mr. Cummins in a very low voice, shaking his head.

"I never heard of such a case in all my experience," said Mr. Cox.

"Eight hundred a year, and as nice a house as any gentleman could wish to hang up his hat in," said Mr. Cummins.

"And an unmarried daughter, I believe," said Mr. Cox, with much moral seriousness in his tone. The Archdeacon only sighed as each separate wail was uttered, and shook his head, signifying that the fatuity of some people was past belief.

"I'll tell you what he might do," said Mr. Cummins, brightening up. "I'll tell you how you might save it. Let him exchange."

"Exchange where?" said the Archdeacon.

"Exchange for a living. There's Quiverful, of Puddingdale. He has twelve children, and would be delighted to get the hospital. To be sure Puddingdale is only four hundred, but that would be saving something out of the fire. Mr. Harding would have a curate, and still keep three hundred or three hundred and fifty."

The Archdeacon opened his eyes and listened. He really thought the scheme might do.

"The newspapers," continued Mr. Cummins, "might hammer away at Quiverful every day for the next six months without his minding them."

The Archdeacon took up his hat and returned to his hotel, thinking the matter over deeply. At any rate he would sound Quiverful. A man with twelve children would do much to double his income.

CHAPTER XX

FAREWELL

On the morning after Mr. Harding's return home he received a note from the Bishop full of affection, condolence, and praise. "Pray come to me at once," wrote the Bishop, "that we may see what had better be done. As to the hospital, I will not say a word to dissuade you, but I don't like your going to Crabtree. At any rate, come to me at once."

Mr. Harding did go to him at once, and long and confidential was the consultation between the two old friends. There they sat together the whole long day, plotting to get the better of the Archdeacon and to carry out little schemes of their own, which they knew would be opposed by the whole weight of his authority.

The Bishop's first idea was that Mr. Harding, if left to himself, would certainly starve—not in the figurative sense in which so many of our ladies and gentlemen do starve on incomes from one to five hundred a year, not that he would be starved as regarded dress coats, port wine, and pocket money—but that he would positively perish of inanition for want of bread.

"How is a man to live when he gives up all his income?" said the Bishop to himself. And then the good-natured little man began to consider how his friend might be best rescued from a death so horrid and painful.

His first proposition to Mr. Harding was that they should live together at the palace. He, the Bishop, positively assured Mr. Harding that he wanted another resident chaplain—not a young, working chaplain, but a steady, middle-aged chaplain, one who would dine and drink a glass of wine with him, talk about the Archdeacon, and poke the fire. The Bishop did not positively name all these duties, but he gave Mr. Harding to understand that such would be the nature of the service required.

It was not without much difficulty that Mr. Harding made his friend see that this would not suit him, that he could not throw up the Bishop's preferment and then come and hang on at the Bishop's table, that he could not allow people to say of him that it was an easy matter to abandon his own income, as he was able to sponge on that of another person. He succeeded, however, in explaining that the plan would not do, and then the Bishop brought forward another which he had in his sleeve. He, the Bishop, had in his will left certain moneys to Mr. Harding's two daughters, imagining that Mr. Harding would himself want no such assistance during his own lifetime. This legacy amounted to three thousand pounds each, duty-free, and he now pressed it as a gift on his friend.

"The girls, you know," said he, "will have it just the same when you're gone—and they won't want it sooner—and as for the interest during my lifetime, it isn't worth talking about. I have more than enough."

With much difficulty and heartfelt sorrow, Mr. Harding refused also this offer. No, his wish was to support himself, however poorly, not to be supported on the charity of anyone. It was hard to make the Bishop understand this, it was hard to make him comprehend that the only real favor he could confer was the continuation of his independent friendship. But at last even this was done. At any rate, thought the Bishop, he will come and dine with me from time to time, and if he be absolutely starving I shall see it.

Touching the precentorship, the Bishop was clearly of opinion that it could be held without the other situation, an opinion from which no one differed; and it was therefore soon settled among all the parties concerned that Mr. Harding should still be the Precentor of the cathedral.

On the day following Mr. Harding's return, the Archdeacon reached Plumstead full of Mr. Cummins's scheme regarding Puddingdale and Mr. Quiverful. On the very next morning he drove over to Puddingdale, and obtained the full consent of the wretched clerical Priam, who was endeavoring to feed his poor Hecuba and a dozen of Hectors on the small proceeds of his ecclesiastical kingdom. Mr. Quiverful had no doubts as to the legal rights of the Warden, his conscience would be quite clear as to accepting the income, and as to the *Jupiter*, he begged to assure the Archdeacon that he was quite indifferent to any emanations from the profane portion of the periodical press.

Having so far succeeded, he next sounded the Bishop, but here he was astonished by most unexpected resistance. The Bishop did not think it would do. "Not do? Why not?" And seeing that his father was not shaken, he repeated the question in a severer form. "Why not do, my lord?"

His lordship looked very unhappy, and shuffled about in his chair, but still didn't give way. He thought Puddingdale wouldn't do for Mr. Harding. It was too far from Barchester.

"Oh, of course he'll have a curate!"

The Bishop also thought that Mr. Quiverful wouldn't do for the hospital. Such an exchange wouldn't look well at such a time, and when pressed harder, he declared he didn't think Mr. Harding would accept of Puddingdale under any circumstances.

"How is he to live?" demanded the Archdeacon.

The Bishop, with tears in his eyes, declared that he had not the slightest conception how life was to be sustained within him at all.

The Archdeacon then left his father and went down to the hospital, but Mr. Harding wouldn't listen at all to the Puddingdale scheme. To his eyes it had no attraction. It savored of simony, and was likely to bring down upon him harder and more deserved strictures than any he had yet received. He positively declined to become Vicar of Puddingdale under any circumstances.

The Archdeacon waxed wroth, talked big, and looked bigger. He said something about dependence and beggary, spoke of the duty every man was under to earn his bread, made passing allusions to the follies of youth and waywardness of age, as though Mr. Harding were afflicted by both, and ended by declaring that he had done. He felt that he had left no stone unturned to arrange matters on the best and easiest footing, that he had, in fact, so arranged them, that he had so managed that there was no further need of any anxiety in the matter. And how had he been paid? His advice had been systematically rejected. He had been not only slighted, but distrusted and avoided. He and his measures had been utterly thrown over, as had been Sir Abraham, who, he had reason to know, was much pained at what had occurred. He now found it was useless to interfere any further, and he should retire. If any further assistance were required from him, he would probably be called on, and should be again happy to come forward. And so he left the hospital, and has not since entered it from that day to this.

And here we must take leave of Archdeacon Grantly. We fear that he is represented in these pages as being worse than he is, but we have had to do with his foibles and not with his virtues. We have seen only the weak side of the man, and have lacked the opportunity of bringing him forward on his strong ground. That he is a man somewhat too fond of his own way, and not sufficiently scrupulous in his manner of achieving it, his best friends cannot deny. That he is bigoted in favor not so much of his doctrines as of his cloth, is also true. And it is true that the possession of a large income is a desire that sits near his heart.

Nevertheless, the Archdeacon is a gentleman and a man of conscience. He spends his money liberally, and does the work he has to do with the best of his ability. He improves the tone of society of those among whom he lives. His aspirations are of a healthy, if not of the highest, kind. Though never an austere man, he upholds propriety of conduct both by example and precept. He is generous to the poor and hospitable to the rich. In matters of religion he is sincere and yet no Pharisee, he is in earnest and yet no fanatic. On the whole, the Archdeacon of Barchester is a man doing more good than harm—a man to be furthered and supported, though perhaps also to be controlled. And it is matter of regret to us that the course of our narrative has required that we should see more of his weakness than his strength.

Mr. Harding allowed himself no rest till everything was prepared for his departure from the hospital. It may be as well to mention that he was not driven to the stern necessity of selling all his furniture. He had been quite in earnest in his intention to do so, but it was soon made known to him that the claims of Messrs. Cox and Cummins made no such step obligatory. The Archdeacon had thought it wise to make use of the threat of the lawyer's bill to frighten his father-in-law into compliance, but he had no intention to saddle Mr. Harding with costs which had been incurred by no means exclusively for his benefit. The amount of the bill was added to the diocesan account, and was, in fact, paid out of the Bishop's pocket, without any consciousness on the part of his lordship. A great part of his furniture he did resolve to sell, having no other means to dispose of it, and the ponies and carriage were transferred by private contract to the use of an old maiden lady in the city.

For his present use Mr. Harding took a lodging in Barchester, and thither were conveyed such articles as he wanted for daily use—his music, books, and instruments, his own armchair, and Eleanor's pet sofa, her teapoy and his cellaret, and also the slender but still sufficient contents of his wine cellar. Mrs. Grantly had much wished that her sister would reside at Plumstead till her father's house at Crabtree should be ready for her, but Eleanor herself strongly resisted this proposal. It was in vain urged upon her that a lady in lodgings cost more than a gentleman, and that under her father's present circumstances such an expense should be avoided. Eleanor had not pressed her father to give up the hospital in order that she might live at Plumstead Rectory, and he alone in his Barchester lodgings. Nor did Eleanor think that she would be treating a certain gentleman very fairly if she betook herself to the house which he would be the least desirous of entering of any in the county. So she got a little bedroom for herself behind the sitting-room, and just over the little back parlor of the chemist with whom they were to lodge. There was somewhat of a savor of senna softened by peppermint about the place, but on the whole the lodgings were clean and comfortable.

The day had been fixed for the migration of the ex-Warden, and all Barchester were in a state of excitement on the subject. Opinion was much divided as to the propriety of Mr. Harding's conduct. The mercantile part of the community, the mayor and corporation and council, also most of the ladies, were loud in his praise. Nothing could be more noble, nothing more generous, nothing more upright. But the gentry were of a different way of thinking—especially the lawyers and the clergymen. They said such conduct was weak and undignified, that Mr. Harding evinced a lamentable want of esprit de corps as well as courage, and that such an abdication must do much harm and could do but little good.

On the evening before he left, he summoned all the bedesmen into his parlor to wish them good-by. With Bunce he had been in frequent communication since his return from London, and had been at much pains to explain to the old man the cause of his resignation, without in any way prejudicing the position of his successor. The others also he had seen more or less frequently, and had heard from most of them separately some expression of regret at his departure, but he had postponed his farewell till the last evening.

He now bade the maid put wine and glasses on the table, and had the chairs arranged around the room, and sent Bunce to each of the men to request they would come and say farewell to their late Warden. Soon the noise of aged scuffling feet was heard upon the gravel and in the little hall, and the eleven men who were enabled to leave their rooms were assembled.

"Come in, my friends, come in," said the Warden. He was still Warden then. "Come in, and sit down." And he took the hand of Abel Handy, who was the nearest to him, and led the limping grumbler to a chair. The others followed slowly and bashfully, the infirm, the lame, and the blind. Poor wretches! Who had been so happy had they but known it! Now their aged faces were covered with shame, and every kind word from their master was a coal of fire burning on their heads.

When first the news had reached them that Mr. Harding was going to leave the hospital, it had been received with a kind of triumph. His departure was, as it were, a prelude to success. He had admitted his want of right to the money about which they were disputing, and as it did not belong to him, of course it did to them. The one hundred a year to each of them was actually becoming a reality. Abel Handy was a hero, and Bunce a fainthearted sycophant, worthy neither honor nor fellowship. But other tidings soon made their way into the old men's rooms. It was first notified to them that the income abandoned by Mr. Harding would not come to them, and these accounts were confirmed by Attorney Finney. They were then informed that Mr. Harding's place would be at once filled by another. That the new warden could not be a kinder man they all knew, that he would be a less friendly one most suspected. And then came the bitter information that from the moment of Mr. Harding's departure, the twopence a day, his own peculiar gift, must of necessity be withdrawn.

And this was to be the end of all their mighty struggle, of their fight for their rights, of their petition, and their debates and their hopes! They were to change the best of masters for a possible bad one, and to lose twopence a day each man! No, unfortunate as this was, it was not the worst, or nearly the worst, as will just now be seen.

"Sit down, sit down, my friends," said the Warden. "I want to say a word to you, and to drink your healths, before I leave you. Come up here, Moody, here is a chair for you. Come, Jonathan Crumple." And by degrees he got the men to be seated. It was not surprising that they should hang back with faint hearts, having returned so much kindness with such deep ingratitude. Last of all of them came Bunce, and with sorrowful mien and slow step got into his accustomed seat near the fireplace.

When they were all in their places, Mr. Harding rose to address them, and then finding himself not quite at home on his legs, he sat down again. "My dear old friends," said he, "you all know that I am going to leave you."

There was a sort of murmur ran round the room, intended, perhaps, to express regret at his departure, but it was but a murmur and might have meant that or anything else.

"There has been lately some misunderstanding between us. You have thought, I believe, that you did not get all that you were entitled to, and that the funds of the hospital have not been properly disposed of. As for me, I cannot say what should be the disposition of these moneys, or how they should be managed, and I have therefore thought it best to go."

"We never wanted to drive Your Reverence out of it," said Handy.

"No, indeed, Your Reverence," said Skulpit. "We never thought it would come to this. When I signed the petition—that is, I didn't sign it, because——"

"Let His Reverence speak, can't you?" said Moody.

"No," continued Mr. Harding, "I am sure you did not wish to turn me out, but I thought it best to leave you. I am not a very good hand at a lawsuit, as you may all guess, and when it seemed necessary that our ordinary quiet mode of living should be disturbed, I thought it better to go. I am neither angry nor offended with any man in the hospital."

Here Bunce uttered a kind of groan, very clearly expressive of disagreement.

"I am neither angry nor displeased with any man in the hospital," repeated Mr. Harding emphatically. "If any man has been wrong—and I don't say any man has—he has erred through wrong advice. In this country all are entitled to look for their own rights, and you have done no more. As long as your interests and my interests were at variance, I could give you no counsel on this subject. But the connection between us has ceased, my income can no longer depend on your doings, and therefore, as I leave you, I venture to offer you my advice."

The men all declared that they would from henceforth be entirely guided by Mr. Harding's opinion in their affairs.

"Some gentleman will probably take my place here very soon, and I strongly advise you to be prepared to receive him in a kindly spirit, and to raise no further question among yourselves as to the amount of his income. Were you to succeed in lessening what he has to receive, you would not increase your own allowance. The surplus would not go to you. Your wants are adequately provided for, and your position could hardly be improved."

"God bless Your Reverence, we knows it," said Spriggs.

"It's all true, Your Reverence," said Skulpit. "We sees it all now."

"Yes, Mr. Harding," said Bunce, opening his mouth for the first time. "I believe they do understand it now—now that they've driven from under the same roof with them such a master as not one of them will ever know again. Now that they're like to be in sore want of a friend."

"Come, come, Bunce," said Mr. Harding, blowing his nose and maneuvering to wipe his eyes at the same time.

"Oh, as to that," said Handy, "we none of us never wanted to do Mr. Harding no harm. If he's going now, it's not along of us, and I don't see for what Mr. Bunce speaks up agen us that way."

"You've ruined yourselves, and you've ruined me too, and that's why," said Bunce.

"Nonsense, Bunce," said Mr. Harding, "there's nobody ruined at all. I hope you'll let me leave you all friends. I hope you'll all drink a glass of wine in friendly feeling with me and with one another. You'll have a good friend, I don't doubt, in your new warden. And if ever you want any other, why, after all I'm not going so far off but that I shall sometimes see you." Then, having finished his speech, Mr. Harding filled all the glasses and himself handed each a glass to the men round him, and raising his own, said:

"God bless you all! You have my heartfelt wishes for your welfare. I hope you may live contented, and die trusting in the Lord Jesus Christ, and thankful to Almighty God for the good things he has given you. God bless you, my friends!" And Mr. Harding drank his wine.

Another murmur, somewhat more articulate than the first, passed round the circle, and this time it was intended to imply a blessing on Mr. Harding.

It had, however, but little cordiality in it. Poor old men! How could they be cordial with their sore consciences and shamed faces? How could they bid God bless him with hearty voices and a true benison, knowing, as they did, that their vile cabal had driven him from his happy home and sent him in his old age to seek shelter under a strange rooftree? They did their best, however. They drank their wine, and withdrew.

As they left the hall door, Mr. Harding shook hands with each of the men, and spoke a kind word to them about their individual cases and ailments. And so they departed, answering his questions in the fewest words, and retreated to their dens, a sorrowful repentant crew.

All but Bunce, who still remained to make his own farewell. "There's poor old Bell," said Mr. Harding. "I mustn't go without saying a word to him. Come through with me, Bunce, and bring the wine with you." And so they went through to the men's cottages, and found the old man propped up as usual in his bed.

"I've come to say good-by to you, Bell," said Mr. Harding, speaking loud, for the old man was deaf.

"And are you going away, then, really?" asked Bell.

"Indeed I am, and I've brought you a glass of wine, so that we may part friends, as we lived, you know."

The old man took the proffered glass in his shaking hands and drank it eagerly. "God bless you, Bell!" said Mr. Harding. "Good-by, my old friend."

"And so you're really going?" the man again asked.

"Indeed I am, Bell."

The poor old bedridden creature still kept Mr. Harding's hand in his own, and the Warden thought that he had met with something like warmth of feeling in the one of all his subjects from whom it was the least likely to be expected, for poor old Bell had nearly outlived all human feelings. "And Your Reverence," said he, and then he paused, while his old palsied head shook horribly and his shriveled cheeks sank lower within his jaws and his glazy eye gleamed with a momentary light, "and Your Reverence, shall we get the hundred a year, then?"

How gently did Mr. Harding try to extinguish the false hope of money which had been so wretchedly raised to disturb the quiet of the dying man! One other week and his mortal coil would be shuffled off. In one short week would God resume his soul, and set it apart for its irrevocable doom. Seven more tedious days and nights of senseless inactivity and all would be over for poor Bell in this world. And yet with his last audible words he was demanding his moneyed rights, and asserting himself to be the proper heir of John Hiram's bounty? Not on him, poor sinner as he was, be the load of such sin!

Mr. Harding returned to his parlor, meditating with a sick heart on what he had seen, and Bunce with him. We will not describe the parting of these two good men, for good men they were. It was in vain that the late Warden

endeavored to comfort the heart of the old bedesman. Poor old Bunce felt
that his days of comfort were gone. The hospital had to him been a happy
home, but it could be so no longer. He had had honor there, and friend
ship. He had recognized his master, and been recognized. All his wants
both of soul and body, had been supplied, and he had been a happy man
He wept grievously as he parted from his friend, and the tears of an old
man are bitter. "It is all over for me in this world," said he as he gave the
last squeeze to Mr. Harding's hand. "I have now to forgive those who have
injured me—and to die."

And so the old man went out, and then Mr. Harding gave way to his
grief and wept aloud.

CHAPTER XXI

CONCLUSION

OUR tale is now done, and it only remains to us to collect the scattered
threads of our little story and to tie them into a seemly knot. This will
not be a work of labor, either to the author or to his readers. We have no
to deal with many personages, or with stirring events, and were it not fo
the custom of the thing, we might leave it to the imagination of all con
cerned to conceive how affairs at Barchester arranged themselves.

On the morning after the day last alluded to, Mr. Harding at an early
hour walked out of the hospital, with his daughter under his arm, and sa
down quietly to breakfast at his lodgings over the chemist's shop. There
was no parade about his departure. No one, not even Bunce, was there to
witness it. Had he walked to the apothecary's thus early to get a piece o
court plaster, or a box of lozenges, he could not have done it with less
appearance of an important movement. There was a tear in Eleanor's eye
as she passed through the big gateway and over the bridge, but Mr. Har
ding walked with an elastic step, and entered his new abode with a pleasan
face.

"Now, my dear," said he, "you have everything ready, and you can make
tea here just as nicely as in the parlor at the hospital." So Eleanor took of
her bonnet and made the tea. After this manner did the late Warden o
Barchester Hospital accomplish his flitting, and change his residence.

It was not long before the Archdeacon brought his father to discuss the
subject of a new warden. Of course he looked upon the nomination as his
own, and he had in his eye three or four fitting candidates, seeing that Mr
Cummins's plan as to the living of Puddingdale could not be brought to
bear. How can I describe the astonishment which confounded him when
his father declared that he would appoint no successor to Mr. Harding

If we can get the matter set to rights, Mr. Harding will return," said the Bishop. "And if we cannot, it will be wrong to put any other gentleman into so cruel a position."

It was in vain that the Archdeacon argued and lectured, and even threatened. In vain he my-lorded his poor father in his sternest manner. In vain his "good heavens!" were ejaculated in a tone that might have moved a whole synod, let alone one weak and aged bishop. Nothing could induce his father to fill up the vacancy caused by Mr. Harding's retirement.

Even John Bold would have pitied the feelings with which the Archdeacon returned to Plumstead. The Church was falling—nay, already in ruins. Its dignitaries were yielding without a struggle before the blows of its antagonists, and one of its most respected bishops, his own father—the man considered by all the world as being in such matters under his, Dr. Grantly's, control—had positively resolved to capitulate, and own himself vanquished!

And how fared the hospital under this resolve of its visitor? Badly indeed. It is now some years since Mr. Harding left it, and the warden's house is still tenantless. Old Bell has died, and Bill Gazy. The one-eyed Spriggs has drunk himself to death, and three others of the twelve have been gathered into the churchyard mold. Six have gone, and the six vacancies remain unfilled! Yes, six have died with no kind friend to solace their last moments, with no wealthy neighbor to administer comforts and ease the stings of death. Mr. Harding, indeed, did not desert them. From him they had such consolation as a dying man may receive from his Christian pastor, but it was the occasional kindness of a stranger which ministered to them, and not the constant presence of a master, a neighbor, and a friend.

Nor were those who remained better off than those who died. Dissensions rose among them, and contests for pre-eminence, and then they began to understand that soon one among them would be the last—some one wretched being would be alone there in that now comfortless hospital, the miserable relic of what had once been so good and so comfortable.

The building of the hospital itself has not been allowed to go to ruin. Mr. Chadwick, who still holds his stewardship and pays the accruing rents into an account opened at a bank for the purpose, sees to that, but the whole place has become disordered and ugly. The warden's garden is a wretched wilderness, the drive and paths are covered with weeds, the flower beds are bare, and the unshorn lawn is now a mass of long damp grass and unwholesome moss. The beauty of the place is gone, its attractions have withered. Alas! a very few years since it was the prettiest spot in Barchester, and now it is a disgrace to the city.

Mr. Harding did not go out to Crabtree Parva. An arrangement was made which respected the homestead of Mr. Smith and his happy family and put Mr. Harding into possession of a small living within the walls of the city. It is the smallest possible parish, containing a part of the cathedral close and a few old houses adjoining. The church is a singular little Gothic

building perched over a gateway through which the close is entered, and
is approached by a flight of stone steps which leads down under the arch-
way of the gate. It is no bigger than an ordinary room—perhaps twenty-
seven feet long by eighteen wide—but still it is a perfect church. It contains
an old carved pulpit and reading desk, a tiny altar under a window filled
with dark old colored glass, a font, some half-dozen pews, and perhaps a
dozen seats for the poor, and also a vestry. The roof is high-pitched and of
black old oak, and the three large beams which support it run down to the
side walls and terminate in grotesquely carved faces—two devils and an
angel on one side, two angels and a devil on the other. Such is the church
of St. Cuthbert at Barchester, of which Mr. Harding became rector, with
a clear income of seventy-five pounds a year.

Here he performs afternoon service every Sunday, and administers the
sacrament once in every three months. His audience is not large, and had
they been so, he could not have accommodated them. But enough come to
fill his six pews, and on the front seat of those devoted to the poor is
always to be seen our old friend Mr. Bunce, decently arrayed in his bedesman's gown.

Mr. Harding is still Precentor of Barchester, and it is very rarely the case
that those who attend the Sunday morning service miss the gratification
of hearing him chant the litany as no other man in England can do it.
He is neither a discontented nor an unhappy man. He still inhabits the lodgings to which he went on leaving the hospital, but he now has them to
himself. Three months after that time Eleanor became Mrs. Bold, and of
course removed to her husband's house.

There were some difficulties to be got over on the occasion of the marriage. The Archdeacon, who could not so soon overcome his grief, would
not be persuaded to grace the ceremony with his presence, but he allowed
his wife and children to be there. The marriage took place in the cathedral,
and the Bishop himself officiated. It was the last occasion on which he ever
did so, and though he still lives, it is not probable that he will ever do
so again.

Not long after the marriage, perhaps six months, when Eleanor's bridal
honors were fading and persons were beginning to call her Mrs. Bold without twittering, the Archdeacon consented to meet John Bold at a dinner
party, and since that time they have become almost friends. The Archdeacon firmly believes that his brother-in-law was, as a bachelor, an infidel,
an unbeliever in the great truths of our religion, but that matrimony has
opened his eyes, as it has those of others. And Bold is equally inclined to
think that time has softened the asperities of the Archdeacon's character.
Friends though they are, they do not often revert to the feud of the hospital.

Mr. Harding, we say, is not an unhappy man. He keeps his lodgings, but
they are of little use to him, except as being the one spot on earth which he
calls his own. His time is spent chiefly at his daughter's or at the palace.
He is never left alone, even should he wish to be so, and within a twelve-

month of Eleanor's marriage his determination to live at his own lodging had been so far broken through and abandoned that he consented to have his violoncello permanently removed to his daughter's house.

Every other day a message is brought to him from the Bishop. "The Bishop's compliments, and his lordship is not very well today, and he hopes Mr. Harding will dine with him." This bulletin as to the old man's health is a myth, for though he is over eighty he is never ill, and will probably die some day as a spark goes out, gradually and without a struggle. Mr. Harding does dine with him very often, which means going to the palace at three and remaining till ten. And whenever he does not the Bishop whines, and says that the port wine is corked, and complains that nobody attends to him, and frets himself off to bed an hour before his time.

It was long before the people of Barchester forgot to call Mr. Harding by his long well-known name of Warden. It had become so customary to say Mr. Warden that it was not easily dropped. "No, no," he always says when so addressed, "not Warden now, only Precentor."

BARCHESTER TOWERS

CHAPTER I

WHO WILL BE THE NEW BISHOP?

IN the latter days of July in the year 185–, a most important question was for ten days hourly asked in the cathedral city of Barchester, and answered every hour in various ways—Who was to be the new bishop?

The death of old Dr. Grantly, who had for many years filled that chair with meek authority, took place exactly as the Ministry of Lord——was going to give place to that of Lord——. The illness of the good old man was long and lingering, and it became at last a matter of intense interest to those concerned whether the new appointment should be made by a Conservative or Liberal government.

It was pretty well understood that the outgoing Premier had made his selection, and that if the question rested with him, the miter would descend on the head of Archdeacon Grantly, the old Bishop's son. The Archdeacon had long managed the affairs of the diocese, and for some months previous to the demise of his father rumor had confidently assigned to him the reversion of his father's honors.

Bishop Grantly died as he had lived, peaceably, slowly, without pain and without excitement. The breath ebbed from him almost imperceptibly, and for a month before his death it was a question whether he were alive or dead.

A trying time was this for the Archdeacon, for whom was designed the reversion of his father's see by those who then had the giving away of episcopal thrones. I would not be understood to say that the Prime Minister had in so many words promised the bishopric to Dr. Grantly. He was too discreet a man for that. The then Prime Minister was all in all at Oxford, and had lately passed a night at the house of the Master of Lazarus. Now the Master of Lazarus—which is, by the by, in many respects the most comfortable as well as the richest college at Oxford—was the Archdeacon's most intimate friend and most trusted counselor. On the occasion of the Prime Minister's visit, Dr. Grantly was of course present, and the meeting was very gracious. On the following morning Dr. Gwynne, the Master, told the Archdeacon that in his opinion the thing was settled.

At this time the Bishop was quite on his last legs, but the Ministry also were tottering. Dr. Grantly returned from Oxford happy and elated, to resume his place in the palace and to continue to perform for the father the last duties of a son, which, to give him his due, he performed with more tender care than was to be expected from his usual somewhat worldly manners.

The Ministry were to be out within five days, his father was to be dead within——No, he rejected that view of the subject. The Ministry were to be out, and the diocese might probably be vacant at the same period. There was much doubt as to the names of the men who were to succeed to power, and a week must elapse before a Cabinet was formed.

He tried to keep his mind away from the subject, but he could not. The race was so very close, and the stakes were so very high. The old Bishop slept during twenty of the twenty-four hours, but during the short periods of his waking moments he knew both his son and his dear old friend Mr. Harding, the Archdeacon's father-in-law, and would thank them tenderly for their care and love. Now he lay sleeping like a baby. Nothing could be easier than the old man's passage from this world to the next.

But by no means easy were the emotions of him who sat there watching. He knew it must be now or never. He was already over fifty, and there was little chance that his friends who were now leaving office would soon return to it. No probable British Prime Minister but he who was now in, he who was so soon to be out, would think of making a bishop of Dr. Grantly. Thus he thought long and sadly, in deep silence, and then gazed at that still living face, and then at last dared to ask himself whether he really longed for his father's death.

The effort was a salutary one, and the question was answered in a moment. The proud, wishful, worldly man sank on his knees by the bedside and, taking the Bishop's hand within his own, prayed eagerly that his sins might be forgiven him.

His face was still buried in the clothes when the door of the bedroom opened noiselessly and Mr. Harding entered with a velvet step. Mr. Harding's attendance at that bedside had been nearly as constant as that of the Archdeacon, and his ingress and egress was as much a matter of course as that of his son-in-law. He was standing close beside the Archdeacon before he was perceived, and would also have knelt in prayer had he not feared that his doing so might have caused some sudden start, and have disturbed the dying man. Dr. Grantly, however, instantly perceived him, and rose from his knees. As he did so Mr. Harding took both his hands, and pressed them warmly. There was more fellowship between them at that moment than there had ever been before, and it so happened that aftercircumstances greatly preserved the feeling. As they stood there pressing each other's hands, the tears rolled freely down their cheeks.

"God bless you, my dears," said the Bishop with feeble voice as he woke. —"God bless you—may God bless you both, my dear children." And so he died.

"You cannot but rejoice that it is over," said Mr. Harding, consoling his friend. The Archdeacon's mind, however, had already traveled from the death chamber to the closet of the Prime Minister. He had brought himself to pray for his father's life, but now that that life was done, minutes were too precious to be lost. It was now useless to dally with the fact of the Bishop's death—useless to lose perhaps everything for the pretense of a foolish sentiment.

"No, I suppose not," said he at last. "We have all expected it so long."

Mr. Harding took him by the arm and led him from the room. "We will see him again tomorrow morning," said he. "We had better leave the room now to the women." And so they went downstairs.

It was already evening, and nearly dark. It was most important that the Prime Minister should know that night that the diocese was vacant. Everything might depend on it, and so, in answer to Mr. Harding's further consolation, the Archdeacon suggested that a telegraph message should be immediately sent off to London.

"Yes," said Dr. Grantly, collecting himself and shaking off his weakness, "we must send a message at once. We don't know what might be the consequence of delay. Will you do it?"

"I! Oh, yes, certainly. I'll do anything, only I don't know exactly what it is you want."

Dr. Grantly sat down before a writing table and, taking pen and ink, wrote on a slip of paper as follows:

By Electric Telegraph
For the Earl of——, Downing Street, or elsewhere
The Bishop of Barchester is dead.
Message sent by the Rev. Septimus Harding

"There," said he, "just take that to the telegraph office at the railway station and give it in as it is. They'll probably make you copy it on to one of their own slips. That's all you'll have to do. Then you'll have to pay them half a crown." And the Archdeacon put his hand in his pocket and pulled out the necessary sum.

Mr. Harding felt very much like an errand boy, and also felt that he was called on to perform his duties as such at rather an unseemly time, but he said nothing and took the slip of paper and the proffered coin.

"But you've put my name into it, Archdeacon."

"Yes," said the other. "There should be the name of some clergyman you know, and what name so proper as that of so old a friend as yourself? The Earl won't look at the name, you may be sure of that. But my dear Mr. Harding, pray don't lose any time."

Mr. Harding got as far as the library door on his way to the station when he suddenly remembered the news with which he was fraught when he entered the poor Bishop's bedroom.

"But, Archdeacon," said he, turning back, "I forgot to tell you.—The Ministry are out."

"Out!" ejaculated the Archdeacon, in a tone which too plainly showed his anxiety and dismay, although under the circumstances of the moment he endeavored to control himself. "Out! Who told you so?"

Mr. Harding explained that news to this effect had come down by electric telegraph. The Archdeacon sat silent for awhile meditating, and Mr. Harding stood looking at him.

"Never mind," said the Archdeacon at last, "send the message all the same. The news must be sent to someone, and there is at present no one else in a position to receive it."

Mr. Harding went out, and sent the message, and it may be as well that we should follow it to its destination. Within thirty minutes of its leaving Barchester it reached the Earl of —— in his inner library. He opened the cover in which the message was enclosed, and having read it, he took his pen and wrote on the back of it:

> For the Earl of——,
> With the Earl of——'s compliments,

and sent it off again on its journey.

Thus terminated our unfortunate friend's chance of possessing the glories of a bishopric.

The names of many divines were given in the papers as that of the bishop-elect. The merits of all these candidates were discussed and somewhat irreverently disposed of, and then the *Jupiter* declared that Dr. Proudie was to be the man. Dr. Proudie was the man. Just a month after the demise of the late Bishop, Dr. Proudie kissed the Queen's hand as his successor-elect.

We must beg to be allowed to draw a curtain over the sorrows of the Archdeacon as he sat, somber and sad at heart, in the study of his parsonage at Plumstead Episcopi.

CHAPTER II

HIRAM'S HOSPITAL ACCORDING TO ACT OF PARLIAMENT

It is hardly necessary that I should here give to the public any lengthened biography of Mr. Harding up to the period of the commencement of this tale. The public cannot have forgotten how ill that sensitive gentleman bore the attack that was made on him in the columns of the *Jupiter* with reference to the income which he received as Warden of Hiram's Hospital in the city of Barchester. Nor can it yet be forgotten that a lawsuit was instituted against him on the matter of that charity by Mr. John Bold, who afterward married his, Mr. Harding's, younger and then only unmarried daughter.

Under pressure of these attacks, Mr. Harding had resigned his wardenship, though strongly recommended to abstain from doing so both by his friends and by his lawyers. He did, however, resign it, and betook himself manfully to the duties of the small parish of St. Cuthbert's in the city, of which he was Vicar, continuing also to perform those of Precentor of the cathedral, a situation of a small emolument which had hitherto been supposed to be joined as a matter of course to the wardenship of the hospital above spoken of.

When he left the hospital from which he had been so ruthlessly driven, and settled himself down in his own modest manner in the High Street of Barchester, he had not expected that others would make more fuss about it than he was inclined to do himself. The extent of his hope was that the movement might have been made in time to prevent any further paragraphs in the *Jupiter*. His affairs, however, were not allowed to subside thus quietly, and people were quite as much inclined to talk about the disinterested sacrifice he had made as they had before been to upbraid him for his cupidity.

The most remarkable thing that occurred was the receipt of an autograph letter from the Archbishop of Canterbury, in which the Primate very warmly praised his conduct, and begged to know what his intentions were for the future. Mr. Harding replied that he intended to be rector of St. Cuthbert's in Barchester, and so that matter dropped. Then the newspapers took up his case, the *Jupiter* among the rest, and wafted his name in eulogistic strains through every reading room in the nation. It was discovered also, that he was the author of that great musical work, *Harding's Church Music*—and a new edition was spoken of, though I believe never printed.

Mr. Harding had spent much of his time with his friend the Bishop, much with his daughter Mrs. Bold—now alas! a widow—and had almost daily visited the wretched remnant of his former subjects, the few surviving bedesmen now left at Hiram's Hospital. Six of them were still living. The number, according to old Hiram's will, should always have been twelve. But after the abdication of their Warden, the Bishop had appointed no successor to him, no new occupants of the charity had been nominated, and it appeared as though the hospital at Barchester would fall into abeyance unless the powers that be should take some steps towards putting it once more into working order.

During the past five years, the powers that be had not overlooked Hiram's Hospital, and sundry political doctors had taken the matter in hand. A political pamphleteer had produced a few dozen pages which he called "Who Are John Hiram's heirs?" intending to give an infallible rule for the governance of all such establishments, and at last a member of the Government promised that in the next session a short bill should be introduced for regulating the affairs of Barchester, and other kindred concerns.

The next session came and, contrary to custom, the bill came also, was read and reread, and in some undistinguished manner passed through its eleven stages without appeal or dissent. What would John Hiram have said in the matter could he have predicted that some forty-five gentlemen would take on themselves to make a law altering the whole purport of his will without in the least knowing at the moment of their making it what it was that they were doing?

The bill, however, did pass, and at the time at which this history is supposed to commence, it had been ordained that there should be, as heretofore, twelve old men in Barchester Hospital, each with 1s. 4d. a day; that there should also be twelve old women, to be located in a house to be built, each with 1s. 2d. a day; that there should be a matron, with a house and £70 a year, a steward with £150 a year, and a Warden with £450 a year, who should have the spiritual guidance of both establishments and the temporal guidance of that appertaining to the male sex. The bishop, dean, and warden were, as formerly, to appoint in turn the recipients of the charity, and the bishop was to appoint the officers. There was nothing said as to the wardenship being held by the Precentor of the cathedral, nor a word as to Mr. Harding's right to the situation.

It was not, however, till some months after the death of the old Bishop, and almost immediately consequent on the installation of his successor, that notice was given that the reform was about to be carried out. The new law and the new Bishop were among the earliest works of a new Ministry, and the death of Dr. Grantly occurred, as we have seen, exactly at the period of the change.

Poor Eleanor Bold! How well does that widow's cap become her, and the solemn gravity with which she devotes herself to her new duties. Poor Eleanor!

Poor Eleanor! I cannot say that with me John Bold was ever a favorite. I never thought him worthy of the wife he had won. But in her estimation he was most worthy. Hers was one of those feminine hearts which cling to a husband not with idolatry, for worship can admit of no defect in its idol, but with the perfect tenacity of ivy. As the parasite plant will follow even the defects of the trunk which it embraces, so did Eleanor cling to and love the very faults of her husband. She had once declared that whatever her father did should in her eyes be right. She then transferred her allegiance, and became ever ready to defend the worst failings of her lord and master.

And John Bold was a man to be loved by a woman. He was himself affectionate, he was confiding and manly. And that arrogance of thought, unsustained by first-rate abilities, that attempt at being better than his neighbors which jarred so painfully on the feelings of his acquaintance, did not injure him in the estimation of his wife.

Could she even have admitted that he had a fault, his early death would have blotted out the memory of it. She wept as for the loss of the most perfect treasure with which mortal woman had ever been endowed. For weeks after he was gone the idea of future happiness in this world was hateful to her. Consolation, as it is called, was insupportable, and tears and sleep were her only relief.

But God tempers the wind to the shorn lamb. She knew that she had within her the living source of other cares. She knew that there was to be created for her another subject of weal or woe, of unutterable joy or despairing sorrow, as God in His mercy might vouchsafe to her. Just eight months after the father's death a second John Bold was born, and if the worship of one creature can be innocent in another, let us hope that the adoration offered over the cradle of the fatherless infant may not be imputed as a sin.

It will not be worth our while to define the character of the child, or to point out in how far the faults of the father were redeemed within that little breast by the virtues of the mother. The baby, as a baby, was all that was delightful, and I cannot foresee that it will be necessary for us to inquire into the facts of his afterlife. Our present business at Barchester will not occupy us above a year or two at the furthest, and I will leave it to some other pen to produce, if necessary, the biography of John Bold the Younger.

The baby was really delightful. He took his food with a will, struck out his toes merrily whenever his legs were uncovered, and did not have fits. These are supposed to be the strongest points of baby perfection, and in all these our baby excelled.

And thus the widow's deep grief was softened, and a sweet balm was poured into the wound which she had thought nothing but death could heal.

I would not, however, have it imagined that Mrs. Bold forgot her husband. She daily thought of him with all conjugal love, and enshrined his memory in the innermost center of her heart. But yet she was happy in her baby. And so Eleanor's bosom became tranquil, and she set about her new duties eagerly and gratefully.

As regards the concerns of the world, John Bold had left his widow in prosperous circumstances. He had bequeathed to her all that he possessed, and that comprised an income much exceeding what she or her friends thought necessary for her. It amounted to nearly a thousand a year, and when she reflected on its extent, her dearest hope was to hand it over, not only unimpaired but increased, to her husband's son, to her own darling, to the little man who now lay sleeping on her knee happily ignorant of the cares which were to be accumulated in his behalf.

When John Bold died she earnestly implored her father to come and live with her, but this Mr. Harding declined, though for some weeks he remained with her as a visitor. He could not be prevailed upon to forgo the possession of some small home of his own, and so remained in the lodgings he had first selected over a chemist's shop in the High Street of Barchester.

CHAPTER III

DR. AND MRS. PROUDIE

THIS narrative is supposed to commence immediately after the installation of Dr. Proudie. I will not describe the ceremony, as I do not precisely understand its nature. I am ignorant whether a bishop be chaired like a Member of Parliament, or carried in a gilt coach like a Lord Mayor, or sworn in like a Justice of Peace, or introduced like a peer to the upper house, or led between two brethren like a Knight of the Garter. But I do know that everything was properly done, and that nothing fit or becoming to a young bishop was omitted on the occasion.

Dr. Proudie was not the man to allow anything to be omitted that might be becoming to his new dignity. He understood well the value of forms, and knew that the due observance of rank could not be maintained unless the exterior trappings belonging to it were held in proper esteem. He was a man born to move in high circles—at least so he thought himself, and circumstances had certainly sustained him in this view. He was the nephew of an Irish baron by his mother's side, and his wife was the niece of a Scotch earl. He had for years held some clerical office appertaining to courtly matters, which had enabled him to live in London and to entrust his parish to his curate. He had been preacher to the Royal Beefeaters, curator of theological manuscripts in the Ecclesiastical Courts, chaplain to the Queen's Yeomanry Guard, and almoner to his Royal Highness the Prince of Rappe-Blankenberg.

His residence in the metropolis, rendered necessary by the duties thus entrusted to him, his high connections, and the peculiar talents and nature of the man recommended him to persons in power, and Dr. Proudie became known as a useful and rising clergyman.

Dr. Proudie was one among those who early in life adapted himself to the views held by the Whigs on most theological and religious subjects. He bore with the idolatry of Rome, tolerated even the infidelity of Socinianism, and was hand and glove with the Presbyterian synods of Scotland and Ulster.

Such a man at such a time was found to be useful, and Dr. Proudie's name began to appear in the newspapers. He was made one of a commission who went over to Ireland to arrange matters preparative to the working of the national board; he became honorary secretary to another commission nominated to inquire into the revenues of cathedral chapters, and had had something to do with both the regium donum and the Maynooth grant.

It must not on this account be taken as proved that Dr. Proudie was a man of great mental powers, or even of much capacity for business, for such qualities had not been required in him. In the arrangement of those church reforms with which he was connected, the ideas and original conception of the work to be done were generally furnished by the Liberal statesman of the day, and the labor of the details was borne by officials of a lower rank. It was, however, thought expedient that the name of some clergyman should appear in such matters, and as Dr. Proudie had become known as a tolerating divine, great use of this sort was made of his name. If he did not do much active good, he never did any harm. He was amenable to those who were really in authority, and at the sittings of the various boards to which he belonged maintained a kind of dignity which had its value.

He was certainly possessed of sufficient tact to answer the purpose for which he was required without making himself troublesome. But it must not therefore be surmised that he doubted his own power, or failed to believe that he could himself take a high part in high affairs when his own turn came. He was biding his time, and patiently looking forward to the days when he himself would sit authoritative at some board and talk and direct and rule the roast while lesser stars sat round and obeyed, as he had so well accustomed himself to do.

His reward and his time had now come. He was selected for the vacant bishopric, and on the next vacancy which might occur in any diocese would take his place in the House of Lords, prepared to give not a silent vote in all matters concerning the weal of the Church Establishment. Toleration was to be the basis on which he was to fight his battles, and in the honest courage of his heart he thought no evil would come to him in encountering even such foes as his brethren of Exeter and Oxford.

Dr. Proudie was an ambitious man, and before he was well consecrated Bishop of Barchester, he had begun to look up to archiepiscopal splendor and the glories of Lambeth, or at any rate of Bishopsthorpe. He was comparatively young, and had, as he fondly flattered himself, been selected as possessing such gifts, natural and acquired, as must be sure to recommend him to a yet higher notice now that a higher sphere was opened to him. Dr. Proudie was therefore quite prepared to take a conspicuous part in all theological affairs appertaining to these realms, and having such views, by no means intended to bury himself at Barchester as his predecessor had done. No. London should still be his ground. A comfortable mansion in a provincial city might be well enough for the dead months of the year. Indeed Dr. Proudie had always felt it necessary to his position to retire from London when other great and fashionable people did so. But London should still be his fixed residence, and it was in London that he resolved to exercise that hospitality so peculiarly recommended to all bishops by St. Paul. How otherwise could he keep himself before the world? How else give to the Government, in matters theological, the full benefit of his weight and talents?

This resolution was no doubt a salutary one as regarded the world at large, but was not likely to make him popular either with the clergy or people of Barchester. Dr. Grantly had always lived there. And in truth it was hard for a bishop to be popular after Dr. Grantly. His income had averaged £9000 a year, his successor was to be rigidly limited to £5000. He had but one child on whom to spend his money, Dr. Proudie had seven or eight. He had been a man of few personal expenses, and they had been confined to the tastes of a moderate gentleman, but Dr. Proudie had to maintain a position in fashionable society and had that to do with comparatively small means. Dr. Grantly had certainly kept his carriage, as became a bishop, but his carriage, horses, and coachman, though they did very well for Barchester, would have been almost ridiculous at Westminster. Mrs. Proudie determined that her husband's equipage should not shame her, and things on which Mrs. Proudie resolved were generally accomplished.

From all this it was likely to result that Dr. Proudie would not spend much money at Barchester, whereas his predecessor had dealt with the tradesmen of the city in a manner very much to their satisfaction. The Grantlys, father and son, had spent their money like gentlemen, but it soon became whispered in Barchester that Dr. Proudie was not unacquainted with those prudent devices by which the utmost show of wealth is produced from limited means.

In person Dr. Proudie is a good-looking man, spruce and dapper, and very tidy. He is somewhat below middle height, being about five feet four, but he makes up for the inches which he wants by the dignity with which he carries those which he has. It is no fault of his own if he has not a commanding eye, for he studies hard to assume it. His features are well formed, though perhaps the sharpness of his nose may give to his face in the eyes of some people an air of insignificance. If so, it is greatly redeemed by his mouth and chin, of which he is justly proud.

Dr. Proudie may well be said to have been a fortunate man, for he was not born to wealth, and he is now Bishop of Barchester. But nevertheless he has his cares. He has a large family, of whom the three eldest are daughters, now all grown up and fit for fashionable life. And he has a wife. It is not my intention to breathe a word against the character of Mrs. Proudie, but still I cannot think that with all her virtues she adds much to her husband's happiness. The truth is that in matters domestic she rules supreme over her titular lord, and rules with a rod of iron. Nor is this all. Things domestic Dr. Proudie might have abandoned to her, if not voluntarily, yet willingly. But Mrs. Proudie is not satisfied with such home dominion, and stretches her power over all his movements, and will not even abstain from things spiritual. In fact, the Bishop is henpecked.

The Archdeacon's wife, in her happy home at Plumstead, knows how to assume the full privileges of her rank and express her own mind in becoming tone and place. But Mrs. Grantly's sway, if sway she has, is easy and beneficent. She never shames her husband. Before the world she is a pattern of obedience. Her voice is never loud, nor her looks sharp. Doubtless she values power, and has not unsuccessfully striven to acquire it, but she knows what should be the limits of a woman's rule.

Not so Mrs. Proudie. This lady is habitually authoritative to all, but to her poor husband she is despotic. Successful as has been his career in the eyes of the world, it would seem that in the eyes of his wife he is never right. All hope of defending himself has long passed from him. Indeed he rarely even attempts self-justification, and is aware that submission produces the nearest approach to peace which his own house can ever attain.

Mrs. Proudie has not been able to sit at the boards and committees to which her husband has been called by the state, nor, as he often reflects, can she make her voice heard in the House of Lords. It may be that she will refuse to him permission to attend to this branch of a bishop's duties. It may be that she will insist on his close attendance to his own closet. He has never whispered a word on the subject to living ears, but he has already made his fixed resolve. Should such an attempt be made, he will rebel. Dogs have turned against their masters, and even Neapolitans against their rulers, when oppression has been too severe. And Dr. Proudie feels within himself that if the cord be drawn too tight, he also can muster courage and resist.

The state of vassalage in which our Bishop has been kept by his wife has not tended to exalt his character in the eyes of his daughters, who assume in addressing their father too much of that authority which is not properly belonging, at any rate, to them. They are, on the whole, fine engaging young ladies. They are tall and robust like their mother, whose high cheekbones, and—we may say auburn hair, they all inherit. They think somewhat too much of their grand-uncles, who have not hitherto returned the compliment by thinking much of them. But now that their father is a bishop, it is probable that family ties will be drawn closer. Dr. Proudie's sons are still at school.

One other marked peculiarity in the character of the Bishop's wife must be mentioned. Though not averse to the society and manners of the world, she is in her own way a religious woman, and the form in which this tendency shows itself in her is by a strict observance of Sabbatarian rule. Dissipation and low dresses during the week are, under her control, atoned for by three services, an evening sermon read by herself, and a perfect abstinence from any cheering employment on the Sunday. Unfortunately for those under her roof to whom the dissipation and low dresses are not extended—her servants, namely, and her husband—the compensating strictness of the Sabbath includes all. Woe betide the recreant housemaid who is found to have been listening to the honey of a sweetheart in the Regent's Park instead of the soul-stirring evening discourse of Mr. Slope. Not only is she sent adrift, but she is so sent with a character which leaves her little hope of a decent place. Woe betide the six-foot hero who escorts Mrs. Proudie to her pew in red-plush breeches if he slips away to the neighboring beer shop instead of falling into the back seat appropriated to his use. Mrs. Proudie has the eyes of Argus for such offenders. Occasional drunkenness in the week may be overlooked, for six feet on low wages are hardly to be procured if the morals are always kept at a high pitch. But not even for grandeur or economy will Mrs. Proudie forgive a desecration of the Sabbath.

In such matters Mrs. Proudie allows herself to be often guided by that eloquent preacher, the Reverend Mr. Slope, and as Dr. Proudie is guided by his wife, it necessarily follows that the eminent man we have named has obtained a good deal of control over Dr. Proudie in matters concerning religion. Mr. Slope's only preferment has hitherto been that of reader and preacher in a London district church, and on the consecration of his friend the new Bishop, he readily gave this up to undertake the onerous but congenial duties of domestic chaplain to his lordship.

Mr. Slope, however, on his first introduction must not be brought before the public at the tail of a chapter.

CHAPTER IV

THE BISHOP'S CHAPLAIN

OF the Reverend Mr. Slope's parentage I am not able to say much. I have heard it asserted that he is lineally descended from that eminent physician who assisted at the birth of Mr. T. Shandy, and that in early years he added an "e" to his name for the sake of euphony, as other great men have done before him. If this be so, I presume he was christened Obadiah—for that is his name—in commemoration of the conflict in which his ancestor so distinguished himself. All my researches on the subject have, however, failed in enabling me to fix the date on which the family changed its religion.

He had been a sizar at Cambridge, and had there conducted himself at any rate successfully, for in due process of time he was an M.A., having university pupils under his care. From thence he was transferred to London, and became preacher at a new district church built on the confines of Baker Street. He was in this position when congenial ideas on religious subjects recommended him to Mrs. Proudie, and the intercourse had become close and confidential.

Having been thus familiarly thrown among the Misses Proudie, it was no more than natural that some softer feeling than friendship should be engendered. There have been some passages of love between him and the eldest hope, Olivia, but they have hitherto resulted in no favorable arrangement. In truth, Mr. Slope, having made a declaration of affection, afterward withdrew it on finding that the Doctor had no immediate worldly funds with which to endow his child. And it may easily be conceived that Miss Proudie after such an announcement on his part was not readily disposed to receive any further show of affection. On the appointment of Dr. Proudie to the bishopric of Barchester, Mr. Slope's views were in truth somewhat altered. Bishops, even though they be poor, can provide for clerical children, and Mr. Slope began to regret that he had not been more disinterested. He no sooner heard the tidings of the Doctor's elevation than he recommenced his siege, not violently, indeed, but respectfully, and at a distance. Olivia Proudie, however, was a girl of spirit. She had the blood of two peers in her veins, and better still, she had another lover on her books. So Mr. Slope sighed in vain, and the pair soon found it convenient to establish a mutual bond of inveterate hatred.

It may be thought singular that Mrs. Proudie's friendship for the young clergyman should remain firm after such an affair, but to tell the truth, she had known nothing of it. Though very fond of Mr. Slope herself, she had never conceived the idea that either of her daughters would become so, and remembering their high birth and social advantages, expected for them matches of a different sort. Neither the gentleman nor the lady found it necessary to enlighten her. Olivia's two sisters had each known of the affair, so had all the servants, so had all the people living in the adjoining houses on either side, but Mrs. Proudie had been kept in the dark.

Mr. Slope soon comforted himself with the reflection that as he had been selected as chaplain to the Bishop, it would probably be in his power to get the good things in the Bishop's gift without troubling himself with the Bishop's daughter, and he found himself able to endure the pangs of rejected love. As he sat himself down in the railway carriage confronting the Bishop and Mrs. Proudie as they started on their first journey to Barchester, he began to form in his own mind a plan of his future life. He knew well his patron's strong points, but he knew the weak ones as well. He understood correctly enough to what attempts the new Bishop's high spirit would soar, and he rightly guessed that public life would better suit the great man's taste than the small details of diocesan duty.

He, therefore, he, Mr. Slope, would in effect be Bishop of Barchester. Such was his resolve, and to give Mr. Slope his due, he had both courage and spirit to bear him out in his resolution. He knew that he should have a hard battle to fight, for the power and patronage of the see would be equally coveted by another great mind—Mrs. Proudie would also choose to be Bishop of Barchester. Mr. Slope, however, flattered himself that he could outmaneuver the lady. She must live much in London, while he would always be on the spot. She would necessarily remain ignorant of much, while he would know everything belonging to the diocese. At first, doubtless, he must flatter and cajole, perhaps yield in some things, but he did not doubt of ultimate triumph. If all other means failed, he could join the Bishop against his wife, inspire courage into the unhappy man, lay an ax to the root of the woman's power, and emancipate the husband.

Such were his thoughts as he sat looking at the sleeping pair in the railway carriage, and Mr. Slope is not the man to trouble himself with such thoughts for nothing. He is possessed of more than average abilities, and is of good courage. Though he can stoop to fawn, and stoop low indeed if need be, he has still within him the power to assume the tyrant, and with the power he has certainly the wish. His acquirements are not of the highest order, but such as they are they are completely under control, and he knows the use of them. He is gifted with a certain kind of pulpit eloquence, not likely indeed to be persuasive with men but powerful with the softer sex. In his sermons he deals greatly in denunciations, excites the minds of his weaker hearers with a not unpleasant terror, and leaves an impression on their minds that all mankind are in a perilous state, and all womankind too, except those who attend regularly to the evening lectures in Baker Street. His looks and tones are extremely severe, so much so that one cannot but fancy that he regards the greater part of the world as being infinitely too bad for his care. As he walks through the streets, his very face denotes his horror of the world's wickedness, and there is always an anathema lurking in the corner of his eye.

In doctrine, he, like his patron, is tolerant of Dissent, if so strict a mind can be called tolerant of anything. With Wesleyan Methodists he has something in common, but his soul trembles in agony at the iniquities of the Puseyites. His aversion is carried to things outward as well as inward. His gall rises at a new church with a high-pitched roof. A full-breasted black-silk waistcoat is with him a symbol of Satan. And a profane jestbook would not, in his view, more foully desecrate the church seat of a Christian than a book of prayer printed with red letters and ornamented with a cross on the back. Most active clergymen have their hobby, and Sunday observances are his. Sunday, however, is a word which never pollutes his mouth—it is always "the Sabbath." The "desecration of the Sabbath," as he delights to call it, is to him meat and drink. He thrives upon that as policemen do on the general evil habits of the community. It is the loved subject of all his evening discourses, the source of all his eloquence, the secret of all his power over the female heart. To him the revelation of God appears only in that one law given for Jewish observance. To him the mercies of our Saviour speak in vain, to him in vain has been preached that sermon which fell from divine lips on the mountain—"Blessed are the meek, for they shall inherit the earth"—"Blessed are the merciful, for they shall obtain mercy." To him the New Testament is comparatively of little moment, for from it can he draw no fresh authority for that dominion which he loves to exercise over at least a seventh part of man's allotted time here below.

Mr. Slope is tall, and not ill-made. His feet and hands are large, as has ever been the case with all his family, but he has a broad chest and wide shoulders to carry off these excrescences, and on the whole his figure is good. His countenance, however, is not specially prepossessing. His hair is lank, and of a dull pale-reddish hue. It is always formed into three straight lumpy masses, each brushed with admirable precision and cemented with much grease. Two of them adhere closely to the sides of his face, and the other lies at right angles above them. He wears no whiskers, and is always punctiliously shaven. His face is nearly of the same color as his hair, though perhaps a little redder. It is not unlike beef—beef, however, one would say, of a bad quality. His forehead is capacious and high, but square and heavy, and unpleasantly shining. His mouth is large, though his lips are thin and bloodless, and his big, prominent, pale-brown eyes inspire anything but confidence. His nose, however, is his redeeming feature. It is pronounced straight and well formed, though I myself should have liked it better did it not possess a somewhat spongy, porous appearance, as though it had been cleverly formed out of a red-colored cork.

I never could endure to shake hands with Mr. Slope. A cold, clammy perspiration always exudes from him, the small drops are ever to be seen standing on his brow, and his friendly grasp is unpleasant.

Such is Mr. Slope—such is the man who has suddenly fallen into the midst of Barchester close, and is destined there to assume the station which has heretofore been filled by the son of the late Bishop. Think, oh, my meditative reader, what an associate we have here for those comfortable prebendaries, those gentlemanlike clerical doctors, those happy, well-used, well-fed minor canons, who have grown into existence at Barchester under the kindly wings of Bishop Grantly!

But not as a mere associate for these does Mr. Slope travel down to Barchester with the Bishop and his wife. He intends to be, if not their master, at least the chief among them. He intends to lead, and to have followers. He intends to hold the pursestrings of the diocese, and draw round him an obedient herd of his poor and hungry brethren.

And here we can hardly fail to draw a comparison between the Archdeacon and our new private chaplain, and despite the manifold faults of the former, one can hardly fail to make it much to his advantage.

Both men are eager, much too eager, to support and increase the power of their order. Both are anxious that the world should be priest-governed, though they have probably never confessed so much, even to themselves. Both begrudge any other kind of dominion held by man over man. Dr. Grantly, if he admits the Queen's supremacy in things spiritual, only admits it as being due to the quasi priesthood conveyed in the consecrating qualities of her coronation, and he regards things temporal as being by their nature subject to those which are spiritual. Mr. Slope's ideas of sacerdotal rule are of quite a different class. He cares nothing, one way or the other, for the Queen's supremacy. These to his ears are empty words, meaning nothing. Forms he regards but little, and such titular expressions

as "supremacy," "consecration," "ordination," and the like convey of themselves no significance to him. Let him be supreme who can. The temporal
king, judge, or gaoler can work but on the body. The spiritual master, if
he have the necessary gifts and can duly use them, has a wider field
of empire. He works upon the soul. If he can make himself be believed, he
can be all-powerful over those who listen. If he be careful to meddle with
none who are too strong in intellect, or too weak in flesh, he may indeed
be supreme. And such was the ambition of Mr. Slope.

Dr. Grantly interfered very little with the worldly doings of those who
were in any way subject to him. I do not mean to say that he omitted
to notice misconduct among his clergy, immorality in his parish, or omis-
sions in his family, but he was not anxious to do so where the necessity
could be avoided. He was not troubled with a propensity to be curious,
and as long as those around him were tainted with no heretical leaning towards Dissent, as long as they fully and freely admitted the efficacy
of Mother Church, he was willing that that mother should be merciful
and affectionate, prone to indulgence, and unwilling to chastise. He himself
enjoyed the good things of this world, and liked to let it be known that
he did so. He cordially despised any brother rector who thought harm of
dinner parties or dreaded the dangers of a moderate claret jug. Consequently
dinner parties and claret jugs were common in the diocese. He liked to give
laws and to be obeyed in them implicitly, but he endeavored that his
ordinances should be within the compass of the man, and not unpalatable
to the gentleman. He had ruled among his clerical neighbors now for sundry
years, and as he had maintained his power without becoming unpopular,
it may be presumed that he had exercised some wisdom.

Of Mr. Slope's conduct much cannot be said, as his grand career is yet
to commence, but it may be premised that his tastes will be very different
from those of the Archdeacon. He conceives it to be his duty to know all
the private doings and desires of the flock entrusted to his care. From the
poorer classes he exacts an unconditional obedience to set rules of conduct, and if disobeyed he has recourse, like his great ancestor, to the fulmi-
nations of an Ernulfus: "Thou shalt be damned in thy going in and in thy
coming out—in thy eating and thy drinking," &c., &c., &c. With the rich,
experience has already taught him that a different line of action is necessary. Men in the upper walks of life do not mind being cursed, and the
women, presuming that it be done in delicate phrase, rather like it. But he
has not therefore given up so important a portion of believing Christians.
With the men, indeed, he is generally at variance. They are hardened
sinners, on whom the voice of the priestly charmer too often falls in vain.
But with the ladies, old and young, firm and frail, devout and dissipated,
he is, as he conceives, all-powerful. He can reprove faults with so much
flattery, and utter censure in so caressing a manner, that the female heart,
if it glow with a spark of Low Church susceptibility, cannot withstand him.
In many houses he is thus an admired guest. The husbands, for their wives'

sake, are fain to admit him, and when once admitted it is not easy to shake him off. He has, however, a pawing, greasy way with him which does not endear him to those who do not value him for their souls' sake, and he is not a man to make himself at once popular in a large circle such as is now likely to surround him at Barchester.

CHAPTER V

A MORNING VISIT

It was known that Dr. Proudie would immediately have to reappoint to the wardenship of the hospital under the Act of Parliament to which allusion has been made, but no one imagined that any choice was left to him—no one for a moment thought that he could appoint any other than Mr. Harding. Mr. Harding himself, when he heard how the matter had been settled, without troubling himself much on the subject considered it as certain that he would go back to his pleasant house and garden. And though there would be much that was melancholy—nay, almost heartrending —in such a return, he still was glad that it was to be so. His daughter might probably be persuaded to return there with him. She had, indeed, all but promised to do so, though she still entertained an idea that the greatest of mortals, that important atom of humanity, that little god upon earth, Johnny Bold her baby, ought to have a house of his own over his head.

Such being the state of Mr. Harding's mind in the matter, he did not feel any peculiar personal interest in the appointment of Dr. Proudie to the bishopric. He, as well as others at Barchester, regretted that a man should be sent among them who they were aware was not of their way of thinking. But Mr. Harding himself was not a bigoted man on points of church 'doctrine, and he was quite prepared to welcome Dr. Proudie to Barchester in a graceful and becoming manner. He had nothing to seek and nothing to fear. He felt that it behooved him to be on good terms with his bishop, and he did not anticipate any obstacle that would prevent it.

In such a frame of mind he proceeded to pay his respects at the palace the second day after the arrival of the Bishop and his chaplain. But he did not go alone. Dr. Grantly proposed to accompany him, and Mr. Harding was not sorry to have a companion who would remove from his shoulders the burden of the conversation in such an interview. In the affair of the consecration Dr. Grantly had been introduced to the Bishop, and Mr. Harding had also been there. He had, however, kept himself in the background, and he was now to be presented to the great man for the first time.

The Archdeacon's feelings were of a much stronger nature. He was not exactly the man to overlook his own slighted claims, or to forgive the preference shown to another. Nevertheless it behooved him also to conduct himself toward the intruder as an old Archdeacon should conduct himself to an incoming bishop, and though he was well aware of all Dr. Proudie's abominable opinions as regarded Dissenters, church reform, the hebdomadal council, and suchlike, though he disliked the man and hated the doctrines, still he was prepared to show respect to the station of the Bishop. So he and Mr. Harding called together at the palace.

His lordship was at home, and the two visitors were shown through the accustomed hall into the well-known room where the good old Bishop used to sit. The furniture had been bought at a valuation, and every chair and table, every bookshelf against the wall, and every square in the carpet was as well known to each of them as their own bedrooms. Nevertheless they at once felt that they were strangers there. The furniture was for the most part the same, yet the place had been metamorphosed. A new sofa had been introduced, a horrid chintz affair, most unprelatical and almost irreligious—such a sofa as never yet stood in the study of any decent High Church clergyman of the Church of England. The old curtains had also given way. They had, to be sure, become dingy, and that which had been originally a rich and goodly ruby had degenerated into a reddish brown. Mr. Harding, however, thought the old reddish brown much preferable to the gaudy buff-colored trumpery moreen which Mrs. Proudie had deemed good enough for her husband's own room in the provincial city of Barchester.

Our friends found Dr. Proudie sitting on the old Bishop's chair, looking very nice in his new apron. They found, too, Mr. Slope standing on the hearthrug, persuasive and eager, just as the Archdeacon used to stand. But on the sofa they also found Mrs. Proudie, an innovation for which a precedent might in vain be sought in all the annals of the Barchester bishopric!

There she was, however, and they could only make the best of her. The introductions were gone through in much form. The Archdeacon shook hands with the Bishop, and named Mr. Harding, who received such an amount of greeting as was due from a bishop to a precentor. His lordship then presented them to his lady wife, the Archdeacon first, with archidiaconal honors, and then the Precentor with diminished parade. After this Mr. Slope presented himself. The Bishop, it is true, did mention his name, and so did Mrs. Proudie too, in a louder tone, but Mr. Slope took upon himself the chief burden of his own introduction. He had great pleasure in making himself acquainted with Dr. Grantly. He had heard much of the Archdeacon's good works in that part of the diocese in which his duties as Archdeacon had been exercised (thus purposely ignoring the Archdeacon's hitherto unlimited dominion over the diocese at large). He was aware that his lordship depended greatly on the assistance which Dr. Grantly would be able to give him in that portion of his diocese. He then thrust out his hand, and grasping that of his new foe, bedewed it unmercifully. Dr. Grantly in return bowed, looked stiff, contracted his eyebrows, and wiped his hand with his pocket handkerchief. Nothing abashed, Mr. Slope then noticed the Precentor, and descended to the grade of the lower clergy. He gave him a squeeze of the hand, damp indeed but affectionate, and was very glad to make the acquaintance of Mr.— Oh, yes, Mr. Harding, he had not exactly caught the name. "Precentor in the cathedral," surmised Mr. Slope. Mr. Harding confessed that such was the humble sphere of his work. "Some parish duty as well," suggested Mr. Slope. Mr. Harding acknowledged the diminutive incumbency of St. Cuthbert's. Mr. Slope then left him alone, having condescended sufficiently, and joined the conversation among the higher powers.

There were four persons there, each of whom considered himself the most important personage in the diocese—himself, indeed, or herself, as Mrs. Proudie was one of them—and with such a difference of opinion it was not probable that they would get on pleasantly together. The Bishop himself actually wore the visible apron, and trusted mainly to that—to that and his title, both being facts which could not be overlooked. The Archdeacon knew his subject, and really understood the business of bishoping, which the others did not, and this was his strong ground. Mrs. Proudie had her sex to back her, and her habit of command, and was nothing daunted by the high tone of Dr. Grantly's face and figure. Mr. Slope had only himself and his own courage and tact to depend on, but he nevertheless was perfectly self-assured, and did not doubt but that he should soon get the better of weak men who trusted so much to externals as both Bishop and Archdeacon appeared to do.

"Do you reside in Barchester, Dr. Grantly?" asked the lady with her sweetest smile.

Dr. Grantly explained that he lived in his own parish of Plumstead Episcopi, a few miles out of the city. Whereupon the lady hoped that the distance was not too great for country visiting, as she would be so glad to make the acquaintance of Mrs. Grantly. She would take the earliest opportunity, after the arrival of her horses at Barchester. Their horses were at present in London. Their horses were not immediately coming down, as the Bishop would be obliged, in a few days, to return to town.

The Archdeacon made his fifth bow—he had made one at each mention of the horses—and promised that Mrs. Grantly would do herself the honor of calling at the palace on an early day. Mrs. Proudie declared that she would be delighted. She hadn't liked to ask, not being quite sure whether Mrs. Grantly had horses. Besides, the distance might have been, &c. &c.

Dr. Grantly again bowed, but said nothing. He could have bought every individual possession of the whole family of the Proudies, and have restored them as a gift, without much feeling the loss, and had kept a separate

pair of horses for the exclusive use of his wife since the day of his marriage. Whereas Mrs. Proudie had been hitherto jobbed about the streets
of London at so much a month during the season, and at other times had
managed to walk, or hire a smart fly from the livery stables.

"Are the arrangements with reference to the Sabbath-day schools generally pretty good in your archdeaconry?" asked Mr. Slope.

"Sabbath-day schools!" repeated the Archdeacon with an affectation of
surprise. "Upon my word, I can't tell. It depends mainly on the parson's
wife and daughters. There is none at Plumstead."

This was almost a fib on the part of the Archdeacon, for Mrs. Grantly
has a very nice school. To be sure it is not a Sunday school exclusively,
and is not so designated. But that exemplary lady always attends there
an hour before church, and hears the children say their catechism, and
sees that they are clean and tidy for church, with their hands washed and
their shoes tied. And Grisel and Florinda, her daughters, carry thither a
basket of large buns, baked on the Saturday afternoon, and distribute them
to all the children not especially under disgrace, which buns are carried
home after church with considerable content, and eaten hot at tea, being
then split and toasted. The children of Plumstead would indeed open their
eyes if they heard their venerated pastor declare that there was no Sunday
school in his parish.

Mr. Slope merely opened his eyes wider, and slightly shrugged his shoulders. He was not, however, prepared to give up his darling project.

"I fear there is a great deal of Sabbath traveling here," said he. "On looking at the Bradshaw, I see that there are three trains in and three out
every Sabbath. Could nothing be done to induce the company to withdraw them? Don't you think, Dr. Grantly, that a little energy might
diminish the evil?"

"Not being a director, I really can't say. But if you can withdraw the
passengers, the company I dare say will withdraw the trains," said the
Doctor. "It's merely a question of dividends."

"But surely, Dr. Grantly," said the lady, "surely we should look at it
differently. You and I, for instance, in our position. Surely we should do
all that we can to control so grievous a sin. Don't you think so, Mr. Harding?" And she turned to the Precentor, who was sitting mute and unhappy.

Mr. Harding thought that all porters and stokers, guards, breaksmen,
and pointsmen, ought to have an opportunity of going to church, and he
hoped that they all had.

"But surely, surely," continued Mrs. Proudie, "surely that is not enough.
Surely that will not secure such an observance of the Sabbath as we are
taught to conceive is not only expedient but indispensable. Surely——"

Come what come might, Dr. Grantly was not to be forced into a dis-
sertation on a point of doctrine with Mrs. Proudie, nor yet with Mr. Slope,
so without much ceremony he turned his back upon the sofa and began

to hope that Dr. Proudie had found that the palace repairs had been such as to meet his wishes.

"Yes, yes," said his lordship. Upon the whole he thought so—upon the whole, he didn't know that there was much ground for complaint. The architect, perhaps, might have—— But his double, Mr. Slope, who had sidled over to the Bishop's chair, would not allow his lordship to finish his ambiguous speech.

"There is one point I would like to mention, Mr. Archdeacon. His lordship asked me to step through the premises, and I see that the stalls in the second stable are not perfect."

"Why, there's standing there for a dozen horses," said the Archdeacon.

"Perhaps so," said the other. "Indeed, I've no doubt of it. But visitors, you know, often require so much accommodation. There are so many of the Bishop's relatives who always bring their own horses."

Dr. Grantly promised that due provision for the relatives' horses should be made, as far at least as the extent of the original stable building would allow. He would himself communicate with the architect.

"And the coach house, Dr. Grantly," continued Mr. Slope. "There is really hardly room for a second carriage in the large coach house, and the smaller one of course holds only one."

"And the gas," chimed in the lady. "There is no gas through the house, none whatever but in the kitchen and passages. Surely the palace should have been fitted through with pipes for gas, and hot water too. There is no hot water laid on anywhere above the ground floor. Surely there should be the means of getting hot water in the bedrooms without having it brought in jugs from the kitchen."

The Bishop had a decided opinion that there should be pipes for hot water. Hot water was very essential for the comfort of the palace. It was, indeed, a requisite in any decent gentleman's house.

Mr. Slope had remarked that the coping on the garden wall was in many places imperfect.

Mrs. Proudie had discovered a large hole, evidently the work of rats, in the servants' hall.

The Bishop expressed an utter detestation of rats. There was nothing, he believed, in this world that he so much hated as a rat.

Mr. Slope had, moreover, observed that the locks of the outhouses were very imperfect. He might specify the coal cellar and the woodhouse.

Mrs. Proudie had also seen that those on the doors of the servants' bedrooms were in an equally bad condition. Indeed the locks all through the house were old-fashioned and unserviceable.

The Bishop thought that a great deal depended on a good lock, and quite as much on the key. He had observed that the fault very often lay with the key, especially if the wards were in any way twisted.

Mr. Slope was going on with his catalogue of grievances when he was somewhat loudly interrupted by the Archdeacon, who succeeded in explaining that the diocesan architect, or rather his foreman, was the person to be addressed on such subjects, and that he, Dr. Grantly, had inquired as to the comfort of the palace merely as a point of compliment. He was sorry, however, that so many things had been found amiss. And then he rose from his chair to escape.

Mrs. Proudie, though she had contrived to lend her assistance in recapitulating the palatial dilapidations, had not on that account given up her hold of Mr. Harding, nor ceased from her cross-examinations as to the iniquity of Sabbatical amusements. Over and over again had she thrown out her "Surely, surely" at Mr. Harding's devoted head, and ill had that gentleman been able to parry the attack.

He had never before found himself subjected to such a nuisance. Ladies hitherto, when they had consulted him on religious subjects, had listened to what he might choose to say with some deference, and had differed, if they differed, in silence. But Mrs. Proudie interrogated him, and then lectured. "Neither thou, nor thy son, nor thy daughter, nor thy manservant, nor thy maidservant," said she, impressively, and more than once, as though Mr. Harding had forgotten the words. She shook her finger at him as she quoted the favorite law, as though menacing him with punishment, and then called upon him categorically to state whether he did not think that traveling on the Sabbath was an abomination and a desecration.

Mr. Harding had never been so hard-pressed in his life. He felt that he ought to rebuke the lady for presuming so to talk to a gentleman and a clergyman many years her senior, but he recoiled from the idea of scolding the Bishop's wife, in the Bishop's presence, on his first visit to the palace. Moreover, to tell the truth, he was somewhat afraid of her. She, seeing him sit silent and absorbed, by no means refrained from the attack.

"I hope, Mr. Harding," said she, shaking her head slowly and solemnly, "I hope you will not leave me to think that you approve of Sabbath traveling." And she looked a look of unutterable meaning into his eyes.

There was no standing this, for Mr. Slope was now looking at him, and so was the Bishop, and so was the Archdeacon, who had completed his adieus on that side of the room. Mr. Harding therefore got up also, and putting out his hand to Mrs. Proudie, said: "If you will come to St. Cuthbert's some Sunday, I will preach you a sermon on that subject."

And so the Archdeacon and the Precentor took their departure, bowing low to the lady, shaking hands with the lord, and escaping from Mr. Slope in the best manner each could. Mr. Harding was again maltreated, but Dr. Grantly swore deeply in the bottom of his heart that no earthly consideration should ever again induce him to touch the paw of that impure and filthy animal.

CHAPTER VI

WAR

"Good heavens!" exclaimed the Archdeacon as he placed his foot on the gravel walk of the close, and raising his hat with one hand, passed the other somewhat violently over his now grizzled locks. Smoke issued forth from the uplifted beaver as it were a cloud of wrath, and the safety valve of his anger opened and emitted a visible steam, preventing positive explosion and probable apoplexy. "Good heavens!"—And the Archdeacon looked up to the gray pinnacles of the cathedral tower, making a mute appeal to that still living witness which had looked down on the doings of so many Bishops of Barchester.

"I don't think I shall ever like that Mr. Slope," said Mr. Harding.

"Like him!" roared the Archdeacon, standing still for a moment to give more force to his voice. "Like him!" All the ravens of the close cawed their assent. The old bells of the tower in chiming the hour echoed the words, and the swallows flying out from their nests mutely expressed a similar opinion. Like Mr. Slope! Why, no, it was not very probable that any Barchester-bred living thing should like Mr. Slope!

"Nor Mrs. Proudie either," said Mr. Harding.

The Archdeacon hereupon forgot himself. I will not follow his example, nor shock my readers by transcribing the term in which he expressed his feeling as to the lady who had been named. The ravens and the last lingering notes of the clock bells were less scrupulous, and repeated in corresponding echoes the very improper exclamation. The Archdeacon again raised his hat, and another salutary escape of steam was effected.

There was a pause, during which the Precentor tried to realize the fact that the wife of a Bishop of Barchester had been thus designated, in the close of the cathedral, by the lips of its own Archdeacon, but he could not do it.

"The Bishop seems to be a quiet man enough," suggested Mr. Harding, having acknowledged to himself his own failure.

"Idiot!" exclaimed the Doctor, who for the nonce was not capable of more than such spasmodic attempts at utterance.

"Well, he did not seem very bright," said Mr. Harding, "and yet he has always had the reputation of a clever man. I suppose he's cautious and not inclined to express himself very freely."

The new Bishop of Barchester was already so contemptible a creature in Dr. Grantly's eyes that he could not condescend to discuss his character. He was a puppet to be played by others, a mere wax doll, done up in an apron and a shovel hat, to be stuck on a throne or elsewhere and pulled about by wires as others chose. Dr. Grantly did not choose to let himself down low enough to talk about Dr. Proudie, but he saw that he would have to talk about the other members of his household, the coadjutor bishops, who had brought his lordship down, as it were, in a box, and were about to handle the wires as they willed. This in itself was a terrible vexation to the Archdeacon. Could he have ignored the chaplain and have fought the Bishop, there would have been at any rate nothing degrading in such a contest. Let the Queen make whom she would Bishop of Barchester. A man, or even an ape, when once a bishop, would be a respectable adversary if he would but fight himself. But what was such a person as Dr. Grantly to do when such another person as Mr. Slope was put forward as his antagonist?

If he, our Archdeacon, refused the combat, Mr. Slope would walk triumphant over the field, and have the diocese of Barchester under his heel. If, on the other hand, the Archdeacon accepted as his enemy the man whom the new puppet Bishop put before him as such, he would have to talk about Mr. Slope, and write about Mr. Slope, and in all matters treat with Mr. Slope, as a being standing, in some degree, on ground similar to his own. He would have to meet Mr. Slope, to—— Bah! The idea was sickening! He could not bring himself to have to do with Mr. Slope.

"He is the most thoroughly bestial creature that ever I set my eyes upon," said the Archdeacon.

"Who—the Bishop?" asked the other innocently.

"Bishop! No—I'm not talking about the Bishop. How on earth such a creature got ordained!—They'll ordain anybody now, I know, but he's been in the Church these ten years, and they used to be a little careful ten years ago."

"Oh, you mean Mr. Slope!"

"Did you ever see any animal less like a gentleman?" asked Dr. Grantly.

"I can't say I felt myself much disposed to like him."

"Like him!" again shouted the Doctor, and the assenting ravens again cawed an echo. "Of course you don't like him. It's not a question of liking. But what are we to do with him?"

"Do with him?" asked Mr. Harding.

"Yes—what are we to do with him? How are we to treat him? There he is, and there he'll stay. He has put his foot in that palace, and he will never take it out again till he's driven. How are we to get rid of him?"

"I don't suppose he can do us much harm."

"Not do harm!—Well, I think you'll find yourself of a different opinion before a month is gone. What would you say, now, if he got himself put into the hospital? Would that be harm?"

Mr. Harding mused awhile, and then said he didn't think the new Bishop would put Mr. Slope into the hospital.

"If he doesn't put him there, he'll put him somewhere else where he'll be as bad. I tell you that that man, to all intents and purposes, will be Bishop of Barchester." And again Dr. Grantly raised his hat and rubbed his hand thoughtfully and sadly over his head.

"Impudent scoundrel!" he continued after a while. "To dare to cross-examine me about the Sunday schools in the diocese, and Sunday traveling too. I never in my life met his equal for sheer impudence. Why, he must have thought we were two candidates for ordination!"

"I declare I thought Mrs. Proudie was the worst of the two," said Mr. Harding.

"When a woman is impertinent, one must only put up with it, and keep out of her way in future. But I am not inclined to put up with Mr. Slope. 'Sabbath traveling!'" And the Doctor attempted to imitate the peculiar drawl of the man he so much disliked. "'Sabbath traveling!' Those are the sort of men who will ruin the Church of England, and make the profession of a clergyman disreputable. It is not the Dissenters or the Papists that we should fear, but the set of canting, low-bred hypocrites who are wriggling their way in among us—men who have no fixed principle, no standard ideas of religion or doctrine, but who take up some popular cry, as this fellow has done about 'Sabbath traveling.'"

Dr. Grantly did not again repeat the question aloud, but he did so constantly to himself: What were they to do with Mr. Slope? How was he openly, before the world, to show that he utterly disapproved of and abhorred such a man?

Hitherto Barchester had escaped the taint of any extreme rigor of church doctrine. The clergymen of the city and neighborhood, though very well inclined to promote High Church principles, privileges, and prerogatives, had never committed themselves to tendencies which are somewhat too loosely called Puseyite practices. They all preached in their black gowns, as their fathers had done before them. They wore ordinary black cloth waistcoats. They had no candles on their altars, either lighted or unlighted. They made no private genuflexions, and were contented to confine themselves to such ceremonial observances as had been in vogue for the last hundred years. The services were decently and demurely read in their parish churches, chanting was confined to the cathedral, and the science of intoning was unknown.

But now the archdeacon began to meditate on some strong measures of absolute opposition. Dr. Proudie and his crew were of the lowest possible order of Church of England clergymen, and therefore it behooved him, Dr. Grantly, to be of the very highest. Dr. Proudie would abolish all forms and ceremonies, and therefore Dr. Grantly felt the sudden necessity of multiplying them. Dr. Proudie would consent to deprive the Church of all collective authority and rule, and therefore Dr. Grantly would stand up for the full power of convocation, and the renewal of all its ancient privileges.

It was true that he could not himself intone the service, but he could procure the co-operation of any number of gentlemanlike curates well trained in the mystery of doing so. He would not willingly alter his own fashion of dress, but he could people Barchester with young clergymen dressed in the longest frocks and in the highest-breasted silk waistcoats. He certainly was not prepared to cross himself, or to advocate the Real Presence, but without going this length there were various observances by adopting which he could plainly show his antipathy to such men as Dr. Proudie and Mr. Slope.

All these things passed through his mind as he paced up and down the close with Mr. Harding. War, war, internecine war was in his heart. He felt that as regarded himself and Mr. Slope, one of the two must be anni-hilated as far as the city of Barchester was concerned. And he did not intend to give way until there was not left to him an inch of ground on which he could stand. He still flattered himself that he could make Barchester too hot to hold Mr. Slope, and he had no weakness of spirit to prevent his bring-ing about such a consummation if it were in his power.

"I suppose Susan must call at the palace," said Mr. Harding.

"Yes, she shall call there, but it shall be once and once only. I dare say 'the horses' won't find it convenient to come out to Plumstead very soon, and when that once is done the matter may drop."

"I don't suppose Eleanor need call. I don't think Eleanor would get on at all well with Mrs. Proudie."

"Not the least necessity in life," replied the Archdeacon, not without the reflection that a ceremony which was necessary for his wife might not be at all binding on the widow of John Bold. "Not the slightest reason on earth why she should do so, if she doesn't like it. For myself, I don't think that any decent young woman should be subjected to the nuisance of being in the same room with that man."

And so the two clergymen parted, Mr. Harding going to his daughter's house and the Archdeacon seeking the seclusion of his brougham.

The new inhabitants of the palace did not express any higher opinion of their visitors than their visitors had expressed of them. Though they did not use quite such strong language as Dr. Grantly had done, they felt as much personal aversion, and were quite as well aware as he was that there would be a battle to be fought, and that there was hardly room for Proudieism in Barchester as long as Grantlyism was predominant.

Indeed it may be doubted whether Mr. Slope had not already within his breast a better-prepared system of strategy, a more accurately defined line of hostile conduct, than the Archdeacon. Dr. Grantly was going to fight because he found that he hated the man. Mr. Slope had predetermined to hate the man because he foresaw the necessity of fighting him. When he had first reviewed the carte du pays, previous to his entry into Barchester, the idea had occurred to him of conciliating the Archdeacon, of cajoling and flattering him into submission, and of obtaining the upper hand by cunning instead of courage. A little inquiry, however, sufficed to convince

him that all his cunning would fail to win over such a man as Dr. Grantly
to such a mode of action as that to be adopted by Mr. Slope, and then he
determined to fall back upon his courage. He at once saw that open battle
against Dr. Grantly and all Dr. Grantly's adherents was a necessity of his
position, and he deliberately planned the most expedient methods of giving
offense.

Soon after his arrival the Bishop had intimated to the Dean that, with
the permission of the canon then in residence, his chaplain would preach
in the cathedral on the next Sunday. The canon in residence happened
to be the Honorable and Reverend Dr. Vesey Stanhope, who at this time
was very busy on the shores of the Lake of Como adding to that unique
collection of butterflies for which he is so famous. Or rather he would
have been in residence but for the butterflies and other such summer-day
considerations. And the Vicar Choral, who was to take his place in the
pulpit, by no means objected to having his work done for him by Mr. Slope.

Mr. Slope accordingly preached, and if a preacher can have satisfaction
in being listened to, Mr. Slope ought to have been gratified. I have reason
to think that he was gratified, and that he left the pulpit with the conviction that he had done what he intended to do when he entered it.

On this occasion the new Bishop took his seat for the first time in the
throne allotted to him. New scarlet cushions and drapery had been prepared, with new gilt binding and new fringe. The old carved oakwood of
the throne, ascending with its numerous grotesque pinnacles halfway up to
the roof of the choir, had been washed, and dusted, and rubbed, and it all
looked very smart.

All Barchester went to hear Mr. Slope—either for that or to gaze at the
new Bishop. All the best bonnets of the city were there, and moreover all
the best glossy clerical hats. Not a stall but had its fitting occupant, for
though some of the prebendaries might be away in Italy or elsewhere, their
places were filled by brethren who flocked into Barchester on the occasion. The Dean was there, a heavy old man, now too old indeed to attend
frequently in his place, and so was the Archdeacon. So also were the
Chancellor, the Treasurer, the Precentor, sundry canons and minor canons,
and every lay member of the choir, prepared to sing the new Bishop in
with due melody and harmonious expression of sacred welcome.

The service was certainly very well performed. Such was always the
case at Barchester, as the musical education of the choir had been good,
and the voices had been carefully selected. The psalms were beautifully
chanted, the Te Deum was magnificently sung, and the litany was given
in a manner which is still to be found at Barchester but, if my taste be
correct, is to be found nowhere else. The litany in Barchester Cathedral
has long been the special task to which Mr. Harding's skill and voice have
been devoted. Crowded audiences generally make good performers, and
though Mr. Harding was not aware of any extraordinary exertion on his

part, yet probably he rather exceeded his usual mark. Others were doing their best, and it was natural that he should emulate his brethren. So the service went on, and at last Mr. Slope got into the pulpit.

He chose for his text a verse from the precepts addressed by St. Paul to Timothy as to the conduct necessary in a spiritual pastor and guide, and it was immediately evident that the good clergy of Barchester were to have a lesson.

"Study to show thyself approved unto God, a workman that needeth not to be ashamed, rightly dividing the word of truth." These were the words of his text, and with such a subject in such a place, it may be supposed that such a preacher would be listened to by such an audience. He was listened to with breathless attention, and not without considerable surprise. Whatever opinion of Mr. Slope might have been held in Barchester before he commenced his discourse, none of his hearers, when it was over, could mistake him either for a fool or a coward.

It would not be becoming were I to travesty a sermon, or even to repeat the language of it in the pages of a novel. In endeavoring to depict the characters of the persons of whom I write, I am to a certain extent forced to speak of sacred things. I trust, however, that I shall not be thought to scoff at the pulpit, though some may imagine that I do not feel all the reverence that is due to the cloth. I may question the infallibility of the teachers, but I hope that I shall not therefore be accused of doubt as to the thing to be taught.

Mr. Slope, in commencing his sermon, showed no slight tact in his ambiguous manner of hinting that, humble as he was himself, he stood there as the mouthpiece of the illustrious divine who sat opposite to him. And having premised so much, he gave forth a very accurate definition of the conduct which that prelate would rejoice to see in the clergymen now brought under his jurisdiction. It is only necessary to say that the peculiar points insisted upon were exactly those which were most distasteful to the clergy of the diocese and most averse to their practice and opinions and that all those peculiar habits and privileges which have always been dear to High Church priests, to that party which is now scandalously called the High and Dry Church, were ridiculed, abused, and anathematized. Now the clergymen of the diocese of Barchester are all of the High and Dry Church.

Having thus, according to his own opinion, explained how a clergyman should show himself approved unto God as a workman that needeth not to be ashamed, he went on to explain how the word of truth should be divided. And here he took a rather narrow view of the question, and fetched his arguments from afar. His object was to express his abomination of all ceremonious modes of utterance, to cry down any religious feeling which might be excited not by the sense but by the sound of words, and in fact to insult cathedral practices. Had St. Paul spoken of rightly pronouncing instead of rightly dividing the word of truth, this part of his sermon would ave been more to the purpose, but the preacher's immediate object was to reach Mr. Slope's doctrine, and not St. Paul's, and he contrived to give he necessary twist to the text with some skill.

He could not exactly say, preaching from a cathedral pulpit, that chanting should be abandoned in cathedral services. By such an assertion he would have overshot his mark and rendered himself absurd, to the delight of his hearers. He could, however, and did allude with heavy denunciations to the practice of intoning in parish churches, although the practice was all but unknown in the diocese. And from thence he came round to he undue preponderance which he asserted music had over meaning in he beautiful service which they had just heard. He was aware, he said, hat the practices of our ancestors could not be abandoned at a moment's otice. The feelings of the aged would be outraged, and the minds of espectable men would be shocked. There were many, he was aware, of ot sufficient caliber of thought to perceive, of not sufficient education to now, that a mode of service which was effective when outward ceremonies were of more moment than inward feelings had become all but arbarous at a time when inward conviction was everything, when each word of the minister's lips should fall intelligibly into the listener's heart. ormerly the religion of the multitude had been an affair of the imagination. Now, in these latter days, it had become necessary that a Christian hould have a reason for his faith—should not only believe, but digest—not nly hear, but understand. The words of our morning service, how beautiful, how apposite, how intelligible they were when read with simple and distinct decorum! But how much of the meaning of the words was lost when they were produced with all the meretricious charms of melody! c. &c.

Here was a sermon to be preached before Mr. Archdeacon Grantly, Mr. Precentor Harding, and the rest of them! Before a whole Dean and Chapter assembled in their own cathedral! Before men who had grown old in he exercise of their peculiar services, with a full conviction of their excellence for all intended purposes! This too from such a man, a clerical parvenu, a man without a cure, a mere chaplain, an intruder among them, a fellow raked up, so said Dr. Grantly, from the gutters of Marylebone! They had to sit through it! None of them, not even Dr. Grantly, could close his ears, nor leave the house of God during the hours of service. They were under an obligation of listening, and that, too, without any immediate power of reply.

There was, at any rate, no tedium felt in listening to Mr. Slope on the occasion in question. His subject came too home to his audience to be dull, and to tell the truth, Mr. Slope had the gift of using words forcibly. He was heard through his thirty minutes of eloquence with mute attention and open ears, but with angry eyes, which glared round from one enraged parson to another, with widespread nostrils from which already burst forth umes of indignation, and with many shufflings of the feet and uneasy

motions of the body which betokened minds disturbed and hearts not at
peace with all the world.

At last the Bishop, who of all the congregation had been most surprised
and whose hair almost stood on end with terror, gave the blessing in a
manner not at all equal to that in which he had long been practicing it in
his own study, and the congregation was free to go their way.

CHAPTER VII

THE DEAN AND CHAPTER TAKE COUNSEL

ALL Barchester was in a tumult. Dr. Grantly could hardly get himself out
of the cathedral porch before he exploded in his wrath. The old Dean
betook himself silently to his deanery, afraid to speak, and there sat half
stupefied, pondering many things in vain. Mr. Harding crept forth solitary
and unhappy and, slowly passing beneath the elms of the close, could
scarcely bring himself to believe that the words which he had heard had
proceeded from the pulpit of Barchester Cathedral. Was he again to be
disturbed? Was his whole life to be shown up as a useless sham a second
time? Would he have to abdicate his precentorship, as he had his wardenship, and to give up chanting, as he had given up his twelve old bedesmen? And what if he did! Some other *Jupiter*, some other Mr. Slope, would
come and turn him out of St. Cuthbert's. Surely he could not have been
wrong all his life in chanting the litany as he had done! He began, however, to have his doubts. Doubting himself was Mr. Harding's weakness.
It is not, however, the usual fault of his order.

Yes, all Barchester was in a tumult! It was not only the clergy who
were affected. The laity also had listened to Mr. Slope's new doctrine, a
with surprise, some with indignation, and some with a mixed feeling i
which dislike of the preacher was not so strongly blended. The old Bishop
and his chaplains, the Dean and his canons and minor canons, the old choir
and especially Mr. Harding, who was at the head of it, had all been popular
in Barchester. They had spent their money and done good, the poor had
not been ground down, the clergy in society had neither been overbearing
nor austere, and the whole repute of the city was due to its ecclesiastical
importance. Yet there were those who had heard Mr. Slope with satisfaction.

It is so pleasant to receive a fillip of excitement when suffering from the
dull routine of everyday life! The anthems and Te Deums were in themselves delightful, but they had been heard so often! Mr. Slope was certainly
not delightful, but he was new, and moreover clever. They had long thought
it slow, so said now many of the Barchesterians, to go on as they had done

n their old humdrum way, giving ear to none of the religious changes which were moving the world without. People in advance of the age now had new ideas, and it was quite time that Barchester should go in advance. Mr. Slope might be right. Sunday had certainly not been strictly kept in Barchester, except as regarded the cathedral services. Indeed the two hours between services had long been appropriated to morning calls and hot luncheons. Then Sunday schools! Really more ought to have been done as to Sunday schools—Sabbath-day schools Mr. Slope had called them. The late Bishop had really not thought of Sunday schools as he should have done. (These people probably did not reflect that catechisms and collects are quite as hard work to the young mind as bookkeeping is to the elderly, and that quite as little feeling of worship enters into the one task as the other.) And then, as regarded that great question of musical services, there might be much to be said on Mr. Slope's side of the question. It certainly was the fact that people went to the cathedral to hear the music, &c. &c.

And so a party absolutely formed itself in Barchester on Mr. Slope's side of the question! This consisted, among the upper classes, chiefly of ladies. No man—that is, no gentleman—could possibly be attracted by Mr. Slope, or consent to sit at the feet of so abhorrent a Gamaliel. Ladies are sometimes less nice in their appreciation of physical disqualification, and provided that a man speak to them well, they will listen though he speak from a mouth never so deformed and hideous. Wilkes was most fortunate as a lover, and the damp, sandy-haired, saucer-eyed, red-fisted Mr. Slope was powerful only over the female breast.

There were, however, one or two of the neighboring clergy who thought it not quite safe to neglect the baskets in which for the nonce were stored the loaves and fishes of the diocese of Barchester. They, and they only, came to call on Mr. Slope after his performance in the cathedral pulpit. Among these Mr. Quiverful, the Rector of Puddingdale, whose wife still continued to present him from year to year with fresh pledges of her love and so to increase his cares and, it is to be hoped, his happiness equally. Who can wonder that a gentleman with fourteen living children and a bare income of £400 a year should look after the loaves and fishes, even when they are under the thumb of a Mr. Slope?

Very soon after the Sunday on which the sermon was preached, the leading clergy of the neighborhood held high debate together as to how Mr. Slope should be put down. In the first place, he should never again preach from the pulpit of Barchester Cathedral. This was Dr. Grantly's earliest dictum, and they all agreed, providing only that they had the power to exclude him. Dr. Grantly declared that the power rested with the Dean and Chapter, observing that no clergyman out of the Chapter had a claim to preach there, saving only the Bishop himself. To this the Dean assented, but alleged that contests on such a subject would be unseemly.

Why silence him at all? suggested Mr. Harding. Let them not be ashamed to hear what any man might have to preach to them, unless he preached false doctrine, in which case, let the Bishop silence him. So spoke our friend—vainly, for human ends must be attained by human means. But the Dean saw a ray of hope out of those purblind old eyes of his. Yes, let them tell the Bishop how distasteful to them was this Mr. Slope. A new Bishop just come to his seat could not wish to insult his clergy while the gloss was yet fresh on his first apron.

Then up rose Dr. Grantly and, having thus collected the scattered wisdom of his associates, spoke forth with words of deep authority.

"It is quite clear that this man must not be allowed to preach again in this cathedral. We all see that, except our dear friend here, the milk of whose nature runs so softly that he would not have the heart to refuse the Pope the loan of his pulpit if the Pope would come and ask it. We must not, however, allow the man to preach again here. It is not because his opinion on church matters may be different from ours—with that one would not quarrel. It is because he has purposely insulted us. When he went up into the pulpit last Sunday, his studied object was to give offense to men who had grown old in reverence of those things of which he dared to speak so slightingly. What! To come here a stranger, a young, unknown and unfriended stranger, and tell us, in the name of the Bishop his master, that we are ignorant of our duties, old-fashioned, and useless! I don't know whether most to admire his courage or his impudence! And one thing I will tell you: That sermon originated solely with the man himself. The Bishop was no more a party to it than was the Dean here. You all know how grieved I am to see a bishop in this diocese holding the latitudinarian ideas by which Dr. Proudie has made himself conspicuous. You all know how greatly I should distrust the opinion of such a man. But in this matter I hold him to be blameless. I believe Dr. Proudie has lived too long among gentlemen to be guilty, or to instigate another to be guilty, of so gross an outrage. No! That man uttered what was untrue when he hinted that he was speaking as the mouthpiece of the Bishop. It suited his ambitious views at once to throw down the gauntlet to us—at once to defy us here in the quiet of our own religious duties—here within the walls of our own loved cathedral—here where we have for so many years exercised our ministry without schism and with good repute. Such an attack upon us, coming from such a quarter, is abominable."

"Abominable," groaned the Dean. "Abominable," re-echoed the Chancellor, uttering the sound from the bottom of his deep chest. "I really think it was," said Mr. Harding.

"Most abominable and most unjustifiable," continued the Archdeacon. "But, Mr. Dean, thank God that pulpit is still our own—your own, I should say. That pulpit belongs solely to the Dean and Chapter of Barchester Cathedral, and as yet Mr. Slope is no part of that Chapter. You, Mr. Dean, have suggested that we should appeal to the Bishop to abstain from forcing this man on us, but what if the Bishop allow himself to be ruled by his chaplain? In my opinion, the matter is in our own hands. Mr. Slope cannot preach there without permission asked and obtained, and let that permission be invariably refused. Let all participation in the ministry of the cathedral service be refused to him. Then if the Bishop choose to interfere, we shall know what answer to make to the Bishop. My friend here has suggested that this man may again find his way into the pulpit by undertaking the duty of some of your minor canons, but I am sure that we may fully trust to these gentlemen to support us when it is known that the Dean objects to any such transfer."

"Of course you may," said the Chancellor.

Such a meeting as that we have just recorded is not held in such a city as Barchester unknown and untold of. Not only was the fact of the meeting talked of in every respectable house, including the palace, but the very speeches of the Dean, the Archdeacon, and Chancellor were repeated—not without many additions and imaginary circumstances, according to the tastes and opinions of the relaters.

All, however, agreed in saying that Mr. Slope was to be debarred from opening his mouth in the cathedral of Barchester. Many believed that the vergers were to be ordered to refuse him even the accommodation of a seat. And some of the most far-going advocates for strong measures declared that his sermon was looked upon as an indictable offense, and that proceedings were to be taken against him for brawling.

The party who were inclined to defend him—the enthusiastically religious young ladies, and the middle-aged spinsters desirous of a move—of course took up his defense the more warmly on account of this attack. If they could not hear Mr. Slope in the cathedral, they would hear him elsewhere. They would leave the dull Dean, the dull old prebendaries, and the scarcely less dull young minor canons, to preach to each other. They would work slippers and cushions and hem bands for Mr. Slope, make him a happy martyr, and stick him up in some new Sion or Bethesda, and put the cathedral quite out of fashion.

Dr. and Mrs. Proudie at once returned to London. They thought it expedient not to have to encounter any personal application from the Dean and Chapter respecting the sermon till the violence of the storm had expended itself. But they left Mr. Slope behind them nothing daunted, and he went about his work zealously, flattering such as would listen to his flattery, whispering religious twaddle into the ears of foolish women, ingratiating himself with the few clergy who would receive him, visiting the houses of the poor, inquiring into all people, prying into everything, and searching with his minutest eye into all palatial dilapidations. He did not, however, make any immediate attempt to preach again in the cathedral.

And so all Barchester was by the ears.

CHAPTER VIII

THE EX-WARDEN REJOICES IN HIS PROBABLE RETURN TO THE
HOSPITAL

AMONG the ladies in Barchester who have hitherto acknowledged Mr. Slope
as their spiritual director must not be reckoned either the Widow Bold or
her sister-in-law. On the first outbreak of the wrath of the denizens of the
close, none had been more animated against the intruder than these two
ladies. And this was natural. Who could be so proud of the musical distinction of their own cathedral as the favorite daughter of the Precentor?
Who would be so likely to resent an insult offered to the old choir? And
in such matters Miss Bold and her sister-in-law had but one opinion.

This wrath, however, has in some degree been mitigated, and I regret to
say that these ladies allowed Mr. Slope to be his own apologist. About a
fortnight after the sermon had been preached, they were both of them
not a little surprised by hearing Mr. Slope announced as the page in but-
tons opened Mrs. Bold's drawing-room door. Indeed, what living man
could, by a mere morning visit, have surprised them more? Here was the
great enemy of all that was good in Barchester coming into their own
drawing-room, and they had no strong arm, no ready tongue, near at hand
for their protection. The widow snatched her baby out of its cradle into
her lap, and Mary Bold stood up ready to die manfully in that baby's
behalf should, under any circumstances, such a sacrifice become necessary.

In this manner was Mr. Slope received. But when he left, he was allowed
by each lady to take her hand, and to make his adieus as gentlemen do who
have been graciously entertained! Yes, he shook hands with them, and was
curtsied out courteously, the buttoned page opening the door as he would
have done for the best canon of them all. He had touched the baby's little
hand and blessed him with a fervid blessing. He had spoken to the widow
of her early sorrows, and Eleanor's silent tears had not rebuked him. He
had told Mary Bold that her devotion would be rewarded, and Mary Bold
had heard the praise without disgust. And how had he done all this? How
had he so quickly turned aversion into at any rate acquaintance? How had
he overcome the enmity with which these ladies had been ready to receive
him, and made his peace with them so easily?

My readers will guess from what I have written that I myself do not
like Mr. Slope, but I am constrained to admit that he is a man of parts.
He knows how to say a soft word in the proper place, he knows how to
adapt his flattery to the ears of his hearers, he knows the wiles of the serpent
and he uses them. Could Mr. Slope have adapted his manners to men as

well as to women, could he ever have learnt the ways of a gentleman, he might have risen to great things.

He commenced his acquaintance with Eleanor by praising her father. He had, he said, become aware that he had unfortunately offended the feelings of a man of whom he could not speak too highly. He would not now allude to a subject which was probably too serious for drawing-room conversation, but he would say that it had been very far from him to utter a word in disparagement of a man of whom all the world, at least the clerical world, spoke so highly as it did of Mr. Harding. And so he went on, unsaying a great deal of his sermon, expressing his highest admiration for the Precentor's musical talents, eulogizing the father and the daughter and the sister-in-law, speaking in that low silky whisper which he always had specially prepared for feminine ears, and, ultimately, gaining his object. When he left, he expressed a hope that he might again be allowed to call, and though Eleanor gave no verbal assent to this, she did not express dissent. And so Mr. Slope's right to visit at the widow's house was established.

The day after this visit Eleanor told her father of it, and expressed an opinion that Mr. Slope was not quite so black as he had been painted. Mr. Harding opened his eyes rather wider than usual when he heard what had occurred, but he said little. He could not agree in any praise of Mr. Slope, and it was not his practice to say much evil of anyone. He did not, however, like the visit, and simple-minded as he was, he felt sure that Mr. Slope had some deeper motive than the mere pleasure of making soft speeches to two ladies.

Mr. Harding, however, had come to see his daughter with other purpose than that of speaking either good or evil of Mr. Slope. He had come to tell her that the place of warden in Hiram's Hospital was again to be filled up, and that in all probability he would once more return to his old home and his twelve bedesmen.

"But," said he, laughing, "I shall be greatly shorn of my ancient glory."

"Why so, Papa?"

"This new Act of Parliament, that is to put us all on our feet again," continued he, "settles my income at four hundred and fifty pounds per annum."

"Four hundred and fifty," said she, "instead of eight hundred! Well, that is rather shabby. But still, Papa, you'll have the dear old house and the garden?"

"My dear," said he, "it's worth twice the money." And as he spoke he showed a jaunty kind of satisfaction in his tone and manner, and in the quick, pleasant way in which he paced Eleanor's drawing-room. "It's worth twice the money. I shall have the house and the garden, and a larger income than I can possibly want."

"At any rate you'll have no extravagant daughter to provide for." And as she spoke, the young widow put her arm within his and made him sit on the sofa beside her. "At any rate you'll not have that expense."

"No, my dear, and I shall be rather lonely without her. But we won't think of that now. As regards income I shall have plenty for all I want. I shall have my old house, and I don't mind owning now that I have felt sometimes the inconveniences of living in a lodging. Lodgings are very nice for young men, but at my time of life there is a want of—— I hardly know what to call it, perhaps not respectability——"

"Oh, Papa! I'm sure there's been nothing like that. Nobody has thought it, nobody in all Barchester has been more respected than you have been since you took those rooms in High Street. Nobody! Not the Dean in his deanery, or the Archdeacon out at Plumstead."

"The Archdeacon would not be much obliged to you if he heard you," said he, smiling somewhat at the exclusive manner in which his daughter confined her illustration to the church dignitaries of the Chapter of Barchester. "But at any rate I shall be glad to get back to the old house. Since I heard that it was all settled, I have begun to fancy that I can't be comfortable without my two sitting-rooms."

"Come and stay with me, Papa, till it is settled—there's a dear Papa."

"Thank ye, Nelly. But no, I won't do that. It would make two movings. I shall be very glad to get back to my old men again. Alas, alas! There have six of them gone in these few last years. Six out of twelve! And the others I fear have had but a sorry life of it there. Poor Bunce, poor old Bunce!"

Bunce was one of the surviving recipients of Hiram's charity, an old man, now over ninety, who had long been a favorite of Mr. Harding's.

"How happy old Bunce will be," said Mrs. Bold, clapping her soft hands softly. "How happy they all will be to have you back again. You may be sure there will soon be friendship among them again when you are there."

"But," said he, half-laughing, "I am to have new troubles, which will be terrible to me. There are to be twelve old women, and a matron. How shall I manage twelve women and a matron!"

"The matron will manage the women, of course."

"And who'll manage the matron?" said he.

"She won't want to be managed. She'll be a great lady herself, I suppose. But, Papa, where will the matron live? She is not to live in the warden's house with you, is she?"

"Well, I hope not, my dear."

"Oh, Papa, I tell you fairly I won't have a matron for a new stepmother."

"You shan't, my dear—that is, if I can help it. But they are going to build another house for the matron and the women, and I believe they haven't even fixed yet on the site of the building."

"And have they appointed the matron?" said Eleanor.

"They haven't appointed the warden yet," replied he.

"But there's no doubt about that, I suppose," said his daughter.

Mr. Harding explained that he thought there was no doubt, that the Archdeacon had declared as much, saying that the Bishop and his chaplain

between them had not the power to appoint anyone else, even if they had
the will to do so and sufficient impudence to carry out such a will. The
Archdeacon was of opinion that though Mr. Harding had resigned his
wardenship, and had done so unconditionally, he had done so under circumstances which left the Bishop no choice as to his reappointment now that
the affair of the hospital had been settled on a new basis by Act of Parliament. Such was the Archdeacon's opinion, and his father-in-law received
it without a shadow of doubt.

Dr. Grantly had always been strongly opposed to Mr. Harding's resignation of the place. He had done all in his power to dissuade him from it.
He had considered that Mr. Harding was bound to withstand the popular
clamor with which he was attacked for receiving so large an income as
eight hundred a year from such a charity, and was not even yet satisfied
that his father-in-law's conduct had not been pusillanimous and undignified.
He looked also on this reduction of the warden's income as a shabby,
paltry scheme on the part of Government for escaping from a difficulty into
which it had been brought by the public press. Dr. Grantly observed that
the Government had no more right to dispose of a sum of four hundred
and fifty pounds a year out of the income of Hiram's legacy than of nine
hundred, whereas, as he said, the Bishop, dean, and Chapter clearly had
a right to settle what sum should be paid. He also declared that the Government had no more right to saddle the charity with twelve old women than
with twelve hundred, and he was therefore very indignant on the matter.
He probably forgot when so talking that Government had done nothing
of the kind, and had never assumed any such might or any such right. He
made the common mistake of attributing to the Government, which in
such matters is powerless, the doings of Parliament, which in such matters
is omnipotent. Still the Archdeacon was too practical a man of the world
to wish that his father-in-law, who had at present little more than £200
per annum for all his wants, should refuse the situation, defiled, undignified,
and commission-ridden as it was.

Mr. Harding had accordingly made up his mind that he would return
to his old home at the hospital, and to tell the truth, had experienced
almost a childish pleasure in the idea of doing so. The diminished income
was to him not even the source of momentary regret. The matron and the
old women did rather go against the grain, but he was able to console himself with the reflection that after all such an arrangement might be of real
service to the poor of the city. The thought that he must receive his reappointment as the gift of the new Bishop, and probably through the hands
of Mr. Slope, annoyed him a little, but his mind was set at rest by the
assurance of the Archdeacon that there would be no favor in such a presentation. The reappointment of the old Warden would be regarded by all
the world as a matter of course. Mr. Harding, therefore, felt no hesitation
in telling his daughter that they might look upon his return to his old
quarters as a settled matter.

"And you won't have to ask for it, Papa."

"Certainly not, my dear. There is no ground on which I could ask for any favor from the Bishop, whom indeed I hardly know. Nor would I ask a favor the granting of which might possibly be made a question to be settled by Mr. Slope. No," said he, moved for a moment by a spirit very unlike his own, "I certainly shall be very glad to go back to the hospital, but I should never go there if it were necessary that my doing so should be the subject of a request to Mr. Slope."

This little outbreak of her father's anger jarred on the present tone of Eleanor's mind. She had not learnt to like Mr. Slope, but she had learnt to think that he had much respect for her father. And she would therefore willingly use her efforts to induce something like good feeling between them.

"Papa," said she, "I think you somewhat mistake Mr. Slope's character."

"Do I?" said he, placidly.

"I think you do, Papa. I think he intended no personal disrespect to you when he preached the sermon which made the Archdeacon and the Dean so angry!"

"I never supposed he did, my dear. I hope I never inquired within myself whether he did or no. Such a matter would be unworthy of any inquiry, and very unworthy of the consideration of the Chapter. But I fear he intended disrespect to the ministration of God's services as conducted in conformity with the rules of the Church of England."

"But might it not be that he thought it his duty to express his dissent from that which you, and the Dean, and all of us here so much approve?"

"It can hardly be the duty of a young man rudely to assail the religious convictions of his elders in the Church. Courtesy should have kept him silent, even if neither charity nor modesty could do so."

"But Mr. Slope would say that on such a subject the commands of his heavenly Master do not admit of his being silent."

"Nor of his being courteous, Eleanor?"

"He did not say that, Papa."

"Believe me, my child, that Christian ministers are never called on by God's word to insult the convictions, or even the prejudices, of their brethren, and that religion is at any rate not less susceptible of urbane and courteous conduct among men than any other study which men may take up. I am sorry to say that I cannot defend Mr. Slope's sermon in the cathedral. But come, my dear, put on your bonnet and let us walk round the dear old gardens at the hospital. I have never yet had the heart to go beyond the courtyard since we left the place. Now I think I can venture to enter."

CHAPTER IX

THE STANHOPE FAMILY

It is now three months since Dr. Proudie began his reign, and changes have already been effected in the diocese which show at least the energy of an active mind. Among other things absentee clergymen have been favored with hints much too strong to be overlooked. Poor dear old Bishop Grantly had on this matter been too lenient, and the Archdeacon had never been inclined to be severe with those who were absent on reputable pretenses and who provided for their duties in a liberal way.

Among the greatest of the diocesan sinners in this respect was Dr. Vesey Stanhope. Years had now passed since he had done a day's duty, and yet there was no reason against his doing duty except a want of inclination on his own part. He held a prebendal stall in the diocese, one of the best residences in the close, and the two large rectories of Crabtree Canonicorum and Stogpingum. Indeed, he had the cure of three parishes, for that of Eiderdown was joined to Stogpingum. He had resided in Italy for twelve years. His first going there had been attributed to a sore throat, and that sore throat, though never repeated in any violent manner, had stood him in such stead that it had enabled him to live in easy idleness ever since.

He had now been summoned home—not, indeed, with rough violence, or by any peremptory command, but by a mandate which he found himself unable to disregard. Mr. Slope had written to him by the Bishop's desire. In the first place, the Bishop much wanted the valuable co-operation of Dr. Vesey Stanhope in the diocese. In the next, the Bishop thought it his imperative duty to become personally acquainted with the most conspicuous of his diocesan clergy. Then the Bishop thought it essentially necessary for Dr. Stanhope's own interests that Dr. Stanhope should, at any rate for a time, return to Barchester. And lastly, it was said that so strong a feeling was at the present moment evinced by the hierarchs of the Church with reference to the absence of its clerical members that it behooved Dr. Vesey Stanhope not to allow his name to stand among those which would probably in a few months be submitted to the councils of the nation.

There was something so ambiguously frightful in this last threat that Dr. Stanhope determined to spend two or three summer months at his residence in Barchester. His rectories were inhabited by his curates, and he felt himself from disuse to be unfit for parochial duty, but his prebendal home was kept empty for him, and he thought it probable that he might be able now and again to preach a prebendal sermon. He arrived, therefore, with all his family at Barchester, and he and they must be introduced to my readers.

The great family characteristic of the Stanhopes might probably be said to be heartlessness, but this want of feeling was, in most of them, accompanied by so great an amount of good nature as to make itself but little noticeable to the world. They were so prone to oblige their neighbors that their neighbors failed to perceive how indifferent to them was the happiness and well-being of those around them. The Stanhopes would visit you in your sickness (provided it were not contagious), would bring you oranges, French novels, and the last new bit of scandal, and then hear of your death or your recovery with an equally indifferent composure. Their conduct to each other was the same as to the world. They bore and forbore—and there was sometimes, as will be seen, much necessity for forbearing—but their love among themselves rarely reached above this. It is astonishing how much each of the family was able to do, and how much each did, to prevent the well-being of the other four.

For there were five in all—the Doctor, namely, and Mrs. Stanhope, two daughters, and one son. The Doctor perhaps was the least singular and most estimable of them all, and yet such good qualities as he possessed were all negative. He was a good-looking, rather plethoric gentleman of about sixty years of age. His hair was snow-white, very plentiful, and somewhat like wool of the finest description. His whiskers were very large and very white, and gave to his face the appearance of a benevolent sleepy old lion. His dress was always unexceptionable. Although he had lived so many years in Italy, it was invariably of a decent clerical hue, but it never was hyperclerical. He was a man not given to much talking, but what little he did say was generally well said. His reading seldom went beyond romances and poetry of the lightest and not always most moral description. He was thoroughly a bon vivant, an accomplished judge of wine, though he never drank to excess, and a most inexorable critic in all affairs touching the kitchen. He had had much to forgive in his own family, and had forgiven everything—except inattention to his dinner. His weakness in that respect was now fully understood, and his temper but seldom tried. As Dr. Stanhope was a clergyman, it may be supposed that his religious convictions made up a considerable part of his character, but this was not so. That he had religious convictions must be believed, but he rarely obtruded them, even on his children. This abstinence on his part was not systematic, but very characteristic of the man. It was not that he had predetermined never to influence their thoughts, but he was so habitually idle that his time for doing so had never come till the opportunity for doing so was gone forever. Whatever conviction the father may have had, the children were at any rate but indifferent members of the Church from which he drew his income.

Such was Dr. Stanhope. The features of Mrs. Stanhope's character were even less plainly marked than those of her lord. The *far niente* of her Italian life had entered into her very soul, and brought her to regard a state of inactivity as the only earthly good. In manner and appearance she was exceedingly prepossessing. She had been a beauty and even now, at fifty-five, she was a handsome woman. Her dress was always perfect. She never dressed but once in the day, and never appeared till between three and four, but when she did appear, she appeared at her best. The structure of her attire was always elaborate, and yet never overlabored. She was rich in apparel, but not bedizened with finery. Her ornaments were costly, rare, and such as could not fail to attract notice, but they did not look as though worn with that purpose. She well knew the great architectural secret of decorating her constructions, and never descended to construct a decoration. But when we have said that Mrs. Stanhope knew how to dress, and used her knowledge daily, we have said all. Other purpose in life she had none. It was something, indeed, that she did not interfere with the purposes of others. In early life she had undergone great trials with reference to the Doctor's dinners, but for the last ten or twelve years her eldest daughter Charlotte had taken that labor off her hands, and she had had little to trouble her—little, that is, till the edict for this terrible English journey had gone forth. Since then, indeed, her life had been laborious enough. For such a one, the toil of being carried from the shores of Como to the city of Barchester is more than labor enough, let the care of the carriers be ever so vigilant. Mrs. Stanhope had been obliged to have every one of her dresses taken in from the effects of the journey.

Charlotte Stanhope was at this time about thirty-five years old, and whatever may have been her faults, she had none of those which belong particularly to old young ladies. She neither dressed young, nor talked young, nor indeed looked young. She appeared to be perfectly content with her time of life, and in no way affected the graces of youth. She was a fine young woman, and had she been a man, would have been a very fine young man. All that was done in the house and that was not done by servants was done by her. She gave the orders, paid the bills, hired and dismissed the domestics, made the tea, carved the meat, and managed everything in the Stanhope household. She, and she alone, could ever induce her father to look into the state of his worldly concerns. She, and she alone, could in any degree control the absurdities of her sister. She, and she alone, prevented the whole family from falling into utter disrepute and beggary. It was by her advice that they now found themselves very unpleasantly situated in Barchester.

So far, the character of Charlotte Stanhope is not unprepossessing. But it remains to be said that the influence which she had in her family, though it had been used to a certain extent for their worldly well-being, had not been used to their real benefit, as it might have been. She had aided her father in his indifference to his professional duties, counseling him that his livings were as much his individual property as the estates of his elder brother were the property of that worthy peer. She had for years past stifled every little rising wish for a return to England which the Doctor had from time to time expressed. She had encouraged her mother in her idleness, in order that she herself might be mistress and manager of the Stanhope household. She had encouraged and fostered the follies of her sister, though she was always willing, and often able, to protect her from their probable result. She had done her best, and had thoroughly succeeded, in spoiling her brother and turning him loose upon the world an idle man without a profession, and without a shilling that he could call his own.

Miss Stanhope was a clever woman, able to talk on most subjects and quite indifferent as to what the subject was. She prided herself on her freedom from English prejudice, and she might have added, from feminine delicacy. On religion she was a pure freethinker, and with much want of true affection, delighted to throw out her own views before the troubled mind of her father. To have shaken what remained of his Church of England faith would have gratified her much, but the idea of his abandoning his preferment in the Church had never once presented itself to her mind. How could he indeed when he had no income from any other source?

But the two most prominent members of the family still remain to be described. The second child had been christened Madeline, and had been a great beauty. We need not say had been, for she was never more beautiful than at the time of which we write, though her person for many years had been disfigured by an accident. It is unnecessary that we should give in detail the early history of Madeline Stanhope. She had gone to Italy when about seventeen years of age, and had been allowed to make the most of her surpassing beauty in the saloons of Milan and among the crowded villas along the shores of the Lake of Como. She had become famous for adventures in which her character was just not lost, and had destroyed the hearts of a dozen cavaliers without once being touched in her own. Blood had flowed in quarrels about her charms, and she heard of these encounters with pleasurable excitement. It had been told of her that on one occasion she had stood by in the disguise of a page and had seen her lover fall.

As is so often the case, she had married the very worst of those who sought her hand. Why she had chosen Paulo Neroni, a man of no birth and no property, a mere captain in the Pope's guard—one who had come up to Milan either simply as an adventurer or else as a spy, a man of harsh temper and oily manners, mean in figure, swarthy in face, and so false in words as to be hourly detected—need not now be told. When the moment for doing so came, she had probably no alternative. He at any rate had become her husband, and after a prolonged honeymoon among the lakes they had gone together to Rome, the papal captain having vainly endeavored to induce his wife to remain behind him.

Six months afterward she arrived at her father's house a cripple, and a mother. She had arrived without even notice, with hardly clothes to cover her, and without one of those many ornaments which had graced her bridal trousseau. Her baby was in the arms of a poor girl from Milan, whom she had taken in exchange for the Roman maid who had accompanied her thus far and who had then, as her mistress said, become homesick and had returned. It was clear that the lady had determined that there should be no witness to tell stories of her life in Rome.

She had fallen, she said, in ascending a ruin, and had fatally injured the sinews of her knee, so fatally that when she stood she lost eight inches of her accustomed height, so fatally that when she essayed to move, she could only drag herself painfully along with protruded hip and extended foot, in a manner less graceful than that of a hunchback. She had consequently made up her mind, once and forever, that she would never stand, and never attempt to move herself.

Stories were not slow to follow her averring that she had been cruelly ill-used by Neroni, and that to his violence had she owed her accident. Be that as it may, little had been said about her husband, but that little had made it clearly intelligible to the family that Signor Neroni was to be seen and heard of no more. There was no question as to readmitting the poor ill-used beauty to her old family rights, no question as to adopting her infant daughter beneath the Stanhope rooftree. Though heartless, the Stanhopes were not selfish. The two were taken in, petted, made much of, for a time all but adored, and then felt by the two parents to be great nuisances in the house. But in the house the lady was, and there she remained, having her own way, though that way was not very conformable with the customary usages of an English clergyman.

Madame Neroni, though forced to give up all motion in the world, had no intention whatever of giving up the world itself. The beauty of her face was uninjured, and that beauty was of a peculiar kind. Her copious rich brown hair was worn in Grecian bandeaux round her head, displaying as much as possible of her forehead and cheeks. Her forehead, though rather low, was very beautiful from its perfect contour and pearly whiteness. Her eyes were long and large and marvelously bright—might I venture to say bright as Lucifer's, I should perhaps best express the depth of their brilliancy. They were dreadful eyes to look at, such as would absolutely deter any man of quiet mind and easy spirit from attempting a passage of arms with such foes. There was talent in them, and the fire of passion, and the play of wit, but there was no love. Cruelty was there instead, and courage, a desire of masterhood, cunning, and a wish for mischief. And yet, as eyes, they were very beautiful. The eyelashes were long and perfect, and the long, steady, unabashed gaze with which she would look into the face of her admirer fascinated while it frightened him. She was a basilisk from whom an ardent lover of beauty could make no escape. Her nose and mouth and teeth and chin and neck and bust were perfect, much more so at twenty-eight than they had been at eighteen. What wonder that with such charms still glowing in her face, and with such deformity destroying her figure, she should resolve to be seen, but only to be seen reclining on a sofa.

Her resolve had not been carried out without difficulty. She had still frequented the opera at Milan, she had still been seen occasionally in the saloons of the noblesse, she had caused herself to be carried in and out from her carriage, and that in such a manner as in no wise to disturb her charms, disarrange her dress, or expose her deformities. Her sister always accompanied her and a maid, a manservant also, and on state occasions, two. It was impossible that her purpose could have been achieved with less, and yet, poor as she was, she had achieved her purpose. And then again the more dissolute Italian youths of Milan frequented the Stanhope villa and surrounded her couch, not greatly to her father's satisfaction. Sometimes his spirit would rise, a dark spot would show itself on his cheek, and he would rebel. But Charlotte would assuage him with some peculiar triumph of her culinary art, and all again would be smooth for a while.

Madeline affected all manner of rich and quaint devices in the garniture of her room, her person, and her feminine belongings. In nothing was this more apparent than in the visiting card which she had prepared for her use. For such an article one would say that she, in her present state, could have but small need, seeing how improbable it was that she should make a morning call. But not such was her own opinion. Her card was surrounded by a deep border of gilding. On this she had imprinted, in three lines:

La Signora Madeline
Vesey Neroni
—Nata Stanhope.

And over the name she had a bright gilt coronet, which certainly looked very magnificent. How she had come to concoct such a name for herself it would be difficult to explain. Her father has been christened Vesey as another man is christened Thomas, and she had no more right to assume it than would have the daughter of a Mr. Josiah Jones to call herself Mrs. Josiah Smith on marrying a man of the latter name. The gold coronet was equally out of place, and perhaps inserted with even less excuse. Paulo Neroni had had not the faintest title to call himself a scion of even Italian nobility. Had the pair met in England, Neroni would probably have been a count, but they had met in Italy, and any such pretense on his part would have been simply ridiculous. A coronet, however, was a pretty ornament, and if it could solace a poor cripple to have such on her card, who would begrudge it to her?

Of her husband, or of his individual family, she never spoke. But with her admirers she would often allude in a mysterious way to her married life and isolated state and, pointing to her daughter, would call her the last of the blood of the emperors, thus referring Neroni's extraction to the old Roman family from which the worst of the Caesars sprang.

The "Signora" was not without talent, and not without a certain sort of industry. She was an indomitable letter-writer, and her letters were worth the postage. They were full of wit, mischief, satire, love, latitudinarian philosophy, free religion, and sometimes, alas! loose ribaldry. The subject, however, depended entirely on the recipient, and she was prepared to correspond with anyone but moral young ladies or stiff old women. She wrote also a kind of poetry, generally in Italian, and short romances, generally in French. She read much of a desultory sort of literature, and as a modern linguist had really made great proficiency. Such was the lady who had now come to wound the hearts of the men of Barchester.

Ethelbert Stanhope was in some respects like his younger sister, but he was less inestimable as a man than she as a woman. His great fault was an entire absence of that principle which should have induced him, as the son of a man without fortune, to earn his own bread. Many attempts had been made to get him to do so, but these had all been frustrated, not so much by idleness on his part as by a disinclination to exert himself in any way not to his taste. He had been educated at Eton, and had been been intended for the Church, but had left Cambridge in disgust after a single term and notified to his father his intention to study for the bar. Preparatory to that, he thought it well that he should attend a German university, and consequently went to Leipsic. There he remained two years, and brought away a knowledge of German and a taste for the fine arts. He still, however, intended himself for the bar, took chambers, engaged himself to sit at the feet of a learned pundit, and spent a season in London. He there found that all his aptitudes inclined him to the life of an artist, and he determined to live by painting. With this object he returned to Milan and had himself rigged out for Rome. As a painter he might have earned his bread, for he wanted only diligence to excel, but when at Rome his mind was carried away by other things. He soon wrote home for money, saying that he had been converted to the Mother Church, that he was already an acolyte of the Jesuits, and that he was about to start with others to Palestine on a mission for converting Jews. He did go to Judea, but being unable to convert the Jews, was converted by them. He again wrote home to say that Moses was the only giver of perfect laws to the world, that the coming of the true Messiah was at hand, that great things were doing in Palestine.

It is needless to tell how the father swore that he would send no more money and receive no Jew, nor how Charlotte declared that Ethelbert could not be left penniless in Jerusalem. Ethelbert did not long remain a Jew. He soon reappeared at the villa without prejudices on the subject of his religion, and with a firm resolve to achieve fame and fortune as a sculptor. He brought with him some models which he had originated at Rome, and which really gave such fair promise that his father was induced to go to further expense in furthering these views. Ethelbert opened an establishment, or rather took lodgings and a workshop, at Carrara, and there spoilt much marble and made some few pretty images. Since that period, now four years ago, he had alternated between Carrara and the villa, but his sojourns at the workshop became shorter and shorter and those at the villa longer and longer.

When the family started for England he had resolved not to be left behind, and with the assistance of his elder sister had carried his point against his father's wishes. It was necessary, he said, that he should come to England for orders. How otherwise was he to bring his profession to account?

In personal appearance Ethelbert Stanhope was the most singular of beings. He was certainly very handsome. He had his sister Madeline's eyes without their stare, and without their hard, cunning, cruel firmness. They were also very much lighter, and of so light and clear a blue as to make his face remarkable, if nothing else did so. On entering a room with him, Ethelbert's blue eyes would be the first thing you would see, and on leaving it almost the last you would forget. His light hair was very long and silky, coming down over his coat. His beard had been prepared in Holy Land, and was patriarchal. He never shaved, and rarely trimmed it. It was glossy, soft, clean, and altogether not unprepossessing. It was such that ladies might desire to reel it off and work it into their patterns in lieu of floss silk. His complexion was fair and almost pink, he was small in height and slender in limb, but well-made, and his voice was of peculiar sweetness.

In manner and dress he was equally remarkable. He had none of the *mauvaise honte* of an Englishman. He required no introduction to make himself agreeable to any person. He habitually addressed strangers, ladies as well as men, without any such formality, and in doing so never seemed to meet with rebuke. His costume cannot be described, because it was so various, but it was always totally opposed to every principle of color and construction to the dress of those with whom he for the time consorted.

He was habitually addicted to making love to ladies, and did so without any scruple of conscience, or any idea that such a practice was amiss. He had no heart to touch himself, and was literally unaware that humanity was subject to such an infliction. He had not thought much about it, but had he been asked, would have said that ill-treating a lady's heart meant injuring her promotion in the world. His principles therefore forbade him to pay attention to a girl if he thought any man was present whom it might suit her to marry. In this manner, his good nature frequently interfered with his amusement, but he had no other motive in abstaining from the fullest declarations of love to every girl that pleased his eye.

Bertie Stanhope, as he was generally called, was, however, popular with both sexes, and with Italians as well as English. His circle of acquaintance was very large, and embraced people of all sorts. He had no respect for rank, and no aversion to those below him. He had lived on familiar terms with English peers, German shopkeepers, and Roman priests. All people were nearly alike to him. He was above, or rather below, all prejudices. No virtue could charm him, no vice shock him. He had about him a natural good manner which seemed to qualify him for the highest circles, and yet he was never out of place in the lowest. He had no principle, no regard for others, no self-respect, no desire to be other than a drone in the hive, if only he could as a drone get what honey was sufficient for him. Of honey, in his latter days it may probably be presaged that he will have but short allowance.

Such was the family of the Stanhopes, who at this period suddenly joined themselves to the ecclesiastical circle of Barchester close. Any stranger union it would be impossible perhaps to conceive. And it was not as though they all fell down into the cathedral precincts hitherto unknown and untalked-of. In such case no amalgamation would have been at all probable between the newcomers and either the Proudie set or the Grantly set. But such was far from being the case. The Stanhopes were all known by name in Barchester, and Barchester was prepared to receive them with open arms. The Doctor was one of her prebendaries, one of her rectors, one of her pillars of strength, and was, moreover, counted on as a sure ally both by Proudies and Grantlys.

He himself was the brother of one peer and his wife was the sister of another—and both these peers were lords of Whiggish tendency with whom the new Bishop had some sort of alliance. This was sufficient to give to Mr. Slope high hope that he might enlist Dr. Stanhope on his side before his enemies could outmaneuver him. On the other hand, the old Dean had many many years ago, in the days of the Doctor's clerical energies, been instrumental in assisting him in his views as to preferment. And many many years ago also, the two Doctors, Stanhope and Grantly, had as young parsons been joyous together in the common rooms of Oxford. Dr. Grantly, consequently, did not doubt but that the newcomer would range himself under his banners.

Little did any of them dream of what ingredients the Stanhope family was now composed.

CHAPTER X

MRS. PROUDIE'S RECEPTION—COMMENCED

The Bishop and his wife had only spent three or four days in Barchester on the occasion of their first visit. His lordship had, as we have seen, taken his seat on his throne, but his demeanor there, into which it had been his intention to infuse much hierarchal dignity, had been a good deal disarranged by the audacity of his chaplain's sermon. He had hardly dared to look his clergy in the face and to declare by the severity of his countenance that in truth he meant all that his factotum was saying on his behalf. Nor yet did he dare to throw Mr. Slope over and show to those around him that he was no party to the sermon, and would resent it.

He had accordingly blessed his people in a shambling manner, not at all to his own satisfaction, and had walked back to his palace with his mind very doubtful as to what he would say to his chaplain on the subject. He did not remain long in doubt. He had hardly doffed his lawn when the partner of all his toils entered his study, and exclaimed even before she had seated herself:

"Bishop, did you ever hear a more sublime, more spirit-moving, more appropriate discourse than that?"

"Well, my love, ha—hum—he!" The Bishop did not know what to say.

"I hope, my lord, you don't mean to say you disapprove?"

There was a look about the lady's eye which did not admit of my lord's disapproving at that moment. He felt that if he intended to disapprove, it must be now or never, but he also felt that it could not be now. It was not in him to say to the wife of his bosom that Mr. Slope's sermon was ill-timed, impertinent, and vexatious.

"No, no," replied the Bishop. "No, I can't say I disapprove—a very clever sermon and very well intended, and I dare say will do a great deal of good." This last praise was added seeing that what he had already said by no means satisfied Mrs. Proudie.

"I hope it will," she said. "I am sure it was well deserved. Did you ever in your life, Bishop, hear anything so like play-acting as the way in which Mr. Harding sings the litany? I shall beg Mr. Slope to continue a course of sermons on the subject till all that is altered. We will have at any rate in our cathedral a decent, godly, modest morning service. There must be no more play-acting here now." And so the lady rang for lunch.

The Bishop knew more about cathedrals and deans and precentors and church services than his wife did, and also more of a bishop's powers. But he thought it better at present to let the subject drop.

"My dear," said he, "I think we must go back to London on Tuesday. I find my staying here will be very inconvenient to the Government."

The Bishop knew that to this proposal his wife would not object, and he also felt that by thus retreating from the ground of battle, the heat of the fight might be got over in his absence.

"Mr. Slope will remain here, of course?" said the lady.

"Oh, of course," said the Bishop.

Thus, after less than a week's sojourn in his palace, did the Bishop fly from Barchester, nor did he return to it for two months, the London season being then over. During that time Mr. Slope was not idle, but he did not again essay to preach in the cathedral. In answer to Mrs. Proudie's letters advising a course of sermons, he had pleaded that he would at any rate wish to put off such an undertaking till she was there to hear them.

He had employed his time in consolidating a Proudie and Slope party—or rather a Slope and Proudie party—and he had not employed his time in vain. He did not meddle with the Dean and Chapter, except by giving them little teasing intimations of the Bishop's wishes about this and the Bishop's feelings about that in a manner which was to them sufficiently annoying but which they could not resent. He preached once or twice in a distant church in the suburbs of the city, but made no allusion to the cathedral service. He commenced the establishment of two "Bishop's Barchester Sabbath-day Schools," gave notice of a proposed "Bishop's Barchester Young Men's Sabbath Evening Lecture Room"—and wrote three or four letters to the manager of the Barchester branch railway, informing him how anxious the Bishop was that the Sunday trains should be discontinued.

At the end of two months, however, the Bishop and the lady reappeared, and as a happy harbinger of their return heralded their advent by the promise of an evening party on the largest scale. The tickets of invitation were sent out from London—they were dated from Bruton Street, and were dispatched by the odious Sabbath-breaking railway in a huge brown-paper parcel to Mr. Slope. Everybody calling himself a gentleman, or herself a lady, within the city of Barchester and a circle of two miles round it was included. Tickets were sent to all the diocesan clergy, and also to many other persons of priestly note, of whose absence the Bishop, or at least the Bishop's wife, felt tolerably confident. It was intended, however, to be a thronged and noticeable affair, and preparations were made for receiving some hundreds.

And now there arose considerable agitation among the Grantlyites whether or no they would attend the episcopal bidding. The first feeling with them all was to send the briefest excuses both for themselves and their wives and daughters. But by degrees policy prevailed over passion. The Archdeacon perceived that he would be making a false step if he allowed the cathedral clergy to give the Bishop just ground of umbrage. They all met in conclave and agreed to go. They would show that they were willing to respect the office, much as they might dislike the man. They agreed to go. The old Dean would crawl in, if it were but for half an hour. The Chancellor, Treasurer, Archdeacon, prebendaries, and minor canons would all go, and would all take their wives. Mr. Harding was especially bidden to do so, resolving in his heart to keep himself far removed from Mrs. Proudie. And Mrs. Bold was determined to go, though assured by her father that there was no necessity for such a sacrifice on her part. When all Barchester was to be there, neither Eleanor nor Mary Bold understood why they should stay away. Had they not been invited separately? And had not a separate little note from the chaplain, couched in the most respectful language, been enclosed with the huge episcopal card?

And the Stanhopes would be there, one and all. Even the lethargic mother would so far bestir herself on such an occasion. They had only just arrived. The card was at the residence waiting for them. No one in Barchester had seen them, and what better opportunity could they have of showing themselves to the Barchester world? Some few old friends, such as the Archdeacon and his wife, had called, and had found the Doctor and his eldest daughter, but the élite of the family were not yet known.

The Doctor indeed wished in his heart to prevent the Signora from accepting the Bishop's invitation, but she herself had fully determined that she would accept it. If her father was ashamed of having his daughter carried into a bishop's palace, she had no such feeling.

"Indeed I shall," she had said to her sister, who had gently endeavored to dissuade her by saying that the company would consist wholly of parsons and parsons' wives. "Parsons, I suppose, are much the same as other men if you strip them of their black coats, and as to their wives, I dare say they won't trouble me. You may tell Papa I don't at all mean to be left at home."

Papa was told, and felt that he could do nothing but yield. He also felt that it was useless for him now to be ashamed of his children. Such as they were, they had become such under his auspices. As he had made his bed, so he must lie upon it; as he had sown his seed, so he must reap his corn. He did not indeed utter such reflections in such language, but such was the gist of his thoughts. It was not because Madeline was a cripple that he shrank from seeing her make one of the Bishop's guests, but because he knew that she would practice her accustomed lures, and behave herself in a way that could not fail of being distasteful to the propriety of Englishwomen. These things had annoyed but not shocked him in Italy. There they had shocked no one, but here in Barchester, here among his fellow parsons, he was ashamed that they should be seen. Such had been his feelings, but he repressed them. What if his brother clergymen were shocked! They could not take from him his preferment because the manners of his married daughter were too free.

La Signora Neroni had, at any rate, no fear that she would shock anybody. Her ambition was to create a sensation, to have parsons at her feet, seeing that the manhood of Barchester consisted mainly of parsons, and to send, if possible, every parson's wife home with a green fit of jealousy. None could be too old for her, and hardly any too young. None too sanctified, and none too worldly. She was quite prepared to entrap the Bishop himself, and then to turn up her nose at the Bishop's wife. She did not doubt of success, for she had always succeeded. But one thing was absolutely necessary—she must secure the entire use of a sofa.

The card sent to Dr. and Mrs. Stanhope and family had been so sent in an envelope having on the cover Mr. Slope's name. The Signora soon learnt that Mrs. Proudie was not yet at the palace, and that the chaplain was managing everything. It was much more in her line to apply to him than to the lady, and she accordingly wrote him the prettiest little billet in the world. In five lines she explained everything, declared how impossible it was for her not be desirous to make the acquaintance of such persons as the Bishop of Barchester and his wife, and she might add also of Mr. Slope, depicted her own grievous state, and concluded by being assured that Mrs. Proudie would forgive her extreme hardihood in petitioning to be allowed to be carried to a sofa. She then enclosed one of her beautiful cards. In return she received as polite an answer from Mr. Slope—a sofa should be kept in the large drawing-room, immediately at the top of the grand stairs, especially for her use.

And now the day of the party had arrived. The Bishop and his wife came down from town only on the morning of the eventful day, as behooved such great people to do, but Mr. Slope had toiled day and night to see that everything should be in right order. There had been much to do. No company had been seen in the palace since heaven knows when. New furniture had been required, new pots and pans, new cups and saucers, new dishes and plates. Mrs. Proudie had at first declared that she would condescend to nothing so vulgar as eating and drinking, but Mr. Slope had talked, or rather written, her out of economy! Bishops should be given to hospitality, and hospitality meant eating and drinking. So the supper was conceded. The guests, however, were to stand as they consumed it.

There were four rooms opening into each other on the first floor of the house, which were denominated the drawing-rooms, the reception room, and Mrs. Proudie's boudoir. In olden days one of these had been Bishop Grantly's bedroom, and another his common sitting-room and study. The present Bishop, however, had been moved down into a back parlor, and had been given to understand that he could very well receive his clergy in the dining-room should they arrive in too large a flock to be admitted into his small sanctum. He had been unwilling to yield, but after a short debate had yielded.

Mrs. Proudie's heart beat high as she inspected her suite of rooms. They were really very magnificent, or at least would be so by candlelight, and they had nevertheless been got up with commendable economy. Large rooms when full of people and full of light look well because they are large and are full and are light. Small rooms are those which require costly fittings and rich furniture. Mrs. Proudie knew this, and made the most of it. She had therefore a huge gas lamp with a dozen burners hanging from each of the ceilings.

People were to arrive at ten, supper was to last from twelve till one, and at half-past one everybody was to be gone. Carriages were to come in at the gate in the town and depart at the gate outside. They were desired to take up at a quarter before one. It was managed excellently, and Mr. Slope was invaluable.

At half-past nine the Bishop and his wife and their three daughters entered the great reception room, and very grand and very solemn they were. Mr. Slope was downstairs giving the last orders about the wine. He well understood that curates and country vicars with their belongings did not require so generous an article as the dignitaries of the close. There is a useful gradation in such things, and Marsala at 20s. a dozen did very well for the exterior supplementary tables in the corner.

"Bishop," said the lady as his lordship sat himself down, "don't sit on that sofa, if you please. It is to be kept separate for a lady."

The Bishop jumped up and seated himself on a cane-bottomed chair. "A lady?" he inquired meekly. "Do you mean one particular lady, my dear?"

"Yes, Bishop, one particular lady," said his wife, disdaining to explain.

"She has got no legs, Papa," said the youngest daughter, tittering.

"No legs!" said the Bishop, opening his eyes.

"Nonsense, Netta, what stuff you talk," said Olivia. "She has got legs, but she can't use them. She has always to be kept lying down, and three or four men carry her about everywhere."

"Laws, how odd!" said Augusta. "Always carried about by four men! I'm sure I shouldn't like it. Am I right behind, Mamma? I feel as if I was open." And she turned her back to her anxious parent.

"Open! To be sure you are," said she, "and a yard of petticoat strings hanging out. I don't know why I pay such high wages to Mrs. Richards if she can't take the trouble to see whether or no you are fit to be looked at." And Mrs. Proudie poked the strings here, and twitched the dress there, and gave her daughter a shove and a shake, and then pronounced it all right.

"But," rejoined the Bishop, who was dying with curiosity about the mysterious lady and her legs, "who is it that is to have the sofa? What's her name, Netta?"

A thundering rap at the front door interrupted the conversation. Mrs. Proudie stood up and shook herself gently, and touched her cap on each side as she looked in the mirror. Each of the girls stood on tiptoe and rearranged the bows on their bosoms, and Mr. Slope rushed upstairs three steps at a time.

"But who is it, Netta?" whispered the Bishop to his youngest daughter.

"La Signora Madeline Vesey Neroni," whispered back the daughter. "And mind you don't let anyone sit upon the sofa."

"La Signora Madeline Vicinironi!" muttered to himself the bewildered prelate. Had he been told that the Begum of Oude was to be there, or Queen Pomara of the Western Isles, he could not have been more astonished. La Signora Madeline Vicinironi, who, having no legs to stand on, had bespoken a sofa in his drawing-room!—Who could she be? He however could now make no further inquiry, as Dr. and Mrs. Stanhope were announced. They had been sent on out of the way a little before the time, in order that the Signora might have plenty of time to get herself conveniently packed into the carriage.

The Bishop was all smiles for the prebendary's wife, and the Bishop's wife was all smiles for the prebendary. Mr. Slope was presented, and was delighted to make the acquaintance of one of whom he had heard so much. The Doctor bowed very low, and then looked as though he could not return the compliment as regarded Mr. Slope, of whom, indeed, he had heard nothing. The Doctor, in spite of his long absence, knew an English gentleman when he saw him.

And then the guests came in shoals: Mr. and Mrs. Quiverful and their three grown daughters. The burly Chancellor and his wife and clerical son from Oxford. Mr. Harding with Eleanor and Miss Bold. The Dean leaning on a gaunt spinster, his only child now living with him, a lady very learned in stones, ferns, plants, and vermin, and who had written a book about petals. A wonderful woman in her way was Miss Trefoil. Mr. Finnie, the attorney, with his wife was to be seen, much to the dismay of many who had never met him in a drawing-room before. The five Barchester doctors were all there, and old Scalpen, the retired apothecary and toothdrawer, who was first taught to consider himself as belonging to the higher orders by the receipt of the Bishop's card. Then came the Archdeacon and his wife, with their elder daughter Griselda, a slim, pale, retiring girl of seventeen, who kept close to her mother and looked out on the world with quiet watchful eyes, one who gave promise of much beauty when time should have ripened it.

And so the rooms became full, and knots were formed, and every new-comer paid his respects to my lord and passed on, not presuming to occupy too much of the great man's attention. The Archdeacon shook hands very heartily with Dr. Stanhope, and Mrs. Grantly seated herself by the Doctor's wife. And Mrs. Proudie moved about with well-regulated grace, measuring out the quantity of her favors to the quality of her guests, just as Mr. Slope had been doing with the wine. But the sofa was still empty, and five-and-twenty ladies and five gentlemen had been courteously warned off it by the mindful chaplain.

"Why doesn't she come?" said the Bishop to himself. His mind was so preoccupied with the Signora that he hardly remembered how to behave himself *en bishop*.

At last a carriage dashed up to the hall steps with a very different manner of approach from that of any other vehicle that had been there that evening. A perfect commotion took place. The Doctor, who heard it as he was standing in the drawing-room, knew that his daughter was coming and retired into the furthest corner, where he might not see her entrance. Mrs. Proudie perked herself up, feeling that some important piece of business was in hand. The Bishop was instinctively aware that La Signora Vicinironi was come at last, and Mr. Slope hurried into the hall to give his assistance.

He was, however, nearly knocked down and trampled on by the cortège that he encountered on the hall steps. He got himself picked up as well as he could, and followed the cortège up stairs. The Signora was carried head foremost, her head being the care of her brother and an Italian manservant who was accustomed to the work. Her feet were in the care of the lady's maid and the lady's Italian page. And Charlotte Stanhope followed to see that all was done with due grace and decorum. In this manner they climbed easily into the drawing-room, and a broad way through the crowd having been opened, the Signora rested safely on her couch. She had sent a servant beforehand to learn whether it was a right-or a left-hand sofa, for it required that she should dress accordingly, particularly as regarded her bracelets.

And very becoming her dress was. It was white velvet, without any other garniture than rich white lace worked with pearls across her bosom and the same round the armlets of her dress. Across her brow she wore a band of red velvet, on the center of which shone a magnificent Cupid in mosaic, the tints of whose wings were of the most lovely azure and the color of his chubby cheeks the clearest pink. On the one arm which her position required her to expose she wore three magnificent bracelets, each of different stones. Beneath her on the sofa, and over the cushion and head of it, was spread a crimson-silk mantle or shawl, which went under her whole body and concealed her feet. Dressed as she was and looking as she did, so beautiful and yet so motionless, with the pure brilliancy of her white dress brought out and strengthened by the color beneath it, with that lovely head and those large bold bright staring eyes, it was impossible that either man or woman should do other than look at her.

Neither man nor woman for some minutes did do other.

Her bearers too were worthy of note. The three servants were Italian, and though perhaps not peculiar in their own country, were very much so in the palace at Barchester. The man especially attracted notice, and created a doubt in the mind of some whether he were a friend or a domestic. The same doubt was felt as to Ethelbert. The man was attired in a loose-fitting common black-cloth morning coat. He had a jaunty, fat, well-pleased, clean face, on which no atom of beard appeared, and he wore round his neck a loose black-silk neck handkerchief. The Bishop essayed to make him a bow, but the man, who was well-trained, took no notice of him and walked out of the room quite at his ease, followed by the woman and the boy.

Ethelbert Stanhope was dressed in light blue from head to foot. He had on the loosest possible blue coat, cut square like a shooting coat, and very short. It was lined with silk of azure blue. He had on a blue-satin waistcoat, a blue neck handkerchief which was fastened beneath his throat with a coral ring, and very loose blue trousers which almost concealed his feet. His soft glossy beard was softer and more glossy than ever.

The Bishop, who had made one mistake, thought that he also was a servant, and therefore tried to make way for him to pass. But Ethelbert soon corrected the error.

CHAPTER XI

MRS. PROUDIE'S RECEPTION—CONCLUDED

"BISHOP OF BARCHESTER, I presume?" said Bertie Stanhope, putting out his hand frankly. "I am delighted to make your acquaintance. We are in rather close quarters here, ain't we?"

In truth they were. They had been crowded up behind the head of the sofa, the Bishop in waiting to receive his guest and the other in carrying her, and they now had hardly room to move themselves.

The Bishop gave his hand quickly, and made his little studied bow, and was delighted to make—— He couldn't go on, for he did not know whether his friend was a signor, or a count, or a prince.

"My sister really puts you all to great trouble," said Bertie.

"Not at all!" The Bishop was delighted to have the opportunity of welcoming the Signora Vicinironi—so at least he said—and attempted to force his way round to the front of the sofa. He had at any rate learnt that his strange guests were brother and sister. The man, he presumed, must be Signor Vicinironi—or Count, or Prince, as it might be. It was wonderful what good English he spoke. There was just a twang of foreign accent, and no more.

"Do you like Barchester on the whole?" asked Bertie.

The Bishop, looking dignified, said that he did like Barchester.

"You've not been here very long, I believe," said Bertie.

"No—not long," said the Bishop, and tried again to make his way between the back of the sofa and a heavy rector, who was staring over it at the grimaces of the Signora.

"You weren't a bishop before, were you?"

Dr. Proudie explained that this was the first diocese he had held.

"Ah—I thought so," said Bertie. "But you are changed about sometimes, ain't you?"

"Translations are occasionally made," said Dr. Proudie, "but not so frequently as in former days."

"They've cut them all down to pretty nearly the same figure, haven't they?" said Bertie.

To this the Bishop could not bring himself to make any answer, but again attempted to move the rector.

"But the work, I suppose, is different?" continued Bertie. "Is there much to do here at Barchester?" This was said exactly in the tone that a young Admiralty clerk might use in asking the same question of a brother acolyte at the Treasury.

"The work of a bishop of the Church of England," said Dr. Proudie with considerable dignity, "is not easy. The responsibility which he has to bear is very great indeed."

"Is it?" said Bertie, opening wide his wonderful blue eyes. "Well, I never was afraid of responsibility. I once had thoughts of being a bishop myself."

"Had thoughts of being a bishop!" said Dr. Proudie, much amazed.

"That is, a parson—a parson first, you know, and a bishop afterward. If I had once begun, I'd have stuck to it. But on the whole I like the Church of Rome the best."

The Bishop could not discuss the point, so he remained silent.

"Now there's my father," continued Bertie. "He hasn't stuck to it. I fancy he didn't like saying the same thing over so often. By the by, Bishop, have you seen my father?"

The Bishop was more amazed than ever. Had he seen his father? No, he replied, he had not yet had the pleasure. He hoped he might, and as he said so, he resolved to bear heavy on that fat, immovable rector if ever he had the power of doing so.

"He's in the room somewhere," said Bertie, "and he'll turn up soon. By the by, do you know much about the Jews?"

At last the Bishop saw a way out. "I beg your pardon," said he, "but I'm forced to go round the room."

"Well, I believe I'll follow in your wake," said Bertie. "Terribly hot—isn't it?" This he addressed to the fat rector, with whom he had brought himself into the closest contact. "They've got this sofa into the worst possible part of the room. Suppose we move it. Take care, Madeline."

The sofa had certainly been so placed that those who were behind it found great difficulty in getting out. There was but a narrow gangway, which one person could stop. This was a bad arrangement, and one which Bertie thought it might be well to improve.

"Take care, Madeline," said he, and turning to the fat rector added, "Just help me with a slight push."

The rector's weight was resting on the sofa, and unwittingly lent all its impetus to accelerate and increase the motion which Bertie intentionally originated. The sofa rushed from its moorings and ran halfway into the middle of the room. Mrs. Proudie was standing with Mr. Slope in front of the Signora, and had been trying to be condescending and sociable. But she was not in the very best of tempers, for she found that whenever she spoke to the lady, the lady replied by speaking to Mr. Slope. Mr. Slope was a favorite, no doubt; but Mrs. Proudie had no idea of being less thought of than the chaplain. She was beginning to be stately, stiff, and offended when unfortunately the castor of the sofa caught itself in her lace train, and carried away there is no saying how much of her garniture. Gathers were heard to go, stitches to crack, plaits to fly open, flounces were seen to fall and breadths to expose themselves—a long ruin of rent lace disfigured the carpet and still clung to the vile wheel on which the sofa moved.

We know what was the wrath of Juno when her beauty was despised. We know too what storms of passion even celestial minds can yield. As Juno may have looked at Paris on Mount Ida, so did Mrs. Proudie look on Ethelbert Stanhope when he pushed the leg of the sofa into her lace train.

"Oh, you idiot, Bertie!" said the Signora, seeing what had been done and what were to be the consequences.

"Idiot!" re-echoed Mrs. Proudie, as though the word were not half strong enough to express the required meaning. "I'll let him know——" And then looking round to learn at a glance the worst, she saw that at present it behooved her to collect the scattered debris of her dress.

Bertie, when he saw what he had done, rushed over the sofa and threw himself on one knee before the offended lady. His object, doubtless, was to liberate the torn lace from the castor, but he looked as though he were imploring pardon from a goddess.

"Unhand it, sir!" said Mrs. Proudie. From what scrap of dramatic poetry she had extracted the word cannot be said, but it must have rested on her memory and now seemed opportunely dignified for the occasion.

"I'll fly to the looms of the fairies to repair the damage if you'll only forgive me," said Ethelbert, still on his knees.

"Unhand it, sir!" said Mrs. Proudie with redoubled emphasis and all but furious wrath. This allusion to the fairies was a direct mockery, and intended to turn her into ridicule. So at least it seemed to her. "Unhand it, sir!" she almost screamed.

"It's not me, it's the cursed sofa," said Bertie, looking imploringly in her face and holding up both his hands to show that he was not touching her belongings, but still remaining on his knees.

Hereupon the Signora laughed—not loud, indeed, but yet audibly. And as the tigress bereft of her young will turn with equal anger on any within reach, so did Mrs. Proudie turn upon her female guest.

"Madam!" she said—and it is beyond the power of prose to tell of the fire which flashed from her eyes.

The Signora stared her full in the face for a moment and then, turning to her brother, said playfully, "Bertie, you idiot, get up."

By this time the Bishop, and Mr. Slope, and her three daughters were around her, and had collected together the wide ruins of her magnificence. The girls fell into circular rank behind their mother, and thus following her and carrying out the fragments, they left the reception rooms in a manner not altogether devoid of dignity. Mrs. Proudie had to retire and rearray herself.

As soon as the constellation had swept by, Ethelbert rose from his knees and turning with mock anger to the fat rector, said: "After all it was your doing, sir—not mine. But perhaps you are waiting for preferment, and so I bore it."

Whereupon there was a laugh against the fat rector, in which both the Bishop and the chaplain joined, and thus things got themselves again into order.

"Oh, my lord, I am so sorry for this accident!" said the Signora, putting out her hand so as to force the Bishop to take it. "My brother is so thoughtless. Pray sit down and let me have the pleasure of making your acquaintance. Though I am so poor a creature as to want a sofa, I am not so selfish as to require it all." Madeline could always dispose herself so as to make room for a gentleman, though, as she declared, the crinoline of her lady friends was much too bulky to be so accommodated.

"It was solely for the pleasure of meeting you that I have had myself dragged here," she continued. "Of course, with your occupation, one cannot even hope that you should have time to come to us—that is, in the way of calling. And at your English dinner parties all is so dull and so stately. Do you know, my lord, that in coming to England my only consolation has been the thought that I should know you." And she looked at him with the look of a she-devil.

The Bishop, however, thought that she looked very like an angel and, accepting the proffered seat, sat down beside her. He uttered some platitude as to his deep obligation for the trouble she had taken, and wondered more and more who she was.

"Of course you know my sad story?" she continued.

The Bishop didn't know a word of it. He knew, however, or thought he knew, that she couldn't walk into a room like other people, and so made the most of that. He put on a look of ineffable distress, and said that he was aware how God had afflicted her.

The Signora just touched the corner of her eyes with the most lovely of pocket handkerchiefs. Yes, she said—she had been sorely tried—tried, she thought, beyond the common endurance of humanity. But while her child was left to her, everything was left. "Oh, my lord," she exclaimed, "you must see that infant—the last bud of a wondrous tree. You must let a mother hope that you will lay your holy hands on her innocent head, and consecrate her for female virtues. May I hope it?" said she, looking into the Bishop's eye and touching the Bishop's arm with her hand.

The Bishop was but a man, and said she might. After all, what was it but a request that he would confirm her daughter?—A request, indeed, very unnecessary to make, as he should do so as a matter of course if the young lady came forward in the usual way.

"The blood of Tiberius," said the Signora, in all but a whisper, "the blood of Tiberius flows in her veins. She is the last of the Neros!"

The Bishop had heard of the last of the Visigoths, and had floating in his brain some indistinct idea of the last of the Mohicans, but to have the last of the Neros thus brought before him for a blessing was very staggering. Still, he liked the lady. She had a proper way of thinking, and talked with more propriety than her brother. But who were they? It was now quite

clear that that blue madman with the silky beard was not a Prince Vicinironi.
The lady was married, and was of course one of the Vicinironis by the
right of her husband. So the Bishop went on learning.

"When will you see her?" said the Signora with a start.

"See whom?" said the Bishop.

"My child," said the mother.

"What is the young lady's age?" asked the Bishop.

"She is just seven," said the Signora.

"Oh," said the Bishop, shaking his head, "she is much too young—very
much too young."

"But in sunny Italy, you know, we do not count by years." And the
Signora gave the Bishop one of her sweetest smiles.

"But indeed she is a great deal too young," persisted the Bishop. "We
never confirm before——"

"But you might speak to her, you might let her hear from your consecrated lips that she is not a castaway because she is a Roman, that she
may be a Nero and yet a Christian, that she may owe her black locks and
dark cheeks to the blood of the pagan Caesars and yet herself be a child
of grace. You will tell her this, won't you, my friend?"

The friend said he would, and asked if the child could say her catechism.

"No," said the Signora. "I would not allow her to learn lessons such as
those in a land ridden over by priests and polluted by the idolatry of
Rome. It is here, in Barchester, that she must first be taught to lisp those
holy words. Oh, that you could be her instructor!"

Now Dr. Proudie certainly liked the lady but, seeing that he was a bishop,
it was not probable that he was going to instruct a little girl in the first
rudiments of her catechism, so he said he'd send a teacher.

"But you'll see her yourself, my lord?"

The Bishop said he would, but where should he call?

"At Papa's house," said the Signora, with an air of some little surprise
at the question.

The Bishop actually wanted the courage to ask her who was her papa,
so he was forced at last to leave her without fathoming the mystery. Mrs.
Proudie, in her second-best, had now returned to the rooms, and her
husband thought it as well that he should not remain in too close conversation with the lady whom his wife appeared to hold in such slight esteem.
Presently he came across his youngest daughter.

"Netta," said he, "do you know who is the father of that Signora
Vicinironi?"

"It isn't Vicinironi, Papa," said Netta, "but Vesey Neroni, and she's
Doctor Stanhope's daughter. But I must go and do the civil to Griselda
Grantly. I declare nobody has spoken a word to the poor girl this evening."

Dr. Stanhope! Dr. Vesey Stanhope! Dr. Vesey Stanhope's daughter,
of whose marriage with a dissolute Italian scamp he now remembered
to have heard something! And that impertinent blue cub who had examined

him as to his episcopal bearings was old Stanhope's son, and the lady who had entreated him to come and teach her child the catechism was old Stanhope's daughter—the daughter of one of his own prebendaries! As these things flashed across his mind, he was nearly as angry as his wife had been. Nevertheless he could not but own that the mother of the last of the Neros was an agreeable woman.

Dr. Proudie tripped out into the adjoining room, in which were congregated a crowd of Grantlyite clergymen, among whom the Archdeacon was standing pre-eminent while the old Dean was sitting nearly buried in a huge armchair by the fireplace. The Bishop was very anxious to be gracious, and, if possible, to diminish the bitterness which his chaplain had occasioned. Let Mr. Slope do the fortiter in re, he himself would pour in the suaviter in modo.

"Pray don't stir, Mr. Dean, pray don't stir," he said as the old man essayed to get up. "I take it as a great kindness, your coming to such an omnium-gatherum as this. But we have hardly got settled yet, and Mrs. Proudie has not been able to see her friends as she would wish to do. Well, Mr. Archdeacon, after all we have not been so hard upon you at Oxford."

"No," said the Archdeacon, "you've only drawn our teeth and cut out our tongues—you've allowed us still to breathe and swallow."

"Ha, ha, ha!" laughed the Bishop. "It's not quite so easy to cut out the tongue of an Oxford magnate—and as for teeth,—ha, ha, ha! Why, in the way we've left the matter, it's very odd if the heads of colleges don't have their own way quite as fully as when the hebdomadal board was in all its glory. What do you say, Mr. Dean?"

"An old man, my lord, never likes changes," said the Dean.

"You must have been sad bunglers if it is so," said the Archdeacon. "And indeed, to tell the truth, I think you have bungled it. At any rate you must own this—you have not done the half what you boasted you would do."

"Oh, Mr. Harding," said the Bishop, overtaking the ci-devant Warden. "I wanted to say one word about the hospital. You know, of course, that it is to be filled up."

Mr. Harding's heart beat a little, and he said that he had heard so.

"Of course," continued the Bishop, "there can be only one man whom I could wish to see in that situation. I don't know what your own views may be, Mr. Harding——"

"They are very simply told, my lord," said the other. "To take the place if it be offered me, and to put up with the want of it should another man get it."

The Bishop professed himself delighted to hear it. Mr. Harding might be quite sure that no other man would get it. There were some few circumstances which would in a slight degree change the nature of the duties. Mr. Harding was probably aware of this, and would perhaps not object to discuss the matter with Mr. Slope. It was a subject to which Mr. Slope had given a good deal of attention.

Mr. Harding felt, he knew not why, oppressed and annoyed. What could Mr. Slope do to him? He knew that there were to be changes. The nature of them must be communicated to the Warden through somebody, and through whom so naturally as the Bishop's chaplain? 'Twas thus he tried to argue himself back to an easy mind, but in vain.

Mr. Slope in the meantime had taken the seat which the Bishop had vacated on the Signora's sofa, and remained with that lady till it was time to marshal the folk to supper. Not with contented eyes had Mrs. Proudie seen this. Had not this woman laughed at her distress, and had not Mr. Slope heard it? Was she not an intriguing Italian woman, half wife and half not, full of affectation, airs, and impudence? Was she not horribly bedizened with velvet and pearls, with velvet and pearls, too, which had not been torn off her back? Above all, did she not pretend to be more beautiful than her neighbors? To say that Mrs. Proudie was jealous would give a wrong idea of her feelings. She had not the slightest desire that Mr. Slope should be in love with herself. But she desired the incense of Mr. Slope's spiritual and temporal services, and did not choose that they should be turned out of their course to such an object as Signora Neroni. She considered also that Mr. Slope ought in duty to hate the Signora, and it appeared from his manner that he was very far from hating her.

"Come, Mr. Slope," she said, sweeping by and looking all that she felt, "can't you make yourself useful? Do pray take Mrs. Grantly down to supper."

Mrs. Grantly heard and escaped. The words were hardly out of Mrs. Proudie's mouth before the intended victim had struck her hand through the arm of one of her husband's curates and saved herself. What would the Archdeacon have said had he seen her walking downstairs with Mr. Slope?

Mr. Slope heard also, but was by no means so obedient as was expected. Indeed, the period of Mr. Slope's obedience to Mrs. Proudie was drawing to a close. He did not wish yet to break with her, nor to break with her at all if it could be avoided. But he intended to be master in that palace, and as she had made the same resolution, it was not improbable that they might come to blows.

Before leaving the Signora he arranged a little table before her, and begged to know what he should bring her. She was quite indifferent, she said—nothing—anything. It was now she felt the misery of her position, now that she must be left alone. Well, a little chicken, some ham, and a glass of champagne.

Mr. Slope had to explain, not without blushing for his patron, that there was no champagne.

Sherry would do just as well. And then Mr. Slope descended with the learned Miss Trefoil on his arm. Could she tell him, he asked, whether the ferns of Barsetshire were equal to those of Cumberland? His strongest worldly passion was for ferns—and before she could answer him he left her wedged between the door and the sideboard. It was fifty minutes before she escaped, and even then unfed.

"You are not leaving us, Mr. Slope," said the watchful lady of the house, seeing her slave escaping toward the door with stores of provisions held high above the heads of the guests.

Mr. Slope explained that the Signora Neroni was in want of her supper.

"Pray, Mr. Slope, let her brother take it to her," said Mrs. Proudie, quite out loud. "It is out of the question that you should be so employed. Pray, Mr. Slope, oblige me. I am sure Mr. Stanhope will wait upon his sister."

Ethelbert was most agreeably occupied in the farther corner of the room, making himself both useful and agreeable to Mrs. Proudie's youngest daughter.

"I couldn't get out, madam, if Madeline were starving for her supper," said he. "I'm physically fixed, unless I could fly."

The lady's anger was increased by seeing that her daughter also had gone over to the enemy, and when she saw that in spite of her remonstrances, in the teeth of her positive orders, Mr. Slope went off to the drawing-room, the cup of her indignation ran over and she could not restrain herself. "Such manners I never saw," she said, muttering. "I cannot and will not permit it." And then, after fussing and fuming for a few minutes, she pushed her way through the crowd and followed Mr. Slope.

When she reached the room above, she found it absolutely deserted except by the guilty pair. The Signora was sitting very comfortably up to her supper, and Mr. Slope was leaning over her and administering to her wants. They had been discussing the merits of Sabbath-day schools, and the lady had suggested that as she could not possibly go to the children, she might be indulged in the wish of her heart by having the children brought to her.

"And when shall it be, Mr. Slope?" said she.

Mr. Slope was saved the necessity of committing himself to a promise by the entry of Mrs. Proudie. She swept close up to the sofa so as to confront the guilty pair, stared full at them for a moment, and then said as she passed on to the next room: "Mr. Slope, his lordship is especially desirous of your attendance below. You will greatly oblige me if you will join him." And so she stalked on.

Mr. Slope muttered something in reply and prepared to go downstairs. As for the Bishop's wanting him, he knew his lady patroness well enough to take that assertion at what it was worth, but he did not wish to make himself the hero of a scene, or to become conspicuous for more gallantry than the occasion required.

"Is she always like this?" said the Signora.

"Yes—always, madam," said Mrs. Proudie, returning, "always the same —always equally adverse to impropriety of conduct of every description."

And she stalked back through the room again, following Mr. Slope out of the door.

The Signora couldn't follow her, or she certainly would have done so. But she laughed loud, and sent the sound of it ringing through the lobby and down the stairs after Mrs. Proudie's feet. Had she been as active as Grimaldi, she could probably have taken no better revenge.

"Mr. Slope," said Mrs. Proudie, catching the delinquent at the door, "I am surprised that you should leave my company to attend on such a painted Jezebel as that."

"But she's lame, Mrs. Proudie, and cannot move. Somebody must have waited upon her."

"Lame," said Mrs. Proudie. "I'd lame her if she belonged to me. What business had she here at all?—Such impertinence—such affectation."

In the hall and adjacent rooms all manner of cloaking and shawling was going on, and the Barchester folk were getting themselves gone. Mrs. Proudie did her best to smirk at each and every one as they made their adieus, but she was hardly successful. Her temper had been tried fearfully. By slow degrees the guests went.

"Send back the carriage quick," said Ethelbert as Dr. and Mrs. Stanhope took their departure.

The younger Stanhopes were left to the very last, and an uncomfortable party they made with the Bishop's family. They all went into the dining-room, and then the Bishop, observing that "the lady" was alone in the drawing-room, they followed him up. Mrs. Proudie kept Mr. Slope and her daughters in close conversation, resolving that he should not be indulged, nor they polluted. The Bishop tried to converse with Charlotte Stanhope about the climate of Italy. Bertie and the Signora had no resource but in each other.

"Did you get your supper at last, Madeline?" said the impudent or else mischievous young man.

"Oh, yes," said Madeline. "Mr. Slope was so very kind as to bring it me. I fear, however, he put himself to more inconvenience than I wished."

Mrs. Proudie looked at her, but said nothing. The meaning of her look might have been thus translated: "If ever you find yourself within these walls again, I'll give you leave to be as impudent and affected and as mischievous as you please."

At last the carriage returned with the three Italian servants, and La Signora Madeline Vesey Neroni was carried out as she had been carried in.

The lady of the palace retired to her chamber by no means contented with the result of her first grand party at Barchester.

CHAPTER XII

SLOPE VERSUS HARDING

Two or three days after the party, Mr. Harding received a note begging him to call on Mr. Slope at the palace at an early hour the following morning. There was nothing uncivil in the communication, and yet the tone of it was thoroughly displeasing. It was as follows:

> My dear Mr. Harding, Will you favor me by calling on me at the palace tomorrow morning at 9.30 A.M. The Bishop wishes me to speak to you touching the hospital. I hope you will excuse my naming so early an hour. I do so as my time is greatly occupied. If, however, it is positively inconvenient to you, I will change it to 10. You will, perhaps, be kind enough to let me have a note in reply.
>
> Believe me to be,
My dear Mr. Harding,
Your assured friend,
Obh. Slope
>
> The Palace, Monday morning,
> 20th August, 185—

Mr. Harding neither could nor would believe anything of the sort, and he thought, moreover, that Mr. Slope was rather impertinent to call himself by such a name. His assured friend, indeed! How many assured friends generally fall to the lot of a man in this world? And by what process are they made? And how much of such process had taken place as yet between Mr. Harding and Mr. Slope? Mr. Harding could not help asking himself these questions as he read and reread the note before him. He answered it, however, as follows:

> Dear Sir, I will call at the palace to-morrow at 9.30 A.M. as you desire.
>
> Truly yours,
S. Harding.
>
> High Street, Barchester, Monday

And on the following morning, punctually at half-past nine, he knocked at the palace door and asked for Mr. Slope.

The Bishop had one small room allotted to him on the ground floor, and Mr. Slope had another. Into this latter Mr. Harding was shown, and asked to sit down. Mr. Slope was not yet there. The ex-Warden stood up at the window looking into the garden, and could not help thinking how very short a time had passed since the whole of that house had been open to him as though he had been a child of the family, born and bred in it. He remembered how the old servants used to smile as they opened the door to him, how the familiar butler would say when he had been absent a few hours longer than usual, "A sight of you, Mr. Harding, is good for sore eyes," how the fussy housekeeper would swear that he couldn't have dined, or couldn't have breakfasted, or couldn't have lunched. And then, above all, he remembered the pleasant gleam of inward satisfaction which always spread itself over the old Bishop's face whenever his friend entered his room.

A tear came into each eye as he reflected that all this was gone. What use would the hospital be to him now? He was alone in the world, and getting old. He would soon, very soon have to go and leave it all, as his dear old friend had gone—go, and leave the hospital, and his accustomed place in the cathedral, and his haunts and pleasures, to younger and perhaps wiser men. That chanting of his!—Perhaps, in truth, the time for it had gone by. He felt as though the world were sinking from his feet, as though this, this was the time for him to turn with confidence to those hopes which he had preached with confidence to others. "What," said he to himself, "can a man's religion be worth if it does not support him against the natural melancholy of declining years?" And as he looked out through his dimmed eyes into the bright parterres of the Bishop's garden, he felt that he had the support which he wanted.

Nevertheless, he did not like to be thus kept waiting. If Mr. Slope did not really wish to see him at half-past nine o'clock, why force him to come away from his lodgings with his breakfast in his throat? To tell the truth, it was policy on the part of Mr. Slope. Mr. Slope had made up his mind that Mr. Harding should either accept the hospital with abject submission or else refuse it altogether, and had calculated that he would probably be more quick to do the latter if he could be got to enter upon the subject in an ill-humor. Perhaps Mr. Slope was not altogether wrong in his calculation.

It was nearly ten when Mr. Slope hurried into the room and, muttering something about the Bishop and diocesan duties, shook Mr. Harding's hand ruthlessly and begged him to be seated.

Now the air of superiority which this man assumed did go against the grain of Mr. Harding, and yet he did not know how to resent it. The whole tendency of his mind and disposition was opposed to any contra-assumption of grandeur on his own part, and he hadn't the worldly spirit or quickness necessary to put down insolent pretensions by downright and open rebuke, as the Archdeacon would have done. There was nothing for Mr. Harding but to submit, and he accordingly did so.

"About the hospital, Mr. Harding?" began Mr. Slope, speaking of it as the head of a college at Cambridge might speak of some sizarship which had to be disposed of.

Mr. Harding crossed one leg over another and then one hand over the other on the top of them, and looked Mr. Slope in the face, but he said nothing.

"It's to be filled up again," said Mr. Slope. Mr. Harding said that he had understood so.

"Of course you know the income will be very much reduced," continued Mr. Slope. "The Bishop wished to be liberal, and he therefore told the Government that he thought it ought to be put at not less than £450. I think on the whole the Bishop was right, for though the services required will not be of a very onerous nature, they will be more so than they were before. And it is perhaps well that the clergy immediately attached to the cathedral town should be made as comfortable as the extent of the ecclesiastical means at our disposal will allow. Those are the Bishop's ideas, and I must say mine also."

Mr. Harding sat rubbing one hand on the other, but said not a word.

"So much for the income, Mr. Harding. The house will of course remain to the warden, as before. It should, however, I think, be stipulated that he should paint inside every seven years, and outside every three years, and be subject to dilapidations in the event of vacating, either by death or otherwise. But this is a matter on which the Bishop must yet be consulted."

Mr. Harding still rubbed his hands, and still sat silent, gazing up into Mr. Slope's unprepossessing face.

"Then as to the duties," continued he. "I believe, if I am rightly informed, there can hardly be said to have been any duties hitherto." And he gave a sort of half-laugh, as though to pass off the accusation in the guise of a pleasantry.

Mr. Harding thought of the happy, easy years he had passed in his old home, of the worn-out, aged men whom he had succored, of his good intentions, and of his work, which had certainly been of the lightest. He thought of these things, doubting for a moment whether he did or did not deserve the sarcasm. He gave his enemy the benefit of the doubt, and did not rebuke him. He merely observed, very tranquilly, and perhaps with too much humility, that the duties of the situation, such as they were, had, he believed, been done to the satisfaction of the late Bishop.

Mr. Slope again smiled, and this time the smile was intended to operate against the memory of the late Bishop rather than against the energy of the ex-Warden, and so it was understood by Mr. Harding. The color rose to his cheeks, and he began to feel very angry.

"You must be aware, Mr. Harding, that things are a good deal changed in Barchester," said Mr. Slope.

Mr. Harding said that he was aware of it. "And not only in Barchester, Mr. Harding, but in the world at large. It is not only in Barchester that a new man is carrying out new measures and casting away the useless rubbish of past centuries. The same thing is going on throughout the country. Work is now required from every man who receives wages, and they who have to superintend the doing of work, and the paying of wages, are bound to see that this rule is carried out. New men, Mr. Harding, are now needed, and are now forthcoming in the Church as well as in other professions."

All this was wormwood to our old friend. He had never rated very high his own abilities or activity, but all the feelings of his heart were with the old clergy, and any antipathies of which his heart was susceptible were directed against those new, busy, uncharitable, self-lauding men of whom Mr. Slope was so good an example.

"Perhaps," said he, "the Bishop will prefer a new man at the hospital."

"By no means," said Mr. Slope. "The Bishop is very anxious that you should accept the appointment. But he wishes you should understand beforehand what will be the required duties. In the first place, a Sabbath-day school will be attached to the hospital."

"What! For the old men?" asked Mr. Harding.

"No, Mr. Harding, not for the old men, but for the benefit of the children of such of the poor of Barchester as it may suit. The Bishop will expect that you shall attend this school, and the teachers shall be under your inspection and care."

Mr. Harding slipped his topmost hand off the other and began to rub the calf of the leg which was supported.

"As to the old men," continued Mr. Slope, "and the old women who are to form a part of the hospital, the Bishop is desirous that you shall have morning and evening service on the premises every Sabbath, and one weekday service; that you shall preach to them once at least on Sundays; and that the whole hospital be always collected for morning and evening prayer. The Bishop thinks that this will render it unnecessary that any separate seats in the cathedral should be reserved for the hospital inmates."

Mr. Slope paused, but Mr. Harding still said nothing.

"Indeed it would be difficult to find seats for the women, and on the whole, Mr. Harding, I may as well say at once that for people of that class the cathedral service does not appear to me the most useful—even if it be so for any class of people."

"We will not discuss that, if you please," said Mr. Harding.

"I am not desirous of doing so—at least, not at the present moment. I hope, however, you fully understand the Bishop's wishes about the new establishment of the hospital. And if, as I do not doubt, I shall receive from you an assurance that you accord with his lordship's views, it will give me very great pleasure to be the bearer from his lordship to you of the presentation to the appointment."

"But if I disagree with his lordship's views?" asked Mr. Harding.

"But I hope you do not," said Mr. Slope.

"But if I do?" again asked the other.

"If such unfortunately should be the case, which I can hardly conceive, I presume your own feelings will dictate to you the propriety of declining the appointment."

"But if I accept the appointment and yet disagree with the Bishop, what then?"

This question rather bothered Mr. Slope. It was true that he had talked the matter over with the Bishop, and had received a sort of authority for suggesting to Mr. Harding the propriety of a Sunday school and certain hospital services. But he had no authority for saying that these propositions were to be made peremptory conditions attached to the appointment. The Bishop's idea had been that Mr. Harding would of course consent, and that the school would become, like the rest of those new establishments in the city, under the control of his wife and his chaplain. Mr. Slope's idea had been more correct. He intended that Mr. Harding should refuse the situation, and that an ally of his own should get it. But he had not conceived the possibility of Mr. Harding openly accepting the appointment and as openly rejecting the conditions.

"It is not, I presume, probable," said he, "that you will accept from the hands of the Bishop a piece of preferment, with a fixed predetermination to disacknowledge the duties attached to it."

"If I become warden," said Mr. Harding, "and neglect my duty, the Bishop has means by which he can remedy the grievance."

"I hardly expected such an argument from you, or I may say the suggestion of such a line of conduct," said Mr. Slope, with a great look of injured virtue.

"Nor did I expect such a proposition."

"I shall be glad at any rate to know what answer I am to make to his lordship," said Mr. Slope.

"I will take an early opportunity of seeing his lordship myself," said Mr. Harding.

"Such an arrangement," said Mr. Slope, "will hardly give his lordship satisfaction. Indeed, it is impossible that the Bishop should himself see every clergyman in the diocese on every subject of patronage that may arise. The Bishop, I believe, did see you on the matter, and I really cannot see why he should be troubled to do so again."

"Do you know, Mr. Slope, how long I have been officiating as a clergyman in this city?" Mr. Slope's wish was now nearly fulfilled. Mr. Harding had become angry, and it was probable that he might commit himself.

"I really do not see what that has to do with the question. You cannot think the Bishop would be justified in allowing you to regard as a sinecure a situation that requires an active man merely because you have been employed for many years in the cathedral."

"But it might induce the Bishop to see me, if I asked him to do so. I shall consult my friends in this matter, Mr. Slope; but I mean to be guilty of no subterfuge.—You may tell the Bishop that as I altogether disagree with his views about the hospital, I shall decline the situation if I find that any such conditions are attached to it as those you have suggested." And so saying, Mr. Harding took his hat and went his way.

Mr. Slope was contented. He considered himself at liberty to accept Mr. Harding's last speech as an absolute refusal of the appointment. At least, he so represented it to the Bishop and to Mrs. Proudie.

"That is very surprising," said the Bishop.

"Not at all," said Mrs. Proudie. "You little know how determined the whole set of them are to withstand your authority."

"But Mr. Harding was so anxious for it," said the Bishop.

"Yes," said Mr. Slope, "if he can hold it without the slightest acknowledgment of your lordship's jurisdiction."

"That is out of the question," said the Bishop.

"I should imagine it to be quite so," said the chaplain.

"Indeed I should think so," said the lady.

"I really am sorry for it," said the Bishop.

"I don't know that there is much cause for sorrow," said the lady. "Mr. Quiverful is a much more deserving man, more in need of it, and one who will make himself much more useful in the close neighborhood of the palace."

"I suppose I had better see Quiverful?" said the chaplain.

"I suppose you had," said the Bishop.

CHAPTER XIII

THE RUBBISH CART

Mr. Harding was not a happy man as he walked down the palace pathway and stepped out into the close. His preferment and pleasant house were a second time gone from him, but that he could endure. He had been schooled and insulted by a man young enough to be his son, but that he could put up with. He could even draw from the very injuries which had been inflicted on him some of that consolation which we may believe martyrs always receive from the injustice of their own sufferings, and which is generally proportioned in its strength to the extent of cruelty with which martyrs are treated. He had admitted to his daughter that he wanted the comfort of his old home, and yet he could have returned to his lodgings in the High Street, if not with exultation, at least with satisfaction, had that been all. But the venom of the chaplain's harangue had worked into his blood, and sapped the life of his sweet contentment.

"New men are carrying out new measures, and are carting away the useless rubbish of past centuries!" What cruel words these had been, and how often are they now used with all the heartless cruelty of a Slope! A man is sufficiently condemned if it can only be shown that either in politics or religion he does not belong to some new school established within the last score of years. He may then regard himself as rubbish and expect to be carted away. We must talk, think, and live up to the spirit of the times, and write up to it too, if that cacoethes be upon us, or we are naught. New men and new measures, long credit and few scruples, great success or wonderful ruin, such are now the tastes of Englishmen who know how to live. Alas, alas! under such circumstances Mr. Harding could not but feel that he was an Englishman who did not know how to live. This new doctrine of Mr. Slope and the rubbish cart—new at least at Barchester—sadly disturbed his equanimity.

"The same thing is going on throughout the whole country!" "Work is now required from every man who receives wages!" And had he been living all his life receiving wages and doing no work? Had he in truth so lived as to be now in his old age justly reckoned as rubbish fit only to be hidden away in some huge dust hole? The school of men to whom he professes to belong, the Grantlys, the Gwynnes, and the old high set of Oxford divines, are afflicted with no such self-accusations as these which troubled Mr. Harding. They, as a rule, are as satisfied with the wisdom and propriety of their own conduct as can be any Mr. Slope, or any Dr. Proudie, with his own. But unfortunately for himself Mr. Harding had little of this self-reliance. When he heard himself designated as rubbish by the Slopes of the world, he had no other resource than to make inquiry within his own bosom as to the truth of the designation. Alas, alas! the evidence seemed generally to go against him.

He had professed to himself in the Bishop's parlor that in these coming sources of the sorrow of age, in these fits of sad regret from which the latter years of few reflecting men can be free, religion would suffice to comfort him. Yes, religion could console him for the loss of any worldly good. But was his religion of that active sort which would enable him so to repent of misspent years as to pass those that were left to him in a spirit of hope for the future? And such repentance itself, is it not a work of agony and of tears? It is very easy to talk of repentance, but a man has to walk over hot plowshares before he can complete it, to be skinned alive as was St. Bartholomew, to be stuck full of arrows as was St. Sebastian, to lie broiling on a gridiron like St. Lorenzo! How if his past life required such repentance as this? Had he the energy to go through with it?

Mr. Harding, after leaving the palace, walked slowly for an hour or so beneath the shady elms of the close, and then betook himself to his daughter's house. He had at any rate made up his mind that he would go out to Plumstead to consult Dr. Grantly, and that he would in the first instance tell Eleanor what had occurred.

And now he was doomed to undergo another misery. Mr. Slope had forestalled him at the widow's house. He had called there on the preceding afternoon. He could not, he had said, deny himself the pleasure of telling Mrs. Bold that her father was about to return to the pretty house at Hiram's Hospital. He had been instructed by the Bishop to inform Mr. Harding that the appointment would now be made at once. The Bishop was of course only too happy to be able to be the means of restoring to Mr. Harding the preferment which he had so long adorned. And then by degrees Mr. Slope had introduced the subject of the pretty school which he hoped before long to see attached to the hospital. He had quite fascinated Mrs. Bold by his description of this picturesque, useful, and charitable appendage, and she had gone so far as to say that she had no doubt her father would approve, and that she herself would gladly undertake a class.

Anyone who had heard the entirely different tone, and seen the entirely different manner, in which Mr. Slope had spoken of this projected institution to the daughter and to the father could not have failed to own that Mr. Slope was a man of genius. He said nothing to Mrs. Bold about the hospital sermons and services, nothing about the exclusion of the old men from the cathedral, nothing about dilapidation and painting, nothing about carting away the rubbish. Eleanor had said to herself that certainly she did not like Mr. Slope personally, but that he was a very active, zealous clergyman, and would no doubt be useful in Barchester. All this paved the way for much additional misery to Mr. Harding.

Eleanor put on her happiest face as she heard her father on the stairs, for she thought she had only to congratulate him, but directly she saw his face she knew that there was but little matter for congratulation. She had seen him with the same weary look of sorrow on one or two occasions before, and remembered it well. She had seen him when he first read that attack upon himself in the *Jupiter* which had ultimately caused him to resign the hospital, and she had seen him also when the Archdeacon had persuaded him to remain there against his own sense of propriety and honor. She knew at a glance that his spirit was in deep trouble.

"Oh, Papa, what is it?" said she, putting down her boy to crawl upon the floor.

"I came to tell you, my dear," said he, "that I am going out to Plumstead. You won't come with me, I suppose?"

"To Plumstead, Papa? Shall you stay there?"

"I suppose I shall, tonight. I must consult the Archdeacon about this weary hospital. Ah me! I wish I had never thought of it again."

"Why, Papa, what is the matter?"

"I've been with Mr. Slope, my dear, and he isn't the pleasantest companion in the world—at least not to me." Eleanor gave a sort of half-blush, but she was wrong if she imagined that her father in any way alluded to her acquaintance with Mr. Slope.

"Well, Papa."

"He wants to turn the hospital into a Sunday school and a preaching house, and I suppose he will have his way. I do not feel myself adapted for such an establishment, and therefore I suppose I must refuse the appointment."

"What would be the harm of the school, Papa?"

"The want of a proper schoolmaster, my dear."

"But that would of course be supplied."

"Mr. Slope wishes to supply it by making me his schoolmaster. But as I am hardly fit for such work, I intend to decline."

"Oh, Papa! Mr. Slope doesn't intend that. He was here yesterday, and what he intends——"

"He was here yesterday, was he?" asked Mr. Harding.

"Yes, Papa."

"And talking about the hospital?"

"He was saying how glad he would be, and the Bishop too, to see you back there again. And then he spoke about the Sunday school, and to tell the truth I agreed with him, and I thought you would have done so too. Mr. Slope spoke of a school not inside the hospital, but just connected with it, of which you would be the patron and visitor, and I thought you would have liked such a school as that, and I promised to look after it and to take a class—and it all seemed so very—— But, oh, Papa! I shall be so miserable if I find I have done wrong."

"Nothing wrong at all, my dear," said he, gently, very gently rejecting his daughter's caress. "There can be nothing wrong in your wishing to make yourself useful. Indeed, you ought to do so by all means. Everyone must now exert himself who would not choose to go to the wall." Poor Mr. Harding thus attempted in his misery to preach the new doctrine to his child. "Himself or herself, it's all the same," he continued. "You will be quite right, my dear, to do something of this sort, but——"

"Well, Papa?"

"I am not quite sure that if I were you I would select Mr. Slope for my guide."

"But I have never done so, and never shall."

"It would be very wicked of me to speak evil of him, for to tell the truth I know no evil of him, but I am not quite sure that he is honest. That he is not gentlemanlike in his manners, of that I am quite sure."

"I never thought of taking him for my guide, Papa."

"As for myself, my dear," continued he, "we know the old proverb—'It's bad teaching an old dog tricks.' I must decline the Sunday school, and shall therefore probably decline the hospital also. But I will first see your brother-in-law." So he took up his hat, kissed the baby, and withdrew, leaving Eleanor in as low spirits as himself.

All this was a great aggravation to his misery. He had so few with whom to sympathize that he could not afford to be cut off from the one whose sympathy was of the most value to him. And yet it seemed probable that this would be the case. He did not own to himself that he wished his daughter to hate Mr. Slope, yet had she expressed such a feeling there would have been very little bitterness in the rebuke he would have given her for so uncharitable a state of mind. The fact, however, was that she was on friendly terms with Mr. Slope, that she coincided with his views, adhered at once to his plans, and listened with delight to his teaching. Mr. Harding hardly wished his daughter to hate the man, but he would have preferred that to her loving him.

When Mr. Harding reached the parsonage he found that the Archdeacon was out and would not be home till dinnertime, so he began his complaint to his elder daughter. Mrs. Grantly entertained quite as strong an antagonism to Mr. Slope as did her husband. She was also quite as alive to the necessity of combating the Proudie faction, of supporting the old church interest of the close, of keeping in her own set such of the loaves and fishes as duly belonged to it, and was quite as well prepared as her lord to carry on the battle without giving or taking quarter. Not that she was a woman prone to quarreling, or ill-inclined to live at peace with her clerical neighbors. But she felt, as did the Archdeacon, that the presence of Mr. Slope in Barchester was an insult to everyone connected with the late Bishop, and that his assumed dominion in the diocese was a spiritual injury to her husband. Hitherto people had little guessed how bitter Mrs. Grantly could be. She lived on the best of terms with all the rectors' wives around her. She had been popular with all the ladies connected with the close. Though much the wealthiest of the ecclesiastical matrons of the county, she had so managed her affairs that her carriage and horses had given umbrage to none. She had never thrown herself among the county grandees so as to excite the envy of other clergymen's wives. She had never talked too loudly of earls and countesses, or boasted that she gave her governess sixty pounds a year, or her cook seventy. Mrs. Grantly had lived the life of a wise, discreet, peacemaking woman, and the people of Barchester were surprised at the amount of military vigor she displayed as general of the feminine Grantlyite forces.

Mrs. Grantly soon learnt that her sister Eleanor had promised to assist Mr. Slope in the affairs of the hospital, and it was on this point that her attention soon fixed itself.

"How can Eleanor endure him?" said she.

"He is a very crafty man," said her father, "and his craft has been successful in making Eleanor think that he is a meek, charitable, good clergyman. God forgive me if I wrong him, but such is not his true character in my opinion."

"His true character indeed!" said she, with something approaching to scorn for her father's moderation. "I only hope he won't have craft enough to make Eleanor forget herself and her position."

"Do you mean marry him?" said he, startled out of his usual demeanor by the abruptness and horror of so dreadful a proposition.

"What is there so improbable in it? Of course that would be his own object if he thought he had any chance of success. Eleanor has a thousand a year entirely at her own disposal, and what better fortune could fall to Mr. Slope's lot than the transferring of the disposal of such a fortune to himself?"

"But you can't think she likes him, Susan?"

"Why not?" said Susan. "Why shouldn't she like him? He's just the sort of man to get on with a woman left as she is, with no one to look after her."

"Look after her!" said the unhappy father. "Don't we look after her?"

"Ah, Papa, how innocent you are! Of course it was to be expected that Eleanor should marry again. I should be the last to advise her against it, if she would only wait the proper time, and then marry at least a gentleman."

"But you don't really mean to say that you suppose Eleanor has ever thought of marrying Mr. Slope? Why, Mr. Bold has only been dead a year."

"Eighteen months," said his daughter. "But I don't suppose Eleanor has ever thought about it. It is very probable, though, that he has, and that he will try and make her do so. And that he will succeed too, if we don't take care what we are about."

This was quite a new phase of the affair to poor Mr. Harding. To have thrust upon him as his son-in-law, as the husband of his favorite child, the only man in the world whom he really positively disliked, would be a misfortune which he felt he would not know how to endure patiently. But then, could there be any ground for so dreadful a surmise? In all worldly matters he was apt to look upon the opinion of his eldest daughter as one generally sound and trustworthy. In her appreciation of character, of motives, and the probable conduct both of men and women, she was usually not far wrong. She had early foreseen the marriage of Eleanor and John Bold, she had at a glance deciphered the character of the new Bishop and his chaplain. Could it possibly be that her present surmise should ever come forth as true?

"But you don't think that she likes him?" said Mr. Harding again.

"Well, Papa, I can't say that I think she dislikes him as she ought to do. Why is he visiting there as a confidential friend when he never ought to have been admitted inside the house? Why is it that she speaks to him about your welfare and your position, as she clearly has done? At the Bishop's party the other night, I saw her talking to him for half an hour at a stretch."

"I thought Mr. Slope seemed to talk to nobody there but that daughter of Stanhope's," said Mr. Harding, wishing to defend his child.

"Oh, Mr. Slope is a cleverer man than you think of, Papa, and keeps more than one iron in the fire."

To give Eleanor her due, any suspicion as to the slightest inclination on her part toward Mr. Slope was a wrong to her. She had no more idea of marrying Mr. Slope than she had of marrying the Bishop, and the idea that Mr. Slope would present himself as a suitor had never occurred to her. Indeed, to give her her due again, she had never thought about suitors since her husband's death. But nevertheless it was true that she had overcome all that repugnance to the man which was so strongly felt for him by the rest of the Grantly faction. She had forgiven him his sermon. She had forgiven him his Low Church tendencies, his Sabbath schools and puritanical observances. She had forgiven his pharisaical arrogance, and even his greasy face and oily vulgar manners. Having agreed to overlook such offenses as these, why should she not in time be taught to regard Mr. Slope as a suitor?

And as to him, it must also be affirmed that he was hitherto equally inno-cent of the crime imputed to him. How it had come to pass that a man whose eyes were generally so widely open to everything around him had not perceived that this young widow was rich as well as beautiful cannot prob-ably now be explained. But such was the fact. Mr. Slope had ingratiated himself with Mrs. Bold merely as he had done with other ladies, in order to strengthen his party in the city. He subsequently amended his error, but it was not till after the interview between him and Mr. Harding.

CHAPTER XIV

THE NEW CHAMPION

THE Archdeacon did not return to the parsonage till close upon the hour of dinner, and there was therefore no time to discuss matters before that important ceremony. He seemed to be in an especial good humor, and wel-comed his father-in-law with a sort of jovial earnestness that was usual with him when things on which he was intent were going on as he would have them.

"It's all settled, my dear," said he to his wife as he washed his hands in his dressing-room while she, according to her wont, sat listening in the bed-room. "Arabin has agreed to accept the living. He'll be here next week." And the Archdeacon scrubbed his hands and rubbed his face with violent alacrity, which showed that Arabin's coming was a great point gained.

"Will he come here to Plumstead?" said the wife.

"He has promised to stay a month with us," said the Archdeacon, "so that he may see what his parish is like. You'll like Arabin very much. He's a gentleman in every respect, and full of humor."

"He's very queer, isn't he?" asked the lady.

"Well, he is a little odd in some of his fancies, but there's nothing about him you won't like. He is as stanch a churchman as there is at Oxford. I really don't know what we should do without Arabin. It's a great thing for me to have him so near me, and if anything can put Slope down, Arabin will do it."

The Reverend Francis Arabin was a fellow of Lazarus, the favored dis-ciple of the great Dr. Gwynne, a High Churchman at all points—so high, indeed, that at one period of his career he had all but toppled over into the cesspool of Rome, a poet and also a polemical writer, a great pet in the common rooms at Oxford, an eloquent clergyman, a droll, odd, humorous, energetic, conscientious man, and, as the Archdeacon had boasted of him, a thorough gentleman. As he will hereafter be brought more closely to our notice, it is now only necessary to add that he had just been presented to the vicarage of St. Ewold by Dr. Grantly, in whose gift as Archdeacon the living lay. St. Ewold is a parish lying just without the city of Barchester. The suburbs of the new town indeed are partly within its precincts, and the pretty church and parsonage are not much above a mile distant from the city gate.

St. Ewold is not a rich piece of preferment—it is worth some three or four hundred a year at most, and has generally been held by a clergyman attached to the cathedral choir. The Archdeacon, however, felt when the living on this occasion became vacant that it imperatively behooved him to aid the force of his party with some tower of strength, if any such tower could be got to occupy St. Ewold's. He had discussed the matter with his brethren in Barchester, not in any weak spirit as the holder of patronage to be used for his own or his family's benefit, but as one to whom was committed a trust on the due administration of which much of the Church's welfare might depend. He had submitted to them the name of Mr. Arabin as though the choice had rested with them all in conclave, and they had unanimously admitted that if Mr. Arabin would accept St. Ewold's, no better choice could possibly be made.

If Mr. Arabin would accept St. Ewold's! There lay the difficulty. Mr. Arabin was a man standing somewhat prominently before the world: that is, before the Church of England world. He was not a rich man, it is true, for he held no preferment but his fellowship, but he was a man not overanxious for riches, not married of course, and one whose time was greatly taken up in discussing, both in print and on platforms, the privileges and practices of the Church to which he belonged. As the Archdeacon had done battle for its temporalities, so did Mr. Arabin do battle for its spiritualities, and both had done so conscientiously—that is, not so much each for his own benefit as for that of others.

Holding such a position as Mr. Arabin did, there was much reason to doubt whether he would consent to become the parson of St. Ewold's, and Dr. Grantly had taken the trouble to go himself to Oxford on the matter. Dr. Gwynne and Dr. Grantly together had succeeded in persuading this eminent divine that duty required him to go to Barchester. There were wheels within wheels in this affair. For some time past Mr. Arabin had been engaged in a tremendous controversy with no less a person than Mr. Slope, respecting the apostolic succession. These two gentlemen had never seen each other, but they had been extremely bitter in print. Mr. Slope had endeavored to strengthen his cause by calling Mr. Arabin an owl, and Mr. Arabin had retaliated by hinting that Mr. Slope was an infidel. This battle had been commenced in the columns of the daily *Jupiter*, the manager of which was very friendly to Mr. Slope's view of the case. The matter, however, had become too tedious for the readers of the *Jupiter*, and a little note had therefore been appended to one of Mr. Slope's most telling rejoinders in which it had been stated that no further letters from the reverend gentlemen could be inserted except as advertisements.

Other methods of publication were, however, found less expensive than advertisements in the *Jupiter*, and the war went on merrily. Mr. Slope declared that the main part of the consecration of a clergyman was the self-devotion of the inner man to the duties of the ministry. Mr. Arabin contended that a man was not consecrated at all, had indeed no single attribute of a clergyman, unless he became so through the imposition of some bishop's hands who had become a bishop through the imposition of other hands, and so on in a direct line to one of the Apostles. Each had repeatedly hung the other on the horns of a dilemma, but neither seemed to be a whit the worse for the hanging, and so the war went on merrily.

Whether or no the near neighborhood of the foe may have acted in any way as an inducement to Mr. Arabin to accept the living of St. Ewold we will not pretend to say, but it had at any rate been settled in Dr. Gwynne's library at Lazarus that he would accept it, and that he would lend his assistance toward driving the enemy out of Barchester, or at any rate silencing him while he remained there. Mr. Arabin intended to keep his rooms at Oxford, and to have the assistance of a curate at St. Ewold, but he promised to give as much time as possible to the neighborhood of Barchester, and from so great a man Dr. Grantly was quite satisfied with such a promise. It was no small part of the satisfaction derivable from such an arrangement that Bishop Proudie would be forced to institute into a living immediately under his own nose the enemy of his favorite chaplain.

All through dinner the Archdeacon's good humor shone brightly in his face. He ate of the good things heartily, he drank wine with his wife and daughter, he talked pleasantly of his doings at Oxford, told his father-in-law that he ought to visit Dr. Gwynne at Lazarus, and launched out again in praise of Mr. Arabin.

"Is Mr. Arabin married, Papa?" asked Griselda.

"No, my dear. The fellow of a college is never married."

"Is he a young man, Papa?"

"About forty, I believe," said the Archdeacon.

"Oh!" said Griselda. Had her father said eighty, Mr. Arabin would not have appeared to her to be very much older.

When the two gentlemen were left alone over their wine, Mr. Harding told his tale of woe. But even this, sad as it was, did not much diminish the Archdeacon's good humor, though it greatly added to his pugnacity.

"He can't do it," said Dr. Grantly over and over again as his father-in-law explained to him the terms on which the new warden of the hospital was to be appointed. "He can't do it. What he says is not worth the trouble of listening to. He can't alter the duties of the place."

"Who can't?" asked the ex-Warden.

"Neither the Bishop nor the chaplain, nor yet the Bishop's wife, wh I take it has really more to say to such matters than either of the othe two. The whole body corporate of the palace together have no powe to turn the warden of the hospital into a Sunday-schoolmaster."

"But the Bishop has the power to appoint whom he pleases, and——"

"I don't know that. I rather think he'll find he has no such power. Le him try it, and see what the press will say. For once we shall have th popular cry on our side. But Proudie, ass as he is, knows the world to well to get such a hornet's nest about his ears."

Mr. Harding winced at the idea of the press. He had had enough c that sort of publicity, and was unwilling to be shown up a second tim either as a monster or as a martyr. He gently remarked that he hoped th newspapers would not get hold of his name again, and then suggested tha perhaps it would be better that he should abandon his object. "I am gettin old," said he, "and after all I doubt whether I am fit to undertake ne duties."

"New duties!" said the Archdeacon. "Don't I tell you there shall be n new duties?"

"Or perhaps old duties either," said Mr. Harding. "I think I will remai content as I am." The picture of Mr. Slope carting away the rubbish wa still present to his mind.

The Archdeacon drank off his glass of claret, and prepared himself t be energetic. "I do hope," said he, "that you are not going to be so wea as to allow such a man as Mr. Slope to deter you from doing what yo know it is your duty to do. You know it is your duty to resume you place at the hospital now that Parliament has so settled the stipend as t remove those difficulties which induced you to resign it. You cannot den this, and should your timidity now prevent you from doing so, your con science will hereafter never forgive you." And as he finished this claus of his speech, he pushed over the bottle to his companion.

"Your conscience will never forgive you," he continued. "You resigne the place from conscientious scruples, scruples which I greatly respecte though I did not share them. All your friends respected them, and you le your old house as rich in reputation as you were ruined in fortune. It now expected that you will return. Dr. Gwynne was saying only the othe day——"

"Dr. Gwynne does not reflect how much older a man I am now tha when he last saw me."

"Old—nonsense!" said the Archdeacon. "You never thought yourself ol till you listened to the impudent trash of that coxcomb at the palace."

"I shall be sixty-five if I live till November," said Mr. Harding.

"And seventy-five if you live till November ten years," said the Arch deacon. "And you bid fair to be as efficient then as you were ten yea ago. But for heaven's sake let us have no pretense in this matter. Your ple of old age is only a pretense. But you're not drinking your wine. It is onl

pretense. The fact is you are half-afraid of this Slope, and would rather
abject yourself to comparative poverty and discomfort than come to blows
with a man who will trample on you if you let him."

"I certainly don't like coming to blows, if I can help it."

"Nor I neither—but sometimes we can't help it. This man's object is to
induce you to refuse the hospital, that he may put some creature of his
own into it, that he may show his power and insult us all by insulting you,
whose cause and character are so intimately bound up with that of the
Chapter. You owe it to us all to resist him in this, even if you have no
solicitude for yourself. But surely, for your own sake you will not be so
lily-livered as to fall into this trap which he has baited for you, and let
him take the very bread out of your mouth without a struggle."

Mr. Harding did not like being called lily-livered, and was rather in-
lined to resent it. "I doubt there is any true courage," said he, "in squab-
bling for money."

"If honest men did not squabble for money in this wicked world of ours,
the dishonest men would get it all, and I do not see that the cause of virtue
would be much improved. No—we must use the means which we have. If
we were to carry your argument home we might give away every shilling
of revenue which the Church has, and I presume you are not prepared to
say that the Church would be strengthened by such a sacrifice." The Archdeacon filled his glass and then emptied it, drinking with much reverence
a silent toast to the well-being and permanent security of those temporalities
which were so dear to his soul.

"I think all quarrels between a clergyman and his bishop should be
avoided," said Mr. Harding.

"I think so too, but it is quite as much the duty of the bishop to look
to that as of his inferior. I tell you what, my friend, I'll see the Bishop in
this matter—that is, if you will allow me—and you may be sure I will not
compromise you. My opinion is that all this trash about the Sunday schools
and the sermons has originated wholly with Slope and Mrs. Proudie, and
that the Bishop knows nothing about it. The Bishop can't very well refuse
to see me, and I'll come upon him when he has neither his wife nor his
chaplain by him. I think you'll find that it will end in his sending you the
appointment without any condition whatever. And as to the seats in the
cathedral, we may safely leave that to Mr. Dean. I believe the fool positively
thinks that the Bishop could walk away with the cathedral if he pleased."

And so the matter was arranged between them. Mr. Harding had come
expressly for advice, and therefore felt himself bound to take the advice
given him. He had known, moreover, beforehand that the Archdeacon would
not hear of his giving the matter up, and accordingly, though he had in
perfect good faith put forward his own views, he was prepared to yield.

They therefore went into the drawing-room in good humor with each
other, and the evening passed pleasantly in prophetic dicussions on the
future wars of Arabin and Slope. The frogs and the mice would be

nothing to them, nor the angers of Agamemnon and Achilles. How the Archdeacon rubbed his hands, and plumed himself on the success of his last move! He could not himself descend into the arena with Slope, but Arabin would have no such scruples. Arabin was exactly the man for such work, and the only man whom he knew that was fit for it.

The Archdeacon's good humor and high buoyancy continued till, when reclining on his pillow, Mrs. Grantly commenced to give him her view of the state of affairs at Barchester. And then certainly he was startled. The last words he said that night were as follows:

"If she does, by heaven, I'll never speak to her again. She dragged me into the mire once, but I'll not pollute myself with such filth as that——" And the Archdeacon gave a shudder which shook the whole room, so violently was he convulsed with the thought which then agitated his mind.

Now in this matter the Widow Bold was scandalously ill-treated by her relatives. She had spoken to the man three or four times, and had expressed her willingness to teach in a Sunday school. Such was the full extent of her sins in the matter of Mr. Slope. Poor Eleanor! But time will show.

CHAPTER XV

THE WIDOW'S SUITORS

Mr. Slope lost no time in availing himself of the Bishop's permission to see Mr. Quiverful, and it was in his interview with this worthy pastor that he first learned that Mrs. Bold was worth the wooing. He rode out to Puddingdale to communicate to the embryo warden the goodwill of the Bishop in his favor, and during the discussion on the matter it was not unnatural that the pecuniary resources of Mr. Harding and his family should become the subject of remark.

Mr. Quiverful with his fourteen children and his four hundred a year was a very poor man, and the prospect of this new preferment, which was to be held together with his living, was very grateful to him. To what clergyman so circumstanced would not such a prospect be very grateful? But Mr. Quiverful had long been acquainted with Mr. Harding, and had received kindness at his hands, so that his heart misgave him as he thought of supplanting a friend at the hospital. Nevertheless he was extremely civil, cringingly civil, to Mr. Slope, treated him quite as the great man, entreated this great man to do him the honor to drink a glass of sherry—at which, as it was very poor Marsala, the now pampered Slope turned up his nose—and ended by declaring his extreme obligation to the Bishop and Mr. Slope, and his great desire to accept the hospital if—if it were certainly the case that Mr. Harding had refused it. What man as needy as Mr. Quiverful would have been more disinterested?

"Mr. Harding did positively refuse it," said Mr. Slope, with a certain air of offended dignity, "when he heard of the conditions to which the appointment is now subjected. Of course you understand, Mr. Quiverful, that the same conditions will be imposed on yourself."

Mr. Quiverful cared nothing for the conditions. He would have undertaken to preach any number of sermons Mr. Slope might have chosen to dictate, and to pass every remaining hour of his Sundays within the walls of a Sunday school. What sacrifices, or at any rate, what promises, would have been too much to make for such an addition to his income, and for such a house! But his mind still recurred to Mr. Harding.

"To be sure," said he, "Mr. Harding's daughter is very rich, and why should he trouble himself with the hospital?"

"You mean Mrs. Grantly," said Slope.

"I meant his widowed daughter," said the other. "Mrs. Bold has twelve hundred a year of her own, and I suppose Mr. Harding means to live with her."

"Twelve hundred a year of her own!" said Slope, and very shortly afterward took his leave, avoiding, as far as it was possible for him to do, any further allusion to the hospital. "Twelve hundred a year," said he to himself as he rode slowly home. If it were the fact that Mrs. Bold had twelve hundred a year of her own, what a fool would he be to oppose her father's return to his old place! The train of Mr. Slope's ideas will probably be plain to all my readers. Why should he not make the twelve hundred a year his own? And if he did so, would it not be well for him to have a father-in-law comfortably provided with the good things of this world? Would it not, moreover, be much more easy for him to gain the daughter if he did all in his power to forward the father's views?

These questions presented themselves to him in a very forcible way, and yet there were many points of doubt. If he resolved to restore to Mr. Harding his former place, he must take the necessary steps for doing so at once. He must immediately talk over the Bishop, quarrel on the matter with Mrs. Proudie, whom he knew he could not talk over, and let Mr. Quiverful know that he had been a little too precipitate as to Mr. Harding's positive refusal. That he could effect all this he did not doubt, but he did not wish to effect it for nothing. He did not wish to give way to Mr. Harding and then be rejected by the daughter. He did not wish to lose one influential friend before he had gained another.

And thus he rode home meditating many things in his mind. It occurred to him that Mrs. Bold was sister-in-law to the Archdeacon, and that not even for twelve hundred a year would he submit to that imperious man. A rich wife was a great desideratum to him, but success in his profession was still greater. There were, moreover, other rich women who might be willing to become wives, and after all, this twelve hundred a year might, when inquired into, melt away into some small sum utterly beneath his notice. Then also he remembered that Mrs. Bold had a son.

Another circumstance also much influenced him, though it was one which may almost be said to have influenced him against his will. The vision of the Signora Neroni was perpetually before his eyes. It would be too much to say that Mr. Slope was lost in love, but yet he thought, and kept continually thinking, that he had never seen so beautiful a woman. He was a man whose nature was open to such impulses, and the wiles of the Italianized charmer had been thoroughly successful in imposing upon his thoughts. We will not talk about his heart—not that he had no heart, but because his heart had little to do with his present feelings. His taste had been pleased, his eyes charmed, and his vanity gratified. He had been dazzled by a sort of loveliness which he had never before seen, and had been caught by an easy, free, voluptuous manner which was perfectly new to him. He had never been so tempted before, and the temptation was now irresistible. He had not owned to himself that he cared for this woman more than for others around him, but yet he thought often of the time when he might see her next and made, almost unconsciously, little cunning plans for seeing her frequently.

He had called at Dr. Stanhope's house the day after the Bishop's party, and then the warmth of his admiration had been fed with fresh fuel. If the Signora had been kind in her manner and flattering in her speech when lying upon the Bishop's sofa, with the eyes of so many on her, she had been much more so in her mother's drawing-room, with no one present but her sister to repress either her nature or her art. Mr. Slope had thus left her quite bewildered, and could not willingly admit into his brain any scheme a part of which would be the necessity of his abandoning all further special friendship with this lady.

And so he slowly rode along very meditative.

And here the author must beg it to be remembered that Mr. Slope was not in all things a bad man. His motives, like those of most men, were mixed, and though his conduct was generally very different from that which we would wish to praise, it was actuated perhaps as often as that of the majority of the world by a desire to do his duty. He believed in the religion which he taught, harsh, unpalatable, uncharitable as that religion was. He believed those whom he wished to get under his hoof, the Grantlys and Gwynnes of the Church, to be the enemies of that religion. He believed himself to be a pillar of strength, destined to do great things. And with that subtle, selfish, ambiguous sophistry to which the minds of all men are so subject, he had taught himself to think that in doing much for the promotion of his own interests he was doing much also for the promotion of religion. But Mr. Slope had never been an immoral man. Indeed, he had resisted temptations to immorality with a strength of purpose that was creditable to him. He had early in life devoted himself to works which were not compatible with the ordinary pleasures of youth, and he had abandoned such pleasures not without a struggle. It must therefore be conceived that he did not admit to himself that he warmly admired the beauty of a married woman without heartfelt stings of conscience, and to pacify that conscience he had to teach himself that the nature of his admiration was innocent.

And thus he rode along meditative and ill at ease. His conscience had not a word to say against his choosing the widow and her fortune. That he looked upon as a godly work rather than otherwise, as a deed which, if carried through, would redound to his credit as a Christian. On that side lay no future remorse, no conduct which he might probably have to forget, no inward stings. If it should turn out to be really the fact that Mrs. Bold had twelve hundred a year at her own disposal, Mr. Slope would rather look upon it as a duty which he owed his religion to make himself the master of the wife and the money—as a duty, too, in which some amount of self-sacrifice would be necessary. He would have to give up his friendship with the Signora, his resistance to Mr. Harding, his antipathy—no, he found on mature self-examination that he could not bring himself to give up his antipathy to Dr. Grantly. He would marry the lady as the enemy of her brother-in-law if such an arrangement suited her. If not, she must look elsewhere for a husband.

It was with such resolve as this that he reached Barchester. He would at once ascertain what the truth might be as to the lady's wealth, and having done this he would be ruled by circumstances in his conduct respecting the hospital. If he found that he could turn round and secure the place for Mr. Harding without much self-sacrifice, he would do so, but if not, he would woo the daughter in opposition to the father. But in no case would he succumb to the Archdeacon.

He saw his horse taken round to the stable, and immediately went forth to commence his inquiries. To give Mr. Slope his due, he was not a man who ever let much grass grow under his feet.

Poor Eleanor! She was doomed to be the intended victim of more schemes than one. About the time that Mr. Slope was visiting the Vicar of Puddingdale a discussion took place respecting her charms and wealth at Dr. Stanhope's house in the close. There had been morning callers there, and people had told some truth and also some falsehood respecting the property which John Bold had left behind him. By degrees the visitors went, and Charlotte Stanhope and her brother were left together. He was sitting idly at the table scrawling caricatures of Barchester notables, then yawning, then turning over a book or two, and evidently at a loss how to kill his time without much labor.

"You haven't done much, Bertie, about getting any orders," said his sister.

"Orders!" said he. "Who on earth is there at Barchester to give one orders? Who among the people here could possibly think it worth his while to have his head done into marble?"

"Then you mean to give up your profession," said she.

"No, I don't," said he, going on with some absurd portrait of the Bishop. "Look at that, Lotte. Isn't it the little man all over, apron and all? I'd go on with my profession at once, as you call it, if the Governor would set me up with a studio in London. But as to sculpture at Barchester—I suppose half the people here don't know what a torso means."

"The Governor will not give you a shilling to start you in London," said Lotte. "Indeed, he can't give you what would be sufficient, for he has not got it. But you might start yourself very well, if you pleased."

"How the deuce am I to do it?" said he.

"To tell you the truth, Bertie, you'll never make a penny by any profession."

"That's what I often think myself," said he, not in the least offended. "Some men have a great gift of making money, but they can't spend it. Others can't put two shillings together, but they have a great talent for all sorts of outlay. I begin to think that my genius is wholly in the latter line."

"How do you mean to live, then?" asked the sister.

"I suppose I must regard myself as a young raven, and look for heavenly manna. Besides, we all got something when the Governor goes."

"Yes—you'll have enough to supply yourself with gloves and boots. I wonder, Bertie, at your indifference, that you, with your talents and personal advantages, should never try to settle yourself in life. I look forward with dread to the time when the Governor must go. Mother and Madeline and I—we shall be poor enough, but you will have absolutely nothing."

"Sufficient for the day is the evil thereof," said Bertie.

"Will you take my advice?" said his sister.

"*Cela dépend*," said the brother.

"Will you marry a wife with money?"

"At any rate," said he, "I won't marry one without. Wives with money ain't so easy to get nowadays, the parsons pick them all up."

"And a parson will pick up the wife I mean for you if you do not look quickly about it. The wife I mean is Mrs. Bold."

"Whew-w-w-w!" whistled Bertie. "A widow!"

"She is very beautiful," said Charlotte.

"With a son and heir all ready to my hand," said Bertie.

"A baby that will very likely die," said Charlotte.

"I don't see that," said Bertie. "But, however, he may live for me—I don't wish to kill him. Only it must be owned that a ready-made family is a drawback."

"There is only one after all," pleaded Charlotte.

"And that a very little one, as the maidservant said," rejoined Bertie.

"Beggars mustn't be choosers, Bertie. You can't have everything."

"God knows I am not unreasonable," said he, "nor yet opinionated, and if you'll arrange it all for me, Lotte, I'll marry the lady. Only mark this—the money must be sure, and the income at my own disposal, at any rate for the lady's life."

Charlotte was explaining to her brother that he must make love for himself if he meant to carry on the matter, and was encouraging him to do so by warm eulogiums on Eleanor's beauty, when the Signora was brought into the drawing-room. When at home, and subject to the gaze of none but her own family, she allowed herself to be dragged about by two persons, and her two bearers now deposited her on her sofa.

"Well, Madeline, so I'm going to be married," Bertie began as soon as the servants had withdrawn.

"There's no other foolish thing left that you haven't done," said Madeline, "and therefore you are quite right to try that."

"Oh, you think it's a foolish thing, do you?" said he. "There's Lotte advising me to marry by all means. But on such a subject your opinion ought to be the best—you have experience to guide you."

"Yes, I have," said Madeline, with a sort of harsh sadness in her tone which seemed to say—What is it to you if I am sad? I have never asked your sympathy.

Bertie was sorry when he saw that she was hurt by what he said, and he came and squatted on the floor close before her face to make his peace with her.

"Come, Mad, I was only joking, you know that. But in sober earnest Lotte is advising me to marry. She wants me to marry this Mrs. Bold. She's a widow with lots of tin, a fine baby, a beautiful complexion, and the George and Dragon hotel up in the High Street. By Jove, Lotte, if I marry her, I'll keep the public house myself—it's just the life to suit me."

"What?" said Madeline. "That vapid swarthy creature in the widow's cap, who looked as though her clothes had been stuck on her back with a pitchfork!" The Signora never allowed any woman to be beautiful.

"Instead of being vapid," said Lotte, "I call her a very lovely woman. She was by far the loveliest woman in the rooms the other night—that is, excepting you, Madeline."

Even the compliment did not soften the asperity of the maimed beauty. "Every woman is charming according to Lotte," she said. "I never knew an eye with so little true appreciation. In the first place, what woman on earth could look well in such a thing as that she had on her head?"

"Of course she wears a widow's cap, but she'll put that off when Bertie marries her."

"I don't see any of course in it," said Madeline. "The death of twenty husbands should not make me undergo such a penance. It is as much a relic of paganism as the sacrifice of a Hindu woman at the burning of her husband's body. If not so bloody, it is quite as barbarous, and quite as useless."

"But you don't blame her for that," said Bertie. "She does it because it's the custom of the country. People would think ill of her if she didn't do it."

"Exactly," said Madeline. "She is just one of those English nonentities who would tie her head up in a bag for three months every summer if her mother and her grandmother had tied up their heads before her. It would never occur to her to think whether there was any use in submitting to such a nuisance."

"It's very hard in a country like England for a young woman to set herself in opposition to prejudices of that sort," said the prudent Charlotte.

"What you mean is that it's very hard for a fool not to be a fool," said Madeline.

"But wearing a widow's cap won't lessen her fortune," said Charlotte.

"Or increase it," said Madeline. "Then why on earth does she do it?"

"But Lotte's object is to make her put it off," said Bertie.

"If it be true that she has got twelve hundred a year quite at her own disposal, and she be not utterly vulgar in her manners, I would advise you to marry her. I dare say she is to be had for the asking, and as you are not going to marry her for love, it doesn't much matter whether she is good-looking or not. As to your really marrying a woman for love, I don't believe *you* are fool enough for that."

"Oh, Madeline!" exclaimed her sister.

And "Oh, Charlotte!" said the other.

"You don't mean to say that no man can love a woman unless he be a fool?"

"I mean very much the same thing—that any man who is willing to sacrifice his interest to get possession of a pretty face is a fool. Pretty faces are to be had cheaper than that. I hate your mawkish sentimentality, Lotte. You know as well as I do in what way husbands and wives generally live together. You know how far the warmth of conjugal affection can withstand the trial of a bad dinner, of a rainy day, or of the least privation which poverty brings with it. You know what freedom a man claims for himself, what slavery he would exact from his wife if he could! And you know also how wives generally obey. Marriage means tyranny on one side and deceit on the other. I say that a man is a fool to sacrifice his interests for such a bargain. A woman, too generally, has no other way of living."

"But Bertie has no other way of living," said Charlotte.

"Then in God's name let him marry Mrs. Bold," said Madeline. And so it was settled between them.

But let the gentlehearted reader be under no apprehension whatsoever. It is not destined that Eleanor shall marry Mr. Slope or Bertie Stanhope.

CHAPTER XVI

BABY WORSHIP

"WELL, then, he's his own mother's own darling. Well, he shall—oh, oh—Mary, Mary—did you ever see? What am I to do? My naughty, naughty, naughty, naughty little Johnny." All these energetic exclamations were elicited by the delight of the mother in finding that her son was strong enough, and mischievous enough, to pull all her hair out from under her cap. "He's been and pulled down all Mamma's hair, and he's the naughtiest, naughtiest, naughtiest little man that ever, ever, ever, ever, ever——"

A regular service of baby worship was going on. Mary Bold was sitting on a low easy chair with the boy in her lap, and Eleanor was kneeling before the object of her idolatry. As she tried to cover up the little fellow's face with her long, glossy, dark-brown locks, and permitted him to pull them hither and thither as he would, she looked very beautiful in spite of the widow's cap which she still wore. There was a quiet, enduring, grateful sweetness about her face which grew so strongly upon those who knew her as to make the great praise of her beauty which came from her old friends appear marvelously exaggerated to those who were only slightly acquainted with her. Her loveliness was like that of many landscapes, which require to be often seen to be fully enjoyed. There was a depth of dark, clear brightness in her eyes which was lost upon a quick observer, a character about her mouth which only showed itself to those with whom she familiarly conversed, a glorious form of head the perfect symmetry of which required the eye of an artist for its appreciation. She had none of that dazzling brilliancy, of that voluptuous Rubens beauty, of that pearly whiteness and those vermilion tints, which immediately entranced with the power of a basilisk men who came within reach of Madeline Neroni. It was all but impossible to resist the Signora, but no one was called upon for any resistance toward Eleanor. You might begin to talk to her as though she were your sister, and it would not be till your head was on your pillow that the truth and intensity of her beauty would flash upon you, that the sweetness of her voice would come upon your ear. A sudden half-hour with the Neroni was like falling into a pit, an evening spent with Eleanor like an unexpected ramble in some quiet fields of asphodel.

"We'll cover him up till there sha'n't be a morsel of his little 'ittle 'ittle 'ittle nose to be seen," said the mother, stretching her streaming locks over the infant's face. The child screamed with delight, and kicked till Mary Bold was hardly able to hold him.

At this moment the door opened and Mr. Slope was announced. Up jumped Eleanor, and with a sudden quick motion of her hands pushed back her hair over her shoulders. It would have been perhaps better for her that she had not, for she thus showed more of her confusion than she would have done had she remained as she was. Mr. Slope, however, immediately recognized her loveliness, and thought to himself that irrespective of her fortune she would be an inmate that a man might well desire for his house, a partner for his bosom's care very well qualified to make care lie easy. Eleanor hurried out of the room to readjust her cap, muttering some unnecessary apology about her baby. And while she is gone we will briefly go back and state what had been hitherto the results of Mr. Slope's meditations on his scheme of matrimony.

His inquiries as to the widow's income had at any rate been so far successful as to induce him to determine to go on with the speculation. As regarded Mr. Harding, he had also resolved to do what he could without injury to himself. To Mrs. Proudie he determined not to speak on the matter, at least not at present. His object was to instigate a little rebellion on the part of the Bishop. He thought that such a state of things would be advisable, not only in respect to Messrs. Harding and Quiverful, but also in the affairs of the diocese generally. Mr. Slope was by no means of opinion that Dr. Proudie was fit to rule, but he conscientiously thought it wrong that his brother clergy should be subjected to petticoat government. He therefore made up his mind to infuse a little of his spirit into the Bishop, sufficient to induce him to oppose his wife, though not enough to make him altogether insubordinate.

He had therefore taken an opportunity of again speaking to his lordship about the hospital, and had endeavored to make it appear that after all it would be unwise to exclude Mr. Harding from the appointment. Mr. Slope, however, had a harder task than he had imagined. Mrs. Proudie, anxious to assume to herself as much as possible of the merit of patronage, had written to Mrs. Quiverful requesting her to call at the palace, and had then explained to that matron, with much mystery, condescension, and dignity, the good that was in store for her and her progeny. Indeed Mrs. Proudie had been so engaged at the very time that Mr. Slope had been doing the same with the husband at Puddingdale Vicarage, and had thus in a measure committed herself. The thanks, the humility, the gratitude, the surprise of Mrs. Quiverful had been very overpowering. She had all but embraced the knees of her patroness, and had promised that the prayers of fourteen unprovided babes (so Mrs. Quiverful had described her own family, the eldest of which was a stout young woman of three-and-twenty) should be put up to Heaven morning and evening for the munificent friend whom God had sent to them. Such incense as this was not unpleasing to Mrs. Proudie, and she made the most of it.

Having done this, she thought it prudent to drop a few words before the Bishop letting him know that she had acquainted the Puddingdale family with their good fortune, so that he might perceive that he stood committed to the appointment. The husband well understood the ruse of his wife, but he did not resent it. He knew that she was taking the patronage out of his hands. He was resolved to put an end to her interference, and reassume his powers. But then he thought this was not the best time to do it. He put off the evil hour, as many a man in similar circumstances has done before him.

Such having been the case, Mr. Slope naturally encountered a difficulty in talking over the Bishop, a difficulty indeed which he found could not be overcome except at the cost of a general outbreak at the palace. A general outbreak at the present moment might be good policy, but it also might not. It was at any rate not a step to be lightly taken. He began by whispering to the Bishop that he feared that public opinion would be against him if Mr. Harding did not reappear at the hospital. The Bishop answered with some warmth that Mr. Quiverful had been promised the appointment on Mr. Slope's advice. "Not promised!" said Mr. Slope. "Yes, promised," replied the Bishop, "and Mrs. Proudie has seen Mrs. Quiverful on the subject." This was quite unexpected on the part of Mr. Slope, but his presence of mind did not fail him, and he turned the statement to his own account.

"Ah, my lord," said he, "we shall all be in scrapes if the ladies interfere."

This was too much in unison with my lord's feelings to be altogether unpalatable, and yet such an allusion to interference demanded a rebuke. My lord was somewhat astounded also, though not altogether made miserable, by finding that there was a point of difference between his wife and his chaplain.

"I don't know what you mean by interference," said the Bishop mildly. "When Mrs. Proudie heard that Mr. Quiverful was to be appointed, it was not unnatural that she should wish to see Mrs. Quiverful about the schools. I really cannot say that I see any interference."

"I only speak, my lord, for your own comfort," said Slope, "for your own comfort and dignity in the diocese. I can have no other motive. As far as personal feelings go, Mrs. Proudie is the best friend I have. I must always remember that. But still, in my present position my first duty is to your lordship."

"I'm sure of that, Mr. Slope, I am quite sure of that," said the Bishop, mollified. "And you really think that Mr. Harding should have the hospital?"

"Upon my word, I'm inclined to think so. I am quite prepared to take upon myself the blame of first suggesting Mr. Quiverful's name. But since doing so, I have found that there is so strong a feeling in the diocese in favor of Mr. Harding that I think your lordship should give way. I hear also that Mr. Harding has modified the objections he first felt to your lordship's propositions. And as to what has passed between Mrs. Proudie and Mrs. Quiverful, the circumstance may be a little inconvenient, but I really do not think that that should weigh in a matter of so much moment."

And thus the poor Bishop was left in a dreadfully undecided state as to what he should do. His mind, however, slightly inclined itself to the appointment of Mr. Harding, seeing that by such a step he should have the assistance of Mr. Slope in opposing Mrs. Proudie.

Such was the state of affairs at the palace when Mr. Slope called at Mrs. Bold's house and found her playing with her baby. When she ran out of the room, Mr. Slope began praising the weather to Mary Bold, then he praised the baby and kissed him, and then he praised the mother, and then he praised Miss Bold herself. Mrs. Bold, however, was not long before she came back.

"I have to apologize for calling at so very early an hour," began Mr. Slope, "but I was really so anxious to speak to you that I hope you and Miss Bold will excuse me."

Eleanor muttered something in which the words "certainly," and "of course," and "not early at all" were just audible, and then apologized for her own appearance, declaring with a smile that her baby was becoming such a big boy that he was quite unmanageable.

"He's a great big naughty boy," said she to the child, "and we must send him away to a great big rough romping school, where they have great big rods, and do terrible things to naughty boys who don't do what their own mammas tell them."

"And where the masters don't have such beautiful long hair to be disheveled," said Mr. Slope, taking up the joke and paying a compliment at the same time.

Eleanor thought he might as well have left the compliment alone, but she said nothing and looked nothing, being occupied as she was with the baby.

"Let me take him," said Mary. "His clothes are nearly off his back with his romping." And so saying she left the room with the child. Miss Bold had heard Mr. Slope say he had something pressing to say to Eleanor, and thinking that she might be de trop, took this opportunity of getting herself out of the room.

"Don't be long, Mary," said Eleanor as Miss Bold shut the door.

"I am glad, Mrs. Bold, to have the opportunity of having ten minutes' conversation with you alone," began Mr. Slope. "Will you let me openly ask you a plain question?"

"Certainly," said she.

"And I am sure you will give me a plain and open answer."

"Either that or none at all," said she, laughing.

"My question is this, Mrs. Bold. Is your father really anxious to go back to the hospital?"

"Why do you ask me?" said she. "Why don't you ask himself?"

"My dear Mrs. Bold, I'll tell you why. There are wheels within wheels, all of which I would explain to you, only I fear that there is not time. It is essentially necessary that I should have an answer to this question. Otherwise I cannot know how to advance your father's wishes, and it is quite impossible that I should ask himself. No one can esteem your father more than I do, but I doubt if this feeling is reciprocal." It certainly was not. "I must be candid with you as the only means of avoiding ultimate consequences which may be most injurious to Mr. Harding. I fear there is a feeling, I will not even call it a prejudice, with regard to myself in Barchester which is not in my favor. You remember that sermon——"

"Oh, Mr. Slope, we need not go back to that!" said Eleanor.

"For one moment, Mrs. Bold. It is not that I may talk of myself, but because it is so essential that you should understand how matters stand. That sermon may have been ill-judged,—it was certainly misunderstood. But I will say nothing about that now—only this, that it did give rise to a feeling against myself which your father shares with others. It may be that he has proper cause, but the result is that he is not inclined to meet me on friendly terms. I put it to yourself whether you do not know this to be the case."

Eleanor made no answer, and Mr. Slope, in the eagerness of his address, edged his chair a little nearer to the widow's seat, unperceived by her.

"Such being so," continued Mr. Slope, "I cannot ask him this question as I can ask it of you. In spite of my delinquencies since I came to Barchester, you have allowed me to regard you as a friend." Eleanor made a little motion with her head which was hardly confirmatory, but Mr. Slope, if he noticed it, did not appear to do so. "To you I can speak openly, and explain the feelings of my heart. This your father would not allow. Unfortunately, the Bishop has thought it right that this matter of the hospital should pass through my hands. There have been some details to get up with which he would not trouble himself, and thus it has come to pass that I was forced to have an interview with your father on the matter."

"I am aware of that," said Eleanor.

"Of course," said he. "In that interview Mr. Harding left the impression on my mind that he did not wish to return to the hospital."

"How could that be?" said Eleanor, at last stirred up to forget the cold propriety of demeanor which she had determined to maintain.

"My dear Mrs. Bold, I give you my word that such was the case," said he, again getting a little nearer to her. "And what is more than that, before my interview with Mr. Harding certain persons at the palace—I do not mean the Bishop—had told me that such was the fact. I own I hardly believed it, I own I thought that your father would wish on every account, for conscience' sake, for the sake of those old men, for old association and the memory of dear days long gone by—on every account I thought that he would wish to resume his duties. But I was told that such was not his wish, and he certainly left me with the impression that I had been told the truth."

"Well!" said Eleanor, now sufficiently roused on the matter.

"I hear Miss Bold's step," said Mr. Slope. "Would it be asking too great a favor to beg you to—— I know you can manage anything with Miss Bold."

Eleanor did not like the word "manage," but still she went out and asked Mary to leave them alone for another quarter of an hour.

"Thank you, Mrs. Bold. I am so very grateful for this confidence. Well, I left your father with this impression. Indeed, I may say that he made me understand that he declined the appointment."

"Not the appointment," said Eleanor. "I am sure he did not decline the appointment. But he said that he would not agree—that is, that he did not like the scheme about the schools and the services, and all that. I am quite sure he never said that he wished to refuse the place."

"Oh, Mrs. Bold!" said Mr. Slope, in a manner almost impassioned. "I would not for the world say to so good a daughter a word against so good a father. But you must, for his sake, let me show you exactly how the matter stands at present. Mr. Harding was a little flurried when I told him of the Bishop's wishes about the school. I did so, perhaps, with the less caution because you yourself had so perfectly agreed with me on the same subject. He was a little put out and spoke warmly. 'Tell the Bishop,' said he, 'that I quite disagree with him—and shall not return to the hospital, as such conditions are attached to it.' What he said was to that effect. Indeed, his words were, if anything, stronger than those. I had no alternative but to repeat them to his lordship, who said that he could look on them in no other light than a refusal. He also had heard the report that your father did not wish for the appointment, and putting all these things together, he thought he had no choice but to look for someone else. He has consequently offered the place to Mr. Quiverful."

"Offered the place to Mr. Quiverful!" repeated Eleanor, her eyes suffused with tears. "Then, Mr. Slope, there is an end of it."

"No, my friend—not so," said he. "It is to prevent such being the end of it that I am now here. I may at any rate presume that I have got an answer to my question, and that Mr. Harding is desirous of returning."

"Desirous of returning—of course he is," said Eleanor. "Of course he wishes to have back his house and his income, and his place in the world, to have back what he gave up with such self-denying honesty, if he can have them without restraints on his conduct to which at his age it would be impossible that he should submit. How can the Bishop ask a man of his age to turn schoolmaster to a pack of children?"

"Out of the question," said Mr. Slope, laughing slightly. "Of course no such demand shall be made on your father. I can at any rate promise you that I will not be the medium of any so absurd a requisition. We wished your father to preach in the hospital, as the inmates may naturally be too old to leave it, but even that shall not be insisted on. We wished also to attach a Sabbath-day school to the hospital, thinking that such an establishment could not but be useful under the surveillance of so good a clergyman as Mr. Harding, and also under your own. But, dear Mrs. Bold, we won't talk of these things now. One thing is clear: We must do what we can to annul this rash offer the Bishop has made to Mr. Quiverful. Your father wouldn't see Quiverful, would he? Quiverful is an honorable man, and would not for a moment stand in your father's way."

"What?" said Eleanor. "Ask a man with fourteen children to give up his preferment! I am quite sure he will do no such thing."

"I suppose not," said Slope, and he again drew near to Mrs. Bold, so that now they were very close to each other. Eleanor did not think much about it, but instinctively moved away a little. How greatly would she have increased the distance could she have guessed what had been said about her at Plumstead! "I suppose not. But it is out of the question that Quiverful could supersede your father—quite out of the question. The Bishop has been too rash. An idea occurs to me which may perhaps, with God's blessing, put us right. My dear Mrs. Bold, would you object to seeing the Bishop yourself?"

"Why should not my father see him?" said Eleanor. She had once before in her life interfered in her father's affairs, and then not to much advantage. She was older now, and felt that she should take no step in a matter so vital to him without his consent.

"Why, to tell the truth," said Mr. Slope, with a look of sorrow as though he greatly bewailed the want of charity in his patron, "the Bishop fancies that he has cause of anger against your father. I fear an interview would lead to further ill will."

"Why," said Eleanor, "my father is the mildest, the gentlest man living."

"I only know," said Slope, "that he has the best of daughters. So you would not see the Bishop? As to getting an interview, I could manage that for you without the slightest annoyance to yourself."

"I could do nothing, Mr. Slope, without consulting my father."

"Ah," said he, "that would be useless. You would then only be your father's messenger. Does anything occur to yourself? Something must be done. Your father shall not be ruined by so ridiculous a misunderstanding."

Eleanor said that nothing occurred to her, but that it was very hard, and the tears came to her eyes and rolled down her cheeks. Mr. Slope would have given much to have had the privilege of drying them, but he had tact enough to know that he had still a great deal to do before he could even hope for any privilege with Mrs. Bold.

"It cuts me to the heart to see you so grieved," said he. "But pray let me assure you that your father's interests shall not be sacrificed if it be possible for me to protect them. I will tell the Bishop openly what are the facts. I will explain to him that he has hardly the right to appoint any other than your father, and will show him that if he does so he will be guilty of great injustice. And you, Mrs. Bold, will have the charity at any rate to believe this of me, that I am truly anxious for your father's welfare—for his and for your own."

The widow hardly knew what answer to make. She was quite aware that her father would not be at all thankful to Mr. Slope, she had a strong wish to share her father's feelings, and yet she could not but acknowledge that Mr. Slope was very kind. Her father, who was generally so charitable to all men, who seldom spoke ill of anyone, had warned her against Mr. Slope, and yet she did not know how to abstain from thanking him. What interest could he have in the matter but that which he professed? Nevertheless there was that in his manner which even she distrusted. She felt, she did not know why, that there was something about him which ought to put her on her guard.

Mr. Slope read all this in her hesitating manner just as plainly as though she had opened her heart to him. It was the talent of the man that he could so read the inward feelings of women with whom he conversed. He knew that Eleanor was doubting him, and that if she thanked him she would only do so because she could not help it, but yet this did not make him angry or even annoy him. Rome was not built in a day.

"I did not come for thanks," continued he, seeing her hesitation, "and do not want them—at any rate before they are merited. But this I do want, Mrs. Bold, that I may make to myself friends in this fold to which it has pleased God to call me as one of the humblest of His shepherds. If I cannot do so, my task here must indeed be a sad one. I will at any rate endeavor to deserve them."

"I'm sure," said she, "you will soon make plenty of friends." She felt herself obliged to say something.

"That will be nothing unless they are such as will sympathize with my feelings, unless they are such as I can reverence and admire—and love. If the best and purest turn away from me, I cannot bring myself to be satisfied with the friendship of the less estimable. In such case I must live alone."

"Oh, I'm sure you will not do that, Mr. Slope!" Eleanor meant nothing, but it suited him to appear to think some special allusion had been intended.

"Indeed, Mrs. Bold, I shall live alone, quite alone as far as the heart is concerned, if those with whom I yearn to ally myself turn away from me. But enough of this. I have called you my friend, and I hope you will not contradict me. I trust the time may come when I may also call your father so. May God bless you, Mrs. Bold, you and your darling boy. And tell your father from me that what can be done for his interest shall be done."

And so he took his leave, pressing the widow's hand rather more closely than usual. Circumstances, however, seemed just then to make this intelligible, and the lady did not feel called on to resent it.

"I cannot understand him," said Eleanor to Mary Bold a few minutes afterward. "I do not know whether he is a good man or a bad man—whether he is true or false."

"Then give him the benefit of the doubt," said Mary, "and believe the best."

"On the whole, I think I do," said Eleanor. "I think I do believe that he means well—and if so, it is a shame that we should revile him and make him miserable while he is among us. But, oh, Mary, I fear Papa will be disappointed in the hospital."

CHAPTER XVII

WHO SHALL BE COCK OF THE WALK?

ALL this time things were going on somewhat uneasily at the palace. The hint or two which Mr. Slope had given was by no means thrown away upon the Bishop. He had a feeling that if he ever meant to oppose the now almost unendurable despotism of his wife, he must lose no further time in doing so, that if he ever meant to be himself master in his own diocese, let alone his own house, he should begin at once. It would have been easier to have done so from the day of his consecration than now, but easier now than when Mrs. Proudie should have succeeded in thoroughly mastering the diocesan details. Then the proffered assistance of Mr. Slope was a great thing for him, a most unexpected and invaluable aid. Hitherto he had looked on the two as allied forces, and had considered that as allies they were impregnable. He had begun to believe that his only chance of escape would be by the advancement of Mr. Slope to some distant and rich preferment. But now it seemed that one of his enemies, certainly the least potent of them but nevertheless one very important, was willing to desert his own camp. Assisted by Mr. Slope, what might he not do? He walked up and down his little study, almost thinking that the time might come when he would be able to appropriate to his own use the big room upstairs in which his predecessor had always sat.

As he revolved these things in his mind a note was brought to him from Archdeacon Grantly in which that divine begged his lordship to do him the honor of seeing him on the morrow—would his lordship have the kindness to name an hour? Dr. Grantly's proposed visit would have reference to the reappointment of Mr. Harding to the wardenship of Barchester Hospital. The Bishop, having read his note, was informed that the Archdeacon's servant was waiting for an answer.

Here at once a great opportunity offered itself to the Bishop of acting on his own responsibility. He bethought himself however of his new ally, and rang the bell for Mr. Slope. It turned out that Mr. Slope was not in the house, and then, greatly daring, the Bishop with his own unassisted spirit wrote a note to the Archdeacon saying that he would see him, and naming an hour for doing so. Having watched from his study window that the messenger got safely off from the premises with this dispatch, he began to turn over in his mind what step he should next take.

Tomorrow he would have to declare to the Archdeacon either that Mr. Harding should have the appointment or that he should not have it. The Bishop felt that he could not honestly throw over the Quiverfuls without informing Mrs. Proudie, and he resolved at last to brave the lioness in her den and tell her that circumstances were such that it behooved him to reappoint Mr. Harding. He did not feel that he should at all derogate from his new courage by promising Mrs. Proudie that the very first piece of available preferment at his disposal should be given to Quiverful to atone for the injury done to him. If he could mollify the lioness with such a sop, how happy would he think his first efforts to have been!

Not without many misgivings did he find himself in Mrs. Proudie's boudoir. He had at first thought of sending for her. But it was not at all impossible that she might choose to take such a message amiss, and then also it might be some protection to him to have his daughters present at the interview. He found her sitting with her account books before her nibbling the end of her pencil, evidently mersed in pecuniary difficulties, and harassed in mind by the multiplicity of palatial expenses and the heavy cost of episcopal grandeur. Her daughters were around her. If the Bishop could get the better of his wife in her present mood, he would be a man indeed. He might then consider the victory his own forever. After all, in such cases the matter between husband and wife stands much the same as it does between two boys at the same school, two cocks in the same yard, or two armies on the same continent. The conquerer once is generally the conqueror forever after. The prestige of victory is everything.

"Ahem—my dear," began the Bishop, "if you are disengaged, I wished to speak to you." Mrs. Proudie put her pencil down carefully at the point to which she had dotted her figures, marked down in her memory the sum she had arrived at, and then looked up, sourly enough, into her helpmate's face. "If you are busy, another time will do as well," continued the Bishop, whose courage, like Bob Acres', had oozed out now that he found himself on the ground of battle.

"What is it about, Bishop?" asked the lady.

"Well, it was about those Quiverfuls—but I see you are engaged. Another time will do just as well for me."

"What about the Quiverfuls? It is quite understood, I believe, that they are to come to the hospital. There is to be no doubt about that, is there?"

"Why, my dear, there is a difficulty," said the Bishop.

"A difficulty!" said Mrs. Proudie. "What difficulty? The place has been promised to Mr. Quiverful, and of course he must have it. He has made all his arrangements. He has written for a curate for Puddingdale, he has spoken to the auctioneer about selling his farm, horses, and cows, and in all respects considers the place as his own. Of course he must have it."

Now, Bishop, look well to thyself, and call up all the manhood that is in thee. Think how much is at stake. If now thou art not true to thy guns, no Slope can hereafter aid thee. How can he who deserts his own colors at the first smell of gunpowder expect faith in any ally? Thou thyself hast sought the battlefield. Fight out the battle manfully now thou art there. Courage, Bishop, courage! Frowns cannot kill, nor can sharp words break any bones. After all the apron is thine own. She can appoint no wardens, give away no benefices, nominate no chaplains, an thou art but true to thyself. Up, man, and at her with a constant heart.

Some little monitor within the Bishop's breast so addressed him. But then there was another monitor there which advised him differently, and as follows. Remember, Bishop, she is a woman, and such a woman too as thou well knowest. A battle of words with such a woman is the very mischief. Were it not better for thee to carry on this war, if it must be waged, from behind thine own table in thine own study? Does not every cock fight best on his own dunghill? Thy daughters also are here, the pledges of thy love, the fruits of thy loins. Is it well that they should see thee in the hour of thy victory over their mother? Nay, is it well that they should see thee in the possible hour of thy defeat? Besides, hast thou not chosen thy opportunity with wonderful little skill, indeed with no touch of that sagacity for which thou art famous? Will it not turn out that thou art wrong in this matter, and thine enemy right, that thou hast actually pledged thyself in this matter of the hospital, and that now thou wouldest turn upon thy wife because she requires from thee but the fulfillment of thy promise? Art thou not a Christian bishop, and is not thy word to be held sacred whatever be the result? Return, Bishop, to thy sanctum on the lower floor, and postpone thy combative propensities for some occasion in which at least thou mayest fight the battle against odds less tremendously against thee.

All this passed within the Bishop's bosom while Mrs. Proudie still sat with her fixed pencil, and the figures of her sum still enduring on the tablets of her memory. "£4 17s. 7d.," she said to herself. "Of course Mr. Quiverful must have the hospital," she said out loud to her lord.

"Well, my dear, I merely wanted to suggest to you that Mr. Slope seems to think that if Mr. Harding be not appointed, public feeling in the matter would be against us, and that the press might perhaps take it up."

"Mr. Slope seems to think!" said Mrs. Proudie, in a tone of voice which plainly showed the Bishop that he was right in looking for a breach in that quarter. "And what has Mr. Slope to do with it? I hope, my lord, you are not going to allow yourself to be governed by a chaplain." And now in her eagerness the lady lost her place in her account.

"Certainly not, my dear. Nothing I can assure you is less probable. But still Mr. Slope may be useful in finding how the wind blows, and I really thought that if we could give something else as good to the Quiverfuls——"

"Nonsense," said Mrs. Proudie. "It would be years before you could give them anything else that could suit them half as well, and as for the press and the public and all that, remember there are two ways of telling a story. If Mr. Harding is fool enough to tell his tale, we can also tell ours. The place was offered to him, and he refused it. It has now been given to someone else, and there's an end of it. At least I should think so."

"Well, my dear, I rather believe you are right," said the Bishop, and sneaking out of the room, he went downstairs troubled in his mind as to how he should receive the Archdeacon on the morrow. He felt himself not very well just at present, and began to consider that he might, not improbably, be detained in his room the next morning by an attack of bile. He was, unfortunately, very subject to bilious annoyances.

"Mr. Slope, indeed! I'll Slope him," said the indignant matron to her listening progeny. "I don't know what has come to Mr. Slope. I believe he thinks he is to be Bishop of Barchester himself because I've taken him by the hand and got your father to make him his domestic chaplain."

"He was always full of impudence," said Olivia. "I told you so once before, Mamma." Olivia, however, had not thought him too impudent when once before he had proposed to make her Mrs. Slope.

"Well, Olivia, I always thought you liked him," said Augusta, who at that moment had some grudge against her sister. "I always disliked the man, because I think him thoroughly vulgar."

"There you're wrong," said Mrs. Proudie. "He's not vulgar at all, and what is more, he is a soul-stirring, eloquent preacher. But he must be taught to know his place if he is to remain in this house."

When Mr. Slope got home he soon learnt from the Bishop, as much from his manner as his words, that Mrs. Proudie's behests in the matter of the hospital were to be obeyed. Dr. Proudie let fall something as to "this occasion only," and "keeping all affairs about patronage exclusively in his own hands." But he was quite decided about Mr. Harding, and as Mr. Slope did not wish to have both the prelate and the prelatess against him, he did not at present see that he could do anything but yield.

He merely remarked that he would of course carry out the Bishop's views, and that he was quite sure that if the Bishop trusted to his own judgment things in the diocese would certainly be well ordered. Mr. Slope knew that if you hit a nail on the head often enough, it will penetrate at last.

He was sitting alone in his room on the same evening when a light knock was made on his door, and before he could answer it the door was opened and his patroness appeared. He was all smiles in a moment, but so was not she also. She took, however, the chair that was offered to her, and thus began her expostulations:

"Mr. Slope, I did not at all approve your conduct the other night with that Italian woman. Anyone would have thought that you were her lover."

"Good gracious, my dear madam," said Mr. Slope, with a look of horror. "Why, she is a married woman."

"That's more than I know," said Mrs. Proudie. "However, she chooses to pass for such. But married or not married, such attention as you paid to her was improper. I cannot believe that you would wish to give offense in my drawing-room, Mr. Slope, but I owe it to myself and my daughters to tell you that I disapprove your conduct."

Mr. Slope opened wide his huge protruding eyes and stared out of them with a look of well-feigned surprise. "Why, Mrs. Proudie," said he, "I did but fetch her something to eat when she said she was hungry."

"And you have called on her since," continued she, looking at the culprit with the stern look of a detective policeman in the act of declaring himself.

Mr. Slope turned over in his mind whether it would be well for him to tell this termagant at once that he should call on whom he liked and do what he liked, but he remembered that his footing in Barchester was not yet sufficiently firm, and that it would be better for him to pacify her.

"I certainly called since at Dr. Stanhope's house, and certainly saw Madame Neroni."

"Yes, and you saw her alone," said the episcopal Argus.

"Undoubtedly I did," said Mr. Slope, "but that was because nobody else happened to be in the room. Surely it was no fault of mine if the rest of the family were out."

"Perhaps not, but I assure you, Mr. Slope, you will fall greatly in my estimation if I find that you allow yourself to be caught by the lures of that woman. I know women better than you do, Mr. Slope, and you may believe me that that Signora, as she calls herself, is not a fitting companion for a strict evangelical unmarried, young clergyman."

How Mr. Slope would have liked to laugh at her had he dared! But he did not dare. So he merely said, "I can assure you, Mrs. Proudie, the lady in question is nothing to me."

"Well, I hope not, Mr. Slope. But I have considered it my duty to give you this caution. And now there is another thing I feel myself called on to speak about. It is your conduct to the Bishop, Mr. Slope."

"My conduct to the Bishop," said he, now truly surprised and ignorant what the lady alluded to.

"Yes, Mr. Slope, your conduct to the Bishop. It is by no means what I would wish to see it."

"Has the Bishop said anything, Mrs. Proudie?"

"No, the Bishop has said nothing. He probably thinks that any remarks on the matter would come better from me, who first introduced you to his lordship's notice. The fact is, Mr. Slope, you are a little inclined to take too much upon yourself."

An angry spot showed itself on Mr. Slope's cheeks, and it was with difficulty that he controlled himself. But he did do so, and sat quite silent while the lady went on.

"It is the fault of many young men in your position, and therefore the Bishop is not inclined at present to resent it. You will no doubt soon learn what is required from you, and what is not. If you will take my advice, however, you will be careful not to obtrude advice upon the Bishop in any matter touching patronage. If his lordship wants advice, he knows where to look for it." And then, having added to her counsel a string of platitudes as to what was desirable and what not desirable in the conduct of a strictly evangelical unmarried young clergyman, Mrs. Proudie retreated, leaving the chaplain to his thoughts.

The upshot of his thoughts was this, that there certainly was not room in the diocese for the energies of both himself and Mrs. Proudie, and that it behooved him quickly to ascertain whether his energies or hers were to prevail.

CHAPTER XVIII

EARLY on the following morning Mr. Slope was summoned to the Bishop's dressing-room, and went there fully expecting that he should find his lordship very indignant, and spirited up by his wife to repeat the rebuke which she had administered on the previous day. Mr. Slope had resolved that at any rate from him he would not stand it, and entered the dressing-room in rather a combative disposition, but he found the Bishop in the most placid and gentlest of humors. His lordship complained of being rather unwell, had a slight headache, and was not quite the thing in his stomach, but there was nothing the matter with his temper.

"Oh, Slope," said he, taking the chaplain's proffered hand, "Archdeacon Grantly is to call on me this morning, and I really am not fit to see him. I fear I must trouble you to see him for me." And then Dr. Proudie proceeded to explain what it was that must be said to Dr. Grantly. He was to be told, in fact, in the civilest words in which the tidings could be conveyed, that Mr. Harding having refused the wardenship, the appointment had been offered to Mr. Quiverful and accepted by him.

Mr. Slope again pointed out to his patron that he thought he was perhaps not quite wise in his decision, and this he did sotto voce. But even with this precaution it was not safe to say much, and during the little that he did say, the Bishop made a very slight but still a very ominous gesture with his thumb toward the door which opened from his dressing-room to some inner sanctuary. Mr. Slope at once took the hint, and said no more, but he perceived that there was to be confidence between him and his patron, that the league desired by him was to be made, and that this appointment of Mr. Quiverful was to be the last sacrifice offered on the altar of conjugal obedience. All this Mr. Slope read in the slight motion of the Bishop's thumb, and he read it correctly. There was no need of parchments and seals, of attestations, explanations, and professions. The bargain was understood between them, and Mr. Slope gave the Bishop his hand upon it. The Bishop understood the little extra squeeze, and an intelligible gleam of assent twinkled in his eye.

"Pray be civil to the Archdeacon, Mr. Slope," said he out loud, "but make him quite understand that in this matter Mr. Harding has put it out of my power to oblige him."

It would be calumny on Mrs. Proudie to suggest that she was sitting in her bedroom with her ear at the keyhole during this interview. She had within her a spirit of decorum which prevented her from descending to such baseness. To put her ear to a keyhole or to listen at a chink was a trick for a housemaid. Mrs. Proudie knew this, and therefore she did not do it, but she stationed hrself as near to the door as she well could, that she might, if possible, get the advantage which the housemaid would have had without descending to the housemaid's artifice.

It was little, however, that she heard, and that little was only sufficient to deceive her. She saw nothing of that friendly pressure, perceived nothing of that concluded bargain. She did not even dream of the treacherous resolves which those two false men had made together to upset her in the pride of her station, to dash the cup from her lip before she had drank of it, to sweep away all her power before she had tasted its sweets! Traitors that they were, the husband of her bosom and the outcast whom she had fostered and brought to the warmth of the world's brightest fireside! But neither of them had the magnanimity of this woman. Though two men have thus leagued themselves together against her, even yet the battle is not lost.

Mr. Slope felt pretty sure that Dr. Grantly would decline the honor of seeing him, and such turned out to be the case. The Archdeacon, when the palace door was opened to him, was greeted by a note. Mr. Slope presented his compliments, &c. &c. The Bishop was ill in his room, and very greatly regretted, &c. &c. Mr. Slope had been charged with the Bishop's views, and if agreeable to the Archdeacon, would do himself the honor, &c. &c. The Archdeacon, however, was not agreeable, and having read his note in the hall, crumpled it up in his hand, and muttering something about sorrow for his lordship's illness, took his leave without sending as much as a verbal message in answer to Mr. Slope's note.

"Ill!" said the Archdeacon to himself as he flung himself into his brougham. "The man is absolutely a coward. He is afraid to see me. Ill, indeed!" The Archdeacon was never ill himself, and did not therefore understand that anyone else could in truth be prevented by illness from keeping an appointment. He regarded all such excuses as subterfuges, and in the present instance he was not far wrong.

Dr. Grantly desired to be driven to his father-in-law's lodgings in the High Street, and hearing from the servant that Mr. Harding was at his daughter's, followed him to Mrs. Bold's house, and there found him. The Archdeacon was fuming with rage when he got into the drawing-room, and had by this time nearly forgotten the pusillanimity of the Bishop in the villainy of the chaplain.

"Look at that," said he, throwing Mr. Slope's crumpled note to Mr. Harding. "I am to be told that if I choose I may have the honor of seeing Mr. Slope, and that too after a positive engagement with the Bishop."

"But he says the Bishop is ill," said Mr. Harding.

"Pshaw! You don't mean to say that you are deceived by such an excuse as that. He was well enough yesterday. Now I tell you what, I will see the Bishop, and I will tell him also very plainly what I think of his conduct. I will see him, or else Barchester will soon be too hot to hold him."

Eleanor was sitting in the room, but Dr. Grantly had hardly noticed her in his anger. Eleanor now said to him, with the greatest innocence: "I wish you had seen Mr. Slope, Dr. Grantly, because I think perhaps it might have done good."

The Archdeacon turned on her with almost brutal wrath. Had she at once owned that she had accepted Mr. Slope for her second husband, he could hardly have felt more convinced of her belonging body and soul to the Slope and Proudie party then he now did on hearing her express such a wish as this. Poor Eleanor!

"See him!" said the Archdeacon, glaring at her. "And why am I to be called on to lower myself in the world's esteem and my own by coming in contact with such a man as that? I have hitherto lived among gentlemen, and do not mean to be dragged into other company by anybody."

Poor Mr. Harding well knew what the Archdeacon meant, but Eleanor was as innocent as her own baby. She could not understand how the Archdeacon could consider himself to be dragged into bad company by condescending to speak to Mr. Slope for a few minutes when the interests of her father might be served by his doing so.

"I was talking for a full hour yesterday to Mr. Slope," said she, with some little assumption of dignity, "and I did not find myself lowered by it."

"Perhaps not," said he. "But if you'll be good enough to allow me, I shall judge for myself in such matters. And I tell you what, Eleanor, it will be much better for you if you will allow yourself to be guided also by the advice of those who are your friends. If you do not you will be apt to find that you have no friends left who can advise you."

Eleanor blushed up to the roots of her hair. But even now she had not the slightest idea of what was passing in the Archdeacon's mind. No thought of love-making or love-receiving had yet found its way to her heart since the death of poor John Bold, and if it were possible that such a thought should spring there, the man must be far different from Mr. Slope that could give it birth.

Nevertheless Eleanor blushed deeply, for she felt she was charged with improper conduct, and she did so with the more inward pain because her father did not instantly rally to her side—that father for whose sake and love she had submitted to be the receptacle of Mr. Slope's confidence. She had given a detailed account of all that had passed to her father, and though he had not absolutely agreed with her about Mr. Slope's views touching the hospital, yet he had said nothing to make her think that she had been wrong in talking to him.

She was far too angry to humble herself before her brother-in-law. Indeed, she had never accustomed herself to be very abject before him, and they had never been confidential allies. "I do not the least understand what you mean, Dr. Grantly," said she. "I do not know that I can accuse myself of doing anything that my friends should disapprove. Mr. Slope called here expressly to ask what Papa's wishes were about the hospital, and as I believe he called with friendly intentions I told him."

"Friendly intentions!" sneered the Archdeacon.

"I believe you greatly wrong Mr. Slope," continued Eleanor, "but I have explained this to Papa already, and as you do not seem to approve of what I say, Dr. Grantly, I will with your permission leave you and Papa together." And so saying she walked slowly out of the room.

All this made Mr. Harding very unhappy. It was quite clear that the Archdeacon and his wife had made up their minds that Eleanor was going to marry Mr. Slope. Mr. Harding could not really bring himself to think that she would do so, but yet he could not deny that circumstances made it appear that the man's company was not disagreeable to her. She was now constantly seeing him, and yet she received visits from no other unmarried gentleman. She always took his part when his conduct was canvassed, although she was aware how personally objectionable he was to her friends. Then again, Mr. Harding felt that if she should choose to become Mrs. Slope, he had nothing that he could justly urge against her doing so. She had full right to please herself, and he, as a father, could not say that she would disgrace herself by marrying a clergyman who stood so well before the world as Mr. Slope did. As for quarreling with his daughter on account of such a marriage, and separating himself from her as the Archdeacon had threatened to do, that with Mr. Harding would be out of the question. If she should determine to marry this man, he must get over his aversion as best he could. His Eleanor, his own old companion in their old happy home, must still be the friend of his bosom, the child of his heart. Let who would cast her off, he would not. If it were fated that he should have to sit in his old age at the same table with that man whom of all men he disliked the most, he would meet his fate as best he might. Anything to him would be preferable to the loss of his daughter.

Such being his feelings, he hardly knew how to take part with Eleanor against the Archdeacon, or with the Archdeacon against Eleanor. It will be said that he should never have suspected her. Alas! he never should have done so. But Mr. Harding was by no means a perfect character. In his indecision, his weakness, his proneness to be led by others, his want of self-confidence, he was very far from being perfect. And then it must be remembered that such a marriage as that which the Archdeacon contemplated with disgust, which we who know Mr. Slope so well would regard with equal disgust, did not appear so monstrous to Mr. Harding, because in his charity he did not hate the chaplain as the Archdeacon did, and as we do.

He was, however, very unhappy when his daughter left the room, and he had recourse to an old trick of his that was customary to him in his times of sadness. He began playing some slow tune upon some imaginary violoncello, drawing one hand slowly backward and forward as though he held a bow in it, and modulating the unreal chords with the other.

"She'll marry that man as sure as two and two make four," said the practical Archdeacon.

"I hope not, I hope not," said the father. "But if she does, what can I say to her? I have no right to object to him."

"No right!" exclaimed Dr. Grantly.

"No right as her father. He is in my own profession, and for aught we we know a good man."

To this the Archdeacon would by no means assent. It was not well, however, to argue the case against Eleanor in her own drawing-room, and so they both walked forth and discussed the matter in all its bearings under the elm trees of the close. Mr. Harding also explained to his son-in-law what had been the purport, at any rate the alleged purport, of Mr. Slope's last visit to the widow. He, however, stated that he could not bring himself to believe that Mr. Slope had any real anxiety such as that he had pretended. "I cannot forget his demeanor to myself," said Mr. Harding, "and it is not possible that his ideas should have changed so soon."

"I see it all," said the Archdeacon. "The sly Tartuffe! He thinks to buy the daughter by providing for the father. He means to show how powerful he is, how good he is, and how much he is willing to do for her beaux yeux. Yes, I see it all now. But we'll be too many for him yet, Mr. Harding," he said, turning to his companion with some gravity and pressing his hand upon the other's arm. "It would perhaps be better for you to lose the hospital than get it on such terms."

"Lose it!" said Mr. Harding. "Why, I've lost it already. I don't want it. I've made up my mind to do without it. I'll withdraw altogether. I'll just go and write a line to the Bishop and tell him that I withdraw my claim altogether."

Nothing would have pleased him better than to be allowed to escape from the trouble and difficulty in such a manner. But he was now going too fast for the Archdeacon.

"No—no—no! We'll do no such thing," said Dr. Grantly. "We'll still have the hospital. I hardly doubt but that we'll have it. But not by Mr. Slope's assistance. If that be necessary, we'll lose it, but we'll have it, spite of his teeth, if we can. Arabin will be at Plumstead tomorrow. You must come over and talk to him."

The two now turned into the cathedral library, which was used by the clergymen of the close as a sort of ecclesiastical clubroom, for writing sermons and sometimes letters, also for reading theological works, and sometimes magazines and newspapers. The theological works were not disturbed, perhaps, quite as often as from the appearance of the building the outside public might have been led to expect. Here the two allies settled on their course of action. The Archdeacon wrote a letter to the Bishop, strongly worded but still respectful, in which he put forward his father-in-law's claim to the appointment and expressed his own regret that he had not been able to see his lordship when he called. Of Mr. Slope he made no mention whatsoever. It was then settled that Mr. Harding should go out to Plumstead on the following day, and after considerable discussion on the matter, the Archdeacon proposed to ask Eleanor there also, so as to withdraw her, if possible, from Mr. Slope's attentions. "A week or two," said he, "may teach her what he is, and while she is there she will be out of harm's way. Mr. Slope won't come there after her."

Eleanor was not a little surprised when her brother-in-law came back and very civilly pressed her to go out to Plumstead with her father. She instantly perceived that her father had been fighting her battles for her behind her back. She felt thankful to him, and for his sake she would not show her resentment to the Archdeacon by refusing his invitation. But she could not, she said, go on the morrow. She had an invitation to drink tea at the Stanhopes which she had promised to accept. She would, she added, go with her father on the next day; if he would wait, or she would follow him.

"The Stanhopes!" said Dr. Grantly. "I did not know you were so intimate with them."

"I did not know it myself," said she, "till Miss Stanhope called yesterday. However, I like her very much, and I have promised to go and play chess with some of them."

"Have they a party there?" said the Archdeacon, still fearful of Mr. Slope.

"Oh, no," said Eleanor. "Miss Stanhope said there was to be nobody at all. But she had heard that Mary had left me for a few weeks, and she had learnt from someone that I play chess, and so she came over on purpose to ask me to go in."

"Well, that's very friendly," said the ex-Warden. "They certainly do look more like foreigners than English people, but I dare say they are none the worse for that."

The Archdeacon was inclined to look upon the Stanhopes with favorable eyes, and had nothing to object on the matter. It was therefore arranged that Mr. Harding should postpone his visit to Plumstead for one day, and then take with him Eleanor, the baby, and the nurse.

Mr. Slope is certainly becoming of some importance in Barchester.

CHAPTER XIX

MR. ARABIN

THE Reverend Francis Arabin, fellow of Lazarus, late professor of poetry at Oxford, and present Vicar of St. Ewold in the diocese of Barchester, must now be introduced personally to the reader. Of his doings in the world, and of the sort of fame which he has achieved, enough has been already said. It has also been said that he is forty years of age, and still unmarried. He was the younger son of a country gentleman of small fortune in the north of England. At an early age he went to Winchester, and was intended by his father for New College. But though studious as a boy, he was not studious within the prescribed limits, and at the age of eighteen he left school with a character for talent, but without a scholarship.

From Winchester he went to Oxford, and was entered as a commoner at Balliol. Here his special career very soon commenced. He utterly eschewed the society of fast men, gave no wine parties, kept no horses, rowed no boats, joined no rows, and was the pride of his college tutor. Such at least was his career till he had taken his little go, and then he commenced a course of action which, though not less creditable to himself as a man, was hardly so much to the taste of the tutor. He became a member of a vigorous debating society, and rendered himself remarkable there for humorous energy. Though always in earnest, yet his earnestness was always droll. To be true in his ideas, unanswerable in his syllogisms, and just in his aspirations was not enough for him. He had failed, failed in his own opinion as well as that of others when others came to know him, if he could not reduce the arguments of his opponents to an absurdity, and conquer both by wit and reason. To say that his object was ever to raise a laugh would be most untrue. He hated such common and unnecessary evidence of satisfaction on the part of his hearers. A joke that required to be laughed at was, with him, not worth uttering. He could appreciate by a keener sense than that of his ears the success of his wit, and would see in the eyes of his auditory whether or no he was understood and appreciated.

He had been a religious lad before he left school. That is, he had addicted himself to a party in religion, and having done so had received that benefit which most men do who become partisans in such a cause. As a boy young Arabin took up the cudgels on the side of the Tractarians, and at Oxford he sat for a while at the feet of the great Newman. To this cause he lent all his faculties. For it he concocted verses, for it he made speeches, for it he scintillated the brightest sparks of his quiet wit. For it he ate and drank and dressed, and had his being. In due process of time he took his degree and wrote himself B.A., but he did not do so with any remarkable amount of academical éclat. He had occupied himself too much with High Church matters, and the polemics, politics, and outward demonstrations usually concurrent with High Churchmanship, to devote himself with sufficient vigor to the acquisition of a double first. He was not a double first, nor even a first-class man; but he revenged himself on the university by putting firsts and double firsts out of fashion for the year, and laughing down a species of pedantry which at the age of twenty-three leaves no room in a man's mind for graver subjects than conic sections or Greek accents.

Greek accents, however, and conic sections were esteemed necessaries at Balliol, and there was no admittance there for Mr. Arabin within the list of its fellows. Lazarus, however, the richest and most comfortable abode of Oxford dons, opened its bosom to the young champion of a Church Militant. Mr. Arabin was ordained, and became a fellow soon after taking his degree, and shortly after that was chosen professor of poetry.

And now came the moment of his great danger. After many mental struggles, and an agony of doubt which may be well surmised, the great prophet of the Tractarians confessed himself a Roman Catholic. Mr. Newman left the Church of England, and with him carried many a waverer. He did not carry off Mr. Arabin, but the escape which that gentleman had was a very narrow one. He left Oxford for a while that he might meditate in complete peace on the step which appeared to him to be all but unavoidable, and shut himself up in a little village on the seashore of one of our remotest counties, that he might learn by communing with his own soul whether or no he could with a safe conscience remain within the pale of his Mother Church.

Things would have gone badly with him there had he been left entirely to himself. Everything was against him. All his worldly interests required him to remain a Protestant, and he looked on his worldly interests as a legion of foes, to get the better of whom was a point of extremest honor. In his then state of ecstatic agony such a conquest would have cost him little, he could easily have thrown away all his livelihood, but it cost him much to get over the idea that by choosing the Church of England he should be open in his own mind to the charge that he had been led to such a choice by unworthy motives. Then his heart was against him. He loved with a strong and eager love the man who had hitherto been his guide, and yearned to follow his footsteps. His tastes were against him. The ceremonies and pomps of the Church of Rome, their august feasts and solemn fasts, invited his imagination and pleased his eye. His flesh was against him. How great an aid it would be to a poor, weak, wavering man to be constrained to high moral duties, self-denial, obedience, and chastity by laws which were certain in their enactments, and not to be broken without loud, palpable, unmistakable sin! Then his faith was against him. He required to believe so much, panted so eagerly to give signs of his belief, deemed it so insufficient to wash himself simply in the waters of Jordan, that some great deed, such as that of forsaking everything for a true Church, had for him allurements almost past withstanding.

Mr. Arabin was at this time a very young man, and when he left Oxford for his far retreat was much too confident in his powers of fence, and too apt to look down on the ordinary sense of ordinary people, to expect aid in the battle that he had to fight from any chance inhabitants of the spot which he had selected. But Providence was good to him, and there, in that all but desolate place on the storm-beat shore of that distant sea he met one who gradually calmed his mind, quieted his imagination, and taught him something of a Christian's duty. When Mr. Arabin left Oxford, he was inclined to look upon the rural clergymen of most English parishes almost with contempt. It was his ambition, should he remain within the fold of their Church, to do somewhat toward redeeming and rectifying their inferiority, and to assist in infusing energy and faith into the hearts of Christian ministers who were, as he thought, too often satisfied to go through life without much show of either.

And yet it was from such a one that Mr. Arabin in his extremest need received that aid which he so much required. It was from the poor curate of a small Cornish parish that he first learnt to know that the highest laws for the governance of a Christian's duty must act from within and not from without, that no man can become a serviceable servant solely by obedience to written edicts, and that the safety which he was about to seek within the gates of Rome was no other than the selfish freedom from personal danger which the bad soldier attempts to gain who counterfeits illness on the eve of battle.

Mr. Arabin returned to Oxford a humbler but a better and a happier man, and from that time forth he put his shoulder to the wheel as a clergyman of the Church for which he had been educated. The intercourse of those among whom he familiarly lived kept him stanch to the principles of that system of the Church to which he had always belonged. Since his severance from Mr. Newman, no one had had so strong an influence over him as the head of his college. During the time of his expected apostacy Dr. Gwynne had not felt much predisposition in favor of the young fellow.

When, however, Mr. Arabin returned and professed himself a confirmed Protestant, the Master of Lazarus again opened his arms to him, and gradually he became the pet of the college. For some little time he was saturnine, silent, and unwilling to take any prominent part in university broils. But gradually his mind recovered, or rather made its tone, and he became known as a man always ready at a moment's notice to take up the cudgels in opposition to anything that savoured of an evangelical bearing. He was great in sermons, great on platforms, great at after-dinner conversations, and always pleasant as well as great. He took delight in elections, served on committees, opposed tooth and nail all projects of university reform, and talked jovially over his glass of port of the ruin to be anticipated by the Church, and of the sacrilege daily committed by the Whigs. The ordeal through which he had gone in resisting the blandishments of the lady of Rome had certainly done much toward the strengthening of his character. Although in small and outward matters he was self-confident enough, nevertheless in things affecting the inner man he aimed at a humility of spirit which would never have been attractive to him but for that visit to the coast of Cornwall. This visit he now repeated every year.

Such is an interior view of Mr. Arabin at the time when he accepted the living of St. Ewold. Exteriorly, he was not a remarkable person. He was above the middle height, well made, and very active. His hair, which had been jet-black, was now tinged with gray, but his face bore no sign of years. It would perhaps be wrong to say that he was handsome, but his face was nevertheless pleasant to look upon. The cheekbones were rather too high for beauty, and the formation of the forehead too massive and heavy, but the eyes, nose, and mouth were perfect. There was a continual play of lambent fire about his eyes, which gave promise of either pathos or humor whenever he essayed to speak, and that promise was rarely broken. There was a gentle play about his mouth which declared that his wit never descended to sarcasm, and that there was no ill nature in his repartee.

Mr. Arabin was a popular man among women, but more so as a general than a special favorite. Living as a fellow at Oxford, marriage with him had been out of the question, and it may be doubted whether he had ever allowed his heart to be touched. Though belonging to a Church in which celibacy is not the required lot of its ministers, he had come to regard himself as one of those clergymen to whom to be a bachelor is almost a necessity. He had never looked for parochial duty, and his career at Oxford was utterly incompatible with such domestic joys as a wife and a nursery. He looked on women, therefore, in the same light that one sees them regarded by many Romish priests. He liked to have near him that which was pretty and amusing, but women generally were little more to him than children. He talked to them without putting out all his powers, and listened to them without any idea that what he should hear from them could either actuate his conduct or influence his opinion.

Such was Mr. Arabin, the new Vicar of St. Ewold, who is going to stay with the Grantlys at Plumstead Episcopi.

CHAPTER XX

ST. EWOLD'S PARSONAGE

WHEN Mr. Harding and Mrs. Bold reached the rectory on the following morning, the Archdeacon and his friend were at St. Ewold's. They had gone over that the new Vicar might inspect his church and be introduced to the Squire, and were not expected back before dinner. Mr. Harding rambled out by himself and strolled, as was his wont at Plumstead, about the lawn and round the church, and as he did so, the two sisters naturally fell into conversation about Barchester.

There was not much sisterly confidence between them. Mrs. Grantly was ten years older than Eleanor, and had been married while Eleanor was yet a child. They had never, therefore, poured into each other's ears their hopes and loves, and now that one was a wife and the other a widow, it was not probable that they would begin to do so. They lived too much asunder to be able to fall into that kind of intercourse which makes confidence between sisters almost a necessity, and moreover that which is so easy at eighteen is often very difficult at twenty-eight. Mrs. Grantly knew this, and did not, therefore, expect confidence from her sister, and yet she longed to ask her whether in real truth Mr. Slope was agreeable to her.

It was by no means difficult to turn the conversation to Mr. Slope. That gentleman had become so famous at Barchester, had so much to do with all clergymen connected with the city, and was so specially concerned in the affairs of Mr. Harding, that it would have been odd if Mr. Harding's daughters had not talked about him. Mrs. Grantly was soon abusing him, which she did with her whole heart, and Mrs. Bold was nearly as eager to defend him. She positively disliked the man, would have been delighted to learn that he had taken himself off so that she should never see him again, had indeed almost a fear of him, and yet she constantly found herself taking his part. The abuse of other people, and abuse of a nature that she felt to be unjust, imposed this necessity on her, and at last made Mr. Slope's defense a habitual course of argument with her.

The evening passed off without anything to make it remarkable. Mr. Arabin discussed the parish of St. Ewold with the Archdeacon, and Mrs. Grantly and Mr. Harding, who knew the personages of the parish, joined in. Eleanor also knew them, but she said little. Mr. Arabin did not apparently take much notice of her, and she was not in a humor to receive at that time with any special grace any special favorite of her brother-in-law. Her first idea on reaching her bedroom was that a much pleasanter family party might be met at Dr. Stanhope's than at the rectory. She began to think that she was getting tired of clergymen and their respectable, humdrum, wearisome mode of living, and that after all, people in the outer world, who had lived in Italy, London, or elsewhere, need not necessarily be regarded as atrocious and abominable. The Stanhopes, she had thought, were a giddy, thoughtless, extravagant set of people. But she had seen nothing wrong about them, and had, on the other hand, found that they thoroughly knew how to make their house agreeable. It was a thousand pities, she thought, that the Archdeacon should not have a little of the same savoir vivre.

Mr. Arabin, as we have said, did not apparently take much notice of her, but yet he did not go to bed without feeling that he had been in company with a very pretty woman, and as is the case with most bachelors, and some married men, regarded the prospect of his month's visit at Plumstead in a pleasanter light when he learnt that a very pretty woman was to share it with him.

Before they all retired it was settled that the whole party should drive over on the following day to inspect the parsonage at St. Ewold. The three clergymen were to discuss dilapidations, and the two ladies were to lend their assistance in suggesting such changes as might be necessary for a bachelor's abode.

Accordingly, soon after breakfast the carriage was at the door. There was only room for four inside, and the Archdeacon got upon the box. Eleanor found herself opposite to Mr. Arabin, and was therefore in a manner forced into conversation with him. They were soon on comfortable terms together, and had she thought about it, she would have thought that in spite of his black cloth Mr. Arabin would not have been a bad addition to the Stanhope family party.

Now that the Archdeacon was away they could all trifle. Mr. Harding began by telling them in the most innocent manner imaginable an old legend about Mr. Arabin's new parish. There was, he said, in days of yore, an illustrious priestess of St. Ewold, famed through the whole country for curing all manner of diseases. She had a well, as all priestesses have ever had, which well was extant to this day, and shared in the minds of many of the people the sanctity which belonged to the consecrated ground of the parish church. Mr. Arabin declared that he should look on such tenets on the part of his parishioners as anything but orthodox. And Mrs. Grantly replied that she so entirely disagreed with him as to think that no parish was in a proper state that had not its priestess as well as its priest. "The duties are never well done," said she, "unless they are so divided."

"I suppose, Papa," said Eleanor, "that in the olden times the priestess bore all the sway herself. Mr. Arabin perhaps thinks that such might be too much the case now if a sacred lady were admitted within the parish."

"I think, at any rate," said he, "that it is safer to run no such risk. No priestly pride has ever exceeded that of sacerdotal females. A very lowly curate I might perhaps essay to rule, but a curatess would be sure to get the better of me."

"There are certainly examples of such accidents happening," said Mrs. Grantly. "They do say that there is a priestess at Barchester who is very imperious in all things touching the altar. Perhaps the fear of such a fate as that is before your eyes."

When they were joined by the Archdeacon on the gravel before the vicarage, they descended again to grave dullness. Not that Archdeacon Grantly was a dull man, but his frolic humors were of a cumbrous kind, and his wit, when he was witty, did not generally extend itself to his auditory. On the present occasion he was soon making speeches about wounded roofs and walls, which he declared to be in want of some surgeon's art. There was not a partition that he did not tap, nor a block of chimneys that he did not narrowly examine. All water pipes, flues, cisterns, and sewers underwent an investigation, and he even descended, in the care of his friend, so far as to bore sundry boards in the floors with a bradawl.

Mr. Arabin accompanied him through the rooms, trying to look wise in such domestic matters, and the other three also followed. Mrs. Grantly showed that she had not herself been priestess of a parish twenty years for nothing, and examined the bells and windowpanes in a very knowing way.

"You will at any rate have a beautiful prospect out of your own window, if this is to be your private sanctum," said Eleanor. She was standing at the lattice of a little room upstairs, from which the view certainly was very lovely. It was from the back of the vicarage, and there was nothing to interrupt the eye between the house and the glorious gray pile of the cathedral. The intermediate ground, however, was beautifully studded with timber. In the immediate foreground ran the little river which afterward skirted the city, and just to the right of the cathedral, the pointed gables and chimneys of Hiram's Hospital peeped out of the elms which encompass it.

"Yes," said he, joining her. "I shall have a beautifully complete view of my adversaries. I shall sit down before the hostile town and fire away at them at a very pleasant distance. I shall just be able to lodge a shot in the hospital, should the enemy ever get possession of it, and as for the palace, I have it within full range."

"I never saw anything like you clergymen," said Eleanor. "You are always thinking of fighting each other."

"Either that," said he, "or else supporting each other. The pity is that we cannot do the one without the other. But are we not here to fight? Is not ours a Church Militant? What is all our work but fighting, and hard fighting, if it be well done?"

"But not with each other."

"That's as it may be. The same complaint which you make of me for battling with another clergyman of our own Church the Mohammedan would make against me for battling with the error of a priest of Rome. Yet surely you would not be inclined to say that I should be wrong to do battle with such as him. A pagan, too, with his multiplicity of gods, would think it equally odd that the Christian and the Mohammedan should disagree."

"Ah, but you wage your wars about trifles so bitterly!"

"Wars about trifles," said he, "are always bitter, especially among neighbors. When the differences are great, and the parties comparative strangers, men quarrel with courtesy. What combatants are ever so eager as two brothers?

"It is so easy to condemn," said he. "I know no life that must be so delicious as that of a writer for newspapers, or a leading member of the Opposition —to thunder forth accusations against men in power, to show up the worst side of everything that is produced, to pick holes in every coat, to be indignant, sarcastic, jocose, moral, or supercilious, to damn with faint praise or crush with open calumny! What can be so easy as this when the critic has to be responsible for nothing? You condemn what I do, but put yourself in my position and do the reverse, and then see if I cannot condemn you."

"Oh, Mr. Arabin, I do not condemn you!"

"Pardon me, you do, Mrs. Bold—you as one of the world. You are now the Opposition Member, you are now composing your leading article, and well and bitterly you do it. 'Let dogs delight to bark and bite,' you fitly begin with an elegant quotation, 'but if we are to have a Church at all, in heaven's name let the pastors who preside over it keep their hands from each other's throats. Lawyers can live without befouling each other's names, doctors do not fight duels. Why is it that clergymen alone should indulge themselves in such unrestrained liberty of abuse against each other?' And so you go on reviling us for our ungodly quarrels, our sectarian propensities and scandalous differences. It will, however, give you no trouble to write another article next week in which we, or some of us, shall be twitted with an unseemly apathy in matters of our vocation. It will not fall on you to reconcile the discrepancy. Your readers will never ask you how the poor parson is to be urgent in season and out of season and yet never come in contact with men who think widely differently from him. You, when you condemn this foreign treaty or that official arrangement, will have to incur no blame for the graver faults of any different measure. It is so easy to condemn, and so pleasant too, for eulogy charms no listeners as detraction does."

Eleanor only half followed him in his raillery, but she caught his meaning. "I know I ought to apologize for presuming to criticize you," she said, "but I was thinking with sorrow of the ill will that has lately come among us at Barchester, and I spoke more freely than I should have done."

"Peace on earth and goodwill among men are like Heaven, promises for the future," said he, following rather his own thoughts than hers. "When that prophecy is accomplished, there will no longer be any need for clergymen."

CHAPTER XXI

THE THORNES OF ULLATHORNE

On the following Sunday Mr. Arabin was to read himself in at his new church. It was agreed at the rectory that the Archdeacon should go over with him and assist at the reading desk, and that Mr. Harding should take the Archdeacon's duty at Plumstead Church. Mrs. Grantly had her school and her buns to attend to and professed that she could not be spared, but Mrs. Bold was to accompany them. It was further agreed also that they would lunch at the Squire's house, and return home after the afternoon service.

Wilfred Thorne, Esq., of Ullathorne, was the Squire of St. Ewold's, or rather the Squire of Ullathorne, for the domain of the modern landlord was of wider notoriety than the fame of the ancient saint. He was a fair specimen of what that race has come to in our days which a century ago was, as we are told, fairly represented by Squire Western. If that representation be a true one, few classes of men can have made faster strides in improvement. Mr. Thorne, however, was a man possessed of quite a sufficient number of foibles to lay him open to much ridicule. He was still a bachelor, being about fifty, and was not a little proud of his person. When living at home at Ullathorne there was not much room for such pride, and there therefore he always looked like a gentleman, and like that which he certainly was, the first man in his parish. But during the month or six weeks which he annually spent in London, he tried so hard to look like a great man there also, which he certainly was not, that he was put down as a fool by many at his club. He was a great proficient in all questions of genealogy, and knew enough of almost every gentleman's family in England to say of what blood and lineage were descended all those who had any claim to be considered as possessors of any such luxuries. For blood and lineage he himself had a most profound respect. He counted back his own ancestors to some period long antecedent to the Conquest, and could tell you, if you would listen to him, how it had come to pass that they, like Cedric the Saxon, had been permitted to hold their own among the Norman barons.

Mr. Thorne did not live in solitude at Ullathorne. He had a sister, who was ten years older than himself, and who participated in his prejudices and feelings so strongly that she was a living caricature of all his foibles. She would not open a modern quarterly, did not choose to see a magazine in her drawing-room, and would not have polluted her fingers with a shred of the *Times* for any consideration. She spoke of Addison, Swift, and Steele as though they were still living, regarded De Foe as the best-known novelist of his country, and thought of Fielding as a young but meritorious novice in the fields of romance. In poetry, she was familiar with names as late as Dryden, and had once been seduced into reading the "Rape of the Lock," but she regarded Spenser as the purest type of her country's literature in this line. Genealogy was her favorite insanity.

In religion, Miss Thorne was a pure Druidess. We would not have it understood by that that she did actually in these latter days assist at any human sacrifices, or that she was in fact hostile to the Church of Christ. She had adopted the Christian religion as a milder form of the worship of her ancestors, and always appealed to her doing so as evidence that she had no prejudices against reform, when it could be shown that reform was salutary.

In her person and her dress she was perfect, and well she knew her own perfection. She was a small, elegantly made old woman, with a face from which the glow of her youth had not departed without leaving some streaks of a roseate hue. She was proud of her color, proud of her gray hair, which she wore in short crisp curls peering out all round her face from the dainty white-lace cap. To think of all the money that she spent in lace used to break the heart of poor Mrs. Quiverful with her seven daughters. She was proud of her teeth, which were still white and numerous, proud of her bright cheery eye, proud of her short jaunty step, and very proud of the neat, precise, small feet with which those steps were taken. She was proud also—ay, very proud—of the rich brocaded silk in which it was her custom to ruffle through her drawing-room.

But for all this rich attire Miss Thorne was not indebted to the generosity of her brother. She had a very comfortable independence of her own, which she divided among juvenile relatives, the milliners, and the poor, giving much the largest share to the latter. It may be imagined, therefore, that with all her little follies she was not unpopular. All her follies have, we believe, been told. Her virtues were too numerous to describe, and not sufficiently interesting to deserve description.

While we are on the subject of the Thornes, one word must be said of the house they lived in. It was not a large house, nor a fine house, nor perhaps to modern ideas a very commodious house, but by those who love the peculiar color and peculiar ornaments of genuine Tudor architecture it was considered a perfect gem.

Mr. Thorne's house was called Ullathorne Court, and was properly so called, for the house itself formed two sides of a quadrangle, which was completed on the other two sides by a wall about twenty feet high. This wall was built of cut stone, rudely cut indeed and now much worn, but of a beautiful rich tawny yellow color, the effect of that stonecrop of minute growth which it had taken three centuries to produce. The top of this wall was ornamented by huge round stone balls of the same color as the wall itself. Entrance into the court was had through a pair of iron gates so massive that no one could comfortably open or close them, consequently they were rarely disturbed. From the gateway two paths led obliquely across the court, that to the left reaching the hall door, which was in the corner made by the angle of the house, and that to the right leading to the back entrance, which was at the farther end of the longer portion of the building.

With those who are now adepts in contriving house accommodation, it will militate much against Ullathorne Court, that no carriage could be brought to the hall door. If you enter Ullathorne at all, you must do so, fair reader, on foot, or at least in a Bath chair. No vehicle drawn by horses ever comes within that iron gate.

It is the color of Ullathorne that is so remarkable. It is all of that delicious tawny hue which no stone can give unless it has on it the vegetable richness of centuries. Strike the wall with your hand and you will think that the stone has on it no covering, but rub it carefully and you will find that the color comes off upon your finger. No colorist that ever yet worked from a palette has been able to come up to this rich coloring of years crowding themselves on years.

Ullathorne is a high building for a country house, for it possesses three

stories. Along the top on every side runs a low parapet, which nearly hides
the roof, and at the corners are figures of fawns and satyrs.

Such is Ullathorne House. But we must say one word of the approach
to it, which shall include all the description which we mean to give of the
church also. The picturesque old Church of St. Ewold's stands immediately opposite to the iron gates which open into the court, and is all but
surrounded by the branches of the lime trees which form the avenue leading up to the house from both sides. This avenue is magnificent, but it
would lose much of its value in the eyes of many proprietors by the fact
that the road through it is not private property. It is a public lane between
hedgerows, with a broad grass margin on each side of the road, from
which the lime trees spring. Ullathorne Court, therefore, does not stand
absolutely surrounded by its own grounds, though Mr. Thorne is owner
of all the adjacent land. This, however, is the source of very little annoyance to him. Men when they are acquiring property think much of such
things, but they who live where their ancestors have lived for years do not
feel the misfortune. It never occurred either to Mr. or Miss Thorne that
they were not sufficiently private because the world at large might, if it
so wished, walk or drive by their iron gates. That part of the world which
availed itself of the privilege was however very small.

Such a year or two since were the Thornes of Ullathorne. Such, we
believe, are the inhabitants of many an English country home. May it be
long before their number diminishes.

CHAPTER XXII

MR. ARABIN READS HIMSELF IN AT ST. EWOLD'S

On the Sunday morning the Archdeacon with his sister-in-law and Mr.
Arabin drove over to Ullathorne, as had been arranged. On their way
thither the new Vicar declared himself to be considerably disturbed in his
mind at the idea of thus facing his parishioners for the first time. He had,
he said, been always subject to *mauvaise honte* and an annoying degree of
bashfulness, which often unfitted him for any work of a novel description,
and now he felt this so strongly that he feared he should acquit himself
badly in St. Ewold's reading-desk. He knew, he said, that those sharp little
eyes of Miss Thorne would be on him, and that they would not approve.
All this the Archdeacon greatly ridiculed. He himself knew not, and had
never known, what it was to be shy. He could not conceive that Miss
Thorne, surrounded as she would be by the peasants of Ullathorne and
a few of the poorer inhabitants of the suburbs of Barchester, could in any
way affect the composure of a man well accustomed to address the learned

ongregation of St. Mary's at Oxford, and he laughed accordingly at the
lea of Mr. Arabin's modesty.

They drove up to the iron gates of Ullathorne Court. Mr. and Miss
Thorne were standing ready dressed for church in the hall, and greeted
their clerical visitors with cordiality. The Archdeacon was an old favorite.
The little bell was tinkling, and the rural population of the parish were
standing about the lane, leaning on the church stile, and against the walls
of the old court, anxious to get a look at their new minister as he passed
from the house to the rectory.

They all went forth together, and when the ladies passed into the church
the three gentlemen tarried a moment in the lane, that Mr. Thorne might
name to the Vicar with some kind of one-sided introduction the most
leading among his parishioners.

"Here are our churchwardens, Mr. Arabin—Farmer Greenacre and Mr.
Stiles. Mr. Stiles has the mill as you go into Barchester. And very good
churchwardens they are."

"Not very severe, I hope," said Mr. Arabin. The two ecclesiastical officers
touched their hats, and each made a leg in the approved rural fashion, assur-
ing the Vicar that they were very glad to have the honor of seeing him,
and adding that the weather was very good for the harvest.

Mr. Arabin read the lessons and preached. It was enough to put a man
a little out, let him have been ever so used to pulpit reading, to see the
knowing way in which the farmers cocked their ears and set about a
mental criticism as to whether their new minister did or did not fall short
of the excellence of him who had lately departed from them. A mental
and silent criticism it was for the existing moment, but soon to be made
public among the elders of St. Ewold's over the green graves of their children and forefathers. The excellence, however, of poor old Mr. Goodenough
had not been wonderful, and there were few there who did not deem that
Mr. Arabin did his work sufficiently well, in spite of the slightly nervous
affection which at first impeded him, and which nearly drove the Archdeacon beside himself.

Mr. Arabin succeeded with his sermon even better than with the lessons.
He took for his text two verses out of the Second Epistle of St. John,
"Whosoever transgresseth, and abideth not in the doctrine of Christ, hath
not God. He that abideth in the doctrine of Christ, he hath both the Father
and Son. If there come any unto you, and bring not this doctrine, receive him
not into your house, neither bid him Godspeed." He told them that the
house of theirs to which he alluded was this their church in which he
now addressed them for the first time, that their most welcome and proper
manner of bidding him Godspeed would be their patient obedience to his
teaching of the Gospel, but that he could put forward no claim to such
conduct on their part unless he taught them the great Christian doctrine
of works and faith combined. On this he enlarged, but not very amply,
and after twenty minutes succeeded in sending his new friends home

to their baked mutton and pudding well pleased with their new minister

Then came the lunch at Ullathorne. As soon as they were in the hal Miss Thorne took Mr. Arabin's hand, and assured him that she receivec him into her house, into the temple, she said, in which she worshiped, anc bade him Godspeed with all her heart. Mr. Arabin was touched, anc squeezed the spinster's hand without uttering a word in reply. Then Mr Thorne expressed a hope that Mr. Arabin found the church well adaptec for articulation, and Mr. Arabin having replied that he had no doubt he should as soon as he had learnt to pitch his voice to the building, they al sat down to the good things before them.

And then they took a stroll out among the trim parterres, and Mr. Arabin explained to Mrs. Bold the difference between a naiad and a dryad, anc dilated on vases and the shapes of urns. Miss Thorne busied herself among her pansies, and her brother, finding it quite impracticable to give anything of a peculiarly Sunday tone to the conversation, abandoned the attempt and had it out with the Archdeacon about Bristol guano.

At three o'clock they again went into church, and now Mr. Arabin read the service and the Archdeacon preached. Nearly the same congrega- tion was present, with some adventurous pedestrians from the city who hac not thought the heat of the midday August sun too great to deter them The Archdeacon took his text from the Epistle to Philemon. "I beseech thee for my son Onesimus, whom I have begotten in my bonds." From such a text it may be imagined the kind of sermon which Dr. Grantly preached, and on the whole it was neither dull, nor bad, nor out of place

The Archdeacon's sermon, text, blessing and all, was concluded within the half-hour. Then they shook hands with their Ullathorne friends and returned to Plumstead. 'Twas thus that Mr. Arabin read himself in at St. Ewold's.

CHAPTER XXIII

MR. SLOPE MANAGES MATTERS VERY CLEVERLY AT
PUDDINGDALE

THE next two weeks passed pleasantly enough at Plumstead. The whole party there assembled seemed to get on well together. Eleanor made the house agreeable, and the Archdeacon and Mrs. Grantly seemed to have forgotten her iniquity as regarded Mr. Slope. Mr. Harding had his violon- cello, and played to them while his daughters accompanied him. There had been gaieties too of all sorts. They had dined at Ullathorne, and the Thornes had dined at the rectory. Mr. Arabin had of course been much in his own parish, looking to the doings at his vicarage, calling on his parishioners, and taking on himself the duties of his new calling. But still

ae had been every evening at Plumstead, and Mrs. Grantly was partly
villing to agree with her husband that he was a pleasant inmate in a house.

They had also been at a dinner party at Dr. Stanhope's, of which Mr.
Arabin had made one. He also, mothlike, burnt his wings in the flames
of the Signora's candle. Mrs. Bold too had been there, and had felt some-
vhat displeased with the taste—want of taste, she called it—shown by Mr.
Arabin in paying so much attention to Madame Neroni. It was as infallible
hat Madeline should displease and irritate the women as that she should
charm and captivate the men. The one result followed naturally on the
other. It was quite true that Mr. Arabin had been charmed. He thought
aer a very clever and a very handsome woman. He thought also that her
peculiar affliction entitled her to the sympathy of all. He had never, he said,
net so much suffering joined to such perfect beauty and so clear a mind.
Twas thus he spoke of the Signora coming home in the Archdeacon's
carriage, and Eleanor by no means liked to hear the praise. It was, how-
ver, exceedingly unjust of her to be angry with Mr. Arabin, as she had
aerself spent a very pleasant evening with Bertie Stanhope, who had taken
aer down to dinner and had not left her side for one moment after the
gentlemen came out of the dining-room. It was unfair that she should
muse herself with Bertie and yet begrudge her new friend his license
of amusing himself with Bertie's sister. And yet she did so. She was half-
ngry with him in the carriage, and said something about meretricious
nanners. Mr. Arabin did not understand the ways of women very well, or
lse he might have flattered himself that Eleanor was in love with him.

But Eleanor was not in love with him. How many shades there are be-
ween love and indifference, and how little the graduated scale is under-
tood! She had now been nearly three weeks in the same house with Mr.
Arabin, and had received much of his attention and listened daily to his
conversation. He had usually devoted at least some portion of his evening
o her exclusively. At Dr. Stanhope's he had devoted himself exclusively
o another. It does not require that a woman should be in love to be
rritated at this. It does not require that she should even acknowledge to
aerself that it is unpleasant to her. Eleanor had no such self-knowledge.
She thought in her own heart that it was only on Mr. Arabin's account
hat she regretted that he could condescend to be amused by the Signora.
'I thought he had more mind," she said to herself as she sat watching her
baby's cradle on her return from the party. "After all, I believe Mr. Stan-
aope is the pleasanter man of the two." Alas for the memory of poor John
Bold! Eleanor was not in love with Bertie Stanhope, nor was she in love
vith Mr. Arabin. But her devotion to her late husband was fast fading
vhen she could revolve in her mind over the cradle of his infant the faults
nd failings of other aspirants to her favor.

Will anyone blame my heroine for this? Let him or her rather thank
God for all His goodness—for His mercy endureth forever.

Eleanor, in truth, was not in love, neither was Mr. Arabin. Neither indeed

was Bertie Stanhope, though he had already found occasion to say nearl
as much as that he was. The widow's cap had prevented him from makin
a positive declaration when otherwise he would have considered himse
entitled to do so on the third or fourth interview. It was, after all, but
small cap now, and had but little of the weeping willow left in its construc
tion. It is singular how these emblems of grief fade away by unseen grad
tions. Each pretends to be the counterpart of the forerunner, and yet th
last little bit of crimped white crape that sits so jauntily on the back c
the head is as dissimilar to the first huge mountain of woe which disfigure
the face of the weeper as the state of the Hindu is to the jointure of th
English dowager.

But let it be clearly understood that Eleanor was in love with no on
and that no one was in love with Eleanor. Under these circumstances he
anger against Mr. Arabin did not last long, and before two days were ove
they were both as good friends as ever. She could not but like him, fo
every hour spent in his company was spent pleasantly. And yet she coul
not quite like him, for there was always apparent in his conversation
certain feeling on his part that he hardly thought it worth his while to b
in earnest. It was almost as though he were playing with a child. She knev
well enough that he was in truth a sober, thoughtful man who in som
matters and on some occasions could endure an agony of earnestness. An
yet to her he was always gently playful. Could she have seen his brow onc
clouded, she might have learnt to love him.

So things went on at Plumstead, and on the whole not unpleasantly, ti
a huge storm darkened the horizon and came down upon the inhabitan
of the rectory with all the fury of a waterspout. It was astonishing hov
in a few minutes the whole face of the heavens was changed. The part
broke up from breakfast in perfect harmony, but fierce passions had arise
before the evening which did not admit of their sitting at the same boar
for dinner. To explain this, it will be necessary to go back a little.

It will be remembered that the Bishop expressed to Mr. Slope in h
dressing-room his determination that Mr. Quiverful should be confirme
in his appointment to the hospital, and that his lordship requested Mr. Slop
to communicate this decision to the Archdeacon. It will also be remem
bered that the Archdeacon had indignantly declined seeing Mr. Slop
and had instead written a strong letter to the Bishop, in which he all bu
demanded the situation of warden for Mr. Harding. To this letter the Arch
deacon received an immediate formal reply from Mr. Slope, in which
was stated that the Bishop had received and would give his best considera
tion to the Archdeacon's letter.

The Archdeacon felt himself somewhat checkmated by this reply. Wha
could he do with a man who would neither see him nor argue with hir
by letter, and who had undoubtedly the power of appointing any clergy
man he pleased? He had consulted with Mr. Arabin, who had suggeste
the propriety of calling in the aid of the Master of Lazarus. "If," said h

you and Dr. Gwynne formally declare your intention of waiting upon
he Bishop, the Bishop will not dare to refuse to see you, and if two such
men as you are see him together, you will probably not leave him without
carrying your point."

The Archdeacon did not quite like admitting the necessity of his being
backed by the Master of Lazarus before he could obtain admission into the
episcopal palace of Barchester, but still he felt that the advice was good,
and he resolved to take it. He wrote again to the Bishop expressing a hope
that nothing further would be done in the matter of the hospital till the
consideration promised by his lordship had been given, and then sent off
a warm appeal to his friend the Master, imploring him to come to Plumstead and assist in driving the Bishop into compliance. The Master had
rejoined raising some difficulty, but not declining, and the Archdeacon
had again pressed his point, insisting on the necessity for immediate action.
Dr. Gwynne unfortunately had the gout, and could therefore name no
immediate day, but still agreed to come if it should be finally found necessary. So the matter stood, as regarded the party at Plumstead.

But Mr. Harding had another friend fighting his battle for him, quite
as powerful as the Master of Lazarus, and this was Mr. Slope. Though the
Bishop had so pertinaciously insisted on giving way to his wife in the
matter of the hospital, Mr. Slope did not think it necessary to abandon his
object. He had, he thought, daily more and more reason to imagine that
the widow would receive his overtures favorably, and he could not but
feel that Mr. Harding at the hospital, and placed there by his means, would
be more likely to receive him as a son-in-law than Mr. Harding growling
in opposition and disappointment under the Archdeacon's wing at Plumstead. Moreover, to give Mr. Slope due credit, he was actuated by greater
motives even than these. He wanted a wife, and he wanted money, but he
wanted power more than either. He had fully realized the fact that he must
come to blows with Mrs. Proudie. He had no desire to remain in Barchester as her chaplain. Sooner than do so he would risk the loss of his
whole connection with the diocese. What! Was he to feel within him the
possession of no ordinary talents, was he to know himself to be courageous,
firm, and—in matters where his conscience did not interfere—unscrupulous,
and yet be contented to be the working factotum of a woman prelate? Mr.
Slope had higher ideas of his own destiny. Either he or Mrs. Proudie must
go to the wall, and now had come the time when he would try which it
would be.

The Bishop had declared that Mr. Quiverful should be the new warden.
As Mr. Slope went downstairs prepared to see the Archdeacon if necessary, but fully satisfied that no such necessity would arise, he declared
to himself that Mr. Harding should be warden. With the object of carrying this point, he rode over to Puddingdale and had a further interview
with the worthy expectant of clerical good things. Mr. Quiverful was on
the whole a worthy man. The impossible task of bringing up as ladies and

gentlemen fourteen children on an income which was insufficient to give them with decency the common necessaries of life had had an effect upon him not beneficial either to his spirit or his keen sense of honor. Who can boast that he would have supported such a burden with a different result? Mr. Quiverful was an honest, painstaking, drudging man, anxious indeed for bread and meat, anxious for means to quiet his butcher and cover with returning smiles the now sour countenance of the baker's wife, but anxious also to be right with his own conscience. He was not careful, as another might be who sat on an easier worldly seat, to stand well with those around him, to shun a breath which might sully his name or a rumor which might affect his honor. He could not afford such niceties of conduct, such moral luxuries. It must suffice for him to be ordinarily honest according to the ordinary honesty of the world's ways, and to let men's tongues wag as they would.

He had felt that his brother clergymen, men whom he had known for the last twenty years, looked coldly on him from the first moment that he had shown himself willing to sit at the feet of Mr. Slope. He had seen that their looks grew colder still when it became bruited about that he was to be the Bishop's new warden at Hiram's Hospital. This was painful enough, but it was the cross which he was doomed to bear. He thought of his wife whose last new silk dress was six years in wear. He thought of all his young flock, whom he could hardly take to church with him on Sundays, for there were not decent shoes and stockings for them all to wear. He thought of the well-worn sleeves of his own black coat, and of the stern face of the draper from whom he would fain ask for cloth to make another did he not know that the credit would be refused him. Then he thought of the comfortable house in Barchester, of the comfortable income, of his boys sent to school, of his girls with books in their hands instead of darning needles, of his wife's face again covered with smiles, and of his daily board again covered with plenty. He thought of these things, and do thou also reader, think of them, and then wonder, if thou canst, that Mr. Slope had appeared to him to possess all those good gifts which could grace a Bishop's chaplain. "How beautiful upon the mountains are the feet of him that bringeth good tidings."

Why, moreover, should the Barchester clergy have looked coldly on Mr. Quiverful? Had they not all shown that they regarded with complacency the loaves and fishes of their Mother Church? Had they not all, by some hook or crook, done better for themselves than he had done? They were not burdened as he was burdened. Dr. Grantly had five children and nearly as many thousands a year on which to feed them. It is very well for him to turn up his nose at a new bishop who could do nothing for him, and a chaplain who was beneath his notice. But it was cruel in a man so circumstanced to set the world against the father of fourteen children because he was anxious to obtain for them an honorable support! He, Mr. Quiverful, had not asked for the wardenship, he had not even accepted it till he had been assured that Mr. Harding had refused it. How hard then that he should be blamed for doing that which not to have done would have argued a most insane imprudence.

Thus in this matter of the hospital poor Mr. Quiverful had his trials, and he had also his consolations. On the whole the consolations were the more vivid of the two. The stern draper heard of the coming promotion, and the wealth of his warehouse was at Mr. Quiverful's disposal. Coming events cast their shadows before, and the coming event of Mr. Quiverful's transference to Barchester produced a delicious shadow in the shape of a new outfit for Mrs. Quiverful and her three elder daughters. Such consolations come home to the heart of a man, and quite home to the heart of a woman. Whatever the husband might feel, the wife cared nothing for frowns of Dean, Archdeacon, or prebendary. To her the outsides and insides of her husband and fourteen children were everything. In her bosom every other ambition had been swallowed up in that maternal ambition of seeing them and him and herself duly clad and properly fed. It had come to that with her that life had now no other purpose. She recked nothing of the imaginary rights of others. She had no patience with her husband when he declared to her that he could not accept the hospital unless he knew that Mr. Harding had refused it. Her husband had no right to be quixotic at the expense of fourteen children. The narrow escape of throwing away his good fortune which her lord had had almost paralyzed her. Now, indeed, they had received the full promise not only from Mr. Slope, but also from Mrs. Proudie. Now, indeed, they might reckon with safety on their good fortune. But what if all had been lost? What if her fourteen bairns had been resteeped to the hips in poverty by the morbid sentimentality of their father? Mrs. Quiverful was just at present a happy woman, but yet it nearly took her breath away when she thought of the risk they had run.

"I don't know what your father means when he talks so much of what is due to Mr. Harding," she said to her eldest daughter. "Does he think that Mr. Harding would give him four hundred and fifty pounds a year out of fine feeling? And what signifies it whom he offends as long as he gets the place? He does not expect anything better. It passes me to think how your father can be so soft while everybody around him is so gripping."

Thus while the outer world was accusing Mr. Quiverful of rapacity for promotion and of disregard to his honor, the inner world of his own household was falling foul of him with equal vehemence for his willingness to sacrifice their interest to a false feeling of sentimental pride. It is astonishing how much difference the point of view makes in the aspect of all that we look at!

Such were the feelings of the different members of the family at Puddingdale on the occasion of Mr. Slope's second visit. Mrs. Quiverful, as soon as she saw his horse coming up the avenue from the vicarage gate, hastily packed up her huge basket of needlework and hurried herself and her daughter out of the room in which she was sitting with her husband. "It's Mr. Slope," she said. "He's come to settle with you about the hospital. I do hope we shall now be able to move at once." And she hastened to bid the maid of all work go to the door, so that the welcome great man might not be kept waiting.

Mr. Slope thus found Mr. Quiverful alone. Mrs. Quiverful went off to her kitchen and back settlements with anxious, beating heart, almost dreading that there might be some slip between the cup of her happiness and the lip of her fruition, but yet comforting herself with the reflection that after what had taken place any such slip could hardly be possible.

Mr. Slope was all smiles as he shook his brother clergyman's hand, and said that he had ridden over because he thought it right at once to put Mr. Quiverful in possession of the facts of the matter regarding the wardenship of the hospital. As he spoke, the poor expectant husband and father saw at a glance that his brilliant hopes were to be dashed to the ground, and that his visitor was now there for the purpose of unsaying what on his former visit he had said. There was something in the tone of the voice, something in the glance of the eye, which told the tale. Mr. Quiverful knew it all at once. He maintained his self-possession, however, smiled with a slight unmeaning smile, and merely said that he was obliged to Mr. Slope for the trouble he was taking.

"It has been a troublesome matter from first to last," said Mr. Slope, "and the Bishop has hardly known how to act. Between ourselves—but mind this of course must go no further, Mr. Quiverful."

Mr. Quiverful said that of course it should not. "The truth is that poor Mr. Harding has hardly known his own mind. You remember our last conversation, no doubt."

Mr. Quiverful assured him that he remembered it very well indeed.

"You will remember that I told you that Mr. Harding had refused to return to the hospital."

Mr. Quiverful declared that nothing could be more distinct on his memory.

"And acting on this refusal, I suggested that you should take the hospital," continued Mr. Slope.

"I understood you to say that the Bishop had authorized you to offer it to me."

"Did I? Did I go so far as that? Well, perhaps it may be that in my anxiety in your behalf I did commit myself further than I should have done. So far as my own memory serves me, I don't think I did go quite so far as that. But I own I was very anxious that you should get it, and I may have said more than was quite prudent."

"But," said Mr. Quiverful in his deep anxiety to prove his case, "my wife received as distinct a promise from Mrs. Proudie as one human being could give to another."

Mr. Slope smiled, and gently shook his head. He meant that smile for a pleasant smile, but it was diabolical in the eyes of the man he was speaking to. "Mrs. Proudie!" he said. "If we are to go to what passes between the ladies in these matters, we shall really be in a nest of troubles from which we shall never extricate ourselves. Mrs. Proudie is a most excellent lady, kindhearted, charitable, pious, and in every way estimable. But, my dear Mr. Quiverful, the patronage of the diocese is not in her hands."

Mr. Quiverful for a moment sat panic-stricken and silent. "Am I to understand, then, that I have received no promise?" he said as soon as he had sufficiently collected his thoughts.

"If you will allow me, I will tell you exactly how the matter rests. You certainly did receive a promise conditional on Mr. Harding's refusal. I am sure you will do me the justice to remember that you yourself declared that you could accept the appointment on no other condition than the knowledge that Mr. Harding had declined it."

"Yes," said Mr. Quiverful, "I did say that, certainly."

"Well, it now appears that he did not refuse it."

"But surely you told me, and repeated it more than once, that he had done so in your own hearing."

"So I understood him. But it seems I was in error. But don't for a moment, Mr. Quiverful, suppose that I mean to throw you over. No. Having held out my hand to a man in your position, with your large family and pressing claims, I am not now going to draw it back again. I only want you to act with me fairly and honestly."

"Whatever I do, I shall endeavor at any rate to act fairly," said the poor man, feeling that he had to fall back for support on the spirit of martyrdom within him.

"I am sure you will," said the other. "I am sure you have no wish to obtain possession of an income which belongs by all right to another. No man knows better than you do Mr. Harding's history, or can better appreciate his character. Mr. Harding is very desirous of returning to his old position, and the Bishop feels that he is at the present moment somewhat hampered, though of course he is not bound, by the conversation which took place on the matter between you and me."

"Well," said Mr. Quiverful, dreadfully doubtful as to what his conduct under such circumstances should be, and fruitlessly striving to harden his nerves with some of that instinct of self-preservation which made his wife so bold.

"The wardenship of this little hospital is not the only thing in the Bishop's gift, Mr. Quiverful, nor is it by many degrees the best. And his lordship is not the man to forget anyone whom he has once marked with approval. If you would allow me to advise you as a friend——"

"Indeed I shall be most grateful to you," said the poor Vicar of Puddingdale.

"I should advise you to withdraw from any opposition to Mr. Harding's claims. If you persist in your demand, I do not think you will ultimately succeed. Mr. Harding has all but a positive right to the place. But if you will allow me to inform the Bishop that you decline to stand in Mr. Harding's way, I think I may promise you—though, by the by, it must not be taken as a formal promise—that the Bishop will not allow you to be a poorer man than you would have been had you become warden."

Mr. Quiverful sat in his arm chair silent, gazing at vacancy. What was he to say? All this that came from Mr. Slope was so true. Mr. Harding had a right to the hospital. The Bishop had a great many good things to give away. Both the Bishop and Mr. Slope would be excellent friends and terrible enemies to a man in his position. And then he had no proof of any promise, he could not force the Bishop to appoint him.

"Well, Mr. Quiverful, what do you say about it?"

"Oh, of course, whatever you think fit, Mr. Slope. It's a great disappointment, a very great disappointment. I won't deny that I am a very poor man, Mr. Slope."

"In the end, Mr. Quiverful, you will find that it will have been better for you."

The interview ended in Mr. Slope receiving a full renunciation from Mr. Quiverful of any claim he might have to the appointment in question. It was only given verbally and without witnesses, but then the original promise was made in the same way.

Mr. Slope again assured him that he should not be forgotten, and then rode back to Barchester satisfied that he would now be able to mold the Bishop to his wishes.

CHAPTER XXIV

FOURTEEN ARGUMENTS IN FAVOR OF MR. QUIVERFUL'S
CLAIMS

WE have most of us heard of the terrible anger of a lioness when, surrounded by her cubs, she guards her prey. Few of us wish to disturb the mother of a litter of puppies when mouthing a bone in the midst of her young family. Medea and her children are familiar to us, and so is the grief of Constance. Mrs. Quiverful, when she first heard from her husband the news which he had to impart, felt within her bosom all the rage of a lioness, the rapacity of the hound, the fury of the tragic queen, and the deep despair of the bereaved mother.

Doubting, but yet hardly fearing, what might have been the tenor of Mr. Slope's discourse, she rushed back to her husband as soon as the front door was closed behind the visitor. It was well for Mr. Slope that he so escaped—the anger of such a woman, at such a moment, would have cowed even him.

"Well, my dear, we are not to have it." Such were the words with which her ears were greeted when she entered the parlor still hot from the kitchen fire. And the face of her husband spoke even more plainly than his words.

"What!" said she—and Mrs. Siddons could not have put more passion into a single syllable. "What! Not have it? Who says so?" And she sat opposite to her husband with her elbows on the table, her hands clasped together, and her coarse, solid, but once handsome face stretched over it toward him.

She sat as silent as death while he told his story, and very dreadful to him her silence was. He told it very lamely and badly, but still in such a manner that she soon understood the whole of it.

"And so you have resigned it?" said she.

"I have had no opportunity of accepting it," he replied. "I had no witnesses to Mr. Slope's offer, even if that offer would bind the Bishop. It was better for me, on the whole, to keep on good terms with such men than to fight for what I should never get!"

"Witnesses!" she screamed, rising quickly to her feet, and walking up and down the room. "Do clergymen require witnesses to their words? He made the promise in the Bishop's name, and if it is to be broken, I'll know the reason why. Did he not positively say that the Bishop had sent him to offer you the place?"

"He did, my dear. But that is now nothing to the purpose."

"It is everything to the purpose, Mr. Quiverful. Witnesses indeed! And then to talk of *your* honor being questioned because you wish to provide for fourteen children. It is everything to the purpose, and so they shall know, if I scream it into their ears from the town cross of Barchester."

"You forget, Letitia, that the Bishop has so many things in his gift. We must wait a little longer. That is all."

"Wait! Shall we feed the children by waiting? Will waiting put George, and Tom, and Sam out into the world? Will it enable my poor girls to give up some of their drudgery? Will waiting make Bessy and Jane fit even to be governesses? Will waiting pay for the things we got in Barchester last week?"

"It is all we can do, my dear. The disappointment is as much to me as to you, and yet God knows I feel it more for your sake than my own."

Mrs. Quiverful was looking full into her husband's face, and saw a small hot tear appear on each of those furrowed cheeks. This was too much for her woman's heart. He also had risen, and was standing with his back to the empty grate. She rushed toward him and, seizing him in her arms, sobbed aloud upon his bosom.

"You are too good, too soft, too yielding," she said at last. "These men, when they want you, they use you like a cat's-paw, and when they want you no longer, they throw you aside like an old shoe. This is twice they' have treated you so."

"In one way this will be all for the better," argued he. "It will make the Bishop feel that he is bound to do something for me."

"At any rate he shall hear of it," said the lady, again reverting to her more angry mood. "At any rate he shall hear of it, and that loudly, and so shall she. She little knows Letitia Quiverful if she thinks I will sit quietly with the loss after all that passed between us at the palace. If there's any feeling within her, I'll make her ashamed of herself." And she paced the room again, stamping the floor as she went with her fat, heavy foot. "Good heavens! What a heart she must have within her to treat in such a way as this the father of fourteen unprovided children!"

Mr. Quiverful proceeded to explain that he didn't think that Mrs. Proudie had had anything to do with it.

"Don't tell me," said Mrs. Quiverful. "I know more about it than that. Doesn't all the world know that Mrs. Proudie is Bishop of Barchester, and that Mr. Slope is merely her creature? Wasn't it she that made me the promise, just as though the thing was in her own particular gift? I tell you it was that woman who sent him over here today because, for some reason of her own, she wants to go back from her word."

"My dear, you're wrong——"

"Now, Q, don't be so soft," she continued. "Take my word for it, the Bishop knows no more about it than Jemima does." Jemima was the two-year-old. "And if you'll take my advice, you'll lose no time in going over and seeing him yourself."

Soft, however, as Mr. Quiverful might be, he would not allow himself to be talked out of his opinion on this occasion, and proceeded with much minuteness to explain to his wife the tone in which Mr. Slope had spoken of Mrs. Proudie's interference in diocesan matters. As he did so, a new idea gradually instilled itself into the matron's head, and a new course of conduct presented itself to her judgment. What if, after all, Mrs. Proudie knew nothing of this visit of Mr. Slope's? In that case, might it not be possible that that lady would still be stanch to her in this matter, still stand her friend, and perhaps possibly carry her through in opposition to Mr. Slope? Mrs. Quiverful said nothing as this vague hope occurred to her, but listened with more than ordinary patience to what her husband had to say. While he was still explaining that in all probability the world was wrong in its estimation of Mrs. Proudie's power and authority, she had fully made up her mind as to her course of action. She did not, however, proclaim her intention. She shook her head ominously as he continued his narration, and when he had completed she rose to go, merely observing that it was cruel, cruel treatment. She then asked him if he would mind waiting for a late dinner instead of dining at their usual hour of three, and having received from him a concession on this point, she proceeded to carry her purpose into execution.

She determined that she would at once go to the palace, that she would do so, if possible, before Mrs. Proudie could have had an interview with

Mr. Slope, and that she would be either submissive, piteous, and pathetic or else indignant, violent, and exacting according to the manner in which she was received.

She was quite confident in her own power. Strengthened as she was by the pressing wants of fourteen children, she felt that she could make her way through legions of episcopal servants and force herself, if need be, into the presence of the lady who had so wronged her. She had no shame about it, no *mauvaise honte*, no dread of archdeacons. Mrs. Quiverful, with fourteen children, had given over being shamefaced, and, in some things had given over being decent. If it were intended that she should be ill-used in the manner proposed by Mr. Slope, it should not be done under the rose. All the world should know of it.

In her present mood Mrs. Quiverful was not over careful about her attire. She tied her bonnet under her chin, threw her shawl over her shoulders, armed herself with the old family cotton umbrella, and started for Barchester. A journey to the palace was not quite so easy a thing for Mrs. Quiverful as for our friend at Plumstead. Plumstead is nine miles from Barchester and Puddingdale is but four. But the Archdeacon could order round his brougham, and his high-trotting fast bay gelding would take him into the city within the hour. There was no brougham in the coach house of Puddingdale vicarage, no bay horse in the stables. There was no method of locomotion for its inhabitants but that which nature has assigned to man.

Mrs. Quiverful was a broad, heavy woman, not young, nor given to walking. In her kitchen, and in the family dormitories, she was active enough, but her pace and gait were not adapted for the road. A walk into Barchester and back in the middle of an August day would be to her a terrible task, if not altogether impracticable. There was living in the parish, about a half mile from the vicarage on the road to the city, a decent, kindly farmer, well-to-do as regards this world, and so far mindful of the next that he attended his parish church with decent regularity. To him Mrs. Quiverful had before now appealed in some of her more pressing family troubles, and had not appealed in vain. At his door she now presented herself, and having explained to his wife that most urgent business required her to go at once to Barchester, begged that Farmer Subsoil would take her thither in his tax cart. The farmer did not reject her plan, and, as soon as Prince could be got into his collar they started on their journey.

Mrs. Quiverful did not mention the purpose of her business, nor did the farmer alloy his kindness by any unseemly questions. She merely begged to be put down at the bridge going into the city, and to be taken up again at the same place in the course of two hours. The farmer promised to be punctual to his appointment, and the lady, supported by her umbrella, took the short cut to the close, and in a few minutes was at the Bishop's door.

Hitherto she had felt no dread with regard to the coming interview. She had felt nothing but an indignant longing to pour forth her claims, and declare her wrongs if those claims were not fully admitted. But now the difficulty of her situation touched her a little. She had been at the palace once before, but then she went to give grateful thanks. Those who have thanks to return for favors received find easy admittance to the halls of the great. Such is not always the case with men, or even with women, who have favors to beg. Still less easy is access for those who demand the fulfillment of promises already made.

Mrs. Quiverful had not been slow to learn the ways of the world. She knew all this, and she knew also that her cotton umbrella and all but ragged shawl would not command respect in the eyes of the palatial servants. If she were too humble, she knew well that she would never succeed. To overcome by imperious overbearing with such a shawl as hers upon her shoulders, and such a bonnet on her head, would have required a personal bearing very superior to that with which nature had endowed her. Of this also Mrs. Quiverful was aware. She must make it known that she was the wife of a gentleman and a clergyman, and must yet condescend to conciliate.

The poor lady knew but one way to overcome these difficulties at the very threshold of her enterprise, and to this she resorted. Low as were the domestic funds at Puddingdale, she still retained possession of half a crown, and this she sacrificed to the avarice of Mrs. Proudie's metropolitan sesquipedalian servingman. She was, she said, Mrs. Quiverful of Puddingdale, the wife of the Reverend Mr. Quiverful. She wished to see Mrs. Proudie. It was indeed quite indispensable that she should see Mrs. Proudie. James Fitzplush looked worse than dubious, did not know whether his lady were out or engaged or in her bedroom, thought it most probable she was subject to one of these or to some other cause that would make her invisible, but Mrs. Quiverful could sit down in the waiting-room while inquiry was being made of Mrs. Proudie's maid.

"Look here, my man," said Mrs. Quiverful, "I must see her." And she put her card and half a crown—think of it, my reader, think of it, her last half a crown—into the man's hand, and sat herself down on a chair in the waiting-room.

Whether the bribe carried the day, or whether the Bishop's wife really chose to see the Vicar's wife, it boots not now to inquire. The man returned and, begging Mrs. Quiverful to follow him, ushered her into the presence of the mistress of the diocese.

Mrs. Quiverful at once saw that her patroness was in a smiling humor. Triumph sat throned upon her brow, and all the joys of dominion hovered about her curls. Her lord had that morning contested with her a great point. He had received an invitation to spend a couple of days with the Archbishop. His soul longed for the gratification. Not a word, however, in His Grace's note alluded to the fact of his being a married man, and if he went at all, he must go alone. This necessity would have presented no insurmountable bar to the visit, or have militated much against the pleasure, had he been able to go without any reference to Mrs. Proudie. But this he could not do. He could not order his portmanteau to be packed, and start with his own man, merely telling the lady of his heart that he would probably be back on Saturday. There are men—may we not rather say monsters?—who do such things, and there are wives—may we not rather say slaves?—who put up with such usage. But Dr. and Mrs. Proudie were not among the number.

The Bishop, with some beating about the bush, made the lady understand that he very much wished to go. The lady, without any beating about the bush, made the Bishop understand that she wouldn't hear of it. It would be useless here to repeat the arguments that were used on each side, and needless to record the result. Those who are married will understand very well how the battle was lost and won, and those who are single will never understand it till they learn the lesson which experience alone can give. When Mrs. Quiverful was shown into Mrs. Proudie's room, that lady had only returned a few minutes from her lord. But before she left him she had seen the answer to the Archbishop's note written and sealed. No wonder that her face was wreathed with smiles as she received Mrs. Quiverful.

She instantly spoke of the subject which was so near the heart of her visitor. "Well, Mrs. Quiverful," said she, "is it decided yet when you are to move into Barchester?"

"That woman," as she had an hour or two since been called, became instantly re-endowed with all the graces that can adorn a Bishop's wife. Mrs. Quiverful immediately saw that her business was to be piteous, and that nothing was to be gained by indignation—nothing, indeed, unless she could be indignant in company with her patroness.

"Oh, Mrs. Proudie," she began, "I fear we are not to move to Barchester at all."

"Why not?" said that lady sharply, dropping at a moment's notice her smiles and condescension, and turning with her sharp, quick way to business which she saw at a glance was important.

And then Mrs. Quiverful told her tale. As she progressed in the history of her wrongs she perceived that the heavier she leant upon Mr. Slope, the blacker became Mrs. Proudie's brow, but that such blackness was not injurious to her own cause. When Mr. Slope was at Puddingdale vicarage that morning she had regarded him as the creature of the lady Bishop, now she perceived that they were enemies. She admitted her mistake to herself without any pain or humiliation. She had but one feeling, and that was confined to her family. She cared little how she twisted and turned among these newcomers at the Bishop's palace so long as she could twist her husband into the warden's house. She cared not which was her friend or which was her enemy, if only she could get this preferment which she so sorely wanted.

She told her tale, and Mrs. Proudie listened to it almost in silence. She told how Mr. Slope had cozened her husband into resigning his claim, and had declared that it was the Bishop's will that none but Mr. Harding should be warden. Mrs. Proudie's brow became blacker and blacker. At last she started from her chair, and begging Mrs. Quiverful to sit and wait for her return, marched out of the room.

"Oh, Mrs. Proudie, it's for fourteen children—for fourteen children." Such was the burden that fell on her ear as she closed the door behind her.

CHAPTER XXV

MRS. PROUDIE WRESTLES AND GETS A FALL

It was hardly an hour since Mrs. Proudie had left her husband's apartment victorious, and yet so indomitable was her courage that she now returned thither panting for another combat. She was greatly angry with what she thought was his duplicity. He had so clearly given her a promise on this matter of the hospital. He had been already so absolutely vanquished on that point. Mrs. Proudie began to feel that if every affair was to be thus discussed and battled about twice and even thrice, the work of the diocese would be too much even for her.

Without knocking at the door she walked quickly into her husband's room, and found him seated at his office table, with Mr. Slope opposite to him. Between his fingers was the very note which he had written to the Archbishop in her presence—and it was open! Yes, he had absolutely violated the seal which had been made sacred by her approval. They were sitting in deep conclave, and it was too clear that the purport of the Archbishop's invitation had been absolutely canvassed again, after it had been already debated and decided on in obedience to her behests! Mr. Slope rose from his chair, and bowed slightly. The two opposing spirits looked each other fully in the face, and they knew that they were looking each at an enemy.

"What is this, Bishop, about Mr. Quiverful?" said she, coming to the end of the table and standing there.

Mr. Slope did not allow the Bishop to answer, but replied himself. "I have been out to Puddingdale this morning, ma'am, and have seen Mr. Quiverful. Mr. Quiverful has abandoned his claim to the hospital, because he is now aware that Mr. Harding is desirous to fill his old place. Under these circumstances I have strongly advised his lordship to nominate Mr. Harding."

"Mr. Quiverful has not abandoned anything," said the lady, with a very imperious voice. "His lordship's word has been pledged to him, and it must be respected."

The Bishop still remained silent. He was anxiously desirous of making his old enemy bite the dust beneath his feet. His new ally had told him that nothing was more easy for him than to do so. The ally was there now at his elbow to help him, and yet his courage failed him. It is so hard to conquer when the prestige of former victories is all against one. It is so hard for the cock who has once been beaten out of his yard to resume his courage and again take a proud place upon a dunghill.

"Perhaps I ought not to interfere," said Mr. Slope, "but yet—"

"Certainly you ought not," said the infuriated dame.

"But yet," continued Mr. Slope, not regarding the interruption, "I have thought it my imperative duty to recommend the Bishop not to slight Mr. Harding's claims."

"Mr. Harding should have known his own mind," said the lady.

"If Mr. Harding be not replaced at the hospital, his lordship will have to encounter much ill will, not only in the diocese, but in the world at large. Besides, taking a higher ground, his lordship, as I understand, feels it to be his duty to gratify in this matter so very worthy a man and so good a clergyman as Mr. Harding."

"And what is to become of the Sabbath-day school, and of the Sunday services in the hospital?" said Mrs. Proudie, with something very nearly approaching to a sneer on her face.

"I understand that Mr. Harding makes no objection to the Sabbath-day school," said Mr. Slope. "And as to the hospital services, that matter will be best discussed after his appointment. If he has any permanent objection, then I fear the matter must rest."

"You have a very easy conscience in such matters, Mr. Slope," said she.

"I should not have an easy conscience," he rejoined, "but a conscience very far from being easy, if anything said or done by me should lead the Bishop to act unadvisedly in this matter. It is clear that in the interview I had with Mr. Harding, I misunderstood him—"

"And it is equally clear that you have misunderstood Mr. Quiverful," said she, now at the top of her wrath. "What business have you at all with these interviews? Who desired you to go to Mr. Quiverful this morning? Who commissioned you to manage this affair? Will you answer me, sir?— Who sent you to Mr. Quiverful this morning?"

There was a dead pause in the room. Mr. Slope had risen from his chair, and was standing with his hand on the back of it, looking at first very solemn and now very black. Mrs. Proudie was standing as she had at first placed herself, at the end of the table, and as she interrogated her foe she struck her hand upon it with almost more than feminine vigor. The Bishop was sitting in his easy chair twiddling his thumbs, turning his eyes now to his wife and now to his chaplain, as each took up the cudgels. How comfortable it would be if they could fight it out between them without the necessity of any interference on his part, fight it out so that one should kill the other utterly, as far as diocesan life was concerned, so that he, the Bishop, might know clearly by whom it behooved him to be led. There would be the comfort of quiet in either case, but if the Bishop had a wish as to which might prove the victor, that wish was certainly not antagonistic to Mr. Slope.

"Better the devil you know than the devil you don't know," is an old saying, and perhaps a true one, but the Bishop had not yet realized the truth of it.

"Will you answer me, sir?" she repeated. "Who instructed you to call on Mr. Quiverful this morning?" There was another pause. "Do you intend to answer me, sir?"

"I think, Mrs. Proudie, that under all the circumstances it will be better for me not to answer such a question," said Mr. Slope. Mr. Slope had many tones in his voice, all duly under his command. Among them was a sanctified low tone and a sanctified loud tone, and he now used the former.

"Did anyone send you, sir?"

"Mrs. Proudie," said Mr. Slope, "I am quite aware how much I owe to your kindness. I am aware also what is due by courtesy from a gentleman to a lady. But there are higher considerations than either of those, and I hope I shall be forgiven if I now allow myself to be actuated solely by them. My duty in this matter is to his lordship, and I can admit of no questioning but from him. He has approved of what I have done, and you must excuse me if I say that having that approval and my own, I want none other."

What horrid words were these which greeted the ear of Mrs. Proudie? The matter was indeed too clear. There was premeditated mutiny in the camp. Not only had ill-conditioned minds become insubordinate by the fruition of a little power, but sedition had been overtly taught and preached. The Bishop had not yet been twelve months in his chair, and rebellion had already reared her hideous head within the palace. Anarchy and misrule would quickly follow unless she took immediate and strong measures to put down the conspiracy which she had detected.

"Mr. Slope," she said, with slow and dignified voice, differing much from that which she had hitherto used, "Mr. Slope, I will trouble you, if you please, to leave the apartment. I wish to speak to my lord alone."

Mr. Slope also felt that everything depended on the present interview. Should the Bishop now be repetticoated, his thralldom would be complete and forever. The present moment was peculiarly propitious for rebellion. The Bishop had clearly committed himself by breaking the seal of the answer to the Archbishop. He had therefore fear to influence him. Mr. Slope had told him that no consideration ought to induce him to refuse the Archbishop's invitation. He had therefore hope to influence him. He had accepted Mr. Quiverful's resignation, and therefore dreaded having to renew that matter with his wife. He had been screwed up to the pitch of asserting a will of his own, and might possibly be carried on till by an absolute success he should have been taught how possible it was to succeed. Now was the moment for victory or rout. It was now that Mr. Slope must make himself master of the diocese or else resign his place and begin his search for fortune again. He saw all this plainly. After what had taken place any compromise between him and the lady was impossible. Let him once leave the room at her bidding and leave the Bishop in her hands, and he might at once pack up his portmanteau and bid adieu to episcopal honors, Mrs. Bold, and the Signora Neroni.

And yet it was not so easy to keep his ground when he was bidden by a lady to go, or to continue to make a third in a party between a husband and wife when the wife expressed a wish for a tête-à-tête with her husband.

"Mr. Slope," she repeated, "I wish to be alone with my lord."

"His lordship has summoned me on most important diocesan business," said Mr. Slope, glancing with uneasy eye at Dr. Proudie. He felt that he must trust something to the Bishop, and yet that trust was so woefully ill-placed. "My leaving him at the present moment is, I fear, impossible."

"Do you bandy words with me, you ungrateful man?" said she. "My lord, will you do me the favor to beg Mr. Slope to leave the room?"

My lord scratched his head, but for the moment said nothing. This was as much as Mr. Slope expected from him, and was on the whole, for him, an active exercise of marital rights.

"My lord," said the lady, "is Mr. Slope to leave this room, or am I?"

Here Mrs. Proudie made a false step. She should not have alluded to the possibility of retreat on her part. She should not have expressed the idea that her order for Mr. Slope's expulsion could be treated otherwise than by immediate obedience. In answer to such a question the Bishop naturally said in his own mind that as it was necessary that one should leave the room, perhaps it might be as well that Mrs. Proudie did so. He did say so in his own mind, but externally he again scratched his head and again twiddled this thumbs.

Mrs. Proudie was boiling over with wrath. Alas, alas! Could she but have kept her temper as her enemy did, she would have conquered as she had ever conquered. But divine anger got the better of her, as it has done of other heroines, and she fell.

"My lord," said she, "am I to be vouchsafed an answer or am I not?"

At last he broke his deep silence and proclaimed himself a Slopeite. "Why, my dear," said he, "Mr. Slope and I are very busy."

That was all. There was nothing more necessary. He had gone to the battlefield, stood the dust and heat of the day, encountered the fury of the foe, and won the victory. How easy is success to those who will only be true to themselves!

Mr. Slope saw at once the full amount of his gain, and turned on the vanquished lady a look of triumph which she never forgot and never forgave. Here he was wrong. He should have looked humbly at her, and with meek, entreating eye have deprecated her anger. He should have said by his glance that he asked pardon for his success, and that he hoped forgiveness for the stand which he had been forced to make in the cause of duty. So might he perchance have somewhat mollified that imperious bosom, and prepared the way for future terms. But Mr. Slope meant to rule without terms. Ah, forgetful, inexperienced man! Can you cause that little trembling victim to be divorced from the woman that possesses him? Can you provide that they shall be separated at bed and board? Is he not flesh of her flesh and bone of her bone, and must he not so continue? It is very well now for you to stand your ground, and triumph as she is driven ignominiously from the room, but can you be present when those curtains are drawn, when that awful helmet of proof has been tied beneath the chin, when the small remnants of the Bishop's prowess shall be cowed by the tassel above his head? Can you then intrude yourself when the wife wishes "to speak to my lord alone"?

But for the moment Mr. Slope's triumph was complete, for Mrs. Proudie without further parley left the room, and did not forget to shut the door after her. Then followed a close conference between the new allies, in which was said much which it astonished Mr. Slope to say and the Bishop to hear. And yet the one said it and the other heard it without ill will. There was no mincing of matters now. The chaplain plainly told the Bishop that the world gave him credit for being under the governance of his wife, that his credit and character in the diocese were suffering, that he would surely get himself into hot water if he allowed Mrs. Proudie to interfere in matters which were not suitable for a woman's powers, and in fact that he would become contemptible if he did not throw off the yoke under which he groaned. The Bishop at first hummed and hawed, and affected to deny the truth of what was said. But his denial was not stout and quickly broke down. He soon admitted by silence his state of vassalage, and pledged himself, with Mr. Slope's assistance, to change his courses. Mr. Slope also did not make out a bad case for himself. He explained how it grieved him to run counter to a lady who had always been his patroness, who had befriended him in so many ways, who had, in fact, recommended him to the Bishop's notice. But, as he stated, his duty was now imperative, he held a situation of peculiar confidence, and was immediately and especially attached to the Bishop's person. In such a situation his conscience required that he should regard solely the Bishop's interests, and therefore he had ventured to speak out.

The Bishop took this for what it was worth, and Mr. Slope only intended that he should do so. It gilded the pill which Mr. Slope had to administer and which the Bishop thought would be less bitter than that other pill which he had so long been taking.

"My lord" had his immediate reward, like a good child. He was instructed to write and at once did write another note to the Archbishop accepting His Grace's invitation. This note Mr. Slope, more prudent than the lady, himself took away and posted with his own hands. Thus he made sure that this act of self-jurisdiction should be as nearly as possible a fait accompli. He begged, and coaxed, and threatened the Bishop with a view of making him also write at once to Mr. Harding, but the Bishop, though temporarily emancipated from his wife, was not yet enthralled to Mr. Slope. He said, and probably said truly, that such an offer must be made in some official form, that he was not yet prepared to sign the form, and that he should prefer seeing Mr. Harding before he did so. Mr. Slope might, however, beg Mr. Harding to call upon him. Not disappointed with his achievement, Mr. Slope went his way. He first posted the precious note which he had in his pocket, and then pursued other enterprises in which we must follow him in other chapters.

Mrs. Proudie, having received such satisfaction as was to be derived from slamming her husband's door, did not at once betake herself to Mrs. Quiverful. Indeed for the first few moments after her repulse she felt that she could not again see that lady. She would have to own that she had been beaten, to confess that the diadem had passed from her brow and the scepter from her hand! No, she would send a message to her with the promise of a letter on the next day or the day after. Thus resolving, she betook herself to her bedroom, but here she again changed her mind. The air of that sacred enclosure somewhat restored her courage and gave her more heart. As Achilles warmed at the sight of his armor, as Don Quixote's heart grew strong when he grasped his lance, so did Mrs. Proudie look forward to fresh laurels as her eye fell on her husband's pillow. She would not despair. Having so resolved, she descended with dignified mien and refreshed countenance to Mrs. Quiverful.

This scene in the Bishop's study took longer in the acting than in the telling. We have not, perhaps, had the whole of the conversation. At any rate Mrs. Quiverful was beginning to be very impatient, and was thinking that Farmer Subsoil would be tired of waiting for her when Mrs. Proudie returned.

"Mrs. Quiverful," thus spoke the lady with considerable austerity, and without sitting down herself, "I find that your husband has behaved in this matter in a very weak and foolish manner."

Mrs. Quiverful immediately rose upon her feet, thinking it disrespectful to remain sitting while the wife of the Bishop stood. But she was desired to sit down again, and made to do so, so that Mrs. Proudie might stand and preach over her. Mrs. Quiverful was cowed and uncomfortable, and a second time essayed to rise from her chair.

"Pray be seated, Mrs. Quiverful, pray keep your seat. Your husband, I say, has been most weak and most foolish. It is impossible, Mrs. Quiverful, to help people who will not help themselves. I much fear that I can now do nothing for you in this matter."

"Oh, Mrs. Proudie, don't say so!" said the poor woman, again jumping up.

"Pray be seated, Mrs. Quiverful. I much fear that I can do nothing further for you in this matter. Your husband has, in a most unaccountable manner, taken upon himself to resign that which I was empowered to offer him. As a matter of course, the Bishop expects that his clergy shall know their own minds. What he may ultimately do—what we may finally decide on doing—I cannot now say. Knowing the extent of your family——"

"Fourteen children, Mrs. Proudie, fourteen of them! And barely bread

—barely bread! It's hard for the children of a clergyman, it's hard for one who has always done his duty respectably!" Not a word fell from her about herself, but the tears came streaming down her big coarse cheeks, on which the dust of the August road had left its traces.

Mrs. Proudie has not been portrayed in these pages as an agreeable or an amiable lady. There has been no intention to impress the reader much in her favor. It is ordained that all novels should have a male and a female angel, and a male and a female devil. If it be considered that this rule is obeyed in these pages, the latter character must be supposed to have fallen to the lot of Mrs. Proudie. But she was not all devil. There was a heart inside that stiff-ribbed bodice, though not, perhaps, of large dimensions, and certainly not easily accessible. Mrs. Quiverful, however, did gain access, and Mrs. Proudie proved herself a woman. Whether it was the fourteen children with their probable bare bread and their possible bare backs, or the respectability of the father's work, or the mingled dust and tears on the mother's face, we will not pretend to say. But Mrs. Proudie was touched.

She did not show it as other women might have done. She did not give Mrs. Quiverful eau-de-Cologne, or order her a glass of wine. She did not take her to her toilet table and offer her the use of brushes and combs, towels and water. She did not say soft little speeches and coax her kindly back to equanimity. Mrs. Quiverful, despite her rough appearance, would have been as amenable to such little tender cares as any lady in the land. But none such were forthcoming. Instead of this, Mrs. Proudie slapped one hand upon the other and declared—not with an oath, for as a lady and a Sabbatarian and a she-Bishop, she could not swear, but with an adjuration—that she wouldn't have it done.

The meaning of this was that she wouldn't have Mr. Quiverful's promised appointment cozened away by the treachery of Mr. Slope and the weakness of her husband. This meaning she very soon explained to Mrs. Quiverful.

"Why was your husband such a fool," said she, now dismounted from her high horse and sitting confidentially down close to her visitor, "as to take the bait which that man threw to him? If he had not been so utterly foolish, nothing could have prevented your going to the hospital."

Poor Mrs. Quiverful was ready enough with her own tongue in accusing her husband to his face of being soft, and perhaps did not always speak of him to her children quite so respectfully as she might have done. But she did not at all like to hear him abused by others, and began to vindicate him, and to explain that of course he had taken Mr. Slope to be an emissary from Mrs. Proudie herself, that Mr. Slope was thought to be peculiarly her friend, and that therefore Mr. Quiverful would have been failing in respect to her had he assumed to doubt what Mr. Slope had said.

Thus mollified, Mrs. Proudie again declared that she would not have it done, and at last sent Mrs. Quiverful home with an assurance that, to the furthest stretch of her power and influence in the palace, the appointment of Mr. Quiverful should be insisted on. As she repeated the word "insisted," she thought of the Bishop in his nightcap, and with compressed lips slightly shook her head.

Mrs. Quiverful got home in the farmer's cart, not indeed with a light heart, but satisfied that she had done right in making her visit.

CHAPTER XXVI

A LOVE SCENE

MR. SLOPE, as we have said, left the palace with a feeling of considerable triumph. Not that he thought that his difficulties were all over, he did not so deceive himself. But he felt that he had played his first move well, as well as the pieces on the board would allow, and that he had nothing with which to reproach himself. He first of all posted the letter to the Archbishop, and having made that sure he proceeded to push the advantage which he had gained. Had Mrs. Bold been at home, he would have called on her, but he knew that she was at Plumstead, so he wrote the following note. It was the beginning of what he trusted might be a long and tender series of epistles.

My dear Mrs. Bold, You will understand perfectly that I cannot at present correspond with your father. I heartily wish that I could, and hope that the day may be not long distant when mists shall have cleared away, and we may know each other. But I cannot preclude myself from the pleasure of sending you these few lines to say that Mr. Q has today, in my presence, resigned any title that he ever had to the wardenship of the hospital, and that the Bishop has assured me that it is his intention to offer it to your esteemed father.

Will you, with my respectful compliments, ask him, who I believe is now a fellow visitor with you, to call on the Bishop either on Wednesday or Thursday, between ten and one. *This is by the Bishop's desire.* If you will so far oblige me as to let me have a line naming either day, and the hour which will suit Mr. Harding, I will take care that the servants shall have orders to show him in without delay. Perhaps I should say no more, but still I wish you could make your father understand that no subject will be mooted between his lordship and him which will refer at all to the method in which he may choose to perform his duty. I, for one, am persuaded that no clergyman could perform it more satisfactorily than he did, or than he will do again.

On a former occasion I was indiscreet and much too impatient, considering your father's age and my own. I hope he will not now refuse my apology. I still hope also that, with your aid and sweet pious labors, we may live to attach such a Sabbath school to the old endowment as may, by God's grace and furtherance, be a blessing to the poor of this city.

You will see at once that this letter is confidential. The subject of course makes it so. But, equally of course, it is for your parent's eye as well as for your own, should you think proper to show it to him.

I hope my darling little friend Johnny is as strong as ever—dear little fellow. Does he still continue his rude assaults on those beautiful long silken tresses?

I can assure you your friends miss you from Barchester sorely, but it would be cruel to begrudge you your sojourn among flowers and fields during this truly sultry weather.

Pray believe me, my dear Mrs. Bold,
Yours most sincerely,
OBADIAH SLOPE

Barchester, Friday

Now this letter, taken as a whole, and with the consideration that Mr. Slope wished to assume a great degree of intimacy with Eleanor, would not have been bad but for the allusion to the tresses. Gentlemen do not write to ladies about their tresses unless they are on very intimate terms indeed. But Mr. Slope could not be expected to be aware of this. He longed to put a little affection into his epistle, and yet he thought it injudicious, as the letter would he knew be shown to Mr. Harding. He would have insisted that the letter should be strictly private, and seen by no eyes but Eleanor's own, had he not felt that such an injunction would have been disobeyed. He therefore restrained his passion, did not sign himself "Yours affectionately," and contented himself instead with the compliment to the tresses.

Having finished his letter, he took it to Mrs. Bold's house, and learning there from the servant that things were to be sent out to Plumstead that afternoon, left it, with many injunctions, in her hands.

We will now follow Mr. Slope so as to complete the day with him, and then return to his letter and its momentous fate in the next chapter.

There is an old song which gives us some very good advice about courting:

It's gude to be off with the auld luve
Before ye be on wi' the new.

Of the wisdom of this maxim Mr. Slope was ignorant, and accordingly, having written his letter to Mrs. Bold, he proceeded to call upon the Signora Neroni. Indeed it was hard to say which was the old love and which the new, Mr. Slope having been smitten with both so nearly at the same time. Perhaps he thought it not amiss to have two strings to his bow. But two strings to Cupid's bow are always dangerous to him on whose behalf they are to be used. A man should remember that between two stools he may fall to the ground.

But in sooth Mr. Slope was pursuing Mrs. Bold in obedience to his better instincts, and the Signora in obedience to his worser. Had he won the widow and worn her, no one could have blamed him. You, O reader, and I and Eleanor's other friends would have received the story of such a winning with much disgust and disappointment, but we should have been angry with Eleanor, not with Mr. Slope. Bishop, male and female, Dean and Chapter and diocesan clergy in full congress, could have found nothing to disapprove of in such an alliance. Convocation itself, that mysterious and mighty synod, could in no wise have fallen foul of it. The possession of £1000 a year and a beautiful wife would not at all have hurt the voice of the pulpit charmer, or lessened the grace and piety of the exemplary clergyman.

But not of such a nature were likely to be his dealings with the Signora Neroni. In the first place he knew that her husband was living, and therefore he could not woo her honestly. Then again she had nothing to recommend her to his honest wooing had such been possible. She was not only portionless, but also from misfortune unfitted to be chosen as the wife of any man who wanted a useful mate. Mr. Slope was aware that she was a helpless, hopeless cripple.

But Mr. Slope could not help himself. He knew that he was wrong in devoting his time to the back drawing-room in Dr. Stanhope's house. He knew that what took place there would if divulged utterly ruin him with Mrs. Bold. He knew that scandal would soon come upon his heels and spread abroad among the black coats of Barchester some tidings, exaggerated tidings, of the sighs which he poured into the lady's ears. He knew that he was acting against the recognized principles of his life, against those laws of conduct by which he hoped to achieve much higher success. But as we have said, he could not help himself. Passion, for the first time in his life, passion was too strong for him.

As for the Signora, no such plea can be put forward for her, for in truth she cared no more for Mr. Slope than she did for twenty others who had been at her feet before him. She willingly—nay, greedily—accepted his homage. He was the finest fly that Barchester had hitherto afforded to her web, and the Signora was a powerful spider that made wondrous webs and could in no way live without catching flies. Her taste in this respect was abominable, for she had no use for the victims when caught. She could not eat them matrimonially, as young lady spiders do whose webs are most frequently of their mothers' weaving. Nor could she devour them by any escapade of a less legitimate description. Her unfortunate affliction precluded her from all hope of levanting with a lover. It would be impossible to run away with a lady who required three servants to move her from a sofa.

The Signora was subdued by no passion. Her time for love was gone.

She had lived out her heart, such heart as she had ever had, in her early years, at an age when Mr. Slope was thinking of the second book of Euclid and his unpaid bill at the buttery hatch. In age the lady was younger than the gentleman, but in feelings, in knowledge of the affairs of love, in intrigue, he was immeasurably her junior. It was necessary to her to have some man at her feet. It was the one customary excitement of her life. She delighted in the exercise of power which this gave her, it was now nearly the only food for her ambition. She would boast to her sister that she could make a fool of any man, and the sister, as little imbued with feminine delicacy as herself, good-naturedly thought it but fair that such amusement should be afforded to a poor invalid who was debarred from the ordinary pleasures of life.

Mr. Slope was madly in love, but hardly knew it. The Signora spitted him, as a boy does a cockchafer on a cork, that she might enjoy the energetic agony of his gyrations. And she knew very well what she was doing.

Mr. Slope, having added to his person all such adornments as are possible to a clergyman making a morning visit, such as a clean necktie, clean handkerchief, new gloves, and a soupçon of not unnecessary scent, called about three o'clock at the Doctor's door. At about this hour the Signora was almost always alone in the back drawing-room. The mother had not come down. The Doctor was out or in his own room. Bertie was out, and Charlotte at any rate left the room if anyone called whose object was specially with her sister. Such was her idea of being charitable and sisterly.

Mr. Slope, as was his custom, asked for Mr. Stanhope, and was told, as was the servant's custom, that the Signora was in the drawing-room. Upstairs he accordingly went. He found her, as he always did, lying on her sofa with a French volume before her, and a beautiful little inlaid writing case open on her table. At the moment of his entrance she was in the act of writing.

"Ah, my friend," said she, putting out her left hand to him, across her desk, "I did not expect you today and was this very instant writing to you——"

Mr. Slope, taking the soft fair delicate hand in his—and very soft and fair and delicate it was—bowed over it his huge red head and kissed it. It was a sight to see, a deed to record if the author could fitly do it, a picture to put on canvas. Mr. Slope was big, awkward, cumbrous, and having his heart in his pursuit was ill at ease. The lady was fair, as we have said, and delicate. Everything about her was fine and refined. Her hand in his looked like a rose lying among carrots, and when he kissed it he looked as a cow might do on finding such a flower among her food. She was graceful as a couchant goddess, and moreover as self-possessed as Venus must have been when courting Adonis.

Oh, that such grace and such beauty should have condescended to waste itself on such a pursuit!

"I was in the act of writing to you," said she, "but now my scrawl may go into the basket." And she raised the sheet of gilded note paper from off her desk as though to tear it.

"Indeed it shall not," said he, laying the embargo of half a stone weight of human flesh and blood upon the devoted paper. "Nothing that you write for my eyes, Signora, shall be so desecrated." And he took up the letter, put that also among the carrots and fed on it, and then proceeded to read it.

"Gracious me! Mr. Slope," said she, "I hope you don't mean to say that you keep all the trash I write to you. Half my time I don't know what I write, and when I do, I know it is only fit for the back of the fire. I hope you have not that ugly trick of keeping letters."

"At any rate, I don't throw them into a wastepaper basket. If destruction is their doomed lot, they perish worthily, and are burnt on a pyre, as Dido was of old."

"With a steel pen stuck through them, of course," said she, "to make the simile more complete. Of all the ladies of my acquaintance I think Lady Dido was the most absurd. Why did she not do as Cleopatra did? Why did she not take out her ships and insist on going with him? She could not bear to lose the land she had got by a swindle, and then she could not bear the loss of her lover. So she fell between two stools. Mr. Slope, whatever you do, never mingle love and business."

Mr. Slope blushed up to his eyes, and over his mottled forehead to the very roots of his hair. He felt sure that the Signora knew all about his intentions with reference to Mrs. Bold. His conscience told him that he was detected. His doom was to be spoken, he was to be punished for his duplicity and rejected by the beautiful creature before him. Poor man. He little dreamt that had all his intentions with reference to Mrs. Bold been known to the Signora, it would only have added zest to that lady's amusement. It was all very well to have Mr. Slope at her feet, to show her power by making an utter fool of a clergyman, to gratify her own infidelity by thus proving the little strength which religion had in controlling the passions even of a religious man. But it would be an increased gratification if she could be made to understand that she was at the same time alluring her victim away from another whose love if secured would be in every way beneficent and salutary.

The Signora had indeed discovered with the keen instinct of such a woman that Mr. Slope was bent on matrimony with Mrs. Bold, but in alluding to Dido she had not thought of it. She instantly perceived, however, from her lover's blushes, what was on his mind, and was not slow in taking advantage of it.

She looked him full in the face, not angrily, nor yet with a smile, but with an intense and overpowering gaze, and then holding up her fore-finger and slightly shaking her head, she said:

"Whatever you do, my friend, do not mingle love and business. Either stick to your treasure and your city of wealth, or else follow your love like a true man. But never attempt both. If you do, you'll have to die with a broken heart as did poor Dido. Which is it to be with you, Mr. Slope, love or money?"

Mr. Slope was not so ready with a pathetic answer as he usually was with touching episodes in his extempore sermons. He felt that he ought to say something pretty, something also that should remove the impression on the mind of his ladylove. But he was rather put about how to do it.

"Love," said he, "true overpowering love, must be the strongest passion a man can feel. It must control every other wish, and put aside every other pursuit. But with me love will never act in that way unless it be returned." And he threw upon the Signora a look of tenderness which was intended to make up for all the deficiencies of his speech.

"Take my advice," said she. "Never mind love. After all, what is it? The dream of a few weeks. That is all its joy. The disappointment of a life is its Nemesis. Who was ever successful in true love? Success in love argues that the love is false. True love is always despondent or tragical. Juliet loved, Haidee loved, Dido loved, and what came of it? Troilus loved and ceased to be a man."

"Troilus loved and was fooled," said the more manly chaplain. "A man may love and yet not be a Troilus. All women are not Cressids."

"No, all women are not Cressids. The falsehood is not always on the woman's side. Imogen was true, but how was she rewarded? Her lord believed her to be the paramour of the first he who came near her in his absence. Desdemona was true and was smothered. Ophelia was true and went mad. There is no happiness in love, except at the end of an English novel. But in wealth, money, houses, lands, goods and chattels, in the good things of this world, yes, in them there is something tangible, something that can be retained and enjoyed."

"Oh, no," said Mr. Slope, feeling himself bound to enter some protest against so very unorthodox a doctrine. "This world's wealth will make no one happy."

"And what will make you happy—you—you?" said she, raising herself up and speaking to him with energy across the table. "From what source do you look for happiness? Do not say that you look for none. I shall not believe you. It is a search in which every human being spends an existence."

"And the search is always in vain," said Mr. Slope. "We look for happiness on earth while we ought to be content to hope for it in Heaven."

"Pshaw! You preach a doctrine which you know you don't believe. It is the way with you all. If you know that there is no earthly happiness, why do you long to be a bishop or a dean? Why do you want lands and income?"

"I have the natural ambition of a man," said he.

"Of course you have, and the natural passions, and therefore I say that you don't believe the doctrine you preach. St. Paul was an enthusiast. He believed so that his ambition and passions did not war against his creed. So does the Eastern fanatic who passes half his life erect upon a pillar. As for me, I will believe in no belief that does not make itself manifest by outward signs.

I will think no preaching sincere that is not recommended by the practice of the preacher."

Mr. Slope was startled and horrified, but he felt that he could not answer. How could he stand up and preach the lessons of his Master, being there, as he was, on the Devil's business? He was a true believer, otherwise this would have been nothing to him. He had audacity for most things, but he had not audacity to make a plaything of the Lord's word. All this the Signora understood, and felt much interest as she saw her cockchafer whirl round upon her pin.

"Your wit delights in such arguments," said he, "but your heart and your reason do not go along with them."

"My heart!" said she. "You quite mistake the principles of my composition if you imagine that there is such a thing about me." After all, there was very little that was false in anything that the Signora said. If Mr. Slope allowed himself to be deceived, it was his own fault. Nothing could have been more open than her declarations about herself.

The little writing table with her desk was still standing before her, a barrier, as it were, against the enemy. She was sitting as nearly upright as she ever did, and he had brought a chair close to the sofa, so that there was only the corner of the table between him and her. It so happened that as she spoke her hand lay upon the table, and as Mr. Slope answered her he put his hand upon hers.

"No heart!" said he. "That is a heavy charge which you bring against yourself, and one of which I cannot find you guilty——"

She withdrew her hand, not quickly and angrily, as though insulted by his touch, but gently and slowly.

"You are in no condition to give a verdict on the matter," said she, "as you have not tried me. No, don't say that you intend doing so, for you know you have no intention of the kind, nor indeed have I either. As for you, you will take your vows where they will result in something more substantial than the pursuit of such a ghostlike, ghastly love as mine."

"Your love should be sufficient to satisfy the dream of a monarch," said Mr. Slope, not quite clear as to the meaning of his words.

"Say an archbishop, Mr. Slope," said she. Poor fellow! she was very cruel to him. He went round again upon his cork on this allusion to his profession. He tried, however, to smile, and gently accused her of joking on a matter which was, he said, to him of such vital moment.

"Why, what gulls do you men make of us!" she replied. "How you fool us to the top of our bent, and of all men you clergymen are the most fluent of your honeyed, caressing words. Now look me in the face, Mr. Slope, boldly and openly."

Mr. Slope did look at her with a languishing, loving eye, and as he did so he again put forth his hand to get hold of hers.

"I told you to look at me boldly, Mr. Slope, but confine your boldness to your eyes."

"Oh, Madeline!" he sighed.

"Well, my name is Madeline," said she, "but none except my own family usually call me so. Now look me in the face, Mr. Slope. Am I to understand that you say you love me?"

Mr. Slope never had said so. If he had come there with any formed plan at all, his intention was to make love to the lady without uttering any such declaration. It was, however, quite impossible that he should now deny his love. He had therefore nothing for it but to go down on his knees distractedly against the sofa, and swear that he did love her with a love passing the love of man.

The Signora received the assurance with very little palpitation or appearance of surprise. "And now answer me another question," said she. "When are you to be married to my dear friend Eleanor Bold?"

Poor Mr. Slope went round and round in mortal agony. In such a condition as his it was really very hard for him to know what answer to give. And yet no answer would be his surest condemnation. He might as well at once plead guilty to the charge brought against him.

"And why do you accuse me of such dissimulation?" said he.

"Dissimulation! I said nothing of dissimulation. I made no charge against you, and make none. Pray don't defend yourself to me. You swear that you are devoted to my beauty, and yet you are on the eve of matrimony with another. I feel this to be rather a compliment. It is to Mrs. Bold that you must defend yourself. That you may find difficult, unless, indeed, you can keep her in the dark. You clergymen are cleverer than other men."

"Signora, I have told you that I loved you, and now you rail at me?"

"Rail at you! God bless the man, what would he have? Come, answer me this at your leisure—not without thinking, now, but leisurely and with consideration. Are you not going to be married to Mrs. Bold?"

"I am not," said he. And as he said it, he almost hated, with an exquisite hatred, the woman whom he could not help loving with an exquisite love.

"But surely you are a worshiper of hers?"

"I am not," said Mr. Slope, to whom the word "worshiper" was peculiarly distasteful. The Signora had conceived that it would be so.

"I wonder at that," said she. "Do you not admire her? To my eye she is the perfection of English beauty. And then she is rich too. I should have thought she was just the person to attract you. Come, Mr. Slope, let me give you advice on this matter. Marry the charming widow. She will be a good mother to your children, and an excellent mistress of a clergyman's household."

"Oh, Signora, how can you be so cruel?"

"Cruel," said she, changing the voice of banter which she had been using for one which was expressively earnest in its tone. "Is that cruelty?"

"How can I love another while my heart is entirely your own?"

"If that were cruelty, Mr. Slope, what might you say of me if I were to declare that I returned your passion? What would you think if I bound

ou even by a lover's oath to do daily penance at this couch of mine?
What can I give in return for a man's love? Ah, dear friend, you have not
realized the conditions of my fate."

Mr. Slope was not on his knees all this time. After his declaration of love
he had risen from them as quickly as he thought consistent with the new
position which he now filled, and as he stood was leaning on the back of
his chair. This outburst of tenderness on the Signora's part quite overcame
him, and made him feel for the moment that he could sacrifice everything
to be assured of the love of the beautiful creature before him, maimed, lame,
and already married as she was.

"And can I not sympathize with your lot?" said he, now seating himself
on her sofa and pushing away the table with his foot.

"Sympathy is so near to pity!" said she. "If you pity me, cripple as I
am, I shall spurn you from me."

"Oh, Madeline, I will only love you." And again he caught her hand and
devoured it with kisses. Now she did not draw it from him, but sat there
as he kissed it, looking at him with her great eyes just as a great spider
would look at a great fly that was quite securely caught.

"Suppose Signor Neroni were to come to Barchester," said she. "Would
you make his acquaintance?"

"Signor Neroni!" said he.

"Would you introduce him to the Bishop, and Mrs. Proudie, and the
young ladies?" said she, again having recourse to that horrid quizzing voice
which Mr. Slope so particularly hated.

"Why do you ask such a question?" said he.

"Because it is necessary that you should know that there is a Signor
Neroni. I think you had forgotten it."

"If I thought that you retained for what wretch one particle of the love
of which he was never worthy, I would die before I would distract you by
telling you what I feel. No! Were your husband the master of your heart,
I might perhaps love you, but you should never know it."

"My heart again! How you talk. And you consider, then, that if a
husband be not master of his wife's heart, he has no right to her fealty,
if a wife ceases to love, she may cease to be true. Is that your doctrine on
this matter, as a minister of the Church of England?"

Mr. Slope tried hard within himself to cast off the pollution with which
he felt that he was defiling his soul. He strove to tear himself away from the
noxious siren that had bewitched him. But he could not do it. He could not
be again heart-free. He had looked for rapturous joy in loving this lovely
creature, and he already found that he met with little but disappointment
and self-rebuke. He had come across the fruit of the Dead Sea, so sweet
and delicious to the eye, so bitter and nauseous to the taste. He had put
the apple to his mouth, and it had turned to ashes between his teeth. Yet
he could not tear himself away. He knew, he could not but know, that she
jeered at him, ridiculed his love, and insulted the weakness of his religion.

But she half-permitted his adoration, and that half-permission added such
fuel to his fire that all the fountain of his piety could not quench it. He
began to feel savage, irritated, and revengeful. He meditated some severity
of speech, some taunt that should cut her as her taunts cut him. He reflected
as he stood there for a moment silent before her that if he desired to quell
her proud spirit he should do so by being prouder even than herself, that
if he wished to have her at his feet suppliant for his love it behooved him
to conquer her by indifference. All this passed through his mind. As far as
dead knowledge went, he knew, or thought he knew, how a woman should
be tamed. But when he essayed to bring his tactics to bear, he failed like
a child. What chance has dead knowledge with experience in any of the
transactions between man and man? What possible chance between man
and woman? Mr. Slope loved furiously, insanely, and truly, but he had
never played the game of love. The Signora did not love at all, but she
was up to every move of the board. It was Philidor pitted against a schoolboy.

And so she continued to insult him, and he continued to bear it.

"Sacrifice the world for love!" said she in answer to some renewed vapid
declaration of his passion. "How often has the same thing been said, and
how invariably with the same falsehood!"

"Falsehood," said he. "Do you say that I am false to you? Do you say that
my love is not real?"

"False? Of course it is false, false as the father of falsehood—if indeed
falsehoods need a sire and are not self-begotten since the world began.
You are ready to sacrifice the world for love? Come, let us see what you
will sacrifice. I care nothing for nuptial vows. The wretch—I think you
were kind enough to call him so—whom I swore to love and obey is so
base that he can only be thought of with repulsive disgust. In the
council chamber of my heart I have divorced him. To me that is as good
as though aged lords had gloated for months over the details of his licentious
life. I care nothing for what the world can say. Will you be as frank? Will
you take me to your home as your wife? Will you call me Mrs. Slope
before Bishop, Dean, and prebendaries?" The poor tortured wretch stood
silent, not knowing what to say. "What! You won't do that? Tell me, then,
what part of the world is it that you will sacrifice for my charms?"

"Were you free to marry, I would take you to my house tomorrow and
wish no higher privilege."

"I am free," said she, almost starting up in her energy. For though
there was no truth in her pretended regard for her clerical admirer, there
was a mixture of real feeling in the scorn and satire with which she spoke
of love and marriage generally. "I am free, free as the winds. Come, will
you take me as I am? Have your wish, sacrifice the world, and prove yourself a true man."

Mr. Slope should have taken her at her word. She would have drawn back,
and he would have had the full advantage of the offer. But he did not.

Instead of doing so, he stood wrapt in astonishment, passing his fingers through his lank red hair and thinking as he stared upon her animated countenance that her wondrous beauty grew more and more wonderful as he gazed on it. "Ha! ha! ha!" she laughed out loud. "Come, Mr. Slope, don't talk of sacrificing the world again. People beyond one and twenty should never dream of such a thing. You and I, if we have the dregs of any love left in us, if we have the remnants of a passion remaining in our hearts, should husband our resources better. We are not in our *première jeunesse*. The world is a very nice place. Your world at any rate is so. You have all manner of fat rectories to get, and possible bishoprics to enjoy. Come, confess, on second thoughts you would not sacrifice such things for the smiles of a lame lady."

It was impossible for him to answer this. In order to be in any way dignified, he felt that he must be silent.

"Come," said she, "don't boody with me. Don't be angry because I speak out some home truths. Alas! the world as I have found it has taught me bitter truths. Come, tell me that I am forgiven. Are we not to be friends?" And she again put out her hand to him.

He sat himself down in the chair beside her, and took her proffered hand and leant over her.

"There," said she, with her sweetest softest smile—a smile to withstand which a man should be cased in triple steel. "There, seal your forgiveness on it." And she raised it toward his face. He kissed it again and again, and stretched over her as though desirous of extending the charity of his pardon beyond the hand that was offered to him. She managed, however, to check his ardor. For one so easily allured as this poor chaplain, her hand was surely enough.

"Oh, Madeline," said he, "tell me that you love me—do you—do you love me?"

"Hush," said she. "There is my mother's step. Our tête-à-tête has been of monstrous length. Now you had better go. But we shall see you soon again, shall we not?"

Mr. Slope promised that he would call again on the following day.

"And, Mr. Slope," she continued, "pray answer my note. You have it in your hand, though I declare during these two hours you have not been gracious enough to read it. It is about the Sabbath school and the children. You know how anxious I am to have them here. I have been learning the catechism myself, on purpose. You must manage it for me next week. I will teach them at any rate to submit themselves to their spiritual pastors and masters."

Mr. Slope said but little on the subject of Sabbath schools, but he made his adieu and betook himself home with a sad heart, troubled mind, and uneasy conscience.

CHAPTER XXVII

MRS. BOLD IS ENTERTAINED BY DR. AND MRS. GRANTLY AT PLUMSTEAD

It will be remembered that Mr. Slope, when leaving his billet doux at the house of Mrs. Bold, had been informed that it would be sent out to her at Plumstead that afternoon. The Archdeacon and Mr. Harding had in fact come into town together in the brougham, and it had been arranged that they should call for Eleanor's parcels as they left on their way home. Accordingly they did so call, and the maid, as she handed to the coachman a small basket and large bundle carefully and neatly packed, gave in at the carriage window Mr. Slope's epistle. The Archdeacon, who was sitting next to the window, took it, and immediately recognized the handwriting of his enemy.

"Who left this?" said he.

"Mr. Slope called with it himself, your Reverence," said the girl, "and was very anxious that missus should have it today."

So the brougham drove off, and the letter was left in the Archdeacon's hand. He looked at it as though he held a basket of adders. Poor Mr. Harding, though by no means inclined to forward Mr. Slope's intimacy with his daughter, would have given anything to have kept the letter from his son-in-law. But that was now impossible. There it was in his hand, and he looked as thoroughly disgusted as though he were quite sure that it contained all the rhapsodies of a favored lover.

"Here," said the Archdeacon, handing the offensive missive to his father-in-law, "I am not going to be the bearer of his love letters. You are her father, and may do as you think fit with it."

By doing as he thought fit with it, the Archdeacon certainly meant that Mr. Harding would be justified in opening and reading the letter, and taking any steps which might in consequence be necessary. To tell the truth, Dr. Grantly did feel rather a stronger curiosity than was justified by his outraged virtue to see the contents of the letter. Of course he could not open it himself, but he wished to make Mr. Harding understand that he, as Eleanor's father, would be fully justified in doing so. The idea of such a proceeding never occurred to Mr. Harding. His authority over Eleanor ceased when she became the wife of John Bold. He had not the slightest wish to pry into her correspondence. He consequently put the letter into his pocket, and only wished that he had been able to do so without the Archdeacon's knowledge. They both sat silent during half the journey home, and then Dr. Grantly said: "Perhaps Susan had better give it to her. She can explain to her sister better than either you or I can do how deep is the disgrace of such an acquaintance."

"I think you are very hard upon Eleanor," replied Mr. Harding. "I will not allow that she has disgraced herself, nor do I think it likely that she will do so. She has a right to correspond with whom she pleases, and I shall not take upon myself to blame her because she gets a letter from Mr. Slope."

"I suppose," said Dr. Grantly, "you don't wish her to marry the man. I suppose you'll admit that she would disgrace herself if she did do so."

"I do not wish her to marry him," said the perplexed father. "I do not like him, and do not think he would make a good husband. But if Eleanor chooses to do so, I shall certainly not think that she disgraces herself."

"Good heavens!" exclaimed Dr. Grantly, and threw himself back into the corner of his brougham. Mr. Harding said nothing more, but commenced playing a dirge with an imaginary fiddle bow upon an imaginary violoncello, for which there did not appear to be quite room enough in the carriage, and he continued the tune, with sundry variations, till he arrived at the rectory door.

He wanted to believe her incapable of such a marriage, he wanted to show that he so believed of her, but he wanted also to be able to say hereafter that she had done nothing amiss if she should unfortunately prove herself to be different from what he thought her to be.

Nothing but affection could justify such fickleness, but affection did justify it. There was but little of the Roman about Mr. Harding. He could not sacrifice his Lucretia even though she should be polluted by the accepted addresses of the clerical Tarquin at the palace. If Tarquin could be prevented, well and good, but if not, the father would still open his heart to his daughter and accept her as she presented herself, Tarquin and all.

Dr. Grantly's mind was of a stronger caliber, and he was by no means deficient in heart. He loved with an honest genuine love his wife and children and friends. He loved his father-in-law, and was quite prepared to love Eleanor too if she would be one of his party, if she would be on his side, if she would regard the Slopes and the Proudies as the enemies of mankind and acknowledge and feel the comfortable merits of the Gwynnes and Arabins. He wished to be what he called "safe" with all those whom he had admitted to the penetralia of his house and heart. He could luxuriate in no society that was deficient in a certain feeling of faithful, stanch Highchurchism, which to him was tantamount to free-masonry. He was not strict in his lines of definition. He endured without impatience many different shades of Anglo-Church conservatism, but with the Slopes and Proudies he could not go on all fours.

He was wanting in, moreover, or perhaps it would be more correct to say he was not troubled by, that womanly tenderness which was so peculiar to Mr. Harding. His feelings toward his friends were that while they stuck to him he would stick to them, that he would work with them shoulder and shoulder, that he would be faithful to the faithful. He knew nothing of that beautiful love which can be true to a false friend.

And thus these two men, each miserable enough in his own way, returned to Plumstead. It was getting late when they arrived there, and the ladies had already gone up to dress. Nothing more was said as the two parted in the hall. As Mr. Harding passed to his own room he knocked at Eleanor's door and handed in the letter. The Archdeacon hurried to his own territory, there to unburden his heart to his faithful partner.

Eleanor, when she received the letter from her father's hand, had no idea from whom it came. She had never seen Mr. Slope's handwriting, or if so had forgotten it, and did not think of him as she twisted the letter as people do twist letters when they do not immediately recognize their correspondents either by the writing or the seal. She was sitting at her glass brushing her hair, and rising every other minute to play with her boy, who was sprawling on the bed and who engaged pretty nearly the whole attention of the maid as well as of his mother.

At last, sitting before her toilet table, she broke the seal and turning over the leaf, saw Mr. Slope's name. She first felt surprised, and then annoyed, and then anxious. As she read it she became interested. She was so delighted to find that all obstacles to her father's return to the hospital were apparently removed that she did not observe the fulsome language in which the tidings were conveyed. She merely perceived that she was commissioned to tell her father that such was the case, and she did not realize the fact that such a communication should not have been made, in the first instance, to her by an unmarried young clergyman. She felt, on the whole, grateful to Mr. Slope, and anxious to get on her dress that she might run with the news to her father. Then she came to the allusion to her own pious labors, and she said in her heart that Mr. Slope was an affected ass. Then she went on again and was offended by her boy being called Mr. Slope's darling—he was nobody's darling but her own, or at any rate not the darling of a disagreeable stranger like Mr. Slope. Lastly she arrived at the tresses and felt a qualm of disgust. She looked up in the glass, and there they were before her, long and silken, certainly, and very beautiful. I will not say but that she knew them to be so, but she felt angry with them and brushed them roughly and carelessly. She crumpled the letter up with angry violence, and resolved, almost without thinking of it, that she would not show it to her father. She would merely tell him the contents of it.

When she entered the drawing-room the whole party were there, including Mr. Arabin, and the whole party looked glum and sour. The two girls sat silent and apart as though they were aware that something was wrong. Even Mr. Arabin was solemn and silent. Eleanor had not seen him since breakfast. He had been the whole day at St. Ewold's, and such having been the case, it was natural that he should tell how matters were going on there. He did nothing of the kind, however, but remained solemn and

ilent. They were all solemn and silent. Eleanor knew in her heart that they
had been talking about her, and her heart misgave her as she thought of
Mr. Slope and his letter. At any rate she felt it to be quite impossible to
peak to her father alone while matters were in this state.

Dinner was soon announced, and Dr. Grantly, as was his wont, gave
Eleanor his arm. But he did so as though the doing it were an outrage on
his feelings rendered necessary by sternest necessity. With quick sympathy
Eleanor felt this, and hardly put her fingers on his coat sleeve. It may
be guessed in what way the dinner hour was passed. Dr. Grantly said
. few words to Mr. Arabin, Mr. Arabin said a few words to Mrs. Grantly,
he said a few words to her father, and he tried to say a few words to
Eleanor. She felt that she had been tried and found guilty of something,
hough she knew not what. She longed to say out to them all, "Well, what is
t that I have done? Out with it, and let me know my crime, for heaven's
ake let me hear the worst of it." But she could not. She could say nothing,
but sat there silent, half-feeling that she was guilty and trying in vain to pre-
end even to eat her dinner.

At last the cloth was drawn, and the ladies were not long following it.
When they were gone the gentlemen were somewhat more sociable but
not much so. They could not of course talk over Eleanor's sins. The Archdeacon had indeed so far betrayed his sister-in-law as to whisper into Mr.
Arabin's ear in the study as they met there before dinner a hint of
what he feared. He did so with the gravest and saddest of fears, and Mr.
Arabin became grave and apparently sad enough as he heard it. He opened
his eyes and his mouth and said in a sort of whisper, "Mr. Slope!" in the
same way as he might have said "The cholera!" had his friend told him
that that horrid disease was in his nursery. "I fear so, I fear so," said the
Archdeacon, and then together they left the room.

We will not accurately analyze Mr. Arabin's feelings on receipt of such
astounding tidings. It will suffice to say that he was surprised, vexed,
sorrowful, and ill at ease. He had not perhaps thought very much about
Eleanor, but he had appreciated her influence, and had felt that close
intimacy with her in a country house was pleasant to him, and also beneficial.
He had spoken highly of her intelligence to the Archdeacon, and had
walked about the shrubberies with her carrying her boy on his back. When
Mr. Arabin had called Johnny his darling, Eleanor was not angry.

Thus the three men sat over their wine all thinking of the same subject,
but unable to speak of it to each other. So we will leave them, and follow
the ladies into the drawing-room.

Mrs. Grantly had received a commission from her husband, and had
undertaken it with some unwillingness. He had desired her to speak gravely
to Eleanor, and to tell her that if she persisted in her adherence to Mr.
Slope, she could no longer look for the countenance of her present friends.
Mrs. Grantly probably knew her sister better than the Doctor did, and
assured him that it would be in vain to talk to her. The only course likely

to be of any service in her opinion was to keep Eleanor away from Bar chester. Perhaps she might have added, for she had a very keen eye in suc things, that there might also be ground for hope in keeping Eleanor nea Mr. Arabin. Of this, however, she said nothing. But the Archdeacon woul not be talked over. He spoke much of his conscience, and declared that : Mrs. Grantly would not do it he would. So instigated, the lady undertoo the task, stating, however, her full conviction that her interference woul be worse than useless. And so it proved.

As soon as they were in the drawing-room Mrs. Grantly found som excuse for sending her girls away and then began her task. She kne well that she could exercise but very slight authority over her sister. Thei various modes of life, and the distance between their residences, had pre vented any very close confidence. They had hardly lived together sinc Eleanor was a child. Eleanor had moreover, especially in latter years, re sented in a quiet sort of way the dictatorial authority which the Arch deacon seemed to exercise over her father, and on this account had bee unwilling to allow the Archdeacon's wife to exercise authority over hersel

"You got a note just before dinner, I believe," began the eldest siste

Eleanor acknowledged that she had done so, and felt that she turned re as she acknowledged it. She would have given anything to have kept he color, but the more she tried to do so, the more signally she failed.

"Was it not from Mr. Slope?"

Eleanor said that the letter was from Mr. Slope.

"Is he a regular correspondent of yours, Eleanor?"

"Not exactly," said she, already beginning to feel angry at the cros examination. She determined, and why it would be difficult to say, tha nothing should induce her to tell her sister Susan what was the subject o the letter. Mrs. Grantly she knew was instigated by the Archdeacon, an she would not plead to any arraignment made against her by him.

"But, Eleanor dear, why do you get letters from Mr. Slope at all, knowing as you do, he is a person so distasteful to Papa, and to the Archdeacon, an indeed to all your friends?"

"In the first place, Susan, I don't get letters from him. And in the nex place, as Mr. Slope wrote the one letter which I have got, and as I onl received it, which I could not very well help doing, as Papa handed it t me, I think you had better ask Mr. Slope instead of me."

"What was his letter about, Eleanor?"

"I cannot tell you," said she, "because it was confidential. It was o business respecting a third person."

"It was in no way personal to yourself, then?"

"I won't exactly say that, Susan," said she, getting more and more angr at her sister's questions.

"Well, I must say it's rather singular," said Mrs. Grantly, affecting t laugh, "that a young lady in your position should receive a letter fro an unmarried gentleman of which she will not tell the contents, and which she is ashamed to show to her sister."

"I am not ashamed," said Eleanor blazing up. "I am not ashamed of anything in the matter, only I do not choose to be cross-examined as to my letters by anyone."

"Well, dear," said the other, "I cannot but tell you that I do not think Mr. Slope a proper correspondent for you."

"If he be ever so improper, how can I help his having written to me? But you are all prejudiced against him to such an extent that that which would be kind and generous in another man is odious and impudent in him. I hate a religion that teaches one to be so one-sided in one's charity."

"I am sorry, Eleanor, that you hate the religion you find here, but surely you should remember that in such matters the Archdeacon must know more of the world than you do. I don't ask you to respect or comply with me, although I am, unfortunately, so many years your senior. But surely in such a matter as this you might consent to be guided by the Archdeacon. He is most anxious to be your friend if you will let him."

"In such a matter as what?" said Eleanor very testily. "Upon my word I don't know what this is all about."

"We all want you to drop Mr. Slope."

"You all want me to be as illiberal as yourselves. That I shall never be. I see no harm in Mr. Slope's acquaintance, and I shall not insult the man by telling him that I do. He has thought it necessary to write to me, and I do not want the Archdeacon's advice about the letter. If I did I would ask it."

"Then, Eleanor, it is my duty to tell you," and now she spoke with a tremendous gravity, "that the Archdeacon thinks that such a correspondence is disgraceful, and that he cannot allow it to go on in his house."

Eleanor's eyes flashed fire as she answered her sister, jumping up from her seat as she did so. "You may tell the Archdeacon that wherever I am I shall receive what letters I please and from whom I please. And as for the word 'disgraceful,' if Dr. Grantly has used it of me he has been unmanly and inhospitable." And she walked off to the door. "When Papa comes from the dining-room I will thank you to ask him to step up to my bedroom. I will show him Mr. Slope's letter, but I will show it to no one else." And so saying she retreated to her baby.

She had no conception of the crime with which she was charged. The idea that she could be thought by her friends to regard Mr. Slope as a lover had never flashed upon her. She conceived that they were all prejudiced and illiberal in their persecution of him, and therefore she would not join in the persecution, even though she greatly disliked the man.

Eleanor was very angry as she seated herself in a low chair by her open window at the foot of her child's bed. "To dare to say I have disgraced myself," she repeated to herself more than once. "How Papa can put up with that man's arrogance! I will certainly not sit down to dinner in his house again unless he begs my pardon for that word." And then a thought struck her that Mr. Arabin might perchance hear of her "disgraceful" correspondence with Mr. Slope, and she turned crimson with pure vexation. Oh, if she had known the truth! If she could have conceived that Mr. Arabin had been informed as a fact that she was going to marry Mr. Slope!

She had not been long in her room before her father joined her. As he left the drawing-room Mrs. Grantly took her husband into the recess of the window and told him how signally she had failed.

"I will speak to her myself before I go to bed," said the Archdeacon.

Mr. Harding looked worn and woebegone as he entered his daughter's room. These sorrows worried him sadly. He felt that if they were continued he must go to the wall in the manner so kindly prophesied to him by the chaplain. He knocked gently at his daughter's door, waited till he was distinctly bade to enter, and then appeared as though he and not she were the suspected criminal.

Eleanor's arm was soon within his, and she had soon kissed his forehead and caressed him, not with joyous but with eager love. "Oh, Papa," she said, "I do so want to speak to you. They have been talking about me downstairs tonight, don't you know they have, Papa?"

Mr. Harding confessed with a sort of murmur that the Archdeacon had been speaking of her.

"I shall hate Dr. Grantly soon——"

"Oh, my dear!"

"Well, I shall. I cannot help it. He is so uncharitable, so unkind, so suspicious of everyone that does not worship himself. And then he is so monstrously arrogant to other people who have a right to their opinions as well as he has to his own."

"He is an earnest, eager man, my dear, but he never means to be unkind."

"He is unkind, Papa, most unkind. There, I got that letter from Mr. Slope before dinner. It was you yourself who gave it to me. There, pray read it. It is all for you. It should have been addressed to you. You know how they have been talking about it downstairs. You know how they behaved to me at dinner. And since dinner Susan has been preaching to me till I could not remain in the room with her. Read it, Papa, and then say whether that is a letter that need make Dr. Grantly so outrageous."

Mr. Harding took his arm from his daughter's waist and slowly read the letter. She expected to see his countenance lit with joy as he learnt that his path back to the hospital was made so smooth, but she was doomed to disappointment, as had once been the case before on a somewhat similar occasion. His first feeling was one of unmitigated disgust that Mr. Slope should have chosen to interfere in his behalf. He had been anxious to get back to the hospital, but he would have infinitely sooner resigned all pretensions to the place than have owed it in any manner to Mr. Slope's influence in his favor. Then he thoroughly disliked the tone of Mr. Slope's letter. It was unctuous, false, and unwholesome, like the man. He saw, which Eleanor had failed to see, that much more had been intended than was expressed. The appeal to Eleanor's pious labors as separate from his own grated sadly against his feelings as a father. And then when he came to the "darling boy" and the "silken tresses," he slowly closed and folded the letter in despair. It was impossible that Mr. Slope should so write unless he had been encouraged. It was impossible Eleanor should have received such a letter, and have received it without annoyance, unless she were willing to encourage him. So at least Mr. Harding argued to himself.

How hard it is to judge accurately of the feelings of others! Mr. Harding, as he came to the close of the letter, in his heart condemned his daughter for indelicacy, and it made him miserable to do so. She was not responsible for what Mr. Slope might write. True. But then she expressed no disgust at it. She had rather expressed approval of the letter as a whole. She had given it to him to read as a vindication for herself and also for him. The father's spirits sank within him as he felt that he could not acquit her.

And yet it was the true feminine delicacy of Eleanor's mind which brought on her this condemnation. Listen to me, ladies, and I beseech *you* to acquit her. She thought of this man, this lover of whom she was so unconscious, exactly as her father did, exactly as the Grantlys did. At least she esteemed him personally as they did. But she believed him to be in the main an honest man, and one truly inclined to assist her father. She felt herself bound, after what had passed, to show this letter to Mr. Harding. She thought it necessary that he should know what Mr. Slope had to say. But she did not think it necessary to apologize for, or condemn, or even allude to the vulgarity of, the man's tone, which arose, as does all vulgarity, from ignorance. It was nauseous to her to have a man like Mr. Slope commenting on her personal attractions, and she did not think it necessary to dilate with her father upon what was nauseous. She never supposed they could disagree on such a subject. It would have been painful for her to point it out, painful for her to speak strongly against a man of whom, on the whole, she was anxious to think and speak well. In encountering such a man she had encountered what was disagreeable, as she might do in walking the streets. But in such encounters she never thought it necessary to dwell on what disgusted her.

And he, foolish, weak, loving man, would not say one word, though one word would have cleared up everything. There would have been a deluge of tears, and in ten minutes everyone in the house would have understood how matters really were. The father would have been delighted. The sister would have kissed her sister and begged a thousand pardons. The Archdeacon would have apologized and wondered, and raised his eyebrows, and gone to bed a happy man. And Mr. Arabin—Mr. Arabin would have dreamt of Eleanor, have awoke in the morning with ideas of love, and retired to rest the next evening with schemes of marriage. But, alas! all this was not to be.

Mr. Harding slowly folded the letter, handed it back to her, kissed her forehead, and bade God bless her. He then crept slowly away to his own room.

As soon as he had left the passage another knock was given at Eleanor's door, and Mrs. Grantly's very demure own maid, entering on tiptoe, wanted to know would Mrs. Bold be so kind as to speak to the Archdeacon for two minutes in the Archdeacon's study, if not disagreeable. The Archdeacon's compliments, and he wouldn't detain her two minutes.

Eleanor thought it was very disagreeable. She was tired and fagged and sick at heart, her present feelings toward Dr. Grantly were anything but those of affection. She was, however, no coward, and therefore promised to be in the study in five minutes. So she arranged her hair, tied on her cap, and went down with a palpitating heart.

CHAPTER XXVIII

A SERIOUS INTERVIEW

THERE are people who delight in serious interviews, especially when to them appertains the part of offering advice or administering rebuke, and perhaps the Archdeacon was one of these. Yet on this occasion he did not prepare himself for the coming conversation with much anticipation of pleasure. Whatever might be his faults, he was not an inhospitable man, and he almost felt that he was sinning against hospitality in upbraiding Eleanor in his own house. Then also, he was not quite sure that he would get the best of it. His wife had told him that he decidedly would not, and he usually gave credit to what his wife said. He was, however, so convinced of what he considered to be the impropriety of Eleanor's conduct, and so assured also of his own duty in trying to check it, that his conscience would not allow him to take his wife's advice and go to bed quietly.

Eleanor's face as she entered the room was not such as to reassure him. As a rule she was always mild in manner and gentle in conduct, but there was that in her eye which made it not an easy task to scold her. In truth she had been little used to scolding. No one since her childhood had tried it but the Archdeacon, and he had generally failed when he did try it. He had never done so since her marriage, and now when he saw her quiet easy step as she entered his room, he almost wished that he had taken his wife's advice.

He began by apologizing for the trouble he was giving her. She begged him not to mention it, assured him that walking downstairs was no trouble to her at all, and then took a seat and waited patiently for him to begin his attack.

"My dear Eleanor," he said, "I hope you believe me when I assure you that you have no sincerer friend than I am." To this Eleanor answered nothing, and therefore he proceeded. "If you had a brother of your own I should not probably trouble you with what I am going to say. But as it is I cannot but think that it must be a comfort to you to know that you have near you one who is as anxious for your welfare as any brother of your own could be."

"I never had a brother," said she.

"I know you never had, and it is therefore that I speak to you."

"I never had a brother," she repeated, "but I have hardly felt the want. Papa has been to me both father and brother."

"Your father is the fondest and most affectionate of men. But——"

"He is—the fondest and most affectionate of men, and the best of counselors. While he lives I can never want advice."

This rather put the Archdeacon out. He could not exactly contradict what his sister-in-law said about her father, and yet he did not at all agree with her. He wanted her to understand that he tendered his assistance because her father was a soft, good-natured gentleman not sufficiently knowing in the ways of the world, but he could not say this to her. So he had to rush into the subject matter of his proffered counsel without any acknowledgment on her part that she could need it, or would be grateful for it.

"Susan tells me that you received a letter this evening from Mr. Slope."

"Yes, Papa brought it in the brougham. Did he not tell you?"

"And Susan says that you objected to let her know what it was about."

"I don't think she asked me. But had she done so I should not have told her. I don't think it nice to be asked about one's letters. If one wishes to show them one does so without being asked."

"True. Quite so. What you say is quite true. But is not the fact of your receiving letters from Mr. Slope which you do not wish to show to your friends a circumstance which must excite some—some surprise—some suspicion——"

"Suspicion!" said she, not speaking above her usual voice, speaking still in a soft womanly tone, but yet with indignation. "Suspicion! And who suspects me, and of what?" And then there was a pause, for the Archdeacon was not quite ready to explain the ground of his suspicion. "No, Dr. Grantly, I did not choose to show Mr. Slope's letter to Susan. I could not show it to anyone till Papa had seen it. If you have any wish to read it now, you can do so." And she handed the letter to him over the table.

This was an amount of compliance which he had not at all expected, and which rather upset him in his tactics. However, he took the letter, perused it carefully, and then, refolding it, kept it on the table under his hand. To him it appeared to be in almost every respect the letter of a declared lover. It seemed to corroborate his worst suspicions, and the fact of Eleanor's showing it to him was all but tantamount to a declaration on her part that it was her pleasure to receive love letters from Mr. Slope. He almost entirely overlooked the real subject matter of the epistle, so intent was he on the forthcoming courtship and marriage.

"I'll thank you to give it me back, if you please, Dr. Grantly."

He took it in his hand and held it up, but made no immediate overture to return it. "And Mr. Harding has seen this?" said he.

"Of course he has," said she. "It was written that he might see it. It refers solely to his business—of course I showed it to him."

"And, Eleanor, do you think that that is a proper letter for you—for a person in your condition—to receive from Mr. Slope?"

"Quite a proper letter," said she, speaking perhaps a little out of obstinacy, probably forgetting at the moment the objectionable mention of her silken curls.

"Then, Eleanor, it is my duty to tell you that I wholly differ from you."

"So I suppose," said she, instigated now by sheer opposition and determination not to succumb. "You think Mr. Slope is a messenger direct from Satan. I think he is an industrious, well-meaning clergyman. It's a pity that we differ as we do. But as we do differ, we had probably better not talk about it."

Here Eleanor undoubtedly put herself in the wrong. She might probably have refused to talk to Dr. Grantly on the matter in dispute without any impropriety, but having consented to listen to him, she had no business to tell him that he regarded Mr. Slope as an emissary from the Evil One. Nor was she justified in praising Mr. Slope, seeing that in her heart of hearts she did not think well of him. She was, however, wounded in spirit, and angry and bitter. She had been subjected to contumely and cross-questioning and ill-usage through the whole evening. No one, not even Mr. Arabin, not even her father, had been kind to her. All this she attributed to the prejudice and conceit of the Archdeacon, and therefore she resolved to set no bounds to her antagonism to him. She would neither give nor take quarter. He had greatly presumed in daring to question her about her correspondence, and she was determined to show that she thought so.

"Eleanor, you are forgetting yourself," said he, looking very sternly at her. "Otherwise you would never tell me that I conceive any man to be a messenger from Satan."

"But you do," said she. "Nothing is too bad for him. Give me that letter, if you please." And she stretched out her hand and took it from him. "He has been doing his best to serve Papa, doing more than any of Papa's friends could do, and yet because he is the chaplain of a bishop whom you don't like, you speak of him as though he had no right to the usage of a gentleman."

"He has done nothing for your father."

"I believe that he has done a great deal, and as far as I am concerned, I am grateful to him. Nothing that you can say can prevent my being so.

I judge people by their acts, and his, as far as I can see them, are good."
She then paused for a moment. "If you have nothing further to say, I shall
be obliged by being permitted to say good night—I am very tired."

Dr. Grantly had, as he thought, done his best to be gracious to his sister-
in-law. He had endeavored not to be harsh to her, and had striven to pluck
the sting from his rebuke. But he did not intend that she should leave him
without hearing him.

"I have something to say, Eleanor, and I fear I must trouble you to hear
it. You profess that it is quite proper that you should receive from Mr.
Slope such letters as that you have in your hand. Susan and I think very
differently. You are, of course, your own mistress, and much as we both
must grieve should anything separate you from us, we have no power
to prevent you from taking steps which may lead to such a separation. If
you are so willful as to reject the counsel of your friends, you must be
allowed to cater for yourself. But Eleanor, I may at any rate ask you this.
Is it worth your while to break away from all those you have loved—from
all who love you—for the sake of Mr. Slope?"

"I don't know what you mean, Dr. Grantly. I don't know what you're
talking about. I don't want to break away from anybody."

"But you will do so if you connect yourself with Mr. Slope. Eleanor,
I must speak out to you. You must choose between your sister and myself
and our friends, and Mr. Slope and his friends. I say nothing of your father,
as you may probably understand his feelings better than I do."

"What do you mean, Dr. Grantly? What am I to understand? I never
heard such wicked prejudice in my life."

"It is no prejudice, Eleanor. I have known the world longer than you
have done. Mr. Slope is altogether beneath you. You ought to know and
feel that he is so. Pray—pray think of this before it is too late."

"Too late!"

"Or if you will not believe me, ask Susan. You cannot think she is prejudiced against you. Or even consult your father. He is not prejudiced
against you. Ask Mr. Arabin——"

"You haven't spoken to Mr. Arabin about this!" said she, jumping up and
standing before him.

"Eleanor, all the world in and about Barchester will be speaking of it
soon."

"But have you spoken to Mr. Arabin about me and Mr. Slope?"

"Certainly I have, and he quite agrees with me."

"Agrees with what?" said she. "I think you are trying to drive me mad."

"He agrees with me and Susan that it is quite impossible you should be
received at Plumstead as Mrs. Slope."

Not being favorites with the tragic muse, we do not dare to attempt any
description of Eleanor's face when she first heard the name of Mrs. Slope
pronounced as that which would or should or might at some time appertain
to herself. The look, such as it was, Dr. Grantly did not soon forget. For

a moment or two she could find no words to express her deep anger and deep disgust, and indeed at this conjuncture words did not come to her very freely.

"How dare you be so impertinent?" at last she said, and then hurried out of the room without giving the Archdeacon the opportunity of uttering another word. It was with difficulty she contained herself till she reached her own room, and then, locking the door, she threw herself on her bed and sobbed as though her heart would break.

But even yet she had no conception of the truth. She had no idea that her father and her sister had for days past conceived in sober earnest the idea that she was going to marry this man. She did not even then believe that the Archdeacon thought she would do so. By some maneuver of her brain she attributed the origin of the accusation to Mr. Arabin, and as she did so her anger against him was excessive, and the vexation of her spirit almost unendurable. She could not bring herself to think that the charge was made seriously. It appeared to her most probable that the Archdeacon and Mr. Arabin had talked over her objectionable acquaintance with Mr. Slope, that Mr. Arabin, in his jeering, sarcastic way, had suggested the odious match as being the severest way of treating with contumely her acquaintance with his enemy, and that the Archdeacon, taking the idea from him, thought proper to punish her by the allusion. The whole night she lay awake thinking of what had been said, and this appeared to be the most probable solution.

But the reflection that Mr. Arabin should have in any way mentioned her name in connection with that of Mr. Slope was overpowering. And the spiteful ill nature of the Archdeacon in repeating the charge to her made her wish to leave his house almost before the day had broken. One thing was certain: Nothing should make her stay there beyond the following morning, and nothing should make her sit down to breakfast in company with Dr. Grantly. When she thought of the man whose name had been linked with her own, she cried from sheer disgust. It was only because she would be thus disgusted, thus pained and shocked and cut to the quick, that the Archdeacon had spoken the horrid word. He wanted to make her quarrel with Mr. Slope, and therefore he had outraged her by his abominable vulgarity. She determined that at any rate he should know that she appreciated it.

Nor was the Archdeacon a bit better satisfied with the result of his serious interview than was Eleanor. He gathered from it, as indeed he could hardly fail to do, that she was very angry with him. But he thought that she was thus angry not because she was suspected of an intention to marry Mr. Slope, but because such an intention was imputed to her as a crime. Dr. Grantly regarded this supposed union with disgust, but it never occurred to him that Eleanor was outraged because she looked at it exactly in the same light.

He returned to his wife vexed and somewhat disconsolate, but nevertheless confirmed in his wrath against his sister-in-law. "Her whole behavior," said he, "has been most objectionable. She handed me his love letter to read as though she were proud of it. And she is proud of it. She is proud of having this slavering, greedy man at her feet. She will throw herself and John Bold's money into his lap. She will ruin her boy, disgrace her father and you, and be a wretched, miserable woman."

On the following morning Eleanor's maid was commissioned to send word into the dining-room that her mistress was not well enough to attend prayers, and that she would breakfast in her own room. Here she was visited by her father, and declared to him her intention of returning immediately to Barchester. He was hardly surprised by the announcement. All the household seemed to be aware that something had gone wrong. Everyone walked about with subdued feet, and people's shoes seemed to creak more than usual. There was a look of conscious intelligence on the faces of the women, and the men attempted, but in vain, to converse as though nothing were the matter. All this had weighed heavily on the heart of Mr. Harding, and when Eleanor told him that her immediate return to Barchester was a necessity, he merely sighed piteously and said that he would be ready to accompany her.

But here she objected strenuously. She had a great wish, she said, to go alone, a great desire that it might be seen that her father was not implicated in her quarrel with Dr. Grantly. To this at last he gave way, but not a word passed between them about Mr. Slope—not a word was said, not a question asked, as to the serious interview on the preceding evening. There was, indeed, very little confidence between them, though neither of them knew why it should be so. Eleanor once asked him why he would not call upon the Bishop, but he answered rather tartly that he did not know—he did not think he should, but he could not say just at present. And so they parted. Each was miserably anxious for some show of affection, for some return of confidence, for some sign of the feeling that usually bound them together. But none was given. The father could not bring himself to question his daughter about her supposed lover, and the daughter would not sully her mouth by repeating the odious word with which Dr. Grantly had roused her wrath. And so they parted.

There was some trouble in arranging the method of Eleanor's return. She begged her father to send for a post chaise, but when Mrs. Grantly heard of this, she objected strongly. If Eleanor would go away in dudgeon with the Archdeacon, why should she let all the servants and all the neighborhood know that she had done so? So at last Eleanor consented to make use of the Plumstead carriage, and as the Archdeacon had gone out immediately after breakfast and was not to return till dinnertime, she also consented to postpone her journey till after lunch, and to join the family at that time. As to the subject of the quarrel not a word was said by anyone. The affair of the carriage was arranged by Mr. Harding, who acted as Mercury between the two ladies. They, when they met, kissed each other very lovingly and then sat down each to her crochet work as though nothing was amiss in all the world.

CHAPTER XXIX

ANOTHER LOVE SCENE

BUT there was another visitor at the rectory whose feelings in this unfortunate matter must be somewhat strictly analyzed. Mr. Arabin had heard from his friend of the probability of Eleanor's marriage with Mr. Slope with amazement, but not with incredulity. It has been said that he was not in love with Eleanor, and up to this period this certainly had been true. But as soon as he heard that she loved someone else he began to be very fond of her himself. He did not make up his mind that he wished to have her for his wife. He had never thought of her, and did not now think of her, in connection with himself. But he experienced an inward indefinable feeling of deep regret, a gnawing sorrow, an unconquerable depression of spirits, and also a species of self-abasement that he—he, Mr. Arabin—had not done something to prevent that other he, that vile he whom he so thoroughly despised, from carrying off this sweet prize.

Whatever man may have reached the age of forty unmarried without knowing something of such feelings must have been very successful or else very coldhearted.

Mr. Arabin had never thought of trimming the sails of his bark so that he might sail as convoy to this rich argosy. He had seen that Mrs. Bold was beautiful, but he had not dreamt of making her beauty his own. He knew that Mrs. Bold was rich, but he had had no more idea of appropriating her wealth than that of Dr. Grantly. He had discovered that Mrs. Bold was intelligent, warmhearted, agreeable, sensible—all, in fact, that a man could wish his wife to be. But the higher were her attractions, the greater her claims to consideration, the less had he imagined that he might possibly become the possessor of them. Such had been his instinct rather than his thoughts, so humble and so diffident. Now his diffidence was to be rewarded by his seeing this woman, whose beauty was to his eyes perfect, whose wealth was such as to have deterred him from thinking of her, whose widowhood would have silenced him had he not been so deterred, by his seeing her become the prey of—Obadiah Slope!

He had but an uneasy ride of it that morning, and little good did he do at St. Ewold's.

The necessary alterations in his house were being fast completed, and he walked through the rooms and went up and down the stairs and rambled through the garden, but he could not wake himself to much interest about them. He stood still at every window to look out and think upon Mr. Slope. At almost every window he had before stood and chatted with Eleanor. She and Mrs. Grantly had been there continually, and while Mrs. Grantly had been giving orders and seeing that orders had been complied with, he and Eleanor had conversed on all things appertaining to a clergyman's profession. He thought how often he had laid down the law to her, and how sweetly she had borne with his somewhat dictatorial decrees. He remembered her listening intelligence, her gentle but quick replies, her interest in all that concerned the Church, in all that concerned him. And then he struck his riding whip against the window sill and declared to himself that it was impossible that Eleanor Bold should marry Mr. Slope.

And yet he did not really believe, as he should have done, that it was impossible. He should have known her well enough to feel that it was truly impossible. He should have been aware that Eleanor had that within her which would surely protect her from such degradation. But he, like so many others, was deficient in confidence in woman. He said to himself over and over again that it was impossible that Eleanor Bold should become Mrs. Slope, and yet he believed that she would do so. And so he rambled about, and could do and think of nothing. He was thoroughly uncomfortable, thoroughly ill at ease, cross with himself and everybody else, and feeding in his heart on animosity toward Mr. Slope. This was not as it should be, as he knew and felt, but he could not help himself. In truth Mr. Arabin was now in love with Mrs. Bold, though ignorant of the fact himself. He was in love, and though forty years old, was in love without being aware of it. He fumed and fretted, and did not know what was the matter, as a youth might do at one-and-twenty. And so, having done no good at St. Ewold's, he rode back much earlier than was usual with him, instigated by some inward unacknowledged hope that he might see Mrs. Bold before she left.

Eleanor had not passed a pleasant morning. She was irritated with everyone, and not least with herself. She felt that she had been hardly used, but she felt also that she had not played her own cards well. She should have held herself so far above suspicion as to have received her sister's innuendoes and the Archdeacon's lecture with indifference. She had not done this, but had shown herself angry and sore, and was now ashamed of her own petulance, and yet unable to discontinue it.

The greater part of the morning she had spent alone, but after a while her father joined her. He had fully made up his mind that, come what come might, nothing should separate him from his younger daughter. It was a hard task for him to reconcile himself to the idea of seeing her at the head of Mr. Slope's table, but he got through it. Mr. Slope, as he argued to himself, was a respectable man and a clergyman, and he, as Eleanor's father, had no right even to endeavor to prevent her from marrying such a one. He longed to tell her how he had determined to prefer her to all the world, how he was prepared to admit that she was not wrong, how thoroughly he differed from Dr. Grantly. But he could not bring himself to mention Mr. Slope's name. There was yet a chance that they were all wrong in their surmise! And being thus in doubt, he could not bring himself to speak openly to her on the subject.

He was sitting with her in the drawing-room, with his arm round her waist, saying every now and then some little soft words of affection and working hard with his imaginary fiddle bow, when Mr. Arabin entered the room. He immediately got up, and the two made some trite remarks to each other, neither thinking of what he was saying, while Eleanor kept her seat on the sofa mute and moody. Mr. Arabin was included in the list of those against whom her anger was excited. He too had dared to talk about her acquaintance with Mr. Slope. He too had dared to blame her for not making an enemy of his enemy. She had not intended to see him before her departure, and was now but little inclined to be gracious.

There was a feeling through the whole house that something was wrong. Mr. Arabin, when he saw Eleanor, could not succeed in looking or in speaking as though he knew nothing of all this. He could not be cheerful and positive and contradictory with her, as was his wont. He had not been two minutes in the room before he felt that he had done wrong to return, and the moment he heard her voice, he thoroughly wished himself back at St. Ewold's. Why indeed should he have wished to have aught further to say to the future wife of Mr. Slope?

"I am sorry to hear that you are to leave us so soon," said he, striving in vain to use his ordinary voice. In answer to this she muttered something about the necessity of her being in Barchester, and betook herself most industriously to her crochet work.

Then there was a little more trite conversation between Mr. Arabin and Mr. Harding, trite, and hard, and vapid, and senseless. Neither of them had anything to say to the other, and yet neither at such a moment liked to remain silent. At last Mr. Harding, taking advantage of a pause, escaped out of the room, and Eleanor and Mr. Arabin were left together.

"Your going will be a great breakup to our party," said he.

She again muttered something which was all but inaudible, but kept her eyes fixed upon her work.

"We have had a very pleasant month here," said he. "At least I have, and I am sorry it should be so soon over."

"I have already been from home longer than I intended," said she, "and it is time that I should return."

"Well, pleasant hours and pleasant days must come to an end. It is a pity that so few of them are pleasant, or perhaps rather——"

"It is a pity, certainly, that men and women do so much to destroy the pleasantness of their days," said she, interrupting him. "It is a pity that there should be so little charity abroad."

"Charity should begin at home," said he. And he was proceeding to explain that he as a clergyman could not be what she would call charitable at the expense of those principles which he considered it his duty to teach when he remembered that it would be worse than vain to argue on such a matter with the future wife of Mr. Slope. "But you are just leaving us," he continued, "and I will not weary your last hour with another lecture. As it is, I fear I have given you too many."

"You should practice as well as preach, Mr. Arabin!"

"Undoubtedly I should. So should we all. All of us who presume to teach are bound to do our utmost towards fulfilling our own lessons. I thoroughly allow my deficiency in doing so, but I do not quite know now to what you allude. Have you any special reason for telling me now that I should practice as well as preach?"

Eleanor made no answer. She longed to let him know the cause of her anger, to upbraid him for speaking of her disrespectfully, and then at last to forgive him and so part friends. She felt that she would be unhappy to leave him in her present frame of mind, but yet she could hardly bring herself to speak to him of Mr. Slope. And how could she allude to the innuendo thrown out by the Archdeacon, and thrown out, as she believed, at the instigation of Mr. Arabin? She wanted to make him know that he was wrong, to make him aware that he had ill-treated her, in order that the sweetness of her forgiveness might be enhanced. She felt that she liked him too well to be contented to part with him in displeasure, and yet she could not get over her deep displeasure without some explanation, some acknowledgment on his part, some assurance that he would never again so sin against her.

"Why do you tell me that I should practice what I preach?" continued he.

"All men should do so."

"Certainly. That is as it were understood and acknowledged. But you do not say so to all men, or to all clergymen. The advice, good as it is, is not given except in allusion to some special deficiency. If you will tell me my special deficiency, I will endeavor to profit by the advice."

She paused for a while and then, looking full in his face, she said: "You are not bold enough, Mr. Arabin, to speak out to me openly and plainly, and yet you expect me, a woman, to speak openly to you. Why did you speak calumny of me to Dr. Grantly behind my back?"

"Calumny!" said he, and his whole face became suffused with blood. "What calumny? If I have spoken calumny of you, I will beg your pardon, and his to whom I spoke it, and God's pardon also. But what calumny have I spoken of you to Dr. Grantly?"

She also blushed deeply. She could not bring herself to ask him whether he had not spoken of her as another man's wife. "You know that best yourself," said she; "but I ask you as a man of honor if you have not spoken of me as you would not have spoken of your own sister. Or rather I will not ask you," she continued, finding that he did not immediately answer her. "I will not put you to the necessity of answering such a question. Dr. Grantly has told me what you said."

"Dr. Grantly certainly asked me for my advice, and I gave it. He asked me——"

"I know he did, Mr. Arabin. He asked you whether he would be doing right to receive me at Plumstead if I continued my acquaintance with a gentleman who happens to be personally disagreeable to yourself and to him."

"You are mistaken, Mrs. Bold. I have no personal knowledge of Mr. Slope, I never met him in my life."

"You are not the less individually hostile to him. It is not for me to question the propriety of your enmity, but I had a right to expect that my name should not have been mixed up in your hostilities. This has been done, and been done by you in a manner the most injurious and the most distressing to me as a woman. I must confess, Mr. Arabin, that from you I expected a different sort of usage."

As she spoke she with difficulty restrained her tears, but she did restrain them. Had she given way and sobbed aloud, as in such cases a woman should do, he would have melted at once, implored her pardon, perhaps knelt at her feet and declared his love. Everything would have been explained, and Eleanor would have gone back to Barchester with a contented mind. How easily would she have forgiven and forgotten the Archdeacon's suspicions had she but heard the whole truth from Mr. Arabin! But then where would have been my novel? She did not cry, and Mr. Arabin did not melt.

"You do me an injustice," said he. "My advice was asked by Dr. Grantly, and I was obliged to give it."

"Dr. Grantly has been most officious, most impertinent. I have as complete a right to form my acquaintance as he has to form his. What would you have said had I consulted you as to the propriety of my banishing Dr. Grantly from my house because he knows Lord Tattenham Corner? I am sure Lord Tattenham is quite as objectionable an acquaintance for a clergyman as Mr. Slope is for a clergyman's daughter."

"I do not know Lord Tattenham Corner."

"No, but Dr. Grantly does. It is nothing to me if he knows all the young lords on every racecourse in England. I shall not interfere with him, nor shall he with me."

"I am sorry to differ with you, Mrs. Bold, but as you have spoken to me on this matter, and especially as you blame me for what little I said on the subject, I must tell you that I do differ from you. Dr. Grantly's position as a man in the world gives him a right to choose his own acquaintances, subject to certain influences. If he chooses them badly, those influences will be used. If he consorts with persons unsuitable to him, his bishop will interfere. What the bishop is to Dr. Grantly, Dr. Grantly is to you."

"I deny it. I utterly deny it," said Eleanor, jumping from her seat and literally flashing before Mr. Arabin as she stood on the drawing-room floor.

He had never seen her so excited, he had never seen her look half so beautiful.

"I utterly deny it," said she. "Dr. Grantly has no sort of jurisdiction over me whatsoever. Do you and he forget that I am not altogether alone in the world? Do you forget that I have a father? Dr. Grantly I believe always has forgotten it.

"From you, Mr. Arabin," she continued, "I would have listened to advice because I should have expected it to have been given as one friend may advise another, not as a schoolmaster gives an order to a pupil. I might have differed from you, on this matter I should have done so, but had you spoken to me in your usual manner and with your usual freedom I should not have been angry. But now—was it manly of you, Mr. Arabin, to speak of me in this way—so disrespectful—so——? I cannot bring myself to repeat what you said. You must understand what I feel. Was it just of you to speak of me in such a way, and to advise my sister's husband to turn me out of my sister's house because I chose to know a man of whose doctrine you disapprove?"

"I have no alternative left to me, Mrs. Bold," said he, standing with his back to the fireplace looking down intently at the carpet pattern, and speaking with a slow, measured voice, "but to tell you plainly what did take place between me and Dr. Grantly."

"Well," said she, finding that he paused for a moment.

"I am afraid that what I may say may pain you."

"It cannot well do so more than what you have already done," said she.

"Dr. Grantly asked me whether I thought it would be prudent for him to receive you in his house as the wife of Mr. Slope, and I told him that I thought it would be imprudent. Believing it to be utterly impossible that Mr. Slope and——"

"Thank you, Mr. Arabin, that is sufficient. I do not want to know your reasons," said she, speaking with a terribly calm voice. "I have shown to this gentleman the commonplace civility of a neighbor. And because I have done so, because I have not indulged against him in all the rancor and hatred which you and Dr. Grantly consider due to all clergymen who do not agree with yourselves, you conclude that I am to marry him. Or rather you do not conclude so—no rational man could really come to such an outrageous conclusion without better ground, you have not thought so—but as I am in a position in which such an accusation must be peculiarly painful, it is made in order that I may be terrified into hostility against this enemy of yours."

As she finished speaking, she walked to the drawing-room window and stepped out into the garden. Mr. Arabin was left in the room, still occupied in counting the pattern on the carpet. He had, however, distinctly heard and accurately marked every word that she had spoken. Was it not clear from what she had said that the Archdeacon had been wrong in imputing to her any attachment to Mr. Slope? Was it not clear that Eleanor was still free to make another choice? It may seem strange that he should for a moment have had a doubt, and yet he did doubt. She had not absolutely denied the charge, she had not expressly said that it was untrue. Mr. Arabin understood little of the nature of a woman's feelings or he would have known how improbable it was that she should make any clearer declaration than she had done. Few men do understand the nature of a woman's heart till years have robbed such understanding of its value. And it is well that it should be so, or men would triumph too easily.

Mr. Arabin stood counting the carpet, unhappy, wretchedly unhappy, at the hard words that had been spoken to him, and yet happy, exquisitely happy, as he thought that after all the woman whom he so regarded was not to become the wife of the man whom he so much disliked. As he stood there he began to be aware that he was himself in love. Forty years had passed over his head, and as yet woman's beauty had never given him an uneasy hour. His present hour was very uneasy.

Not that he remained there for half or a quarter of that time. In spite of what Eleanor had said, Mr. Arabin was in truth a manly man. Having ascertained that he loved this woman, and having now reason to believe that she was free to receive his love, at least if she pleased to do so, he followed her into the garden to make such wooing as he could.

He was not long in finding her. She was walking to and fro beneath the avenue of elms that stood in the Archdeacon's grounds, skirting the churchyard. What had passed between her and Mr. Arabin had not, alas! tended to lessen the acerbity of her spirit. She was very angry, more angry with him than with anyone. How could he have so misunderstood her?

As she passed along the avenue, every now and then an unbidden tear would force itself on her cheek, and as she raised her hand to brush it away she stamped with her little foot upon the sward with very spite to think that she had been so treated.

Mr. Arabin was very near to her when she first saw him, and she turned short round and retraced her steps down the avenue, trying to rid her cheeks of all trace of the telltale tears. It was a needless endeavor, for Mr. Arabin was in a state of mind that hardly allowed him to observe such trifles. He followed her down the walk and overtook her just as she reached the end of it.

He had not considered how he would address her, he had not thought what he would say. He had only felt that it was wretchedness to him to quarrel with her, and that it would be happiness to be allowed to love her. And yet he could not lower himself by asking her pardon. He had done her no wrong. He had not calumniated her, not injured her, as she had accused him of doing. He could not confess sins of which he had not been guilty. He could only let the past be past, and ask her as to her and his hopes for the future.

"I hope we are not to part as enemies?" said he.

"There shall be no enmity on my part," said Eleanor. "I endeavor to avoid all enmities. It would be a hollow pretense were I to say that there can be true friendship between us after what has just passed. People cannot make their friends of those whom they despise."

"And am I despised?"

"*I* must have been so before you could have spoken of me as you did. And I was deceived, cruelly deceived. I believed that you thought well of me, I believed that you esteemed me."

"Thought well of you and esteemed you!" said he. "In justifying myself before you I must use stronger words than those." He paused for a moment, and Eleanor's heart beat with painful violence within her bosom as she waited for him to go on. "I have esteemed, do esteem, you as I never yet esteemed any woman. Think well of you! I never thought to think so well, so much, of any human creature. Speak calumny of you! Insult you! Willfully injure you! I wish it were my privilege to shield you from calumny, insult, and injury. Calumny! Ah, me. 'Twere almost better that it were so. Better than to worship with a sinful worship, sinful and vain also." And then he walked along beside her, with his hands clasped behind his back, looking down on the grass beneath his feet and utterly at a loss how to express his meaning. And Eleanor walked beside him determined at least to give him no assistance.

"Ah, me!" he uttered at last, speaking rather to himself than to her. "Ah, me! These Plumstead walks were pleasant enough if one could have but heartsease, but without that the dull dead stones of Oxford were far preferable, and St. Ewold's too. Mrs. Bold, I am beginning to think that I mistook myself when I came hither. A Romish priest now would have escaped all this. O Father of Heaven! How good for us would it be if Thou couldest vouchsafe to us a certain rule."

"And have we not a certain rule, Mr. Arabin?"

"Yes—yes, surely—'Lead us not into temptation, but deliver us from evil.' But what is temptation? What is evil? Is this evil—is this temptation?"

Poor Mr. Arabin! It would not come out of him, that deep true love of his. He could not bring himself to utter it in plain language that would require and demand an answer.

And yet Eleanor understood him as thoroughly as though he had declared his passion with all the elegant fluency of a practiced Lothario. With a woman's instinct she followed every bend of his mind as he spoke of the pleasantness of Plumstead and the stones of Oxford, as he alluded to the safety of the Romish priest and the hidden perils of temptation. She knew that it all meant love. She knew that this man at her side, this accomplished scholar, this practiced orator, this great polemical combatant, was striving and striving in vain to tell her that his heart was no longer his own.

She knew this, and felt a sort of joy in knowing it, and yet she would not come to his aid. He had offended her deeply, had treated her unworthily, the more unworthily seeing that he had learnt to love her, and Eleanor could not bring herself to abandon her revenge. She did not ask herself whether or no she would ultimately accept his love. She did not even acknowledge to herself that she now perceived it with pleasure. At the present moment it did not touch her heart, it merely appeased her pride and flattered her vanity. Mr. Arabin had dared to associate her name with that of Mr. Slope, and now her spirit was soothed by finding that he would fain associate it with his own. And so she walked on beside him inhaling incense, but giving out no sweetness in return.

"Answer me this," said Mr. Arabin, stopping suddenly in his walk and stepping forward so that he faced his companion. "Answer me this one question. You do not love Mr. Slope? You do not intend to be his wife?"

Mr. Arabin certainly did not go the right way to win such a woman as Eleanor Bold. Just as her wrath was evaporating, as it was disappearing before the true warmth of his untold love, he rekindled it by a most useless repetition of his original sin. Had he known what he was about he should never have mentioned Mr. Slope's name before Eleanor Bold till he had made her all his own. Then, and not till then, he might have talked of Mr. Slope with as much triumph as he chose.

"I shall answer no such question," said she. "And what is more, I must tell you that nothing can justify your asking it. Good morning!"

And so saying she stepped proudly across the lawn, and passing through the drawing-room window, joined her father and sister at lunch in the dining-room. Half an hour afterward she was in the carriage, and so she left Plumstead without again seeing Mr. Arabin.

His walk was long and sad among the somber trees that overshadowed the churchyard. He left the Archdeacon's grounds that he might escape attention, and sauntered among the green hillocks under which lay at rest so many of the once loving swains and forgotten beauties of Plumstead. To his ears Eleanor's last words sounded like a knell never to be reversed. He could not comprehend that she might be angry with him, indignant with him, remorseless with him, and yet love him. He could not make up his mind whether or no Mr. Slope was in truth a favored rival. If not, why should she not have answered his question?

Poor Mr. Arabin—untaught, illiterate, boorish, ignorant man! That at forty years of age you should know so little of the workings of a woman's heart!

CHAPTER XXX

THE BISHOP'S LIBRARY

DURING Eleanor's drive into Barchester she had not much opportunity of reflecting on Mr. Arabin. She had been constrained to divert her mind both from his sins and his love by the necessity of conversing with her sister and maintaining the appearance of parting with her on good terms. When the carriage reached her own door, and while she was in the act of giving her last kiss to her sister and nieces, Mary Bold ran out and exclaimed,

"Oh, Eleanor, have you heard?—Oh, Mrs. Grantly, have you heard what has happened? The poor Dean!"

"Good heavens!" said Mrs. Grantly. "What—what has happened?"

"This morning at nine he had a fit of apoplexy, and he has not spoken since. I very much fear that by this time he is no more."

Mrs. Grantly had been very intimate with the Dean, and was therefore much shocked. Eleanor had not known him so well, nevertheless she was sufficiently acquainted with his person and manners to feel startled and grieved also at the tidings she now received. "I will go at once to the deanery," said Mrs. Grantly. "The Archdeacon I am sure will be there. If there is any news to send you I will let Thomas call before he leaves town." And so the carriage drove off, leaving Eleanor and her baby with Mary Bold.

Mrs. Grantly had been quite right. The Archdeacon was at the deanery. He had come into Barchester that morning by himself, not caring to intrude himself upon Eleanor, and he also immediately on his arrival had heard of the Dean's fit. There was, as we have before said, a library or reading room connecting the cathedral with the Dean's house. This was generally called the bishop's library, because a certain Bishop of Barchester was supposed to have added it to the cathedral. It was built immediately over a portion of the cloisters, and a flight of stairs descended from it into the room in which the cathedral clergymen put their surplices on and off. As it also opened directly into the Dean's house, it was the passage through which that dignitary usually went to his public devotions. Who had or had not the right of entry into it, it might be difficult to say, but the people of Barchester believed that it belonged to the Dean and the clergymen of Barchester believed that it belonged to the Chapter.

On the morning in question most of the resident clergymen who constituted the Chapter, and some few others, were here assembled, and among them as usual the Archdeacon towered with high authority. He had heard of the Dean's fit before he was over the bridge which led into the town, and had at once come to the well-known clerical trysting place. He had been there by eleven o'clock, and had remained ever since. From time to time the medical men who had been called in came through from the deanery into the library, uttered little bulletins, and then returned. There was, it appears, very little hope of the old man's rallying, indeed no hope of anything like a final recovery. The only question was whether he must die at once, speechless, unconscious, stricken to death by his first heavy fit, or whether by due aid of medical skill he might not be so far brought back to this world as to become conscious of his state and enabled to address one prayer to his Maker before he was called to meet Him face to face at the judgment seat.

The Archdeacon alone of the attendant clergy had been admitted for a moment into the sick man's chamber. He had crept in with creaking shoes, had said with smothered voice a word of consolation to the sorrowing daughter, had looked on the distorted face of his old friend with solemn but yet eager, scrutinizing eye, as though he said in his heart "And so some day it will probably be with me," and then, having whispered an unmeaning word or two to the doctors, had creaked his way back again into the library.

"He'll never speak again, I fear," said the Archdeacon as he noiselessly closed the door, as though the unconscious dying man, from whom all sense had fled, would have heard in his distant chamber the spring of the lock which was now so carefully handled.

"When a man over seventy has a stroke of apoplexy, it seldom comes very lightly," said the burly Chancellor.

"He was an excellent, sweet-tempered man," said one of the Vicars Choral. "Heaven knows how we shall repair his loss."

"He was indeed," said a minor canon, "and a great blessing to all those privileged to take a share of the services of our cathedral. I suppose the Government will appoint, Mr. Archdeacon. I trust we may have no stranger."

"We will not talk about his successor," said the Archdeacon, "while there is yet hope."

"Oh no, of course not," said the minor canon. "It would be exceedingly indecorous! But——"

"I know of no man," said the meager little prebendary, "who has better interest with the present government than Mr. Slope."

"Mr. Slope!" said two or three at once almost sotto voce. "Mr. Slope Dean of Barchester!"

"Pooh!" exclaimed the burly Chancellor.

"The Bishop would do anything for him," said the little prebendary.

"And so would Mrs. Proudie," said the Vicar Choral.

"Pooh!" said the Chancellor.

The Archdeacon had almost turned pale at the idea. What if Mr. Slope should become Dean of Barchester? To be sure there was no adequate ground, indeed no ground at all, for presuming that such a desecration could even be contemplated. But nevertheless it was on the cards. Dr. Proudie had interest with the Government, and the man carried as it were Dr. Proudie in his pocket. How should they all conduct themselves if Mr. Slope were to become Dean of Barchester? The bare idea for a moment struck even Dr. Grantly dumb.

"It would certainly not be very pleasant for us to have Mr. Slope at the deanery," said the little prebendary, chuckling inwardly at the evident consternation which his surmise had created.

"About as pleasant and as probable as having you in the palace," said the Chancellor.

"I should think such an appointment highly improbable," said the minor canon, "and moreover extremely injudicious. Should not you, Mr. Arch-deacon?"

"I should presume such a thing to be quite out of the question," said the Archdeacon. "But at the present moment I am thinking rather of our poor friend who is lying so near us than of Mr. Slope."

At this moment the door opened and in came Dr. Fillgrave.

"How is he?" "Is he conscious?" "Can he speak?" "I hope not dead?" "No worse news, Doctor, I trust?" "I hope, I trust, something better, Doctor?" said half a dozen voices all at once, each in a tone of extremest anxiety. It was pleasant to see how popular the good old Dean was among his clergy.

"No change, gentlemen, not the slightest change. But a telegraphic message has arrived—Sir Omicron Pie will be here by the 9.15 P.M. train. If any man can do anything Sir Omicron Pie will do it. But all that skill can do has been done."

Just at this period Mrs. Grantly's carriage drove into the close, and the Archdeacon went down to confirm the news which she had heard before.

By the 9.15 P.M. train Sir Omicron Pie did arrive. And in the course of the night a sort of consciousness returned to the poor old Dean. Whether this was due to Sir Omicron Pie is a question on which it may be well not to offer an opinion. Dr. Fillgrave was very clear in his own mind, but Sir Omicron himself is thought to have differed from that learned Doctor. At any rate Sir Omicron expressed an opinion that the Dean had yet some days to live.

For the eight or ten next days, accordingly, the poor Dean remained in the same state, half-conscious and half-comatose, and the attendant clergy began to think that no new appointment would be necessary for some few months to come.

CHAPTER XXXI

A NEW CANDIDATE FOR ECCLESIASTICAL HONORS

THE Dean's illness occasioned much mental turmoil in other places besides the deanery and adjoining library, and the idea which occurred to the meager little prebendary about Mr. Slope did not occur to him alone.

The Bishop was sitting listlessly in his study when the news reached him of the Dean's illness. It was brought to him by Mr. Slope, who of course was not the last person in Barchester to hear it. It was also not slow in finding its way to Mrs. Proudie's ears. It may be presumed that there was not just then much friendly intercourse between these two rival claimants for his lordship's obedience. Indeed, though living in the same house, they had not met since the stormy interview between them in the Bishop's study on the preceding day.

On that occasion Mrs. Proudie had been defeated. That the prestige of
continual victory should have been torn from her standards was a subject
of great sorrow to that militant lady, but though defeated, she was not
overcome. She felt that she might yet recover her lost ground, that she
might yet hurl Mr. Slope down to the dust from which she had picked him,
and force her sinning lord to sue for pardon in sackcloth and ashes.

On that memorable day, memorable for his mutiny and rebellion against
her high behests, he had carried his way with a high hand, and had really
begun to think it possible that the days of his slavery were counted. He
had begun to hope that he was now about to enter into a free land, a land
delicious with milk which he himself might quaff, and honey which would
not tantalize him by being only honey to the eye. When Mrs. Proudie
banged the door as she left his room, he felt himself every inch a bishop.
To be sure his spirit had been a little cowed by his chaplain's subsequent
lecture, but on the whole he was highly pleased with himself, and flattered
himself that the worst was over. "*Ce n'est que le premier pas qui coûte*,"
he reflected, and now that the first step had been so magnanimously taken,
all the rest would follow easily.

He met his wife as a matter of course at dinner, where little or nothing
was said that could ruffle the Bishop's happiness. His daughters and the
servants were present and protected him.

He made one or two trifling remarks on the subject of his projected
visit to the Archbishop, in order to show to all concerned that he intended
to have his own way, and the very servants, perceiving the change, transferred a little of their reverence from their mistress to their master. All
which the master perceived, and so also did the mistress. But Mrs. Proudie
bided her time.

After dinner he returned to his study, where Mr. Slope soon found him,
and there they had tea together and planned many things. For some few
minutes the Bishop was really happy, but as the clock on the chimney-
piece warned him that the stilly hours of night were drawing on, as he
looked at his chamber candlestick and knew that he must use it, his heart
sank within him again. He was as a ghost all whose power of wandering
free through these upper regions ceases at cockcrow, or rather he was
the opposite of a ghost, for till cockcrow he must again be a serf. And
would that be all? Could he trust himself to come down to breakfast a free
man in the morning?

He was nearly an hour later than usual when he betook himself to his
rest. Rest! What rest? However, he took a couple of glasses of sherry, and
mounted the stairs. Far be it from us to follow him thither. There are some
things which no novelist, no historian, should attempt, some few scenes in
life's drama which even no poet should dare to paint. Let that which passed
between Dr. Proudie and his wife on this night be understood to be among
them.

He came down the following morning a sad and thoughtful man. He was attenuated in appearance, one might almost say emaciated. I doubt whether his now grizzled locks had not palpably become more gray than on the preceding evening. At any rate he had aged materially.

He came down and breakfasted alone. Mrs. Proudie, being indisposed, took her coffee in her bedroom, and her daughters waited upon her there. He ate his breakfast alone and then, hardly knowing what he did, he betook himself to his usual seat in his study. He was thus seated when Mr. Slope made his appearance, with breathless impatience.

"My lord, the Dean is dead."

"Good heavens!" exclaimed the Bishop, startled out of his apathy by an announcement so sad and so sudden.

"He is either dead or now dying. He has had an apoplectic fit, and I am told that there is not the slightest hope. Indeed I do not doubt that by this time he is no more."

Bells were rung, and servants were immediately sent to inquire. In the course of the morning the Bishop, leaning on his chaplain's arm, himself called at the deanery door. Mrs. Proudie sent to Miss Trefoil all manner of offers of assistance. The Miss Proudies sent also, and there was immense sympathy between the palace and the deanery. The answer to all inquiries was unvaried. The Dean was just the same, and Sir Omicron Pie was expected down by the 9.15 P.M. train.

And then Mr. Slope began to meditate, as others also had done, as to who might possibly be the new dean. And it occurred to him, as it had also occurred to others, that it might be possible that he should be the new dean himself. And then the question as to the twelve hundred, or fifteen hundred, or two thousand ran in his mind, as it had run through those of the other clergymen in the cathedral library.

Whether it might be two thousand, or fifteen or twelve hundred, it would in any case undoubtedly be a great thing for him, if he could get it. The gratification to his ambition would be greater even than that of his covetousness. How glorious to outtop the Archdeacon in his own cathedral city, to sit above prebendaries and canons, and have the cathedral pulpit and all the cathedral services altogether at his own disposal!

But it might be easier to wish for this than to obtain it. Mr. Slope, however, was not without some means of forwarding his views, and he at any rate did not let the grass grow under his feet. In the first place he thought—and not vainly—that he could count upon what assistance the Bishop could give him. He immediately changed his views with regard to his patron. He made up his mind that if he became dean, he would hand his lordship back again to his wife's vassalage, and he thought it possible that his lordship might not be sorry to rid himself of one of his mentors. Mr. Slope had also taken some steps toward making his name known to other men in power.

But it was incumbent on Mr. Slope first to secure the Bishop. He specially felt that it behooved him to do this before the visit to the Archbishop was made. It was really quite providential that the Dean should have fallen ill just at the very nick of time. If Dr. Proudie could be instigated to take the matter up warmly, he might manage a good deal while staying at the Archbishop's palace. Feeling this very strongly, Mr. Slope determined to sound the Bishop that very afternoon. He was to start on the following morning to London, and therefore not a moment could be lost with safety.

He went into the Bishop's study about five o'clock and found him still sitting alone. It might have been supposed that he had hardly moved since the little excitement occasioned by his walk to the Dean's door. He still wore on his face that dull, dead look of half-unconscious suffering. He was doing nothing, reading nothing, thinking of nothing, but simply gazing on vacancy when Mr. Slope for the second time that day entered his room.

"Well, Slope," said he, somewhat impatiently, for to tell the truth he was not anxious just at present to have much conversation with Mr. Slope.

"Your lordship will be sorry to hear that as yet the poor Dean has shown no sign of amendment."

"Oh—ah—hasn't he? Poor man! I'm sure I'm very sorry. I suppose Sir Omicron has not arrived yet?"

"No, not till the 9.15 P.M. train."

"I wonder they didn't have a special. They say Dr. Trefoil is very rich."

"Very rich, I believe," said Mr. Slope. "But the truth is all the doctors in London can do no good, no other good than to show that every possible care has been taken. Poor Dr. Trefoil is not long for this world, my lord."

"I suppose not—I suppose not."

"Oh, no. Indeed, his best friends could not wish that he should outlive such a shock, for his intellects cannot possibly survive it."

"Poor man! Poor man!" said the Bishop.

"It will naturally be a matter of much moment to your lordship who is to succeed him," said Mr. Slope. "It would be a great thing if you could secure the appointment for some person of your own way of thinking on important points. The party hostile to us are very strong here in Barchester—much too strong."

"Yes, yes. If poor Dr. Trefoil is to go, it will be a great thing to get a good man in his place."

"It will be everything to your lordship to get a man on whose co-operation you can reckon. Only think what trouble we might have if Dr. Grantly, or Dr. Hyandry, or any of that way of thinking were to get it."

"It is not very probable that Lord —— will give it to any of that school. Why should he?"

"No. Not probable, certainly not, but it's possible. Great interest will probably be made. If I might venture to advise your lordship, I would suggest that you should discuss the matter with His Grace next week.

I have no doubt that your wishes, if made known and backed by His Grace, would be paramount with Lord ——."

"Well, I don't know that. Lord —— has always been very kind to me, very kind. But I am unwilling to interfere in such matters unless asked. And indeed if asked, I don't know whom at this moment I should recommend."

Mr. Slope, even Mr. Slope, felt at the present rather abashed. He hardly knew how to frame his little request in language sufficiently modest. He had recognized and acknowledged to himself the necessity of shocking the Bishop in the first instance by the temerity of his application, and his difficulty was how best to remedy that by his adroitness and eloquence. "I doubted myself," said he, "whether your lordship would have anyone immediately in your eye, and it is on this account that I venture to submit to you an idea that I have been turning over in my own mind. If poor Dr. Trefoil must go, I really do not see why, with your lordship's assistance, I should not hold the preferment myself."

"You!" exclaimed the Bishop, in a manner that Mr. Slope could hardly have considered complimentary.

The ice was now broken, and Mr. Slope became fluent enough. "I have been thinking of looking for it. If your lordship will press the matter on the Archbishop, I do not doubt but I shall succeed. You see I shall be the first to move, which is a great matter. Then I can count upon assistance from the public press. My name is known, I may say somewhat favorably known, to that portion of the press which is now most influential with the Government, and I have friends also in the Government But nevertheless it is to you, my lord, that I look for assistance. It is from your hands that I would most willingly receive the benefit. And, which should ever be the chief consideration in such matters, you must know better than any other person whatsoever what qualifications I possess."

The Bishop sat for a while dumfounded. Mr. Slope Dean of Barchester! The idea of such a transformation of character would never have occurred to his own unaided intellect. At first he went on thinking why, for what reasons, on what account, Mr. Slope should be Dean of Barchester. But by degrees the direction of his thoughts changed, and he began to think why, for what reasons, on what account, Mr. Slope should not be Dean of Barchester. As far as he himself, the Bishop, was concerned, he could well spare the services of his chaplain. That little idea of using Mr. Slope as a counterpoise to his wife had well-nigh evaporated. He had all but acknowledged the futility of the scheme. If indeed he could have slept in his chaplain's bedroom instead of his wife's, there might have been something in it. But—— And thus as Mr. Slope was speaking the Bishop began to recognize the idea that that gentleman might become Dean of Barchester without impropriety—not moved, indeed, by Mr. Slope's eloquence, for he did not follow the tenor of his speech, but led thereto by his own cogitations.

"I need not say," continued Mr. Slope, "that it would be my chief desire to act in all matters connected with the cathedral as far as possible in accordance with your views. I know your lordship so well (and I hope you know me well enough to have the same feelings) that I am satisfied that my being in that position would add materially to your own comfort, and enable you to extend the sphere of your useful influence. As I said before, it is most desirable that there should be but one opinion among the dignitaries of the same diocese. I doubt much whether I would accept such an appointment in any diocese in which I should be constrained to differ from the bishop. In this case there would be a delightful uniformity of opinion."

Mr. Slope perfectly well perceived that the Bishop did not follow a word that he said, but nevertheless he went on talking. He knew it was necessary that Dr. Proudie should recover from his surprise, and he knew also that he must give him the opportunity of appearing to have been persuaded by argument. So he went on and produced a multitude of fitting reasons all tending to show that no one on earth could make so good a Dean of Barchester as himself, that the Government and the public would assuredly coincide in desiring that he, Mr. Slope, should be Dean of Barchester, but that for high considerations of ecclesiastical polity it would be especially desirable that this piece of preferment should be so bestowed through the instrumentality of the Bishop of the diocese.

"But I really don't know what I could do in the matter," said the Bishop.

"If you would mention it to the Archbishop, if you could tell His Grace that you consider such an appointment very desirable, that you have it much at heart with a view to putting an end to schism in the diocese. If you did this with your usual energy, you would probably find no difficulty in inducing His Grace to promise that he would mention it to Lord ——. Of course you would let the Archbishop know that I am not looking for the preferment solely through his intervention, that you do not exactly require him to ask it as a favor, that you expect that I shall get it through other sources, as is indeed the case, but that you are very anxious that His Grace should express his approval of such an arrangement to Lord ——."

It ended in the Bishop promising to do as he was bid. Not that he so promised without a stipulation. "About that hospital," he said in the middle of the conference. "I was never so troubled in my life." Which was about the truth. "You haven't spoken to Mr. Harding since I saw you?"

Mr. Slope assured his patron that he had not.

"Ah well, then—I think upon the whole it will be better to let Quiverful have it. It has been half-promised to him, and he has a large family and is very poor. I think on the whole it will be better to make out the nomination for Mr. Quiverful."

"But, my lord," said Mr. Slope, still thinking that he was bound to make a fight for his own view on this matter, and remembering that it still behooved him to maintain his lately acquired supremacy over Mrs. Proudie, lest he should fail in his views regarding the deanery. "But, my lord, I am really much afraid——"

"Remember, Mr. Slope," said the Bishop, "I can hold out no sort of hope to you in this matter of succeeding poor Dr. Trefoil. I will certainly speak to the Archbishop, as you wish it, but I cannot think——"

"Well, my lord," said Mr. Slope, fully understanding the Bishop, and in his turn interrupting him, "perhaps your lordship is right about Mr. Quiverful. I have no doubt I can easily arrange matters with Mr. Harding, and I will make out the nomination for your signature as you direct."

"Yes, Slope, I think that will be best. And you may be sure that any little that I can do to forward your views shall be done."

And so they parted.

CHAPTER XXXII

MRS. PROUDIE VICTRIX

THE next week passed over at Barchester with much apparent tranquillity. The hearts, however, of some of the inhabitants were not so tranquil as the streets of the city. The poor old Dean still continued to live. The Bishop still remained away. He had stayed a day or two in town, and had also remained longer at the Archbishop's than he had intended.

Mrs. Bold was thrown much with the Stanhopes, of whom she became fonder and fonder. If asked, she would have said that Charlotte Stanhope was her especial friend, and so she would have thought. But to tell the truth, she liked Bertie nearly as well. She had no more idea of regarding him as a lover than she would have had of looking at a big tame dog in such a light. She admitted him to a kind of familiarity which she had never known with anyone else, and of which she by no means understood the danger. She blushed once at finding that she had called him Bertie, and on the same day only barely remembered her position in time to check herself from playing upon him some personal practical joke to which she was instigated by Charlotte.

In all this Eleanor was perfectly innocent, and Bertie Stanhope could hardly be called guilty. But every familiarity into which Eleanor was entrapped was deliberately planned by his sister. She knew well how to play her game, and played it without mercy. She knew, none so well, what was her brother's character, and she would have handed over to him the young widow, and the young widow's money, and the money of the widow's child, without remorse. With her pretended friendship and warm cordiality, she strove to connect Eleanor so closely with her brother as to make it impossible that she should go back even if she wished it. But Charlotte

Stanhope knew really nothing of Eleanor's character, did not even understand that there were such characters. She did not comprehend that a young
and pretty woman could be playful and familiar with a man such as Bertie
Stanhope and yet have no idea in her head, no feeling in her heart, that
she would have been ashamed to own to all the world. Charlotte Stanhope did not in the least conceive that her new friend was a woman whom
nothing could entrap into an inconsiderate marriage, whose mind would
have revolted from the slightest impropriety had she been aware that any
impropriety existed.

Miss Stanhope, however, had tact enough to make herself and her father's
house very agreeable to Mrs. Bold. There was with them all an absence
of stiffness and formality which was peculiarly agreeable to Eleanor
after the great dose of clerical arrogance which she had lately been constrained to take. She played chess with them, walked with them, and drank
tea with them, studied or pretended to study astronomy, assisted them in
writing stories in rhyme, in turning prose tragedy into comic verse, or
comic stories into would-be tragic poetry. She had no idea before that
she had any such talents. She had not conceived the possibility of her doing
such things as she now did. She found with the Stanhopes new amusements
and employments, new pursuits, which in themselves could not be wrong
and which were exceedingly alluring.

But during all this time Eleanor by no means forgot Mr. Arabin, nor
did she forget Mr. Slope. She had parted from Mr. Arabin in her anger.
She was still angry at what she regarded as his impertinent interference,
but nevertheless she looked forward to meeting him again, and also looked
forward to forgiving him. The words that Mr. Arabin had uttered still
sounded in her ears. She knew that if not intended for a declaration of love,
they did signify that he loved her, and she felt also that if he ever did
make such a declaration, it might be that she should not receive it unkindly.
She was still angry with him, very angry with him—so angry that she
would bite her lip and stamp her foot as she thought of what he had said
and done. But nevertheless she yearned to let him know that he was forgiven.
All that she required was that he should own that he had sinned.

She was to meet him at Ullathorne on the last day of the present month.
Miss Thorne had invited all the country round to a breakfast on the lawn.
There were to be tents, and archery, and dancing for the ladies on the
lawn, and for the swains and girls in the paddock. There were to be
fiddlers and fifers, races for the boys, poles to be climbed, ditches full
of water to be jumped over, horse collars to be grinned through (this latter
amusement was an addition of the stewards, and not arranged by Miss
Thorne in the original program), and every game to be played which,
in a long course of reading, Miss Thorne could ascertain to have been
played in the good days of Queen Elizabeth. Everything of more modern
growth was to be tabooed, if possible.

This party at Ullathorne had been planned in the first place as a sort of welcoming to Mr. Arabin on his entrance into St. Ewold's parsonage. An intended harvest-home gala for the laborers and their wives and children had subsequently been amalgamated with it, and thus it had grown to its present dimensions. All the Plumstead party had of course been asked, and at the time of the invitation Eleanor had intended to have gone with her sister. Now her plans were altered, and she was going with the Stanhopes. The Proudies were also to be there, and as Mr. Slope had not been included in the invitation to the palace, the Signora, whose impudence never deserted her, asked permission of Miss Thorne to bring him.

This permission Miss Thorne gave, having no other alternative, but she did so with a trembling heart, fearing Mr. Arabin would be offended. Immediately on his return she apologized, almost with tears, so dire an enmity was presumed to rage between the two gentlemen. But Mr. Arabin comforted her by an assurance that he should meet Mr. Slope with the greatest pleasure imaginable, and made her promise that she would introduce them to each other.

But this triumph of Mr. Slope's was not so agreeable to Eleanor, who since her return to Barchester had done her best to avoid him. She would not give way to the Plumstead folk when they so ungenerously accused her of being in love with this odious man, but nevertheless, knowing that she was so accused, she was fully alive to the expediency of keeping out of his way and dropping him by degrees. She had seen very little of him since her return. Her servant had been instructed to say to all visitors that she was out. She could not bring herself to specify Mr. Slope particularly, and in order to avoid him she had thus debarred herself from all her friends. She had excepted Charlotte Stanhope, and by degrees a few others also.

Nevertheless the Stanhopes were pledged to take Mr. Slope with them to Ullathorne. An arrangement was therefore necessarily made which was very disagreeable to Eleanor. Dr. Stanhope, with herself, Charlotte, and Mr. Slope, were to go together, and Bertie was to follow with his sister Madeline. It was clearly visible by Eleanor's face that this assortment was very disagreeable to her, and Charlotte, who was much encouraged thereby in her own little plan, made a thousand apologies.

"I see you don't like it, my dear," said she, "but we could not manage otherwise. Bertie would give his eyes to go with you, but Madeline cannot possibly go without him. Nor could we possibly put Mr. Slope and Madeline in the same carriage without anyone else. They'd both be ruined forever, you know, and not admitted inside Ullathorne gates, I should imagine, after such an impropriety."

"Of course that wouldn't do," said Eleanor. "But couldn't I go in the carriage with the Signora and your brother?"

"Impossible!" said Charlotte. "When she is there, there is only room for two." The Signora, in truth, did not care to do her traveling in the presence of strangers.

"Well, then," said Eleanor, "you are all so kind, Charlotte, and so good to me, that I am sure you won't be offended, but I think I'll not go at all."

"Not go at all!—What nonsense!—Indeed you shall." It had been absolutely determined in family council that Bertie should propose on that very occasion.

"Or I can take a fly," said Eleanor. "You know I am not embarrassed by so many difficulties as you young ladies. I can go alone."

"Nonsense, my dear! Don't think of such a thing. After all it is only for an hour or so, and to tell the truth, I don't know what it is you dislike so. I thought you and Mr. Slope were great friends. What is it you dislike?"

"Oh, nothing particular," said Eleanor. "Only I thought it would be a family party."

"Of course it would be much nicer, much more snug, if Bertie could go with us. It is he that is badly treated. I can assure you he is much more afraid of Mr. Slope than you are. But you see Madeline cannot go out without him—and she, poor creature, goes out so seldom! I am sure you don't begrudge her this, though her vagary does knock about our own party a little."

Of course Eleanor made a thousand protestations, and uttered a thousand hopes that Madeline would enjoy herself. And of course she had to give way and undertake to go in the carriage with Mr. Slope. In fact, she was driven either to do this or to explain why she would not do so. Now she could not bring herself to explain to Charlotte Stanhope all that had passed at Plumstead.

But it was to her a sore necessity. She thought of a thousand little schemes for avoiding it. She would plead illness, and not go at all. She would persuade Mary Bold to go although not asked, and then make a necessity of having a carriage of her own to take her sister-in-law. Anything, in fact, she could do rather than be seen by Mr. Arabin getting out of the same carriage with Mr. Slope. However, when the momentous morning came she had no scheme matured, and then Mr. Slope handed her into Dr. Stanhope's carriage, and following her steps, sat opposite to her.

The Bishop returned on the eve of the Ullathorne party, and was received at home with radiant smiles by the partner of all his cares. On his arrival he crept up to his dressing-room with somewhat of a palpitating heart. He had overstayed his allotted time by three days, and was not without much fear of penalties. Nothing, however, could be more affectionately cordial than the greeting he received. The girls came out and kissed him in a manner that was quite soothing to his spirit, and Mrs. Proudie, "albeit unused to the melting mood," squeezed him in her arms, and almost in words called him her dear, darling, good, pet, little Bishop. All this was a very pleasant surprise.

Mrs. Proudie had somewhat changed her tactics. Not that she had seen any cause to disapprove of her former line of conduct, but she had now brought matters to such a point that she calculated that she might safely do so. She had got the better of Mr. Slope, and she now thought well to show her husband that when allowed to get the better of everybody, when obeyed by him and permitted to rule over others, she would take care that he should have his reward. Mr. Slope had not a chance against her. Not only could she stun the poor Bishop by her midnight anger, but she could assuage and soothe him, if she so willed, by daily indulgences. She could furnish his room for him, turn him out as smart a bishop as any on the bench, give him good dinners, warm fires, and an easy life. All this she would do if he would but be quietly obedient. But if not——! To speak sooth, however, his sufferings on that dreadful night had been so poignant as to leave him little spirit for further rebellion.

As soon as he had dressed himself she returned to his room. "I hope you enjoyed yourself at ——," said she, seating herself on one side of the fire while he remained in his armchair on the other, stroking the calves of his legs. It was the first time he had had a fire in his room since the summer, and it pleased him, for the good Bishop loved to be warm and cozy. Yes, he said, he had enjoyed himself very much. Nothing could be more polite than the Archbishop, and Mrs. Archbishop had been equally charming.

Mrs. Proudie was delighted to hear it. Nothing, she declared, pleased her so much as to think

"Her baïrn respectit like the lave."

She did not put it precisely in these words, but what she said came to the same thing. And then, having petted and fondled her little man sufficiently, she proceeded to business.

"The poor Dean is still alive," said she.

"So I hear, so I hear," said the Bishop. "I'll go to the deanery directly after breakfast tomorrow."

"We are going to this party at Ullathorne tomorrow morning, my dear. We must be there early, you know—by twelve o'clock, I suppose."

"Oh—ah!" said the Bishop. "Then I'll certainly call the next day."

"Was much said about it at ——?" asked Mrs. Proudie.

"About what?" said the Bishop.

"Filling up the Dean's place," said Mrs. Proudie. As she spoke a spark of the wonted fire returned to her eye, and the Bishop felt himself to be a little less comfortable than before.

"Filling up the Dean's place—that is, if the Dean dies?—Very little, my dear. It was mentioned, just mentioned."

"And what did you say about it, Bishop?"

"Why, I said that I thought that if—that is, should—should the Dean die—that is, I said I thought——" As he went on stammering and floundering, he saw that his wife's eye was fixed sternly on him. Why should he encounter such evil for a man whom he loved so slightly as Mr. Slope? Why should he give up his enjoyments and his ease, and such dignity as might be allowed to him, to fight a losing battle for a chaplain? The chaplain after all, if successful, would be as great a tyrant as his wife. Why fight at all? Why contend? Why be uneasy? From that moment he determined to fling Mr. Slope to the winds, and take the goods the gods provided.

"I am told," said Mrs. Proudie, speaking very slowly, "that Mr. Slope is looking to be the new dean."

"Yes—certainly, I believe he is," said the Bishop.

"And what does the Archbishop say about that?" asked Mrs. Proudie.

"Well, my dear, to tell the truth, I promised Mr. Slope to speak to the Archbishop. Mr. Slope spoke to me about it. It is very arrogant of him, I must say—but that is nothing to me."

"Arrogant!" said Mrs. Proudie. "It is the most impudent piece of pretension I ever heard of in my life. Mr. Slope Dean of Barchester indeed! And what did you do in the matter, Bishop?"

"Why, my dear, I did speak to the Archbishop."

"You don't mean to tell me," said Mrs. Proudie, "that you are going to make yourself ridiculous by lending your name to such a preposterous attempt as this? Mr. Slope Dean of Barchester indeed!" And she tossed her head, and put her arms akimbo, with an air of confident defiance that made her husband quite sure that Mr. Slope never would be Dean of Barchester. In truth, Mrs. Proudie was all but invincible. Had she married Petruchio, it may be doubted whether that arch wife-tamer would have been able to keep her legs out of those garments which are presumed by men to be peculiarly unfitted for feminine use.

"It is preposterous, my dear."

"Then why have you endeavored to assist him?"

"Why—my dear, I haven't assisted him—much."

"But why have you done it at all? Why have you mixed your name up in anything so ridiculous? What was it you did say to the Archbishop?"

"Why, I just did mention it. I just did say that—that in the event of the poor Dean's death, Mr. Slope would—would——"

"Would what?"

"I forget how I put it—would take it if he could get it, something of that sort. I didn't say much more than that."

"You shouldn't have said anything at all. And what did the Archbishop say?"

"He didn't say anything. He just bowed and rubbed his hands. Somebody else came up at the moment, and as we were discussing the new parochial universal school committee, the matter of the new dean dropped. After that I didn't think it wise to renew it."

"Renew it! I am very sorry you ever mentioned it. What will the Archbishop think of you?"

"You may be sure, my dear, the Archbishop thought very little about it."

"But why did you think about it, Bishop? How could you think of making such a creature as that Dean of Barchester?—Dean of Barchester! I suppose he'll be looking for a bishopric some of these days—a man that hardly knows who his own father was, a man that I found without bread to his mouth or a coat to his back. Dean of Barchester indeed! I'll dean him."

Mrs. Proudie considered herself to be in politics a pure Whig, all her family belonged to the Whig party. Now among all ranks of Englishmen and Englishwomen (Mrs. Proudie should, I think, be ranked among the former, on the score of her great strength of mind) no one is so hostile to lowly-born pretenders to high station as the pure Whig.

The Bishop thought it necessary to exculpate himself. "Why, my dear," said he, "it appeared to me that you and Mr. Slope did not get on quite so well as you used to do."

"Get on!" said Mrs. Proudie, moving her foot uneasily on the hearthrug and compressing her lips in a manner that betokened much danger to the subject of their discourse.

"I began to find that he was objectionable to you"—Mrs. Proudie's foot worked on the hearthrug with great rapidity—"and that you would be more comfortable if he was out of the palace."—Mrs. Proudie smiled, as a hyena may probably smile before he begins his laugh.—"And therefore I thought that if he got this place, and so ceased to be my chaplain, you might be pleased at such an arrangement."

And then the hyena laughed out. Pleased at such an arrangement! Pleased at having her enemy converted into a dean with twelve hundred a year! Mr. Slope had no mercy to expect. She would pick him to the very last bone.

"Oh, yes, my dear, of course he'll cease to be your chaplain," said she. "After what has passed that must be a matter of course. I couldn't for a moment think of living in the same house with such a man. Besides, he has shown himself quite unfit for such a situation—making broils and quarrels among the clergy, getting you, my dear, into scrapes, and taking upon himself as though he were as good as Bishop himself. Of course he'll go. But because he leaves the palace, that is no reason why he should get into the deanery."

"Oh, of course not!" said the Bishop. "But to save appearances, you know, my dear——"

"I don't want to save appearances. I want Mr. Slope to appear just what he is—a false, designing, mean, intriguing man. I have my eye on him. He little knows what I see. He is misconducting himself in the most disgraceful way with that lame Italian woman. That family is a disgrace to Barchester, and Mr. Slope is a disgrace to Barchester! If he doesn't look well to it, he'll have his gown stripped off his back instead of having a dean's hat on his head. Dean, indeed! The man has gone mad with arrogance."

The Bishop said nothing further to excuse either himself or his chaplain, and having shown himself passive and docile was again taken into favor. They soon went to dinner, and he spent the pleasantest evening he had had in his own house for a long time. His daughter played and sang to him as he sipped his coffee and read his newspaper, and Mrs. Proudie asked good-natured little questions about the Archbishop. And then he went happily to bed, and slept as quietly as though Mrs. Proudie had been Griselda herself. While shaving himself in the morning and preparing for the festivities of Ullathorne, he fully resolved to run no more tilts against a warrior so fully armed at all points as was Mrs. Proudie.

CHAPTER XXXIII

OXFORD—THE MASTER AND TUTOR OF LAZARUS

MR. ARABIN, as we have said, had but a sad walk of it under the trees of Plumstead churchyard. He did not appear to any of the family till dinnertime, and then he seemed, as far as their judgment went, to be quite himself. He had, as was his wont, asked himself a great many questions and given himself a great many answers, and the upshot of this was that he had set himself down for an ass. He had determined that he was much too old and much too rusty to commence the maneuvers of love-making, that he had let the time slip through his hands which should have been used for such purposes, and that now he must lie on his bed as he had made it. Then he asked himself whether in truth he did love this woman. And he answered himself, not without a long struggle, but at last honestly, that he certainly did love her. He then asked himself whether he did not also love her money, and he again answered himself that he did so. But here he did not answer honestly. It was and ever had been his weakness to look for impure motives for his own conduct. No doubt, circumstanced as he was, with a small living and a fellowship, accustomed as he had been to collegiate luxuries and expensive comforts, he might have hesitated to marry a penniless woman had he felt ever so strong a predilection for the woman herself. No doubt Eleanor's fortune put all such difficulties out of the question. But it was equally without doubt that his love for her had crept upon him without the slightest idea on his part that he could ever benefit his own condition by sharing her wealth.

When he had stood on the hearthrug counting the pattern, and counting also the future chances of his own life, the remembrance of Mrs. Bold's comfortable income had not certainly damped his first assured feeling of love for her. And why should it have done so? Need it have done so with the purest of men? Be that as it may, Mr. Arabin decided against himself. He decided that it had done so in his case, and that he was not the purest of men.

He also decided, which was more to his purpose, that Eleanor did not care a straw for him, and that very probably she did care a straw for his rival. Then he made up his mind not to think of her any more, and went on thinking of her till he was almost in a state to drown himself in the little brook which ran at the bottom of the Archdeacon's grounds.

And ever and again his mind would revert to the Signora Neroni, and he would make comparisons between her and Eleanor Bold, not always in favor of the latter. The Signora had listened to him, and flattered him, and believed in him—at least she had told him so. Mrs. Bold had also listened to him, but had never flattered him, had not always believed in him, and now had broken from him in violent rage. The Signora, too, was the more lovely woman of the two, and had also the additional attraction of her affection, for to him it was an attraction.

But he never could have loved the Signora Neroni as he felt that he now loved Eleanor, and so he flung stones into the brook instead of flinging in himself, and sat down on its margin as sad a gentleman as you shall meet in a summer's day.

He heard the dinner bell ring from the churchyard, and he knew that it was time to recover his self-possession. He felt that he was disgracing himself in his own eyes, that he had been idling his time and neglecting the high duties which he had taken upon himself to perform. He should have spent this afternoon among the poor at St. Ewold's instead of wandering about at Plumstead an ancient lovelorn swain, dejected and sighing, full of imaginary sorrows and Wertherian grief. He was thoroughly ashamed of himself and determined to lose no time in retrieving his character, so damaged in his own eyes.

Thus when he appeared at dinner he was as animated as ever, and was the author of most of the conversation which graced the Archdeacon's board on that evening. Mr. Harding was ill at ease and sick at heart, and did not care to appear more comfortable than he really was. What little he did say was said to his daughter. He thought that the Archdeacon and Mr. Arabin had leagued together against Eleanor's comfort, and his wish now was to break away from the pair, and undergo in his Barchester lodgings whatever Fate had in store for him. He hated the name of the hospital, his attempt to regain his lost inheritance there had brought upon him so much suffering. As far as he was concerned Mr. Quiverful was now welcome to the place.

And the Archdeacon was not very lively. The poor Dean's illness was of course discussed in the first place. Dr. Grantly did not mention Mr. Slope's name in connection with the expected event of Dr. Trefoil's death. He did not wish to say anything about Mr. Slope just at present, nor did he wish to make known his sad surmises. But the idea that his enemy might possibly become Dean of Barchester made him very gloomy. Should such an event take place, such a dire catastrophe come about, there would be an end to his life as far as his life was connected with the city of Barchester. He must give up all his old haunts, all his old habits, and live quietly as a retired rector at Plumstead. It had been a severe trial for him to have Dr.

Proudie in the palace, but with Mr. Slope also in the deanery he felt that he should be unable to draw his breath in Barchester close.

Thus it came to pass that in spite of the sorrow at his heart, Mr. Arabin was apparently the gayest of the party. Both Mr. Harding and Mrs. Grantly were in a slight degree angry with him on account of his want of gloom. To the one it appeared as though he were triumphing at Eleanor's banishment, and to the other that he was not affected as he should have been by all the sad circumstances of the day: Eleanor's obstinacy, Mr. Slope's success, and the poor Dean's apoplexy. And so they were all at cross-purposes.

Mr. Harding left the room almost together with the ladies, and then the Archdeacon opened his heart to Mr. Arabin. He still harped upon the hospital. "What did that fellow mean," said he, "by saying in his letter to Mrs. Bold that if Mr. Harding would call on the Bishop it would be all right? Of course I would not be guided by anything he might say, but still it may be well that Mr. Harding should see the Bishop. It would be foolish to let the thing slip through our fingers because Mrs. Bold is determined to make a fool of herself."

Mr. Arabin hinted that he was not quite so sure that Mrs. Bold would make a fool of herself. He said that he was not convinced that she did regard Mr. Slope so warmly as she was supposed to do. The Archdeacon questioned and cross-questioned him about this, but elicited nothing, and at last remained firm in his own conviction that he was destined, *malgré lui,* to be the brother-in-law of Mr. Slope. Mr. Arabin strongly advised that Mr. Harding should take no step regarding the hospital in connection with, or in consequence of, Mr. Slope's letter. "If the Bishop really means to confer the appointment on Mr. Harding," argued Mr. Arabin, "he will take care to let him have some other intimation than a message conveyed through a letter to a lady. Were Mr. Harding to present himself at the palace he might merely be playing Mr. Slope's game." And thus it was settled that nothing should be done till the great Dr. Gwynne's arrival, or at any rate without that potentate's sanction.

It was droll to observe how these men talked of Mr. Harding as though he were a puppet, and planned their intrigues and small ecclesiastical maneuvers in reference to Mr. Harding's future position without dreaming of taking him into their confidence. There was a comfortable house and income in question, and it was very desirable and certainly very just that Mr. Harding should have them. But that at present was not the main point—it was expedient to beat the Bishop, and if possible to smash Mr. Slope. Mr. Slope had set up, or was supposed to have set up, a rival candidate. Of all things the most desirable would have been to have had Mr. Quiverful's appointment published to the public and then annulled by the clamor of an indignant world loud in the defense of Mr. Harding's rights. But of such an event the chance was small. A slight fraction only of the world would be indignant, and that fraction would be one not accustomed to loud speaking. And then the preferment had in a sort of way been offered to Mr. Harding, and had in a sort of way been refused by him.

Mr. Slope's wicked, cunning hand had been peculiarly conspicuous in the way in which this had been brought to pass, and it was the success of Mr. Slope's cunning which was so painfully grating to the feelings of the Archdeacon. That which of all things he most dreaded was that he should be outgeneraled by Mr. Slope, and just at present it appeared probable that Mr. Slope would turn his flank, steal a march on him, cut off his provisions, carry his strong town by a coup de main, and at last beat him thoroughly in a regular pitched battle. The Archdeacon felt that his flank had been turned when desired to wait on Mr. Slope instead of the Bishop, that a march had been stolen when Mr. Harding was induced to refuse the Bishop's offer, that his provisions would be cut off when Mr. Quiverful got the hospital, that Eleanor was the strong town doomed to be taken, and that Mr. Slope, as Dean of Barchester, would be regarded by all the world as the conqueror in the final conflict.

Dr. Gwynne was the deus ex machinâ who was to come down upon the Barchester stage and bring about deliverance from these terrible evils. Two or three days after Eleanor's departure, Mr. Arabin went to Oxford, and soon found himself closeted with the august head of his college. It was quite clear that Dr. Gwynne was not very sanguine as to the effects of his journey to Barchester, and not overanxious to interfere with the Bishop. He had had the gout, but was very nearly convalescent, and Mr. Arabin at once saw that had the mission been one of which the Master thoroughly approved, he would before this have been at Plumstead.

As it was, Dr. Gwynne was resolved on visiting his friend, and willingly promised to return to Barchester with Mr. Arabin. He could not bring himself to believe that there was any probability that Mr. Slope would be made Dean of Barchester. Rumor, he said, had reached even his ears not at all favorable to that gentleman's character, and he expressed himself strongly of opinion that any such appointment was quite out of the question.

CHAPTER XXXIV

MISS THORNE'S FÊTE CHAMPÊTRE

The day of the Ullathorne party arrived and all the world were there, or at least so much of the world as had been included in Miss Thorne's invitation. As we have said, the Bishop returned home on the previous evening, and on the same evening, and by the same train, came Dr. Gwynne and Mr. Arabin from Oxford. The Archdeacon with his brougham was in waiting for the Master of Lazarus, so that there was a goodly show of church dignitaries on the platform of the railway.

The Stanhope party was finally arranged in the odious manner already described, and Eleanor got into the Doctor's carriage full of apprehension and presentiment of further misfortune.

The order of the day was to be as follows. The quality, as the upper classes in rural districts are designated by the lower with so much true discrimination, were to eat a breakfast, and the nonquality were to eat a dinner. Two marquees had been erected for these two banquets, that for the quality on the esoteric or garden side of a certain deep haha, and that for the nonquality on the exoteric or paddock side of the same. Both were of huge dimensions. That on the outer side was, one may say, on an egregious scale.

No one who has not had a hand in the preparation of such an affair can understand the manifold difficulties which Miss Thorne encountered in her project. Had she not been made throughout of the very finest whalebone, riveted with the best Yorkshire steel, she must have sunk under them.

In the first place, there was a dreadful line to be drawn. Who were to dispose themselves within the haha, and who without? To this the unthinking will give an offhand answer, as they will to every ponderous question. Oh, the Bishop and suchlike within the haha, and Farmer Greenacre and suchlike without. True, my unthinking friend, but who shall define these suchlikes? It is in such definitions that the whole difficulty of society consists. To seat the Bishop on an armchair on the lawn and place Farmer Greenacre at the end of a long table in the paddock is easy enough. But where will you put Mrs. Lookaloft, whose husband, though a tenant on the estate, hunts in a red coat, whose daughters go to a fashionable seminary in Barchester, who calls her farmhouse Rosebank, and who has a pianoforte in her drawing-room?

And now the morning arrived. The Ullathorne household was early on the move. Cooks were cooking in the kitchen long before daylight, and men were dragging out tables and hammering red baize onto benches at the earliest dawn. With what dread eagerness did Miss Thorne look out at the weather as soon as the parting veil of night permitted her to look at all! In this respect at any rate there was nothing to grieve her. The glass had been rising for the last three days, and the morning broke with that dull, chill, steady gray haze which in autumn generally presages a clear and dry day. By seven she was dressed and down. Miss Thorne knew nothing of the modern luxury of déshabilles. She would as soon have thought of appearing before her brother without her stockings as without her stays, and Miss Thorne's stays were no trifle.

Miss Thorne had fondly thought that when she called on her friends to come at twelve, and specially begged them to believe that she meant it, she would be able to see them comfortably seated in their tents at two. Vain woman—or rather ignorant woman—ignorant of the advances of that civilization which the world had witnessed while she was growing old. At twelve she found herself alone, dressed in all the glory of the newest of her many suits of raiment, with strong shoes, however, and a serviceable bonnet on her head and a warm rich shawl on her shoulders. Thus clad she peered out into the tent, went to the haha, and satisfied herself that at any rate the youngsters were amusing themselves, spoke a word to Mrs. Greenacre over the ditch, and took one look at the quintain. Three or four young farmers were turning the machine round and round, and poking at the bag of flour in a manner not at all intended by the inventor of the game, but no mounted sportsmen were there. Miss Thorne looked at her watch. It was only fifteen minutes past twelve.

Miss Thorne returned to her drawing-room rather quicker than was her wont, fearing that the Countess might come and find none to welcome her. She need not have hurried, for no one was there. At half-past twelve she peeped into the kitchen. At a quarter to one she was joined by her brother, and just then the first fashionable arrival took place. Mrs. Clantantram was announced.

No announcement was necessary, indeed, for the good lady's voice was heard as she walked across the courtyard to the house scolding the unfortunate postilion who had driven her from Barchester. At the moment, Miss Thorne could not but be thankful that the other guests were more fashionable and were thus spared the fury of Mrs. Clantantram's indignation.

"Oh Miss Thorne, look here!" said she as soon as she found herself in the drawing-room. "Do look at my roquelaure! It's clean spoilt, and forever. I wouldn't but wear it because I knew you wished us all to be grand today, and yet I had my misgivings. Oh, dear, oh, dear! It was five and twenty shillings a yard."

The Barchester post horses had misbehaved in some unfortunate manner just as Mrs. Clantantram was getting out of the chaise, and had nearly thrown her under the wheel. Mrs. Clantantram belonged to other days, and therefore, though she had but little else to recommend her, Miss Thorne was to a certain extent fond of her. She sent the roquelaure away to be cleaned, and lent her one of her best shawls out of her own wardrobe.

The next comer was Mr. Arabin, who was immediately informed of Mrs. Clantantram's misfortune, and of her determination to pay neither master nor postboy, although, as she remarked, she intended to get her lift home before she made known her mind upon that matter. Then a good deal of rustling was heard in the sort of lobby that was used for the ladies' outside cloaks, and the door having been thrown wide open, the servant announced, not in the most confident of voices, Mrs. Lookaloft and the Miss Lookalofts and Mr. Augustus Lookaloft.

Poor man!—We mean the footman. He knew, none better, that Mrs. Lookaloft had no business there, that she was not wanted there, and would not be welcome. But he had not the courage to tell a stout lady with a low dress, short sleeves, and satin at eight shillings a yard that she had come to the wrong tent. He had not dared to hint to young ladies with white dancing shoes and long gloves that there was a place ready for them in the paddock. And thus Mrs. Lookaloft carried her point, broke through the guards, and made her way into the citadel. That she would have to pass an uncomfortable time there she had surmised before. But nothing now could rob her of the power of boasting that she had consorted on the lawn with the Squire and Miss Thorne, with a Countess, a Bishop, and the county grandees while Mrs. Greenacre and suchlike were walking about with the plowboys in the park. It was a great point gained by Mrs. Lookaloft, and it might be fairly expected that from this time forward the tradesmen of Barchester would, with undoubting pens, address her husband as T. Lookaloft, Esq.

Mrs. Lookaloft's pluck carried her through everything, and she walked triumphant into the Ullathorne drawing-room, but her children did feel a little abashed at the sort of reception they met with. It was not in Miss Thorne's heart to insult her own guests, but neither was it in her disposition to overlook such effrontery.

"Oh, Mrs. Lookaloft, is this you," said she, "and your daughters and son? Well, we're very glad to see you, but I'm sorry you've come in such low dresses, as we are all going out of doors. Could we lend you anything?"

"Oh, dear no! Thank ye, Miss Thorne," said the mother. "The girls and myself are quite used to low dresses when we're out."

"Are you indeed?" said Miss Thorne, shuddering, but the shudder was lost on Mrs. Lookaloft.

"And where's Lookaloft?" said the master of the house, coming up to welcome his tenant's wife. Let the faults of the family be what they would, he could not but remember that their rent was well paid. He was therefore not willing to give them a cold shoulder.

"Such a headache, Mr. Thorne!" said Mrs. Lookaloft. "In fact, he couldn't stir, or you may be certain on such a day he would not have absented hisself."

"Dear me," said Miss Thorne. "If he is so ill, I'm sure you'd wish to be with him."

"Not at all!" said Mrs. Lookaloft. "Not at all, Miss Thorne. It is only bilious, you know, and when he's that way he can bear nobody nigh him."

The fact however was that Mr. Lookaloft, having either more sense or less courage than his wife, had not chosen to intrude on Miss Thorne's drawing-room. And as he could not very well have gone among the plebeians while his wife was with the patricians, he thought it most expedient to remain at Rosebank.

Mrs. Lookaloft soon found herself on a sofa, and the Miss Lookalofts on two chairs, while Mr. Augustus stood near the door, and here they remained till in due time they were seated all four together at the bottom of the dining-room table.

Then the Grantlys came, the Archdeacon and Mrs. Grantly and the two girls, and Dr. Gwynne and Mr. Harding. And as ill-luck would have it, they were closely followed by Dr. Stanhope's carriage. As Eleanor looked out of the carriage window she saw her brother-in-law helping the ladies out, and threw herself back into her seat, dreading to be discovered. She had had an odious journey. Mr. Slope's civility had been more than ordinarily greasy, and now, though he had not in fact said anything which she could notice, she had for the first time entertained a suspicion that he was intending to make love to her. Was it after all true that she had been conducting herself in a way that justified the world in thinking that she liked the man? After all, could it be possible that the Archdeacon and Mr. Arabin were right and that she was wrong? Charlotte Stanhope had also been watching Mr. Slope, and had come to the conclusion that it behooved her brother to lose no further time if he meant to gain the widow. She almost regretted that it had not been contrived that Bertie should be at Ullathorne before them.

Dr. Grantly did not see his sister-in-law in company with Mr. Slope, but Mr. Arabin did. Mr. Arabin came out with Mr. Thorne to the front door to welcome Mrs. Grantly, and he remained in the courtyard till all their party had passed on. Eleanor hung back in the carriage as long as she well could, but she was nearest to the door, and when Mr. Slope, having alighted, offered her his hand, she had no alternative but to take it. Mr. Arabin, standing at the open door while Mrs. Grantly was shaking hands with someone within, saw a clergyman alight from the carriage whom he at once knew to be Mr. Slope, and then he saw this clergyman hand out Mrs. Bold. Having seen so much, Mr. Arabin, rather sick at heart, followed Mrs. Grantly into the house.

Eleanor was, however, spared any further immediate degradation, for Dr. Stanhope gave her his arm across the courtyard, and Mr. Slope was fain to throw away his attention upon Charlotte.

They had hardly passed into the house, and from the house to the lawn, when, with a loud rattle and such noise as great men and great women are entitled to make in their passage through the world, the Proudies drove up. It was soon apparent that no everyday comer was at the door. One servant whispered to another that it was the Bishop, and the word soon ran through all the hangers-on and strange grooms and coachmen about the place. There was quite a little cortège to see the Bishop and his "lady" walk across the courtyard, and the good man was pleased to see that the Church was held in such respect in the parish of St. Ewold's.

And now the guests came fast and thick, and the lawn began to be crowded and the room to be full. Voices buzzed, silk rustled against silk, and muslin crumpled against muslin. Miss Thorne became more happy than she had been.

Eleanor left Dr. Stanhope as soon as she could do so civilly, and went in quest of her father, whom she found on the lawn in company with Mr. Arabin. She was not sorry to find them together. She was anxious to disabuse at any rate her father's mind as to this report which had got abroad respecting her, and would have been well pleased to have been able to do the same with regard to Mr. Arabin. She put her own through her father's arm, coming up behind his back, and then tendered her hand also to the Vicar of St. Ewold's.

"And how did you come?" said Mr. Harding when the first greeting was over.

"The Stanhopes brought me," said she. "Their carriage was obliged to come twice, and has now gone back for the Signora." As she spoke she caught Mr. Arabin's eye, and saw that he was looking pointedly at her with a severe expression. She understood at once the accusation contained in his glance. It said as plainly as an eye could speak: "Yes, you came with the Stanhopes, but you did so in order that you might be in company with Mr. Slope."

"Our party," said she, still addressing her father, "consisted of the Doctor and Charlotte Stanhope, myself, and Mr. Slope." As she mentioned the last name she felt her father's arm quiver slightly beneath her touch. At the same moment Mr. Arabin turned away from them, and joining his hands behind his back, strolled slowly away by one of the paths.

"Papa," said she, "it was impossible to help coming in the same carriage with Mr. Slope, it was quite impossible. I had promised to come with them before I dreamt of his coming, and afterward I could not get out of it without explaining and giving risk to talk. You weren't at home, you know. I couldn't possibly help it." She said all this so quickly that by the time her apology was spoken she was quite out of breath.

"I don't know why you should have wished to help it, my dear," said her father.

"Yes, Papa, you do. You must know, you do know, all the things they said at Plumstead. I am sure you do. You know all the Archdeacon said. How unjust he was, and Mr. Arabin too. He's a horrid man, a horrid odious man, but——"

"Who is an odious man, my dear? Mr. Arabin?"

"No, but Mr. Slope. You know I mean Mr. Slope. He's the most odious man I ever met in my life, and it was most unfortunate my having to come here in the same carriage with him. But how could I help it?"

A great weight began to move itself off Mr. Harding's mind. So after all the Archdeacon with all his wisdom, and Mrs. Grantly with all her tact, and Mr. Arabin with all his talent were in the wrong. His own child, his Eleanor, the daughter of whom he was so proud, was not to become the wife of a Mr. Slope. He had been about to give his sanction to the marriage, so certified had he been of the fact, and now he learnt that this imputed lover of Eleanor's was at any rate as much disliked by her as by anyone of the family. Mr. Harding, however, was by no means sufficiently a man of the world to conceal the blunder he had made. He could not pretend that he had entertained no suspicion, he could not make-believe that he had never joined the Archdeacon in his surmises. He was greatly surprised, and gratified beyond measure, and he could not help showing that such was the case.

"My darling girl," said he, "I am so delighted, so overjoyed. My own child, you have taken such a weight off my mind."

"But surely, Papa, *you* didn't think——"

"I didn't know what to think, my dear. The Archdeacon told me that——"

"The Archdeacon!" said Eleanor, her face lighting up with passion. "A man like the Archdeacon might, one would think, be better employed than in traducing his sister-in-law and creating bitterness between a father and his daughter!"

"He didn't mean to do that, Eleanor."

"What did he mean, then? Why did he interfere with me, and fill your mind with such falsehood?"

"Never mind it now, my child, never mind it now. We shall all know you better now."

"Oh, Papa, that you should have thought it! That you should have suspected me!"

"I don't know what you mean by suspicion, Eleanor. There would be nothing disgraceful, you know, nothing wrong, in such a marriage. Nothing that could have justified my interfering as your father." And Mr. Harding would have proceeded in his own defense to make out that Mr. Slope after all was a very good sort of man, and a very fitting second husband for a young widow, had he not been interrupted by Eleanor's greater energy.

"It would be disgraceful," said she. "It would be wrong, it would be abominable. Could I do such a horrid thing, I should expect no one to speak to me. Ugh——" And she shuddered as she thought of the matrimonial torch which her friends had been so ready to light on her behalf. "I don't wonder at Dr. Grantly, I don't wonder at Susan, but, oh, Papa, I do wonder at you. How could you, how could you believe it?" Poor Eleanor, as she thought of her father's defalcation, could resist her tears no longer, and was forced to cover her face with her handkerchief.

The place was not very opportune for her grief. They were walking through the shrubberies and there were many people near them. Poor Mr. Harding stammered out his excuse as best he could, and Eleanor with an effort controlled her tears and returned her handkerchief to her pocket. She did not find it difficult to forgive her father, nor could she altogether refuse to join him in the returning gaiety of spirit to which her present avowal gave rise. It was such a load off his heart to think that he should not be called on to welcome Mr. Slope as his son-in-law. It was such a relief to him to find that his daughter's feelings and his own were now, as they ever had been, in unison. He had been so unhappy for the last six weeks about this wretched Mr. Slope! He was so indifferent as to the loss of the hospital, so thankful for the recovery of his daughter, that, strong as was the ground for Eleanor's anger, she could not find it in her heart to be long angry with him.

"Dear Papa," she said, hanging closely to his arm, "never suspect me again. Promise me that you never will. Whatever I do, you may be sure I shall tell you first, you may be sure I shall consult you."

And Mr. Harding did promise, and owned his sin, and promised again. And so while he promised amendment and she uttered forgiveness they returned together to the drawing-room windows.

And what had Eleanor meant when she declared that *whatever she did*, she would tell her father first? What was she thinking of doing?

CHAPTER XXXV

THE SIGNORA NERONI, THE COUNTESS DE COURCY, AND MRS. PROUDIE MEET EACH OTHER AT ULLATHORNE

AND now there were new arrivals. Just as Eleanor reached the drawing-room the Signora was being wheeled into it. She had been brought out of the carriage into the dining-room and there placed on a sofa, and was now in the act of entering the other room, by the joint aid of her brother and sister, Mr. Arabin, and two servants in livery. She was all in her glory, and looked so pathetically happy, so full of affliction and grace, was so beautiful, so pitiable, and so charming, that it was almost impossible not to be glad she was there.

Miss Thorne was unaffectedly glad to welcome her. In fact, the Signora was a sort of lion, and though there was no drop of the Leohunter blood in Miss Thorne's veins, she nevertheless did like to see attractive people at her house. The Signora was attractive, and on her first settlement in the dining-room she had whispered two or three soft feminine words into Miss Thorne's ear which, at the moment, had quite touched that lady's heart.

"Oh, Miss Thorne, where is Miss Thorne?" she said as soon as her attendants had placed her in her position just before one of the windows from whence she could see all that was going on upon the lawn. "How am I to thank you for permitting a creature like me to be here? But if you knew the pleasure you give me, I am sure you would excuse the trouble I bring with me." And as she spoke she squeezed the spinster's little hand between her own.

"We are delighted to see you here," said Miss Thorne. "You give us no trouble at all, and we think it a great favor conferred by you to come and see us, don't we, Wilfred?"

"A very great favor indeed," said Mr. Thorne, with a gallant bow but of a somewhat less cordial welcome than that conceded by his sister. Mr. Thorne had heard perhaps more of the antecedents of his guest than his sister had done, and had not as yet undergone the power of the Signora's charms.

But while the mother of the last of the Neros was thus in her full splendor, with crowds of people gazing at her and the élite of the company standing round her couch, her glory was paled by the arrival of the Countess De Courcy. Miss Thorne had now been waitiing three hours for the Countess, and could not therefore but show very evident gratification when the arrival at last took place. She and her brother of course went off to welcome the titled grandees, and with them, alas! went many of the Signora's admirers.

"Oh, Mr. Thorne," said the Countess while in the act of being disrobed of her fur cloaks and rerobed in her gauze shawls, "what dreadful roads you have, perfectly frightful."

It happened that Mr. Thorne was waywarden for the district and, not liking the attack, began to excuse his roads.

"Oh, yes, indeed they are," said the Countess, not minding him in the least, "perfectly dreadful, are they not, Margaretta? Why, my dear Miss Thorne, we left Courcy Castle just at eleven—it was only just past eleven, was it not, John? and——"

"Just past one, I think you mean," said the Honorable John, turning from the group and eyeing the Signora through his glass. The Signora gave him back his own, as the saying is, and more with it, so that the young nobleman was forced to avert his glance and drop his glass.

"I say, Thorne," whispered he, "who the deuce is that on the sofa?"

"Dr. Stanhope's daughter," whispered back Mr. Thorne. "Signora Neroni, she calls herself."

"Whew-ew-ew!" whistled the Honorable John. "The devil she is. I have heard no end of stories about that filly. You must positively introduce me, Thorne, you positively must."

Mr. Thorne, who was respectability itself, did not quite like having a guest about whom the Honorable John De Courcy had heard no end of stories, but he couldn't help himself. He merely resolved that before he went to bed he would let his sister know somewhat of the history of the lady she was so willing to welcome. The innocence of Miss Thorne, at her time of life, was perfectly charming, but even innocence may be dangerous.

"John may say what he likes," continued the Countess, urging her excuses to Miss Thorne, "I am sure we were past the castle gate before twelve, weren't we, Margaretta?"

"Upon my word I don't know," said the Lady Margaretta, "for I was half-asleep. But I do know that I was called sometime in the middle of the night, and was dressing myself before daylight."

Poor Miss Thorne was altogether overcome. She knew very well that she had been ill-treated, and yet she found herself making apologies to Lady De Courcy. To do her ladyship justice, she received them very graciously, and allowed herself with her train of daughters to be led toward the lawn.

There were two windows in the drawing-room wide-open for the Countess to pass through, but she saw that there was a woman on a sofa at the third window, and that that woman had, as it were, a following attached to her. Her ladyship therefore determined to investigate the woman. The De Courcys were hereditarily shortsighted, and had been so for thirty centuries at least. So Lady De Courcy, who when she entered the family had adopted the family habits, did as her son had done before her, and taking her glass to investigate the Signora Neroni pressed in among the gentlemen who surrounded the couch, and bowed slightly to those whom she chose to honor by her acquaintance.

In order to get to the window she had to pass close to the front of the couch, and as she did so she stared hard at the occupant. The occupant in return stared hard at the Countess. The Countess, who since her countess-ship commenced had been accustomed to see all eyes not royal, ducal, or marquesal fall before her own, paused as she went on, raised her eyebrows, and stared even harder than before. But she had now to do with one who cared little for Countesses. It was, one may say, impossible for mortal man or woman to abash Madeline Neroni. She opened her large bright lustrous eyes wider and wider, till she seemed to be all eyes. She gazed up into the lady's face, not as though she did it with an effort, but as if she delighted in doing it. She used no glass to assist her effrontery, and needed none. The faintest possible smile of derision played round her mouth, and her nostrils were slightly dilated, as if in sure anticipation of her triumph. And it was sure. The Countess De Courcy, in spite of her thirty centuries and De Courcy castle, and the fact that Lord De Courcy was grand master of the ponies to the Prince of Wales, had not a chance with her. At first the little circlet of gold wavered in the Countess's hand, then the hand shook, then the circlet fell, the Countess's head tossed itself into the air, and the Count-ess's feet shambled out to the lawn. She did not however go so fast but what she heard the Signora's voice asking:

"Who on earth is that woman, Mr. Slope?"

"That is Lady De Courcy."

"Oh, ah. I might have supposed so. Ha, ha, ha! Well, that's as good as a play."

It was as good as a play to any there who had eyes to observe it, and wit to comment on what they observed.

But the Lady De Courcy soon found a congenial spirit on the lawn. There she encountered Mrs. Proudie, and as Mrs. Proudie was not only the wife of a bishop but was also the cousin of an earl, Lady De Courcy considered her to be the fittest companion she was likely to meet in that assemblage. They were accordingly delighted to see each other. Mrs. Proudie by no means despised a countess, and as this Countess lived in the county and within a sort of extensive visiting distance of Barchester, she was glad to have this opportunity of ingratiating herself.

"My dear Lady De Courcy, I am so delighted," said she, looking as little grim as it was in her nature to do. "I hardly expected to see you here. It is such a distance, and then you know, such a crowd."

"And such roads, Mrs. Proudie! I really wonder how the people ever get about. But I don't suppose they ever do."

"Well, I really don't know, but I suppose not. The Thornes don't, I know," said Mrs. Proudie. "Very nice person, Miss Thorne, isn't she?"

"Oh, delightful, and so queer. I've known her these twenty years. A great pet of mine is dear Miss Thorne. She is so very strange, you know. She always makes me think of the Eskimos and the Indians. Isn't her dress quite delightful?"

"Delightful," said Mrs. Proudie. "I wonder now whether she paints. Did you ever see such color?"

"Oh, of course," said Lady De Courcy. "That is, I have no doubt she does. But, Mrs. Proudie, who is that woman on the sofa by the window? Just step this way and you'll see her, there——" And the Countess led her to a spot where she could plainly see the Signora's well-remembered face and figure.

She did not however do so without being equally well seen by the Signora. "Look, look," said that lady to Mr. Slope, who was still standing near to her. "See the high spiritualities and temporalities of the land in league together, and all against poor me. I'll wager my bracelet, Mr. Slope, against your next sermon that they've taken up their position there on purpose to pull me to pieces. Well, I can't rush to the combat, but I know how to protect myself if the enemy come near me."

But the enemy knew better. They could gain nothing by contact with the Signora Neroni, and they could abuse her as they pleased at a distance from her on the lawn.

"She's that horrid Italian woman, Lady De Courcy. You must have heard of her."

"What Italian woman?" said her ladyship, quite alive to the coming story. "I don't think I've heard of any Italian woman coming into the country. She doesn't look Italian, either."

"Oh, you must have heard of her," said Mrs. Proudie. "No, she's not absolutely Italian. She's Dr. Stanhope's daughter—Dr. Stanhope the prebendary—and she calls herself the Signora Neroni."

"Oh-h-h-h!" exclaimed the Countess.

"I was sure you had heard of her," continued Mrs. Proudie. "I don't know anything about her husband. They do say that some man named Neroni is still alive. I believe she did marry such a man abroad, but I do not at all know who or what he was."

"Ah-h-h-h!" said the Countess, shaking her head with much intelligence as every additional "h" fell from her lips. "I know all about it now. I have heard George mention her. George knows all about her. George heard about her in Rome."

"She's an abominable woman, at any rate," said Mrs. Proudie.

"Insufferable," said the Countess.

"She made her way into the palace once, before I knew anything about her, and I cannot tell you how dreadfully indecent her conduct was."

"Was it?" said the delighted Countess.

"Insufferable," said the prelatess.

"But why does she lie on a sofa?" asked Lady De Courcy.

"She has only one leg," replied Mrs. Proudie.

"Only one leg!" said Lady De Courcy, who felt to a certain degree dissatisfied that the Signora was thus incapacitated. "Was she born so?"

"Oh, no," said Mrs. Proudie, and her ladyship felt somewhat recomforted by the assurance, "she had two. But that Signor Neroni beat her, I believe, till she was obliged to have one amputated. At any rate, she entirely lost the use of it."

"Unfortunate creature!" said the Countess, who herself knew something of matrimonial trials.

"Yes," said Mrs. Proudie, "one would pity her in spite of her past bad conduct if she now knew how to behave herself. But she does not. She is the most insolent creature I ever put my eyes on."

"Indeed she is," said Lady De Courcy.

"And her conduct with men is so abominable that she is not fit to be admitted into any lady's drawing-room."

"Dear me!" said the Countess, becoming again excited, happy, and merciless.

"You saw that man standing near her—the clergyman with the red hair?"

"Yes, yes."

"She has absolutely ruined that man. The Bishop, or I should rather take the blame on myself, for it was I—I brought him down from London to Barchester. He is a tolerable preacher, an active young man, and I therefore introduced him to the Bishop. That woman, Lady De Courcy, has got hold of him, and has so disgraced him that I am forced to require that he shall leave the palace, and I doubt very much whether he won't lose his gown!"

"Why, what an idiot the man must be!" said the Countess.

"You don't know the intriguing villainy of that woman," said Mrs. Proudie, remembering her torn flounces.

"But you say she has only got one leg!"

"She is as full of mischief as though she had ten. Look at her eyes, Lady De Courcy. Did you ever see such eyes in a decent woman's head?"

"Indeed I never did, Mrs. Proudie."

"And her effrontery, and her voice. I quite pity her poor father, who is really a good sort of man."

"Dr. Stanhope, isn't he?"

"Yes, Dr. Stanhope. He is one of our prebendaries—a good, quiet sort of man himself. But I am surprised that he should let his daughter conduct herself as she does."

"I suppose he can't help it," said the Countess.

"But a clergyman, you know, Lady De Courcy! He should at any rate prevent her from exhibiting in public, if he cannot induce her to behave at home. But he is to be pitied. I believe he has a desperate life of it with the lot of them. That apish-looking man there, with the long beard and the loose trousers,—he is the woman's brother. He is nearly as bad as she is. They are both of them infidels."

"Infidels!" said Lady De Courcy. "And their father a prebendary!"

"Yes, and likely to be the new dean too," said Mrs. Proudie.

"Oh, yes, poor dear Dr. Trefoil!" said the Countess, who had once in her life spoken to that gentleman. "I was so distressed to hear it, Mrs. Proudie. And so Dr. Stanhope is to be the new dean! He comes of an excellent family, and I wish him success in spite of his daughter. Perhaps, Mrs. Proudie, when he is dean they'll be better able to see the error of their ways."

To this Mrs. Proudie said nothing. Her dislike of the Signora Neroni was too deep to admit of her even hoping that that lady should see the error of her ways. Mrs. Proudie looked on the Signora as one of the lost,—one of those beyond the reach of Christian charity—and was therefore able to enjoy the luxury of hating her without the drawback of wishing her eventually well out of her sins.

Any further conversation between these congenial souls was prevented by the advent of Mr. Thorne, who came to lead the Countess to the tent. Indeed, he had been desired to do so some ten minutes since, but he had been delayed in the drawing-room by the Signora. She had contrived to detain him, to get him near to her sofa, and at last to make him seat himself on a chair close to her beautiful arm. The fish took the bait, was hooked, and caught, and landed.

And now the eating and drinking began in earnest. Dr. Grantly, to his great horror, found himself leagued to Mrs. Clantantram. Dr. Gwynne got a baronet's wife, and Mrs. Grantly fell to the lot of a baronet. Charlotte Stanhope attached herself to Mr. Harding in order to make room for Bertie, who succeeded in sitting down in the dining-room next to Mrs. Bold. To speak sooth, now that he had love in earnest to make, his heart almost failed him.

Eleanor had been right glad to avail herself of his arm, seeing that Mr. Slope was hovering nigh her. In striving to avoid that terrible Charybdis of a Slope she was in great danger of falling into an unseen Scylla on the other hand, that Scylla being Bertie Stanhope. Nothing could be more gracious than she was to Bertie. She almost jumped at his proffered arm. Charlotte perceived this from a distance, and triumphed in her heart. Bertie felt it, and was encouraged. Mr. Slope saw it, and glowered with jealousy. Eleanor and Bertie sat down to table in the dining-room, and as she took her seat at his right hand, she found that Mr. Slope was already in possession of the chair at her own.

As these things were going on in the dining-room, Mr. Arabin was hanging enraptured and alone over the Signora's sofa, and Eleanor from her seat could look through the open door and see that he was doing so.

CHAPTER XXXVI

THE BISHOP BREAKFASTS, AND THE DEAN DIES

THE Bishop of Barchester said grace over the well-spread board in the Ullathorne dining-room, and while he did so the last breath was flying from the Dean of Barchester as he lay in his sickroom in the deanery. When the Bishop of Barchester raised his first glass of champagne to his lips, the deanship of Barchester was a good thing in the gift of the Prime Minister. Before the Bishop of Barchester had left the table, the Minister of the day was made aware of the fact at his country seat in Hampshire, and had already turned over in his mind the names of five very respectable aspirants for the preferment. It is at present only necessary to say that Mr. Slope's name was not among the five.

" 'Twas merry in the hall when the beards wagged all," and the clerical beards wagged merrily in the hall of Ullathorne that day. It was not till after the last cork had been drawn, the last speech made, the last nut cracked, that tidings reached and were whispered about that the poor Dean was no more. It was well for the happiness of the clerical beards that this little delay took place, as otherwise decency would have forbidden them to wag at all.

But there was one sad man among them that day. Mr. Arabin's beard did not wag as it should have done. He had come there hoping the best, striving to think the best, about Eleanor, turning over in his mind all the words he remembered to have fallen from her about Mr. Slope and trying to gather from them a conviction unfavorable to his rival. He had not exactly resolved to come that day to some decisive proof as to the widow's intention, but he had meant, if possible, to recultivate his friendship with Eleanor. And in his present frame of mind any such recultivation must have ended in a declaration of love.

He had passed the previous night alone at his new parsonage, and it was the first night that he had so passed. It had been dull and somber enough. Mrs. Grantly had been right in saying that a priestess would be wanting at St. Ewold's. He had sat there alone with his glass before him, and then with his teapot, thinking about Eleanor Bold. As is usual in such meditations, he did little but blame her—blame her for liking Mr. Slope and blame her for not liking him, blame her for her cordiality to himself and blame her for her want of cordiality, blame her for being stubborn, headstrong, and passionate. And yet the more he thought of her, the higher she rose in his affection. If only it should turn out, if only it could be made to turn out, that she had defended Mr. Slope not from love, but on principle, all would be right. Such principle in itself would be admirable, lovable, womanly. He felt that he could be pleased to allow Mr. Slope just so much favor as that. But if—— And then Mr. Arabin poked his fire most unnecessarily, spoke crossly to his new parlormaid who came in for the tea things, and threw himself back in his chair determined to go to sleep. Why had she been so stiff-necked when asked a plain question? She could not but have known in what light he regarded her. Why had she not answered a plain question, and so put an end to his misery? Then, instead of going to sleep in his arm-chair, Mr. Arabin walked about the room as though he had been possessed.

On the following morning, when he attended Miss Thorne's behests, he was still in a state of confused uncertainty, hope, and doubt when he saw Mr. Slope, with his most polished smile, handing Eleanor out of her carriage. He thought of nothing more. He never considered whether the carriage belonged to her or to Mr. Slope, or to anyone else to whom they might both be mutually obliged without any concert between themselves. This sight in his present state of mind was quite enough to upset him and his resolves. It was clear as noonday. Had he seen her handed into a carriage by Mr. Slope at a church door with a white veil over her head, the truth could not be more manifest. He went into the house, and, as we have seen, soon found himself walking with Mr. Harding. Shortly afterward Eleanor came up, and then he had to leave his companion and either go about alone or find another. While in this state he was encountered by the Archdeacon.

"I wonder," said Dr. Grantly, "if it be true that Mr. Slope and Mrs. Bold came here together. Susan says she is almost sure she saw their faces in the same carriage as she got out of her own."

Mr. Arabin had nothing for it but to bear his testimony to the correctness of Mrs. Grantly's eyesight.

"It is perfectly shameful," said the Archdeacon. "Or I should rather say shameless. She was asked here as my guest, and if she be determined to disgrace herself, she should have feeling enough not to do so before my immediate friends. I wonder how that man got himself invited. I wonder whether she had the face to bring him."

To this Mr. Arabin could answer nothing, nor did he wish to answer anything. Though he abused Eleanor to himself, he did not choose to abuse her to anyone else, nor was he well pleased to hear anyone else speak ill of her. Dr. Grantly, however, was very angry, and did not spare his sister-in-law. Mr. Arabin therefore left him as soon as he could, and wandered back into the house.

He had not been there long when the Signora was brought in. For some time he kept himself out of temptation and merely hovered round her at a distance, but as soon as Mr. Thorne had left her he yielded himself up to the basilisk and allowed himself to be made prey of.

It is impossible to say how the knowledge had been acquired, but the Signora had a sort of instinctive knowledge that Mr. Arabin was an admirer of Mrs. Bold. Men hunt foxes by the aid of dogs, and are aware that they do so by the strong organ of smell with which the dog is endowed. They do not, however, in the least comprehend how such a sense can work with such acuteness. The organ by which women instinctively, as it were, know and feel how other women are regarded by men, and how also men are regarded by other women, is equally strong and equally incomprehensible. A glance, a word, a motion, suffices. By some such acute exercise of her feminine senses the Signora was aware that Mr. Arabin loved Eleanor Bold, and therefore, by a further exercise of her peculiar feminine propensities, it was quite natural for her to entrap Mr. Arabin into her net.

The work was half-done before she came to Ullathorne, and when could she have a better opportunity of completing it? She had had almost enough of Mr. Slope, though she could not quite resist the fun of driving a very sanctimonious clergyman to madness by a desperate and ruinous passion.

But Mr. Arabin was game of another sort. The Signora was herself possessed of quite sufficient intelligence to know that Mr. Arabin was a man more than usually intellectual. She knew also that as a clergyman he was of a much higher stamp than Mr. Slope. She would never have attempted to drive Mr. Arabin into ridiculous misery as she did Mr. Slope.

Such were her reflections about Mr. Arabin. As to Mr. Arabin, it cannot be said that he reflected at all about the Signora. He knew that she was beautiful, and he felt that she was able to charm him. He required charming in his present misery, and therefore he went and stood at the head of her couch. She knew all about it. Such were her peculiar gifts. It was her nature to see that he required charming, and it was her province to charm him. As the Eastern idler swallows his dose of opium, as the London reprobate swallows his dose of gin, so with similar desires and for similar reasons did Mr. Arabin prepare to swallow the charms of the Signora Neroni.

"Why ain't you shooting with bows and arrows, Mr. Arabin?" said she when they were nearly alone together in the drawing-room. "Or talking with young ladies in shady bowers, or turning your talents to account in some way? What was a bachelor like you asked here for? Don't you mean to earn your cold chicken and champagne? Were I you, I should be ashamed to be so idle."

Mr. Arabin murmured some sort of answer. Though he wished to be charmed, he was hardly yet in a mood to be playful in return.

"Why, what ails you, Mr. Arabin?" said she. "Here you are in your own parish, Miss Thorne tells me that her party is given expressly in your honor and yet you are the only dull man at it. Your friend Mr. Slope was with me a few minutes since, full of life and spirits. Why don't you rival him?"

It was not difficult for so acute an observer as Madeline Neroni to see that she had hit the nail on the head and driven the bolt home. Mr. Arabin winced visibly before her attack, and she knew at once that he was jealous of Mr. Slope.

"But I look on you and Mr. Slope as the very antipodes of men," said she. "There is nothing in which you are not each the reverse of the other, except in belonging to the same profession, and even in that you are so unlike as perfectly to maintain the rule. He is gregarious, you are given to solitude. He is active, you are passive. He works, you think. He likes women, you despise them. He is fond of position and power, and so are you, but for directly different reasons. He loves to be praised, you very foolishly abhor it. He will gain his rewards, which will be an insipid useful wife, a comfortable income, and a reputation for sanctimony. You will also gain yours."

"Well, and what will they be?" said Mr. Arabin, who knew that he was being flattered and yet suffered himself to put up with it. "What will be my rewards?"

"The heart of some woman whom you will be too austere to own that you love, and the respect of some few friends which you will be too proud to own that you value."

"Rich rewards," said he, "but of little worth if they are to be so treated."

"Oh, you are not to look for such success as awaits Mr. Slope. He is born to be a successful man. He suggests to himself an object and then starts for it with eager intention. Nothing will deter him from his pursuit. He will have no scruples, no fears, no hesitation. His desire is to be a bishop with a rising family. The wife will come first, and in due time the apron. You will see all this, and then——"

"Well, and what then?"

"Then you will begin to wish that you had done the same."

Mr. Arabin looked placidly out at the lawn, and resting his shoulder on the head of the sofa, rubbed his chin with his hand. It was a trick he had when he was thinking deeply, and what the Signora said made him think. Was it not all true? Would he not hereafter look back, if not at Mr. Slope, at some others, perhaps not equally gifted with himself, who had risen in the world while he had lagged behind, and then wish that he had done the same?

"Is not such the doom of all speculative men of talent?" said she. "Do they not all sit rapt as you now are, cutting imaginary silken cords with their fine edges, while those not so highly tempered sever the everyday Gordian knots of the world's struggle and win wealth and renown? Steel too highly polished, edges too sharp, do not do for this world's work, Mr. Arabin."

Who was this woman that thus read the secrets of his heart and re-uttered to him the unwelcome bodings of his own soul? He looked full into her face when she had done speaking and said, "Am I one of those foolish blades, too sharp and too fine to do a useful day's work?"

"Why do you let the Slopes of the world outdistance you?" said she. "Is not the blood in your veins as warm as his? Does not your pulse beat as fast? Has not God made you a man, and intended you to do a man's work here— ay, and to take a man's wages also?"

Mr. Arabin sat ruminating and rubbing his face, and wondering why these things were said to him, but he replied nothing. The Signora went on:

"The greatest mistake any man ever made is to suppose that the good things of the world are not worth the winning. And it is a mistake so opposed to the religion which you preach! Why does God permit His bishops one after another to have their five thousands and ten thousands a year if such wealth be bad and not worth having? Why are beautiful things given to us, and luxuries and pleasant enjoyments, if they be not intended to be used? They must be meant for someone, and what is good for a layman cannot surely be bad for a clerk. You try to despise these good things, but you only try, you don't succeed."

"Don't I?" said Mr. Arabin, still musing, and not knowing what he said.

"I ask you the question. Do you succeed?"

Mr. Arabin looked at her piteously. It seemed to him as though he were being interrogated by some inner spirit of his own, to whom he could not refuse an answer and to whom he did not dare to give a false reply.

"Come, Mr. Arabin, confess—do you succeed? Is money so contemptible? Is worldly power so worthless? Is feminine beauty a trifle to be so slightly regarded by a wise man?"

"Feminine beauty!" said he, gazing into her face as though all the feminine beauty in the world were concentrated there. "Why do you say I do not regard it?"

"If you look at me like that, Mr. Arabin, I shall alter my opinion—or should do so, were I not of course aware that I have no beauty of my own worth regarding."

The gentleman blushed crimson, but the lady did not blush at all. A slightly increased color animated her face, just so much so as to give her an air of special interest. She expected a compliment from her admirer, but she was rather grateful than otherwise by finding that he did not pay it to her. Messrs. Slope and Thorne, Messrs. Brown, Jones, and Robinson, they all paid her compliments. She was rather in hopes that she would ultimately succeed in inducing Mr. Arabin to abuse her.

"But your gaze," said she, "is one of wonder and not of admiration. You wonder at my audacity in asking you such questions about yourself."

"Well, I do rather," said he.

"Nevertheless I expect an answer, Mr. Arabin. Why were women made beautiful if men are not to regard them?"

"But men do regard them," he replied.

"And why not you?"

"You are begging the question, Madame Neroni."

"I am sure I shall beg nothing, Mr. Arabin, which you will not grant, and I do beg for an answer. Do you not as a rule think women below your

otice as companions? Let us see. There is the Widow Bold looking round
t you from her chair this minute. What would you say to her as a com-
anion for life?"

Mr. Arabin, rising from his position, leaned over the sofa and looked
hrough the drawing-room door to the place where Eleanor was seated
etween Bertie Stanhope and Mr. Slope. She at once caught his glance,
nd averted her own. She was not pleasantly placed in her present position.
Mr. Slope was doing his best to attract her attention, and she was striving to
revent his doing so by talking to Mr. Stanhope, while her mind was intently
xed on Mr. Arabin and Madame Neroni. Bertie Stanhope endeavored to
ake advantage of her favors, but he was thinking more of the manner in
which he would by-and-by throw himself at her feet than of amusing her
t the present moment.

"There," said the Signora. "She was stretching her beautiful neck to
ook at you, and now you have disturbed her. Well, I declare I believe I
m wrong about you, I believe that you do think Mrs. Bold a charming
oman. Your looks seem to say so, and by her looks I should say that she
 jealous of me. Come, Mr. Arabin, confide in me, and if it is so, I'll do
l in my power to make up the match."

It is needless to say that the Signora was not very sincere in her offer.
he was never sincere on such subjects. She never expected others to be
, nor did she expect others to think her so. Such matters were her play-
ings, her billiard table, her hounds and hunters, her waltzes and polkas, her
cnics and summer-day excursions. She had little else to amuse her, and
erefore played at love-making in all its forms. She was now playing at it
ith Mr. Arabin, and did not at all expect the earnestness and truth of his
nswer.

"All in your power would be nothing," said he, "for Mrs. Bold is, I
magine, already engaged to another."

"Then you own the impeachment yourself."

"You cross-question me rather unfairly," he replied, "and I do not know
hy I answer you at all. Mrs. Bold is a very beautiful woman, and as
telligent as beautiful. It is impossible to know her without admiring her."

"So you think the widow a very beautiful woman?"

"Indeed I do."

"And one that would grace the parsonage of St. Ewold's."

"One that would well grace any man's house."

"And you really have the effrontery to tell me this," said she—"to tell me,
ho, as you very well know, set up to be a beauty myself, and who am at
is very moment taking such an interest in your affairs—you really have
e effrontery to tell me that Mrs. Bold is the most beautiful woman you
now."

"I did not say so," said Mr. Arabin. "You are more beautiful——"

"Ah, come now, that is something like. I thought you could not be so un-
eling."

"You are more beautiful, perhaps more clever."

"Thank you, thank you, Mr. Arabin. I knew that you and I should b
friends."

"But——"

"Not a word further. I will not hear a word further. If you talk till mid
night, you cannot improve what you have said."

"But, Madame Neroni, Mrs. Bold——"

"I will not hear a word about Mrs. Bold. Dread thoughts of strychnin
did pass across my brain, but she is welcome to the second place."

"Her place——"

"I won't hear anything about her or her place. I am satisfied, and that
enough. But, Mr. Arabin, I am dying with hunger. Beautiful and cleve
as I am, you know I cannot go to my food, and yet you do not bring it t
me."

This at any rate was so true as to make it necessary that Mr. Arabin shoul
act upon it, and he accordingly went into the dining-room and supplied th
Signora's wants.

"And yourself?" said she.

"Oh," said he, "I am not hungry. I never eat at this hour."

"Come, come, Mr. Arabin, don't let love interfere with your appetit
It never does with mine. Give me half a glass more champagne, and the
go to the table. Mrs. Bold will do me an injury if you stay talking to m
any longer."

Mr. Arabin did as he was bid. He took her plate and glass from her an
going into the dining-room, helped himself to a sandwich from the crowde
table and began munching it in a corner.

As he was doing so Miss Thorne, who had hardly sat down for a momen
came into the room, and seeing him standing, was greatly distressed.

"Oh, my dear Mr. Arabin," said she, "have you never sat down ye
I am so distressed. You of all men, too."

Mr. Arabin assured her that he had only just come into the room.

"That is the very reason why you should lose no more time. Com
I'll make room for you. Thank 'ee, my dear," she said, seeing that Mr
Bold was making an attempt to move from her chair, "but I would n
for worlds see you stir, for all the ladies would think it necessary to follo
But perhaps if Mr. Stanhope has done—just for a minute, Mr. Stanhope—t
I can get another chair."

And so Bertie had to rise to make way for his rival. This he did, as h
did everything, with an air of good-humored pleasantry which made
impossible for Mr. Arabin to refuse the proffered seat.

"His bishopric let another take," said Bertie, the quotation being certain
not very appropriate either for the occasion or the person spoken to. "I ha
eaten and am satisfied. Mr. Arabin, pray take my chair. I wish for yo
sake that it really was a bishop's seat."

Mr. Arabin did sit down, and as he did so, Mrs. Bold got up as though to follow her neighbor.

"Pray, pray don't move," said Miss Thorne, almost forcing Eleanor back into her chair. "Mr. Stanhope is not going to leave us. He will stand behind you like a true knight as he is. And now I think of it, Mr. Arabin, let me introduce you to Mr. Slope. Mr. Slope, Mr. Arabin." And the two gentlemen bowed stiffly to each other across the lady whom they both intended to marry, while the other gentleman who also intended to marry her stood behind, watching them.

The two had never met each other before, and the present was certainly not a good opportunity for much cordial conversation, even if cordial conversation between them had been possible. As it was, the whole four who formed the party seemed as though their tongues were tied. Mr. Slope, who was wide-awake to what he hoped was his coming opportunity, was not much concerned in the interest of the moment. His wish was to see Eleanor move, that he might pursue her. Bertie was not exactly in the same frame of mind. The evil day was near enough, there was no reason why he should precipitate it. He had made up his mind to marry Eleanor Bold if he could, and was resolved today to take the first preliminary step toward doing so. But there was time enough before him. He was not going to make an offer of marriage over the tablecloth. Having thus good-naturedly made way for Mr. Arabin, he was willing also to let him talk to the future Mrs. Stanhope as long as they remained in their present position.

Mr. Arabin, having bowed to Mr. Slope, began eating his food without saying a word further. He was full of thought, and though he ate he did so unconsciously.

But poor Eleanor was the most to be pitied. The only friend on whom she thought she could rely was Bertie Stanhope, and he, it seemed, was determined to desert her. Mr. Arabin did not attempt to address her. She said a few words in reply to some remarks from Mr. Slope, and then, feeling the situation too much for her, started from her chair in spite of Miss Thorne and hurried from the room. Mr. Slope followed her, and young Stanhope lost the occasion.

Madeline Neroni, when she was left alone, could not help pondering much on the singular interview she had had with this singular man. It was quite clear that Mr. Arabin was heartily in love with Mrs. Bold, and the Signora, with very unwonted good nature, began to turn it over in her mind whether she could not do him a good turn. Of course Bertie was to have the first chance. It was an understood family arrangement that her brother was, if possible, to marry the Widow Bold. Madeline knew too well his necessities and what was due to her sister to interfere with so excellent a plan as long as it might be feasible. But she had strong suspicion that it was not feasible. She did not think it likely that Mrs. Bold would accept a man in her brother's position, and she had frequently said so to Charlotte. She was inclined to believe that Mr. Slope had more chance of success, and with her it would be a labor of love to rob Mr. Slope of his wife.

And so the Signora resolved, should Bertie fail, to do a good-natured act for once in her life, and give up Mr. Arabin to the woman whom he loved.

CHAPTER XXXVII

ULLATHORNE SPORTS—ACT II

"THAT which has made them drunk has made me bold." 'Twas thus that Mr. Slope encouraged himself as he left the dining-room in pursuit of Eleanor. He had not indeed seen in that room any person really intoxicated, but there had been a good deal of wine drunk, and Mr. Slope had not hesitated to take his share in order to screw himself up to the undertaking which he had in hand. He is not the first man who has thought it expedient to call in the assistance of Bacchus on such an occasion.

Eleanor was out through the window and on the grass before she perceived that she was followed. Just at that moment the guests were nearly all occupied at the tables. Here and there were to seen a constant couple or two who preferred their own sweet discourse to the jingle of glasses, or the charms of rhetoric which fell from the mouths of the Honorable George and the Bishop of Barchester, but the grounds were as nearly vacant as Mr. Slope could wish them to be.

Eleanor saw that she was pursued, and as a deer, when escape is no longer possible, will turn to bay and attack the hounds, so did she turn upon Mr. Slope.

"Pray don't let me take you from the room," said she, speaking with all the stiffness which she knew how to use. "I have come out to look for a friend. I must beg of you, Mr. Slope, to go back."

But Mr. Slope would not be thus entreated. He had observed all day that Mrs. Bold was not cordial to him, and this had to a certain extent oppressed him. But he did not deduce from this any assurance that his aspirations were in vain. He saw that she was angry with him. Might she not be so because he had so long tampered with her feelings? Might it not arise from his having, as he knew was the case, caused her name to be bruited about in conjunction with his own without having given her the opportunity of confessing to the world that henceforth their names were to be one and the same? Poor lady! He had within him a certain Christian conscience-stricken feeling of remorse on this head. It might be that he had wronged her by his tardiness. He had, however, at the present moment imbibed too much of Mr. Thorne's champagne to have any inward misgivings. He was right in repeating the boast of Lady Macbeth—he was not drunk, but he was bold enough for anything. It was a pity that in such a state he could not have encountered Mrs. Proudie.

"You must permit me to attend you," said he. "I could not think of allowing you to go alone."

"Indeed you must, Mr. Slope," said Eleanor, still very stiffly, "for it is my special wish to be alone."

The time for letting the great secret escape him had already come. Mr. Slope saw that it must be now or never, and he was determined that it should be now. This was not his first attempt at winning a fair lady. He had been on his knees, looked unutterable things with his eyes, and whispered honeyed words before this. Indeed he was somewhat an adept at these things, and had only to adapt to the perhaps different taste of Mrs. Bold the well-remembered rhapsodies which had once so much gratified Olivia Proudie.

"Do not ask me to leave you, Mrs. Bold," said he with an impassioned look, impassioned and sanctified as well—with that sort of look which is not uncommon with gentlemen of Mr. Slope's school, and which may perhaps be called the tender-pious. "Do not ask me to leave you till I have spoken a few words with which my heart is full, which I have come hither purposely to say."

Eleanor saw how it was now. She knew directly what it was she was about to go through, and very miserable the knowledge made her. Of course she could refuse Mr. Slope, and there would be an end of that, one might say. But there would not be an end of it as far as Eleanor was concerned. The very fact of Mr. Slope's making an offer to her would be a triumph to the Archdeacon, and in a great measure a vindication of Mr. Arabin's conduct. The widow could not bring herself to endure with patience the idea that she had been in the wrong. She had defended Mr. Slope, she had declared herself quite justified in admitting him among her acquaintance, had ridiculed the idea of his considering himself as more than an acquaintance, and had resented the Archdeacon's caution in her behalf. Now it was about to be proved to her in a manner sufficiently disagreeable that the Archdeacon had been right and she herself had been entirely wrong.

"I don't know what you can have to say to me, Mr. Slope, that you could not have said when we were sitting at table just now." And she closed her lips, and steadied her eyeballs, and looked at him in a manner that ought to have frozen him.

But gentlemen are not easily frozen when they are full of champagne, and it would not at any time have been easy to freeze Mr. Slope.

"There are things, Mrs. Bold, which a man cannot well say before a crowd, which perhaps he cannot well say at any time,—which indeed he may most fervently desire to get spoken, and which he may yet find it almost impossible to utter. It is such things as these that I now wish to say to you." And then the tender-pious look was repeated, with a little more emphasis even than before.

Eleanor had not found it practicable to stand stock-still before the dining-room window and there receive his offer in full view of Miss Thorne's guests. She had therefore in self-defense walked on, and thus Mr. Slope had gained his object of walking with her. He now offered her his arm.

"Thank you, Mr. Slope, I am much obliged to you, but for the very short time that I shall remain with you I shall prefer walking alone."

"And must it be so short?" said he. "Must it be——"

"Yes," said Eleanor, interrupting him, "as short as possible, if you please, sir."

"I had hoped, Mrs. Bold—I had hoped——"

"Pray hope nothing, Mr. Slope, as far as I am concerned, pray do not. I do not know, and need not know, what hope you mean. Our acquaintance is very slight, and will probably remain so. Pray, pray let that be enough. There is at any rate no necessity for us to quarrel."

Mrs. Bold was certainly treating Mr. Slope rather cavalierly, and he felt it so. She was rejecting him before he had offered himself, and informed him at the same time that he was taking a great deal too much on himself to be so familiar. She did not even make an attempt

> From such a sharp and waspish word as "no"
> To pluck the sting.

He was still determined to be very tender and very pious, seeing that in spite of all Mrs. Bold had said to him he not yet abandoned hope, but he was inclined also to be somewhat angry. The widow was bearing herself, as he thought, with too high a hand, was speaking of herself in much too imperious a tone. She had clearly no idea that an honor was being conferred on her. Mr. Slope would be tender as long as he could, but he began to think if that failed, it would not be amiss if he also mounted himself for a while on his high horse. Mr. Slope could undoubtedly be very tender, but he could be very savage also, and he knew his own abilities.

"That is cruel," said he, "and unchristian too. The worst of us are all still bidden to hope. What have I done that you should pass on me so severe a sentence?" And then he paused a moment, during which the widow walked steadily on with measured step, saying nothing further.

"Beautiful woman," at last he burst forth, "beautiful woman, you cannot pretend to be ignorant that I adore you. Yes, Eleanor, yes, I love you. I love you with the truest affection which a man can bear to woman. Next to my hopes of Heaven are my hopes of possessing you." (Mr. Slope's memory here played him false, or he would not have omitted the deanery.) "How sweet to walk to Heaven with you by my side, with you for my guide, mutual guides. Say, Eleanor, dearest Eleanor, shall we walk that sweet path together?"

Eleanor had no intention of ever walking together with Mr. Slope on any other path than that special one of Miss Thorne's which they now occupied, but as she had been unable to prevent the expression of Mr.

Slope's wishes and aspirations, she resolved to hear him out to the end before she answered him.

"Ah! Eleanor," he continued, and it seemed to be his idea that as he had once found courage to pronounce her Christian name he could not utter it often enough. "Ah! Eleanor, will it not be sweet, with the Lord's assistance, to travel hand in hand through this mortal valley which His mercies will make pleasant to us, till hereafter we shall dwell together at the foot of His throne?" And then a more tenderly pious glance than ever beamed from the lover's eyes. "Ah! Eleanor——"

"My name, Mr. Slope, is Mrs. Bold," said Eleanor, who, though determined to hear out the tale of his love, was too much disgusted by his blasphemy to be able to bear much more of it.

"Sweetest angel, be not so cold," said he, and as he said it the champagne broke forth, and he contrived to pass his arm round her waist. He did this with considerable cleverness, for up to this point Eleanor had contrived with tolerable success to keep her distance from him. They had got into a walk nearly enveloped by shrubs, and Mr. Slope therefore no doubt considered that as they were now alone it was fitting that he should give her some outward demonstration of that affection of which he talked so much. It may perhaps be presumed that the same stamp of measures had been found to succeed with Olivia Proudie. Be this as it may, it was not successful with Eleanor Bold.

She sprang from him as she would have jumped from an adder, but she did not spring far—not, indeed, beyond arm's length. And, then, quick as thought, she raised her little hand and dealt him a box on the ear with such right goodwill that it sounded among the trees like a miniature thunderclap. The provocation was too much for her, the temptation to instant resentment of the insult too strong.

"I never, never will speak another word to you," she said, gasping with emotion and the loss of breath which her exertion and violent feelings occasioned her, and so saying she put foot to the ground and ran quickly back along the path to the house.

We will not attempt to tell with what mighty surgings of the inner heart Mr. Slope swore to revenge himself on the woman who had disgraced him, nor will we vainly strive to depict his deep agony of soul.

There he is, however, alone in the garden walk, and we must contrive to bring him out of it. He was not willing to come forth quite at once. His cheek was stinging with the weight of Eleanor's fingers, and he fancied that everyone who looked at him would be able to see on his face the traces of what he had endured. He stood awhile, becoming redder and redder with rage. He stood motionless, undecided, glaring with his eyes, thinking of the pains and penalties of Hades, and meditating how he might best devote his enemy to the infernal gods with all the passion of his accustomed eloquence. He longed in his heart to be preaching at her. 'Twas thus that he was ordinarily avenged of sinning mortal men and women. Could he at once have ascended his Sunday rostrum and fulminated at her such denunciations as his spirit delighted in, his bosom would have been greatly eased.

And then he began to feel a righteous disgust at the wickedness of the doings around him. He had been justly chastised for lending, by his presence, a sanction to such worldly lures. The gaiety of society, the mirth of banquets, the laughter of the young, and the eating and drinking of the elders were, for a while, without excuse in his sight. What had he now brought down upon himself by sojourning thus in the tents of the heathen? He had consorted with idolaters round the altars of Baal, and therefore a sore punishment had come upon him. He then thought of the Signora Neroni, and his soul within him was full of sorrow. He had an ink-ling—a true inkling—that he was a wicked, sinful man, but it led him in no right direction. He could admit no charity in his heart. He felt debasement coming on him, and he longed to shake it off, to rise up in his stirrup, to mount to high places and great power, that he might get up into a mighty pulpit and preach to the world a loud sermon against Mrs. Bold.

There he stood fixed to the gravel for about ten minutes. Fortune favored him so far that no prying eyes came to look upon him in his misery. Then a shudder passed over his whole frame, he collected himself and slowly wound his way round to the lawn, advancing along the path and not returning in the direction which Eleanor had taken. When he reached the tent he found the Bishop standing there in conversation with the Master of Lazarus. His lordship had come out to air himself after the exertion of his speech.

"This is very pleasant—very pleasant, my lord, is it not?" said Mr. Slope with his most gracious smile, and pointing to the tent. "Very pleasant. It is delightful to see so many persons enjoy themselves so thoroughly."

Mr. Slope thought he might force the Bishop to introduce him to Dr. Gwynne. A very great example had declared and practiced the wisdom of being everything to everybody, and Mr. Slope was desirous of following it. His maxim was never to lose a chance. The Bishop, however, at the present moment was not very anxious to increase Mr. Slope's circle of acquaintance among his clerical brethren. He had his own reasons for dropping any marked allusion to his domestic chaplain, and he therefore made his shoulder rather cold for the occasion.

"Very, very," said he without turning round, or even deigning to look at Mr. Slope. "And therefore, Dr. Gwynne, I really think that you will find that the hebdomadal board will exercise as wide and as general an authority as at the present moment."

Suddenly an interruption came, not altogether unwelcome to Mr. Slope. One of the Bishop's servants came up to his master's shoulder with a long, grave face, and whispered into the Bishop's ear.

"What is it, John?" said the Bishop.

"The Dean, my lord. He is dead."

CHAPTER XXXVIII

MRS. BOLD CONFIDES HER SORROW TO HER FRIEND MISS STANHOPE

WHEN Mrs. Bold came to the end of the walk and faced the lawn, she began to bethink herself what she should do. Was she to wait there till Mr. Slope caught her, or was she to go in among the crowd with tears in her eyes and passion in her face? She might in truth have stood there long enough without any reasonable fear of further immediate persecution from Mr. Slope, but we are all inclined to magnify the bugbears which frighten us. In her present state of dread she did not know of what atrocity he might venture to be guilty. Had anyone told her a week ago that he would have put his arm round her waist at this party of Miss Thorne's, she would have been utterly incredulous. Had she been informed that he would be seen on the following Sunday walking down the High Street in a scarlet coat and top boots, she would not have thought such phenomenon more improbable.

But this improbable iniquity he had committed, and now there was nothing she could not believe of him. In the first place, it was quite manifest that he was tipsy. In the next place, it was to be taken as proved that all his religion was sheer hypocrisy. And finally, the man was utterly shameless. She therefore stood watching for the sound of his footfall, not without some fear that he might creep out at her suddenly from among the bushes.

As she thus stood, she saw Charlotte Stanhope at a little distance from her walking quickly across the grass. Eleanor's handkerchief was in her hand, and putting it to her face so as to conceal her tears, she ran across the lawn and joined her friend.

"Oh, Charlotte," she said, almost too much out of breath to speak very plainly, "I am so glad I have found you."

"Glad you have found me!" said Charlotte, laughing. "That's a good joke. Why, Bertie and I have been looking for you everywhere. He swears that you have gone off with Mr. Slope, and is now on the point of hanging himself."

"Oh, Charlotte, don't," said Mrs. Bold.

"Why, my child, what on earth is the matter with you!" said Miss Stanhope, perceiving that Eleanor's hand trembled on her own arm, and finding also that her companion was still half-choked by tears. "Goodness heaven! something has distressed you. What is it? What can I do for you?"

Eleanor answered her only by a sort of spasmodic gurgle in her throat. She was a good deal upset, as people say, and could not at the moment collect herself.

"Come here, this way, Mrs. Bold. Come this way, and we shall not be seen. What has happened to vex you so? What can I do for you? Can Bertie do anything?"

"Oh, no, no, no, no," said Eleanor. "There is nothing to be done. Only that horrid man——"

"What horrid man?" asked Charlotte.

There are some moments in life in which both men and women feel themselves imperatively called on to make a confidence, in which not to do so requires a disagreeable resolution and also a disagreeable suspicion. There are people of both sexes who never make confidences, who are never tempted by momentary circumstances to disclose their secrets, but such are generally dull, close, unimpassioned spirits, "gloomy gnomes, who live in cold dark mines." There was nothing of the gnome about Eleanor, and she therefore resolved to tell Charlotte Stanhope the whole story about Mr. Slope.

"That horrid man, that Mr. Slope," said she. "Did you not see that he followed me out of the dining-room?"

"Of course I did, and was sorry enough, but I could not help it. I knew you would be annoyed. But you and Bertie managed it badly between you."

"It was not his fault, nor mine either. You know how I disliked the idea of coming in the carriage with that man."

"I am sure I am very sorry if that has led to it."

"I don't know what has led to it," said Eleanor, almost crying again. "But it has not been my fault."

"But what has he done, my dear?"

"He's an abominable, horrid, hypocritical man, and it would serve him right to tell the Bishop all about it."

"Believe me, if you want to do him an injury, you had far better tell Mrs. Proudie. But what did he do, Mrs. Bold?"

"Ugh!" exclaimed Eleanor.

"Well, I must confess he's not very nice," said Charlotte Stanhope.

"Nice!" said Eleanor. "He is the most fulsome, fawning, abominable man I ever saw. What business had he to come to me?—I that never gave him the slightest tittle of encouragement—I that always hated him, though I did take his part when others ran him down."

"That's just where it is, my dear. He has heard that, and therefore fancied that of course you were in love with him."

This was wormwood to Eleanor. It was in fact the very thing which all her friends had been saying for the last month past, and which experience now proved to be true. Eleanor resolved within herself that she would never again take any man's part. The world with all its villainy, and all its ill-nature, might wag as it liked. She would not again attempt to set crooked things straight.

"But what did he do, my dear?" said Charlotte, who was really rather interested in the subject.

"He–he–he——"

"Well, come, it can't have been anything so very horrid, for the man was not tipsy."

"Oh, I am sure he was," said Eleanor. "I am sure he must have been tipsy."

"Well, I declare I didn't observe it. But what was it, my love?"

"Why, I believe I can hardly tell you. He talked such horrid stuff that you never heard the like—about religion, and Heaven, and love.—Oh, dear, he is such a nasty man."

"I can easily imagine the sort of stuff he would talk. Well,—and then——?"

"And then—he took hold of me."

"Took hold of you?"

"Yes—he somehow got close to me, and took hold of me——"

"By the waist?"

"Yes," said Eleanor, shuddering.

"And then——"

"Then I jumped away from him, and gave him a slap on the face, and ran away along the path till I saw you."

"Ha, ha, ha!" Charlotte Stanhope laughed heartily at the finale to the tragedy. It was delightful to her to think that Mr. Slope had had his ears boxed. She did not quite appreciate the feeling which made her friend so unhappy at the result of the interview. To her thinking, the matter had ended happily enough as regarded the widow, who indeed was entitled to some sort of triumph among her friends. Whereas to Mr. Slope would be due all those gibes and jeers which would naturally follow such an affair. His friends would ask him whether his ears tingled whenever he saw a widow, and he would be cautioned that beautiful things were made to be looked at and not to be touched.

Such were Charlotte Stanhope's views on such matters, but she did not at the present moment clearly explain them to Mrs. Bold. Her object was to endear herself to her friend, and therefore, having had her laugh, she was ready enough to offer sympathy. Could Bertie do anything? Should Bertie speak to the man and warn him that in future he must behave with more decorum? Bertie, indeed, she declared, would be more angry than anyone else when he heard to what insult Mrs. Bold had been subjected.

"But you won't tell him?" said Mrs. Bold, with a look of horror.

"Not if you don't like it," said Charlotte. "But considering everything, I would strongly advise it. If you had a brother, you know it would be unnecessary. But it is very right that Mr. Slope should know that you have somebody by you that will and can protect you."

"But my father is here."

"Yes, but it is so disagreeable for clergymen to have to quarrel with each other, and circumstanced as your father is just at this moment, it would be very inexpedient that there should be anything unpleasant between him

and Mr. Slope. Surely you and Bertie are intimate enough for you t
permit him to take your part."

Charlotte Stanhope was very anxious that her brother should at onc
on that very day, settle matters with his future wife. Things had now com
to that point between him and his father, and between him and h
creditors, that he must either do so or leave Barchester—either do that c
go back to his unwashed associates, dirty lodgings, and poor living at Ca
rara.

Such being the state of the case, it was very necessary that no more tim
should be lost. Charlotte had seen her brother's apathy when he neglecte
to follow Mrs. Bold out of the room, with anger which she could hardl
suppress. It was grievous to think that Mr. Slope should have so distance
him. Charlotte felt that she had played her part with sufficient skill. She ha
brought them together and induced such a degree of intimacy that he
brother was really relieved from all trouble and labor in the matter. An
moreover it was quite plain that Mrs. Bold was very fond of Bertie. An
now it was plain enough also that he had nothing to fear from his riva
Mr. Slope.

There was certainly an awkwardness in subjecting Mrs. Bold to a secon
offer on the same day. It would have been well perhaps to have put th
matter off for a week, could a week have been spared. But circumstance
are frequently too peremptory to be arranged as we would wish to arrang
them, and such was the case now. This being so, could not this affair o
Mr. Slope's be turned to advantage? Could it not be made the excus
for bringing Bertie and Mrs. Bold into still closer connection, into suc
close connection that they could not fail to throw themselves into eac
other's arms? Such was the game which Miss Stanhope now at a moment'
notice resolved to play.

And very well she played it. In the first place, it was arranged that Mr
Slope should not return in the Stanhopes' carriage to Barchester. It s
happened that Mr. Slope was already gone, but of that of course they
knew nothing. The Signora should be induced to go first, with only the
servants and her sister, and Bertie should take Mr. Slope's place in the
second journey. Bertie was to be told in confidence of the whole affair
and when the carriage was gone off with its first load, Eleanor was to
be left under Bertie's special protection, so as to ensure her from any
further aggression from Mr. Slope. While the carriage was getting ready,
Bertie was to seek out that gentleman and make him understand that he
must provide himself with another conveyance back to Barchester. Their
immediate object should be to walk about together in search of Bertie.
Bertie, in short, was to be the Pegasus on whose wings they were to ride
out of their present dilemma.

There was a warmth of friendship and cordial kindliness in all this that
was very soothing to the widow, but yet, though she gave way to it, she
was hardly reconciled to doing so. It never occurred to her that now that

he had killed one dragon another was about to spring up in her path. She
ad no remote idea that she would have to encounter another suitor in her
roposed protector. But she hardly liked the thought of putting herself
o much into the hands of young Stanhope. She felt that if she wanted
rotection, she should go to her father. She felt that she should ask him
o provide a carriage for her back to Barchester. She knew that she should
ot throw herself entirely upon friends whose friendship dated as it were
ut from yesterday. But yet she could not say no to one who was so
isterly in her kindness, so eager in her good nature, so comfortably sym-
athetic, as Charlotte Stanhope. And thus she gave way to all the propo-
itions made to her.

They first went into the dining-room looking for their champion, and
rom thence to the drawing-room. Here they found Mr. Arabin still
anging over the Signora's sofa, or rather they found him sitting near her
ead, as a physician might have sat had the lady been his patient. There
vas no other person in the room.

All that had passed and was passing between Mr. Arabin and the lady
t is unnecessary to give in detail. She was doing with him as she did with
ll others. It was her mission to make fools of men, and she was pursuing
er mission with Mr. Arabin. She had almost got him to own his love for
Mrs. Bold, and had subsequently almost induced him to acknowledge a
assion for herself. He, poor man, was hardly aware what he was doing
or saying, hardly conscious whether he was in Heaven or in Hell. So
ittle had he known of female attractions of that peculiar class which the
Signora owned that he became affected with a kind of temporary delirium
when first subjected to its power. He lost his head rather than his heart,
and toppled about mentally, reeling in his ideas as a drunken man does on his
egs. She had whispered to him words that really meant nothing, but which
coming from such beautiful lips, and accompanied by such lustrous glances,
seemed to have a mysterious significance, which he felt though he could
not understand.

In being thus besirened, Mr. Arabin behaved himself very differently
from Mr. Slope. The Signora had said truly, that the two men were the
contrasts of each other, that the one was all for action, the other all for
thought. Mr. Slope, when this lady laid upon his senses the overpowering
breath of her charms, immediately attempted to obtain some fruition, to
achieve some mighty triumph. He began by catching at her hand, and
progressed by kissing it. He made vows of love, and asked for vows in return.
He promised everlasting devotion, knelt before her, and swore that had she
been on Mount Ida, Juno would have had no cause to hate the offspring
of Venus. But Mr. Arabin uttered no oaths, kept his hand mostly in his
trousers pocket, and had no more thought of kissing Madame Neroni than
of kissing the Countess De Courcy.

As soon as Mr. Arabin saw Mrs. Bold enter the room, he blushed and
rose from his chair, then he sat down again, and then again got up. The

Signora saw the blush at once, and smiled at the poor victim, but Eleanor was too much confused to see anything.

"Oh, Madeline," said Charlotte, "I want to speak to you particularly. We must arrange about the carriage, you know." And she stooped down to whisper to her sister. Mr. Arabin immediately withdrew to a little distance, and as Charlotte had in fact much to explain before she could make the new carriage arrangement intelligible, he had nothing to do but to talk to Mrs. Bold.

"We have had a very pleasant party," said he, using the tone he would have used had he declared that the sun was shining very brightly or the rain falling very fast.

"Very," said Eleanor, who never in her life had passed a more unpleasant day.

"I hope Mr. Harding has enjoyed himself."

"Oh, yes, very much," said Eleanor, who had not seen her father since she parted from him soon after her arrival.

"He returns to Barchester tonight, I suppose."

"Yes, I believe so—that is, I think he is staying at Plumstead."

"Oh, staying at Plumstead," said Mr. Arabin.

"He came from there this morning. I believe he is going back. He didn't exactly say, however."

"I hope Mrs. Grantly is quite well."

"She seemed to be quite well. She is here—that is, unless she has gone away."

"Oh, yes, to be sure. I was talking to her. Looking very well indeed." Then there was a considerable pause, for Charlotte could not at once make Madeline understand why she was to be sent home in a hurry without her brother.

"Are you returning to Plumstead, Mrs. Bold?" Mr. Arabin merely asked this by way of making conversation, but he immediately perceived that he was approaching dangerous ground.

"No," said Mrs. Bold, very quietly, "I am going home to Barchester."

"Oh, ah, yes. I had forgotten that you had returned." And then Mr. Arabin, finding it impossible to say anything further, stood silent until Charlotte had completed her plans, and Mrs. Bold stood equally silent, intently occupied, as it appeared, in the arrangement of her rings.

And yet these two people were thoroughly in love with each other. And though one was a middle-aged clergyman and the other a lady at any rate past the wishy-washy bread-and-butter period of life, they were as unable to tell their own minds to each other as any Damon and Phillis whose united ages would not make up that to which Mr. Arabin had already attained.

Madeline Neroni consented to her sister's proposal, and then the two ladies again went off in quest of Bertie Stanhope.

CHAPTER XXXIX

ULLATHORNE SPORTS—ACT III

AND now Miss Thorne's guests were beginning to take their departure, and the amusement of those who remained was becoming slack. It was getting dark, and ladies in morning costumes were thinking that if they were to appear by candlelight they ought to readjust themselves. Some young gentlemen had been heard to talk so loud that prudent mammas determined to retire judiciously, and the more discreet of the male sex, whose libations had been moderate, felt that there was not much more left for them to do.

The Countess and her noble brood were among the first to leave. Mrs. Proudie could not stay when the Countess was gone. So the Bishop was searched for by the Reverend Messrs. Grey and Green, and found in one corner of the tent enjoying himself thoroughly in a disquisition on the hebdomadal board. He obeyed, however, the behests of his lady without finishing the sentence in which he was promising to Dr. Gwynne that his authority at Oxford should remain unimpaired, and the episcopal horses turned their noses toward the palatial stables. Then the Grantlys went. Before they did so, Mr. Harding managed to whisper a word into his daughter's ear. Of course, he said, he would undeceive the Grantlys as to that foolish rumor about Mr. Slope.

"No, no, no," said Eleanor. "Pray do not—pray wait till I see you. You will be home in a day or two, and then I will explain to you everything."

"I shall be home tomorrow," said he.

"I am so glad," said Eleanor. "You will come and dine with me, and then we shall be so comfortable."

Mr. Harding promised. He did not exactly know what there was to be explained, or why Dr. Grantly's mind should not be disabused of the mistake into which he had fallen, but nevertheless he promised. He owed some reparation to his daughter, and he thought that he might best make it by obedience.

And thus the people were thinning off by degrees as Charlotte and Eleanor walked about in quest of Bertie. Their search might have been long had they not happened to hear his voice. He was comfortably ensconced in the haha, with his back to the sloping side, smoking a cigar and eagerly engaged in conversation with some youngster from the farther side of the county whom he had never met before, who was also smoking under Bertie's pupilage and listening with open ears to an account given by his companion of some of the pastimes of Eastern clime.

"Bertie, I am seeking you everywhere," said Charlotte. "Come up here at once."

Bertie looked up out of the haha and saw the two ladies before him. A
there was nothing for him but to obey, he got up and threw away hi
cigar. From the first moment of his acquaintance with her he had like
Eleanor Bold. Had he been left to his own devices, had she been penniless
and had it then been quite out of the question that he should marry he
he would most probably have fallen violently in love with her. But no
he could not help regarding her somewhat as he did the marble workshop
at Carrara, as he had done his easel and palette, as he had done the lawyer'
chambers in London—in fact, as he had invariably regarded everything b
which it had been proposed to him to obtain the means of living. Eleano
Bold appeared before him no longer as a beautiful woman, but as a ne
profession called matrimony. Bertie did not dislike money, but he hate
the very thought of earning it. He was now called away from his pleasan
cigar to earn it by offering himself as a husband to Mrs. Bold. The wor
indeed was made easy enough, for in lieu of his having to seek the widow
the widow had apparently come to seek him.

He made some sudden absurd excuse to his auditor, and then, throwin
away his cigar, climbed up the wall of the haha and joined the ladies o
the lawn.

"Come and give Mrs. Bold an arm," said Charlotte, "while I set you o
a piece of duty which, as a preux chevalier, you must immediately perform
Your personal danger will, I fear, be insignificant, as your antagonist is ;
clergyman."

Bertie immediately gave his arm to Eleanor, walking between her and hi
sister. The little history of Mr. Slope's misconduct was then told to Berti
by his sister, Eleanor's ears tingling the while. And well they might tingle
If it were necessary to speak of the outrage at all, why should it be spoken
of to such a person as Mr. Stanhope, and why in her own hearing? She
knew she was wrong, and was unhappy and dispirited, and yet she could
think of no way to extricate herself, no way to set herself right. Charlotte
spared her as much as she possibly could, spoke of the whole thing as though
Mr. Slope had taken a glass of wine too much, said that of course there
would be nothing more about it, but that steps must be taken to exclude
Mr. Slope from the carriage.

"Mrs. Bold need be under no alarm about that," said Bertie, "for Mr.
Slope has gone this hour past. He told me that business made it necessary
that he should start at once for Barchester."

"He is not so tipsy, at any rate, but what he knows his fault," said Charlotte. "Well, my dear, that is one difficulty over. Now I'll leave you with
your true knight, and get Madeline off as quickly as I can. The carriage
is here, I suppose, Bertie?"

"It has been here for the last hour."

"That's well. Good-by, my dear. Of course you'll come in to tea. I shall
trust to you to bring her, Bertie, even by force if necessary." And so saying,
Charlotte ran off across the lawn leaving her brother alone with the widow.

As Miss Stanhope went off, Eleanor bethought herself that as Mr. Slope had taken his departure, there no longer existed any necessity for separating Mr. Stanhope from his sister Madeline, who so much needed his aid. She said as much.

"Oh, let Charlotte have her own way," said he. "She has arranged it, and there will be no end of confusion if we make another change. Charlotte always arranges everything in our house, and rules us like a despot."

"But the Signora?" said Eleanor.

"Oh, the Signora can do very well without me. Indeed, she will have to do without me," he added, thinking rather of his studies in Carrara than of his Barchester hymeneals.

"Why, you are not going to leave us?" asked Eleanor.

It has been said that Bertie Stanhope was a man without principle. He certainly was so. He had no power of using active mental exertion to keep himself from doing evil. Evil had no ugliness in his eyes, virtue no beauty. He was void of any of those feelings which actuate men to do good. But he was perhaps equally void of those which actuate men to do evil. He got into debt with utter recklessness, thinking nothing as to whether the tradesmen would ever be paid or not. But he did not invent active schemes of deceit for the sake of extracting the goods of others. If a man gave him credit, that was the man's lookout, Bertie Stanhope troubled himself nothing further. In borrowing money he did the same. He gave people references to "his Governor," told them that the "old chap" had a good income, and agreed to pay sixty per cent for the accommodation. All this he did without a scruple of conscience, but then he never contrived active villainy.

In this affair of his marriage, it had been represented to him as a matter of duty that he ought to put himself in possession of Mrs. Bold's hand and fortune, and at first he had so regarded it. About her he had thought but little. It was the customary thing for men situated as he was to marry for money, and there was no reason why he should not do what others around him did. And so he consented. But now he began to see the matter in another light. He was setting himself down to catch this woman as a cat sits to catch a mouse. He was to catch her, and swallow her up, her and her child, and her houses and land, in order that he might live on her instead of on his father. There was a cold, calculating, cautious cunning about this quite at variance with Bertie's character. The prudence of the measure was quite as antagonistic to his feelings as the iniquity.

And then, should he be successful, what would be the reward? Having satisfied his creditors with half of the widow's fortune, he would be allowed to sit down quietly at Barchester, keeping economical house with the remainder. His duty would be to rock the cradle of the late Mr. Bold's child, and his highest excitement a demure party at Plumstead rectory, should it ultimately turn out that the Archdeacon would be sufficiently reconciled to receive him.

There was very little in the program to allure such a man as Bertie Stanhope. Would not the Carrara workshop, or whatever worldly career fortune might have in store for him, would not almost anything be better than this? The lady herself was undoubtedly all that was desirable, but the most desirable lady becomes nauseous when she has to be taken as a pill. He was pledged to his sister, however, and let him quarrel with whom he would, it behooved him not to quarrel with her. If she were lost to him, all would be lost that he could ever hope to derive henceforward from the paternal rooftree. Could not some happy deceit bring him through in this matter so that he might save appearances with his sister and yet not betray the widow to her ruin? What if he made a confederate of Eleanor? 'Twas in this spirit that Bertie Stanhope set about his wooing.

"But you are not going to leave Barchester?" asked Eleanor.

"I do not know," he replied. "I hardly know yet what I am going to do. But it is at any rate certain that I must do something."

"You mean about your profession?" said she.

"Yes, about my profession, if you can call it one."

"And is it not one?" said Eleanor. "Were I a man, I know none I should prefer to it, except painting. And I believe the one is as much in your power as the other."

"Yes, just about equally so," said Bertie, with a little touch of inward satire directed at himself. He knew in his heart that he would never make a penny by either.

"I have often wondered, Mr. Stanhope, why you do not exert yourself more," said Eleanor, who felt a friendly fondness for the man with whom she was walking. "But I know it is very impertinent in me to say so."

"Impertinent!" said he. "Not so, but much too kind. It is much too kind in you to take any interest in so idle a scamp."

"But you are not a scamp, though you are perhaps idle. And I do take an interest in you, a very great interest," she added, in a voice which almost made him resolve to change his mind. "And when I call you idle, I know you are only so for the present moment. Why can't you settle steadily to work here in Barchester?"

"And make busts of the Bishop, Dean and Chapter? Or perhaps, if I achieve a great success, obtain a commission to put up an elaborate tombstone over a prebendary's widow, a dead lady with a Grecian nose, a bandeau, and an intricate lace veil—lying of course on a marble sofa, from among the legs of which Death will be creeping out and poking at his victim with a small toasting fork."

Eleanor laughed, but yet she thought that if the surviving prebendary paid the bill, the object of the artist as a professional man would in a great measure be obtained.

"I don't know about the Dean and Chapter and the prebendary's widow," said Eleanor. "Of course you must take them as they come. But the fact of your having a great cathedral in which such ornaments are required could not but be in your favor."

"No real artist could descend to the ornamentation of a cathedral," said Bertie, who had his ideas of the high ecstatic ambition of art, as indeed all artists have who are not in receipt of a good income. "Buildings should be fitted to grace the sculpture, not the sculpture to grace the building."

"Yes, when the work of art is good enough to merit it. Do you, Mr. Stanhope, do something sufficiently excellent, and we ladies of Barchester will erect for it a fitting receptacle. Come, what shall the subject be?"

"I'll put you in your pony chair, Mrs. Bold, as Dannecker put Ariadne on her lion. Only you must promise to sit for me."

"My ponies are too tame, I fear, and my broad-brimmed straw hat will not look so well in marble as the lace veil of the prebendary's wife."

"If you will not consent to that, Mrs. Bold, I will consent to try no other subject in Barchester."

"You are determined, then, to push your fortune in other lands?"

"I am determined," said Bertie, slowly and significantly, as he tried to bring up his mind to a great resolve, "I am determined in this matter to be guided wholly by you."

"Wholly by me!" said Eleanor, astonished at, and not quite liking, his altered manner.

"Wholly by you," said Bertie, dropping his companion's arm and standing before her on the path. In their walk they had come exactly to the spot in which Eleanor had been provoked into slapping Mr. Slope's face. Could it be possible that this place was peculiarly unpropitious to her comfort? Could it be possible that she should here have to encounter yet another amorous swain?

"If you will be guided by me, Mr. Stanhope, you will set yourself down to steady and persevering work, and you will be ruled by your father as to the place in which it will be most advisable for you to do so."

"Nothing could be more prudent, if only it were practicable. But now, if you will let me, I will tell you how it is that I will be guided by you, and why. Will you let me tell you?"

"I really do not know what you can have to tell."

"No—you cannot know. It is impossible that you should. But we have been very good friends, Mrs. Bold, have we not?"

"Yes, I think we have," said she, observing in his demeanor an earnestness very unusual with him.

"You were kind enough to say just now that you took an interest in me, and I was perhaps vain enough to believe you."

"There is no vanity in that. I do so as your sister's brother—and as my own friend also."

"Well, I don't deserve that you should feel so kindly toward me," said Bertie, "but upon my word I am very grateful for it." And he paused awhile, hardly knowing how to introduce the subject that he had in hand.

And it was no wonder that he found it difficult. He had to make known to his companion the scheme that had been prepared to rob her of her wealth. He had to tell her that he had intended to marry her without loving her, or else that he loved her without intending to marry her. And he had also to bespeak from her not only his own pardon, but also that of his sister and induce Mrs. Bold to protest in her future communion with Charlotte that an offer had been duly made to her and duly rejected.

Bertie Stanhope was not prone to be very diffident of his own conversational powers, but it did seem to him that he was about to tax them almost too far. He hardly knew where to begin, and he hardly knew where he should end.

By this time Eleanor was again walking on slowly by his side, not taking his arm as she had heretofore done, but listening very intently for whatever Bertie might have to say to her.

"I wish to be guided by you," said he, "and, indeed in this matter there is no one else who can set me right."

"Oh, that must be nonsense," said she.

"Well, listen to me now, Mrs. Bold, and if you can help it, pray don't be angry with me."

"Angry!" said she.

"Oh, indeed you will have cause to be so. You know how very much attached to you my sister Charlotte is."

Eleanor acknowledged that she did.

"Indeed she is. I never knew her to love anyone so warmly on so short an acquaintance. You know also how well she loves me?"

Eleanor now made no answer, but she felt the blood tingle in her cheek as she gathered from what he said the probable result of this double-barreled love on the part of Miss Stanhope.

"I am her only brother, Mrs. Bold, and it is not to be wondered at that she should love me. But you do not yet know Charlotte—you do not know how entirely the well-being of our family hangs on her. Without her to manage for us, I do not know how we should get on from day to day. You cannot yet have observed all this."

Eleanor had indeed observed a good deal of this. She did not however now say so, but allowed him to proceed with his story.

"You cannot therefore be surprised that Charlotte should be most anxious to do the best for us all."

Eleanor said that she was not at all surprised.

"And she has had a very difficult game to play, Mrs. Bold—a very difficult game. Poor Madeline's unfortunate marriage and terrible accident, my mother's ill-health, my father's absence from England, and last, and worst perhaps, my own roving, idle spirit have almost been too much for her. You cannot wonder if among all her cares one of the foremost is to see me settled in the world."

Eleanor on this occasion expressed no acquiescence. She certainly supposed that a formal offer was to be made, and could not but think that so singular an exordium was never before made by a gentleman in a similar osition. Mr. Slope had annoyed her by the excess of his ardor. It was quite clear that no such danger was to be feared from Mr. Stanhope. Prudential motives alone actuated him. Not only was he about to make love because his sister told him, but he also took the precaution of explaining all this before he began. 'Twas thus, we may presume, that the matter presented itself to Mrs. Bold.

When he had got so far, Bertie began poking the gravel with a little cane which he carried. He still kept moving on, but very slowly, and his companion moved slowly by his side, not inclined to assist him in the task the performance of which appeared to be difficult to him.

"Knowing how fond she is of yourself, Mrs. Bold, cannot you imagine what scheme should have occurred to her?"

"I can imagine no better scheme, Mr. Stanhope, than the one I proposed to you just now."

"No," said he, somewhat lackadaisically. "I suppose that would be the best, but Charlotte thinks another plan might be joined with it.—She wants me to marry you."

A thousand remembrances flashed across Eleanor's mind all in a moment—how Charlotte had talked about and praised her brother, how she had continually contrived to throw the two of them together, how she had encouraged all manner of little intimacies, how she had with singular cordiality persisted in treating Eleanor as one of the family. All this had been done to secure her comfortable income for the benefit of one of the family! She had enjoyed the society of the Stanhopes, she had greatly liked the cordiality of Charlotte, and had been happy in her new friends. Now she saw the cause of all this kindness, and her mind was opened to a new phase of human life.

"Miss Stanhope," said she, haughtily, "has been contriving for me a great deal of honor, but she might have saved herself the trouble. I am not sufficiently ambitious."

"Pray don't be angry with her, Mrs. Bold," said he, "or with me either."

"Certainly not with you, Mr. Stanhope," said she, with considerable sarcasm in her tone. "Certainly not with you."

"No—nor with her," said he, imploringly.

"And why, may I ask you, Mr. Stanhope, have you told me this singular story? For I may presume I may judge by your manner of telling it, that—that—that you and your sister are not exactly of one mind on the subject."

"No, we are not."

"And if so," said Mrs. Bold, who was now really angry with the unnecessary insult which she thought had been offered to her, "and if so, why has it been worth your while to tell me all this?"

"I did once think, Mrs. Bold—that you—that you——"

The widow now again became entirely impassive, and would not lend the slightest assistance to her companion.

"I did once think that you perhaps might—might have been taught to regard me as more than a friend."

"Never," said Mrs. Bold, "never! If I have ever allowed myself to do anything to encourage such an idea I have been very much to blame—very much to blame indeed."

"You never have," said Bertie, who really had a good-natured anxiety to make what he said as little unpleasant as possible. "You never have, and I have seen for some time that I had no chance, but my sister's hopes ran higher. I have not mistaken you, Mrs. Bold, though perhaps she has."

"Then why have you said all this to me?"

"Because I must not anger her."

"And will not this anger her? Upon my word, Mr. Stanhope, I do not understand the policy of your family. Oh, how I wish I was at home!" And as she expressed the wish, she could restrain herself no longer, but burst into a flood of tears.

Poor Bertie was greatly moved. "You shall have the carriage to yourself going home," said he, "at least you and my father. As for me, I can walk, or for the matter of that it does not much signify what I do." He perfectly understood that part of Eleanor's grief arose from the apparent necessity of her going back to Barchester in the carriage with her second suitor.

This somewhat mollified her. "Oh, Mr. Stanhope," said she, "why should you have made me so miserable? What will you have gained by telling me all this?"

He had not even yet explained to her the most difficult part of his proposition. He had not told her that she was to be a party to the little deception which he intended to play off upon his sister. This suggestion had still to be made, and as it was absolutely necessary, he proceeded to make it.

We need not follow him through the whole of his statement. At last, and not without considerable difficulty, he made Eleanor understand why he had let her into his confidence, seeing that he no longer intended her the honor of a formal offer. At last he made her comprehend the part which she was destined to play in this little family comedy.

But when she did understand it, she was only more angry with him than ever—more angry not only with him, but with Charlotte also. Her fair name was to be bandied about between them in different senses, and each sense false. She was to be played off by the sister against the father, and then by the brother against the sister. Her dear friend Charlotte, with all her agreeable sympathy and affection, was striving to sacrifice her for the Stanhope family welfare. And Bertie, who, as he now proclaimed himself, was over head and ears in debt, completed the compliment of owning that he did not care to have his debts paid at so great a sacrifice of himself. Then she was asked to conspire together with this unwilling suitor for the sake of making the family believe that he had in obedience to their commands done his best to throw himself thus away!

She lifted up her face when he had finished, and looking at him with much dignity, even through her tears, she said:

"I regret to say it, Mr. Stanhope, but after what has passed, I believe that all intercourse between your family and myself had better cease."

"Well, perhaps it had," said Bertie naïvely. "Perhaps that will be better, at any rate for a time, and then Charlotte will think you are offended at what I have done."

"And now I will go back to the house, if you please," said Eleanor. "I can find my way by myself, Mr. Stanhope. After what has passed," she added, "I would rather go alone."

"But I must find the carriage for you, Mrs. Bold, and I must tell my father that you will return with him alone, and I must make some excuse to him for not going with you, and I must bid the servant put you down at your own house, for I suppose you will not now choose to see them again in the close."

There was a truth about this, and a perspicuity in making arrangements for lessening her immediate embarrassment, which had some effect in softening Eleanor's anger. So she suffered herself to walk by his side over the now deserted lawn till they came to the drawing-room window. There was something about Bertie Stanhope which gave him, in the estimation of everyone, a different standing from that which any other man would occupy under similar circumstances. Angry as Eleanor was, and great as was her cause for anger, she was not half as angry with him as she would have been with anyone else. He was apparently so simple, so good-natured, so unaffected and easy to talk to, that she had already half-forgiven him before he was at the drawing-room window.

When they arrived there, Dr. Stanhope was sitting nearly alone with Mr. and Miss Thorne. One or two other unfortunates were there who from one cause or another were still delayed in getting away, but they were every moment getting fewer in number.

As soon as he had handed Eleanor over to his father, Bertie started off to the front gate in search of the carriage, and there waited leaning patiently against the front wall, and comfortably smoking a cigar, till it came up. When he returned to the room Dr. Stanhope and Eleanor were alone with their hosts.

"At last, Miss Thorne," said he cheerily, "I have come to relieve you. Mrs. Bold and my father are the last roses of the very delightful summer you have given us, and desirable as Mrs. Bold's society always is, now at least you must be glad to see the last flowers plucked from the tree."

Miss Thorne declared that she was delighted to have Mrs. Bold and Dr. Stanhope still with her, and Mr. Thorne would have said the same had he not been checked by a yawn which he could not suppress.

"Father, will you give your arm to Mrs. Bold?" said Bertie. And so the last adieus were made, and the prebendary led out Mrs. Bold, followed by his son.

"I shall be home soon after you," said he as the two got into the carriage
"Are you not coming in the carriage?" said the father.

"No, no, I have someone to see on the road, and shall walk. John, mind
you drive to Mrs. Bold's house first."

CHAPTER XL

MR. AND MRS. QUIVERFUL ARE MADE HAPPY. MR. SLOPE
IS ENCOURAGED BY THE PRESS

BEFORE she started for Ullathorne, Mrs. Proudie, careful soul, caused two
letters to be written, one by herself and one by her lord, to the inhabitants
of Puddingdale vicarage, which made happy the hearth of those within it.

As soon as the departure of the horses left the Bishop's stable groom free
for other services, that humble denizen of the diocese started on the Bishop's
own pony with the two dispatches. That from the Bishop was simply a
request that Mr. Quiverful would wait upon his lordship the next morning
at 11 A.M., and that from the lady was as simply a request that Mrs. Quiverful would do the same by her, though it was couched in somewhat longer
and more grandiloquent phraseology.

It had become a point of conscience with Mrs. Proudie to urge the settlement of this great hospital question. She was resolved that Mr. Quiverful
should have it. She was resolved that there should be no more doubt or
delay, no more refusals and resignations, no more secret negotiations carried
on by Mr. Slope on his own account in opposition to her behests.

"Bishop," she said immediately after breakfast on the morning of that
eventful day, "have you signed the appointment yet?"

"No, my dear, not yet. It is not exactly signed as yet."

"Then do it," said the lady.

The Bishop did it, and a very pleasant day indeed he spent at Ullathorne.

Much perturbation and flutter, high expectation and renewed hopes,
were occasioned at Puddingdale by the receipt of these episcopal dispatches.
Mrs. Quiverful, whose careful ear caught the sound of the pony's feet as
he trotted up to the vicarage kitchen door, brought them in hurriedly to her
husband. She was at the moment concocting the Irish stew destined to satisfy
the noonday wants of fourteen young birds, let alone the parent couple.
She had taken the letters from the man's hands between the folds of her
capacious apron, so as to save them from the contamination of the stew, and
in this guise she brought them to her husband's desk.

They at once divided the spoil, each taking that addressed to the other.
"Quiverful," said she with impressive voice, "you are to be at the palace
at eleven tomorrow."

"And so are you, my dear," said he, almost gasping with the importance of the tidings. And then they exchanged letters.

"She'd never have sent for me again," said the lady, "if it wasn't all right."

"Oh, my dear, don't be too certain!" said the gentleman. "Only think if it should be wrong."

"She'd never have sent for me, Q, if it wasn't all right," again argued the lady. "She's stiff and hard and proud as piecrust, but I think she's right at bottom." Such was Mrs. Quiverful's verdict about Mrs. Proudie, to which in aftertimes she always adhered. People when they get their income doubled usually think that those through whose instrumentality this little ceremony is performed are right at bottom.

"Oh, Letty!" said Mr. Quiverful, rising from his wellworn seat.

"Oh, Q!" said Mrs. Quiverful. And then the two, unmindful of the kitchen apron, the greasy fingers, and the adherent Irish stew, threw themselves warmly into each other's arms.

"For heaven's sake don't let anyone cajole you out of it again," said the wife.

"Let me alone for that," said the husband with a look of almost fierce determination, pressing his fist as he spoke rigidly on his desk as though he had Mr. Slope's head below his knuckles, and meant to keep it there.

"I wonder how soon it will be," said she.

"I wonder whether it will be at all," said he, still doubtful.

"Well, I won't say too much," said the lady. "The cup has slipped twice before, and it may fall altogether this time, but I'll not believe it. He'll give you the appointment tomorrow. You'll find he will."

"Heaven send he may," said Mr. Quiverful, solemnly. And who that considers the weight of the burden on this man's back will say that the prayer was an improper one? There were fourteen of them—fourteen of them living, as Mrs. Quiverful had so powerfully urged in the presence of the Bishop's wife. As long as promotion cometh from any human source, whether north or south, east or west, will not such a claim as this hold good, in spite of all our examination tests, *detur dignioris,* and optimist tendencies? It is fervently to be hoped that it may. Till we can become divine we must be content to be human, lest in our hurry for a change we sink to something lower.

And then the pair, sitting down lovingly together, talked over all their difficulties, as they so often did, and all their hopes, as they so seldom were enabled to do.

And the last in all Barchester to mar their hopes, had he heard and seen all that passed at Puddingdale that day, would have been Mr. Harding. What wants had he to set in opposition to those of such a regiment of young ravens? There are fourteen of them living! With him at any rate, let us say that that argument would have been sufficient for the appointment of Mr. Quiverful.

In the morning, Q and his wife kept their appointments with that punctuality which bespeaks an expectant mind. The friendly farmer's gig was borrowed, and in that they went, discussing many things by the way. They had instructed the household to expect them back by one, and injunctions were given to the eldest pledge to have ready by that accustomed hour the remainder of the huge stew which the provident mother had prepared on the previous day. The hands of the kitchen clock came round to two, three, four, before the farmer's gig wheels were again heard at the vicarage gate. With what palpitating hearts were the returning wanderers greeted!

"I suppose, children, you all thought we were never coming back any more?" said the mother as she slowly let down her solid foot till it rested on the step of the gig. "Well, such a day as we've had!" And then, leaning heavily on a big boy's shoulder, she stepped once more on terra firma.

There was no need for more than the tone of her voice to tell them that all was right. The Irish stew might burn itself to cinders now.

Then there was such kissing and hugging, such crying and laughing. Mr. Quiverful could not sit still at all, but kept walking from room to room, then out into the garden, then down the avenue into the road, and then back again to his wife. She, however, lost no time so idly.

"We must go to work at once, girls, and that in earnest. Mrs. Proudie expects us to be in the hospital house on the fifteenth of October."

Had Mrs. Proudie expressed a wish that they should all be there on the next morning, the girls would have had nothing to say against it.

"And when will the pay begin?" asked the eldest boy.

"Today, my dear," said the gratified mother.

"Oh—that is jolly," said the boy.

The Quiverfuls had hardly left the palace, and Mrs. Proudie was still holding forth on the matter to her husband, when another visitor was announced in the person of Dr. Gwynne. The Master of Lazarus had asked for the Bishop, and not for Mrs. Proudie, and therefore when he was shown into the study he was surprised rather than rejoiced to find the lady there.

But we must go back a little—and it shall be but a little—for a difficulty begins to make itself manifest in the necessity of disposing of all our friends in the small remainder of this one volume.

Going home in the carriage that evening from Ullathorne, Dr. Gwynne had not without difficulty brought round his friend the Archdeacon to a line of tactics much less bellicose than that which his own taste would have preferred. "It will be unseemly in us to show ourselves in a bad humor. And moreover we have no power in this matter, and it will therefore be bad policy to act as though we had." 'Twas thus the Master of Lazarus argued. "If," he continued, "the Bishop be determined to appoint another to the hospital, threats will not prevent him, and threats should not be lightly used by an archdeacon to his bishop. If he will place a stranger in the hospital, we can only leave him to the indignation of others. It is probable that such a step may not eventually injure your father-in-law. I will see the Bishop, if you will allow me—alone." At this the Archdeacon winced visibly. "Yes, alone, for so I shall be calmer. And then I shall at any rate learn what he does mean to do in the matter."

The Archdeacon puffed and blew, put up the carriage window and then put it down again, argued the matter up to his own gate, and at last gave way. Everybody was against him, his own wife, Mr. Harding, and Dr. Gwynne.

"Pray keep him out of hot water, Dr. Gwynne," Mrs. Grantly had said to her guest. "My dearest madam, I'll do my best," the courteous Master had replied. 'Twas thus he did it, and earned for himself the gratitude of Mrs. Grantly.

And now we may return to the Bishop's study.

Dr. Gwynne had certainly not foreseen the difficulty which here presented itself. He—together with all the clerical world of England—had heard it rumored about that Mrs. Proudie did not confine herself to her wardrobes, stillrooms, and laundries, but yet it had never occurred to him that if he called on a bishop at one o'clock in the day, he could by any possibility find him closeted with his wife. Or that if he did so, the wife would remain longer than necessary to make her curtsy. It appeared, however, as though in the present case Mrs. Proudie had no idea of retreating.

The Bishop had been very much pleased with Dr. Gwynne on the preceding day, and of course thought that Dr. Gwynne had been as much pleased with him. He attributed the visit solely to compliment, and thought it an extremely gracious and proper thing for the Master of Lazarus to drive over from Plumstead specially to call at the palace so soon after his arrival in the county. The fact that they were not on the same side either in politics or doctrines made the compliment the greater. The Bishop, therefore, was all smiles. And Mrs. Proudie, who liked people with good handles to their names, was also very well disposed to welcome the Master of Lazarus.

"We had a charming party at Ullathorne, Master, had we not?" said she. "I hope Mrs. Grantly got home without fatigue."

Dr. Gwynne said that they had all been a little tired, but were none the worse this morning.

"An excellent person, Miss Thorne," suggested the Bishop.

"And an exemplary Christian, I am told," said Mrs. Proudie.

Dr. Gwynne declared that he was very glad to hear it.

"I have not seen her Sabbath-day schools yet," continued the lady, "but I shall make a point of doing so before long."

Dr. Gwynne merely bowed at this intimation. He had heard something of Mrs. Proudie and her Sunday schools, both from Dr. Grantly and Mr. Harding.

"By the by, Master," continued the lady, "I wonder whether Mrs. Grantly would like me to drive over and inspect her Sabbath-day school. I hear that it is most excellently kept."

Dr. Gwynne really could not say. He had no doubt Mrs. Grantly would be most happy to see Mrs. Proudie any day Mrs. Proudie would do her the honor of calling—that was, of course, if Mrs. Grantly should happen to be at home.

A slight cloud darkened the lady's brow. She saw that her offer was not taken in good part. This generation of unregenerated vipers was still perverse, stiff-necked, and hardened in their iniquity. "The Archdeacon, I know," said she, "sets his face against these institutions."

At this Dr. Gwynne laughed slightly. It was but a smile. Had he given his cap for it he could not have helped it.

Mrs. Proudie frowned again. " 'Suffer little children, and forbid them not,' " said she. "Are we not to remember that, Dr. Gwynne? 'Take heed that ye despise not one of these little ones.' Are we not to remember that, Dr. Gwynne?" And at each of these questions she raised at him her menacing forefinger.

"Certainly, madam, certainly," said the Master, "and so does the Archdeacon, I am sure, on weekdays as well as on Sundays."

"On weekdays you can't take heed not to despise them," said Mrs. Proudie, "because then they are out in the fields. On weekdays they belong to their parents, but on Sundays they ought to belong to the clergyman." And the finger was again raised.

The Master began to understand and to share the intense disgust which the Archdeacon always expressed when Mrs. Proudie's name was mentioned. What was he to do with such a woman as this? To take his hat and go would have been his natural resource, but then he did not wish to be foiled in his object.

"My lord," said he, "I wanted to ask you a question on business, if you could spare me one moment's leisure. I know I must apologize for so disturbing you, but in truth I will not detain you five minutes."

"Certainly, Master, certainly," said the Bishop. "My time is quite yours—pray make no apology, pray make no apology."

"You have a great deal to do just at the present moment, Bishop. Do not forget how extremely busy you are at present," said Mrs. Proudie, whose spirit was now up, for she was angry with her visitor.

"I will not delay his lordship much above a minute," said the Master of Lazarus, rising from his chair and expecting that Mrs. Proudie would now go, or else that the Bishop would lead the way into another room.

But neither event seemed likely to occur, and Dr. Gwynne stood for a moment silent in the middle of the room.

"Perhaps it's about Hiram's Hospital?" suggested Mrs. Proudie.

Dr. Gwynne, lost in astonishment, and not knowing what else on earth to do, confessed that his business with the Bishop was connected with Hiram's Hospital.

"His lordship has finally conferred the appointment on Mr. Quiverful this morning," said the lady.

Dr. Gwynne made a simple reference to the Bishop, and finding that the lady's statement was formally confirmed, he took his leave. "That comes of the Reform Bill," he said to himself as he walked down the Bishop's avenue.

CHAPTER XLI

MRS. BOLD AT HOME

Poor Mrs. Bold, when she got home from Ullathorne on the evening of Miss Thorne's party, was very unhappy, and moreover very tired. Nothing fatigues the body so much as weariness of spirit, and Eleanor's spirit was indeed weary.

Dr. Stanhope had civilly but not very cordially asked her in to tea, and her manner of refusal convinced the worthy Doctor that he need not repeat the invitation. He had not exactly made himself a party to the intrigue which was to convert the late Mr. Bold's patrimony into an income for his hopeful son, but he had been well aware what was going on. And he was well aware also when he perceived that Bertie declined accompanying them home in the carriage that the affair had gone off.

Eleanor was very much afraid that Charlotte would have darted out upon her as the prebendary got out at his own door, but Bertie had thoughtfully saved her from this by causing the carriage to go round by her own house. This also Dr. Stanhope understood, and allowed to pass by without remark.

When she got home, she found Mary Bold in the drawing-room with the child in her lap. She rushed forward and, throwing herself on her knees, kissed the little fellow till she almost frightened him.

"Oh, Mary, I am so glad you did not go. It was an odious party."

Now the question of Mary's going had been one greatly mooted between them. Mrs. Bold, when invited, had been the guest of the Grantlys, and Miss Thorne, who had chiefly known Eleanor at the hospital or at Plumstead rectory, had forgotten all about Mary Bold. Her sister-in-law had implored her to go under her wing, and had offered to write to Miss Thorne, or to call on her. But Miss Bold had declined. In fact, Mr. Bold had not been very popular with such people as the Thornes, and his sister would not go among them unless she were specially asked to do so.

"Well, then," said Mary cheerfully, "I have the less to regret."

"You have nothing to regret, but oh! Mary, I have—so much—so much."
—And then she began kissing her boy, whom her caresses had roused from his slumbers. When she raised her head, Mary saw that the tears were running down her cheeks.

"Good heavens, Eleanor, what is the matter?—What has happened to you?—Eleanor—dearest Eleanor—what is the matter?" And Mary got up with the boy still in her arms.

"Give him to me—give him to me," said the young mother. "Give him to me, Mary." And she almost tore the child out of her sister's arms. The poor little fellow murmured somewhat at the disturbance, but nevertheless nestled himself close into his mother's bosom.

"Here, Mary, take the cloak from me. My own, own darling, darling, darling jewel. You are not false to me. Everybody else is false, everybody else is cruel. Mamma will care for nobody, nobody, nobody, but her own, own own little man." And she again kissed and pressed the baby, and cried till the tears ran down over the child's face.

"Who has been cruel to you, Eleanor?" said Mary. "I hope I have not."

Now in this matter Eleanor had great cause for mental uneasiness. She could not certainly accuse her loving sister-in-law of cruelty, but she had to do that which was more galling—she had to accuse herself of imprudence against which her sister-in-law had warned her. Miss Bold had never encouraged Eleanor's acquaintance with Mr. Slope, and she had positively discouraged the friendship of the Stanhopes as far as her usual gentle mode of speaking had permitted. Eleanor had only laughed at her, however, when she said that she disapproved of married women who lived apart from their husbands, and suggested that Charlotte Stanhope never went to church. Now, however, Eleanor must either hold her tongue, which was quite impossible, or confess herself to have been utterly wrong, which was nearly equally so. So she staved off the evil day by more tears, and consoled herself by inducing little Johnny to rouse himself sufficiently to return her caresses.

"He is a darling—as true as gold. What would Mamma do without him? Mamma would lie down and die if she had not her own Johnny Bold to give her comfort." This and much more she said of the same kind, and for a time made no other answer to Mary's inquiries.

This kind of consolation from the world's deceit is very common. Mothers obtain it from their children, and men from their dogs. Some men even do so from their walking sticks, which is just as rational. How is it that we can take joy to ourselves in that we are not deceived by those who have not attained the art to deceive us? In a true man, if such can be found, or a true woman, much consolation may indeed be taken.

In the caresses of her child, however, Eleanor did receive consolation, and may ill befall the man who would begrudge it to her. The evil day, however, was only postponed. She had to tell her disagreeable tale to Mary, and she had also to tell it to her father. Must it not, indeed, be told to the whole circle of her acquaintance before she could be made to stand all right with them? At the present moment there was no one to whom she could turn for comfort. She hated Mr. Slope. That was a matter of course, in that feeling she reveled. She hated and despised the Stanhopes, but that feeling distressed her greatly. She had, as it were, separated herself from her old friends to throw herself into the arms of this family, and then how had they intended to use her? She could hardly reconcile herself to her own father, who had believed ill of her. Mary Bold had turned mentor.

That she could have forgiven had the mentor turned out to be in the wrong, but mentors in the right are not to be pardoned. She could not but hate the Archdeacon, and now she hated him worse than ever, for she must in some sort humble herself before him. She hated her sister, for she was part and parcel of the Archdeacon. And she would have hated Mr. Arabin if she could. He had pretended to regard her, and yet before her face he had hung over that Italian woman as though there had been no beauty in the world but hers—no other woman worth a moment's attention. And Mr. Arabin would have to learn all this about Mr. Slope! She told herself that she hated him, and she knew that she was lying to herself as she did so. She had no consolation but her baby, and of that she made the most. Mary, though she could not surmise what it was that had so violently affected her sister-in-law, saw at once that her grief was too great to be kept under control, and waited patiently till the child should be in his cradle.

"You'll have some tea, Eleanor," she said.

"Oh, I don't care," said she, though in fact she must have been very hungry, for she had eaten nothing at Ullathorne.

Mary quietly made the tea and buttered the bread, laid aside the cloak, and made things look comfortable.

"He's fast asleep," said she. "You're very tired. Let me take him up to bed."

But Eleanor would not let her sister touch him. She looked wistfully at her baby's eyes, saw that they were lost in the deepest slumber, and then made a sort of couch for him on the sofa. She was determined that nothing should prevail upon her to let him out of her sight that night.

"Come, Nelly," said Mary, "don't be cross with me. I at least have done nothing to offend you."

"I ain't cross," said Eleanor.

"Are you angry, then? Surely you can't be angry with me."

"No, I ain't angry, at least not with you."

"If you are not, drink the tea I have made for you. I am sure you must want it."

Eleanor did drink it, and allowed herself to be persuaded. She ate and drank, and as the inner woman was recruited she felt a little more charitable toward the world at large. At last she found words to begin her story, and before she went to bed she had made a clean breast of it and told everything—everything, that is, as to the lovers she had rejected. Of Mr. Arabin she said not a word.

"I know I was wrong," said she, speaking of the blow she had given to Mr. Slope, "but I didn't know what he might do, and I had to protect myself."

"He richly deserved it," said Mary.

"Deserved it!" said Eleanor, whose mind as regarded Mr. Slope was almost bloodthirsty. "Had I stabbed him with a dagger, he would have deserved it. But what will they say about it at Plumstead?"

"I don't think I should tell them," said Mary. Eleanor began to think she would not.

On the next day she did not go out of the house. Barchester she thought would be crowded with Stanhopes and Slopes, perhaps also with Arabins and Grantlys. Indeed there was hardly anyone among her friends whom she could have met without some cause of uneasiness. In the course of the afternoon she heard that the Dean was dead, and she also heard that Mr. Quiverful had been finally appointed to the hospital.

In the evening her father came to her, and then the story, or as much of it as she could bring herself to tell him, had to be repeated. He was not in truth much surprised at Mr. Slope's effrontery, but he was obliged to act as though he had been, to save his daughter's feelings. He was, however, anything but skillful in his deceit, and she saw through it.

"I see," said she, "that you think it only in the common course of things that Mr. Slope should have treated me in this way." She had said nothing to him about the embrace, nor yet of the way in which it had been met.

"I do not think it at all strange," said he, "that anyone should admire my Eleanor."

"It is strange to me," said she, "that any man should have so much audacity without ever having received the slightest encouragement."

To this Mr. Harding answered nothing. With the Archdeacon it would have been the text for a rejoinder which would not have disgraced Bildad the Shuhite.

"But you'll tell the Archdeacon?" asked Mr. Harding.

"Tell him what?" said she sharply.

"Or Susan?" continued Mr. Harding. "You'll tell Susan. You'll let them know that they wronged you in supposing that this man's addresses would be agreeable to you."

"They may find that out their own way," said she. "I shall not ever willingly mention Mr. Slope's name to either of them."

"But I may."

"I have no right to hinder you from doing anything that may be necessary to your own comfort, but pray do not do it for my sake. Dr. Grantly never thought well of me, and never will. I don't know now that I am even anxious that he should do so."

And then they went to the affair of the hospital. "But is it true, Papa?"

"What, my dear?" said he. "About the Dean? Yes, I fear quite true. Indeed I know there is no doubt about it."

"Poor Miss Trefoil. I am so sorry for her. But I did not mean that," said Eleanor. "But about the hospital, Papa?"

"Yes, my dear. I believe it is true that Mr. Quiverful is to have it."

"Oh, what a shame!"

"No, my dear, not at all, not at all a shame. I am sure I hope it will suit him."

"But, Papa, you know it is a shame. After all your hopes, all your expectations to get back to your old house, to see it given away in this way to a perfect stranger!"

"My dear, the Bishop had a right to give it to whom he pleased."

"I deny that, Papa. He had no such right. It is not as though you were a candidate for a new piece of preferment. If the Bishop has a grain of justice——"

"The Bishop offered it to me on his terms, and as I did not like the terms, I refused it. After that I cannot complain."

"Terms! He had no right to make terms."

"I don't know about that, but it seems he had the power. But to tell you the truth, Nelly, I am as well satisfied as it is. When the affair became the subject of angry discussion I thoroughly wished to be rid of it altogether."

"But you did want to go back to the old house, Papa. You told me so yourself."

"Yes, my dear, I did. For a short time I did wish it. And I was foolish in doing so. I am getting old now, and my chief worldly wish is for peace and rest. Had I gone back to the hospital, I should have had endless contentions with the Bishop, contentions with his chaplain, and contentions with the Archdeacon. I am not up to this now, I am not able to meet such troubles, and therefore I am not ill-pleased to find myself left to the little Church of St. Cuthbert's. I shall never starve," added he, laughing, "as long as you are here."

"But will you come and live with me, Papa?" she said earnestly, taking him by both his hands. "If you will do that, if you will promise that, I will own that you are right."

"I will dine with you today, at any rate."

"No, but live here altogether. Give up that close, odious little room in High Street."

"My dear, it's a very nice little room, and you are really quite uncivil."

"Oh, Papa, don't joke. It's not a nice place for you. You say you are growing old, though I am sure you are not."

"Am not I, my dear?"

"No, Papa, not old—not to say old. But you are quite old enough to feel the want of a decent room to sit in. You know how lonely Mary and I are here. You know nobody ever sleeps in the big front bedroom. It is really unkind of you to remain up there alone when you are so much wanted here."

"Thank you, Nelly—thank you. But, my dear——"

"If you had been living here, Papa, with us, as I really think you ought to have done, considering how lonely we are, there would have been none of all this dreadful affair about Mr. Slope."

Mr. Harding, however, did not allow himself to be talked over into giving up his own and only little pied-à-terre in the High Street. He promised to come and dine with his daughter, and stay with her, and visit her, and do everything but absolutely live with her. It did not suit the peculiar feelings of the man to tell his daughter that though she had rejected Mr. Slope, and been ready to reject Mr. Stanhope, some other more favored suitor would probably soon appear, and that on the appearance of such a suitor the big front bedroom might perhaps be more frequently in requisition than at present. But doubtless such an idea crossed his mind and added its weight to the other reasons which made him decide on still keeping the close, odious little room in High Street.

The evening passed over quietly and in comfort. Eleanor was always happier with her father than with anyone else. He had not, perhaps, any natural taste for baby worship, but he was always ready to sacrifice himself and therefore made an excellent third in a trio with his daughter and Mary Bold in singing the praises of the wonderful child.

They were standing together over their music in the evening, the baby having again been put to bed upon the sofa, when the servant brought in a very small note in a beautiful pink envelope. It quite filled the room with perfume as it lay upon the small salver. Mary Bold and Mrs. Bold were both at the piano, and Mr. Harding was sitting close to them with the violoncello between his legs, so that the elegancy of the epistle was visible to them all.

"Please, ma'am, Dr. Stanhope's coachman says he is to wait for an answer," said the servant.

Eleanor got very red in the face as she took the note in her hand. She had never seen the writing before. Charlotte's epistles, to which she was well accustomed, were of a very different style and kind. She generally wrote on large note paper, she twisted up her letters into the shape and sometimes into the size of cocked hats, she addressed them in a sprawling manly hand, and not unusually added a blot or a smudge, as though such were her own peculiar sign manual. The address of this note was written in a beautiful female hand, and the gummed wafer bore on it an impress of a gilt coronet. Though Eleanor had never seen such a one before, she guessed that it came from the Signora. Such epistles were very numerously sent out from any house in which the Signora might happen to be dwelling, but they were rarely addressed to ladies. When the coachman was told by the lady's maid to take the letter to Mrs. Bold, he openly expressed his opinion that there was some mistake about it. Whereupon the lady's maid boxed the coachman's ears. Had Mr. Slope seen in how meek a spirit the coachman took the rebuke, he might have learnt a useful lesson, both in philosophy and religion.

The note was as follows:

MY DEAR MRS. BOLD, May I ask you, as a great favor, to call on me tomorrow? You can say what hour will best suit you, but quite early, if you can. I need hardly say that if I could call upon you I should not take this liberty with you.

I partly know what occurred the other day, and I promise you that you shall meet with no annoyance if you will come to me. My brother leaves us for London today, from thence he goes to Italy.

It will probably occur to you that I should not thus intrude on you unless I had that to say to you which may be of considerable moment. Pray therefore excuse me, even if you do not grant my request.

And believe me,
Very sincerely yours,
M. VESEY NERONI

Thursday Evening

The three of them sat in consultation on this epistle for some ten or fifteen minutes, and then decided that Eleanor should write a line saying that she would see the Signora the next morning at twelve o'clock.

CHAPTER XLII

THE STANHOPES AT HOME

WE must now return to the Stanhopes, and see how they behaved themselves on their return from Ullathorne.

Charlotte, who came back in the first homeward journey with her sister, waited in palpitating expectation till the carriage drove up to the door a second time. She did not run down or stand at the window, or show in any outward manner that she looked for anything wonderful to occur. But when she heard the carriage wheels, she stood up with erect ears, listening for Eleanor's footfall on the pavement or the cheery sound of Bertie's voice welcoming her in. Had she heard either, she would have felt that all was right, but neither sound was there for her to hear. She heard only her father's slow step as he ponderously let himself down from the carriage and slowly walked along the hall till he got into his own private room on the ground floor. "Send Miss Stanhope to me," he said to the servant.

"There's something wrong now," said Madeline, who was lying on her sofa in the back drawing-room.

"It's all up with Bertie," replied Charlotte. "I know, I know," she said to the servant, as he brought up the message. "Tell my father I will be with him immediately."

"Bertie's wooing has gone astray," said Madeline. "I knew it would."

"It has been his own fault, then. She was ready enough, I am quite sure," said Charlotte, with that sort of ill nature which is not uncommon when one woman speaks of another.

"What will you say to him now?" By "him" the Signora meant their father.

"That will be as I find him. He was ready to pay two hundred pounds for Bertie, to stave off the worst of his creditors, if this marriage had gone on. Bertie must now have the money instead, and go and take his chance."

"Where is he now?"

"Heaven knows! Smoking in the bottom of Mr. Thorne's haha, or philandering with some of those Miss Chadwicks. Nothing will ever make an impression on him. But he'll be furious if I don't go down."

"No, nothing ever will. But don't be long, Charlotte, for I want my tea."

And so Charlotte went down to her father. There was a very black cloud on the old man's brow, blacker than his daughter could ever yet remember to have seen there. He was sitting in his own armchair, not comfortably over the fire in the middle of the room, waiting till she should come and listen to him.

"What has become of your brother?" he said as soon as the door was shut.

"I should rather ask you," said Charlotte. "I left you both at Ullathorne when I came away. What have you done with Mrs. Bold?"

"Mrs. Bold! Nonsense. The woman has gone home as she ought to do. And heartily glad I am that she should not be sacrificed to so heartless a reprobate."

"Oh, Papa!"

"A heartless reprobate! Tell me now where he is, and what he is going to do. I have allowed myself to be fooled between you. Marriage, indeed! Who on earth that has money, or credit, or respect in the world to lose would marry him?"

"It is no use your scolding me, Papa. I have done the best I could for him and you."

"And Madeline is nearly as bad," said the prebendary, who was in truth very, very angry.

"Oh, I suppose we are all bad," replied Charlotte.

The old man emitted a huge leonine sigh. If they were all bad, who had made them so? If they were unprincipled, selfish, and disreputable, who was to be blamed for the education which had had so injurious an effect?

"I know you'll ruin me among you," said he.

"Why, Papa, what nonsense that is. You are living within your income this minute, and if there are any new debts, I don't know of them. I am sure there ought to be none, for we are dull enough here."

"Are those bills of Madeline's paid?"

"No, they are not. Who was to pay them?"

"Her husband may pay them."

"Her husband! Would you wish me to tell her you say so? Do you wish to turn her out of your house?"

"I wish she would know how to behave herself."

"Why, what on earth has she done now? Poor Madeline! Today is only the second time she has gone out since we came to this vile town."

He then sat silent for a time, thinking in what shape he would declare his resolve. "Well, Papa," said Charlotte, "shall I stay here, or may I go upstairs and give Mamma her tea?"

"You are in your brother's confidence. Tell me what he is going to do."

"Nothing, that I am aware of."

"Nothing—nothing! Nothing but eat and drink, and spend every shilling of my money he can lay his hands upon. I have made up my mind, Charlotte. He shall eat and drink no more in this house."

"Very well. Then I suppose he must go back to Italy."

"He may go where he pleases."

"That's easily said, Papa, but what does it mean? You can't let him——"

"It means this," said the Doctor, speaking more loudly than was his wont, and with wrath flashing from his eyes, "that as sure as God rules in Heaven I will not maintain him any longer in idleness."

"Oh, ruling in Heaven!" said Charlotte. "It is no use talking about that. You must rule him here on earth, and the question is how you can do it. You can't turn him out of the house penniless, to beg about the street."

"He may beg where he likes."

"He must go back to Carrara. That is the cheapest place he can live at, and nobody there will give him credit for above two or three hundred pauls. But you must let him have the means of going."

"As sure as——"

"Oh, Papa, don't swear. You know you must do it. You were ready to pay two hundred pounds for him if this marriage came off. Half that will start him to Carrara."

"What? Give him a hundred pounds!"

"You know we are all in the dark, Papa," she said, thinking it expedient to change the conversation. "For anything we know, he may be at this moment engaged to Mrs. Bold."

"Fiddlestick," said the father, who had seen the way in which Mrs. Bold had got into the carriage while his son stood apart without even offering her his hand.

"Well, then, he must go to Carrara," said Charlotte.

Just at this moment the lock of the front door was heard, and Charlotte's quick ears detected her brother's catlike step in the hall. She said nothing, feeling that for the present Bertie had better keep out of her father's way. But Dr. Stanhope also heard the sound of the lock.

"Who's that?" he demanded. Charlotte made no reply, and he asked again: "Who is that that has just come in? Open the door. Who is it?"

"I suppose it is Bertie."

"Bid him come here," said the father. But Bertie, who was close to the door and heard the call, required no further bidding, but walked in with a perfectly unconcerned and cheerful air. It was this peculiar insouciance which angered Dr. Stanhope even more than his son's extravagance.

"Well, sir?" said the Doctor.

"And how did you get home, sir, with your fair companion?" said Bertie. "I suppose she is not upstairs, Charlotte?"

"Bertie," said Charlotte, "Papa is in no humor for joking. He is very angry with you."

"Angry!" said Bertie, raising his eyebrows as though he had never yet given his parent cause for a single moment's uneasiness.

"Sit down, if you please, sir," said Dr. Stanhope very sternly, but not now very loudly. "And I'll trouble you to sit down too, Charlotte. Your mother can wait for her tea a few minutes."

Charlotte sat down on the chair nearest to the door, in somewhat of a perverse sort of manner, as much as though she would say—Well, here I am. You shan't say I don't do what I am bid, but I'll be whipped if I give way to you. And she was determined not to give way. She too was angry with Bertie, but she was not the less ready on that account to defend him from his father. Bertie also sat down. He drew his chair close to the library table, upon which he put his elbow, and then, resting his face comfortably on one hand, he began drawing little pictures on a sheet of paper with the other. Before the scene was over he had completed admirable figures of Miss Thorne, Mrs. Proudie, and Lady De Courcy, and begun a family piece to comprise the whole set of the Lookalofts.

"Would it suit you, sir," said the father, "to give me some idea as to what your present intentions are—what way of living you propose to yourself?"

"I'll do anything you can suggest, sir," replied Bertie.

"No, I shall suggest nothing further. My time for suggesting has gone by. I have only one order to give, and that is that you leave my house."

"Tonight?" said Bertie, and the simple tone of the question left the Doctor without any adequately dignified method of reply.

"Papa does not quite mean tonight," said Charlotte. "At least I suppose not."

"Tomorrow, perhaps," suggested Bertie.

"Yes, sir, tomorrow," said the Doctor. "You shall leave this tomorrow."

"Very well, sir. Will the 4.30 P.M. train be soon enough?" And Bertie, as he asked, put the finishing touch to Miss Thorne's high-heeled boots.

"You may go how and when and where you please, so that you leave my house tomorrow. You have disgraced me, sir, you have disgraced yourself, and me, and your sisters."

"I am glad at least, sir, that I have not disgraced my mother," said Bertie.

Charlotte could hardly keep her countenance, but the Doctor's brow grew still blacker than ever. Bertie was executing his chef d'œuvre in the delineation of Mrs. Proudie's nose and mouth.

"You are a heartless reprobate, sir, a heartless, thankless, good-for-nothing reprobate. I have done with you. You are my son—that I cannot help—but you shall have no more part or parcel in me as my child, nor I in you as your father."

"Oh, Papa, Papa, you must not, shall not, say so!" said Charlotte.

"I will say so, and do say so," said the father, rising from his chair. "And now leave the room, sir."

"Stop, stop," said Charlotte. "Why don't you speak, Bertie? Why don't you look up and speak? It is your manner that makes Papa so angry."

"He is perfectly indifferent to all decency, to all propriety," said the Doctor. And then he shouted out: "Leave the room, sir! Do you hear what I say?"

"Papa, Papa, I will not let you part so. I know you will be sorry for it." And then she added, getting up and whispering into his ear: "Is he only to blame? Think of that. We have made our own bed, and such as it is we must lie on it. It is no use for us to quarrel among ourselves." And as she finished her whisper Bertie finished off the Countess's bustle, which was so well done that it absolutely seemed to be swaying to and fro on the paper with its usual lateral motion.

"My father is angry at the present time," said Bertie, looking up for a moment from his sketches, "because I am not going to marry Mrs. Bold. What can I say on the matter? It is true that I am not going to marry her. In the first place——"

"That is not true, sir," said Dr. Stanhope, "but I will not argue with you."

"You were angry just this moment because I would not speak," said Bertie, going on with a young Lookaloft.

"Give over drawing," said Charlotte, going up to him and taking the paper from under his hand. The caricatures, however, she preserved, and showed them afterward to the friends of the Thornes, the Proudies, and De Courcys. Bertie, deprived of his occupation, threw himself back in his chair and waited further orders.

"I think it will certainly be for the best that Bertie should leave this at once, perhaps tomorrow," said Charlotte, "but pray, Papa, let us arrange some scheme together."

"If he will leave this tomorrow, I will give him ten pounds and he shall be paid five pounds a month by the banker at Carrara as long as he stays permanently in that place."

"Well, sir, it won't be long," said Bertie, "for I shall be starved to death in about three months."

"He must have marble to work with," said Charlotte.

"I have plenty there in the studio to last me three months," said Bertie. "It will be no use attempting anything large in so limited a time—unless I do my own tombstone."

Terms, however, were ultimately come to somewhat more liberal than those proposed, and the Doctor was induced to shake hands with his son, and bid him good night. Dr. Stanhope would not go up to tea, but had it brought to him in his study by his daughter.

But Bertie went upstairs and spent a pleasant evening. He finished the Lookalofts, greatly to the delight of his sisters, though the manner of portraying their décolleté dresses was not the most refined. Finding how matters were going, he by degrees allowed it to escape from him that he had not pressed his suit upon the widow in a very urgent way.

"I suppose, in point of fact, you never proposed at all?" said Charlotte.

"Oh, she understood that she might have me if she wished," said he.

"And she didn't wish," said the Signora.

"You have thrown me over in the most shameful manner," said Charlotte. "I suppose you told her all about my little plan?"

"Well, it came out somehow, at least the most of it."

"There's an end of that alliance," said Charlotte, "but it doesn't matter much. I suppose we shall all be back at Como soon."

"I am sure I hope so," said the Signora. "I'm sick of the sight of black coats. If that Mr. Slope comes here any more he'll be the death of me."

"You've been the ruin of him, I think," said Charlotte.

"And as for a second black-coated lover of mine, I am going to make a present of him to another lady with most singular disinterestedness."

The next day, true to his promise, Bertie packed up and went off by the 4.30 P.M. train, with £20 in his pocket, bound for the marble quarries of Carrara. And so he disappears from our scene.

At twelve o'clock on the day following that on which Bertie went, Mrs. Bold, true also to her word, knocked at Dr. Stanhope's door with a timid hand and a palpitating heart. She was at once shown up to the back drawing-room, the folding doors of which were closed, so that in visiting the Signora Eleanor was not necessarily thrown into any communion with those in the front room. As she went up the stairs she saw none of the family, and was so far saved much of the annoyance which she had dreaded.

"This is very kind of you, Mrs. Bold, very kind after what has happened," said the lady on the sofa with her sweetest smile.

"You wrote in such a strain that I could not but come to you."

"I did, I did. I wanted to force you to see me."

"Well, Signora, I am here."

"How cold you are to me! But I suppose I must put up with that. I know you think you have reason to be displeased with us all. Poor Bertie! If you knew all, you would not be angry with him."

"I am not angry with your brother—not in the least. But I hope you did not send for me here to talk about him."

"If you are angry with Charlotte, that is worse, for you have no warmer friend in all Barchester. But I did *not* send for you to talk about this.— Pray bring your chair nearer, Mrs. Bold, so that I may look at you. It is so unnatural to see you keeping so far off from me."

Eleanor did as she was bid, and brought her chair close to the sofa.

"And now, Mrs. Bold, I am going to tell you something which you may perhaps think indelicate, but yet I know that I am right in doing so."

Hereupon Mrs. Bold said nothing, but felt inclined to shake in her chair. The Signora, she knew, was not very particular, and that which to her appeared to be indelicate might to Mrs. Bold appear to be extremely indecent.

"I believe you know Mr. Arabin?"

Mrs. Bold would have given the world not to blush, but her blood was not at her own command. She did blush up to her forehead, and the Signora, who had made her sit in a special light in order that she might watch her, saw that she did so.

"Yes—I am acquainted with him. That is, slightly. He is an intimate friend of Dr. Grantly, and Dr. Grantly is my brother-in-law."

"Well, if you know Mr. Arabin, I am sure you must like him. I know and like him much. Everybody that knows him must like him."

Mrs. Bold felt it quite impossible to say anything in reply to this. Her blood was rushing about her body she knew not how or why. She felt as though she were swinging in her chair, and she knew that she was not only red in the face but also almost suffocated with heat. However, she sat still and said nothing.

"How stiff you are with me, Mrs. Bold," said the Signora. "And I the while am doing for you all that one woman can do to serve another."

A kind of thought came over the widow's mind that perhaps the Signora's friendship was real, and that at any rate it could not hurt her. And another kind of thought, a glimmering of a thought, came to her also— that Mr. Arabin was too precious to be lost. She despised the Signora, but might she not stoop to conquer? It should be but the smallest fraction of a stoop!

"I don't want to be stiff," she said, "but your questions are so very singular."

"Well, then, I will ask you one more singular still," said Madeline Neroni, raising herself on her elbow and turning her own face full upon her companion's. "Do you love him, love him with all your heart and soul, with all the love your bosom can feel? For I can tell you that he loves you, adores you, worships you, thinks of you and nothing else, is now thinking of you as he attempts to write his sermon for next Sunday's preaching. What would I not give to be loved in such a way by such a man—that is, if I were an object fit for any man to love!"

Mrs. Bold got up from her seat and stood speechless before the woman who was now addressing her in this impassioned way. When the Signora thus alluded to herself, the widow's heart was softened, and she put her own hand, as though caressingly, on that of her companion which was resting on the table. The Signora grasped it and went on speaking.

"What I tell you is God's own truth, and it is for you to use it as may be best for your own happiness. But you must not betray me. He knows nothing of this. He knows nothing of my knowing his inmost heart. He is simple as a child in these matters. He told me his secret in a thousand ways because he could not dissemble, but he does not dream that he has told it. You know it now, and I advise you to use it."

Eleanor returned the pressure of the other's hand with an infinitesimal soupçon of a squeeze.

"And remember," continued the Signora, "he is not like other men. You must not expect him to come to you with vows and oaths and pretty presents, to kneel at your feet and kiss your shoestrings. If you want that, there are plenty to do it, but he won't be one of them." Eleanor's bosom nearly burst with a sigh, but Madeline, not heeding her, went on. "With him, yea will stand for yea and nay for nay. Though his heart should break for it, the woman who shall reject him once will have rejected him once and for all. Remember that. And now, Mrs. Bold, I will not keep you, for you are fluttered. I partly guess what use you will make of what I have said to you. If ever you are a happy wife in that man's house, we shall be far away, but I shall expect you to write me one line to say that you have forgiven the sins of the family."

Eleanor half-whispered that she would, and then, without uttering another word, crept out of the room and down the stairs, opened the front door for herself without hearing or seeing anyone, and found herself in the close.

It would be difficult to analyze Eleanor's feelings as she walked home. She was nearly stupefied by the things that had been said to her. She felt sore that her heart should have been so searched and riddled by a comparative stranger, by a woman whom she had never liked and never could like. She was mortified that the man whom she owned to herself that she loved should have concealed his love from her and shown it to another. There was much to vex her proud spirit. But there was nevertheless an understratum of joy in all this which buoyed her up wondrously. She tried if she could disbelieve what Madame Neroni had said to her, but she found that she could not. It was true, it must be true. She could not, would not, did not doubt it.

On one point she fully resolved to follow the advice given her. If it should ever please Mr. Arabin to put such a question to her as that suggested, her yea should be yea. Would not all her miseries be at an end if she could talk of them to him openly, with her head resting on his shoulder?

CHAPTER XLIII

MR. SLOPE'S PARTING INTERVIEW WITH THE SIGNORA

On the following day the Signora was in her pride. She was dressed in her brightest of morning dresses, and had quite a levee round her couch. It was a beautifully bright October afternoon. All the gentlemen of the neighborhood were in Barchester, and those who had the entry of Dr.

Stanhope's house were in the Signora's back drawing-room. Charlotte and Mrs. Stanhope were in the front room, and such of the lady's squires as could not for the moment get near the center of attraction had to waste their fragrance on the mother and sister.

The first who came and the last to leave was Mr. Arabin. This was the second visit he had paid to Madame Neroni since he had met her at Ullathorne. He came he knew not why, to talk about he knew not what. But in truth the feelings which now troubled him were new to him, and he could not analyze them. It may seem strange that he should thus come dangling about Madame Neroni because he was in love with Mrs. Bold, but it was nevertheless the fact, and though he could not understand why he did so, Madame Neroni understood it well enough.

She had been gentle and kind to him, and had encouraged his staying. Therefore he stayed on. She pressed his hand when he first greeted her, she made him remain near her and whispered to him little nothings. And then her eye, brilliant and bright, now mirthful, now melancholy, and invincible in either way! What man with warm feelings, blood unchilled, and a heart not guarded by a triple steel of experience could have withstood those eyes! The lady, it is true, intended to do him no mortal injury. She merely chose to inhale a slight breath of incense before she handed the casket over to another. Whether Mrs. Bold would willingly have spared even so much is another question.

And then came Mr. Slope. All the world now knew that Mr. Slope was a candidate for the deanery, and that he was generally considered to be the favorite. Mr. Slope therefore walked rather largely upon the earth. He gave to himself a portly air, such as might become a dean, spoke but little to other clergymen, and shunned the Bishop as much as possible.

Mr. Slope, great as he was with embryo grandeur, still came to see the Signora. Indeed, he could not keep himself away. He dreamed of that soft hand which he had kissed so often, and of that imperial brow which his lips had once pressed, and he then dreamed also of further favors.

And Mr. Thorne was there also. It was the first visit he had ever paid to the Signora, and he made it not without due preparation. Mr. Thorne was a gentleman usually precise in his dress, and prone to make the most of himself in an unpretending way. The gray hairs in his whiskers were eliminated perhaps once a month, those on his head were softened by a mixture which we will not call a dye—it was only a wash. His tailor lived in St. James's Street, and his bootmaker at the corner of that street and Piccadilly. He was particular in the article of gloves, and the getting-up of his shirts was a matter not lightly thought of in the Ullathorne laundry. On the occasion of the present visit he had rather overdone his usual efforts, and caused some little uneasiness to his sister, who had not hitherto received very cordially the proposition for a lengthened visit from the Signora at Ullathorne.

There were others also there—young men about the city who had not much to do and who were induced by the lady's charms to neglect that little. But all gave way to Mr. Thorne, who was somewhat of a grand seigneur, as a country gentleman always is in a provincial city.

"Oh, Mr. Thorne, this is so kind of you!" said the Signora. "You promised to come, but I really did not expect it. I thought you country gentlemen never kept your pledges."

"Oh yes, sometimes," said Mr. Thorne, looking rather sheepish, and making his salutations a little too much in the style of the last century.

"You deceive none but your consti—stit—stit—what do you call the people that carry you about in chairs and pelt you with eggs and apples when they make you a Member of Parliament?"

"One another also, sometimes, Signora," said Mr. Slope, with a deanish sort of smirk on his face. "Country gentlemen do deceive one another sometimes, don't they, Mr. Thorne?"

Mr. Thorne gave him a look which undeaned him completely for the moment, but he soon remembered his high hopes and, recovering himself quickly, sustained his probable coming dignity by a laugh at Mr. Thorne's expense.

"I never deceive a lady, at any rate," said Mr. Thorne, "especially when the gratification of my own wishes is so strong an inducement to keep me true, as it now is." *

Mr. Thorne went on thus awhile with antediluvian grimaces and compliments which he had picked up from Sir Charles Grandison, and the Signora at every grimace and at every bow smiled a little smile and bowed a little bow. Mr. Thorne, however, was kept standing at the foot of the couch, for the new Dean sat in the seat of honor near the table. Mr. Arabin the while was standing with his back to the fire, his coattails under his arms, gazing at her with all his eyes—not quite in vain, for every now and again a glance came up at him, bright as a meteor out of Heaven.

"Oh, Mr. Thorne, you promised to let me introduce my little girl to you. Can you spare a moment—will you see her now?"

Mr. Thorne assured her that he could, and would see the young lady with the greatest pleasure in life. "Mr. Slope, might I trouble you to ring the bell?" said she. And when Mr. Slope got up she looked at Mr. Thorne and pointed to the chair. Mr. Thorne, however, was much too slow to understand her, and Mr. Slope would have recovered his seat had not the Signora, who never chose to be unsuccessful, somewhat summarily ordered him out of it.

"Oh, Mr. Slope, I must ask you to let Mr. Thorne sit here just for a moment or two. I am sure you will pardon me. We can take a liberty with you this week. Next week, you know, when you move into the Dean's house, we shall all be afraid of you."

Mr. Slope, with an air of much indifference, rose from his seat and, walking into the next room, became greatly interested in Mrs. Stanhope's worsted work.

And then the child was brought in. She was a little girl about eight years of age, like her mother only that her enormous eyes were black, and her hair quite jet. Her complexion, too, was very dark, and bespoke her foreign blood. She was dressed in the most outlandish and extravagant way in which clothes could be put on a child's back. She had great bracelets on her naked little arms, a crimson fillet braided with gold round her head, and scarlet shoes with high heels. Her dress was all flounces, and stuck out from her as though the object were to make it lie off horizontally from her little hips. It did not nearly cover her knees, but this was atoned for by a loose pair of drawers, which seemed made throughout of lace, then she had on pink-silk stockings. It was thus that the last of the Neros was habitually dressed at the hour when visitors were wont to call.

"Julia, my love," said the mother—Julia was ever a favorite name with the ladies of that family. "Julia, my love, come here. I was telling you about the beautiful party poor Mamma went to. This is Mr. Thorne. Will you give him a kiss, dearest?"

Julia put up her face to be kissed, as she did to all her mother's visitors, and then Mr. Thorne found that he had got her and, which was more terrific to him, all her finery, into his arms. The lace and starch crumpled against his waistcoat and trousers, the greasy black curls hung upon his cheek, and one of the bracelet clasps scratched his ear. He did not at all know how to hold so magnificent a lady, nor holding her what to do with her. However, he had on other occasions been compelled to fondle little nieces and nephews, and now set about the task in the mode he always had used.

"Diddle, diddle, diddle, diddle," said he, putting the child on one knee and working away with it as though he were turning a knife-grinder's wheel with his foot.

"Mamma, Mamma," said Julia, crossly, "I don't want to be diddle-diddled. Let me go, you naughty old man you."

Poor Mr. Thorne put the child down quietly on the ground and drew back his chair. Mr. Slope, who had returned to the polestar that attracted him, laughed aloud, Mr. Arabin winced and shut his eyes, and the Signora pretended not to hear her daughter.

"Go to Aunt Charlotte, lovy," said the Mamma, "and ask her if it is not time for you to go out."

But little Miss Julia, though she had not exactly liked the nature of Mr. Thorne's attention, was accustomed to be played with by gentlemen, and did not relish the idea of being sent so soon to her aunt.

"Julia, go when I tell you, my dear." But Julia still went pouting about the room. "Charlotte, do come and take her," said the Signora. "She must go out, and the days get so short now." And thus ended the interview between Mr. Thorne and the last of the Neros.

Mr. Thorne recovered from the child's crossness sooner than from Mr. Slope's laughter. He could put up with being called an old man by an infant, but he did not like to be laughed at by the Bishop's chaplain, even though that chaplain was about to become a dean. He said nothing, but he showed plainly enough that he was angry.

The Signora was ready enough to avenge him. "Mr. Slope," said she, "I hear that you are triumphing on all sides."

"How so?" said he, smiling. He did not dislike being talked to about the deanery, though of course he strongly denied the imputation.

"You carry the day both in love and war." Mr. Slope hereupon did not look quite so satisfied as he had done.

"Mr. Arabin," continued the Signora, "don't you think Mr. Slope is a very lucky man?"

"Not more so than he deserves, I am sure," said Mr. Arabin.

"Only think, Mr. Thorne, he is to be our new dean. Of course we all know that."

"Indeed, Signora," said Mr. Slope, "we all know nothing about it. I can assure you I myself——"

"He *is* to be the new dean—there is no manner of doubt of it, Mr. Thorne."

"Hum!" said Mr. Thorne.

"Passing over the heads of old men like my father and Archdeacon Grantly——"

"Oh—oh!" said Mr. Slope.

"The Archdeacon would not accept it," said Mr. Arabin, whereupon Mr. Slope smiled abominably, and said as plainly as a look could speak that the grapes were sour.

"Going over all our heads," continued the Signora, "for of course I consider myself one of the Chapter."

"If I am ever dean," said Mr. Slope—"that is, were I ever to become so, I should glory in such a canoness."

"Oh, Mr. Slope, stop, I haven't half done. There is another canoness for you to glory in. Mr. Slope is not only to have the deanery, but a wife to put in it."

Mr. Slope again looked disconcerted.

"A wife with a large fortune, too. It never rains but it pours, does it, Mr. Thorne?"

"No, never," said Mr. Thorne, who did not quite relish talking about Mr. Slope and his affairs.

"When will it be, Mr. Slope?"

"When will what be?" said he.

"Oh, we know when the affair of the dean will be—a week will settle that! The new hat, I have no doubt, has been already ordered. But when will the marriage come off?"

"Do you mean mine or Mr. Arabin's?" said he, striving to be facetious.

"Well, just then I meant yours, though perhaps after all Mr. Arabin's may be first. But we know nothing of him. He is too close for any of us.

Now all is open and aboveboard with you, which, by the by, Mr. Arabin, I beg to tell you I like much the best. He who runs can read that Mr. Slope is a favored lover. Come, Mr. Slope, when is the widow to be made Mrs. Dean?"

To Mr. Arabin this badinage was peculiarly painful, and yet he could not tear himself away and leave it. He believed, still believed with that sort of belief which the fear of the thing engenders, that Mrs. Bold would probably become the wife of Mr. Slope. Of Mr. Slope's little adventure in the garden he knew nothing. For aught he knew, Mr. Slope might have had an adventure of quite a different character. He might have thrown himself at the widow's feet, been accepted, and then returned to town a jolly thriving wooer. The Signora's jokes were bitter enough to Mr. Slope, but they were quite as bitter to Mr. Arabin. He still stood leaning against the fireplace, fumbling with his hands in his trousers pockets.

"Come, come, Mr. Slope, don't be so bashful," continued the Signora. "We all know that you proposed to the lady the other day at Ullathorne. Tell us with what words she accepted you. Was it with a simple 'yes,' or with two 'no, no's,' which make an affirmative? Or did silence give consent? Or did she speak out with that spirit which so well becomes a widow, and say openly, 'By my troth, sir, you shall make me Mrs. Slope as soon as it is your pleasure to do so'?"

Mr. Slope had seldom in his life felt himself less at his ease. There sat Mr. Thorne laughing silently. There stood his old antagonist Mr. Arabin gazing at him with all his eyes. There round the door between the two rooms were clustered a little group of people, including Miss Stanhope and the Reverend Messrs. Gray and Green, all listening to his discomfiture. He knew that it depended solely on his own wit whether or no he could throw the joke back upon the lady. He knew that it stood him to do so if he possibly could, but he had not a word. " 'Tis conscience that makes cowards of us all." He felt on his cheek the sharp points of Eleanor's fingers, and did not know who might have seen the blow, who might have told the tale to this pestilent woman who took such delight in jeering him. He stood there, therefore, red as a carbuncle and mute as a fish, grinning just sufficiently to show his teeth, an object of pity.

But the Signora had no pity, she knew nothing of mercy. Her present object was to put Mr. Slope down, and she was determined to do it thoroughly now that she had him in her power.

"What, Mr. Slope, no answer? Why, it can't possibly be that the woman has been fool enough to refuse you? She can't surely be looking out after a bishop. But I see how it is, Mr. Slope. Widows are proverbially cautious. You should have let her alone till the new hat was on your head, till you could show her the key of the deanery."

"Signora," said he at last, trying to speak in a tone of dignified reproach, "you really permit yourself to talk on solemn subjects in a very improper way."

"Solemn subjects—what solemn subject? Surely a dean's hat is not such a solemn subject."

"I have no aspirations such as those you impute to me. Perhaps you will drop the subject."

"Oh, certainly, Mr. Slope, but one word first. Go to her again with the Prime Minister's letter in your pocket. I'll wager my shawl to your shovel she does not refuse you then."

"I must say, Signora, that I think you are speaking of the lady in a very unjustifiable manner."

"And one other piece of advice, Mr. Slope, I'll only offer you one other." And then she commenced singing:

> "It's gude to be merry and wise, Mr. Slope,
> It's gude to be honest and true.
> It's gude to be off with the old love—Mr. Slope,
> Before you are on with the new.—

"Ha, ha, ha!"

And the Signora, throwing herself back on her sofa, laughed merrily. She little recked how those who heard her would, in their own imaginations, fill up the little history of Mr. Slope's first love. She little cared that some among them might attribute to her the honor of his earlier admiration. She was tired of Mr. Slope and wanted to get rid of him. She had ground for anger with him, and she chose to be revenged.

How Mr. Slope got out of that room he never himself knew. He did succeed ultimately, and probably with some assistance, in getting his hat and escaping into the air. At last his love for the Signora was cured. Whenever he again thought of her in his dreams, it was not as of an angel with azure wings. He connected her rather with fire and brimstone, and though he could still believe her to be a spirit, he banished her entirely out of Heaven, and found a place for her among the infernal gods. When he weighed in the balance, as he not seldom did, the two women to whom he had attached himself in Barchester, the pre-eminent place in his soul's hatred was usually allotted to the Signora.

CHAPTER XLIV

THE DEAN ELECT

During the entire next week Barchester was ignorant who was to be its new dean. On Sunday morning Mr. Slope was decidedly the favorite, but he did not show himself in the cathedral, and then he sank a point or two in the betting. On Monday he got a scolding from the Bishop in the hearing of the servants, and down he went till nobody would have him at any price. But on Tuesday he received a letter in an official cover marked "Private," by which he fully recovered his place in the public favor. On Wednesday he was said to be ill, and that did not look well, but on Thursday morning he went down to the railway station, with a very jaunty air, and when it was ascertained that he had taken a first-class ticket for London, there was no longer any room for doubt on the matter.

While matters were in this state of ferment at Barchester, there was not much mental comfort at Plumstead. Our friend the Archdeacon had many grounds for inward grief. He was much displeased at the result of Dr. Gwynne's diplomatic mission to the palace, and did not even scruple to say to his wife that had he gone himself, he would have managed the affair much better. His wife did not agree with him, but that did not mend the matter.

Mr. Quiverful's appointment to the hospital was, however, a fait accompli, and Mr. Harding's acquiescence in that appointment was not less so. Nothing would induce Mr. Harding to make a public appeal against the Bishop, and the Master of Lazarus quite approved of his not doing so.

"I don't know what has come to the Master," said the Archdeacon over and over again. "He used to be ready enough to stand up for his order."

"My dear Archdeacon," Mrs. Grantly would say in reply, "what is the use of always fighting? I really think the Master is right." The Master, however, had taken steps of his own of which neither the Archdeacon nor his wife knew anything.

Then Mr. Slope's successes were henbane to Dr. Grantly, and Mrs. Bold's improprieties were as bad. What would be all the world to Archdeacon Grantly if Mr. Slope should become Dean of Barchester and marry his wife's sister! He talked of it and talked of it till he was nearly ill. Mrs. Grantly almost wished that the marriage was done and over, so that she might hear no more about it.

And there was yet another ground of misery which cut him to the quick, nearly as closely as either of the others. That paragon of a clergyman whom he had bestowed upon St. Ewold's, that college friend of whom he had boasted so loudly, that ecclesiastical knight before whose lance Mr. Slope was to fall and bite the dust, that worthy bulwark of the Church as it should be, that honored representative of Oxford's best spirit, was—so at least his wife had told him half a dozen times—misconducting himself!

Nothing had been seen of Mr. Arabin at Plumstead for the last week, but a good deal had, unfortunately, been heard of him. As soon as Mrs. Grantly had found herself alone with the Archdeacon on the evening of the Ullathorne party, she had expressed herself very forcibly as to Mr. Arabin's conduct on that occasion. He had, she declared, looked and acted and talked very unlike a decent parish clergyman. At first the Archdeacon had laughed at this, and assured her that she need not trouble herself, that

Mr. Arabin would be found to be quite safe. But by degrees he began to find that his wife's eyes had been sharper than his own. Other people coupled the Signora's name with that of Mr. Arabin. The meager little prebendary who lived in the close told him to a nicety how often Mr. Arabin had visited at Dr. Stanhope's, and how long he had remained on the occasion of each visit. He had asked after Mr. Arabin at the cathedral library, and an officious little Vicar Choral had offered to go and see whether he could be found at Dr. Stanhope's. Rumor, when she has contrived to sound the first note on her trumpet, soon makes a loud peal audible enough. It was too clear that Mr. Arabin had succumbed to the Italian woman, and that the Archdeacon's credit would suffer fearfully if something were not done to rescue the brand from the burning. Besides, to give the Archdeacon his due, he was really attached to Mr. Arabin, and grieved greatly at his backsliding.

They were sitting talking over their sorrows in the drawing-room before dinner on the day after Mr. Slope's departure for London, and on this occasion Mrs. Grantly spoke out her mind freely. She had opinions of her own about parish clergymen, and now thought it right to give vent to them.

"If you would have been led by me, Archdeacon, you would never have put a bachelor into St. Ewold's."

"But, my dear, you don't mean to say that all bachelor clergymen misbehave themselves."

"I don't know that clergymen are so much better than other men," said Mrs. Grantly. "It's all very well with a curate whom you have under your own eye, and whom you can get rid of if he persists in improprieties."

"But Mr. Arabin was a fellow, and couldn't have had a wife."

"Then I would have found someone who could."

"But, my dear, are fellows never to get livings?"

"Yes, to be sure they are—when they get engaged. I never would put a young man into a living unless he were married, or engaged to be married. Now here is Mr. Arabin. The whole responsibility lies upon you."

"There is not at this moment a clergyman in all Oxford more respected for morals and conduct than Arabin."

"Oh, Oxford!" said the lady, with a sneer. "What men choose to do at Oxford nobody ever hears of. A man may do very well at Oxford who would bring disgrace on a parish, and to tell you the truth, it seems to me that Mr. Arabin is just such a man."

The Archdeacon groaned deeply, but he had no further answer to make.

"You really must speak to him, Archdeacon. Only think what the Thornes will say if they hear that their parish clergyman spends his whole time philandering with this woman."

The Archdeacon groaned again. He was a courageous man, and knew well enough how to rebuke the younger clergymen of the diocese when necessary. But there was that about Mr. Arabin which made the Doctor feel that it would be very difficult to rebuke him with good effect.

"You can advise him to find a wife for himself, and he will understand well enough what that means," said Mrs. Grantly.

The Archdeacon had nothing for it but groaning. There was Mr. Slope—he was going to be made dean, he was going to take a wife, he was about to achieve respectability and wealth, an excellent family mansion, and a family carriage. He would soon be among the comfortable elite of the ecclesiastical world of Barchester, whereas his own protégé, the true scion of the true Church, by whom he had sworn, would be still but a poor vicar, and that with a very indifferent character for moral conduct! It might be all very well recommending Mr. Arabin to marry, but how would Mr. Arabin when married support a wife?

Things were ordering themselves thus in Plumstead drawing-room when Dr. and Mrs. Grantly were disturbed in their sweet discourse by the quick rattle of a carriage and pair of horses on the gravel sweep. The sound was not that of visitors whose private carriages are generally brought up to country-house doors with demure propriety, but betokened rather the advent of some person or persons who were in a hurry to reach the house, and had no intention of immediately leaving it. Guests invited to stay a week, and who were conscious of arriving after the first dinner bell, would probably approach in such a manner. So might arrive an attorney with the news of a grand-uncle's death, or a son from college with all the fresh honors of a double first. No one would have had himself driven up to the door of a country house in such a manner who had the slightest doubt of his own right to force an entry.

"Who is it?" said Mrs. Grantly, looking at her husband.

"Who on earth can it be?" said the Archdeacon to his wife. He then quietly got up and stood with the drawing-room door open in his hand. "Why, it's your father!"

It was indeed Mr. Harding, and Mr. Harding alone. He had come by himself in a post chaise with a couple of horses from Barchester, arriving almost after dark, and evidently full of news. His visits had usually been made in the quietest manner. He had rarely presumed to come without notice, and had always been driven up in a modest old green fly, with one horse, that hardly made itself heard as it crawled up to the hall door.

"Good gracious, Warden, is it you?" said the Archdeacon, forgetting in his surprise the events of the last few years. "But come in. Nothing the matter, I hope."

"We are very glad you are come, Papa," said his daughter. "I'll go and get your room ready at once."

"I ain't Warden, Archdeacon," said Mr. Harding. "Mr. Quiverful is Warden."

"Oh, I know, I know," said the Archdeacon, petulantly. "I forgot all about it at the moment. Is anything the matter?"

"Don't go this moment, Susan," said Mr. Harding. "I have something to tell you."

"The dinner bell will ring in five minutes," said she.

"Will it?" said Mr. Harding. "Then perhaps I had better wait." He was big with news which he had come to tell, but which he knew could not be told without much discussion. He had hurried away to Plumstead as fast as two horses could bring him, and now, finding himself there, he was willing to accept the reprieve which dinner would give him.

"If you have anything of moment to tell us," said the Archdeacon, "pray let us hear it at once. Has Eleanor gone off?"

"No, she has not," said Mr. Harding, with a look of great displeasure.

"Has Slope been made dean?"

"No, he has not, but——"

"But what?" said the Archdeacon, who was becoming very impatient.

"They have——"

"They have what?" said the Archdeacon.

"They have offered it to me," said Mr. Harding, with a modesty which almost prevented his speaking.

"Good heavens!" said the Archdeacon, and sank back exhausted in an easy chair.

"My dear, dear father," said Mrs. Grantly, and threw her arms round her father's neck.

"So I thought I had better come out and consult with you at once," said Mr. Harding.

"Consult?" shouted the Archdeacon. "But, my dear Harding, I congratulate you with my whole heart—with my whole heart, I do indeed. I never heard anything in my life that gave me so much pleasure." And he got hold of both his father-in-law's hands and shook them as though he were going to shake them off, and walked round and round the room, twirling a copy of the *Jupiter* over his head to show his extreme exultation.

"But——" began Mr. Harding.

"But me no buts," said the Archdeacon. "I never was so happy in my life. It was just the proper thing to do. Upon my honor I'll never say another word against Lord —— the longest day I have to live."

"That's Dr. Gwynne's doing, you may be sure," said Mrs. Grantly, who greatly liked the Master of Lazarus, he being an orderly married man with a large family.

"I suppose it is," said the Archdeacon.

"Oh, Papa, I am so truly delighted!" said Mrs. Grantly, getting up and kissing her father.

"But, my dear——" said Mr. Harding. It was all in vain that he strove to speak, nobody would listen to him.

"Well, Mr. Dean," said the Archdeacon, triumphing, "the deanery gardens will be some consolation for the hospital elms. Well, poor Quiverful! I won't begrudge him his good fortune any longer."

"No, indeed," said Mrs. Grantly. "Poor woman, she has fourteen children. I am sure I am very glad they have got it."

"So am I," said Mr. Harding.

"I would give twenty pounds," said the Archdeacon, "to see how Mr. Slope will look when he hears it." The idea of Mr. Slope's discomfiture formed no small part of the Archdeacon's pleasure.

At last Mr. Harding was allowed to go upstairs and wash his hands, having, in fact, said very little of all that he had come out to Plumstead on purpose to say. Nor could anything more be said till the servants were gone after dinner. The joy of Dr. Grantly was so uncontrollable that he could not refrain from calling his father-in-law Mr. Dean before the men, and therefore it was soon matter of discussion in the lower regions how Mr. Harding, instead of his daughter's future husband, was to be the new dean, and various were the opinions on the matter. The cook and butler, who were advanced in years, thought that it was just as it should be, but the footman and lady's maid, who were younger, thought it was a great shame that Mr. Slope should lose his chance.

"He's a mean chap all the same," said the footman, "and it ain't along of him that I says so. But I always did admire the missus's sister, and she'd well become the situation."

While these were the ideas downstairs, a very great difference of opinion existed above. As soon as the cloth was drawn and the wine on the table, Mr. Harding made for himself an opportunity of speaking. It was, however, with much inward troubling that he said:

"It's very kind of Lord ——, very kind, and I feel it deeply, most deeply. I am, I must confess, gratified by the offer——"

"I should think so," said the Archdeacon.

"But, all the same, I am afraid that I can't accept it."

The decanter almost fell from the Archdeacon's hand upon the table, and the start he made was so great as to make his wife jump up from her chair. Not accept the deanship! If it really ended in this, there would be no longer any doubt that his father-in-law was demented. The question now was whether a clergyman with low rank, and preferment amounting to less than £200 a year, should accept high rank, £1200 a year, and one of the most desirable positions which his profession had to afford!

"What!" said the Archdeacon, gasping for breath and staring at his guest as though the violence of his emotion had almost thrown him into a fit. "What!"

"I do not find myself fit for new duties," urged Mr. Harding.

"New duties! What duties?" said the Archdeacon, with unintended sarcasm.

"Oh, Papa," said Mrs. Grantly, "nothing can be easier than what a dean has to do. Surely you are more active than Dr. Trefoil."

"He won't have half as much to do as he has at present," said Dr. Grantly. "Did you see what the *Jupiter* said the other day about young men?"

"Yes, and I saw that the *Jupiter* said all that it could to induce the appointment of Mr. Slope. Perhaps you would wish to see Mr. Slope made dean."

Mr. Harding made no reply to this rebuke, though he felt it strongly. He had not come over to Plumstead to have further contention with his son-in-law about Mr. Slope, so he allowed it to pass by.

"I know I cannot make you understand my feeling," he said, "for we have been cast in different molds. I may wish that I had your spirit and energy and power of combating, but I have not. Every day that is added to my life increases my wish for peace and rest."

"And where on earth can a man have peace and rest if not in a deanery?" said the Archdeacon.

"People will say that I am too old for it."

"Good heavens! People! What people? What need you care for any people?"

"But I think myself I am too old for any new place."

"Dear Papa," said Mrs. Grantly, "men ten years older than you are appointed to new situations day after day."

"My dear," said he, "it is impossible that I should make you understand my feelings, nor do I pretend to any great virtue in the matter. The truth is, I want the force of character which might enable me to stand against the spirit of the times. The call on all sides now is for young men, and I have not the nerve to put myself in opposition to the demand. Were the *Jupiter*, when it hears of my appointment, to write article after article setting forth my incompetency, I am sure it would cost me my reason. I ought to be able to bear with such things, you will say. Well, my dear, I own that I ought. But I feel my weakness, and I know that I can't. And, to tell you the truth, I know no more than a child what the dean has to do."

"Pshaw!" exclaimed the Archdeacon.

"Don't be angry with me, Archdeacon. Don't let us quarrel about it, Susan. If you knew how keenly I feel the necessity of having to disoblige you in this matter, you would not be angry with me."

This was a dreadful blow to Dr. Grantly. Nothing could possibly have suited him better than having Mr. Harding in the deanery. Though he had never looked down on Mr. Harding on account of his recent poverty, he did fully recognize the satisfaction of having those belonging to him in comfortable positions. It would be much more suitable that Mr. Harding should be Dean of Barchester than Vicar of St. Cuthbert's and Precentor to boot. And then the great discomfiture of that archenemy of all that was respectable in Barchester, of that new Low Church clerical parvenu that had fallen amongst them—that alone would be worth more, almost, than the situation itself. It was frightful to think that such unhoped-for good fortune should be marred by the absurd crotchets and unwholesome hallucinations by which Mr. Harding allowed himself to be led astray. To have the cup so near his lips and then to lose the drinking of it was more than Dr. Grantly could endure.

And yet it appeared as though he would have to endure it. In vain he threatened and in vain he coaxed. Mr. Harding did not indeed speak with perfect decision of refusing the proffered glory, but he would not speak with anything like decision of accepting it. When pressed again and again, he would again and again allege that he was wholly unfitted to new duties. It was in vain that the Archdeacon tried to insinuate, though he could not plainly declare, that there were no new duties to perform. It was in vain he hinted that in all cases of difficulty he, he the Archdeacon, was willing and able to guide a weak-minded dean. Mr. Harding seemed to have a foolish idea not only that there were new duties to do, but that no one should accept the place who was not himself prepared to do them.

The conference ended in an understanding that Mr. Harding should at once acknowledge the letter he had received from the Minister's private secretary, and should beg that he might be allowed two days to make up his mind, and that during those two days the matter should be considered.

On the following morning the Archdeacon was to drive Mr. Harding back to Barchester.

CHAPTER XLV

MISS THORNE SHOWS HER TALENT AT MATCHMAKING

ON Mr. Harding's return to Barchester from Plumstead, which was effected by him in due course in company with the Archdeacon, more tidings of a surprising nature met him. He was during the journey subjected to such a weight of unanswerable argument, all of which went to prove that it was his bounden duty not to interfere with the paternal Government that was so anxious to make him a dean, that when he arrived at the chemist's door in High Street, he hardly knew which way to turn himself in the matter. But, perplexed as he was, he was doomed to further perplexity. He found a note there from his daughter begging him most urgently to come to her immediately. But we must again go back a little in our story.

Miss Thorne had not been slow to hear the rumors respecting Mr. Arabin which had so much disturbed the happiness of Mrs. Grantly. And she also was unhappy to think that her parish clergyman should be accused of worshiping a strange goddess. She also was of opinion that rectors and vicars should all be married, and with that good-natured energy which was characteristic of her, she put her wits to work to find a fitting match for Mr. Arabin. Mrs. Grantly, in this difficulty, could think of no better remedy than a lecture from the Archdeacon. Miss Thorne thought that a young lady, marriageable and with a dowry, might be of more efficacy. In looking through the catalogue of her unmarried friends who might possibly be in want of a husband, and might also be fit for such promotion as a country parsonage affords, she could think of no one more eligible than Mrs. Bold. Consequently, losing no time, she went into Barchester on the day of Mr. Slope's discomfiture, the same day that her brother had had his interesting interview with the last of the Neros, and invited Mrs. Bold to bring her nurse and baby to Ullathorne and make them a protracted visit.

Miss Thorne suggested a month or two, intending to use her influence afterward in prolonging it so as to last out the winter, in order that Mr. Arabin might have an opportunity of becoming fairly intimate with his intended bride. "We'll have Mr. Arabin too," said Miss Thorne to herself, "and before the spring they'll know each other, and in twelve or eighteen months' time, if all goes well, Mrs. Bold will be domiciled at St. Ewold's." And then the kindhearted lady gave herself some not undeserved praise for her matchmaking genius.

Eleanor was taken a little by surprise, but the matter ended in her promising to go to Ullathorne for at any rate a week or two, and on the day previous to that on which her father drove out to Plumstead she had had herself driven out to Ullathorne.

Miss Thorne would not perplex her with her embryo lord on that same evening, thinking that she would allow her a few hours to make herself at home. But on the following morning Mr. Arabin arrived. "And now," said Miss Thorne to herself, "I must contrive to throw them in each other's way." That same day, after dinner Eleanor, with an assumed air of dignity which she could not maintain, with tears that she could not suppress, with a flutter which she could not conquer and a joy which she could not hide, told Miss Thorne that she was engaged to marry Mr. Arabin, and that it behooved her to get back home to Barchester as quick as she could.

To say simply that Miss Thorne was rejoiced at the success of the scheme would give a very faint idea of her feelings on the occasion. My readers may probably have dreamt before now that they have had before them some terribly long walk to accomplish, some journey of twenty or thirty miles, an amount of labor frightful to anticipate, and that immediately on starting they have ingeniously found some accommodating short cut which has brought them without fatigue to their work's end in five minutes. Miss Thorne's waking feelings were somewhat of the same nature.

It cannot be denied that when Eleanor accepted Miss Thorne's invitation, she remembered that Ullathorne was in the parish of St. Ewold's. Since her interview with the Signora she had done little else than think about Mr. Arabin, and the appeal that had been made to her. She could not bring herself to believe or try to bring herself to believe that what she had been told was untrue. Think of it how she would, she could not but accept it as a fact that Mr. Arabin was fond of her. And then when she went further, and asked herself the question, she could not but accept it as a fact also that she was fond of him. If it were destined for her to be the partner of his hopes and sorrows, to whom could she look for friendship so properly as to Miss Thorne? This invitation was like an ordained step toward the fulfillment of her destiny, and when she also heard that Mr. Arabin was expected to be at Ullathorne on the following day, it seemed as though all the world were conspiring in her favor. Well, did she not deserve it? In that affair of Mr. Slope, had not all the world conspired against her?

She could not, however, make herself easy and at home. When in the evening after dinner Miss Thorne expatiated on the excellence of Mr. Arabin's qualities, and hinted that any little rumor which might be ill-naturedly spread abroad concerning him really meant nothing, Mrs. Bold found herself unable to answer. When Miss Thorne went a little further and declared that she did not know a prettier vicarage house in the county than St. Ewold's, Mrs. Bold still held her tongue, though her ears tingled with the conviction that all the world knew that she was in love with Mr. Arabin. Well, what would that matter if they could only meet and tell each other what each now longed to tell?

And they did meet. Mr. Arabin came early in the day, and found the two ladies together at work in the drawing-room. Miss Thorne, who had she known all the truth would have vanished into air at once, had no conception that her immediate absence would be a blessing, and remained chatting with them till luncheon time. Mr. Arabin could talk about nothing but the Signora Neroni's beauty, would discuss no people but the Stanhopes. This was very distressing to Eleanor, and not very satisfactory to Miss Thorne. But yet there was evidence of innocence in his open avowal of admiration.

And then they had lunch, and then Mr. Arabin went out on parish duty, and Eleanor and Miss Thorne were left to take a walk together.

"Do you think the Signora Neroni is so lovely as people say?" Eleanor asked as they were coming home.

"She is very beautiful certainly, very beautiful," Miss Thorne answered, "but I do not know that anyone considers her lovely. She is a woman all men would like to look at, but few I imagine would be glad to take her to their hearths, even were she unmarried and not afflicted as she is."

There was some little comfort in this. Eleanor made the most of it till she got back to the house. She was then left alone in the drawing-room, and just as it was getting dark Mr. Arabin came in.

It was a beautiful afternoon in the beginning of October, and Eleanor was sitting in the window to get the advantage of the last daylight for her novel. There was a fire in the comfortable room, but the weather was not cold enough to make it attractive, and as she could see the sun from where she sat, she was not very attentive to her book.

Mr. Arabin when he entered stood awhile with his back to the fire in his usual way, merely uttering a few commonplace remarks about the beauty of the weather while he plucked up courage for more interesting converse. It cannot probably be said that he had resolved then and there to make an offer to Eleanor. Men, we believe, seldom make such resolves. Mr. Slope and Mr. Stanhope had done so, it is true, but gentlemen generally propose without any absolutely defined determination as to their doing so. Such was now the case with Mr. Arabin.

"It is a lovely sunset," said Eleanor, answering him on the dreadfully trite subject which he had chosen.

Mr. Arabin could not see the sunset from the hearthrug, so he had to go close to her.

"Very lovely," said he, standing modestly so far away from her as to avoid touching the flounces of her dress. Then it appeared that he had nothing further to say, so after gazing for a moment in silence at the brightness of the setting sun, he returned to the fire.

Eleanor found that it was quite impossible for herself to commence a conversation. In the first place she could find nothing to say. Words, which were generally plenty enough with her, would not come to her relief. And moreover, do what she would, she could hardly prevent herself from crying.

"Do you like Ullathorne?" said Mr. Arabin, speaking from the safely distant position which he had assumed on the hearthrug.

"Yes, indeed, very much!"

"I don't mean Mr. and Miss Thorne. I know you like them, but the style of the house. There is something about old-fashioned mansions, built as this is, and old-fashioned gardens, that to me is especially delightful."

"I like everything old-fashioned," said Eleanor. "Old-fashioned things are so much the honestest."

"I don't know about that," said Mr. Arabin, gently laughing. "That is an opinion on which very much may be said on either side. It is strange how widely the world is divided on a subject which so nearly concerns us all, and which is so close beneath our eyes. Some think that we are quickly progressing toward perfection, while others imagine that virtue is disappearing from the earth."

"And you, Mr. Arabin, what do you think?" said Eleanor. She felt somewhat surprised at the tone which his conversation was taking, and yet she was relieved at his saying something which enabled herself to speak without showing her own emotion.

"What do I think, Mrs. Bold?" And then he rumbled his money with his hands in his trousers pockets and looked and spoke very little like a thriving lover. "It is the bane of my life that on important subjects I acquire no fixed opinion. I think, and think, and go on thinking, and yet my thoughts are running ever in different directions. I hardly know whether or no we do lean more confidently than our fathers did on those high hopes to which we profess to aspire."

"I think the world grows more worldly every day," said Eleanor.

"That is because you see more of it than when you were younger. But we should hardly judge by what we see—we see so very very little." There was then a pause for a while, during which Mr. Arabin continued to turn over his shillings and half-crowns. "If we believe in Scripture, we can hardly think that mankind in general will now be allowed to retrograde."

Eleanor, whose mind was certainly engaged otherwise than on the general state of mankind, made no answer to this. She felt thoroughly dissatisfied with herself. She could not force her thoughts away from the topic on which the Signora had spoken to her in so strange a way, and yet she knew that she could not converse with Mr. Arabin in an unrestrained, natural tone till she did so. She was most anxious not to show to him any special emotion, and yet she felt that if he looked at her he would at once see that she was not at ease.

But he did not look at her. Instead of doing so, he left the fireplace and began walking up and down the room. Eleanor took up her book resolutely, but she could not read, for there was a tear in her eye, and do what she would, it fell on her cheek. When Mr. Arabin's back was turned to her she wiped it away, but another was soon coursing down her face in its place. They would come, not a deluge of tears that would have betrayed her at once, but one by one, single monitors. Mr. Arabin did not observe her closely, and they passed unseen.

Mr. Arabin, thus pacing up and down the room, took four or five turns before he spoke another word, and Eleanor sat equally silent with her face bent over her book. She was afraid that her tears would get the better of her, and was preparing for an escape from the room when Mr. Arabin in his walk stood opposite to her. He did not come close up, but stood exactly on the spot to which his course brought him, and then, with his hands under his coattails, thus made his confession.

"Mrs. Bold," said he, "I owe you retribution for a great offense of which I have been guilty toward you." Eleanor's heart beat so that she could not trust herself to say that he had never been guilty of any offense. So Mr. Arabin thus went on.

"I have thought much of it since, and I am now aware that I was wholly unwarranted in putting to you a question which I once asked you. It was indelicate on my part, and perhaps unmanly. No intimacy which may exist between myself and your connection Dr. Grantly could justify it. Nor could the acquaintance which existed between ourselves." This word "acquaintance" struck cold on Eleanor's heart. Was this to be her doom after all? "I therefore think it right to beg your pardon in a humble spirit, and I now do so."

What was Eleanor to say to him? She could not say much, because she was crying, and yet she must say something. She was most anxious to say that something graciously, kindly, and yet not in such a manner as to betray herself. She had never felt herself so much at a loss for words.

"Indeed I took no offense, Mr. Arabin."

"Oh, but you did! And had you not done so, you would not have been yourself. You were as right to be offended as I was wrong so to offend you. I have not forgiven myself, but I hope to hear that you forgive me."

She was now past speaking calmly, though she still continued to hide her tears, and Mr. Arabin, after pausing a moment in vain for her reply, was walking off toward the door. She felt that she could not allow him to go unanswered without grievously sinning against all charity, so, rising from her seat, she gently touched his arm and said: "Oh, Mr. Arabin, do not go till I speak to you! I do forgive you. You know that I forgive you."

He took the hand that had so gently touched his arm, and then gazed into her face as if he would peruse there, as though written in a book, the whole future destiny of his life. And as he did so, there was a sober, sad seriousness in his own countenance which Eleanor found herself unable to sustain. She could only look down upon the carpet, let her tears trickle as they would, and leave her hand within his.

It was but for a minute that they stood so, but the duration of that minute was sufficient to make it ever memorable to them both. Eleanor was sure now that she was loved. No words, be their eloquence what it might, could be more impressive than that eager, melancholy gaze.

Why did he look so into her eyes? Why did he not speak to her? Could it be that he looked for her to make the first sign?

And he, though he knew but little of women, even he knew that he was loved. He had only to ask and it would be all his own, that inexpressible loveliness, those ever speaking but yet now mute eyes, that feminine brightness and eager, loving spirit which had so attracted him since first he had encountered it at St. Ewold's. It might, must, be all his own now. On no other supposition was it possible that she should allow her hand to remain thus clasped within his own. He had only to ask. Ah, but that was the difficulty! Did a minute suffice for all this? Nay, perhaps it might be more than a minute.

"Mrs. Bold——" at last he said, and then stopped himself.

If he could not speak, how was she to do so? He had called her by her name, the same name that any merest stranger would have used! She withdrew her hand from his, and moved as though to return to her seat. "Eleanor!" he then said, in his softest tone, as though the courage of a lover were as yet but half-assumed, as though he were still afraid of giving offense by the freedom which he took. She looked slowly, gently, almost piteously up into his face. There was at any rate no anger there to deter him.

"Eleanor!" he again exclaimed, and in a moment he had her clasped to his bosom. How this was done—whether the doing was with him or her, whether she had flown thither conquered by the tenderness of his voice, or he with a violence not likely to give offense had drawn her to his breast—neither of them knew, nor can I declare. There was now that sympathy between them which hardly admitted of individual motion. They were one and the same—one flesh—one spirit—one life.

"Eleanor, my own Eleanor, my own, my wife!" She ventured to look up at him through her tears, and he, bowing his face down over hers, pressed his lips upon her brow—his virgin lips, which since a beard first

grew upon his chin had never yet tasted the luxury of a woman's cheek.
She had been told that her yea must be yea or her nay, nay, but she was
called on for neither the one nor the other. She told Miss Thorne that she
was engaged to Mr. Arabin, but no such words had passed between them,
no promises had been asked or given.

"Oh, let me go," said she, "let me go now. I am too happy to remain—
let me go, that I may be alone." He did not try to hinder her, he did not
repeat the kiss, he did not press another on her lips. He might have done
so had he been so minded. She was now all his own. He took his arm from
round her waist, his arm that was trembling with a new delight, and let her
go. She fled like a roe to her own chamber, and then, having turned the
bolt, she enjoyed the full luxury of her love. She idolized, almost worshiped, this man who had so meekly begged her pardon. And he was now
her own. Oh, how she wept and cried and laughed as the hopes and fears
and miseries of the last few weeks passed in remembrance through her mind!

Mr. Slope! That anyone should have dared to think that she who had
been chosen by him could possibly have mated herself with Mr. Slope!
That they should have dared to tell him also, and subject her bright happiness to such needless risk! And then she smiled with joy as she thought of
all the comforts that she could give him—not that he cared for comforts,
but that it would be so delicious for her to give.

She got up and rang for her maid that she might tell her little boy of
his new father, and in her own way she did tell him. She desired her maid
to leave her, in order that she might be alone with her child, and then while
he lay sprawling on the bed she poured forth the praises, all unmeaning to
him, of the man she had selected to guard his infancy.

She could not be happy, however, till she had made Mr. Arabin take the
child to himself and thus, as it were, adopt him as his own. The moment
the idea struck her she took the baby up in her arms and, opening her door,
ran quickly down to the drawing-room. She at once found, by his step still
pacing on the floor, that he was there, and a glance within the room told
her that he was alone. She hesitated a moment, and then hurried in with
her precious charge.

Mr. Arabin met her in the middle of the room. "There," said she, breathless with her haste. "There, take him—take him and love him."

Mr. Arabin took the little fellow from her, and kissing him again and
again, prayed God to bless him. "He shall be all as my own—all as my
own," said he. Eleanor, as she stooped to take back her child, kissed the
hand that held him, and then rushed back with her treasure to her chamber.

It was thus that Mr. Harding's younger daughter was won for the second
time. At dinner neither she nor Mr. Arabin were very bright, but their
silence occasioned no remark. In the drawing-room, as we have before said,
she told Miss Thorne what had occurred. The next morning she returned to
Barchester, and Mr. Arabin went over with his budget of news to the Archdeacon. As Dr. Grantly was not there, he could only satisfy himself by tell-

ing Mrs. Grantly that he intended himself the honor of becoming her brother-in-law. In the ecstasy of her joy at hearing such tidings, Mrs. Grantly vouchsafed him a warmer welcome than any he had yet received from Eleanor.

"Good heavens!" she exclaimed—it was the general exclamation of the rectory. "Poor Eleanor! Dear Eleanor! What a monstrous injustice has been done her!—Well, it shall all be made up now." And then she thought of the Signora. "What lies people tell," she said to herself.

But people in this matter had told no lies at all.

CHAPTER XLVI

THE BELZEBUB COLT

When Miss Thorne left the dining-room, Eleanor had formed no intention of revealing to her what had occurred, but when she was seated beside her hostess on the sofa the secret dropped from her almost unawares. Eleanor was but a bad hypocrite, and she found herself quite unable to continue talking about Mr. Arabin as though he were a stranger while her heart was full of him. When Miss Thorne, pursuing her own scheme with discreet zeal, asked the young widow whether in her opinion it would not be a good thing for Mr. Arabin to get married, she had nothing for it but to confess the truth. "I suppose it would," said Eleanor, rather sheepishly. Whereupon Miss Thorne amplified on the idea. "Oh, Miss Thorne," said Eleanor, "he is going to be married. I am engaged to him."

Now Miss Thorne knew very well that there had been no such engagement when she had been walking with Mrs. Bold in the morning. She had also heard enough to be tolerably sure that there had been no preliminaries to such an engagement. She was therefore taken a little by surprise. But nevertheless she embraced her guest, and cordially congratulated her.

Eleanor had no opportunity of speaking another word to Mr. Arabin that evening, except such words as all the world might hear, and these, as may be supposed, were few enough. Miss Thorne did her best to leave them in privacy, but Mr. Thorne, who knew nothing of what had occurred, and another guest, a friend of his, entirely interfered with her good intentions. So poor Eleanor had to go to bed without one sign of affection. Her state, nevertheless, was not to be pitied.

The next morning she was up early. It was probable, she thought, that by going down a little before the usual hour of breakfast, she might find Mr. Arabin alone in the dining-room. Might it not be that he also would calculate that an interview would thus be possible? Thus thinking, Eleanor was dressed a full hour before the time fixed in the Ullathorne household for morning prayers. She did not at once go down. She was afraid to seem to be too anxious to meet her lover, though heaven knows her anxiety was intense enough. She therefore sat herself down at her window, and repeatedly looking at her watch, nursed her child till she thought she might venture forth.

When she found herself at the dining-room door, she stood a moment, hesitating to turn the handle, but when she heard Mr. Thorne's voice inside she hesitated no longer. Her object was defeated, and she might now go in as soon as she liked without the slightest imputation on her delicacy. Mr. Thorne and Mr. Arabin were standing on the hearthrug discussing the merits of the Belzebub colt, or rather Mr. Thorne was discussing and Mr. Arabin was listening. That interesting animal had rubbed the stump of his tail against the wall of his stable, and occasioned much uneasiness to the Ullathorne master of the horse. Had Eleanor but waited another minute, Mr. Thorne would have been in the stables.

Mr. Thorne, when he saw his lady guest, repressed his anxiety. The Belzebub colt must do without him. And so the three stood, saying little or nothing to each other, till at last the master of the house, finding that he could no longer bear his present state of suspense respecting his favorite young steed, made an elaborate apology to Mrs. Bold and escaped. As he shut the door behind him, Eleanor almost wished that he had remained. It was not that she was afraid of Mr. Arabin, but she hardly yet knew how to address him.

He, however, soon relieved her from her embarrassment. He came up to her, and taking both her hands in his, he said: "So, Eleanor, you and I are to be man and wife. Is it so?"

She looked up into his face, and her lips formed themselves into a single syllable. She uttered no sound, but he could read the affirmative plainly in her face.

"It is a great trust," said he, "a very great trust."

"It is—it is," said Eleanor, not exactly taking what he had said in the sense that he had meant. "It is a very, very great trust, and I will do my utmost to deserve it."

"And I also will do my utmost to deserve it," said Mr. Arabin, very solemnly. And then, winding his arm round her waist, he stood there gazing at the fire and she, with her head leaning on his shoulder, stood by him, well satisfied with her position. They neither of them spoke, or found any want of speaking. All that was needful for them to say had been said. The yea, yea had been spoken by Eleanor in her own way—and that way had been perfectly satisfactory to Mr. Arabin.

And now it remained to them each to enjoy the assurance of the other's love. And how great that luxury is! How far it surpasses any other pleasure which God has allowed to his creatures! And to a woman's heart how doubly delightful.

There is a feeling still half-existing, but now half-conquered by the force of human nature, that a woman should be ashamed of her love till the husband's right to her compels her to acknowledge it. We would fain preach a different doctrine. A woman should glory in her love, but on that account let her take the more care that it be such as to justify her glory.

Eleanor did glory in hers, and she felt, and had cause to feel, that it deserved to be held as glorious. She could have stood there for hours with his arm round her had fate and Mr. Thorne permitted it. Each moment she crept nearer to his bosom, and felt more and more certain that there was her home. What now to her was the Archdeacon's arrogance, her sister's coldness, or her dear father's weakness? What need she care for the duplicity of such friends as Charlotte Stanhope? She had found the strong shield that should guard her from all wrongs, the trusty pilot that should henceforward guide her through the shoals and rocks. She would give up the heavy burden of her independence, and once more assume the position of a woman, and the duties of a trusting and loving wife.

And he too stood there fully satisfied with his place. They were both looking intently on the fire, as though they could read there their future fate, till at last Eleanor turned her face toward his. "How sad you are," she said, smiling, and indeed his face was, if not sad, at least serious. "How sad you are, love!"

"Sad," said he, looking down at her. "No, certainly not sad." Her sweet loving eyes were turned toward him, and she smiled softly as he answered her. The temptation was too strong even for the demure propriety of Mr. Arabin, and bending over her, he pressed his lips to hers.

Immediately after this Mr. Thorne appeared, and they were both delighted to hear that the tail of the Belzebub colt was not materially injured.

It had been Mr. Harding's intention to hurry over to Ullathorne as soon as possible after his return to Barchester, in order to secure the support of his daughter in his meditated revolt against the Archdeacon as touching the deanery, but he was spared the additional journey by hearing that Mrs. Bold had returned unexpectedly home. As soon as he had read her note he started off, and found her waiting for him in her own house.

How much each of them had to tell the other, and how certain each was that the story which he or she had to tell would astonish the other!

"My dear, I am so anxious to see you," said Mr. Harding, kissing his daughter.

"Oh, Papa, I have so much to tell you!" said the daughter, returning the embrace.

"My dear, they have offered me the deanery!" said Mr. Harding, anticipating by the suddenness of the revelation the tidings which Eleanor had to give him.

"Oh, Papa," said she, forgetting her own love and happiness in her joy at the surprising news, "oh, Papa, can it be possible? Dear Papa, how thoroughly, thoroughly happy that makes me!"

"But, my dear, I think it best to refuse it."

"Oh, Papa!"

"I am sure you will agree with me, Eleanor, when I explain it to you. You know, my dear, how old I am. If I live, I——"

"But, Papa, I must tell you about myself."

"Well, my dear."

"I do so wonder how you'll take it."

"Take what?"

"If you don't rejoice at it, if it doesn't make you happy, if you don't encourage me, I shall break my heart."

"If that be the case, Nelly, I certainly will encourage you."

"But I fear you won't. I do so fear you won't. And yet you can't but think I am the most fortunate woman living on God's earth."

"Are you, dearest? Then I certainly will rejoice with you. Come, Nelly, come to me, and tell me what it is."

"I am going——"

He led her to the sofa, and seating himself beside her, took both her hands in his. "You are going to be married, Nelly. Is not that it?"

"Yes," she said, faintly. "That is, if you will approve." And then she blushed as she remembered the promise which she had so lately volunteered to him, and which she had so utterly forgotten in making her engagement with Mr. Arabin.

Mr. Harding thought for a moment who the man could be whom he was to be called upon to welcome as his son-in-law. A week since he would have had no doubt whom to name. In that case he would have been prepared to give his sanction, although he would have done so with a heavy heart. Now he knew that at any rate it would not be Mr. Slope, though he was perfectly at a loss to guess who could possibly have filled the place. For a moment he thought that the man might be Bertie Stanhope, and his very soul sank within him.

"Well, Nelly?"

"Oh, Papa, promise to me that, for my sake, you will love him."

"Come, Nelly, come, tell me who it is."

"But will you love him, Papa?"

"Dearest, I must love anyone that you love." Then she turned her face to his and whispered into his ear the name of Mr. Arabin.

No man that she could have named could have more surprised or more delighted him. Had he looked round the world for a son-in-law to his taste, he could have selected no one whom he would have preferred to Mr. Arabin. He was a clergyman; he held a living in the neighborhood, he was of a set to which all Mr. Harding's own partialities most closely adhered, he was the great friend of Dr. Grantly, and he was moreover a man of whom Mr. Harding knew nothing but what he approved. Nevertheless, his surprise was so great as to prevent the immediate expression of his joy. He had never thought of Mr. Arabin in connection with his daughter, he had never imagined that they had any feeling in common. He had feared that his daughter had been made hostile to clergymen of Mr. Arabin's stamp by her intolerance of the Archdeacon's pretensions. Had he been put to wish, he might have wished for Mr. Arabin for a son-in-law, but had he been put to guess, the name would never have occurred to him.

"Mr. Arabin!" he exclaimed. "Impossible!"

"Oh, Papa, for heaven's sake don't say anything against him! If you love me, don't say anything against him. Oh, Papa, it's done, and mustn't be undone—oh, Papa!"

Fickle Eleanor! Where was the promise that she would make no choice for herself without her father's approval? She had chosen, and now demanded his acquiescence. "Oh, Papa, isn't he good? Isn't he noble? Isn't he religious, high-minded, everything that a good man possibly can be?" And she clung to her father, beseeching him for his consent.

"My Nelly, my child, my own daughter! He is, he is noble and good and high-minded. He is all that a woman can love and a man admire. He shall be my son, my own son. He shall be as close to my heart as you are. My Nelly, my child, my happy, happy child!"

We need not pursue the interview any further. By degrees they returned to the subject of the new promotion. Eleanor tried to prove to him, as the Grantlys had done, that his age could be no bar to his being a very excellent dean, but those arguments had now even less weight on him than before. He said little or nothing, but sat meditative. Every now and then he would kiss his daughter, and say "Yes," or "No," or "Very true," or "Well, my dear, I can't quite agree with you there," but he could not be got to enter sharply into the question of "to be, or not to be" Dean of Barchester. Of her and her happiness, of Mr. Arabin and his virtues, he would talk as much as Eleanor desired, and to tell the truth, that was not a little, but about the deanery he would now say nothing further. He had got a new idea into his head—Why should not Mr. Arabin be the new dean?

CHAPTER XLVII

THE ARCHDEACON IS SATISFIED WITH THE STATE OF AFFAIRS

THE Archdeacon, in his journey into Barchester, had been assured by Mr. Harding that all their prognostications about Mr. Slope and Eleanor were groundless. Mr. Harding, however, had found it very difficult to shake his son-in-law's faith in his own acuteness. The matter had, to Dr. Grantly, been so plainly corroborated by such patent evidence, borne out by such endless circumstances, that he at first refused to take as true the positive statement which Mr. Harding made to him of Eleanor's own disavowal of the impeachment. But at last he yielded in a qualified way. He brought himself to admit that he would at the present regard his past convictions as a mistake, but in doing this he so guarded himself that if, at any future time, Eleanor should come forth to the world as Mrs. Slope, he might still be able to say: "There, I told you so. Remember what you said and what I said, and remember also for coming years that I was right in this matter—as in all others."

He carried, however, his concession so far as to bring himself to undertake to call at Eleanor's house, and he did call accordingly, while the father and daughter were yet in the middle of their conference. Mr. Harding had had so much to hear and to say that he had forgotten to advertise Eleanor of the honor that awaited her, and she heard her brother-in-law's voice in the hall while she was quite unprepared to see him.

"There's the Archdeacon," she said, springing up.

"Yes, my dear. He told me to tell you that he would come and see you, but to tell the truth, I had forgotten all about it."

Eleanor fled away, regardless of all her father's entreaties. She could not now, in the first hours of her joy, bring herself to bear all the Archdeacon's retractions, apologies, and congratulations. He would have so much to say, and would be so tedious in saying it. Consequently the Archdeacon, when he was shown into the drawing-room, found no one there but Mr. Harding.

"You must excuse Eleanor," said Mr. Harding.

"Is anything the matter?" asked the Doctor, who at once anticipated that the whole truth about Mr. Slope had at last come out.

"Well, something is the matter. I wonder now whether you will be much surprised?"

The Archdeacon saw by his father-in-law's manner that after all he had nothing to tell him about Mr. Slope. "No," said he, "certainly not—nothing will ever surprise me again." Very many men nowadays, besides the Archdeacon, adopt or affect to adopt the nil-admirari doctrine, but nevertheless, to judge from their appearance, they are just as subject to sudden emotions as their grandfathers and grandmothers were before them.

"What do you think Mr. Arabin has done?"

"Mr. Arabin! It's nothing about that daughter of Stanhope's, I hope?"

"No, not that woman," said Mr. Harding, enjoying his joke in his sleeve.

"Not that woman! Is he going to do anything about any woman? Why can't you speak out if you have anything to say? There is nothing I hate so much as these sort of mysteries."

"There shall be no mystery with you, Archdeacon, though of course it must go no further at present."

"Well."

"Except Susan. You must promise me you'll tell no one else."

"Nonsense!" exclaimed the Archdeacon, who was becoming angry in his suspense. "You can't have any secret about Mr. Arabin."

"Only this—that he and Eleanor are engaged."

It was quite clear to see by the Archdeacon's face that he did not believe a word of it. "Mr. Arabin! It's impossible."

"Eleanor, at any rate, has just now told me so."

"It's impossible," repeated the Archdeacon.

"Well, I can't say I think it impossible. It certainly took me by surprise, but that does not make it impossible."

"She must be mistaken."

Mr. Harding assured him that there was no mistake, that he would find on returning home that Mr. Arabin had been at Plumstead with the express object of making the same declaration, that even Miss Thorne knew all about it. And that, in fact, the thing was as clearly settled as any such arrangement between a lady and a gentleman could well be.

"Good heavens!" said the Archdeacon, walking up and down Eleanor's drawing-room. "Good heavens! Good heavens!"

Now, these exclamations certainly betokened faith. Mr. Harding properly gathered from them that at last Dr. Grantly did believe the fact. The first utterance clearly evinced a certain amount of distaste at the information he had received, the second simply indicated surprise, in the tone of the third Mr. Harding fancied that he could catch a certain gleam of satisfaction.

The Archdeacon had truly expressed the workings of his mind. He could not but be disgusted to find how utterly astray he had been in all his anticipations. Had he only been lucky enough to have suggested this marriage himself when he first brought Mr. Arabin into the county, his character for judgment and wisdom would have received an addition which would have classed him at any rate next to Solomon. And why had he not done so? Might he not have foreseen that Mr. Arabin would want a wife in his parsonage? He had foreseen that Eleanor would want a husband, but should he not also have perceived that Mr. Arabin was a man much more likely to attract her than Mr. Slope? The Archdeacon found that he had been at fault, and of course could not immediately get over his discomfiture.

Then his surprise was intense. How sly this pair of young turtledoves had been with him. How egregiously they had hoaxed him. He had preached to Eleanor against her fancied attachment to Mr. Slope at the very time that she was in love with his own protégé, Mr. Arabin, and had absolutely taken that same Mr. Arabin into his confidence with reference to his dread of Mr. Slope's alliance. It was very natural that the Archdeacon should feel surprise.

But there was also great ground for satisfaction. Looking at the match by itself, it was the very thing to help the Doctor out of his difficulties. In the first place, the assurance that he should never have Mr. Slope for his brother-in-law was in itself a great comfort. Then Mr. Arabin was, of all men, the one with whom it would best suit him to be so intimately connected. But the crowning comfort was the blow which this marriage would give to Mr. Slope. He had now certainly lost his wife, rumor beginning to whisper that he might possibly lose his position in the palace, and if Mr. Harding would only be true, the great danger of all would be surmounted. In such case it might be expected that Mr. Slope would own himself vanquished, and take himself altogether away from Barchester. And so the Archdeacon would again be able to breathe pure air.

"Well, well," said he. "Good heavens! Good heavens!" And the tone of the fifth exclamation made Mr. Harding fully aware that content was reigning in the Archdeacon's bosom.

And then slowly, gradually, and craftily Mr. Harding propounded his own new scheme. Why should not Mr. Arabin be the new dean?

Slowly, gradually, and thoughtfully Dr. Grantly fell into his father-in-law's views. Much as he liked Mr. Arabin, sincere as was his admiration for that gentleman's ecclesiastical abilities, he would not have sanctioned a measure which would rob his father-in-law of his fairly earned promotion were it at all practicable to induce his father-in-law to accept the promotion which he had earned. But the Archdeacon had on a former occasion received proof of the obstinacy with which Mr. Harding could adhere to his own views in opposition to the advice of all his friends. He knew tolerably well that nothing would induce the meek, mild man before him to take the high place offered to him if he thought it wrong to do so. Knowing this, he also said to himself more than once: "Why should not Mr. Arabin be Dean of Barchester?" It was at last arranged between them that they would together start to London by the earliest train on the following morning, making a little detour to Oxford on their journey. Dr. Gwynne's counsels, they imagined, might perhaps be of assistance to them.

These matters settled, the Archdeacon hurried off, that he might return to Plumstead and prepare for his journey. The day was extremely fine, and he came into the city in an open gig. As he was driving up the High Street he encountered Mr. Slope at a crossing. Had he not pulled up rather sharply, he would have run over him. The two had never spoken to each other since they had met on a memorable occasion in the Bishop's study. They did not speak now, but they looked each other full in the face, and Mr. Slope's countenance was as impudent, as triumphant, as defiant as ever. Had Dr. Grantly not known to the contrary, he would have imagined that his enemy had won the deanship, the wife, and all the rich honors for which he had been striving. As it was, he had lost everything that he had in the world, and had just received his congé from the Bishop.

In leaving the town the Archdeacon drove by the well-remembered entrance of Hiram's Hospital. There at the gate was a large, untidy farmer's wagon laden with untidy-looking furniture, and there, inspecting the arrival, was good Mrs. Quiverful—not dressed in her Sunday best—not very clean in her apparel—not graceful as to her bonnet and shawl, or indeed with many feminine charms as to her whole appearance. She was busy at domestic work in her new house, and had just ventured out, expecting to see no one on the arrival of the family chattels. The Archdeacon was down upon her before she knew where she was.

Her acquaintance with Dr. Grantly or his family was very slight indeed. The Archdeacon, as a matter of course, knew every clergyman in the archdeaconry, it may almost be said in the diocese, and had some acquaintance, more or less intimate, with their wives and families. With Mr. Quiverful he had been concerned on various matters of business, but of Mrs. Q he had seen very little. Now, however, he was in too gracious a mood to pass her by unnoticed. The Quiverfuls, one and all, had looked for the bitterest hostility from Dr. Grantly. They knew his anxiety that Mr. Harding should return to his old home at the hospital, and they did not know that a new home had been offered to him at the deanery. Mrs. Quiverful was therefore not a little surprised, and not a little rejoiced also, at the tone in which she was addressed.

"How do you do, Mrs. Quiverful—how do you do?" said he, stretching his left hand out of the gig as he spoke to her. "I am very glad to see you employed in so pleasant and useful a manner, very glad indeed."

Mrs. Quiverful thanked him, and shook hands with him, and looked into his face suspiciously. She was not sure whether the congratulations and kindness were or were not ironical.

"Pray tell Mr. Quiverful from me," he continued, "that I am rejoiced at his appointment. It's a comfortable place, Mrs. Quiverful, and a comfortable house, and I am very glad to see you in it. Good-by—good-by." And he drove on, leaving the lady well pleased and astonished at his good nature. On the whole things were going well with the Archdeacon, and he could afford to be charitable to Mrs. Quiverful. He looked forth from his gig smilingly on all the world, and forgave everyone in Barchester their sins, excepting only Mrs. Proudie and Mr. Slope. Had he seen the Bishop, he would have felt inclined to pat even him kindly on the head.

He determined to go home by St. Ewold's. This would take him some three miles out of his way, but he felt that he could not leave Plumstead comfortably without saying one word of good-fellowship to Mr. Arabin. When he reached the parsonage the Vicar was still out, but from what he had heard he did not doubt but that he would meet him on the road between their two houses. He was right in this, for about halfway home, at a narrow turn, he came upon Mr. Arabin, who was on horseback.

"Well, well, well, well," said the Archdeacon, loudly, joyously, and with supreme good humor. "Well, well, well, well, so after all we have no further cause to fear Mr. Slope."

"I hear from Mrs. Grantly that they have offered the deanery to Mr. Harding," said the other.

"Mr. Slope has lost more than the deanery, I find." And then the Archdeacon laughed jocosely. "Come, come, Arabin, you have kept your secret well enough. I know all about it now."

"I have had no secret, Archdeacon," said the other with a quiet smile. "None at all—not for a day. It was only yesterday that I knew my own good fortune, and today I went over to Plumstead to ask your approval. From what Mrs. Grantly has said to me, I am led to hope that I shall have it."

"With all my heart, with all my heart," said the Archdeacon cordially, holding his friend fast by the hand. "It's just as I would have it. She is an excellent young woman, she will not come to you empty-handed, and I think she will make you a good wife. If she does her duty by you as her sister does by me, you'll be a happy man, that's all I can say." And as he finished speaking a tear might have been observed in each of the Doctor's eyes.

Mr. Arabin warmly returned the Archdeacon's grasp, but he said little. His heart was too full for speaking, and he could not express the gratitude which he felt. Dr. Grantly understood him as well as though he had spoken for an hour.

"And mind, Arabin," said he, "no one but myself shall tie the knot. We'll get Eleanor out to Plumstead, and it shall come off there. I'll make Susan stir herself, and we'll do it in style. I must be off to London tomorrow on special business. Harding goes with me. But I'll be back before your bride has got her wedding dress ready." And so they parted.

On his journey home the Archdeacon occupied his mind with preparations for the marriage festivities. He made a great resolve that he would atone to Eleanor for all the injury he had done her by the munificence of his future treatment. He would show her what was the difference in his eyes between a Slope and an Arabin. On one other thing also he decided with a firm mind—if the affair of the dean should not be settled in Mr. Arabin's favor, nothing should prevent him putting a new front and bow window to the dining-room at St. Ewold's parsonage.

"So we're sold after all, Sue," said he to his wife, accosting her with a kiss as soon as he entered his house. He did not call his wife Sue above twice or thrice in a year, and these occasions were great high days.

"Eleanor has had more sense than we gave her credit for," said Mrs. Grantly.

And there was great content in Plumstead rectory that evening, and Mrs. Grantly promised her husband that she would now open her heart and take Mr. Arabin into it. Hitherto she had declined to do so.

CHAPTER XLVIII

MR. SLOPE BIDS FAREWELL TO THE PALACE AND ITS INHABITANTS

WE must now take leave of Mr. Slope, and of the Bishop also, and of Mrs. Proudie. These leave-takings in novels are as disagreeable as they are in real life—not so sad, indeed, for they want the reality of sadness, but quite as perplexing, and generally less satisfactory. What novelist, what Fielding, what Scott, what George Sand, or Sue, or Dumas, can impart an interest to the last chapter of his fictitious history? Promises of two children and superhuman happiness are of no avail, nor assurance of extreme respectability carried to an age far exceeding that usually allotted to mortals. The sorrows of our heroes and heroines, they are your delight, oh public!—their sorrows, or their sins, or their absurdities, not their virtues, good sense, and consequent rewards. When we begin to tint our final pages with couleur de rose, as in accordance with fixed rule we must do, we altogether extinguish our own powers of pleasing. When we become dull we offend your intellect, and we must become dull or we should offend your taste. A late writer, wishing to sustain his interest to the last page, hung his hero at the end of the third volume. The consequence was that no one would read his novel. And who can apportion out and dovetail his incidents, dialogues, characters, and descriptive morsels so as to fit them all exactly into 462 pages, without either compressing them unnaturally, or extending them artificially at the end of his labor? Do I not myself know that I am at this moment in want of a dozen pages, and that I am sick with cudgeling my brains to find them? And then when everything is done, the kindest-hearted critic of them all invariably twits us with the incompetency and lameness of our conclusion. We have either become idle and neglected it, or tedious and overlabored it. It is insipid or unnatural, overstrained or imbecile. It means nothing, or attempts too much. The last scene of all, as all last scenes we fear must be,

> Is second childishness, and mere oblivion,
> San teeth, sans eyes, sans taste, sans everything.

I can only say that if some critic who thoroughly knows his work, and has labored on it till experience has made him perfect, will write the last fifty pages of a novel in the way they should be written, I, for one, will in future do my best to copy the example. Guided by my own lights only, I confess that I despair of success.

For the last week or ten days, Mr. Slope had seen nothing of Mrs. Proudie, and very little of the Bishop. He still lived in the palace, and still went through his usual routine work, but the confidential doings of the diocese had passed into other hands. He had seen this clearly, and marked it well, but it had not much disturbed him. He had indulged in other hopes till the Bishop's affairs had become dull to him, and he was moreover aware that as regarded the diocese Mrs. Proudie had checkmated him. It has been explained in the beginning of these pages how three or four were contending together as to who in fact should be Bishop of Barchester. Each of these had now admitted to himself (or boasted to herself) that Mrs. Proudie was victorious in the struggle. They had gone through a competitive examination of considerable severity, and she had come forth the winner, facile princeps. Mr. Slope had for a moment run her hard, but it was only for a moment. It had become, as it were, acknowledged that Hiram's Hospital should be the testing point between them, and now Mr. Quiverful was already in the hospital, the proof of Mrs. Proudie's skill and courage.

All this did not break down Mr. Slope's spirit, because he had other hopes. But, alas! at last there came to him a note from his friend Sir Nicholas, informing him that the deanship was disposed of. Let us give Mr. Slope his due. He did not lie prostrate under this blow, or give himself up to vain lamentations. He did not henceforward despair of life, and call upon gods above and gods below to carry him off. He sat himself down in his chair, counted out what monies he had in hand for present purposes and what others were coming in to him, bethought himself as to the best sphere for his future exertions, and at once wrote off a letter to a rich sugar-refiner's wife in Baker Street who, as he well knew, was much given to the entertainment and encouragement of serious young evangelical clergymen. He was again, he said, "upon the world, having found the air of a cathedral town, and the very nature of cathedral services, uncongenial to his spirit." And then he sat awhile making firm resolves as to his manner of parting from the Bishop, and also as to his future conduct.

> At last he rose, and twitched his mantle blue (black),
> Tomorrow to fresh woods and pastures new.

Having received a formal command to wait upon the Bishop, he rose and proceeded to obey it. He rang the bell and desired the servant to inform his master that if it suited his lordship, he, Mr. Slope, was ready to wait upon him. The servant, who well understood that Mr. Slope was no longer in the ascendant, brought back a message saying that his lordship desired that Mr. Slope would attend him immediately in his study. Mr. Slope waited about ten minutes more to prove his independence, and then he went into the Bishop's room. There, as he had expected, he found Mrs. Proudie, together with her husband.

"Hum, ha—Mr. Slope, pray take a chair," said the gentleman Bishop.

"Pray be seated, Mr. Slope," said the lady Bishop.

"Thank ye, thank ye," said Mr. Slope, and walking round to the fire, he threw himself into one of the armchairs that graced the hearthrug.

"Mr. Slope," said the Bishop, "it has become necessary that I should speak to you definitely on a matter that has for some time been pressing itself on my attention."

"May I ask whether the subject is in any way connected with myself?" said Mr. Slope.

"It is so—certainly—yes, it certainly is connected with yourself, Mr. Slope."

"Then, my lord, if I may be allowed to express a wish, I would prefer that no discussion on the subject should take place between us in the presence of a third person."

"Don't alarm yourself, Mr. Slope," said Mrs. Proudie. "No discussion is at all necessary. The Bishop merely intends to express his own wishes."

"I merely intend, Mr. Slope, to express my own wishes—no discussion will be at all necessary," said the Bishop, reiterating his wife's words.

"That is more, my lord, than we any of us can be sure of," said Mr. Slope. "I cannot, however, force Mrs. Proudie to leave the room, nor can I refuse to remain here if it be your lordship's wish that I should do so."

"It is his lordship's wish, certainly," said Mrs. Proudie.

"Mr. Slope," began the Bishop in a solemn, serious voice, "it grieves me to have to find fault. It grieves me much to have to find fault with a clergyman, but especially so with a clergyman in your position."

"Why, what have I done amiss, my lord?" demanded Mr. Slope boldly.

"What have you done amiss, Mr. Slope?" said Mrs. Proudie, standing erect before the culprit and raising that terrible forefinger. "Do you dare to ask the Bishop what you have done amiss? Does not your conscience——"

"Mrs. Proudie, pray let it be understood, once for all, that I will have no words with you."

"Ah, sir, but you will have words," said she, "you must have words. Why have you had so many words with that Signora Neroni? Why have you disgraced yourself, you a clergyman too, by constantly consorting with such a woman as that—with a married woman,—with one altogether unfit for a clergyman's society?"

"At any rate, I was introduced to her in your drawing-room," retorted Mr. Slope.

"And shamefully you behaved there," said Mrs. Proudie, "most shamefully. I was wrong to allow you to remain in the house a day after what I then saw. I should have insisted on your instant dismissal."

"I have yet to learn, Mrs. Proudie, that you have the power to insist either on my going from hence or on my staying here."

"What!" said the lady. "I am not to have the privilege of saying who shall and who shall not frequent my own drawing-room! I am not to save my servants and dependents from having their morals corrupted by improper conduct! I am not to save my own daughters from impurity! I will let you see, Mr. Slope, whether I have the power or whether I have not. You will have the goodness to understand that you no longer fill any situation about the Bishop, and as your room will be immediately wanted in the palace for another chaplain, I must ask you to provide yourself with apartments as soon as may be convenient to you."

"My lord," said Mr. Slope, appealing to the Bishop and so turning his back completely on the lady, "will you permit me to ask that I may have from your own lips any decision that you may have come to on this matter?"

"Certainly, Mr. Slope, certainly," said the Bishop. "That is but reasonable. Well, my decision is that you had better look out for some other preferment. For the situation which you have lately held I do not think that you are well suited."

"And what, my lord, has been my fault?"

"That Signora Neroni is one fault," said Mrs. Proudie, "and a very abominable fault she is—very abominable and very disgraceful. Fie, Mr. Slope, fie! You an evangelical clergyman indeed!"

"My lord, I desire to know for what fault I am turned out of your lordship's house."

"You hear what Mrs. Proudie says," said the Bishop.

"When I publish the history of this transaction, my lord, as I decidedly shall do in my own vindication, I presume you will not wish me to state that you have discarded me at your wife's bidding—because she has objected to my being acquainted with another lady, the daughter of one of the prebendaries of the Chapter?"

"You may publish what you please, sir," said Mrs. Proudie. "But you will not be insane enough to publish any of your doings in Barchester. Do you think I have not heard of your kneelings at that creature's feet—that is, if she has any feet—and of your constant slobbering over her hand? I advise you to beware, Mr. Slope, of what you do and say. Clergymen have been unfrocked for less than what you have been guilty of."

"My lord, if this goes on I shall be obliged to indict this woman—Mrs. Proudie I mean—for defamation of character."

"I think, Mr. Slope, you had better now retire," said the Bishop. "I will enclose to you a check for any balance that may be due to you, and under the present circumstances it will of course be better for all parties that you should leave the palace at the earliest possible moment. I will allow you for your journey back to London, and for your maintenance in Barchester for a week from this date."

"If, however, you wish to remain in this neighborhood," said Mrs. Proudie, "and will solemnly pledge yourself never again to see that woman, and will promise also to be more circumspect in your conduct, the Bishop will mention your name to Mr. Quiverful, who now wants a curate at Puddingdale. The house is, I imagine, quite sufficient for your requirements, and there will moreover be a stipend of fifty pounds a year."

"May God forgive you, madam, for the manner in which you have treated me," said Mr. Slope, looking at her with a very heavenly look. "And remember this, madam, that you yourself may still have a fall." And he looked at her with a very worldly look. "As to the Bishop, I pity him!" And so saying, Mr. Slope left the room. Thus ended the intimacy of the Bishop of Barchester with his first confidential chaplain.

Mrs. Proudie was right in this; namely, that Mr. Slope was not insane enough to publish to the world any of his doings in Barchester. He was aware that it would be wise in him to drop for the future all allusions to his doings in the cathedral city. Soon after the interview just recorded he left Barchester, shaking the dust off his feet as he entered the railway carriage, and he gave no longing, lingering look after the cathedral towers as the train hurried him quickly out of their sight.

It is well known that the family of the Slopes never starve. They always fall on their feet like cats, and let them fall where they will, they live on the fat of the land. Our Mr. Slope did so. On his return to town he found that the sugar-refiner had died and that his widow was inconsolable, or, in other words, in want of consolation. Mr. Slope consoled her, and soon found himself settled with much comfort in the house in Baker Street. He possessed himself also, before long, of a church in the vicinity of the New Road, and became known to fame as one of the most eloquent preachers and pious clergymen in that part of the metropolis. There let us leave him.

Of the Bishop and his wife very little further need be said. From that time forth nothing material occurred to interrupt the even course of their domestic harmony. Very speedily, a further vacancy on the bench of bishops gave to Dr. Proudie the seat in the House of Lords which he at first so anxiously longed for. But by this time he had become a wiser man. He did certainly take his seat, and occasionally registered a vote in favor of government views on ecclesiastical matters. But he had thoroughly learnt that his proper sphere of action lay in close contiguity with Mrs. Proudie's wardrobe. He never again aspired to disobey, or seemed even to wish for autocratic diocesan authority. If ever he thought of freedom, he did so as men think of the millennium, as of a good time which may be coming but which nobody expects to come in their day. Mrs. Proudie might be said still to bloom, and was at any rate strong, and the Bishop had no reason to apprehend that he would be speedily visited with the sorrows of a widower's life.

He is still Bishop of Barchester. He has so graced that throne that the Government has been averse to translate him, even to higher dignities. There may he remain, under safe pupilage, till the newfangled manners of the age have discovered him to be superannuated, and bestowed on him a pension. As for Mrs. Proudie, our prayers for her are that she may live forever.

CHAPTER XLIX

THE NEW DEAN TAKES POSSESSION OF THE DEANERY, AND THE NEW WARDEN OF THE HOSPITAL

Mr. Harding and the Archdeacon together made their way to Oxford, and there, by dint of cunning argument, they induced the Master of Lazarus also to ask himself this momentous question: "Why should not Mr. Arabin be Dean of Barchester?" He of course for a while tried his hand at persuading Mr. Harding that he was foolish, overscrupulous, self-willed, and weak-minded, but he tried in vain. If Mr. Harding would not give way to Dr. Grantly, it was not likely he would give way to Dr. Gwynne, more especially now that so admirable a scheme as that of inducting Mr. Arabin into the deanery had been set on foot. When the Master found that his eloquence was vain, and heard also that Mr. Arabin was about to become Mr. Harding's son-in-law, he confessed that he also would under such circumstances be glad to see his old friend and protégé, the fellow of his college, placed in the comfortable position that was going a-begging.

"It might be the means, you know, Master, of keeping Mr. Slope out," said the Archdeacon with grave caution.

"He has no more chance of it," said the Master, "than our college chaplain. I know more about it than that."

Mrs. Grantly had been right in her surmise. It was the Master of Lazarus who had been instrumental in representing in high places the claims which Mr. Harding had upon the Government, and he now consented to use his best endeavors toward getting the offer transferred to Mr. Arabin. The three of them went on to London together, and there they remained a week, to the great disgust of Mrs. Grantly and most probably also of Mrs. Gwynne. The Minister was out of town in one direction and his private secretary in another. The clerks who remained could do nothing in such a matter as this, and all was difficulty and confusion. The two Doctors seemed to have plenty to do. They bustled here and they bustled there, and complained at their club in the evenings that they had been driven off their legs. But Mr. Harding had no occupation. Once or twice he suggested that he might perhaps return to Barchester. His request, however, was peremptorily refused, and he had nothing for it but to while away his time in Westminster Abbey.

At length an answer from the great man came. The Master of Lazarus had made his proposition through the Bishop of Belgravia. Now this bishop, though but newly gifted with his diocesan honors, was a man of much weight in the clericopolitical world. He was, if not as pious, at any rate as wise, as St. Paul, and had been with so much effect all things to all men that though he was great among the dons of Oxford, he had been selected for the most favorite seat on the bench by a Whig Prime Minister. To him Dr. Gwynne had made known his wishes and his arguments, and the Bishop had made them known to the Marquis of Kensington-Gore. The Marquis, who was Lord High Steward of the Pantry Board, and who by most men was supposed to hold the highest office out of the Cabinet, trafficked much in affairs of this kind. He not only suggested the arrangement to the Minister over a cup of coffee, standing on a drawing-room rug in Windsor Castle, but he also favorably mentioned Mr. Arabin's name in the ear of a distinguished person.

And so the matter was arranged. The answer of the great man came, and Mr. Arabin was made Dean of Barchester. The three clergymen who had come up to town on this important mission dined together with great glee on the day on which the news reached them. In a silent, decent, clerical manner, they toasted Mr. Arabin with full bumpers of claret. The satisfaction of all of them was supreme. The Master of Lazarus had been successful in his attempt, and success is dear to us all. The Archdeacon had trampled upon Mr. Slope, and had lifted to high honors the young clergyman whom he had induced to quit the retirement and comfort of the university. So at last the Archdeacon thought, though, to speak sooth, not he but circumstances had trampled on Mr. Slope. But the satisfaction of Mr. Harding was of all perhaps the most complete. He laid aside his usual melancholy manner, and brought forth little quiet jokes from the inmost mirth of his heart. He poked his fun at the Archdeacon about Mr. Slope's marriage, and quizzed him for his improper love for Mrs. Proudie. On the following day they all returned to Barchester.

It was arranged that Mr. Arabin should know nothing of what had been done till he received the Minister's letter from the hands of his embryo father-in-law. In order that no time might be lost, a message had been sent to him by the preceding night's post begging him to be at the deanery at the hour that the train from London arrived. There was nothing in this which surprised Mr. Arabin. It had somehow got about through all Barchester that Mr. Harding was the new dean, and all Barchester was prepared to welcome him with pealing bells and full hearts. Mr. Slope had certainly had a party, there had certainly been those in Barchester who were prepared to congratulate him on his promotion with assumed sincerity, but even his own party was not brokenhearted by his failure. The inhabitants of the city, even the high-souled ecstatic young ladies of thirty-five, had begun to comprehend that their welfare, and the welfare of the place, was connected in some mysterious manner with daily chants and biweekly anthems. The expenditure of the palace had not added much to the popularity of the Bishop's side of the question, and on the whole there was a strong reaction. When it became known to all the world that Mr. Harding was to be the new dean, all the world rejoiced heartily.

Mr. Arabin, we have said, was not surprised at the summons which called him to the deanery. He had not as yet seen Mr. Harding since Eleanor had accepted him, nor had he seen him since he had learnt his future father-in-law's preferment. There was nothing more natural, more necessary, than that they should meet each other at the earliest possible moment. Mr. Arabin was waiting in the deanery parlor when Mr. Harding and Dr. Grantly were driven up from the station.

There was some excitement in the bosoms of them all as they met and shook hands, by far too much to enable either of them to begin his story and tell it in a proper equable style of narrative. Mr. Harding was some minutes quite dumfounded, and Mr. Arabin could only talk in short, spasmodic sentences about his love and good fortune. He slipped in, as best he could, some sort of congratulation about the deanship, and then went on with his hopes and fears—hopes that he might be received as a son, and fears that he hardly deserved such good fortune. Then he went back to the dean. It was the most thoroughly satisfactory appointment, he said, of which he had ever heard.

"But! but! but——" said Mr. Harding, and then, failing to get any further, he looked imploringly at the Archdeacon.

"The truth is, Arabin," said the Doctor, "that after all you are not destined to be son-in-law to a dean. Nor am I either, more's the pity."

Mr. Arabin looked at him for explanation. "Is not Mr. Harding to be the new dean?"

"It appears not," said the Archdeacon. Mr. Arabin's face fell a little, and he looked from one to the other. It was plainly to be seen from them both that there was no cause of unhappiness in the matter, at least not of unhappiness to them, but there was as yet no elucidation of the mystery.

"Think how old I am," said Mr. Harding, imploringly.

"Fiddlestick!" said the Archdeacon.

"That's all very well, but it won't make a young man of me," said Mr. Harding.

"And who is to be dean?" asked Mr. Arabin.

"Yes, that's the question," said the Archdeacon. "Come, Mr. Precentor, since you obstinately refuse to be anything else, let us know who is to be the man. He has got the nomination in his pocket."

With eyes brimful of tears, Mr. Harding pulled out the letter and handed it to his future son-in-law. He tried to make a little speech, but failed altogether. Having given up the document, he turned round to the wall, feigning to blow his nose, and then sat himself down on the old Dean's dingy horsehair sofa. And here we find it necessary to bring our account of the interview to an end.

Nor can we pretend to describe the rapture with which Mr. Harding was received by his daughter. She wept with grief and wept with joy, with grief that her father should in his old age still be without that rank and worldly position which, according to her ideas, he had so well earned, and with joy in that he, her darling father, should have bestowed on that other dear one the good things of which he himself would not open his hand to take possession. And here Mr. Harding again showed his weakness. In the melee of this exposal of their loves and reciprocal affection, he found himself unable to resist the entreaties of all parties that the lodgings in the High Street should be given up. Eleanor would not live in the deanery, she said, unless her father lived there also. Mr. Arabin would not be Dean unless Mr. Harding would be co-Dean with him. The Archdeacon declared that his father-in-law should not have his own way in everything, and Mrs. Grantly carried him off to Plumstead, that he might remain there till Mr. and Mrs. Arabin were in a state to receive him in their own mansion.

Pressed by such arguments as these, what could a weak old man do but yield?

But there was yet another task which it behooved Mr. Harding to do before he could allow himself to be at rest. Little has been said in these pages of the state of those remaining old men who had lived under his sway at the hospital. But not on this account must it be presumed that he had forgotten them, or that in their state of anarchy and in their want of due government he had omitted to visit them. He visited them constantly, and had latterly given them to understand that they would soon be required to subscribe their adherence to a new master. There were now but five of them, one of them having been but quite lately carried to his rest—but five of the full number which had hitherto been twelve, and which was now to be raised to twenty-four, including women. Of these old Bunce, who for many years had been the favorite of the late Warden, was one, and Abel Handy, who had been the humble means of driving that Warden from his home, was another.

Mr. Harding now resolved that he himself would introduce the new Warden to the hospital. He felt that many circumstances might conspire to make the men receive Mr. Quiverful with aversion and disrespect. He felt also that Mr. Quiverful might himself feel some qualms of conscience if he entered the hospital with an idea that he did so in hostility to his predecessor. Mr. Harding therefore determined to walk in arm in arm with Mr. Quiverful, and to ask from these men their respectful obedience to their new master.

On returning to Barchester, he found that Mr. Quiverful had not yet slept in the hospital house, or entered on his new duties. He accordingly made known to that gentleman his wishes, and his proposition was not rejected.

It was on a bright clear morning, though in November, that Mr. Harding and Mr. Quiverful, arm in arm, walked through the hospital gate. It was one trait in our old friend's character that he did nothing with parade. He omitted, even in the more important doings of his life, that sort of parade by which most of us deem it necessary to grace our important doings. We have housewarmings, christenings, and gala days; we keep, if not our own birthdays, those of our children; we are apt to fuss ourselves if called upon to change our residences, and have, almost all of us, our little state occasions. Mr. Harding had no state occasions. When he left his old house, he went forth from it with the same quiet composure as though he were merely taking his daily walk, and now that he re-entered it with another Warden under his wing, he did so with the same quiet step and calm demeanor. He was a little less upright than he had been five years—nay, it was now nearly six years—ago, he walked perhaps a little slower, his footfall was perhaps a thought less firm. Otherwise one might have said that he was merely returning with a friend under his arm.

This friendliness was everything to Mr. Quiverful. To him, even in his poverty, the thought that he was supplanting a brother clergyman so kind and courteous as Mr. Harding had been very bitter. Under his circumstances it had been impossible for him to refuse the proffered boon. He could not reject the bread that was offered to his children, or refuse to ease the heavy burden that had so long oppressed that poor wife of his. Nevertheless it had been very grievous to him to think that in going to the hospital he might encounter the ill will of his brethren in the diocese. All this Mr. Harding had fully comprehended. It was for such feelings as these, for the nice comprehension of such motives, that his heart and intellect were peculiarly fitted. In most matters of worldly import the Archdeacon set down his father-in-law as little better than a fool. And perhaps he was right. But in some other matters, equally important if they be rightly judged, Mr. Harding, had he been so minded, might with as much propriety have set down his son-in-law for a fool. Few men, however, are constituted as was Mr. Harding. He had that nice appreciation of the feelings of others which belongs of right exclusively to women.

Arm in arm they walked into the inner quadrangle of the building, and there the five old men met them. Mr. Harding shook hands with them all, and then Mr. Quiverful did the same. With Bunce Mr. Harding shook hands twice, and Mr. Quiverful was about to repeat the same ceremony, but the old man gave him no encouragement.

"I am very glad to know that at last you have a new Warden," said Mr. Harding in a very cheery voice.

"We be very old for any change," said one of them, "but we do suppose it be all for the best."

"Certainly—certainly it is for the best," said Mr. Harding. "You will again have a clergyman of your own Church under the same roof with you, and a very excellent clergyman you will have. It is a great satisfaction to me to know that so good a man is coming to take care of you, and that it is no stranger, but a friend of my own, who will allow me from time to time to come in and see you."

"We be very thankful to your Reverence," said another of them.

"I need not tell you, my good friends," said Mr. Quiverful, "how extremely grateful I am to Mr. Harding for his kindness to me—I must say his uncalled-for, unexpected kindness."

"He be always very kind," said a third.

"What I can do to fill the void which he left here I will do. For your sake and my own I will do so, and especially for his sake. But to you who have known him, I can never be the same well-beloved friend and father that he has been."

"No, sir, no," said old Bunce, who hitherto had held his peace, "no one can be that. Not if the new Bishop sent a hangel to us out of Heaven. We doesn't doubt you'll do your best, sir, but you'll not be like the old master, not to us old ones."

"Fie, Bunce, fie! How dare you talk in that way?" said Mr. Harding, but as he scolded the old man he still held him by his arm, and pressed it with warm affection.

There was no getting up any enthusiasm in the matter. How could five old men tottering away to their final resting-place be enthusiastic on the reception of a stranger? What could Mr. Quiverful be to them, or they to Mr. Quiverful? Had Mr. Harding indeed come back to them, some last flicker of joyous light might have shone forth on their aged cheeks, but it was in vain to bid them rejoice because Mr. Quiverful was about to move his fourteen children from Puddingdale into the hospital house. In reality they did no doubt receive advantage, spiritual as well as corporal, but this they could neither anticipate nor acknowledge.

It was a dull affair enough, this introduction of Mr. Quiverful, but still it had its effect. The good which Mr. Harding intended did not fall to the ground. All the Barchester world, including the five old bedesmen, treated Mr. Quiverful with the more respect because Mr. Harding had thus walked in arm in arm with him on his first entrance to his duties.

And here in their new abode we will leave Mr. and Mrs. Quiverful and their fourteen children. May they enjoy the good things which Providence has at length given to them!

CHAPTER L

CONCLUSION

THE end of a novel, like the end of a children's dinner party, must be made up of sweetmeats and sugarplums. There is now nothing else to be told but the gala doings of Mr. Arabin's marriage, nothing more to be described than the wedding dresses, no further dialogue to be recorded than that which took place between the Archdeacon who married them and Mr. Arabin and Eleanor who were married. "Wilt thou have this woman to thy wedded wife?" and "Wilt thou have this man to thy wedded husband, to live together according to God's ordinance?" Mr. Arabin and Eleanor each answered, "I will." We have no doubt that they will keep their promises, the more especially as the Signora Neroni had left Barchester before the ceremony was performed.

Mrs. Bold had been somewhat more than two years a widow before she was married to her second husband, and little Johnnie was then able with due assistance to walk on his own legs into the drawing-room to receive the salutations of the assembled guests. Mr. Harding gave away the bride, the Archdeacon performed the service, and the two Miss Grantlys, who were joined in their labors by other young ladies of the neighborhood, performed the duties of bridesmaids with equal diligence and grace. Mrs. Grantly superintended the breakfast and bouquets, and Mary Bold distributed the cards and cake. The Archdeacon's three sons had also come home for the occasion. The eldest was great with learning, being regarded by all who knew him as a certain future double first. The second, however, bore the palm on this occasion, being resplendent in a new uniform. The third was just entering the university, and was probably the proudest of the three.

But the most remarkable feature in the whole occasion was the excessive liberality of the Archdeacon. He literally made presents to everybody. As Mr. Arabin had already moved out of the parsonage of St. Ewold's, that scheme of elongating the dining-room was of course abandoned, but he would have refurnished the whole deanery had he been allowed. He sent down a magnificent piano by Erard, gave Mr. Arabin a cob which any dean in the land might have been proud to bestride, and made a special present to Eleanor of a new pony chair that had gained a prize in the Exhibition. Nor did he even stay his hand here. He bought a set of cameos for his wife and a sapphire bracelet for Miss Bold, showered pearls and workboxes on his daughters, and to each of his sons he presented a cheque for £20. On Mr. Harding he bestowed a magnificent violoncello with all the new-fashioned arrangements and expensive additions, which on account of these novelties, that gentleman could never use with satisfaction to his audience or pleasure to himself.

Those who knew the Archdeacon well perfectly understood the cause of his extravagance. 'Twas thus that he sang his song of triumph over Mr. Slope. This was his paean, his hymn of thanksgiving, his loud oration. He had girded himself with his sword, and gone forth to the war. Now he was returning from the field laden with the spoils of the foe. The cob and the cameos, the violoncello and the pianoforte, were all as it were trophies reft from the tent of his now conquered enemy.

The Arabins after their marriage went abroad for a couple of months, according to the custom in such matters now duly established, and then commenced their deanery life under good auspices. And nothing can be more pleasant than the present arrangement of ecclesiastical affairs in Barchester. The titular Bishop never interferes and Mrs. Proudie not often. Her sphere is more extended, more noble, and more suited to her ambition than that of a cathedral city. As long as she can do what she pleases with the diocese, she is willing to leave the Dean and Chapter to themselves. Mr. Slope tried his hand at subverting the old-established customs of the close, and from his failure she has learnt experience. The burly Chancellor and the meager little prebendary are not teased by any application respecting Sabbath-day schools, the Dean is left to his own dominions, and the intercourse between Mrs. Proudie and Mrs. Arabin is confined to a yearly dinner given by each to the other. At these dinners Dr. Grantly will not take a part, but he never fails to ask for and receive a full account of all that Mrs. Proudie either does or says.

His ecclesiastical authority has been greatly shorn since the palmy days in which he reigned supreme as mayor of the palace to his father, but nevertheless such authority as is now left to him he can enjoy without interference. He can walk down the High Street of Barchester without feeling that those who see him are comparing his claims with those of Mr. Slope. The intercourse between Plumstead and the deanery is of the most constant and familiar description. Since Eleanor has been married to a clergyman, and especially to a dignitary of the Church, Mrs. Grantly has found many more points of sympathy with her sister, and on a coming occasion, which is much looked forward to by all parties, she intends to spend a month or two at the deanery. She never thought of spending a month in Barchester when little Johnnie Bold was born!

The two sisters do not quite agree on matters of church doctrine, though their differences are of the most amicable description. Mr. Arabin's Church is two degrees higher than that of Mrs. Grantly. This may seem strange to those who will remember that Eleanor was once accused of partiality to Mr. Slope, but it is no less the fact. She likes her husband's silken vest, she likes his adherence to the rubric, she specially likes the eloquent philosophy of his sermons, and she likes the red letters in her own prayer book. It must not be presumed that she has a taste for candles, or that she is at all astray about the Real Presence, but she has an inkling that way. She sent a handsome subscription toward certain very heavy ecclesiastical legal expenses which have lately been incurred in Bath, her name of course not appearing. She assumes a smile of gentle ridicule when the Archbishop of Canterbury is named, and she has put up a memorial window in the cathedral.

Mrs. Grantly, who belongs to the High and Dry Church, the High Church as it was some fifty years since, before tracts were written and young clergymen took upon themselves the highly meritorious duty of cleaning churches, rather laughs at her sister. She shrugs her shoulders, and tells Miss Thorne that she supposes Eleanor will have an oratory in the deanery before she has done. But she is not on that account a whit displeased. A few High Church vagaries do not, she thinks, sit amiss on the shoulders of a young dean's wife. It shows at any rate that her heart is in the subject, and it shows moreover that she is removed, wide as the poles asunder, from that cesspool of abomination in which it was once suspected that she would wallow and grovel. Anathema maranatha! Let anything else be held as blessed so that that be well cursed. Welcome kneelings and bowings, welcome matins and complines, welcome bell, book, and candle, so that Mr. Slope's dirty surplices and ceremonial Sabbaths be held in due execration!

If it be essentially and absolutely necessary to choose between the two, we are inclined to agree with Mrs. Grantly that the bell, book, and candle are the lesser evil of the two. Let it however be understood that no such necessity is admitted in these pages.

Dr. Arabin (we suppose he must have become a doctor when he became a dean) is more moderate and less outspoken on doctrinal points than his wife, as indeed in his station it behooves him to be. He is a studious, thoughtful, hard-working man. He lives constantly at the deanery, and preaches nearly every Sunday. His time is spent in sifting and editing old ecclesiastical literature, and in producing the same articles new. At Oxford he is generally regarded as the most promising clerical ornament of the age. He and his wife live together in perfect mutual confidence. There is but one secret in her bosom which he has not shared. He has never yet learned how Mr. Slope had his ears boxed.

The Stanhopes soon found that Mr. Slope's power need no longer operate to keep them from the delight of their Italian villa. Before Eleanor's marriage they had all migrated back to the shores of Como. They had not been resettled long before the Signora received from Mrs. Arabin a very pretty though very short epistle, in which she was informed of the fate of the writer. This letter was answered by another, bright, charming, and witty, as the Signora's letters always were, and so ended the friendship between Eleanor and the Stanhopes.

One word of Mr. Harding, and we have done.

He is still Precentor of Barchester, and still pastor of the little Church of St. Cuthbert's. In spite of what he has so often said himself, he is not even yet an old man. He does such duties as fall to his lot well and conscientiously, and is thankful that he has never been tempted to assume others for which he might be less fitted.

The author now leaves him in the hands of his readers—not as a hero, not as a man to be admired and talked of, not as a man who should be toasted at public dinners and spoken of with conventional absurdity as a perfect divine, but as a good man without guile, believing humbly in the religion which he has striven to teach, and guided by the precepts which he has striven to learn.